By Robert Ludlum

The critics on Robert Ludlum

'Robert Ludlum is an ingenious storyteller with a wonderful and convincing imagination. His place as a bestselling novelist is assured'
Mario Puzo, author of *The Godfather*

'Robert Ludlum has the storytelling gift' *TLS*

'Robert Ludlum is, of course, the bestselling thriller writer of all time, having sold more than two hundred million copies of his twenty-two novels, and he has become known for the sweep and intricacy of his plots ... Now he brings us *The Prometheus Deception* ... his most ingenious novel yet ... Ludlum transcends the genre' *The New Yorker*

'The pace is fast, the action plentiful ... a must read' *Booklist*

'Don't ever begin a Ludlum novel if you have to go to work the next day' *Chicago Sun-Times*

'Ludlum stuffs more surprises into his novels than any other six pack of thriller writers combined'
New York Times

'Ludlum is light years beyond his literary competition in piling plot twist upon plot twist, until the mesmerized reader is held captive' *Chicago Tribune*

'Robert Ludlum is an acknowledged superstar of the political thriller' Amazon.co.uk

'A typically baroque concoction boasting more twists than a packet of pretzels ... a hugely enjoyable caper'
Sunday Times

'Olympic style, all-out espionage ... Good news for Ludlum's countless fans' *Daily Express*

'Huge in scope ... Ludlum spins it all together with lots of suspense' *Sunday Telegraph*

Robert Ludlum is the author of 29 novels, published in 32 languages and 40 countries, and at one time was the world's bestselling author with his blend of sophisticated plotting and extreme pace. There are more than 210 million copies of his books in print. He is best known for *The Scarlatti Inheritance*, *The Chancellor Manuscript* and the Jason Bourne series – *The Bourne Identity, The Bourne Supremacy* and *The Bourne Ultimatum* – among others.

The Road to Gandolfo

———

The Road to Omaha

ROBERT LUDLUM

ORION

The Road to Gandolfo
First published in Great Britain by Hart-Davis, MacGibbon Ltd in
1976
under the author's pseudonym of Michael Shepherd
First published by Orion Books Ltd in 2004

The Road to Omaha
First published in Great Britain in 1992 by Harper Collins Publishers
First published by Orion Books Ltd in 2004

This omnibus edition published in 2006
by Orion Books Ltd,
Orion House, 5 Upper St Martin's Lane,
London WC2H 9EA

A CIP catalogue record for this book is available from the British
Library.

ISBN 1 89880 193 2

Printed and bound in Great Britain by
Mackays of Chatham Ltd, Chatham Kent

For John Patrick

A distinguished writer, an honoured man, a
good friend. Whose idea this was.
With affection

A large part of this story took
place a while back. And quite a bit of
it tomorrow.
Such is the poetic licence of
Liturgical Drama.

A WORD FROM THE AUTHOR

The Road to Gandolfo is one of those rare if insane accidents that can happen to a writer perhaps once or twice in his lifetime. Through divine or demonic providence a concept is presented that fuels the fires of his imagination. He is convinced it is truly a *staggering* premise which will serve as the spine of a truly *staggering* tale. Visions of one powerful scene after another parade across his inner screen, each exploding with drama and meaning and ... well, damn it, they're just plain *staggering!*

Out come reams of paper. The typewriter is dusted and pencils are sharpened; doors are closed and heady music is played to drown out the sounds of man and nature beyond the cell of staggering creation. Fury takes over. The premise which will be the spinal thunderbolt of an incredible tale begins to take on substance as characters emerge with faces and bodies, personalities and conflicts. The plot surges forward, complex gears mesh and strip and make a hell of a lot of noise – drowning out the work of true masters like that Mozart fellow and what's-his-name Handel.

But suddenly something is wrong. I mean *wrong!*

The author is giggling. He can't *stop* giggling.

That's horrible! Staggering premises should be accorded awed respect ... heaven knows not chuckles!

But try as he may the poor fool telling the tale is trapped, bombarded by a fugue of voices all repeating an old *ars antigua* phrase: *You've-got-to-be-kidding.*

Poor fool looks to his muses. Why are they winking? Is that *The Messiah* he's hearing or is it *Mairzy-Dotes*? What happened to the staggering thunderbolt? Why is it spiraling out of whack in a clear blue sky, hiccuping its way to a diminished . . . *giggle?*

Poor fool is bewildered; he gives up. Or rather, he gives in because by now he's having a lot of fun. After all, it *was* the time of Watergate, and nobody could invent *that* scenario! I mean it simply wouldn't play in Peoria. At that point-in-time, that is.

So poor fool plunges along, enjoying himself immensely, vaguely wondering who will sign the commitment papers, figuring his wife will stop them because the oaf does the dishes now and then and makes a damn good martini.

The *oeuvre* is finally presented and, most gratefully for poor fool, the closeted sound of laughter is heard. Followed by screams of revolt and threats of beyond-salvage termination with extreme-prejudice.

'Not under *your* name!'

Time mandates change, and change is cleansing.

Now it's under my name, and I hope you enjoy it. I *did* have a lot of fun.

Robert Ludlum
Connecticut Shore, 1982

PART ONE

Behind each corporation must be the singular force, or motive, that sets it apart from any other corporate structure and gives it its particular identity.

Shepherd's Laws of Economics:
Book XXXII, Chapter 12

PROLOGUE

The crowds gathered in St Peter's Square. Thousands upon thousands of the faithful waited in hushed anticipation for the pontiff to emerge on the balcony and raise his hands in benediction. The fasting and the prayers were over; the Feast of San Gennaro would be ushered in with the pealing of the twilight Angelus echoing throughout the Vatican. And the bells would be heard throughout all Rome, heralding merriment and good feeling. The blessing of Pope Francesco the First would be the signal to begin.

There would be dancing in the streets, and torches and candlelight and music and wine. In the Piazza Navonna, the Trevi, even sections of the Palatine, long tables were heaped with pasta and fruit and all manner of home-produced pastries. For had not this pontiff, the beloved Francesco, given the lesson? Open your hearts and your cupboards to your neighbour. And his to you. Let all men high and low understand that we are one family. In these times of hardship and chaos and high prices, what better way to overcome but to enter into the spirit of the Lord and truly show love for thy neighbour?

For a few days let rancours subside and divisions be healed. Let the word go forth that all men are brothers, all women sisters; and all together brothers and sisters and very much each other's keepers. For but a few days let charity and grace and concern rule the hearts of everyone, sharing the sweet and the sad, for there is no evil that can withstand the force of good.

Embrace, raise the wine; show laughter and tears and

accept one another in expressions of love. Let the world see there is no shame in the exultation of the spirit. And once having touched, having heard the voices of brother and sister, carry forth the sweet memories beyond the Feast of San Gennaro, and let life be guided by the principles of Christian benevolence. The earth can be a better place; it is up to the living to make it so. That was the lesson of Francesco I.

A hush fell over the tens of thousands in St Peter's Square. Any second now the figure of the beloved *Papa* would walk with strength and dignity and great love on to the balcony and raise his hands in benediction. And for the Angelus to begin.

Within the high-ceilinged Vatican chambers above the square, cardinals, monsignors, and priests talked among themselves in groups, their eyes continually straying to the figure of the pontiff seated in the corner. The room was resplendent with vivid colours: scarlets, purples, immaculate whites. Robes and cassocks and head pieces – symbols of the highest offices in the Church – swayed and were turned, giving the illusion of a constantly moving fresco.

And in the corner, seated in a wing chair of ivory and blue velvet, was the Vicar of Christ, Pope Francesco I. He was a plain man of wide girth, and the strong yet gentle features of a *campagnuolo*, a man of the earth. Standing beside him was his personal secretary, a young Black priest from America, from the archdiocese of New York. It was like Francesco to have such a papal aide.

The two were talking quietly, the pontiff turning his enormous head, his huge, soft brown eyes looking up at the young priest in serene composure.

'*Mannaggi*'!' whispered Francesco, his large peasant hand covering his lips. 'This is crazy! The entire city will be drunk for a week! Everyone will be making love in the streets. Are you sure we have it right?'

'I double-checked. Do you want to argue with him?' replied the Black, bending down in tranquil solicitousness.

4

'My God, no! He was always the smartest one in the villages!'

A cardinal approached the pontiff's chair and leaned forward. 'Holy Father, it is time. The multitudes await you,' he said softly.

'Who—? Yes, of course. In a minute, my good friend.'

The cardinal smiled under his enormous hat; his eyes were filled with adoration. Francesco always called him his good friend. 'Thank you, your Holiness.' The cardinal backed away.

The Vicar of Christ began humming. Then words emerged. '*Che gelida . . . manina . . . a rigido esanime . . . ah, la, la-laa – tra-la la, la-laaa . . .*'

'What are you *doing*?' The young papal aide from the archdiocese of New York, Harlem district, was visibly upset.

'Rodolfo's aria. Ah, that Puccini! It helps me to sing when I am nervous.'

'Well, cut it out, man! Or pick a Gregorian chant. At least a litany.'

'I don't know any. Your Italian's getting better, but it's still not so good.'

'I'm trying, brother. You're not the easiest to learn with. Come on, now. Let's go. Out to the balcony.'

'Don't push! I go. Let's see, I raise the hand, then up and down and right to left—'

'*Left to right!*' whispered the priest harshly. 'Don't you listen? If we're going on with this honkey charade, for God's sake learn the fundamentals!'

'I thought if I was standing, giving – not taking – I should reverse it.'

'Don't mess. Just do what's natural.'

'Then I sing.'

'Not that natural! Come on.'

'All right, all *right*.' The pontiff rose from his chair and smiled benignly at all in the room. He turned once again to his aide and spoke softly so that none could hear. 'In case anyone should ask, which one is San Gennaro?'

'Nobody will ask. If someone does, use your standard reply.'

'Ah, yes. "Study the scriptures, my son." You know, this is all crazy!'

'Walk slowly and stand up straight. And smile, for God's sake! You're *happy*.'

'I'm *miserable*, you African!'

Pope Francesco I, Vicar of Christ, walked through the enormous doors out on to the balcony to be greeted by a thunderous roar that shook the very foundations of St Peter's. Thousands upon thousands of the faithful raised their voices in the exultation of the spirit.

'Il Papa! Il Papa! Il Papa!'

And as the Holy Father walked out into the myriad reflections of the orange sun setting in the west, there were many in the chambers who heard the muted strains of the chant emerging from the holy lips. Each believed it had to be some obscure early musical work, unknown to all but the most scholarly. For such was the knowledge of the *erudito*, Pope Francesco.

'Che . . . gelida . . . manina . . . a rigido esanimeee . . . ah, la, la-laaa . . . tra-la, la, la . . . la-la-laaa . . .'

6

CHAPTER ONE

'That son of a bitch!' Brigadier General Arnold Symington brought the paperweight down on the thick layer of glass on his Pentagon desk. The glass shattered; fragments shot through the air in all directions. *'He couldn't!'*

'He did, sir,' replied the frightened lieutenant, shielding his eyes from the office shrapnel. 'The Chinese are very upset. The premier himself dictated the complaint to the diplomatic mission. They're running editorials in the *Red Star* and broadcasting them over Radio Peking.'

'How the hell *can* they?' Symington removed a piece of glass from his little finger. 'What the hell are they saying? "We interrupt this programme to announce that the American military representative, General MacKenzie Hawkins, *shot the balls* off a ten-foot jade statue in Son Tai Square"? – Bullshit! Peking wouldn't allow that; it's too goddamned undignified.'

'They're phrasing it a bit differently, sir. They say he destroyed an historic monument of precious stone in the Forbidden City. They say it's as though someone blew up the Lincoln Memorial.'

'It's a different kind of statue! Lincoln's got clothes on; his balls don't show! It's not the same!'

'Nevertheless, the White House thinks the parallel is justified, sir. The President wants Hawkins removed. More than removed, actually; he wants him cashiered. Court-martial and all. Publicly.'

'Oh, for Christ's sake, that's out of the question.' Symington leaned back in his chair and breathed deeply, trying to control himself. He reached out for the report on his desk. 'We'll transfer him. With a reprimand. We'll send transcripts of the – censure, we'll call it a censure – to Peking.'

'That's not strong enough, sir. The State Department made it clear. The President concurs. We have trade agreements pending—'

'For Christ's sake, Lieutenant!' interrupted the brigadier. 'Will someone tell that spinning top in the Oval Office that he can't have it on all points of the compass! Mac Hawkins was *selected*. From twenty-seven candidates. I remember exactly what the President said. Exactly. "That mother's *perfect*!" That's what he said.'

'That's inoperative now, sir. He feels the trade agreements take precedence over prior considerations.' The lieutenant was beginning to perspire.

'You bastards kill me,' said Symington, lowering his voice ominously. 'You really frost my apricots. How do you figure to do that? Make it "inoperative", I mean. Hawkins may be a sharp pain in your diplomatic ass right now, but that doesn't wash away what *was operative*. He was a fucking teenage hero at the Battle of the Bulge *and* West Point football; *and* if they gave medals for what he did in Southeast Asia, even Mac Hawkins isn't strong enough to wear all that hardware! He makes John Wayne look like a pansy! He's *real*; that's why that Oval Yo-yo picked him!'

'I really think the office of the presidency – regardless of what he may think of the man – as commander in chief he—'

'*Horse-shit!*' The brigadier general roared again, separating the words in equal emphasis, giving the crudity of his oath the sound of a military cadence. 'I'm simply explaining to you – in the strongest terms I know – that you don't publicly court-martial a MacKenzie Hawkins to satisfy a Peking complaint, no matter how many goddamned trade agreements are floating around. Do you know *why*, Lieutenant?'

The young officer replied softly, sure of his accuracy. 'Because he would make an issue of it. Publicly.'

'Bing-go.' Symington's comment sprang out in a high-pitched monotone. 'The Hawkinses of this country have a constituency, Lieutenant. That's precisely *why* our commander in chief picked him! He's a political palliative. And if you don't think Mac Hawkins knows it, well – you didn't have to recruit him. I did.'

'We are prepared for that reaction, General.' The lieutenant's words were barely audible.

The brigadier leaned forward, careful not to put his elbows in the shattered glass. 'I didn't get that.'

'The State Department anticipated a hard-line counter-thrust. Therefore we must institute an aggressive counter-reaction *to* that thrust. The White House regrets the necessity but at this point in time recognizes the crisis quotient.'

'That's what I thought I was going to get.' Symington's words were less audible than the lieutenant's. 'Spell it out. How are you going to ream him?'

The lieutenant hesitated. 'Forgive me, sir, but the object is not to – ream General Hawkins. We are in a provocatively delicate position. The People's Republic demands satisfaction. Rightly so; it was a crude, vulgar act on General Hawkins's part. Yet he refuses to make a public apology.'

Symington looked at the report still in his right hand. 'Does it say why in here?'

'General Hawkins claims it was a trap. His statement's on page three.'

The brigadier flipped to the page and read. The lieutenant drew out a handkerchief and blotted his chin. Symington put down the report carefully on the shattered glass and looked up.

'If what Mac says is true, it *was* a trap. Broadcast *his* side of the story.'

'He has no side, General. He was drunk.'

'Mac says *drugged*. Not drunk, Lieutenant.'

'They were drinking, sir.'

'And he was drugged. I'd guess Hawkins would know the difference. I've seen him sweat sour mash.'

'He does not deny the charge, however.'

'He denies the responsibility of his actions. Hawkins was the finest intelligence strategist in Indochina. He's drugged couriers and pouch men in Cambodia, Laos, both Vietnams, and probably across the Manchurian borders. He knows the goddamned difference.'

'I'm afraid his knowing it doesn't *make* any difference, sir. The crisis quotient demands our acceding to Peking's wishes. The trade agreements are paramount. Frankly, sir, we need gas.'

'Jesus! I figured that was one thing you *had*.'

The lieutenant replaced the handkerchief in his pocket and smiled wanly. 'The levity is called for, I realize that. However, we have just ten days to bring everything into focus; to make our inputs and come up with a positive print.'

Symington stared at the young officer; his expression that of a grown man about to cry. 'What does that mean?'

'It's a harsh thing to say, but General Hawkins has placed his own interests above those of his duty. We'll have to make an example. For everybody's sake.'

'An example? For wanting the truth out?'

'There's a higher duty, General.'

'I know,' said the brigadier wearily. 'To the – trade agreements. To the gas.'

'Quite frankly, yes. There are times when symbols have to be traded off for pragmatic objectives. Team players understand.'

'All right. But Mac won't lie down and play busted symbol for you. So what's the – *input*?'

'The inspector general,' said the lieutenant, as an obnoxious student might, holding up a severed tapeworm in Biology I. 'We're running an in-depth data trace on him. We know he was involved in questionable activities in Indochina. We have reason to believe he violated international codes of conduct.'

'You bet your ass he did! He was one of the best!'

'There's no statute on those codes. The IG specialists have caseloads going back much further than General

Hawkins's *ex-officio* activities.' The lieutenant smiled. It was a genuine smile; he was a happy person.

'So you're going to hang him with clandestine operations that half the joint chiefs and most of the CIA know would bring him a truckload of citations – if they could talk about them. You bastards kill me.' Symington nodded his head, agreeing with himself.

'Perhaps you could save us time, General. Can you provide us with some specifics?'

'Oh, no! You want to crucify the son of a bitch, you build your own cross!'

'You do understand the situation, don't you, sir?'

The brigadier moved his chair back and kicked fragments of glass from under his feet. 'I'll tell you something,' he said. 'I haven't understood anything since nineteen forty-five.' He glared at the young officer. 'I know you're with Sixteen-hundred, but are you regular army?'

'No, sir. Reserve status, temporary assignment. I'm on a leave of absence from Y, J, and B. To put out fires before they burn up the flagpoles, as it were.'

'Y, J, and B. I don't know that division.'

'Not a division, sir. Youngblood, Jakel, and Blowe, Los Angeles. We're the top ad agency on the Coast.'

General Arnold Symington's face slowly took on the expression of a distressed basset hound. 'The uniform looks real nice, Lieutenant.' The brigadier paused, then shook his head. 'Nineteen forty-five,' he said.

Major Sam Devereaux, field investigator for the Office of the Inspector General, looked across the room at the calendar on his wall. He got up from the chair behind his desk, walked over to it, and Xed the day's date. One month and three days and he would be a civilian again.

Not that he was ever a soldier. Not really; certainly not spiritually. He was a military accident. A fracture compounded by a huge mistake that resulted in an extension of his tour of service. It had been a simple choice of alternatives: Re-enlistment or Leavenworth.

Sam was a lawyer, a damn fine attorney specializing in criminal law. Years ago he had held a series of Selective Service deferments. Through Harvard College and Harvard Law School; then two years of postgraduate specialization and clerking; finally into the fourteenth month of practice with the prestigious Boston law firm of Aaron Pinkus Associates.

The army had faded into a vaguely disagreeable shadow across his life; he had forgotten about the long series of deferments.

The United States Army, however, did not forget.

During one of those logistic crunches that episodically grip the military, the Pentagon discovered it had a sudden dearth of lawyers. The Department of Military Justice was in a bind – hundreds of courts-martial on bases all over the globe were suspended for lack of judge advocates and defence attorneys. The stockades were crowded. So the Pentagon scoured the long-forgotten series of deferments and scores of young unattached, childless lawyers – obtainable meat – were sent unrefusable invitations in which was explained the meaning of the word 'deferment' as opposed to the word 'annulment'.

That was the accident. Devereaux's mistake came later. Much later. Seven thousand miles away on the converging borders of Laos, Burma, and Thailand.

The Golden Triangle.

Devereaux – for reasons known only to God and military logistics – never saw a court-martial, much less tried one. He was assigned to the Legal Investigations Division of the Office of the Investigator General and sent to Saigon to see what laws were being violated.

There were so many, there was no way to count. And since drugs took precedence over the black market – there were simply too many American entrepreneurs in the latter – his inquiries took him to the Golden Triangle where one-fifth of the world's narcotics were being funnelled out, courtesy of powerful men in Saigon, Washington, Vientiane, and Hong Kong.

Sam was conscientious. He didn't like drug peddlers and he threw the investigatory books at them, careful to make sure his briefs to Saigon were transmitted operationally within the confused chain of command.

No report signatures. Just names and violations. After all, he could get shot or knifed – at least, ostracized for such behaviour. It was an education in covert activities.

His trophies included seven ARVN generals, thirty-one representatives in Thieu's congress, twelve US Army colonels – light and full – three brigadiers, and fifty-eight assorted majors, captains, lieutenants, and master sergeants. Added to these were five congressmen, four senators, a member of the President's cabinet, eleven corporation executives with American companies overseas – six of which already had enough trouble in the area of campaign contributions – and a square-jawed Baptist minister with a large national following.

To the best of Sam's knowledge, one second lieutenant and two master sergeants were indicted. The rest were – 'pending'.

So Sam Devereaux committed his mistake. He was so incensed that the wheels of Southeast Asian justice spun off the tracks at the first hint of influence that he decided to trap a very big fish in the corruption net and make an example. He chose a major general in Bangkok. A man named Heseltine Brokemichael. Major General Heseltine Brokemichael, West Point '43.

Sam had the evidence, mounds of it. Through a series of elaborate entrapments in which he himself acted as the 'connection', a participant who could swear under oath to the general's malfeasance, he built his case thoroughly. There could not possibly be two General Brokemichaels, and Sam was an avenging angel of a prosecutor, circling in for his kill.

But there were. Two. Two major generals named Brokemichael – one Heseltine, one Ethelred! Apparently cousins. And the one in Bangkok – Heseltine – was not the one in Vientiane – Ethelred. The Vientiane Brokemichael was the felon. Not his cousin. Further, the Brokemichael in Bangkok was more an avenger than Sam. He believed *he* was gathering evidence on a corrupt IG investigator. And he was. Devereaux had violated most of the international contraband laws and *all* of the United States government's.

Sam was arrested by the MPs, thrown into a maximum security cell, and told he could look forward to the better part of his lifetime in Leavenworth.

Fortunately, a superior officer in the inspector general's command, who did not really understand a sense of justice that made Sam commit so many crimes, but did understand Sam's legal and investigatory contributions to the cause of the inspector general, came to Sam's aid. Devereaux had actually filed more evidentiary material than any other legal officer in Southeast Asia; his work in the field made up for a great deal of inactivity in Washington.

So the superior officer allowed a little unofficial plea bargaining in Sam's case. If Sam would accept disciplinary action at the hands of a furious Major General Heseltine Brokemichael in Bangkok, constituting a six-month loss of pay – no criminal charges would be brought. There was just one more condition: to continue his work for the inspector general's office for an additional two years beyond the expiration of his army commitment. By that time, reasoned the superior officer, the mess in Indochina would be turned over to those messing, and the IG caseloads reduced or conveniently buried.

Re-enlistment or Leavenworth.

So Major Sam Devereaux, patriotic citizen-soldier, extended his tour of duty. And the mess in Indochina was in no way lessened, but indeed turned over to the participants, and Devereaux was transferred back to Washington, D.C.

One month and three days to go, he mused, as he looked out his office window and watched the MPs at the guardhouse check the automobiles driving out. It was after five; he had to catch a plane at Dulles in two hours. He had packed that morning and brought his suitcase to the office.

The four years were coming to an end. Two plus two.

14

The time spent, he reflected, might be resented, but it had not been wasted. The abyss of corruption that was Southeast Asia reached into the hierarchical corridors of Washington. The inhabitants of these corridors knew who he was; he had more offers from prestigious law firms than he could reply to, much less consider. And he did not want to consider them; he disapproved of them. Just as he disapproved of the current investigation on his desk.

The manipulators were at it again. This time it was the thorough discrediting of a career officer named Hawkins. Lieutenant General MacKenzie Hawkins.

At first Sam had been stunned. MacKenzie Hawkins was an original. A legend. The stuff of which cults were born. Cults slightly to the political right of Attila the Hun.

Hawkins's place in the military firmament was secure. Bantam Books published his biography – serialization and *Reader's Digest* rights had been sold before a word was on paper. Hollywood gave obscene amounts of money to film his life story. And the anti-militarists made him an object of fascist-hatred.

The biography was not overly successful because the subject was not overly cooperative. Apparently there were certain personal idiosyncrasies that did not enhance the image, four wives paramount among them. The motion picture was less than triumphant insofar as it comprised endless battle scenes with little or no hint of the man other than an actor squinting through the battle dust, yelling to his men in a peculiar lisp to 'get those Godless . . . [Roar of cannon] . . . who would tear down Old Glory! At 'em, boys!'

Hollywood, too, had discovered the four wives and certain other peculiarities of the studio's on-the-set technical adviser. MacKenzie Hawkins went through starlets three at a time and had intercourse with the producer's wife in the producer's swimming pool while the producer watched in fury from the living room window.

He did not stop the picture, however. For Christ's sake, it was costing damn near *six mill*!

These misfired endeavours might have caused another

15

man to fade, if only from embarrassment, but not so Mac Hawkins. In private, among his peers, he ridiculed those responsible and regaled his associates with stories of Manhattan and Hollywood.

He was sent to the war college with a new specialization: intelligence, clandestine operations. His peers felt a little more secure with the charismatic Hawkins consigned to covert activities. And the colonel became a brigadier and absorbed all there was to learn of his new speciality. He spent two years grinding away, studying every phase of intelligence work until the instructors had no more to instruct him.

So he was sent to Saigon where the escalating hostilities had blossomed into a full-scale war. And in Vietnam – both Vietnams, and Laos, and Cambodia, and Thailand, and Burma – Hawkins corrupted the corruptors and the ideologues alike. Reports of his behind-the-lines and across-the-neutral-borders activities made 'protective reaction' seem like a logical strategy. So unorthodox, so blatantly criminal were his methods of operation that G-2, Saigon, found itself denying his existence. After all, there were limits. Even for clandestine activities.

If *America First* was a maxim – and it was – Hawkins saw no reason why it should not apply to the filthy world of covert operations.

And for Hawkins, America *was* first. Ir-re-fucking-gardless!

So Sam Devereaux thought it was all a little sad that such a man was about to be knocked out of the box by the manipulators who got to where they were by draping the flag so gloriously and generously around themselves. Hawkins was now an offending lion in the diplomatic arena and had to be eliminated in the cause of double-think. The men who should have been upholding the general's point of honour were doing their best to sink him fast – in ten days, to be precise.

Normally Sam would have taken pleasure out of building a case against a messianic ass like Hawkins; and regardless of

16

his feelings to the contrary, he would build a case against him. It was his last file for the inspector general's office, and he was not going to risk another two-year alternative. But he was still sad. The Hawk, as he was known – misguided fanatic as he might be – deserved better than what he was getting.

Perhaps, thought Sam, his depression was brought about by the last 'operative' instruction from the White House: find something in the morals area Hawkins can't deny. Check to see if he was ever in the care of a psychiatrist.

A psychiatrist! Jesus! They *never* learned.

In the meantime, Sam had dispatched a team of IG investigators to Saigon to see if they could dig up a few negative specifics. And he was off to Dulles airport to catch a plane to Los Angeles.

All of Hawkins's ex-wives lived within a radius of thirty miles of each other, from Malibu to Beverly Hills. They'd be better than any psychiatrist. Christ! A psychiatrist!

At 1600 Pennsylvania Avenue, Washington, D.C. they were all novacained above the shoulders.

17

CHAPTER TWO

'My name is Lin Shoo,' said the uniformed Communist softly, slant-eyeing the large, dishevelled American soldier who sat in a leather chair, holding a glass of whisky in one hand and a well-chewed cigar in the other. 'I am commander of the People's Police, Peking. And you are under house arrest at this moment. There is no point in being abusive, these are merely formalities.'

'Formalities for what?' MacKenzie Hawkins shouted from his armchair – the only occidental piece of furniture in the oriental house. He put his heavy boot on a black lacquered table and flung his hand over the leather back, the lighted cigar dangerously close to a silk screen room divider. 'There aren't any goddamned formalities except through the diplomatic mission. Go down there and make your complaints. You'll probably have to get in line.'

Hawkins chuckled and drank from his glass.

'You have chosen to reside outside the mission,' continued the Chinese named Lin Shoo, his eyes darting between the cigar and the screen. 'Therefore you are not technically within United States territory. So you are subject to the disciplines of the People's Police. However, we know you will not go anywhere, General. That is why I say it is a formality.'

'What have you got out there?' Hawkins waved his cigar towards the thin, rectangular windows.

'There are two patrols on each side of your residence. Eight in all.'

'That's a big fucking guard detail for someone who's not going anywhere.'

'Small liberties. Photographically, two is more desirable than one and three is menacing.'

'You taking liberties?' Hawkins drew on his cigar and again rested his hand over the back of the leather chair. The lighted butt was no more than an inch from the silk.

'The Ministry of Education has done so, yes. You will admit, General, your place of isolation is most pleasant, is it not? This is a lovely house on a lovely hill. So very peaceful, and with a fine view.' Lin Shoo walked around the chair and unobtrusively moved the panel of the silk screen away from Hawkins's cigar. It was too late; the heat of the butt had caused a small circular burn in the fabric.

'It's a high-rent district,' replied Hawkins. 'Somebody in this people's paradise, where nobody owns anything but everyone owns everything, is making a fast buck. Four hundred of 'em every month.'

'You were fortunate to find it. Property can be purchased by collectives. A collective is not private ownership.' The police officer walked to the narrow opening that led to the single sleeping room of the house. It was dark; where sunlight should have been streaming through the wide window there was a blanket nailed across the frame into the thin surrounding wall. On the floor a number of mats had been piled one on top of another; wrappings from American candy bars were scattered about and there was a distinct odour of whisky.

'Why the photographs?'

The Chinese turned from the unpleasant sight. 'To show the world that we are treating you better than you treated us. This house is not a tiger cage in Saigon, nor is it a dungeon in the shark-infested waters of Holcotaz.'

'Alcatraz. The Indians got it.'

'I beg your pardon?'

'Nothing. You're making a big splash with this thing, aren't you?'

Lin Shoo was silent for a moment; it was the pause before

19

profundity. 'Should someone – who has for years publicly denounced the deeply felt objectives of your beloved motherland – dynamite your Lin-Kolon Memorial inside your Washington Square within your state of Columbia, the robed barbarians on your Court of Supreme Justice would, no doubt, have executed him by now.' The Chinese smiled and smoothed the tunic of his Mao uniform. 'We do not behave in such primitive ways. All life is precious. Even a diseased dog, such as you.'

'And you gooks never denounced anybody, is that it?'

'Our leaders reveal only truth. That is common knowledge throughout the world; the lessons of the infallible chairman. Truth is not denunciation, General. It is merely truth. All knowing.'

'Like my state of Columbia,' muttered Hawkins, removing his foot from the lacquered table. 'Why the hell did you pick me out? A lot of people have done a lot of goddamned denouncing. Why am I so special?'

'Because they are not so famous. Or infamous, if you will—. Although I did enjoy the film of your life. Very artistic; a poem of violence.'

'You saw that, huh?'

'Privately. Certain portions were extracted. Those showing the actor portraying you murdering our heroic youth. Very savage, General.' The Communist circled the black lacquered table and smiled again. 'Yes, you are an infamous man. And now you have insulted us by destroying a revered monument—'

'Come off it. I don't even know what happened. I was drugged and you goddamned well know it. I was with your General Lu Sin. With *his* broads, in *his* house.'

'You must give us our honour back again, General Hawkins. Can't you see that?' Lin Shoo spoke quietly, as though Hawkins had not interrupted. 'It would be a simple matter for you to render an apology. A ceremony has been planned. With a small contingent of the press in attendance. We have written out the words for you.'

'*Oh, boy!*' Hawkins sprang out of the chair, towering over

the policeman. 'We're back to that again! How many times do I have to tell you bastards? *Americans don't crawl!* In any goddamned ceremony, with or without the goddamned press! Read that straight, you puke-skinned dwarf!'

'Do not upset yourself. You place far too much emphasis on a mere ceremonial function; you place everyone – *all of us* – in most difficult positions. A small ceremony; so little, so simple—'

'Not to me it isn't! I represent the armed forces of the United States and nothing's little or simple to us! We don't trip easy, buddy boy; we march straight to the drums!'

'I beg your pardon?'

Hawkins shrugged, a touch bewildered by his own words. 'Never mind. The answer's no. You may scare the lace-pants boys down at the mission, but you don't shake me.'

'*They* appealed to you because they were instructed to do so. Certainly that must have occurred to you.'

'Double bullshit!' Hawkins walked around to the fire-place, drank from his glass and placed it on the mantel next to a brightly coloured box. 'Those fags were cooking up something with that group of queens at State. Wait'll the White House – wait'll the *Pentagon* reads *my* report. Oh, boy! You bowlegged runts will hightail it to the mountains and then we'll blow *them* up!' Hawkins grinned, his eyes bright.

'You are so abusive,' said Lin Shoo quietly, shaking his head sadly. He picked up the brightly coloured box next to the general's glass. 'Tsing Taow firecrackers. The finest made in the world. So loud, so bright with white light when they go *bang, bang, bang*. Very lovely to watch and to hear.'

'Yeah,' agreed Hawkins, slightly confused by the change of subject. 'Lu Sin gave 'em to me. We shot off a motherload the other night. Before the fucker drugged me.'

'Very beautiful, General Hawkins. They are a fine gift.'

'Christ knows he owed me *something*.'

'But do you not see?' continued the police officer. 'They sound like – explosives. Look like – detonating ammunition, but they are neither. They are only show. Semblances of something else. Real in themselves but only an *illusion* of *another* reality. Not dangerous at all.'

'So?'

'That is precisely what you are being asked to give. The semblance, not the reality. You have only to *pretend*. In a short, simple ceremony with but a few words that *you* know are only an illusion. Not dangerous at all. And very polite.'

'Wrong-o!' roared Hawkins. 'Everybody knows what a firecracker is; *nobody'll* know I'm pretending.'

'Between the two of us, I must differ. It is nothing more than diplomatic ritual. Everyone will understand, take my word for it.'

'Yeah? How the hell do you know that? You're a Peking cop, not a Kissing-ass.'

The Communist fingered the box of firecrackers and sighed audibly. 'I apologize for the minor deception, General. I am not with the People's Police. I am second vice-prefect for the Ministry of Education. I am here to make an appeal to you. An appeal to your reason. However, the rest is quite true. You *are* under house arrest, and the patrols outside *are* policemen.'

'I'll be goddamned! They sent me a lace-pants.' Hawkins grinned again. 'You boys are worried, real worried, aren't you?'

The Communist sighed once more. 'Yes. The idiots who started this thing have been shipped to mining collectives in Outer Mongolia. It was lunacy; although I'll grant them you were a temptation, General Hawkins. Have you any *idea* the volumes of scurrilous attacks you've made on every Marxist, Socialist, and, forgive me, even vaguely democratically oriented nation on the face of this earth? The worst examples – I should say *best* examples of demagoguery!'

'A lot of that crap was written by the people who paid me to speak,' said Hawkins, a bit reflectively. And then he quickly added, 'Not that I didn't believe it! Goddamn, I *believe!*'

'You're impossible!' Lin Shoo stamped his foot as a child might. 'You're as insane as Lu Sin and his band of growling paper lions! May they all crack many rocks and fornicate with Mongolian sheep! You are simply impossible!'

Hawkins stared at the Communist – both at the furious expression on his face and the brightly coloured box of firecrackers in his hand. He had made a decision and both of them knew it.

'I'm also something else, slant eyes,' said the lieutenant general, approaching Lin Shoo.

'No! *No!* No *violence*, you idiot—' It was too late for the Communist to scream. Hawkins grabbed the cloth of his tunic, pulled him swiftly off his feet and chopped Lin Shoo beneath the mandible.

The vice-prefect of the Ministry of Education slumped instantly into unconsciousness.

Hawkins grabbed the box of firecrackers out of Lin Shoo's hand and raced around the lacquered table into the sleeping quarters. He grabbed the blanket nailed across the window, folded back a tiny section on the edge and looked outside at the rear of the house. There were the two policemen chatting calmly, their rifles at their sides. Beyond them was the sloping hill that led down to the village.

Hawkins released the blanket and ran back into the main room, dropping immediately to his hands and knees and scrambling obstacle-style towards the front door. He stood up and silently opened it a crack. The two flanking policemen were about forty feet away and were as relaxed as the troops in the rear. What's more, they were looking down the descending road, their attention *not* on the house.

MacKenzie took the brightly coloured box of firecrackers from under his arm, ripped off the lightweight paper and shook out the connecting strings of cylinders. He wound two separate strands together, twisted both fuses into one, and removed his World War II Zippo from his pocket.

He stopped; he sucked his breath, angry with himself. Then, holding the strands of firecrackers at his side, he walked casually past the windows into the bedroom and removed his holster and cartridge belt from another nail in the thin wall. He strapped the apparatus around his waist,

23

removed the Colt .45 and checked the magazine. Satisfied, he shoved the weapon into its leather casing as he walked out of the bedroom. He circled the armchair in front of the Han Shu mantel, stepped over the immobile Lin Shoo, and returned to the front door.

He ignited the Zippo, and held the flame beneath the twisted fuse, then opened the door and threw the entwined strands on to the grass beyond the porch.

Closing and bolting the door softly and swiftly, Hawkins dragged a small red lacquered chest from the foyer and forced it against the thick, carved panel. Then he raced into the sleeping quarters and pulled back a small section of the window blanket and waited.

The explosions were even louder than he remembered; made so, he guessed, by the combined strands bursting against one another.

The guards at the rear of the house were jolted out of their lethargy; their weapons collided in midair as each whipped his off the ground. Rifles in waist-firing position, the two men raced towards the front of the house.

The moment they were out of sight, Hawkins yanked down the blanket, crashed his foot into the thin strips of wood and thinner panes of glass, shattering the entire window. He leaped through on to the grass and started running towards the fields and the sloping hill.

CHAPTER THREE

At the base of the hill was the main dirt road that circled the village. Like spokes from a wheel, numerous offshoots headed directly into the small marketplace, in the centre of the town. A semi-paved thoroughfare branched outward tangentially from the circling road and connected with a paved highway about four miles to the east. The American diplomatic mission was twelve miles down that highway within Peking proper.

What he needed was a vehicle, preferably an automobile, but automobiles were practically non-existent outside the highest official circles. The People's Police had automobiles, of course; it had crossed his mind to double back around the hill to find Lin Shoo's, but that was too risky. Even if he found it and stole it, it would be a marked vehicle.

Hawkins circled the village, keeping to the high ground above the road. They would be coming after him. He could stay in the hills indefinitely; that didn't bother him. He had bivouacked underground in the mountains of Cong-Sol and Lai Tai in Cambodia for months at a time; he could live in the forests better than most animals. Goddamn, he was a *pro*!

But it was also pointless. He had to get to the mission and let the Free World know what kind of enemy it was sucking up to. Enough was enough, goddamn it! They could send out radio messages, barricade the whole complex, and fight it out until the offshore carriers sent in air strikes to pinpoint pulverize, even if it meant blowing up half of Peking. Then the copters could come in and get them out.

Of course, the civilians would shit in their pants, but he

would control them. Teach the fancy pants how to fight. *Fight! Not talk!*

MacKenzie stopped his fantasizing. Below to the right, coming around the bend in the road a quarter of a mile away was a lone motorcycle. On it was a *shee-san* police official, a kind of Chinese state trooper. The answer to a prayer!

Hawkins rose from the tall grass and started scrambling down the hill. In less than a minute he was at the edge of the dirt border. The bike was still around the curve out of sight, but he heard it coming closer. He threw himself down in the dirt in the middle of the road, drawing his legs up to appear smaller than he was, and lay perfectly still.

The motorcycle's engine roared as the driver came around the curve, then sputtered as it skidded to a stop. The *shee-san* got off the bike and whipped out the kick-stand. Hawkins could hear and feel the quick footsteps as the trooper approached.

The *shee-san* bent over him and touched his shoulder, recoiling at the recognition of the American uniform. Mac moved. The *shee-san* shrieked.

Five minutes later Hawkins had stretched the *shee-san*'s tunic and pants over his rolled-up trousers and shirt. He slipped the trooper's goggles over his eyes and put on the ludicrously tiny visor hat, using the chin strap to hold it in place, a cloth pimple sitting on the crew-cut, greyish black hair. Fortunately for his sense of well-being, he had a cigar. He chewed the end to its desired juiciness and lighted up.

He was ready to ride.

The diplomatic attaché ran into the director's office without saying a word to the secretary or even knocking at the door. The director was threading his teeth with dental floss.

'Excuse me, sir. I've just received the instructions from Washington! I knew you'd have to read them!'

The director of the diplomatic mission, Peking, reached for the cable and read it. His eyes widened and his mouth opened in astonishment. A long strand of dental floss, caught in his teeth, extended down to the desk.

He saw the road-block cutting off his entry on to the Peking highway. It was about three quarters of a mile down the semi-paved thoroughfare; a single *shee-san* patrol car and a line of troopers stretching across the road was all he could distinguish through the fogged-up goggles.

As he drew nearer, he could see that the guards were shouting to each other. One trooper stepped in front of the line and began waving his rifle in the air – hysterically – back and forth, a signal for the approaching rider to stop.

There was only one thing for it, thought Hawkins. If you're going to buy a goddamned grave, buy it *big*! Go out with all weapons on repeat-fire, blazing barrels of thunder and lightning; go out with the screams of the Commie bastards ringing in your ears!

Goddamn! He couldn't see for the fucking dust, and his goddamn *foot* kept slipping off the tiny fucking gas pedal.

He slapped his hand to his holster and pulled out the .45.

He couldn't focus worth shit, but by *Christ*, he could squeeze the trigger! He did so repeatedly.

To his astonishment the *shee-san* did not fire back; instead they dived into the mounds of dirt and sand, screaming like hysterical piglets, scampering into and over the mounds of dirt burying their asses from the fire-power of his single .45 weapon.

Goddamn! *Disgraceful!*

Unless his goggles were playing tricks with the dirt and cigar smoke and the onrushing blurs, even the trooper in front – an officer, by Christ; he had to be – even *he* didn't have the balls to fight back.

An *officer*!

MacKenzie kept the bike at top-throttle and exhausted the clip of the .45. He careened up and over a mound of dirt and sand and cascaded on to a sloping hill of grass. As the bike was in midair he glimpsed the blurs of screaming heads beneath him and wished to hell he had more ammo. He twisted the handlebars violently so he could angle down and zoom diagonally back towards the road.

Goddamn! He hit the surface again! He'd broken through the barricade! He was barrel-assing on to the Peking highway!

The flat concrete was a joy. The spinning wheels of the motorcycle hummed; the wind rushed against his face – clear, intoxicating blasts of clean, dustless air which forced the smoke of his cigar into whirling pockets around his ears. Even the goggles were clear now.

He took the next nine miles like a star-spangled meteor through an unknowing Chincom sky. Another mile and he would turn into the northern side streets of Peking. Goddamn! He was going to make it! And then, by Christ, the Commie bastards would find out what an American counter-strike was!

He raced the bike through the crowded streets and careened off the kerb at the entrance to Glorious Flower Square, the final stretch of the mission which stood at the end of the small plaza, fronting the street in alabaster, Oriental splendour. There were, as usual, crowds of Peking-ers and out-of-towners milling about, waiting to catch glimpses of the strange, huge pink people that came and went through the white steel doors inside the medium-sized compound.

It wasn't much of a compound at that; there was no brick wall or high metal fence surrounding the mission. Only a thin latticework of decorative wood, lacquered against the elements, enclosing the clipped grass lawn that fronted the steps.

The protection was in the windows and doors: iron grillework and steel.

MacKenzie revved the bike's engine to maximum, figuring the noise would part the throngs of onlookers.

It did.

The Chinese scattered as he raced down the street.

And Hawkins damn near fell off the bike's saddle at what he saw in front of him; what – in a sense – was rushing towards him at goddamn near fifty miles an hour on that short stretch of pavement in Glorious Flower Square.

There were *three sets of wooden barricades* – elongated horses – in front of the closed latticework gate! Each horizontal plank was a foot or so above the other, forming a receding escalator wall of thick boards backed up by the delicate, filigreed fence.

Standing in a line at port-arms were a dozen or so soldiers, flanked by two officers, all staring straight ahead. At him.

This is it, thought MacKenzie, nothing left but the gesture, the motion – the act itself.

Total defiance!

Goddamn! If he only had some ammo left!

He crouched and headed the bike right into the centre of the barricade; he twisted the bar accelerator to the maximum and pressed the foot choke all the way down.

The speedometer's needle wavered in a violence of its own as it quivered and shot up swiftly towards the end of the dial; man and machine burst through the air corridor like a strange, huge bullet of flesh and steel.

Amid the screams of the hysterical crowds and the scattering of the panicked soldiers, Hawkins yanked the handlebars furiously back and slapped the weight of his body against the rear of the saddle. The front wheel rose off the ground like an abstract, spinning phoenix – followed by a mad extension of tail and rider – and crashed into the upper section of the barricade.

There was a thunderous shattering of wood and latticework as MacKenzie Hawkins shot up, into – and through – the tiers of obstructions, a maniacally effective human cannonball that dragged the rest of the weapon with him.

The bike plummeted down into the path of washed pebbles that led to the steps of the mission. As it did so, MacKenzie was hurled forward, somersaulting over the bars, rolling on the tiny stones until he thudded into the base of the short flight of steps to the white steel door, the cigar still gripped between his teeth.

Any second now the Chincoms would regroup, the fusillade would begin, and the sharp chops of icelike pain would commence, giving him, perhaps, only seconds before oblivion came.

But the firing did not begin. Only louder and louder screaming from the crowds and the soldiers. Oriental heads peered over the mass of wreckage, above the shattered planks, in front of the smashed latticework. Most of the soldiers who had thrown themselves on the ground were now on their hands and knees.

Yet no one fired a weapon. Then MacKenzie understood: he was, technically, within US territory. If he was shot inside the compound it might be construed as an execution on American soil. It could become an international incident. *Goddamn!* He was protected by lacepants fol-de-rol! Diplomatic niceties were keeping him alive!

He scrambled to his feet, ran up the steps to the white steel door and began punching the bell and pounding his hand on the metal panel.

There was no response.

He banged louder and kept his free hand on the bell. He yelled to those inside and after what seemed like minutes, the single rectangular slot in the door was opened.

A pair of wide, frightened eyes peered out.

'For Christ's sake, it's *Hawkins!*' roared MacKenzie, putting his screaming mouth inches in front of the panicked set of eyes. 'Open the goddamned door, you son of a bitch! What the hell are you doing?'

The eyes blinked, but the door did not open.

Hawkins yelled again, and again the eyes blinked. After several seconds the eyes were replaced by trembling lips.

'No one's home, sir,' came the quivering, unbelievable words.

'*What?!*'

'Sorry, General.'

The shaking lips were now replaced by the rapid slamming of metal. The slot was closed.

MacKenzie stood there in temporary shock. Then he started pounding once again and yelling again and punching the bell buttons so hard the Bakelite cracked.

Nothing.

He looked back at the crowds and the soldiers, and became aware of the screams and grins and wave after wave of giggles.

Hawkins jumped down the set of steps and began running across the lawn in front of the building. All the windows were not only shut, but the iron inner shutters had been closed behind the grillework. The whole goddamn mission was sealed tight, an enormous white, rectangular clam.

He raced around the side. It was the same everywhere: closed windows, iron shutters, grillework.

He rounded the back lawn and ran to the large rear entrance. He began pounding the door and yelling louder than he thought he had ever yelled in his life.

Finally the slot opened and another set of eyes appeared – less frightened than those in front but nevertheless wide and disturbed.

'Open this fucking door, goddamn it!'

Once more lips appeared, and now MacKenzie could see the grey moustache. It was the ambassador.

'Get away from here, Hawkins,' said the deep, anglicized voice, cultivated in the Eastern Establishment. 'You're just not operative!'

And the slot was closed.

MacKenzie stood there immobilized. Time and space fused into nothingness. He was vaguely aware that the crowds and the soldiers had moved around the latticework fence at the sides and the rear of the mission.

Without really thinking, he backed away from the entrance and looked up at the outside wall of the building and at the roof.

He could do it, using the grillework of the windows. He jumped to the first window and climbed up the grillework until he reached the next protrusion of crisscrossing bars.

In several minutes he had scaled the side of the building and pulled himself over the edge of the sloping tiled roof.

He trudged up to the apex and looked around.

The flagpole was centred in the grass on the lawn to the

left of the gravel path. The gently waving cloth of Old Glory undulated in the breeze in isolated splendour.

Lieutenant General MacKenzie Hawkins tested the wind and then unzipped his fly.

CHAPTER FOUR

Devereaux smiled at the doorman of the Beverly Hills Hotel, then walked around the huge automobile to the driver's side, tipped the parking attendant, and climbed in behind the wheel, the glare of the sunlight bouncing off the hood. It was all so Southern California: doormen, parking attendants, silent tips, oversized cars, and blinding sunlight.

As was the telephone conversation he had held two hours ago with the first Mrs MacKenzie Hawkins.

He had decided to begin logically, piecing together a progressive disintegration of the man. Surely a pattern would emerge; it would be easier to document this contemporary version of the Rake's Progress if he started with the subject's introduction to the really corrupt world: soft silks and money as opposed to mere killing, torture, and West Point arrogance.

Regina Sommerville Hawkins was that introduction. According to the data banks, Regina was Virginia Hunt Country, spoiled-rich out of Foxcroft and Finch. She had set her cotillion bonnet for the trophy called Hawkins in 1947, when the celebrated youthful warrior of the Bulge had further impressed the nation with dazzling feats on the gridiron. Since Daddy Sommerville owned most of Virginia Beach, and Ginny was an authentic Southern belle – money *and* magnolia, not just the fragrance – the match was easily arranged. The heroic up-from-the-ranks West Pointer was met, overwhelmed, and temporarily subdued by the lilting drawl, large breasts, and indigenous conveniences of this soft but persistent daughter of the Confederacy.

Daddy knew a lot of people in Washington, so, combined with Hawkins's own talents and track record, Regina expected to be a general's wife within six months. A year at best.

In Washington. Or Newport News. Or New York. Or perhaps lovely Hawaii. With servants and uniforms and dances and more servants and . . .

However, Hawkins was peculiar, and Daddy did not know *that* many people who could curb his odd behaviour. The Hawk did not want the la-de-da life of Washington, Newport News, or New York. He wanted to be with his troops. And there was a congressional on his sheet; requests were not denied lightly. Regina found herself in out-of-the-way army camps where her husband furiously trained disinterested draftees for a war that wasn't. So she decided to shed her trophy. Daddy did know enough people to make that easy. Hawkins was transferred to West Germany and Regina's doctors made it clear she could not take the climate. The distance between them just made it feasible to call the whole thing quietly off.

Now, nearly thirty years later, Regina Sommerville Hawkins Clark Madison Greenberg was living in a suburb of Los Angeles called Tarzana with her fourth husband, Emmanuel Greenberg, motion picture producer. On the phone two hours ago she had said to Sam Devereaux:

'Listen, lover, you want to talk about Mac? I'll get the girls together. We usually meet on Thursdays, but what the hell is a day?'

So Sam wrote down the directions to Tarzana and was now on his way in a rented car to Regina's manse. The car radio played *Muddied Waters*, which seemed appropriate.

He found the driveway of the Greenberg residence and entered it, ascending, he was sure, the final crest of the hills. Halfway into the property was an iron gate, operated electrically; it swung open as he approached.

He parked in front of a four-car garage. On the flat asphalt surface there were two Cadillacs, a Silver Cloud Rolls and, in rather obvious counterpoint, a Maserati. Two uniformed chauffeurs were talking idly, leaning against the Rolls. Sam got out of the car with his attaché case and closed the door. 'I'm Mrs Greenberg's broker,' he said to the chauffeurs.

'This is the *place*, man,' laughed the younger chauffeur. 'Merrill, Lynch, and The Girls. That's what they ought to call it.'

'Maybe they will some day. Is that the path to the door?' Sam gestured towards a flagstone walk that seemed to disappear into a short forest of California fern and miniature orange trees.

'Yes, sir,' said the older, dignified chauffeur, as if it were important to cut short the younger man's informality. 'To the right. You'll see it.'

Sam walked down the path to the front door. He had never seen a pink door before, but if he had to see one, he knew it would be in Southern California. He pushed the doorbell and heard the chimes ring out the opening notes of the *Love Story* theme. He wondered if Regina knew the ending.

The door opened and she stood in the foyer, dressed in tight-fitting shorts and an equally tight, translucent shirt that made her huge breasts burst forward in an absolutely challenging fashion.

Though in her forties, Regina was dark haired, tanned, unlined, and lovely, and she carried her frontage with the assurance of youth.

'You're the *may*jor?' she asked, the rank emerging in the low, slow, flat *A* of the Hunt Country.

'Major Sam Devereaux,' he confirmed. It was silly to state the name so formally but his attention was on her two titanic challenges.

'Come on in. I reckon you figured we'd all take offence at a uniform.'

'Something like that, I guess.' Devereaux smiled foolishly, forced his eyes away from the shirt and walked into the foyer.

The foyer was short; the entrance to a huge sunken living

35

room, the far wall of which was nothing but glass. Beyond the glass was a kidney-shaped pool surrounded by a terrace of Italian tile, bordered by an ornate iron fence overlooking the valley.

All this he noticed after, say, fifteen seconds. The first quarter minute was taken up observing three additional pairs of breasts.

Each pair was magnificent in its individual style. Full and Round. Narrow and Pointed. Sloping yet Argumentative.

They belonged in turn to Madge, Lillian, and Anne; Regina Greenberg made the introductions swiftly and pleasantly. And Sam automatically related the breasts – the girls – to the data in his attaché case.

Lillian was number three. Palo Alto, California.

Madge was number two. Tuckahoe, New York.

Ann was number four. Detroit, Michigan.

A nice cross-section of America.

Regina – Ginny – was obviously the oldest, not so much in appearance as in authority. For in truth, all the girls were in that vague age range between middle thirties and the next decade – a span Southern California was expert in obscuring. And each was attractive and commanding in a way slightly different from the others. And each was dressed in sexy Southern California: casual but minutely engineered for that effect.

MacKenzie Hawkins was a man whose tastes and abilities were to be envied.

The courtesies were got over with rapidly, courteously. Sam was offered a drink, which he dared not refuse in this company, and seated in a sunken bean bag from which it was impossible to rise. He managed to place the attaché case at his side, but immediately realized that the contortions required to reach over, pick it up, and open it on his lap would tax Plastic Man, so he hoped it would not be necessary.

'Well, here we all are,' drawled Regina Greenberg. 'Hawkins's Harem, as it were. What does the Pentagon want? Testimonials?'

'There's one we'll all give without reservation,' said Lillian brightly.

'Enthusiastically,' said Madge.

'*Ooob*,' said Anne.

'Yes, well. The general's abilities are enormous,' stammered Sam. 'I mean – well, I didn't expect to meet you all at once. Together. In a group.'

'Oh, we're a real sorority, Major.' Madge, Round and Full, sat in a bean bag next to Sam and reached over, touching his arm. 'Ginny told you. Hawkins's—'

'Yes, I understood,' said Devereaux, swiftly interrupting.

'Talk to one of us about Mac, you talk to all of us,' added Lillian – Narrow and Pointed – from across the room in a particularly mellifluous voice.

'That's right,' cooed Anne – Sloping yet Argumentative – standing outrageously in front of the centre pane of glass on the swimming pool wall.

'In the event we don't have a quorum, I act as spokeswoman,' drawled Regina Greenberg from a jaguar-skin couch against the right wall. 'That's because I was there first and have seniority.'

'Not necessarily in years, dear,' said Madge. 'We won't let you malign yourself.'

'It's difficult to know how to begin,' said Sam, who, nevertheless, plunged into the difficulty. He touched first, gently, on the abstract hardships of dealing with a highly individualistic personality. He slowly, gently explained that MacKenzie Hawkins had involved his government in a most delicate situation for which a solution had to be found. And although said government was filled with undeniable and undying gratitude for General Hawkins's extraordinary contributions, it was often necessary to study a man's background to help him – and his government – resolve delicate situations. Frequently the partially negative led to the positive, if only to balance and accentuate the affirmative.

'So you want to screw him,' recapped Regina Greenberg. 'It had to happen, didn't it, girls?'

There was a chorus of yesses and uh-huhs.

Sam knew better than to offer a flat denial; there was more intelligence – or perception – in that room than might have been evident at first. 'Why do you say that?' he asked Ginny.

'Gawd, Mayjor!' replied Titanic. 'Mac's been on a collision course with the high-brass pricky-shits for years! He sees through their manure piles. That's why they like it when those Northern liberals make him out a joke. But Mac's no joke!'

'Nobody thinks he's funny right now, Mrs Greenberg. Let me assure you.'

'What's Mac done?' The question was put defensively by Anne, still silhouetted splendidly at the window.

'He defaced—' Sam stopped; bad choice of word. 'He destroyed a national monument belonging to a government we're trying to maintain a détente with. Like our Lincoln Memorial.'

'Was he drunk?' asked Lillian, eyes and narrow frontage levelled at Sam; two sets of sharp artillery.

'He says he wasn't.'

'Then he wasn't,' stated Madge positively from the bean bag beside him.

'Mac can drink a whole battalion under a mess hall slop shoot.' Ginny Greenberg's drawl was punctuated by her affirmatively nodding head. 'But he never, *never* plays the whisky game to the disadvantage of that uniform.'

'He wouldn't put it into words, Major,' said Lillian, 'but it was a stronger rule than any oath he ever took.'

'For two reasons,' added Ginny. 'He surely didn't want to disgrace his rank, but just as important, he didn't like for the pricky-shits to laugh at him because of booze.'

'So you see,' stated Madge in the bean bag, 'Mac didn't do what they said he did to the Lincoln Memorial. He just wouldn't.'

Sam looked back and forth at the girls. Not one of these ex-Mrs Hawkinses was going to help him; none would utter a negative word about the man.

Why?

He struggled like hell to get out of the bean bag and tried to assume the stance of a cross-examining attorney. A very soft, gentle attorney. He paced slowly in front of the massive window. Anne went to the bean bag.

'Naturally,' he began, smiling, 'these circumstances, this group here, evoke several questions. Not that you're under any obligation to answer, but frankly, speaking personally, I don't understand. Let me explain—'

'Let *me answer*,' interrupted Regina. 'You can't figure out why Hawkins's Harem protects its namesake. Right?'

'Right.'

'As spokeswoman,' continued Ginny, receiving nods of assent from the others, 'I'll be brief and to the point. Mac Hawkins is one great guy – in bed and out, and don't snicker at the bed because most marriages haven't got it. You can't live with the son of a bitch, but that's not his fault.

'Mac gave us something we'll never forget because it's with us every day. He taught us to break our moulds. Sounds simple, doesn't it? "Break your mould." But, lover, it sets you *free*. "You're your own goddamned inventory," he used to say. "There's nothing you *have* to do and nothing you *can't* do; use your inventory and work like hell."

'Now, I don't think that all of us believe that's holy writ. But by gawd, he made each one of us try a lot harder. He set us free before it was chic and we haven't done badly. So, you see, there's not one of us – if Mac came knocking at the door – who wouldn't accommodate him. You dig?'

'I dig,' replied Sam quietly.

The telephone rang. Regina reached behind the couch to the French phone on the marble table. She turned to Sam. 'It's for you.'

Sam looked a bit startled. 'I left your number with the hotel but I didn't expect...' He walked to the table and took the phone.

'He *what*?!' Blood drained from Sam's face. He listened again. 'Jesus! He *didn't*!' And then in the weariness of aftershock: 'Yes, sir. I can see he most certainly did ... I'll

39

go back to the hotel and await instructions. Unless you'd rather turn this over to someone else; my tour is up in a month, sir. I see. Five days at the outside, sir.'

He hung up and turned to Hawkins's Harem. Those four magnificent pairs of mammaries that both invited and defied description.

'We're not going to need you, ladies. Although Mac Hawkins may.'

'I'm your only contact with Sixteen-hundred, Major,' said the young lieutenant as he paced – somewhat childishly, thought Sam – the plush Beverly Hills Hotel room. 'You can refer to me as Lodestone. No names, please.'

'Lieutenant Lodestone, Sixteen-hundred. Has a nice ring to it,' said Devereaux, pouring himself another bourbon.

'I'd go easy on the alcohol.'

'Why don't you go to China instead? Of *me*, that is.'

'You do have a long, long flight.'

'Not if *you* make it, I don't.'

'In a way, I wish I could. Do you realize there are seven hundred million potential consumers over there? I'd really like to get a see-you shot of that market.'

'A who?'

'Close-up look. A real peek-see.'

'Ohh. *C-U*. Not see-you—'

'What an opportunity!' The lieutenant stood by the hotel window, his hands clasped behind his back. *Caveat consumer*.

'Then *go*, for Christ's sake! In thirty-two days I've got a permit to get out of this Disneyland and I don't want to trade my uniform in for a Chinese smock!'

'I'm afraid I can't, sir. Sixteen-hundred needs pro-PR now. All the other slambangs are gone. Some are turning out a crackerjack house organ at Dannemora ... Damn!' The lieutenant turned from the window and walked to the writing-desk where there were half a dozen photographs, five by seven. 'It's all here, Major. All you need. They're a little hazy, but they show Brand X, all right! He certainly can't deny it now.'

Sam looked at the blurred but definable telephotos from Peking. 'He almost reached, didn't he?'

'Disgraceful!' The lieutenant winced as he studied the photographs. 'There's nothing left to be said.'

'Except that he almost made it.' Sam crossed to an armchair and sat down with his bourbon. The lieutenant followed him.

'Your head IG investigator in Saigon will fly his reports directly to you in Tokyo. Take them with you to Peking. They've got a lot of real dirt.' The young officer smiled his genuine smile. 'Just in case you need some final stickum for the coffin.'

'Gee, you're a nice kid. Ever meet your father?' Sam drank a great deal of his bourbon.

'You mustn't personalize it, Major. It's an objective operation and we have the input. It's all part of the—'

'Don't say again—'

'. . . game plan.' Lodestone swallowed the words. 'Sorry. And anyway, if you do personalize it, what more do you want? The man's a maniac. A dangerous egotistical madman who's interfering violently with peaceful pursuits.'

'I'm a lawyer, Lieutenant, not an avenging angel. Your maniac made several contributions to other – game plans. He's got a lot of people in his corner. I met with eight – *four* – this afternoon.' Sam looked at his glass; where did the bourbon go?

'Not any more, he doesn't,' said the officer flatly.

'He doesn't what?'

'Whatever constituency he had will disappear.'

'Constituency? He's a politician?' Sam decided he needed another drink. He couldn't follow this Buster Brown any longer. So why not get really drunk?

'He *peed* on the Stars and Stripes! That's a Peoria no-no!'

'Did he really reach?'

'We're sending you to China,' continued Lodestone, overlooking the question, 'in the fastest way possible. Phantom jet aircraft over the northern route, stops in Juneau and the Aleutians, into Tokyo. From there a supply carrier to Peking. I've brought all the papers you need from Washington.'

Devereaux mumbled into his bourbon. 'I don't like moo goo gai pan and I hate egg rolls . . .'

'May I suggest you get some rest, sir? It's almost twenty-three hundred and we have to leave for the airbase at oh four hundred. You take off at dawn.'

'Wish I'd said that, Lodestone. Nice ring to it. Five hours. And you're down the hall but not *in here*.'

'Sir?' The young man cocked his head.

'I'm going to give you an order. Go away. I don't want to see you until you come to sew in my name tags.'

'What?'

'Get the hell out of here.' And then Sam remembered and his eyes – though slightly glazed – were laughing. 'You know what you are, Lieutenant? You're a pricky-shit. A real, honest-to-God pricky-shit. Now I know what it means!'

Four hours . . . He wondered.

It was worth a try. But first he needed another drink.

He poured it and walked to the writing-desk and laughed at the Peking telephotos. The son of a bitch had flair, no question about it. But he was not at the desk to look at the photographs; he opened the drawer and took out his notebook. He turned the pages and did his best to focus on his own handwriting. He walked to the telephone by the bed, dialled nine, and then the number on the page.

'Hello?' The voice was magnolia-soft and Sam could actually smell the oleander blossoms.

'Mrs Greenberg? This is Sam Devereaux—'

'Well, how're *you*?' Regina's greeting was positively enthusiastic; there was no attempt to conceal her pleasure that the caller was a man. 'We were all wondering which one you'd call. I'm really flattered, *May*jor! I mean, actually, I'm the elder stateswoman. I'm really touched.'

Her husband was probably out, thought Sam through the bourbon, warmed by the memory of her challenging, translucent shirt.

'That's very kind of you. You see, in a little while I'm going to go on a long, long trip. Over oceans and mountains and more oceans and islands and . . .' *Jesus!* He hadn't figured out how to put it; he hadn't really been sure he could dial her number. Goddamn bourbon fantasies! 'Well, it's sheecrit – *secret*. Very covert. But I'm going to talk to your – namesake?'

'Of *cawsse*, lover! And naturally, you didn't get half a cha*y*nce to ask all those important government questions. I understand, I *really do*.'

'Well, several items came up, one in particular—'

'It usually does. I do believe I should do all I can to help the government in its delicate situation. You're at the Beverly Hills?'

'Yes, ma'm. Room eight twenty.'

'Wait a sec.' She put her hand over the receiver, but Sam could hear her calling out. '*Manny!* There's a national emergency. I have to go to town.'

CHAPTER FIVE

'Major! Major Devereaux! Your phone is off the hook. That's a no-no.'

An incessant, ridiculously loud knocking accompanied Lodestone's nasal screams.

'What the gawd-almighty hell is *that*?' asked Regina Greenberg, nudging Sam under the covers. 'It sounds like an unoiled piston.'

Devereaux opened his eyes into the visual abyss of a hangover. 'That, dear patron saint of Tarzana, is the voice of the evil people. They surface when the earth churns.'

'Do you know what time it is? Call the hotel police, for heaven's sake.'

'No,' said Sam, reluctantly getting out of bed. 'Because if I do, that gentleman will call the joint chiefs of staff. I think they're scared to death of him. They're merely professional killers; he's in advertising.'

And before Devereaux could really focus, hands had dressed him, cars had driven him, men had yelled at him, and he was strapped into an Air Force Phantom jet.

They all smiled. Everyone in China smiled. With their lips more than their eyes, thought Sam.

He was met at the Peking airfield by an American diplomatic vehicle, escorted by two flanking Chinese army cars and eight Chinese army officers. All smiling; even the vehicles.

The two nervous Americans that came with the diplomatic car were attachés. They were anxious to get back to the mission; neither was comfortable around the Chinese troops.

Nor did either attaché care to discuss very much of anything except the weather, which was dull and overcast. Whenever Sam brought up the subject of MacKenzie Hawkins – and why not? he had relieved himself on *their* roof – their mouths became taut and they shook their heads in short, lateral jerks and pointed their fingers below the windows at various areas of the automobile. And laughed at nothing.

Finally Devereaux realized they were convinced that the diplomatic car was bugged. So Sam laughed, too. At nothing.

If the automobile *was* fitted with electronic surveillance, and if someone *was* listening, thought Devereaux, that person was probably conjuring up a picture of three adult males passing dirty comics back and forth.

And if the ride from the airfield seemed strange to Sam, his half-hour meeting with the ambassador at the diplomatic mission in Glorious Flower Square was ludicrous.

He was ushered into the building by his cackling escorts, greeted solemnly by a group of serious-faced Americans who had gathered in the hallway like onlookers in a zoological laboratory – unsure of their safety but fascinated by the new animal brought in for observation – and propelled quickly down a corridor to a large door that was obviously the entrance to the ambassador's office. Once inside, the ambassador greeted him with a rapid handshake, simultaneously raising a finger over his slightly quivering moustache. One of the escorts removed a small metal device about the size of a pack of cigarettes and began waving it around the windows as though blessing the panes of glass. The ambassador watched the man.

'I can't be sure,' whispered the attaché.

'Why not?' asked the diplomat.

'The needle moved a touch, but it could be the loud-speakers in the square.'

'Damn! We have to get more sophisticated scanners.

Scramble a memo to Washington.' The ambassador took Sam's elbow, leading him back to the door. 'Come with me, General.'

'I'm a major.'

'That's nice.'

The ambassador propelled Sam out of the office, across the corridor to another door, which he opened, and then preceded Devereaux down a steep flight of stone steps into a large basement. There was a single light bulb on the wall; the ambassador snapped it on and led Sam past a number of wooden crates to another door in the barely visible wall. It was heavy and the diplomat had to put his foot against the surrounding cement in order to pull it open.

Inside was a long-out-of-use, walk-in refrigerator, now serving as a wine cellar.

The ambassador entered and struck a match. On one of the racks was a candle, half burned down. The ambassador held the flame to the wick, and the light swelled flickeringly against the walls and the racks. The wine was not the best, observed Devereaux silently.

The ambassador reached out and yanked Sam into the centre of the small enclosure and then pulled the heavy door almost shut, but not completely.

His lean, aristocratic features accentuated by the wavering flame of the candle, the ambassador smiled apologetically.

'We may strike you as a touch paranoid, but it's not the case at all, I can assure you.'

'Oh, no, sir. This is very cosy. And quiet.'

Sam tried to return the ambassador's smile. And for the next thirty minutes he received his last instructions from his government. It was an appropriate place to get them: deep underground, the surrounding earth inhabited by worms that never saw the light of day.

Armed with his briefcase and no courage whatsoever, Devereaux walked out the mission's white steel door, to be greeted by a Chinese officer who waved at him from the foot of the path. Sam saw for the first time the evidence of wreckage –

large splinters of wood, several angle irons lying about on the lawn.

The officer stood outside the border of the property and grinned a flat grin. 'My name is Lin Shoo, Major Deveroxx. I will escort you to Lieutenant General Hawkins. My car, should you please.'

Sam climbed into the back seat of the army staff vehicle and settled back, his case on his lap. As opposed to the nervous Americans, Lin Shoo was not at all inhibited about talking. The subject quickly became MacKenzie Hawkins.

'A highly volatile individual, Major Deveroxx,' said the Chinese, shaking his head. 'He is possessed by dragons.'

'Has anyone tried reasoning with him?'

'I, myself. With great and charming persuasion.'

'But not with great or charming success, I gather.'

'What can I tell you? He assaulted me. It wasn't proper at all.'

'And you want a full-scale trial because of *that*? The ambassador said you were adamant. A trial or a lot of hazzerai.'

'Hazzerai?'

'It means trouble. It's Jewish.'

'You don't look Jewish . . .'

'What about this trial?' interrupted Sam. 'Are the charges centred on assault?'

'Oh, no. That would not be philosophically consistent. We expect to suffer *physically*. Through struggle and suffering there is strength.' Lin Shoo smiled; Devereaux didn't know why. 'The general will be tried for crimes against the motherland.'

'An extension of the original charge,' said Sam, making a quiet statement.

'Far more complex, however,' replied Lin Shoo, his smile fading into resigned depression. 'Wilful destruction of national shrines – not unlike your Lincoln Memorials. He escaped once, you know. With a stolen truck he ran into the statuary on Son Tai Square. He is now charged with defacement of venerated artistic craftsmanship – the statuary he ran into was sculptured after the designs of the chairman's wife. And there can be no counter-argument concerning drugs for this. He was seen by too many diplomatic people. He made great sums of noise in Son Tai.'

'He'll claim extenuating circumstances.' No harm in testing, thought Devereaux.

'As with assault, there is no such thing.'

'I see.' Sam didn't but there was no point in pursuing it. 'What could he draw?'

'How so? Draw? The sculpture?'

'Prison. What sort of prison sentence? How long?'

'Roughly four thousand, seven hundred and fifty years.'

'*What?* You might as well execute him!'

'Life is precious to the sons and daughters of the motherland. Every living thing is capable of contribution. Even a vicious criminal like your maniac imperialist general. He could have many productive years in Mongolia.'

'Now just hold on!' Devereaux changed his position abruptly to look Lin Shoo full in the face. He could not be sure, but he thought he heard a metallic click from the front seat. Not unlike the springing of a pistol's safety catch.

He decided not to think about it. It was better that way. He returned his attention to Lin Shoo.

'That's *crazy*! You know that's just plain dumb! What the hell are you talking about? Four thousand – *Mongolia*?' Devereaux's attaché case fell out of his lap; he heard – again – the metallic click. 'I mean, let's be reasonable . . .' Devereaux's words drifted off nervously. He picked up the leather case.

'These are the legitimate penalties for the crimes,' said Lin Shoo. 'No foreign government has the right to interfere with the internal discipline of its host nation. It is inconceivable. However, in this particular case, perhaps, it is not entirely unreasonable.'

Sam paused before speaking; he watched the scowl on Lin Shoo's face return slightly, ever so slightly, to its previous polite, unhumorous smile. 'Do I detect the beginnings of an out-of-court settlement?'

'How so? Out of court?'

'A compromise. Do we talk about a compromise?'

Lin Shoo now allowed the scowl to float away. His smile came as close to being genial as Devereaux could imagine. 'Please, yes. A compromise would be enlightening. There is strength, also, in enlightenment.'

'And maybe a little less than four thousand years in Mongolia – in the compromise?'

'Fraught with possibilities. Should you succeed where others have not. After all, it is to our natural advantage to reach a compromise.'

'I hope you know how right you are. Hawkins is a national hero.'

'So was your Speero Agaroo, Major. Your President said so himself.'

'What can you offer? Dispense with the trial?'

Lin Shoo dropped his smile, too suddenly for comfort, thought Sam.

'We cannot do that. The trial has been announced. Too many people in the international community know of it.'

'You want to save face, or do you want to sell gas?' Devereaux sat back; the Chinese officer did want a compromise.

'A little of both is a compromise, is it not?'

'What's your little? In the event I can get Hawkins to be reasonable.'

'A reduction of the sentence would be one consideration.' Lin Shoo's smile returned.

'From four thousand to twenty-five hundred years?' asked Devereaux. 'You're all heart. Let's start with probation; I'll concede acquittal.'

'How so? Probation?'

'I'll explain later; you'll like it. Give me some real incentive to work on Hawkins.' Sam fingered the top of his attaché case, tapping his nails on the leather. It was a silly thing that usually split adversaries' concentration and sometimes produced a hasty concession.

'A Chinese trial takes many forms. Long, ornate, and

quite ritualistic. Or very short, swift, and devoid of excess. Three months or three hours. I can, perhaps, bring about the latter—'

'That *and* probation, I'll buy,' said Sam quickly. 'That's incentive enough to make me want to work real hard. You've got a deal.'

'This probation. You will have to define more legalistically.'

'Basically, you not only save face and sell gas, but you can show how tough you are and *still* be heroes in the world press. All at the same time. What could be better than that?'

Lin Shoo smiled. Devereaux wondered briefly if there wasn't more understanding beyond that smile than the Chinese cared to show. Then he dismissed the thought; Lin Shoo distracted him by asking a question and answering it before Sam could speak.

'What could be better than that? Having General Hawkins out of China. Yes, *that* would be better.'

'What a coincidence. Because that's one insignificant part of probation.'

'Really?' Lin Shoo looked straight ahead.

'You, I can handle,' said Sam, almost reflectively. 'I've still got to worry about Brand X.'

CHAPTER SIX

The cell could be seen clearly through a single pane of unidirectional glass embedded in the heavy steel door. There was a western-style bed, a writing-desk, recessed overhead lights, both a desk lamp and bedside light, and a large rug on the floor. There was an open door on the right wall that led to a small bathroom, and a horizontal clothes rack on the left. The room was no more than ten by twelve feet, but all things considered, far grander than Sam had visualized.

The only thing missing was MacKenzie Hawkins.

'You see,' said Lin Shoo, 'how considerate we are; how well appointed are the general's accommodations?'

'I'm impressed,' replied Devereaux. 'Except I don't see the general.'

'Oh, he is there.' The Chinese smiled and spoke softly. 'He has his little games. He hears the footsteps and conceals himself on either side of the door. Twice the guards were alarmed and made ill-considered entrances. Fortunately, there were several to overcome the general's strength. Now all the shifts are alerted. His meals are delivered through a slot.'

'He's still trying . . .' Sam chuckled. 'He's something.'

'He is many things,' added Lin Shoo enigmatically as he approached a webbed circle beneath the unidirectional glass and pushed a red button. 'General Hawkins? Please, General, show yourself. It is your good and gracious friend, Lin Shoo. I know you are beside the door, General.'

'*Up your ass, slant eyes!*'

Lin Shoo released the button momentarily and turned to Devereaux. 'He is not always the essence of courtesy.' The Chinese returned to the speaker and pushed the button again. 'Please, General, I have a countryman of yours with me. A representative of your government. From the armed forces of your nation—'

'You better check her goddamned purse! Maybe up her skirt! Her lipstick might be a bomb!' came the shout from the unseen general officer.

Lin Shoo turned back to Devereaux in bewilderment. Sam gently moved the Chinese out of the way, pushed the button himself, and yelled into the speaker.

'Get off it, you chicken fucker! You're a goddamn bruise on my prick! Show that hairy ass you call a face or I'll open the slop-shoot and drop in that fucking lipstick! I'll *frag* you, you miserable son of a bitch! – Incidentally, Regina Greenberg says hello.'

The immense head of MacKenzie Hawkins slowly appeared in the pane of unidirectional glass. It emerged from the side, huge, crew-cut, leather-lined. Mac's expression was one of utter consternation. A half-chewed cigar was gripped between his teeth, beneath wide, blood-shot eyes that betrayed disbelieving curiosity.

'How so? What do you say?' Lin Shoo's controlled lips were parted in astonishment.

'It's a highly classified military code,' said Devereaux. 'We only employ it under extreme conditions.'

'I will not pursue the matter; it would not be courteous. If you flip the lever on the side of the glass, General Hawkins will see you. When you feel comfortable, I shall admit you. However, I will remain outside, please.'

Sam pushed the small handle on the side of the glass; there was a click. The large, squinting face reacted with instant hostility. Devereaux had the feeling that Hawkins was observing something very obscene but unimportant: Sam, the military accident.

Devereaux nodded to Lin Shoo. The Chinese reached out with both hands, as if to pull with one and push with the other, and unlatched the door. The heavy steel panel opened; Sam walked in.

To an enormous fist that came rushing towards him, on a direct collision course with his left eye. The impact came; the room, the world, the galaxy spun out of orbit into the shimmering of a hundred thousand splotches of white light.

Sam felt the wet cloth over his face before he felt the pain in his head, especially his eye, and he thought that was strange. He reached up, pulled the cloth away and blinked. All he saw at first was a white ceiling. The centre light hurt his head, especially his left eye. He realized he was on a bed, so he rolled over and everything came back to him.

Hawkins was at the writing-desk, papers and photographs scattered about the top. The general was reading from a sheaf of stapled papers.

Devereaux did not have to move his painful head farther to know that his opened attaché case was somewhere near the general. Nevertheless, he did so and saw it at Hawkins's feet. Open and upside down. Empty. The contents in front of the general.

Sam cleared his throat. He could not think of anything else to do. Hawkins turned; his expression was not pleasant. Somehow absent was that welcoming, manly bond of recognition between comrades at arms.

'You little pricky-shits have been busy, haven't you?'

Painfully, Devereaux swung his legs over the side of the bed and touched his left eye. He touched it gently, mainly because he could barely see out of it. 'I may be a shit, General, but I'm not so little, as one day I hope to prove to you. Christ, I hurt.'

'*You* want to prove something' – Hawkins gestured at the papers and allowed himself the inkling of a cynical grin – 'to *me*? With what you *know* about me? You've got moxie, boy. I'll say that for you.'

'That phrase is about as antediluvian as you are,' muttered Sam as he stood up. Unsteadily. 'You enjoying the reading material?'

'It's some goddamned record! They'll probably want to make another movie about me.'

'Leavenworth Productions. Film processed in the prison laundry. You *are* a bona fide fruitcake.' Devereaux pointed to a blanket draped over the door covering the pane of unidirectional glass. 'Is that smart?' He gestured at the blanket.

'It's not dumb. It confuses them. The oriental mind has two very pronounced pressure points: confusion and embarrassment.' Hawkins's eyes were level.

The statement startled Sam. Perhaps it was Hawkins's choice of words, or maybe the quiet intelligence behind the voice. Whatever it was, it was unexpected. 'I mean it's a little useless; the room is bugged. Bugged, hell! All they have to do is push a red button and they can hear everything we say.'

'Wrong, soldier,' replied the general as he got out of the chair. 'If you *are* a soldier and not a goddamn lace-pants. Come here.' Hawkins walked over to the blanket and folded back, first, a corner on the right, then the opposite section of the cloth on the left. In both small areas were barely visible holes in the wall, now very visible with wet toilet paper shoved into the centres. Hawkins dropped the two sections of the blanket and then pointed to six additional plugs of wet toilet tissue – two on each wall, upper and lower – and grinned his leather-lined grin. 'I've gone over this fucking cell palm-spread by palm-spread. I've blocked out each mike; there aren't any others. Naturally, I didn't touch 'em before. See how careful the goddamn monkeys were? Even got one right over the pillow in case I talked in my sleep. That was the toughest to spot.'

Grudgingly, Sam nodded his approval. And then he thought of the obvious. 'If you *have* plugged every one, they'll race in here and move us. You should realize that.'

'You should think better. Electronic surveillance in close areas is wired terminally into a single unit. First, they'll figure they've got a short in the unit circuit, which will take 'em an hour to trace if they don't have to break down the walls and can do it with sensors and that'll confuse 'em.

Then, if they rule out a short, they'll guess *I* plugged 'em and that'll embarrass 'em. Confusion and embarrassment; the pressure points. It'll take 'em another hour to figure how to get us somewhere else without admitting error. We've got at least two hours. So you better do some pretty fine explaining in that time.'

Devereaux had the distinct feeling that he had better be capable of some pretty fine explaining. Hawkins was a wily pro and Sam did not relish any confrontation. Certainly not physical or, he was beginning to suspect, mental.

'Don't you want to hear about Regina Greenberg?'

'I've read your notes. You've got lousy handwriting.'

'I'm a lawyer; all lawyers have lousy handwriting. It's part of the bar exam. Also I didn't intend to have them typed up.'

'I should hope not,' said Hawkins. 'You've also got a dirty mind.'

'You've got terrific taste.'

'I don't discuss former wives.'

'They've discussed *you*,' countered Sam.

'I know the girls. You didn't get anything you could use. Not from the girls, you didn't. Anything else you got is none of my business.'

'Do I detect a moral position?'

'In my own crude way. I got a little class, boy.' Hawkins pointed to the desk; his arm, hand, and extended finger all were very steady. 'Now, start explaining that stuff.'

'What's there to explain? You've read it, you say. Do I have to tell you that it represents an airtight case of *persona non grata* on one side, and a large embarrassment for the other? If I do, I just have.' Devereaux touched his eye; it hurt like hell, so he sat down again on the bed.

'That stuff in Indochina,' growled Hawkins, walking to the desk and picking up the stapled pages, 'it's written up like I was working for the fucking gooks!'

'I wouldn't go that far. It raises certain questions as to your methods of operation—'

That's going *that* far, boy!' interrupted the general. 'I was either working for 'em or working with *both* sides, or just

55

pocketing half the pouch money in Southeast Asia! *Or* I was so *dumb* I didn't know what I was doing at all!'

'*Ahh!*' sang Sam in a lilting, false tremolo. 'Now we are beginning to understand, said Alice to Cock Robin. A military, really military, man with two Congressional Medals of Honour is a dubious bet for traitor. But all that combat, all those banging noises and that scurrying behind the lines and capture and torture and primitive means of brutal survival – the cumulative effect of all *that* would certainly flip out said hero right into laughing land. Very sad, but the human psyche can take only so much.'

'Horseshit!' roared Hawkins. 'My head's screwed on a hell of a lot tighter than those fuckers who asked for all this crap!'

'Two points for the general,' said Devereaux, holding up his fingers in the *V* sign. 'I hereby state for the record that the general's head is screwed better than anyone at Sixteen-hundred. And, I might add, so is the general.'

'What does that mean, boy?'

'Oh, come on, Hawkins. You're finished! How and why it happened, I don't know. I just know that you got in the way at a rotten time; you made too much noise and you are *expendable*! Not only expendable, but a goddamned pawn that Sixteen-hundred's giving up loud and clear. You're even an *example!*'

'Horseshit, again! Wait'll the Pentagon gets wind of this!'

'They've – *it's* – already got its nostrils full. The brass noses are colliding with each other, running to the deodorant factories. You don't exist, General! Except maybe as a wayward memory.' Sam got up from the bed. The pain in the eye was spreading throughout his head again.

'You can't sell that and I won't buy it,' said Hawkins defensively, his voice indicating a slightly diminished confidence. 'I've got friends. I've got a career sheet that reads like a recruiting poster. Goddamn it, soldier, I'm a general officer who came up from the ranks – from the fucking mud in Belgium! They won't treat me this way!'

'I'm not a soldier. I'm a lawyer and I'm telling you you've

been treated – with several layers of forget-me gas. Those telephotos from your buddies in Peking sealed the whole ball of wax. You've bubbled over.'

'They've got to prove it!'

'They've got that, too. I was given it in a pitch-black wine cellar about an hour ago. By a psychotic holding a candle. A very solid citizen. They've got you.'

Hawkins squinted his eyes and removed the chewed, unlit cigar from his mouth. 'How?'

'"Medical records." That's the hard evidence. Psychiatric and physical. "Stress collapse" is only the beginning. The Defence Department will issue a statement that says, in essence, you were purposely placed in ambivalent situations so they could ascertain the development. "Schizoid progression", I think it's called. Conflicting objectives like the Indochina stuff. Also those pictures of you pissing on the mission's roof have a very complicated psychiatric explanation.'

'I've got a *better* one. I was goddamned angry! Wait'll I give my version.'

'You won't get a chance to tell it. If the game plan becomes an issue, the President plans to go on the air, praise your past, show your current medical records – with heartbreaking reluctance, of course – and ask the country to pray for you.'

'Couldn't happen.' The general shook his head confidentially. '*No* one believes a president anymore.'

'Maybe not, but he's got the buttons. Not his own, maybe, but enough others. You'll be strapped down in a Nike silo, if he says so.' Sam saw that there was a metal mirror in the small cubicle that housed the toilet. He walked towards the door.

'But why should he *do* it? Why would anyone *let* him do it?' Hawkins's cigar was held limply in his hand.

Devereaux looked at the size and hue of the shiner over his left eye. 'Because we need gas,' he replied.

'Huh?' Hawkins dropped his cigar on the rug. Obviously

without thinking, he stepped on it, grinding it into the surface. 'Gas?'

'It's too complicated. Never mind.' Sam pressed the sensitive flesh around his eye with his fingers. He hadn't had a mouse in over fifteen years; he wondered how long it would take for the swelling to recede. 'Just accept the situation for what it is and make the best deal you can. You haven't got much choice.'

'You mean I'm supposed to lie down and *take* it?'

Devereaux walked out of the toilet, stopped and sighed. 'I'd say the immediate objective was to keep you from lying down in Mongolia. For some four thousand-plus years. If you cooperate, maybe I can pull it off.'

'Out of China?'

'Yes.'

'How much cooperation? With the gooks *and* Washington?' Hawkins's squint was very pronounced.

'A lot. All the way down the pike.'

'Out of the army?'

'No point in staying. Is there, really?'

'Goddamn!'

'I agree. But where does it get you? There's a big world out of that uniform. Enjoy it.'

Hawkins crossed back to the desk in angry silence. He picked up one of the photographs, shrugged and dropped it. He reached into his pocket for a fresh cigar. 'Goddamn, boy, you're not thinking again. You're a lawyer, maybe, but like you say, you're no soldier. A field commander sucks in a hostile patrol, he doesn't feed it, he cuts it down. Nobody's going to let me enjoy. They'll put me in that Nike silo you mentioned. To keep me from talking.'

Devereaux exhaled a long breath through his lips. 'It's just possible I can build a shield acceptable to all parties. After you went down the pike over *here*. Full confession, public apology, the works.'

'Goddamn!'

'Mongolia, General . . .'

Hawkins bit into the cigar; the bullet between his teeth, thought Sam.

'What's a "shield"?'

'Off the top of my head, I figure a letter to the secretary of the army, accompanied by a tape of your reading it – verified by voice print. In the letter, *and* the tape, you state that in moments of complete lucidity you're aware of your illness – et cetera, et cetera.'

Hawkins stared at Devereaux. 'You're out of your mind!'

'There are a lot of Nike silos in the Dakotas.'

'Jesus!'

'It's not as bad as it sounds. The letter and the tape will be buried in the Pentagon. Used only if you publicly make waves. Both to be returned, say, in five years. How about it?'

Hawkins reached into his pocket for a book of matches. He struck one and a cloud of pungent smoke nearly fogged out his face; but his voice was clear behind it. 'Down this Chinese pike of yours, there's no talk about that psychiatric bullshit. No one tries to make me out a nut.'

'Hell, no. Nothing like that. Simple fatigue.' Devereaux paced back and forth in the small enclosure as he so often did in conference rooms, weaving the fabric of defence. 'A little booze, maybe; that's sympathetic, even kind of cute when the client's a ballsy type.' Sam stopped, clarifying his thoughts. 'The Chinese would prefer an ideological approach; it'd soften them up. You saw the light. They've been generous to you, nice to you. The People's regime is dandy. *And* tolerant. You didn't realize that. You're really sorry for all those nasty things you've said for a quarter of a century.'

'Goddamn! You make me *bleed*, boy!' With a technique that escaped Sam, Hawkins actually chewed on his cigar as he roared. And then he removed it and lowered his voice. 'I know, I know——. The silos or Mongolia. *Jesus!*'

Devereaux watched the man – painfully. He took several steps towards him and spoke softly. 'You've been squeezed, General. By righteous pieces of plastic; nobody knows that better than I do. I've read your file and I agree with maybe one-fiftieth of what you stand for; in many ways I think you're a menace. But one thing you're not is a manipulator. And you're no joke. Remember what you told the girls? You said everyone's his own inventory. That says a lot to me. So let me help you. I'm no soldier, but I'm a damned good lawyer.'

Hawkins turned away. In embarrassment, thought Sam. When the words came, there was a defencelessness about them that made him wince.

'Don't know why I'm so concerned about what anybody says – or why I don't settle for a silo *or* Mongolia. Goddamn, boy, I've spent thirty-some years in this man's army. You take off the uniform – no matter what you put me into – I'm as naked as a plucked duck. I only *know* the army; I don't know anything else, not trained for anything when you come right down to it. Never spent any time with the technological – except little stuff in G-two, things like that. Don't know anything about fancy doings like "negotiations". All I know how to do is fuck up and trap pouch thieves – those Indochina reports are right about that: I outsmarted the KGU, the CIA, the ARVN, and even the sellouts on the Saigon general staff. But that's different. I can handle personnel, I suppose. But they always gave me the misfits, the stockade products; if they'd been civilians they wouldn't be allowed on the streets. I was always good with them. I could control those devious bastards; I could put myself in their slimy shoes and *use* 'em, *use* their goddamned angling. But there's nothing I can do on the outside.'

'That doesn't sound like the man who said everyone's his own inventory. You're better than that.'

Hawkins turned and faced Sam. He spoke slowly, reflectively. 'Shit, boy. You know what? The only goddamned thing I'm trained for is to be a crook, maybe. And I'd probably fuck that up because I don't give that much of a damn about money.'

'You look for challenges. Talented people always do. Money's a by-product; usually the challenge there is in the amounts, what they represent, not what they can purchase.'

'I guess so.' Hawkins took a deep breath and stretched; his resignation was coming into focus for him, thought Devereaux. He walked past Sam aimlessly, humming the opening notes of *Mairzy-Doats*. Devereaux knew from long experience with clients to let the moment subside, allow the client time to fully accept the decision.

'Wait a minute, boy. *Wait* a minute—.' Hawkins took the cigar out of his mouth and levelled his eyes with Sam. 'Everybody wants my cooperation. The Chinks, those assholes in Washington – probably a dozen gas conglomerates. I mean they not only *want* it, they *need* it. So much so they'll fake records, build a case—. That ball of wax got out of *control*—'

'Now hold on. What we're faced with—'

'No, *you* hold on, boy! I'm not going to give you a hard time. I'll make you a better deal than you thought possible.' Hawkins shoved the cigar between his teeth, his eyes alive, his voice thoughtful yet intense. 'I'll do exactly – *say* exactly, whatever you bastards want me to say and do. Word for word, gesture for gesture. I'll kiss every butt on Son Tai Square, if you want. But *I* want two things. Out of China *and* the army – they go together. And one thing more: three days in the G-two files back in D.C. Just my *own*, nobody else's. What the hell, I wrote *up* the goddamned things! A last look at my contributions, all the guards you want. I'll be making my final evaluations and additions. Standard procedure for discharging intelligence officers. How about it?'

Sam hesitated. 'I don't know. That stuff's classified—'

'Not to the officer who filed it! Clandestine Operations, Regulation seven seven five, Statute of Amendments. Actually, he's *required* to make his final evaluations.'

'Are you *sure*?'

'Never more sure of anything in my life, boy.'

'Well, if it's standard—'

'I just gave you the regulation! It's military bible, boy!'

'Then I can't see any obstacles—'

'I want it in writing. In exchange for that letter and tape that certifies me so fatigued I eat lizard shit. In fact, *I'll* make the ultimatum: D.C. issues me a written order to comply with CO Reg seven seven five upon my return to the States, or I'll opt for all the silos in Mongolia! I've still got a lot of supporters back home. They may be a little squirrelly, but they're also goddamned noisy.'

MacKenzie Hawkins chuckled; his cigar was a mangled pulp of itself. It was Sam's turn to squint.

'What are you thinking of?'

'Not a hell of a lot, boy. You just reminded me of something. Everyone *is* his own inventory. The sum of his parts. There may *be* a big goddamned world out there. And a challenge or two.'

PART TWO

This closely held corporation – that is, the company whose investors are few, regardless of capitalization – must have at its financial core men of generous heart and stout courage, who will infuse the structure with their dedication and sense of purpose.

Shepherd's Laws of Economics:
Book CVI, Chapter 38

CHAPTER SEVEN

The People's trial went brilliantly for all concerned. MacKenzie Hawkins was the image of converted, reformed hostility; he was a manly pussycat, playing his role to perfection. On his arrival at Travis Air Force Base in California, he emerged from the plane a stoic figure and spoke clearly into the cameras, and at the crowds of press and lunatic fringers, charming the media and defusing the screeching superpatriots.

He stated simply that there came a time when old soldiers – even youngish old soldiers – should step aside gracefully; times changed and values with them. What was perfidy a decade ago was, perhaps, a proper course of action today. The military man, the military *mind* was not equipped – nor should it be trained – for great international issues. It was enough that the military man, a simple warrior in his nation's legions – *sic . . . ibid . . . in gloria transit . . .* MacKenzie Hawkins – adhere to the eternal truths as he saw them.

It was all very refreshing.

It was all very heartfelt.

It was all bullshit.

And Mac Hawkins was superb.

It was remarked that the man in the Oval Office watched from deep down in a sunken armchair with his pet 150-pound dog, Python, protectively on his lap. He laughed and clapped his hands over Python's fur and stamped his feet and giggled and had a wonderful time. His family skipped in and laughed and clapped their hands and giggled and stamped their feet just like daddy. They weren't sure why daddy was so happy, but it was the best fun they'd had since daddy shot that awful little spaniel in the stomach.

Sam Devereaux watched the transformation of MacKenzie Hawkins from roaring bear to passive possum with dubious awe. The Hawk had turned into a soft-bellied mushy-beak, and what was basically lacking was the motive. Not that Sam discounted the spectre of imprisonment – Mongolia *or* Leavenworth – but once Hawkins had agreed to the plea of guilty, the public apology, the *letter* and gratuitous photographs of his bowed head during the hundred-year sentence of probation, he could have merely resumed his military bearing and let whatever storms rage that might. Instead, he went to extremes to still any controversy. It seemed as though he really wanted to fade away (terrible phrase, thought Devereaux).

Naturally, it crossed Sam's mind that Hawkins's behaviour was somehow related to Washington's quid pro quo regarding the G-2 files – the CO Regulation 775, and MacKenzie's access to them. If so, it was an unnecessary effort on the general's part; three intelligence services had looked over the files and found nothing to compromise national security. By and large the entries concerned old-hat Saigon conspiracies, some ancient European network speculations, and a slew of conjectures, rumours, and unsubstantiated allegations – dipsy-doodle nonsense.

If Hawkins honestly believed he could make a compromising dollar – and for what other purpose would he insist on CO 775? – from these out-of-date, unconfirmed recordings, there was no harm in it. What with inflation, the reduced pension he would receive, and the overall untouchability of his status, things were going to be rough enough. So nobody much cared what he did with his old files. Besides, if there was any resulting embarrassment there was also *the letter*.

'Goddamn, it's good to talk to you again, young fella.' MacKenzie's voice was loud and enthusiastic over the telephone, causing Sam to jerk the instrument away from his ear. The gesture was part audio-input, part raw fear of association.

Devereaux had left the Hawk over two weeks ago in California, just after the press conference at Travis. Sam had flown back to Washington, his discharge barely three days off, and he had spent the time wrapping up any and all desk matters that might conceivably – even *barely* conceivably – stand in the way of that glorious hour.

Hawkins wasn't a desk matter, but his mere presence was an abstract threat. On general principles.

'Hello, Mac,' said Sam cautiously. They had dispensed with the military titles at the beginning of the Peking trial. 'You in Washington?'

'Where else, boy? Tomorrow I trek over to G-two for my seven seven five. Didn't you know?'

'I've been pretty busy. There's been a lot to close out here. No reason for anyone to tell me about your seven seven five.'

'I think there is,' replied the Hawk. 'You're escorting me. I thought you knew that.'

There was a sudden, huge lump in the middle of Devereaux's stomach. He absently opened his desk drawer and reached for the Maalox as he spoke. '*Escorting* you? Why do you need an escort? Don't you know the address? I'll give you the address, Mac, I've got it right here. Don't go away. *Sergeant!* Get me the address of G-two Archives! Move your *ass*, Sergeant!'

'Hold on, Sam,' came the soothing words of MacKenzie Hawkins. 'It's just military procedure, that's all. Nothing to get uptight over. Anyway, I *know* the address; you should, too, boy and that's a fact.'

'I don't *want* to escort you. I'm a *lousy* escort! I said goodbye to you in California.'

'You can say hello again over dinner. How about it?'

Devereaux breathed deeply. He swallowed the Maalox and waved away the WAC who was his sergeant-secretary. 'Mac, I'm sorry, but I *do* have a number of things to finish up. Maybe at the end of the week; anytime actually – the day after tomorrow. At sixteen hundred hours to be precise.'

'Well, Sam, I thought we ought to go over the G-two routine for tomorrow morning. I mean you *have* to be there, son. It's in the orders. We wouldn't want anything fucked up over there, would we? *Jesus!* They wouldn't let either one of us out then.'

'Where do you want to have dinner?' asked Devereaux. He grimaced. The Maalox bottle was empty.

You're escorting me. I thought you knew that ... It's in the orders. We wouldn't want anything fucked up over there, would we?

No, we certainly would not. Devereaux shook his head. A couple in the next booth were staring at him. He stopped and grinned foolishly; the couple whispered to each other and looked away. Their reaction was clear: You never knew who was being sentenced next.

A tall man came through the curtained arch across the room. It was Sam's turn to stare. In awe.

It was the Hawk. He was sure of it. But the tall man threading his way politely through the crowded room bore little resemblance to the dishevelled, cigar-chewing Mac-Kenzie Hawkins who had squinted at him through the glass of a Peking cell. And even less to the close-cropped Hawkins who stood ramrod straight at all times and took each step as though marching to the tune of a thousand pipers – against a strong wind.

To begin with there was the Van Dyke beard. Granted it was new, but the definition was clear and exceedingly well groomed. As was the hair; it was not only growing out, but it had been shaped by tonsorial hands so that the grey swept over the ears in waves. Very, very distinguished. And the eyes – well, one could not really see the eyes because they were covered by tinted, tortoiseshell glasses, a very light tint that was more academic, or diplomatic, than mysterious.

And the man's walk. Good God! Hawkins's ramrod military posture had been replaced by a tasteful, goddamn it, *elegant grace*. There was a softness about the whole bearing, a kind of casual glide that was more Palm Beach than Fort Benning.

'I saw you watching me,' said the Hawk as he slid into the booth. 'Not bad, eh, boy? Not one of those pricky-shits stopped me. How about that?'

'I'm astonished,' answered Sam.

'You shouldn't be, son. First thing you learn in infiltration is adaptability. Not just terrain, but a good-sized accent on local customs and behaviour. It's a form of psycho-war.'

'What the hell are you talking about?'

'Behind the lines, Sam. This is enemy territory, don't you know that?'

By the time Mac Hawkins had elegantly spooned his iced vichyssoise he had reached the heart – the core – the bombshell of his reason for dinner with Sam. It was explosively capsuled in a single name.

Heseltine Brokemichael. Late Major General of Command, Bangkok. Currently in limbo, Washington, D.C.

'Yes, Sam, old Brokey was with me in Korea and points east and south. Damn fine officer; a little hot-headed, but then he always had to contend with that stupid bastard cousin of his. What's that idiotic name of his? Ethelred? Can you imagine? *Two* Brokemichaels in the same goddamned army, both with freak names!'

'I'm not hungry any more,' said Devereaux quietly. The Hawk continued.

'Yes, sir, you really laid the heavy mortar on Brokey's career. He couldn't get another star on his collar if he bought all the astrologers in the Pentagon. You see, they can never be *sure*; one of the goddamned Brokemichaels is a crook, but, of course, you never proved that, either.'

'They wouldn't let me!' Devereaux's whisper carried farther than he cared to think about. The couple in the next booth stared again. Sam grinned again. 'I had the evidence; I built the case. They made me drop it!'

'And a good man was cut down just when the joint chiefs were looking kindly on him. I tell you, it's a pity.'

'Get off it, Mac. I had that bastard cold—'

'The wrong bastard, boy. And even then you committed serious crimes to get your so-called evidence.'

'I took a calculated risk because I was damned angry. I paid for it with two years of my life in that cockadoodle uniform. And that's *it*. I want out.'

'That's too bad. I mean, I'm sorry to hear you say that because you may have to spend a little more time over at IG if I—'

'*Hold it!*' interrupted Devereaux in a whisper that bordered a roar. 'I'm out the day after tomorrow! Nothing, *nothing's* going to change that!'

'I certainly hope not. Let me finish. You *may* have to spend time if I can't talk old Brokey out of this crazy idea of his. You see, those charges against you in Bangkok weren't actually dropped; they were sort of suspended because of the complicated circumstances, and what with all those peace freaks screaming against the military. Now, Brokey doesn't hold anything against you, Sam, but he'd really like to clarify his own status, you can understand that. He figures that if he resurrects those charges, you can dig up the files and get the *right* Brokemichael – you'd *have* to or be on a rock pile – and he'd have the JCS smiling nicely on him, just like they used to. Wouldn't take more than, say, six or seven months. A year at the outside – *maybe* eighteen months if the trial was a long one, but you'd both get what you want—'

'I want *out*! That's *all* I want!' Sam wrung his napkin so tightly it squeaked. 'I *paid* for my moral indignation. It's *past*.'

'Past for you, boy. Not old Brokey.'

'The facts are *there*. I made a goddamned apology; it's in writing. The day after tomorrow, after sixteen hundred hours, I'll dictate a statement – to a civilian secretary – recapping the whole thing in one-syllable words. I will *not* reopen that case!'

'You will if old Brokey pulls out a certain Bangkok file and issues a directive for your arrest. He *is* a general officer, Sam.

Even though he may have pulled duty cleaning out the fucking high-brass latrines, for all I know.'

Hawkins had pursed his lips, tsking, and shaking his head slowly; the wide, innocent eyes behind the tinted glasses, conveyed anything but innocence.

'All right, Mac. Game time is over. You said, *if* you couldn't talk Brokemichael out of this nonsense. *Can* you talk him out of it?'

'Either talk him out of it, or remove him from the scene for a couple of days. Yes, I can do one or the other. Once you've got that discharge, boy, Brokey'd have a hell of a time convincing anyone to go after you. That paper's sort of a statute of limitations, you know. But I don't have to tell *you* that.'

'No, you don't. Just tell me what rotten thing you want from me.'

The Hawk removed his tinted glasses and, elegantly, wiped the non-prescription lenses as though he were polishing jade. 'Well, as a matter of fact, I've been giving a lot of thought to my immediate future. And I think there's a place for you, but I'm not sure.'

'Don't ever be. Next week I'll be back at my desk in Boston with Aaron Pinkus Associates, the best law firm in the Bay State.'

'Well, you could take an extra few weeks. Say a month, couldn't you? *Jesus*, boy, it's been four years; what's another month?'

'Aaron Pinkus will one day be on the Supreme Court. Every day with him is an education and I'm not giving up thirty years of paid education. What do you mean, you think there's a place for me? Doing what?'

'I may need an attorney. I think you're the best I ever met.'

'I'm probably the only one you've ever met—'

'But you've got a few weak spots, young fella,' interrupted Hawkins, replacing his tinted glasses. 'I'm sorry to say that, but it's a fact. So I don't know whether to hire you or not. I have to ponder some more about you.'

'In the meantime, you'll keep Brokemichael out of the picture?'

'And you'll give some consideration to acting as my attorney? Just for a couple of weeks? You see, I've got a little money saved up—'

'I know exactly how much money you've got,' broke in Devereaux sympathetically. 'I *had* to. You want advice for investments?'

'Sort of—'

'Then without qualification I'll help you. I mean that.' Sam did. After a lifetime of devotion, risk, and service, Mac had managed to amass a sum total of fifty-odd thousand dollars. No other assets whatsoever. No houses, real estate, stocks. Nothing. That and a reduced pension was all he had for the rest of his life. 'And if I can't give you the advice I think you should have, I'll find someone else who can.'

'That's mighty touching, son.'

Was there a hint of a glistening tear in this tough old-line officer's eyes? It was difficult to tell with the tinted glasses.

'It's the least I can do. It may sound corny, but it's the least any taxpayer can do for you. You've given a lot, and you've been shafted by the plastic men. I know that.'

'Well, boy,' said Hawkins, inhaling deeply, heroically, 'everyone does what he has to do in this world. At a given moment of time – *Ouch!* This goddamn faggot suit is tighter than a Memorial Day uniform.' The Hawk pulled out a folded, faded magazine from his breast pocket. The pages showing were dog-eared and marked with red pencil.

'What's that?' asked Devereaux.

'Oh, some Chincom propaganda the slants left in my cell. It's the standard Commie crap, misspelled English and all. This is an article that's supposed to show the kind of injustice that's widespread in organized religion. This here Catholic pope has a first cousin – kind of like the Brokemichaels in a way, except they don't have the same names – but they look alike. Actually they're identical, except that this pope's cousin grows a beard to hide the likeness.'

'I don't understand. Where's the injustice?'

'This cousin is a small-time singer in a minor opera company and half the time he's out of work. The Chincoms make the obvious comparison. The singer sings his heart out for the people's culture and starves half to death, while his pope cousin eats like a guinea gourmet and steals from the poor.'

'It interested you so much you marked it up?'

'Hell, no, boy. I just picked out the inaccuracies to show this priest friend of mine. It may surprise you, but I've been doing a little studying about things I haven't thought much about before. God, and the church, and things like that—. Don't you laugh, now.'

Devereaux smiled gently. 'I'd never laugh at a thing like that. I don't think it's anything to laugh at. A man's religious thoughts are not only his constitutional right, but often his very real sustenance.'

'That's a mighty nice way to phrase it. Real deep, Sam. By the way, just one thing about this Brokemichael business. Tomorrow morning at G-two. Keep your fucking mouth shut and do as I say.'

Hawkins was waiting under the canopy when Sam pulled up to the kerb in front of the hotel. He held what looked like a very expensive briefcase in one hand, opened the car door with his other and slid in. There was a broad grin on his face.

'*Goddamn!* It's a beautiful morning!'

It was not. It was cold and wet and the skies promised a heavy rain.

'Your barometer's a little off.'

'Nonsense! The day – like age – depends on how you feel, boy. And I feel just grand!' Hawkins smoothed the lapels of his tweed suit, adjusted the deep red paisley tie over the modish striped shirt, and ran his fingers delicately over the hair above his ears.

'Glad you're in such good spirits,' said Sam, starting up the car and entering the flow of traffic. 'I don't want to dampen them but you can't take a briefcase with you. You can't remove any papers. Nothing leaves the G-two offices.'

Hawkins laughed. He pulled out a cigar from his shirt pocket. 'Oh, don't worry your legal head about details,' he said, snipping off the end of the cigar with a sterling silver clipper. 'I've taken care of all that.'

'There's nothing to take care of! I'm responsible for you and I've got twenty-four hours to keep my nose clean.' Devereaux took his hostility out on the horn; the sound was returned in good measure by the surrounding vehicles.

'Jesus, you're in a foul temper. You just keep your eyes on the high ground, don't concern yourself with the flanks.'

'*Goddamn* it, doesn't anybody speak English anymore? What goddamned flanks? What does *that* mean?'

'It means what I said last night.' MacKenzie spoke as he lighted his cigar. 'Do as I say and don't make waves. By the way, would you like to know the name of the fella in charge of the G-two archives? Well, no reason for you to know, but he's a bright son of a bitch, a real genius. Didn't know what I was doing for the service when I got him out of that prison camp west of Hanoi a few years back. He's a Pointer, too. Can you beat that? Class of forty-seven. Same as me. Goddamn! The coincidences in this world—'

'No! . . . No, Mac! No! No, no *no*! You can't! I won't let you!' Sam attacked the horn again. Viciously hammering on it. At a crippled old lady who was having a difficult time crossing the intersection. The poor, trembling thing sank her head farther into her quivering shoulders.

'Regulation seven seven five makes it clear that a legal escort is just that. An escort. Not an observer. He takes the clandestine operations officer to and from the place of examination, but he's not permitted inside the room. I guess there're a lot of dishonest lawyers, Sam.' MacKenzie took a long, savouring intake of cigar smoke.

'There's *another* thing that's not allowed in that room, you son of a bitch!' Devereaux slammed his hand in fury on the rim of the horn once more. The crippled old lady was now splayed out in the middle of the street. 'And that's a *briefcase*!'

'It is, if the officer is making his final contributions. *Nobody* can see those but the ranking archivist of G-two. It's classified material.'

'There's nothing in there!' yelled Sam, pointing at his briefcase.

'How do you know? It's locked.'

Upon entering the offices of army intelligence, Hawkins was escorted quietly, professionally, to the specific room selected for his 775, by two flanking military police. Sam took up the rear. It seemed to Devereaux as formal an exercise as an execution, except that Mac was loose and slightly slouched in his modish tweed suit, not ramrod at all. But once the four of them were inside the room, Hawkins straightened up and replaced his warm civilian tones with the harsh bark of a leather-lined general officer. He ordered the MPs to take Sam into the next room and summon their superior. The MP captains saluted, took Devereaux by the elbows silently into the adjacent room, slammed the door, locked it, checked the corridor, and walked in Wehrmacht unison out into the hallway. They locked that door, too.

He had a vague feeling of *déjà vu*; then he remembered. He'd watched a late-night movie on television several weeks ago. *Seven Days in May*. He walked to the single window and looked out. And down. Through the bars. It was four storeys to the street. G-2 wasn't taking any chances with legal escorts from the inspector general's office, he thought.

There was the sound of voices from the next room. And then overly masculine laughter accompanied by eruptions of profanity. Old comrades-in-arms recalling the good old days when everyone got his ass shot off, except the generals. Sam sat down in a chair and picked up a dog-eared, worn-out copy of *Let's Stamp Out V.D. in G-2*, and read.

His reading – which was actually rather fascinating – was suddenly interrupted by the steady repetition of another sound from the examination room.

Therump-chump. Therump-chump. Therump-chump.

Devereaux swallowed several times, annoyed with himself for leaving his antacid tablets in the car. The sound he was hearing could not be confused with any other sound in his frame of reference, no matter how hard he tried. It was a Xerox machine.

Why would an examination room for the processing of eyes-only classified files have a Xerox machine?

On the other hand, why wouldn't it?

The first question was infinitely more logical. A Xerox machine was a contradiction – in spirit and in fact – to the purpose of Regulation 775.

Sam went back to his reading, unable to keep his mind even on the pictures.

An hour and twenty minutes later the *therump-chumping* stopped. Several minutes after that a metallic crack of a lock was heard and the door of the examination room was opened. MacKenzie emerged carrying his expensive brief-case, now bulging and strapped together with shining steel G-2 bands, and a foot-long steel chain dangling from the crossbar.

'What the hell is that?' asked Devereaux from the chair, apprehensively and not at all kindly.

'Nothing,' replied the Hawk casually. 'Just some Fleet-Pac-Com-Sat transfer files.'

'And what the hell is that?'

'*Major*,' continued MacKenzie, raising his voice, standing suddenly very erect. 'I present Brigadier General Beryzfick-oosh! *Atten . . . hut!*'

Devereaux shot up from the chair and snapped his hand in salute as a barrel-chested officer with twelve rows of ribbons, an eye patch and, Sam swore, a fright wig on his head, walked swiftly into the room. The salute was returned with a vibrating flourish; the officer then extended a large, muscular hand.

'Hear you're up for discharge, Major,' said the general gruffly.

'Yes, sir,' answered Devereaux, gripping the outstretched hand.

At which instant Hawkins slapped the briefcase chain over Sam's wrist, securing the triple combination lock between the links, and barked, 'First transfer completed, General!' '*Confirmed*, sir!' shot back the general, still holding Devereaux's hand in an iron grip, his one eye staring at Sam. 'Fleet-Pac-Com-Sat is now in your custody, Major! Prepare for second transfer!'

'For what, General?'

'Say!' The general released Sam's hand. 'Aren't you the legal prick who shafted old Brokey Brokemichael?'

Devereaux's stomach was suddenly in agony; perspiration formed instantly on his forehead, as the heavy briefcase pulled him halfway to the floor. 'There are two sides to that story, sir.'

'Goddamned right!' shouted the general. 'Brokey's and some shit-ass noncombatant's who *should* be on a stockade rock pile!'

'Now, just a minute, General—'

'What, soldier? You being *insubordinate*?'

'No, sir. Not at *all*, sir. I would just like to point out—'

'Point *out*? You point your ass in the direction of that door and secure the transfer of Fleet-Pac-Com-Sat, or I'll point you right into a court-martial! For insubordination *and* incompetence!'

'Yes, sir! Right away, sir!' Sam tried to salute but the chain and the briefcase were too heavy, so he made a rapid about-face and headed for the door, which was miraculously opened by the two MP captains.

The formalities at the entrance desk were over with quickly. The steel G-2 bands securing the briefcase were some kind of symbol of authority. Devereaux signed the checkout book and the miniature camera silently took his photograph.

Out on the street, Sam turned to the Hawk. 'That guy's crazy! Another ten seconds he would have thrown me into solitary! For *what*?'

'Old Brokey's got a lot of friends,' said MacKenzie. 'Here, I'll drive.'

'Thanks.' Devereaux reached awkwardly into his pocket and gave Hawkins the keys, his hand still trembling. They walked to the parking lot and got in the car.

Fifteen minutes later, in the middle of a Washington traffic jam, Sam's nerves began to calm down. His panic at being faced with a weird, apoplectic general screwing up his discharge at the last minute was fading. But that concern was being inexorably replaced with another very genuine fear. Brought about partially by the Hawk's silence.

'Mac, now that this pile of fleet-kumquats is in my custody, what the hell am I supposed to do with them? Where's this second transfer taking place?'

'Don't you know?'

'Of course not.'

'The general thinks you do.'

'Well, I *don't*!'

'You want to go back and ask him, Sam? Personally, I don't recommend it. Not with the way he feels about you. *Jesus!* He might dig up all kinds of very serious violations. And you just got your picture taken. One thing always leads to another, you know what I mean? Like the domino theory. Your trial could last for a year or two.'

'*What the hell's in here, Hawkins?* Don't bullshit me! What *is it*?'

'Sorry, Sam. I'm afraid I can't discuss it. You understand, boy. It's classified.'

Sam sat forward on the couch, his arm stretched out over the coffee table. MacKenzie manipulated the hacksaw back and forth over the chain.

'Once I get this goddamned chain off, we can work on the lock,' said Mac comfortingly. 'It would be easier with a small blowtorch.'

'Not on *my* arteries, you son of a bitch! And thanks for not telling me you didn't have the combination.'

'Now, don't worry, I'll have it off in ten or fifteen minutes. The steel's a touch harder than I figured.'

An hour and fourteen minutes later the last links were severed, leaving one dangling chain and a triple combination lock around Devereaux's wrist.

'I've got to get in touch with my office,' Sam said. 'They'll expect me to check in.'

'No, they won't. You're with me. Covering my seven seven five. That's what the agreement states. One day minimum, three days maximum.'

'But we're not there.'

'We went to lunch . . .' MacKenzie cleared this throat.

'I should still telephone—'

'*Goddamn*, you've no faith in me at *all*! Why the hell do you think I waited until this morning before going to G-two? You've got one day left and *I* account for your time. You can't get in trouble if you're not *there*.'

'Of course not. No trouble – just a firing squad.'

'Nonsense.' Hawkins got up from the floor, carrying the freed briefcase to the hotel writing desk. 'You're safer with me. I know those IG close-outs. You think you're winding everything up and some pricky-shit waltzes in and tells you you're not going anywhere until some brief is completed.'

Devereaux looked over at the general, now snapping the G-2 bands and opening the expensive briefcase. There was logic in Mac's madness. There *was* sure to be some ball-breaking file or other that a confused superior did not care to have left in his lap. A memorandum could be misplaced – or not read. A confrontation, even a discussion, between legal officers could not be overlooked. Hawkins definitely had a point: Sam was safer away from the office.

MacKenzie removed several hundred Xeroxed pages and put them on the desk beside the briefcase. Devereaux pointed to them and spoke cautiously. 'That's all *your* seven seven five?'

'Well, not exactly. A lot of it's open stuff that's never been closed out.'

Sam was suddenly more uncomfortable than he had been

for the past three hours. 'Wait a minute. You said back at G-two that it was just raw material on people you'd run across.'

'Of people *other* people ran across. I added that, son, I really did. You were just so upset you didn't listen.'

'Oh, Christ! You removed raw files on subjects that weren't *yours*?'

'No, Sam,' replied the Hawk as he squared off some pages. '*You* did. It says so right at the security desk. Your signature.'

Devereaux sank back in the couch. 'You devious son of a bitch.'

'That kind of says it,' agreed Hawkins sadly. 'There were times in the field – operating way the hell behind the lines, of course – when I wondered how I could bring myself to do the things I did. But then the answer was always the same. I was trained to survive, boy. And survive I do.' The Hawk now had four piles of Xeroxes neatly to the left of the briefcase on the desk. He tapped his fingers over them as if playing a piano and then looked over at Sam pensively. 'I think you're going to do real fine. You *will* accept the temporary appointment as my attorney, won't you? It won't be for long.'

'And it's a little more complicated than investments, isn't it?' Devereaux remained well back in the couch.

'A mite, I suspect.'

'And if I refuse I don't even have to worry about Brokemichael. He's minor. Now there's a small matter of removing classified files from G-two. No statute of limitations on that little caper.'

'Don't imagine there is.'

'What do you want me to do?'

'Work up some contracts. Pretty simple stuff, I should think. I'm forming a company. A corporation, I guess you'd call it.'

Sam inhaled deeply. 'That's really kind of amusing, if it weren't so sad. Purpose and intent notwithstanding, there's a not-so-minor item called capitalization required when you form a corporation. I know your finances. I hate to disabuse you but you're not exactly in the corporate assets league.'

'No faith, that's your trouble. I expect you'll change.'

'And what does that cryptic remark mean?'

'It means I've got the assets figured out to the dollar, that's what it means.' Hawkins planted his fingers over the Xeroxes in an elongated press. As if he had found the Lost Chord.

'What assets?'

'Forty million dollars.'

'*What!*' In his stunned disbelief, Sam leaped up from the couch. The dangling steel chain followed swiftly and, in a howling instant of pain, the bottom links whipped across his eye.

His left eye.

The room went around and around.

CHAPTER EIGHT

Devereaux ripped open the envelope the instant he closed the hotel door. He pulled out the rectangular slip of heavy paper and stared at it.

It was a cashier's cheque made out to his name. The amount was for ten thousand dollars.

It was absurd.

Everything was absurd; nothing made any sense at all.

He had been a civilian for exactly one week. There had been no hitches regarding his discharge; no Brokemichael surfaced, and no last-minute problems developed in the office because he had not gone to the office until an hour before his formal separation from the army. And when he arrived he not only had a patch over his left eye, but a thick bandage around his right wrist. From burns.

He had moved out of his apartment, sent his belongings to Boston, but did not follow them because a devious son of a bitch named MacKenzie Hawkins stated that he needed 'his attorney' in New York. Therefore Sam had a two-room suite at the Drake Hotel on Park Avenue, reserved and paid for. The suite was leased for a month; Hawkins thought it would be enough time.

For what? Mackenzie was not yet ready to 'spell it out'. However, Sam was not to worry; everything was 'on the expense account'.

Whose expense account?

The corporation's.

What corporation?

The one Sam would soon be forming.

Absurd!

Forty million dollars' worth of delusions that screamed for a frontal lobotomy.

And now a cashier's cheque for ten thousand dollars. Free and clear and no receipt required.

Ridiculous! Hawkins could not afford it. Besides, he had gone too far. People did not send other people (especially lawyers) ten thousand dollars without some kind of explanation. It simply was not healthy.

Sam walked over to the hotel telephone, checked the confusing litany on the pull-out tab beneath the instrument, and placed a call to MacKenzie.

'Goddamn, boy! That's no way to behave! I mean, you might at least say thank you.'

'What the hell for? Accessory to theft? Where did you get ten thousand dollars?'

'Right out of the bank?'

'Your savings?'

'That's right. Didn't steal from anyone but myself.'

'But why?'

There was a slight pause in Washington. 'You used the word, son. I believe you called it a retainer.'

There was a second pause. In New York. 'I think I said I was the only lawyer I knew who had a retainer based in the sort of blackmail that could march me in front of a firing squad.'

'That's what you said. And I wanted to correct that impression. I want you to know I value your services. I surely wouldn't want you to think I didn't appreciate you.'

'Cut it out! You can't afford it and I haven't done anything.'

'Well, boy, I believe I'm in a better position to judge what I can afford. And you *did* do something. You got me out of China some four thousand years before my parole was due.'

'That's different. I mean—'

'And tomorrow's going to be your first day of work,' interrupted the Hawk. 'Not much, but a beginning.'

There was now a long pause in New York. 'Before you say

anything, you should understand that as a member of the bar, I subscribe to a canon of ethics that is very specific. I'll do nothing to jeopardize my standing as an attorney.'

Hawkins replied loudly, with no pause whatsoever, 'I should hope not! Goddamn, boy, I don't want any slippery shyster in *my* corporation. Wouldn't look good on the stationery—'

'*Mac!*' roared Devereaux in exasperation. 'You didn't have stationery printed?'

'No. I just said that. But it's a hell of an idea.'

Sam did his best to control himself. 'Please. *Please*. There's a law firm in Boston and a very nice man who'll be on the Supreme Court someday who expects me back in a couple of weeks. He wouldn't look kindly on my being employed by – somebody else during my leave. And you said my work for you would be finished in three or four weeks. So no stationery.'

'All right,' agreed Hawkins sadly.

'Now, what's on for tomorrow? I'll charge you by the day and deduct it from the ten thousand and return the rest at the end of the month. From Boston.'

'Oh, don't worry about that.'

'I *do* worry. I should also tell you that I'm not licensed to practise in the state of New York. I may have to pay outside attorney's fees; depending upon what you want done. I gather it involves filing for this corporation of yours.'

Devereaux lit a cigarette. He was happy to see that his hands were not shaking.

'Not yet. We'll get to that in a couple of days. Tomorrow I want you to check out a man named Dellacroce. Angelo Dellacroce. He lives in Scarsdale. He's got several companies in New York.'

'What do you mean "check out"?'

'Well, I understand he's had business problems. I'd like to know how serious they are. Or were. Sort of find out what his current state of well-being is.'

'"Well-being"?'

'Yeah. In the sense of his being around and not in jail, or anything like that.'

Devereaux paused, then spoke calmly, as if explaining to a child. 'I'm a lawyer, not a private investigator. Lawyers only do what you're talking about on television.'

Again MacKenzie Hawkins replied quickly. 'I can't believe that. If somebody wants to become part of a corporation, the attorney for the company should find out if the fellow's on the up-and-up, shouldn't he?'

'Well, it would depend on the degree of participation, I suppose.'

'It's considerable.'

'You mean this Angelo Dellacroce has expressed interest?'

'In a way, yes. But I wouldn't want him to think I was being rude by making inquiries, if you know what I mean.'

Devereaux noticed that his hand now trembled slightly. It was a bad sign; better than a pained stomach but still bad. 'I've got that strange feeling again. You're not telling me things you should tell me.'

'All in good time. Can you do what I ask?'

'Well, there's a firm here in the city that my office uses – used to use, anyway. Probably still does. They might be able to help.'

'That's fine. You see them. But don't forget, Sam, we've got a lawyer-client relationship. That's like a doctor or a priest or a good whore; my name doesn't get mentioned.'

'I could do without the last reference,' said Devereaux. Damn it. His stomach growled. He hung up.

'*Angelo Dellacroce!*' Jesse Barton, senior partner, son-of-founder, Barton, Barton, and Whistlewhite, laughed. 'Sam, you've been away too long!'

'*That* bad?'

'Let's put it this way. If our mutual Boston friend and your erstwhile employer – I *assume* he's still your employer – Aaron Pinkus, thought you were seriously considering Dellacroce for some kind of money deal, he'd call your mother.'

'That bad?'

'I'm not kidding. Aaron would question your sanity and personally remove your name from the office door.' Barton leaned forward. 'Dellacroce is Cosa Nostra with a capital Mafia. He's so high in the charity rackets the cardinal invites him to the Alfred E. Smith dinner every year. And naturally, he's untouchable. He drives district attorneys and prosecutors right out of their gourds. They can't get him, but not for lack of trying.'

'Then Aaron mustn't learn of my very innocent inquiry,' replied Sam in confidence.

'Your indiscretion is safe with me. Incidentally, is it an indiscretion? This party of yours, is he really that naïve?'

Sam's stomach began to answer for him. He spoke rapidly to cover the sound. 'In my judgement, yes. I'm paying back a debt, Jesse. My client saved my ass in Indochina.'

'I see.'

'So he's important to me,' continued Sam. 'And according to you he's naïve. About this Dellacroce.'

'Don't take my word for it,' said Barton, reaching for his telephone. 'Miss Dempsey, get me Phil Jensen downtown, please.' Jesse replaced the receiver. 'Jensen's second in command at the prosecutor's office. Federal district, not municipal. Dellacroce's been a target over there ever since Phil joined; that was damn near three years ago. Jensen gave up an easy sixty thou' to go after the evil people.'

'Commendable.'

'Bullshit. He wants to be a senator or better. That's where the real money is—' The telephone rang. Barton picked it up. 'Thank you . . . Hello, Phil? Jesse, I've got an old friend here; he's been away for a few years. He was asking me about Angelo Dellacroce—'

The explosion on the other end of the line reverberated throughout the office. Jesse winced. 'No, for Christ's sake, he's not involved with him. Do you think I'm crazy? . . . I told you he's been away; out of the country, as a matter of fact.' Jesse listened for a moment and looked over at Sam.

'Were you in northern Italy? ... Where, Phil? ... Around Milan?'

Devereaux shook his head. Barton continued, one ear at the telephone, his words directed at Sam.

'Or Marseilles? ... Or Ankara? ... What about Rashid?' Devereaux kept shaking his head.

'*Algiers?* ... Were you in Algiers? ... No, Phil, you're way off. This is very straight. I wouldn't be calling you if it was anything else, now would I? ... Simple investment stuff, very legitimate ... Yes, I know, Phil ... Phil says those bastards will own Disneyland next .... Come on, Phil, that's not kosher; he'll simply walk away from him. I just wanted to confirm Dellacroce's status ... Okay. All right. I've got it. Thanks.'

Barton replaced the phone and leaned back. 'There you are.'

'I touched a raw nerve.'

'The rawest. Dellacroce not only skipped free of an airtight indictment last week, but because of a grand jury leak, the prosecutor's office has to issue a public apology. How does that grab you?'

'I'm glad I'm not Jensen.'

'Jensen's not. His office will lay off Dellacroce for a couple of months then ring him in again. Won't do them any good; Dellacroce's got his ass in butter. He slides in and out of courtrooms.'

'But my client should stay away.' Devereaux did not ask a question.

'Several continents,' replied Barton. 'Clothes don't make the man; his investors do. Ask anyone from Biscayne to San Clemente.'

'Well, goddamn, isn't that interesting? You just can't tell anymore, can you?'

'Stay clear of him,' said Devereaux, shifting the hotel phone and reaching for the glass of bourbon on the other side of the desk. 'He's bad news and you don't want him near you.'

'I see what you mean—'

'I'd rather you said "Yes, Sam, I'll stay away from Angelo Dellacroce." That's what I'd like to hear you say.'

'See what you mean.'

'You're not listening. When you pay a lawyer a retainer you listen to him. Now, repeat after me: "I will not go near—"'

'I know you've had a hard day, but you might put your mind to the next order of business. Just sort of think about it.'

'I'm still thinking about Angelo Dellacroce.'

'That part's finished with—'

'Glad to hear it.'

'—for the time being. Now, I want you to begin roughing out a kind of standard corporation agreement. A real legal document that has blanks for people putting in money.'

'People like Dellacroce?' Devereaux's voice made clear his position.

'*Goddamn*, forget about that guinea bastard!'

'From what I know about him I think you should refer to him as the Roman-blood-royal. But I'd rather you never referred to him again. What kind of corporation? If you want it filed in New York, I'll have to bring in another attorney. I told you that.'

'*No sir, boy!*' Hawkins shouted the words. 'I don't want anyone else involved! Just you!'

'I made it very clear: I'm not licensed to practise here. I can't file in the state of New York.'

'Who said anything about filing? I just want the papers.'

Sam was numb. He was not sure what he was supposed to say; what he could say: 'Do you mean to tell me you retained me for ten thousand dollars to prepare legal papers you are not going to execute – strike, that – *file*?'

'Didn't say I wouldn't sometime. I'm just not going to worry about it now.'

'Then why get a lawyer until you need one? And why the hell am I in New York?'

'Because I don't want you in Washington. For your own good. And when a man raises money for a corporation, he's got to have real legal-looking documents to give for it. I reversed the order of your questions.'

'I'm glad you told me. I won't pursue either one. What kind of corporation?'

'A regular one.'

'There's no such thing. Every company is different.'

'The kind where profits are shared. Among investors.'

'In that they're all the same. Or should be.'

'That's the kind I want. No monkey business.'

'Wait a minute.' Devereaux put down the phone and crossed to the chair where he'd left his attaché case. From it he took out a yellow legal pad and two pencils and returned to the desk. 'I'll need the specifics. I'm going to ask you some questions so I can rough out this not-to-be-filed, unexecuted legal document.'

'Go ahead, boy.'

'What's the title? The corporate name.'

'I thought about that. What do you think of the Shepherd Company?'

'Not a hell of a lot. I don't know what it means. Not that it makes any difference. Call it anything you like.'

'I like the Shepherd Company.'

'Fine.' Sam wrote out the words. 'What's the address?'

'United Nations.'

Devereaux looked at the telephone. 'What?'

'The address. Whatever the United Nations building is.'

'Why?'

'It's . . . symbolic.'

'You can't use a symbolic address.'

'Why not?'

'I forgot. You're not filing. All right. The depository?'

'Who?'

'The bank. Where the corporate funds will be deposited.'

'Leave that blank. A couple of lines. There'll be several banks.'

Sam's pencil involuntarily stopped. He forced it onward. 'What's the purpose of the company?'

There was a pause in Washington. 'Give me some legal-sounding choices.'

Now a longer pause in New York. Devereaux's pencil really objected. 'Let's start with "intent".'

'Obviously, to make money.'

'How?'

'By having something people will pay for.'

'Manufacturing? Production of merchandise?'

'No, not really.'

'Marketing?'

'That's nearer. Keep going.'

'Where?'

'Some more words,' replied Hawkins.

'I'm not a corporate attorney but if I remember the books, a company's purpose – its motive for profit – is in one form or another of production, manufacturing, marketing, acquisition, services—'

'Hold it! That one.'

'Services?'

'That's good, but I mean the one before that.'

Sam exhaled. 'Acquisition?'

'That's it. Acquisition.'

'Acquiring at one price, disposing at a second, higher price. You're in brokerage?'

'That's very good, Sam. That's really using the old noodle.'

Devereaux pushed the pencil against its inanimate will and wrote on the pad. 'If you're a broker, there's got to be a product. Services or real estate or merchandise—'

'Of a deeply religious nature,' interrupted MacKenzie, his voice low and solemn.

'What is?'

'The product.'

Sam inhaled; it was a long breath. When he exhaled it was with a hum. 'Are you saying that you are forming a company to broker the acquisition of religious merchandise?'

'That'll do,' answered Hawkins simply.

'Artifacts?'

'That's even better.'

'For Christ's sake, *what is*?'

'"Broker the acquisition of religious artifacts." Goddamn, boy. Perfect!'

Devereaux borrowed the standard New York State forms for a limited partnership agreement from Barton. It was a relatively simple matter to transcribe his notes into the partnership forms and have the hotel stenographer re-type the pages as though they had been dictated. Things were looking up, thought Sam as he scrutinized the finished product, replete with its blank lines for investors, depositories, amounts; and the inane description of 'brokering the acquisition of religious artifacts'.

But it looked as legal as a chapter in Blackstone. Yes, Sam mused as he balanced the envelope containing the gobbledygook he was about to mail to MacKenzie Hawkins. Things *were* looking up. He'd be back in Boston with Aaron Pinkus Associates in a few days; his 'legal' work for the Hawk was finished. Altogether it had taken him nine days, some three weeks short of the month Mac had figured.

He had agreed to stay at the Drake a day or two longer, giving Mac sufficient opportunity to approve of his labours. There was no question that approval would come, and it did.

'My word, Sam, that's a mighty impressive-looking document,' said the Hawk over the telephone from Washington. 'I'm downright amazed you were able to write it all up so quickly.'

'There are certain guidelines to follow; it wasn't that difficult.'

'You're too modest, young fella.'

'I'm anxious, that's what I am. Anxious to get back to Boston—'

'I can certainly understand that,' broke in Hawkins without the commensurate affirmative that would have curtailed the sudden, growing pain in Devereaux's stomach.

'*Listen*, Mac—'

'I see you made me president of the company. You didn't tell me that.'

'There were no other names. I asked you about the corporate officers and you said leave the lines blank.'

'What are those titles *secretary* and *treasurer*? Are they important?'

'Not if you're not filing.'

'Suppose someday I decided to?'

'The standard procedure is to combine the two. Most states require a minimum of two general partners for a limited partnership agreement.'

'But I could have more if I wanted to, couldn't I?'

'Certainly.'

'I just wanted to know what's right, Sam. Not important. It's never going to be filed. Just passes the time.'

Devereaux thought he detected a note of melancholy in Hawkins's voice. Was Mac beginning to come to grips with his own fantasies? Did he begin to understand that his irrational foray into corporate legalities was simple compensation for the absence of command decision? Sam began to relax. He actually felt sorry for this old warhorse. *Passes the time* was a euphemism for *filling up the days*. 'I'm sure it does, General.'

'Why, Sam, you haven't called me general in weeks.'

'Sorry. A slip.'

'I'll be in touch with you tomorrow, boy. You've worked hard. Have a little fun tonight. Remember, it's on the expense account.'

'As to that ten thou'. It's very generous of you but I don't want it. I don't need it. I'll deduct whatever legal expenses – stenographer, supplies, that kind of thing – and return the rest. Then there's an investment counsellor I know in Washington—'

Devereaux stopped. He realized that the click on the other end of the line had terminated the conversation.

There was no point in not having a good time. He had spent enough weekends in New York to know where the action was: the singles' bars on Third Avenue.

Sam was spectacularly successful. His catch was a nubile young thing who had come out of Omaha, Nebraska – the county seat of Henry Fonda and Marlon Brando – to scale the Broadway heights. She was terribly impressed with a lawyer who did a lot of work for Metro-Goldwyn-Warner-Brothers when he wasn't handling contracts for *Dirty Sally* and *Masterpiece Theatre*.

Sam was impressed, too. All during the night, throughout most of the next morning, well into the following afternoon and (with time out for food and limited discussion) into the next evening.

It was 9.27 when the telephone rang; 9.29 when the nubile young thing spoke sleepily. 'Sam, the phone's on my side.'

'You're very observant.'

'Shall I get it?' she asked.

'Since it's on your side, I'd say yes.'

'You're sure?'

Sam opened his eyes. The girl had raised herself and was stretching; the sheet had fallen away. 'Make it quick,' Devereaux said.

'If you're sure.'

'I have no wife and my mother doesn't know where I am and Aaron Pinkus wouldn't be mad. Get the phone, talk fast, and hang up.'

The girl reached for the instrument; Sam reached for the girl.

'There's a man with a raspy voice who wants to talk to you. He says his name is Angelo Dellacroce.' She handed Sam the receiver.

'Hey, *you*!' The words spat from the telephone. 'You Samuel Deverooze, sec'atary-treasurer of this Shepherd Company?'

CHAPTER NINE

Former Lieutenant General MacKenzie Hawkins, twice awarded the nation's highest honour for extraordinary heroism beyond the call of duty in deadly combat against the enemy, cowered like a frightened boy at the sight of former Major Sam Devereaux, military accident.

Hawkins could see Sam getting out of the taxi at the entrance of the North Hampton Golf Club. The brass lamps on top of the stone posts flanking the drive were the only source of light; it was a cold, cloudy night and no moon could be seen. The lamps, however, gave sufficient illumination to reveal the anguished expression on Devereaux's face.

Sam was furious, MacKenzie realized that. But, he thought to himself, he had not actually lied. Not really. He never told Devereaux he *wouldn't* approach Angelo Dellacroce. Only that he had no reason to do so when Sam pressed him on the point. At that moment. Not *later*.

The secretary-treasurer title was something else. It looked terrific on the partnership agreement: *Samuel Devereaux, Esq., Counsellor-at-law, Suite 4-F, Drake Hotel, New York*, right above the line reserved for the second most important office in the Shepherd Company. It was for Devereaux's own good; he'd understand that soon enough. But at the moment Samuel Devereaux, Esq., was mad as a caged bull fenced off from heifers in heat.

The Hawk had agreed to Dellacroce's rendezvous because it suited him. The Italian was so concerned about surveillance he had insisted on meeting Mac in the middle of the fairway on hole six at the North Hampton Golf Club between the hours of midnight and one in the morning. But if Hawkins had objected and changed the location to the Bell Telephone Company, Dellacroce would have capitulated.

For Dellacroce had no choice. Mac had a folder on the Mafioso that would have guaranteed a jail sentence worthy of a court in the People's Republic.

Still, a meeting at night in terrain surrounded by thick woods and streams and small lakes appealed to Hawkins. He was at home in such territory. It wasn't Cambodia or Laos, but he could sort of keep his hand in, as it were.

He flew up from Washington in the afternoooon and with false identification rented a car and drove out to North Hampton. As soon as it was dark, he circled the golf club and parked at the west perimeter. Dellacroce had told him that the club was closed for the evening and the night watchman would be replaced by one of his men.

Which meant, of course, that Dellacroce would double the patrols everywhere, especially around the area of fairway six.

His pockets stuffed with coils of thin rope and rolls of three-inch adhesive, Hawkins employed an old Ho Chiminh tactic that had served him well in the past. He began his commando assault at the farthest point inside the hostile area and worked his way towards the front.

. At 2300 the enemy patrols started to man their emplacements within the North Hampton Golf Club. There were nine (a few more than Mac had anticipatcd) spaced out in the rough by the edge of the woods on both sides of fairway six, the line of relay extending back to the clubhouse and the driveway.

One by one, Hawkins immobilized eight patrols; he removed all weapons, bound them, taped their faces – all facial muscles, not just the mouths – and rendered them unconscious with *kai-sai* chops at the base of the skull. Then he worked his way back to the ninth patrol who manned the entrance.

He saved for this man a strategy that was particularly

effective against the Pathet Lao. For the guard had to be able to talk.

The man was exceedingly cooperative. Especially after Mac had sliced his trousers from crotch to cuff.

At ten minutes to midnight, Dellacroce's huge black limousine drove swiftly through the gates and up to the wide, pillared porch. In the darkness the ninth patrol, riveted to a pillar, spoke.

'Everything's fine, Mr Dellacroce. All the boys are spread good, like you said.'

The man's voice was a bit high and a little strained, but Hawkins figured rightly that Dellacroce had other things on his mind.

'Okay. Real good,' was the raspy reply as Dellacroce got out of the automobile, flanked by two heavyset bodyguards who walked like gorillas with their hands in their fur. 'Rocco, you stay here with Augie. You, Fingers, you come with me. And, Meat, you get the fuckin' car back in the lot outta sight.'

Before Dellacroce and Fingers had rounded the corner of the building, the ninth patrol was *kai-saied* out of commission. By the time Dellacroce and Fingers had disappeared across the lawn, Rocco had joined Augie in peaceful oblivion.

The gentleman named Meat was Hawkins's next dispatchee. It took nearly five minutes, but only because Meat was an experienced combat man. He did not park the limousine at the edge of the lot; instead, he had pulled to a stop in the centre. It was good positioning, thought Mac. Meat could observe all his flanks unencumbered by visual shadings or sightline obstructions. Meat was good.

But not good enough.

MacKenzie scrambled diagonally out of the parking area, over the first tee, and left through the rough towards fairway six. Since Dellacroce had made it clear he would be alone, Hawkins knew that Fingers would be hiding in the darkness, no doubt at the edge of the woods, and if he had a brain in his head, across the fairway on the east side for a superior line of fire.

But Fingers did not have much savvy. He remained in the west rough, prone in the underbush, eliminating any rear flank observation.

Goddamn, thought MacKenzie, it was not much fun taking an asshole like Fingers.

Nevertheless, he took him. Silently. In eleven seconds.

Leaving Angelo Dellacroce alone in the middle of fairway six, the lighted end of a cigar protruding from his fat mouth, his squat body sagging at ease, his plump hands clasped behind his back as though waiting to be served a plate of linguini in a slow trattoria.

Three minutes later Devereaux's taxi was heard on the deserted back road fronting the golf club, and MacKenzie waited behind the pillar.

As Sam walked haltingly up the drive, Hawkins decided not to tell him about the immobilized patrols. It would only worry the ex-major; better to let him think Dellacroce was true to his word: he was alone on fairway six.

'God*damn!* Hello, Sam!'

Devereaux threw himself to the ground, hugging the gravel for dear life. And then he looked up; MacKenzie took out a small but powerful pencil light from his pocket and flicked it on.

The ex-major was certainly angry. His face was kind of pinched and puffed, as if it might explode right out of his skin.

'You unprincipled son of a bitch!' Sam whispered, fury and fear intermeshed. 'You lowlife! You're the most devious, despicable form of subhuman that ever lived! What the hell have you done, you *bastard*?'

'Now, now, that's no way to talk. Come on, get up; you look silly down there all splayed out . . .' MacKenzie reached for Devereaux's hand.

'*Don't touch me*, you slug worm! Fucking Mongolian sheep is too *good* for you! I should have let Lin Shoo pry out your fingernails, one by one, for four thousand fucking years! Don't *touch* me!' Sam staggered to his feet.

'Look, Major—'

'Don't call me that! I don't own a serial number and I don't want to be addressed *ever* by anything *remotely* military! I'm a lawyer, but I'm not *your* goddamned lawyer! Where the hell are we? How many "torpedoes" have us covered with guns?'

MacKenzie grinned. 'There's nobody, boy. Just Dellacroce standing out on the fairway like a nice uncle at a backyard pasta party.'

'I don't believe you! Do you know what that gorilla told me on the phone when I said I wouldn't come out here? That goddamned hood told me my health would take a sudden turn for the worse! That's what he told me!'

'Oh, don't pay any attention to that sort of thing. Those fat slobs always talk tough.'

'Horseshit!' Devereaux peered into the darkness. 'That maniac said if I was late he'd send a basket of fruit to the hospital – *tomorrow*! And if I tried to leave town, some goon called Meat would find me before the week was up!'

The Hawk shook his head. 'Meat's pretty good, but I think you could take him. I'd put my money on you, boy.'

'I don't *want* to take him – or *any*body! And don't put any money on *me*. You're never going to see me again! I just wanted to get this over with. I want to meet this Dellacroce; tell him the whole thing's a crazy mistake! I had some typing done for you, and that's all!'

'Now listen to me, son. You're over-reacting. There's nothing to worry about at all.' Hawkins started walking across the lawn. Devereaux kept pace, his head snapping in the direction of every noise. 'Mr Dellacroce will be exceedingly cooperative. And there'll be no more tough talk, you'll see.'

'What was that?' There was a squishing sound.

'Relax, will you? I think you stepped on some dog turd. Do me a favour. Don't start explaining anything until I talk with Dellacroce, okay? It won't take me more than three or four minutes.'

'*No!* Absolutely *no*! I don't care to have a promising legal career cut short in the middle of a fairway at some Cosa Nostra golf course! These people don't play games! They use bullets, and chains, and heavy cement! And rivers! What was *that*?' There was a fluttering of wings in the dark trees.

'We alarmed a bird. Let's put it this way. If you just keep your mouth shut until I'm finished, I'll pay you another ten thousand. Free and clear. How about that?'

'You're a lunatic! No, again. Because I can't spend it displacing roots in a Boston cemetery! You could offer ten million; the answer's still no!'

'That's not out of the question—'

'For Christ's sake, have yourself committed before somebody else does!'

'Then I'm afraid I'll have to put it this way. You either shut up until my business with Mr Dellacroce is finished, or tomorrow morning I call the FBI and tell them there's an ex-major walking around peddling raw-file intelligence documents he illegally removed from the G-two archives.'

'Oh, no you don't! Because I'll tell the truth. I'll tell them how you blackmailed me, then conned me, then blackmailed me again. You'd get a lighter prison sentence in Peking!'

'It surely does get complicated, doesn't it? I mean you'd be reopening the Brokemichael business. How would it look? A man violates the espionage laws because he doesn't like spending a little extra time in the service of his country. In a cushy job, not even combat. Pretty weak blackmail, I'd say.'

'You *unprincipled*—'

'I know, I know,' said the Hawk wearily. 'You keep repeating yourself. What you've got to understand is that it doesn't make a whole lot of difference to me. As you said, I've been shafted. How much more shafting can they do?'

Hawkins kept walking. Devereaux followed reluctantly, his eyes darting everywhere, his nerves obviously frayed; a series of whispered squeaks emerged from his throat until he found the words. 'Have you no decency, sir? No sense of compassion? No love of your fellowman within your heart?'

'I surely do,' said the Hawk. They cut across the third tee on to fairway six. 'Now keep that eloquent tongue of yours inactive for a while. If you don't like the way things go, then speak your piece. Can I be fairer than that?'

The overcast sky was thinning out; intermittently the moon shone through. And a hundred yards ahead they could see the squat figure of Angelo Dellacroce, his hands still clasped behind his back, the lighted stub of a cigar in his mouth.

'He must have ashes all over his front,' said Hawkins quietly. Then louder, 'Mr Dellacroce?'

There was a grunt from the obese body in front of them. MacKenzie flicked on his pencil light and held it over his own head, spilling the light on his longish steel-grey hair, throwing shadows down across his precisely barbered Van Dyke.

'You're making us a target!' whispered Sam.

'Who's going to shoot?'

They approached the Italian; Mac extended his hand. Dellacroce made no move to accept it. Hawkins spoke quietly. 'Even when I accepted gook surrenders I got a handshake. Sort of separates us from the animals.'

Reluctantly Dellacroce pulled his hand from behind his back and the two shook. 'I ain't no gook and this ain't no surrender,' said the raspy voice.

'Course it isn't,' answered MacKenzie brightly. 'It's the beginning of a profitable association. By the way, this is my attorney and good friend, Sam Devereaux—'

'*Mac!*'

'Shut up and shake hands,' said Hawkins *sotto voce*. 'Goddamn, boys. I said shake *hands!*'

With even greater reluctance, the two hands inched towards each other, touched briefly and separated as though the owners feared infection.

'That's better,' said the Hawk enthusiastically. 'Now we can talk.'

And MacKenzie did. He started by listing the illegal activities – both foreign and domestic – of Angelo Dellacroce. It took him two minutes.

'Now, Mr Dellacroce, the reason the authorities can't catch up with you is that they don't have access to a single financial clearing house that ties in specifically with all these here sundry enterprises. I realize it will sound strange to you, sir, but I believe I have that access. There's a bank in Geneva, Switzerland; the first three numbers of the account happen to be seven, one, five. In this account is something over sixty-two million dollars—'

'*Basta! Basta!*'

'—and the deposits were made directly from such locales as I've suggested. Now I guess you've studied the new Swiss laws relative to such accounts. They're tricky because fraud in one country may not constitute fraud in Geneva. But goddamn, would you believe there's now a way for Interpol to subpoena the records of those accounts? All the international police have to do is submit a copy of a payment – to a specific account – that's been made by a convicted narcotics dealer. And it surely is wondrous good fortune on my part to have in my possession Xeroxed copies of quite a few such payments—'

'*Basta!* You shut up!' Dellacroce roared. '*Fingers! Manny! Carlo! Dino!* Get out here! *Now!*'

There were only the sounds of the night in reply.

'There's no one there. At least no one that can hear you,' said the Hawk softly.

'*What?* – *Fingers! Figlio della prostituta!* Get out here!'

Nothing.

'Now, you and I, Mr Dellacroce, will step away from my friend and attorney, here, so we can talk real private-like.' MacKenzie touched the Italian's arm, which was instantly yanked away.

'*Meat! Augie! Rocco!* You hear me, boys? Get out here!'

'They're sleeping, too, sir,' said Hawkins kindly. 'They won't wake up for a couple of hours.'

Dellacroce whipped his head towards Mac. 'You got cops here? How many cops you got?' The questions overlapped.

'Nobody. Just me and my good friend and attorney—'

'How many? Alone you couldn't!'

'Alone, I did,' answered the Hawk.

'My best boys!'

'I'd hate like hell to see your support troops.' MacKenzie chuckled. 'Now it's time for our private talk.'

The Hawk led Dellacroce thirty feet away. He talked quietly for exactly four minutes and thirty seconds.

At which point a rasping, ear-splitting scream shattered the stillness of fairway six.

'*Mannnnaaagggiii*'!'

And Angelo Dellacroce fainted right there on the manicured grass.

MacKenzie bent over the man and gently slapped him back into consciousness.

They talked once more with the Hawk holding the obese Italian's neck as though he were a medical corpsman.

The scream came again.

'*Mannnnaaaaggggiii*'!'

And Dellacroce fainted again.

So the Hawk revived him again.

And they talked for two minutes more.

'*Mannnnaaaagggggiiii*'!'

This time MacKenzie lowered the man's head on the grass of fairway six and got up. The moon had broken through the night clouds, revealing a stunned Sam staring at the sight of the fallen Dellacroce. This was it, thought the Hawk, as he walked slowly towards Devereaux. There was no point in procrastinating any longer. Sam would have to be told. There was no other way.

'Well, Sam,' began Mac with quiet confidence in the intermittent moonlight on fairway six, 'it's a pretty good start. Mr Dellacroce was eager to subscribe to the full amount reserved for him. The Shepherd Company has its first ten million dollars.'

Devereaux's knees buckled. The Hawk rushed forward

and caught him before he hit the ground. The ground was not hard but MacKenzie wanted Sam to know he cared; it was always a good idea to let one's superior-adjutant know the commander was concerned for his well-being. 'God-damn, son, you've got to stop this kind of thing! You're behaving no better than Mr Dellacroce! Now that's just not proper; you're cut from a finer tunic!'

Sam's eyes were swimming around and around in the moonlight on fairway six. The words that emerged from his trembling lips were by and large incoherent, but several phrases were repeated often enough to be understood. 'Secretary-treasurer! – Oh, my God, I'm a *sec'atary-treasurer*! Ten million dollars' worth of cement! I'm in ten million dollars' worth of shit! I'll be sunk in concrete pyjamas! I'm *dead*!'

'Now, now, stop your wailin'. You're a big lawyer, fella; you shouldn't act like this.'

'I should never have met you, you squirrelly bastard! That's the only *shouldn't* of my life! Oh, my God! That killer passed out!'

'So did you. Almost. I caught you—'

'*Shhh!* Let's get out of here! I'll send him a letter – I'll get some Bellevue stationery – I'll certify you a fucking lunatic! It was all a lousy joke!'

'Oh, Mr Dellacroce knows better than that, boy!' Hawkins patted Devereaux's cheek with his right hand while, with his left, he kept an iron grip on the base of Sam's skull, inhibiting any movement above the waist. 'Dellacroce's a very religious man, most of these Italian fellas are; doesn't make any difference what they do for a living. That's separate. He knows I told him the truth.'

'What the hell are you talking about? What's religion got to do with anything? Get the fuck off my neck!'

'Religion helps a man recognize the truth. He may not like it; his *religion* may not like it, or even admit it is the truth, but because he's contemplated, the religious man can separate what's real from what's horseshit. You follow me?'

'Not for a goddamned second! My neck hurts!'

'Sorry, I'll ease up, but it's time we talk.' MacKenzie removed his hand. Instantly Devereaux bolted, but the Hawk merely rolled with him, pinning him back to the earth. 'I said we've got to *talk*, boy. You're a reasonable person; you can see the logic in that.'

'The problem,' whispered Sam, straining on the ground, 'is that you're *not* reasonable *or* logical! Do you know what you've done? Guys like that—' He gestured with his head; somehow, he could not use his hands. 'They freeze people for welching on their bookies! They think nothing about paying for the biggest funeral in town – for a *paisan* who held out on a skim! I *know*. I'm from *Boston*.'

'You're over-reacting again. Mr Dellacroce won't do anything like that. He knows where he stands – which is roughly in twenty feet of lye if he doesn't behave. That account in Geneva. He stole from his own people.'

Grudgingly, suspiciously, Devereaux stared at Mac in the moonlight. 'You're sure of that?'

'It was all in the G-two files. Trouble was nobody put it together. I don't think they wanted to; Dellacroce's crowd are big Pentagon supporters, what with government contracts and union affiliations—. Now, will you listen to me?'

With a reluctance born of fear, but with an assent formed in necessity, Sam nodded. The Hawk helped him up and the two men walked into the rough off fairway six. There was a large oak tree whose leaves filtered the moonlight. Sam sat down against the trunk; Mac fell to one knee in front of him, the line officer clarifying orders at a fire base.

'Remember a couple of weeks ago my telling you how I was looking into things I hadn't thought much about before? God and the church and things like that.'

'I remember saying I wouldn't laugh—' Devereaux's reply was flat, wary. A monotone.

'That was very thoughtful, boy. Well, I *was* doing some thinking, but not quite in the way you maybe considered. You and I know that ninety-nine per cent of all Commie propaganda is horseshit; everybody knows that. Ours is only – say, fifty to sixty per cent, so we're way ahead on that score. But that one per cent of the Bolshie feedback got me to wondering. About this Catholic situation. Not what people *believe*, that's their business. But how the organization operates. And it seemed to me that these Vatican fellows got such a good thing going they should spread a little more around. I mean, they got investments, son. When the stock market goes up a couple of points anywhere in the world, they make zillions.'

'And if it goes down, they lose zillions.'

'Not so! The brokers get 'em out in time or they get canned from the Knights of Malta. It's part of the arrangement. And they can't get their pictures taken with the pope.'

'That *is* horseshit.'

'If it is, why do all the Catholic brokers on Wall Street have all those initials after their names. You know of any college degrees that start with the letter K? Malta, Columbus, Lourdes. And the saints! *Jesus!* Knights of Assisi, Knights of Peter, Matthew – it goes on for pages. It's kind of a social order. The more a fellow on the stock exchange does for the Vatican, the better the K after his name. And Wall Street's only one example. It's the same all over the place.'

'I think you've been reading some pretty strange books. The *Ku Klux Klanner*, maybe. Nineteen-twenty edition.'

'Hell, no, I don't cotton to that shit. A man's got a right to believe anything he likes. I'm only talking about the financial part. Then there's real estate. Do you know the sort of real estate the Vatican boys have? I swear they pick up rent from the Ginza to the Gaza strips and most places in between. They own *the* prime properties in New York, Chicago, Hartford, Detroit – 'most every place where the micks, the wops, the Polacks and all those kind of people migrated. They always do it the same way. They go in early – before all the ethnics get settled – and buy up land and build a big church. Naturally, all these Ellis Islanders are nervous being in a strange place and all, so *they* build their houses near the church. In a generation or so the kids are lawyers and dentists and own automobile dealerships. So what do they do? They move out to the suburbs and go to work where they once lived, which is now the centre of *town*, the *business* district. And the church property skyrockets! It's a regular pattern, boy!'

'I'm trying to find something negative here and I can't,' said Sam, staring in the shadows at the excited Hawkins. 'What's wrong with the pattern?'

'I didn't say it was wrong. I said it made for one hell of a centralized portfolio.'

'"Centralized portfolio"? You've got a new vocabulary.'

'Like you said, I've been reading. And not such strange books as you might think. You see, Sam, the product these Vatican boys manufacture – that's not meant disrespectfully, only in a business sense – doesn't change. It may have to adjust a mite now and then, take a tuck here or a nip there, but the basic merchandise stays the same. That reduces a major cost factor and allows for a continuous profit figure with no chance of negative entry—'

'"Negative entry"?'

'That's an accounting term.'

'I know it's an accounting term. How do *you* know – don't tell me. Your reading material.'

'Maggie's drawers, son.'

'What?'

'Never mind. You're on target, that's all. Now, you take an economic situation where the stock exchanges and the real estate markets hold firm, and that means you got the banks, because you control both money *and* land. Prime economic resources. And you add to that a product that requires minimum assembly alterations with maximum purchase growth – hell, boy, it's a worldwide *gold mine*.'

'You have been reading. But if you're right, why's there so much hassle over the parochial schools and *their* costs?'

'That's services, Sam. That's an entirely different entry column. I'm talking about basic portfolios, not annual operating expenditures; they fluctuate with economic conditions. Anyway, it's mostly blackmail.'

'That's succinct. They wouldn't like you in Boston.'

The Hawk shifted his weight and spoke a little more

softly, but with no loss of emphasis. 'You mentioned before about something wrong. Well, I don't like to mention it because it only applies to the pricky-shit high brass and not the troops, but there is something that's got a bit of sting to it.'

'*You* found a *moral* position?'

'Morality and economics should be more related than they have been; everybody knows that. You take this political thing. Nobody's traded fire power with the Reds any better'n I have. God*damn*, nobody's going to bury me! But it strikes me that these Catholic boys in the Vatican – and that means all the powerful dioceses – use the Bolshie excuse a mite too freely to oppose just about everything that could make things better for the peasant slobs scratching a life out of very tough ground.'

Devereaux eyed Hawkins sceptically. 'That position's a little dated. A great many changes are taking place in the Church. This new pope is opening a lot of windows. Like John the Twenty-third did.'

'Not quick enough, Sam. What the Vatican brass needs is a good shake-up in command. Something to jolt their *be*robed asses out of their lethargy.'

'You can't change a two-thousand-year pattern over-night—'

'Oh, I understand that,' interrupted the Hawk. 'And I'm glad you brought up this new pope. This Francesco. Because he's a very popular fellow. Even those who hate his guts – for doing what he's doing – know he's the biggest asset they've got in the whole damn church – that's not meant in a religious sense, of course. I don't take positions that way.'

'What positions? What sense?'

'This Francesco,' continued Mac, overlooking Devereaux's questions, 'is more than just the pope, which is enough to begin with. He's a beloved individual, you know what I'm driving at?'

'I wish you wouldn't say that.'

'He's the sort of person every man jack of a Catholic would really sacrifice for, you see what I mean?'

'I don't like that phrase, either.'

The Hawk changed knees rapidly; it was good to redistribute weight as often as possible when in an immobile position. 'Do you know the estimated total communicant membership of the Catholic Church?'

'The *what*?'

'How many Catholics there are in the world? Never mind, I'll tell you. Four hundred million. Now, taking the median figure of one American dollar – setting a specific date for the rate of exchange; some giving more, most less – that comes to *four hundred million dollars*.'

'What does?'

'The projected gross.'

'What projected gross?'

'Of the Shepherd Company's business services. This here "brokering the acquisition of religious artifacts". It's a clear ratio of ten to one in terms of capitalization, but naturally the profit ratio, as opposed to the gross figure, will be affected by the necessary outlay for equipment and support personnel.'

'What the hell are you babbling about?!'

'We're going to kidnap the pope, Sam.'

'*Whaaat!*'

'I've got a trunkful of books, boy. I've really been studying the tactical problems and I think I've got 'em licked. You see, there's this place called Chiesa di San Tommaso di Villanova in Gandolfo – pardon my lousy Italian – and the route from the Vatican is over a kind of country thorough-fare called the Via Appia Antica. It's the road to this here Gandolfo – Castel Gandolfo, they call it. These Italians, they never use one word when they can use two.'

'*Whaaat?!*'

'Now, don't go over-reacting. You'll wake up Dellacroce.'

'*Whaaat?*'

'But first we have to corral the remaining capitalization. There's thirty million more coming. I believe I've almost narrowed down the three investors, but I've still got some refining to do.' The Hawk clapped his hand over Devereaux's open mouth. 'Now, don't start that again. You keep repeating yourself.'

Devereaux's eyes bulged above MacKenzie's spread hand, but the rest of his body was frozen. Sort of a form of comatose shock, thought Hawkins. He'd seen a lot of that kind of thing when raw recruits got their first taste of a fire fight. At least Sam wasn't screaming. Or struggling. He was just plain still and kind of cold. The Hawk continued; he had only a few words left to say. The in-depth command analyses would come later. In a way he was glad Devereaux's over-reaction was so extreme. In his enthusiasm he had nearly given Sam some tactical information he was not sure he wanted Devereaux to have.

'I didn't choose you lightly. No superior-adjutant is an easy choice for a commander to make, for in many ways the SA is an extension of himself. You got it on *merit*, boy. I don't say you're ideal, you've got deficiencies. I've told you that. But, goddamn, your assets out-point your liabilities. I say that as an honest friend as well as a superior officer.

'Now, there'll be certain executive orders that you'll be asked to carry out, not always knowing precisely why they're vital. You'll just have to accept them. Command is a lonely responsibility; there's not always the time to share the reasons for one's decisions. Ask any frontline officer who sends a battalion into fire. But you'll do splendidly. I just know you will. And if by any chance you're tempted to question the orders of your superior officer, or feel that you cannot in conscience implement them, I think you should know that our investor, Angelo Dellacroce, believes that you alone, as the attorney and secretary-treasurer of the Shepherd Company, compiled that list of his illegal activities and furnished me with them. I believe that's why he didn't care to shake hands with you. Coupled with your G-two espionage violations, I'd say your position was somewhat untenable. But if I were you and had my druthers, I'd choose to fight the government treason charges rather than our investor, Mr Dellacroce. I think that Mafia bastard would cut your balls off, grind 'em up in a blender, and serve 'em as a fancy pâté at your funeral. Like you said earlier, it'd probably be an expensive funeral.'

There was no point in the Hawk holding his hand over his superior-adjutant's mouth any longer. Sam had *merfed* and *gleefed* in a spasm of panic and passed out cold.

The moonlight, filtering through the leaves of the large, sturdy oak rough off fairway six, cut shafts of yellow and white across Sam's young, peaceful, unmistakably strong features.

Goddamn, thought Mackenzie, the boy's going to be fine! He just needed a little time to absorb the facts. Of course, if a person didn't know any better, he'd think the son of a bitch was dead.

CHAPTER TEN

Sam Devereaux sank despondently into the hotel chair and wished he were dead.

Well, not really, but it certainly would solve a lot of problems. Of course, it was entirely possible that the state of his demise might come about whether he desired it or not. Which brought his eyes back to the insane, unfiled but filled-out limited partnership agreement between the Shepherd Company, MacKenzie Hawkins, President, and the North Hampton Corporation, Mrs Angelo Dellacroce, President; Depository: the Great Bank of Geneva, Switzerland. He held the legal document in his hand and wondered absently where his fingernails had gone.

Prominently on the first page, directly under the title of president and above the line reserved for the secretary-treasurer, was his name.

Mr Samuel Devereaux, Counsellor-at-law, Suite 4-F, The Drake Hotel, New York City.

He speculated for a moment whether he could alter the Drake's registry and then abandoned the idea. What was the point? On one flank (*flank?*) was the United States government with very specific espionage laws, and on the other was Angelo Dellacroce and his guards-of-honour with their white ties on white shirts and dark glasses and black suits and very *un*specific methods of dealing with the likes of 'squeals' such as S. Devereaux, counsellor-at-law.

Sam wondered what Aaron Pinkus would do. Then he realized what Aaron would do and abandoned that thought, too.

111

Pinkus would sit *Shiva* for him.

He got out of the chair and wandered aimlessly through the hotel suite. What the hell *was* he going to do? What in God's name *could* he do? His gaze fell on the unsigned, typewritten note on the desk.

Copies of this limited partnership agreement have been sent by messenger to MacKenzie Hawkins, Esquire, President, the Shepherd Company, c/o The Watergate Hotel, Wash. D.C. Instructions cabled: Great Bank of Geneva. Funds transfer awaits presence Sec.-Treas., Shep. Co., Samuel Devereaux in Geneva.

He had been *cabled – internationally*.

In some marble banking hall in Switzerland, a powerful broker of international finance had no doubt already listed him as the bona fide overseer of the transfer of ten million dollars into an account of a nonfiled but very much existing company named Shepherd.

That's what he was going to do whether he liked it or not. It was Geneva, or a lifetime of cracking rocks at Leavenworth, *or* Dellacroce justice – feet-in-cement style.

Kidnap the pope!

My God! That's what the crazy bastard said. He was going to *kidnap the pope*!

All of Mac's other insanities paled by any stretch of comparison! World War Three might be more acceptable! A simple war would be so much – well, simpler. Borders were defined, objectives properly obscured, ideologies flexible. A war was duck soup compared to 400 million hysterical Catholics; and heads of state moaning and groaning their obsequious platitudes, blaming every conceivable inimical faction, extremist or not (secretly glad to be rid of the meddling nuisance in the Vatican) and . . .

My God! World War Three could be a very logical consequence of Hawkins's act!

And with that realization Sam knew what he had to do. He had to stop MacKenzie. But he could not stop him if he were in a maximum security cell in Leavenworth: who would believe him? And he certainly could not stop him if he were at the bottom of one of the deeper sections of the Hudson River, probably upstate, courtesy of Angelo Dellacroce; who would hear him?

No, the only way he could push the Hawk's insanity out of the realm of reality was to find out how the hell MacKenzie intended to pull off his papal score. The most foolish thing here would be to assume he couldn't do it. The Hawk was no joke; anyone who thought he was need only look at a few of Mac's accomplishments – including four extraordinary ex-wives who adored him, and a little matter of an initial capitalization of ten million dollars, to say nothing of military exploits spanning three decades and the same number of wars.

What the Hawk was bringing to the profession of crime were all the strategic resources, the finely honed discipline, and the leadership of an experienced general officer. MacKenzie was starting at the top; no graduate of the lineup he, but instead, a full-fledged criminal commander who had already outsacked a Mafia don in his own backyard.

The son of a bitch had flair. Christ! He had the balls of King Kong smashing the concrete off the Empire State Building as he climbed up the sides.

Kidnap the pope!

Who the hell would believe it?

Samuel Devereaux believed it, that's who believed it. What was left was for S. Devereaux, counsellor-at-law, to figure out how to stop it. And stay both alive and outside prison walls so doing. A vague idea was coming into focus, but it was still too blurred to make sense. Yet there was a core of possibility within the outlines.

'Don't be too confident,' said Sam out loud. 'You're dealing with a living, legal, spinal meningitis!'

But it *was* possible. He could pretend to go along with MacKenzie (always with great reluctance; to act otherwise would be out of character), gather in the diseased money and, at the last moment, convene the investors and blow the whole operation out of the sky. And to save his hide, there'd be a lot of 'in the case of my sudden demise, my own attorneys are instructed to publicly reveal . . .' any number of things.

Including the translation of the Shepherd Company's 'brokering of religious artifacts'.

Who would believe it?

'*Stop that!*' Sam grabbed his wrist, startled by the sound of his own voice. He was further startled by the sound of the telephone. He raced to it like a man facing execution rushing to hear what the governor had to say.

'Goddamn! This must be the attorney *and* secretary *and* treasurer of the Shepherd Company! With assets over ten million dollars! How does that strike you?'

'It's a leading question. I'll not indulge.'

'You know something, boy? You must be a pistol of a lawyer!'

'Are you sure you want to talk over the telephone?' asked Devereaux. 'It's been given a pretty good FCC rating lately.'

'Oh, that's all right. We won't say anything we shouldn't. At least, *I* won't, and I hope to hell you know better. I just wanted to tell you that the additional copies of the partnership agreement are downstairs waiting for you. I sent them up last night with an old master sergeant I used to know—'

'Good *God*, you had *duplicates* made? You damn fool! Those copy places usually keep a set! If they're photostats there'll be negatives!'

'Not where I was. Right down here in the Watergate lobby there's a big machine. You put in a quarter for each page – *Jesus!* You should have seen the crowds gather! They're a little jumpy around here, aren't they? But nobody saw anything. It was kind of weird. Everybody staring; nobody saying anything. Except two guys from the *Washington Post* who came running in from the street—'

'All right!' interrupted Devereaux. 'The copies are downstairs. What the hell am I supposed to do with them?'

'Put 'em in your fancy briefcase, the one I gave you. Take

'em to Geneva. You won't need 'em in Switzerland, of course, but there may be one or two other stops on the way back. Namely, London; that's pretty definite. You'll be at the Savoy for a day or two. Airline tickets and everything will be at the hotel in Geneva. When you're in London a gentleman named Danforth will call you. You'll know what to do.'

'That's a dirty pool. I won't know what to do; I don't know what I'm *doing*!' You can't just put me in this crazy situation and not tell me anything. I'm carrying documents! My *name* is on them! I'm involved with the transfer of ten million dollars!'

'Now, calm down,' said the Hawk with gentle firmness. 'Remember what I told you: There'll be times when, as my adjutant, you'll be asked to carry out orders—'

'*Bullshit!*' roared Sam. 'What am I supposed to *say* to people?'

'Well, what's bullshit to one man may be sugar-coated wheat to another. If anyone presses you, you're just helping an old soldier who's quietly raising a few dollars to spread religious brotherhood.'

'That's absurd,' said Devereaux.

'That's the Shepherd Company,' said the Hawk.

MacKenzie lifted up five specific pages from the Xeroxed G-2 files scattered over the hotel bed and took them to the desk across the room. He sat down, picked up a red crayon, and proceeded to mark each copy on the top left border. One to five.

Goddamn! It was the sequence he had been looking for, the pattern he knew was there because a man can't resist going back to his first method of fortune building if the circumstances appear right. And because time minimizes the problems and pressures a person felt decades ago, especially if the profits remain.

The covert intelligence out of Hanoi three years ago had been confusing but authentic. Authentic, that is, on the bottom line; everything else was distorted.

115

An Englishman was making a killing by brokering hardware and ammunition to North Vietnam.

No big deal; London did not frown on trade to the Commie bloc, although there were specific regulations as to war machinery. But it was a period during that screwed-up, half-assed conflict when the boys in Hanoi *and* Moscow *and* Peking were running slow on the production lines. Money could be made in large bundles by anyone who could divert combat supplies into North Vietnamese ports.

One Lord Sidney Danforth had done just that.

Buying in the United States, West Germany, and France, he sailed under Chilean flag ostensibly for ports in the new African countries. Except the ships did not go anywhere near Africa. They altered their courses in international Pacific waters, sped north, refuelled in the Russian out-islands, and headed south to Haiphong as regulation-bound trading vessels.

G-2 could never prove Danforth's involvement because the Communist payments were made directly to the Chilean companies and Danforth stayed well out of sight. And Washington was not about to provoke an incident. Danforth was a powerful Englishman with a lot of clout in the Foreign Office. Nam wasn't worth it.

What had intrigued MacKenzie, however, were the two keys: Chilean flag and African ports. They were covers that had been used before. Thirty years ago. During World War II.

It was common knowledge in intelligence circles that certain South American companies with outside financing had fed war machinery to the Axis at enormous profit during the early forties. In those hectic wartime days the shipping destinations were always Cape Town and Port Elizabeth because the manifest records in those harbours were chaotic at best, but usually non-existent. Scores of ships that were supposed to dock in South Africa altered courses in the southern Atlantic waters and headed into the Mediterranean. To Italy, generally.

Was it possible that one Lord Sidney Danforth had imitated his own operations of three decades past?

It was one thing to chisel a few million out of Southeast Asia in the seventies, something else again to make a fortune out of the holocaust that tested the courage of the British Lion. A man could get his name taken off the Buckingham Palace guest list pretty quickly for something like that.

It was time for the Hawk to have a transatlantic talk with Lord Sidney Danforth, seventy-two-year-old knighted paragon of British industry. And just about the wealthiest man in England.

Goddamn! The Shepherd Company was attracting some of the most interesting investors.

CHAPTER ELEVEN

The Strand was crowded. It was shortly past five o'clock; the legion of office workers were heading home.

Sam had arrived at Heathrow Airport on the 3.40 flight from Geneva and had wasted no time getting to the relaxed comfort of a Savoy suite. He needed it. Geneva had been a nightmare.

He had realized that for any future record, he had to convey a very specific ignorance as to the objectives of the Shepherd Company, cloaking this lack of knowledge in profound respect for the unnamed principals involved; especially the president, who was motivated by deeply religious convictions.

The Geneva bankers, were, at first, impressed by his humility. My God, ten million United States dollars and the overseeing lawyer only smiled and spoke convivial banalities, demurring when pressed for identities, nodding soulfully about religious brotherhood when the staggering amount was brought up. So they asked him out to lunch, where there were a lot of winks and drinks and offers of bedroom gymnastics of an incredible variety. This was, after all, Switzerland; a buck was a buck and this hard-nosed approach was not to be confused with yodelling and edelweiss and Heidi in her pinafores. Gradually, thought Devereaux, as the lunches evolved into dinners, the Geneva bankers thought he was either the dumbest attorney ever to practise before the American bar or the most implausibly secretive middle-man ever to cross their borders.

He kept up the charade for three days and nights, leaving

behind a half-dozen confused Swiss burgomasters, tearfully frustrated over unrequited confidences and terribly sick to their stomachs after too much industrial lubricant. And the strain on Sam was unbearable. He had reached the point where he could not concentrate on anything but his own rigid, blank smile and the necessary quiet control of his fears. He was so preoccupied with himself that when the vice-president of the Great Bank of Geneva saw him off at the airport, Devereaux just smiled and said 'Thank you' when the banker threw up over his raincoat.

In his anxiety to get the hell out of Geneva, he had left his shaving kit behind, which explained why he was now on The Strand looking for a drugstore. He walked south for a block and a half, opposite the Hippodrome, and went into the Strand Chemists. His purchases made, he headed back to the hotel, anticipating a long, warm bath, a shave, and a good dinner at the Savoy Grill.

'Major Devereaux!' The voice was enthusiastic, American, and feminine. It came from a taxi which stopped in Savoy Court.

It was Sloping yet Argumentative, the fourth Mrs Mac-Kenzie Hawkins, the lovely lady named Anne. She hurled herself at Sam, encircling his neck with her arms, pressing her cheek and various other parts against him.

Instantly she withdrew and rather awkwardly composed herself. 'I'm awfully sorry. Gosh, that was real *forward* of me. Please forgive me. It was just so *terrific* to see a familiar face.'

'Nothing to apologize for,' said Sam, remembering that Sloping yet Argumentative had appeared to him as the most naïve, as well as the youngest, of the four wives. She had *oohed* a lot, if he recalled correctly. 'Are you staying at the Savoy?'

'Yes. I got in last night. I've never been to England before, so I spent the whole day just walking *everywhere*. Gosh, my feet are yelling at me.' She parted her very expensive suede coat and frowned at the lovely legs very much in evidence below her short skirt.

'Well, let's get you off them quickly. Into the bar, I mean.'

'I can't *tell* you! It's so *marvy* to see someone you know!'

'Are you here by yourself?' asked Devereaux.

'Oh yes, Don, he's my husband – now – is so darned busy with his marinas and restaurants and all those other things that he just said to me last week in LA, he said, "Annie, honey, why don't you get your pretty little ass out of the way for a while? This is going to be a heavy month." Well, I thought of Mexico and Palm Springs and all the usual places, and then I figured, damn! Annie, you've never been to London. So off I flew.' She nodded brightly to the Savoy doorman and continued as Sam gestured her through the entrance into the lobby. 'Don thought I was crazy. I mean, who do I know in England? But I think that was part of it, you know? I wanted to go someplace where there weren't all the usual faces. Somewhere really different.'

'I hope I didn't spoil it.'

'How?'

'Well, you said I was a familiar face—'

'Oh, my, no! I said familiar, but I didn't mean *familiar*. I mean, one little short afternoon at Ginny's isn't *that* kind of familiar.'

'I see what you mean. The lounge is right up those stairs.' Sam nodded towards the steps on the left that led to the Savoy's American Bar. But Anne stopped, still holding on to his arm.

'Major,' she began haltingly, 'my feet are still screaming and my neck is sore from looking up and my shoulder's aching from this darned purse strap. I'd really love to spend a little time straightening myself out.'

'Oh, sure,' replied Devereaux. 'I'm being thoughtless. And stupid. As a matter of fact I was going to do some, er, straightening out myself. I left my shaving gear in Switzerland.' He held up the bag from the Strand Chemists.

'Well, then, that's *marvy*!'

'I'll call you in about an hour—'

'Why do that? Have you seen the size of those johnnies upstairs? Wow! They're bigger than some of Don's ladies' rooms. In his restaurants, I mean. There's plenty of room.

120

And those big, groovy towels. I swear they're terry cloth sheets!' She squeezed his arm and smiled ingenuously.

'Well, it *is* a solution—'

'The only one. Come on, we'll get some drinks from room service and *really* relax.' They started for the elevator.

'It's very kind of you—'

'Kind, hell! Ginny told us you called. She positively *lorded* it over us. Now it's my turn. You were in Geneva?'

Sam stopped. 'I said Switzerland—'

'Isn't that Geneva?'

Anne's suite was also on the Thames side, also on the sixth floor, and conveniently no more than fifty feet down the corridor from his.

Switzerland. Isn't that Geneva? Several thoughts crossed Devereaux's mind, but he was entirely too exhausted to dwell on them. And, for the first time in days, entirely too relaxed to let them interfere.

The rooms were very like his own. High ceilings with real mouldings; marvellous old furniture – polished, functional – desks and tables and pictures and chairs and a sofa that would do credit to Parke-Bernet; mantel clocks and lamps that were neither nailed down nor with embedded plastic cards proclaiming ownership; tall casement windows, flanked by regal drapes, that looked out on the river with the lights of small boats, the buildings beyond, and especially Waterloo Bridge.

He was in the sitting room, on the pillowhead sofa, with his shoes off and a tall drink in his hand. The London Philharmonic was on Radio 3, playing a Vivaldi concerto, and the warmth from a heater filled the room with a splendid comfort. Good things came to the deserving, thought Sam.

Anne came out of the bathroom and stopped in the frame of the doorway. Devereaux's glass was suddenly checked on its way to his lips. She was dressed – if that was the word – in a translucent sheath that at once left little to, yet completely provoked, the imagination. Her Sloping yet Argumentative breasts swelled to blushing points beneath the soft, single layer of fabric; her long, light-brown hair fell casually and sensually over her shoulders, framing her extraordinary endowments. Her tapered legs were outlined under the sheath.

Without saying a word, she raised her hand and beckoned him with her finger. He rose from the sofa and followed.

Inside the huge, tiled bathroom, the enormous Savoy tub was filled with steaming water; several thousand bubbles gave off the scent of roses and wet springtime. Anne reached up and removed his tie, and then his shirt, and then unstrapped his buckle, unzipped his trousers and lowered them to the floor. He kicked them free himself.

She placed her hands on both sides of his waist and pulled down his shorts, kneeling as she did so.

He sat on the edge of the warm tub while she pulled off his socks; and she held his left arm as he slid over the side, his body disappearing under the steaming white bubbles.

She stood up, undid a yellow bow at her neck, and the sheath fell to the floor on top of the thick white rug.

She was utterly magnificent.

And she got into the tub with Sam.

'Do you want to go down to dinner?' asked the girl from beneath the covers.

'Sure,' replied Devereaux from under same.

'Do you know we slept for over three hours? It's nearly nine-thirty.' She stretched; Sam watched. 'After we eat, let's go to one of those pubs.'

'If you like,' said Devereaux, still watching her, his head on the pillow. She was sitting up now, the sheet had fallen to her waist. Sloping yet Argumentative were challenging all they surveyed.

'Gosh,' Anne spoke softly, a touch awkwardly, as she turned and looked down at Sam, who could barely see her face. 'I'm being real forward again.'

'Friendly's a better word. I'm friendly, too.'

'You know what I mean.' She bent over him and kissed

him on both eyes. 'You may have other plans; things you have to do or something.'

'Things I want to do,' interrupted Devereaux warmly. 'All plans are completely flexible, subject only to whim and pleasure.'

'That sounds sexy as hell.'

'I feel sexy as hell.'

'Thank you.'

'Thank *you*.' Sam reached above and beyond her soft, lovely back and pulled the sheet over them.

Ten minutes later (it was either ten minutes or several hours, thought Devereaux) they made the decision: They really did need food, preceded, of course, by short, smoky drams of iced whisky, which they had in the sitting room, on the pillowed couch, under two soft, enormous bath towels.

'I think the word is "sybaritic".' Sam adjusted the terry cloth over his lap. Radio 3 was now playing a Noël Coward medley and the smoke from their cigarettes drifted into the sprays of warm orange light from the fireplace. Only two lamps were turned on; the room was dreamed of in a thousand ballads.

'Sybaritic has a selfish meaning,' said the girl. 'We share; that's not selfish.'

Sam looked at her. Hawkins's fourth wife was no idiot. How in hell did he do it? Had he done it? 'The way we share, it's sybaritic, believe me.'

'If you want me to,' she answered, smiling and putting her glass down on the coffee table.

'Its not important. Why don't we dress and go eat?'

'All right. I'll just be a few seconds.' She saw his questioning expression. 'No, I will. I don't dawdle for hours. Mac once said—' She stopped, embarrassed.

'It's okay,' he said gently. 'I'd really like to hear.'

'Well, he once said that if you try to change the outside too much, you can't help but mix up the inside. And you shouldn't do that unless there's a goddamned good reason. Or if you really don't like yourself.' She swung her legs out from under her and rose from the couch, holding the towel around her body. 'One, I don't see any reason; and two, I kind of like me. Mac taught me that, too. I like *us*.'

'So do I,' said Devereaux. 'When you're finished, we'll go down to my room and I'll change.

'Good. I'll button your shirt and tie your tie.' She grinned and dashed through the foyer door into the bedroom. Devereaux got up naked, throwing the long towel over his shoulder, and went to the side table where the bar was set up in a silver tray. He poured a small quantity of Scotch and thought about Mac Hawkins's bathroom philosophy.

Change the outside too much – you mix up the inside.

It wasn't bad, all things considered.

The tiny white light shone between the red and green bulbs on the small panel beside Devereaux's door. Sam and the girl saw it simultaneously as they walked down the corridor and approached his suite. It was the sign that a message was at the front desk for the guest. Devereaux swore under his breath.

Goddamn it! Geneva had not been erased *that* quickly. Or so completely, either. The least Hawkins could do was to let him get a decent night's sleep!

'One of those lights was on for me this afternoon,' said Anne. 'I came back to change my shoes and found it; it means you have a phone call.'

'Or a message.'

'Mine was a call. From Don in Santa Monica. I finally got him back; you know, it was only eight o'clock in the morning in California.'

'Nice of him to get up and phone.'

'Not so. My husband owns two things in Santa Monica: a restaurant and a girl. The restaurant's not open at eight in the morning; forgive my bitchiness. I think Don just wanted to make sure I was really seven thousand miles away.' Anne smiled up at him naïvely. He was not sure how to respond, all things considered.

'Seems like a lot of trouble for, well, for checking up.' Sam snapped on the light switch in his foyer. Beyond, the sitting room lamps were on, as he had left them five hours ago.

'My husband suffers from a mental illness peculiar to cheap strayers. As a lawyer, I'm sure you're familiar with it. He's paranoid about getting caught. Not morally, you understand; when he's juiced up, he flaunts *that* part. Just financially; he's scared to death some court will make him pay big if I opt for out.'

They walked into his sitting room; he wanted to say something but, again, all things considered he was not sure what it should be. He chose the safest. 'I think the man's out of his mind.'

'You're sweet, but you didn't have to say it. On the other hand, I suppose it's the safest thing you *could* say—'

'Let's find another subject,' he interrupted quickly, indicating the couch and the coffee table with the Savoy-supplied newspapers on it. 'Sit down and I'll be with you in a minute. I haven't forgotten: You button the shirt and tie the tie.' Sam started for the bedroom door.

'Aren't you going to call the desk?'

'It can *wait*,' he answered from the bedroom. 'I have no intention of letting anything interfere with a quiet dinner. Or for that matter, showing you a pub or two, if they're still open when we're finished.'

'You really should find out who's trying to reach you. It could be important.'

'*You're* important,' shouted Sam, removing a tan double-knit suit from the awkward hangar in his suitcase.

'It could be something vital,' said the girl from the sitting room.

'*You're vital*,' he replied, selecting a red-striped shirt from the next layer of clothes.

'I can't *ever* not answer a phone, or check for messages, or call back even a name I never heard of; that's being *too* casual.'

'You're not a lawyer. Ever tried to get a lawyer the day after you've hired him? His secretary is trained to lie with the conviction of Aimee Semple McPherson.'

'Why?' Anne was now standing in the bedroom doorway.

'Well, he's got your money; he's scrounging around for another fee. What the hell, your case probably entails an exchange of letters with the opposing attorney, other explanations notwithstanding. He doesn't want complications.'

Anne approached him as he slipped on the red-striped shirt. She nonchalantly began buttoning it. 'You're a very cool Clyde. Here you are in a strange country—'

'Not so strange,' he broke in, smiling. 'I've been here before. I'm your tour guide, remember?'

'I mean, you've just come from Geneva where you obviously had a bad time—'

'Not so bad. I survived.'

'—and now someone is desperately trying to find you—'

'What's desperate? I don't know anybody so desperate.'

'For Christ's sake!' The girl yanked his collar as she fastened it. 'Things like this make me nervous!'

'Why?'

'I feel responsible!'

'You shouldn't.' Devereaux was fascinated. Anne was very serious. He wondered . . .

And the telephone rang.

'Hello?'

'Mr Samuel Devereaux?' asked the precise voice of a male Britisher.

'Yes, this is Sam Devereaux.'

'I've been waiting for your call—'

'I just got in,' interrupted Sam. 'I haven't checked my messages yet. Who is this?'

'At the moment, merely a telephone number.'

Devereaux paused, annoyed. 'Then I should tell you, you would have waited all night. I don't return calls to telephone numbers.'

'Come, sir,' was the agitated reply. 'You're not expecting any other caller of consequence.'

'That's a little presumptuous, I think—'

'Think whatever you like, sir! I'm in a great hurry and quite put out with you. Now, where do you wish to meet?'

'I don't know that I want to. Fuck off, Basil, or whatever the hell your name is.'

The pause was now on the other end of the line. Sam could hear heavy breathing. In seconds the telephone number spoke. 'For God's sake, have pity on an old man. I've done you no harm.'

Sam was suddenly touched. The voice had cracked slightly; the man was desperate. He remembered Hawkins's last conversation. 'Are you—'

'No *names, please!*'

'All right. No names. Are you recognizable?'

'Extremely. I thought you knew that.'

'I didn't. So we meet someplace out of the way.'

'Very much so. I thought you knew that, too.'

'Stop saying that!' Devereaux was as much annoyed with Hawkins as he was with the Englishman on the telephone. 'Then you'd better choose it, unless you want to come to the Savoy.'

'Impossible! That's kind of you. I have several apartment buildings in Belgravia. One's the Hampton Arms; do you know it?'

'I can find it.'

'Good. I'll be there. Flat four seven. It will take me an hour to get into London.'

'Don't hurry. I don't want to meet in an hour.'

'Oh? At what time then?'

'When do the pubs close these days?'

'Midnight. A little over an hour.'

'Shit!'

'I beg your pardon?'

'I'll see you at one o'clock.'

'Very well. The Hampton security will be alerted. Remember, no names. Just flat four seven.'

'Four seven.'

'And, Devereaux. Bring the papers.'

'What papers?'

The pause was longer now, the English breathing heavier. 'That goddamned agreement, you *ass*.'

The girl not only accepted the fact that their dinner would be short and that he had to leave the hotel, but she seemed positively elated.

Sam was wondering less and less. The *why* escaped him, but the *what* was becoming clearer. He agreed to have a nightcap with her when he returned. The hour was unimportant, Anne said; she gave him a key.

The taxi stopped at the kerb in front of the Hampton Arms. At Sam's mention of flat four seven, he was led by a doorman in a series of swift, secretive movements that took him through service doors, a short back staircase, a freight elevator, and the delivery entrance of the flat.

An ominous-looking man with a north country accent asked for identification and then led Sam through a pantry, a large living room, a hallway, and finally to a small dimly lit library where a rather ugly little old man sat in the shadows by the window. The door closed. Devereaux stood, adjusting his eyes to the light and the unattractive ancient in the armchair.

'Mr Devereaux – naturally,' said the wrinkled old man.

'Yes. You must be the Danforth Hawkins spoke of.'

'Lord Sidney Danforth.' The ugly little person spat out the ugly words, then suddenly his voice was syrup. 'I don't know how your employer pieced together what he did, nor do I for a moment admit *anything*; it's all so preposterous. And so long ago. Nevertheless, I am a good man, a charitable man. Quite a *wonderful* man. Give me the damned papers!'

'What?'

'The agreement, you insufferable bastard!'

Stunned, Sam reached into his breast pocket where he had a folded copy of the Shepherd Company's limited partnership. He crossed to the ugly little person and gave it to him. Danforth swung out a portable desk panel from somewhere at the side of the armchair and snapped on a bright worklight at the top of the board. He grabbed the papers and started scanning them.

'Fine!' said Danforth, wheezing, flipping over the pages. 'They say absolutely *nothing*!' The little Britisher reached for a pen and began filling in the black lines. When he had finished, he refolded the papers and handed them distastefully to Devereaux. 'Now, get out! I am a marvellous man, a magnanimous provider; a humble multi-millionaire whom everyone adores. I have richly deserved the extraordinary honours heaped upon my person. Everybody knows that And nobody. I repeat, *nobody* could conceivably associate me with such madness! I am only – spreading brotherhood – do you understand me? *Brotherhood*, I say!'

'I don't understand anything,' said Sam.

'Neither do I,' replied Danforth. 'The transfer will be made in the Cayman Islands. The bank is listed and the ten million will be shifted within forty-eight hours. Then I'm through with you!'

'The Cayman Islands?'

'They're in the Caribbean, you ass.'

CHAPTER TWELVE

He could see the tiny white light shining fifty feet down the Savoy corridor. He did not have to get any closer to know it was the door to his rooms; avoiding it was a second, very good reason to let himself into Annie's suite.

'If that's not you, Sam, I've got problems,' she called from the bedroom.

'It's me. All your problems are happy ones.'

'I like those kind.'

Devereaux walked into the large bedroom with the windows overlooking the river. Anne was sitting up, reading a brightly coloured paperback by the light of the table lamp. 'What's that?' he asked. 'It looks impressive.'

'A marvellous history of Henry the Eighth's wives. I got it at the Tower this morning. That man was a monster!'

'Not really. A lot of his troubles were geopolitical.'

'In his crotch they were!'

'That's more historically sound than you may think. How about a drink?'

'You've got to make a phone call first. I promised; first thing you did when you got back.'

The girl turned a page calmly. Sam was not only astonished, he was curious. 'What did you say?'

'MacKenzie called. All the way from Washington.' She turned another page.

'MacKenzie?' Devereaux could not help himself; he roared. 'Just – *MacKenzie called*! You're sitting there like you heard from room service and tell me MacKenzie called. How do *you* know he called? Did he call *you*?'

'Really, Sam, stop being so uptight.' Cold as ice, she turned another goddamned page. 'It's not as though I didn't know him. I mean, after all—'

'Oh, no! Spare me the odious comparisons! I just want to know about this extraordinary coincidence that has you seven thousand miles from home taking a telephone call from an ex-husband who's calling *me* – three thousand miles from New York.'

'If you'll calm down, I'll tell you. If you won't, I'm just going to keep on reading.'

Devereaux thought about how much he wanted a drink, but he suppressed his anger and spoke quietly. 'I'm calm and I would very much like to have you speak. Please speak.'

Anne put the book down on her lap and looked up at him. 'To begin with, Mac was every bit as uptight as you are when I got on the line.'

'How *did* you get on the line?'

'Because I was worried.'

'That's why, not how.'

'If you recall, and I think you will if you try real hard, you left me at the table downstairs. You were running late and I insisted. I told you I'd sign the check and go upstairs. Am I right so far?'

'I owe you for dinner. Go on.'

'A nice young man in white tie and tails came to the table and said there was an urgent transatlantic call for you. Are they always so dressed up?'

'It's a Savoy custom. What did you say?'

'That you wouldn't be back until very late; I wasn't sure of the time. He seemed upset so I asked him if I could help. He said the caller was a General Hawkins from Washington, and I think the rank and the city made him nervous. Mac always does that; it gets better telephone service. So I told him not to worry about a thing. I'd talk to the old fart. He liked that.' Anne returned to her book. 'Now, go call him. The number's on the desk in the other room. It's also on the desk in your place and also downstairs. I'm very flattered that you got it here first.'

It *was* possible, Sam reflected. Unlikely but within the scope of possibility, as certain radio waves indicated the possibility of additional civilizations in galactic space. 'What did Hawkins say? How was he uptight?'

'Oh, just that I was *here*, I suppose,' said the girl, reluctantly taking her eyes off the page. 'He started swearing and yelling and giving orders. I said, "Mac," I said, "go wash your mouth out with brown soap!" I always used to tell him that. I mean he uses language we stayed away from in Belle Isle. Anyway, he calmed down and started to laugh.' Anne's eyes drifted upward, at nothing. She was remembering, thought Sam, and those memories were not cold ones. 'He asked me if I'd got rid of the fancy gigolo waiter yet – that's what he calls Don – and if not, *why* not. And how you were such a nice fellow. You know, Mac thinks a great deal of you. Anyhow, it is very important that you call him back. I said it'd be awfully late; maybe not until three in the morning. But he said that was all right; it would only be ten o'clock in Washington.'

'Can't it wait until morning?'

'No. Mac was very emphatic. He said if you thought about putting it off I should tell you it had something to do with an Italian gentleman who was asking for you.'

'Did he add that he was in the undertaking business?'

'No. But I think you should call him. If you want privacy, you can use the phone in the other room.'

'Goddamn, boy! Isn't it a real small world! There you are halfway across the globe and who do you run into but little old Annie. Not that she's old, you understand—'

'I understand,' interrupted Sam, 'that you've got greetings for me from Dellacroce. What did you tell your deeply religious friend now? That I crucified Jesus?'

'Hell, no. That was just a little psych-prod, in case you were reluctant to return my call. I haven't even talked to Dellacroce. I don't think he's in favour of any further communications. Does that make you feel better?'

Devereaux lit a cigarette. It helped cover the slight pain

that was developing in his stomach. 'I'll tell you the truth, Mac. It simply makes me nervous that you called me at all. It makes me feel that you are about to say something that will not bring me any closer to Boston, or my mother, or my real employer, Aaron Pinkus; that's the way your psych-prod makes me feel.'

There was a long series of audible tsks from MacKenzie Hawkins in Washington. 'You are a very suspicious person. It must be the lawyer in you. How did everything go with Danforth?'

'He's a madman. He blows out hot and cold like a psycho. He also signed the papers; he's in for ten million for reasons I can't possibly imagine. The bank's in the Cayman Islands, which is, I assume, the reason for your telephone call.'

'You mean you think I'd ask you to go to the Caymans?'

'It crossed my mind.'

'I wouldn't do that. The Caymans aren't any fun. Just dinky little hot spots with lots of banks and pricky-shit bankers. They're trying to make the place into another Switzerland . . . No, I'll fly down there myself and take care of it. And you've got another ten thousand added to your account. Thought you'd like to know that.'

'*Mac!*' Devereaux's stomach experienced a sharp, stinging sensation. 'You can't *do* that!'

'It's easy, boy. You just make the cashier's cheque out for deposit only.'

'That's not what I mean! You have no *right* putting money into my account!'

'The bank didn't argue—'

'The bank wouldn't argue! *I* argue! I *am* arguing! Christ, don't you understand? It means you're paying me!'

'One-tenth of one per cent? Goddamn, boy, I'm cheating you!'

'I don't *want* to be paid! I don't want anything to *do* with any money from you! That makes me an *accessory*!'

'I don't know anything about that, but it's surely not right for one person to call upon the time and the talents of

133

another person and not pay him for it.' Hawkins's voice had the ring of a quiet evangelist.

'Oh, shut up, you son of a bitch,' said Devereaux, recognizing the inevitability of defeat. 'Outside of Danforth, why did you call?'

'Well, now that you mention it, there's a fellow in West Berlin I'd like you to talk with.'

'Wait. Don't tell me,' interrupted Sam wearily. 'The airline tickets and the hotel reservations will be at the Savoy desk before I can say kippered herring.'

'By morning, anyway.'

'Okay, Mac, I know when I'm hung.' He was getting in deeper. Somehow, some way, some time, Sam thought, he would have to climb out.

MacKenzie wrote out the figure numerically.

$20,000,000.00

Then he wrote it in words:

Twenty million dollars.

Strange, but it had no real effect on him. It was merely a means, not an end in itself. Although it had occurred to him that he could easily call it an economic day, wrap it up, and retire to the south of France. Certainly, neither Dellacroce nor Danforth would sue. Not bloody likely. But that wasn't what it was all about; the money was both a conveyance and a by-product. And in its way, a legitimate form of punishment. The two marks deserved their losses.

But time was running short and he could not allow himself to get sidetracked. Summer was only a few months away; there was an enormous amount of work to do. The selection and training of the support personnel would be time-consuming. The leasing and stocking of the manoeuvre site would be difficult, especially the covert purchasing of equipment. The manoeuvres themselves would take a number of weeks. All told, there was a great deal to accomplish in a short time. Because of this it was a natural temptation to veer from the initial strategy and go with less than the full capitalization, but it would be wrong. That's for sure. He had set the figure of forty million not merely for the numerical symmetry to the four hundred million (although it certainly looked proper on the limited partnership agreement, in the blank lines he had filled out), but because forty million took care of *everything*, including last-extremity contingencies.

Otherwise known as quick-witted evacuation of the fire base.

It would have to be forty million. He was just about ready for his third investor.

Heinrich Koenig, Berlin.

Herr Koenig had not been easy. Whereas Sidney Danforth had overworked his modus operandi in Chile, and whereas Angelo Dellacroce had been just plain sloppy with regard to his Mediterranean payments and entirely too ostentatious in his manner of living, Heinrich Koenig had made no obvious errors, and lived the quiet life of a country squire in a peaceful rural town twenty-odd miles from Berlin.

But twenty-two years ago Koenig had played an enormously dangerous game brilliantly. A game that not only netted him a fortune but also ensured the capitalization and ultimate success of his various business enterprises.

During the height of the Cold War, Koenig was a double agent-cum-blackmailer. He began by secretly informing on single agents to both sides, then extorting cash – financed through opposing intelligence channels – from those seeking protection from exposure. Soon he was issued exclusive international, non-tariff 'franchises' for his new companies from scores of countries dependent upon the economic goodwill of both giant factions. Finally, with the grace of Mephistopheles, he forced Washington, London, Berlin, Bonn, and Moscow into declaring his companies *outside* the regulatory legalities that governed other industries. Koenig accomplished this by explaining to each that he would inform the others of its past activities.

And then, to the profound relief of many governments, Koenig retired. He had built his empire on the trampled

135

bodies – deceased and paralysed – of half the bureaucratic and industrial population of Europe and America. He had remained untouchable because of the very real terror of chain reaction-reprisal. What bureaucrat, what under-secretary, what minister or statesman (indeed, what head of a government) would allow access to the horrors of Pandora's box? So, in retirement, Koenig remained as safe as during his halcyon days of furious activity.

Fear was Koenig's clout. But there was no fear or clout if a man didn't give a good goddamn about reaction or reprisals – governmental, industrial, or international.

And naturally this was Hawkins's weapon.

For there was an international army of victims who would quick-march for the kill if they thought they could do so with impunity, if everyone realized his past sins were known to everybody else. Complete disclosure was Mac's threat.

Koenig would certainly see the logic of this approach; it was the absence of it that had guaranteed his fortunes. He surely could foretell the effects of several hundred lengthy cablegrams sent simultaneously to several hundred inhabitants of the corridors of power throughout the world. Oh, yes! Koenig would be convinced, the instant a barrage of names, dates, and activities was rattled off to him.

MacKenzie picked up the raw-file Xeroxes from the bed, keeping the piles in sequence, and carried them to the coffee table in front of the couch. He sat down and with the red crayon he began circling two or three items on each page.

Things were going beautifully. It was all a question of making a realistic appraisal of one's capabilities and the logistics available to complement those abilities. Simple inventory. He picked up the Xeroxes, moved to the desk, and arranged the papers properly in front of the telephone. He was ready to calmly, dispassionately recite a record of international duplicity that would cause Genghis Khan to blush.

Heinrich Koenig would part with ten million dollars.

His eyes rimmed with black circles of exhaustion, Devereaux

went through customs at Berlin's Tempelhof Airport, fully prepared to have his forehead stamped by the officiously barking neo-Nazi who inspected his papers and luggage. Christ, he thought, give a German a rubber stamp and he went wild.

At one point he stared in amazement at the contents of his own suitcase. Everything was folded neatly and arranged tidily as though packed by Bergdorf Goodman, and he simply did not pack suitcases that way. Then through the fog of dislocation, he remembered that Anne had taken care of everything. She not only had packed for him, she had also accompanied him to the cashier's desk and helped him settle his bill.

She had done all this, reflected Sam, because he was not in any condition to do much for himself. The insanity of his predicament had led him into a battle with a bottle of Scotch. He lost. The only thing he did remember to do was to airmail the goddamned limited partnership agreement to Hawkins.

Berlin's Kempinsky Hotel was a Teutonic version of New York's old Sherry-Netherland with a slightly harsher interior; the overstuffed lobby chairs seemed cast more in concrete than leather. Still, it screamed money, polished dark wood, and terribly proper clerks Sam knew hated his weak, democratically oriented, and inferior guts.

The front desk dispensed with him efficiently and swiftly. He was escorted by a disagreeable, ageing SS Oberführer who treated his suitcase as though it contained bagels and lox. Once inside the suite (it was enormous; Mac Hawkins did send him first class) the Oberführer snapped up the shades in the various rooms with the authority of a man used to issuing commands to a firing squad. Devereaux, fearing for his life, grossly overtipped him, saw him to the door as if he were a visiting diplomat and bid him a gracious *auf Wiedersehen*!

He opened his suitcase. Anne had possessed the foresight to wrap a full bottle of Scotch in a Savoy towel. If there was ever time to ingest the indigestible, it was now. Not much; just enough to get the motor running.

There was a knock on the door. Sam was so startled he coughed a mouthful of whisky over the bed. He corked the bottle and furiously looked for a place to hide it.

Under the pillow! Covered by the bedspread! He stopped. What was he doing? What the hell was the matter with him? What was *happening* to him? *Goddamn you, MacKenzie Hawkins!*

He took a deep breath, and calmly placed the bottle on the dresser top. He took another deep breath, opened the door, and promptly, involuntarily, expelled every bit of air in his lungs.

Standing in the door frame was the blonde Aphrodite from Palo Alto, California, catalogued in his memory as Narrow and Pointed. The third Mrs MacKenzie Hawkins. Lillian.

'I knew it was you! I said to the man at the desk that it *had* to be you!'

Sam was not sure why he had catalogued Lillian as Narrow and Pointed. 'Narrow' did the lady an injustice. Perhaps it was a relative adjective, subject to the immediate visual comparison to the other six.

Devereaux was thinking these absurd thoughts and – he was aware – staring like a twelve-year-old at his first *Artists and Models* magazine, while Lillian sat across from him, explaining that she had flown into Berlin three days ago to attend a two-week course in gourmet cooking.

Of course, it was unbelievable. After all, he was a skilled attorney. He had analysed scores of crime-ridden mentalities, stripping away the layers of fraud from sophisticated deceivers on all levels of the social jungle. In spite of his drained mind and body, he was not a man to be conned easily and he would let the third Mrs MacKenzie Hawkins know that – in *spades*! He stared at her harder, then mentally shrugged. What the hell!

'So there we are, Sam. I may call you Sam, mayn't I? It's amazing what an interest in really fine cooking can lead to.'

'But entirely plausible, Lillian! That's what makes coincidences truly – well, coincidental!' Sam laughed quasihysterically, doing his best to control his eyes. He was simply too exhausted to be successful; he just gave up and let his eyes roam freely.

'And I can't think of a better way to see Berlin. If we're lucky, we can find an indoor tennis court! I hear the hotel has a swimming pool; perhaps a gymnasium—' Lillian stopped and Devereaux felt deprived; in his spent condition he was enjoying the soft, breathless, aural massage. 'I may be taking far too much for granted. Are you travelling alone?'

He knew he shouldn't. He *shouldn't*.

'More alone than I've ever been in my life.'

'Well, we certainly can't have that. If you don't mind my saying so, you look dreadfully tired. I think you've been working half to death. You really need someone to look after you.'

'I am only a warm shadow of my substance . . .'

'You poor lamb. Come over here and let me rub your shoulder blades. It does wonders, it really, really does.'

'I am a wasted vestige. I am filled with vacuum and molten lead . . .'

'You're exhausted, my lamb. That's the good boy; stretch out and put your head on Lilly's lap. Oh my, your temples are so warm. And your neck muscles are much too tense. There, that's better; doesn't it feel better?'

It did. He could feel her nimble fingers unbutton his shirt and the gentle hands moving about his chest, caressing his flesh with the touch of angels. What the hell. He opened his eyes, his sight was filled with the unbearable loveliness of two magnificent breasts inches above his face.

'Do you like hot tubs filled with lots of soap bubbles that smell like roses and springtime?' he whispered.

'Not actually,' she whispered back. 'I'm partial to warm showers. Straight up, as it were.'

Sam smiled.

CHAPTER THIRTEEN

The fragrance permeated the air around him; he did not need to open his eyes to know its source.

If he was able to reconstruct the previous evening with any accuracy – and the quiescence below his waist convinced him that he could – they had spent most of the night in the Kempinsky shower.

Sam opened his eyes. Lillian was beside him, sitting up against the pillows with a pair of horn-rimmed glasses perched on her lovely upturned nose. She was reading from an enormous piece of frayed cardboard, the white sheet covering her chest but not for an instant obscuring the shafts beneath.

'Hello,' he said quietly.

'Good morning!' She looked down at him and positively beamed. 'Do you know what time it is?'

The blonde creature *was* a healthy type, he considered. It must be all that California surfboarding, or perhaps Mac-Kenzie Hawkins had taught her to do pushups. 'My watch is under the covers with my wrist. I do not know what time it is.'

'It's twenty after ten. You slept for eleven hours. How do you feel?'

'Are you telling me we went to bed – I was asleep – by eleven-thirty last night?'

'You could be heard at the Brandenburg Gate. I kept shoving you to stop your snoring. You were positively operatic. How's your head?'

'Fairly secure, as a matter of fact. I wonder why?'

'All that steam. And exercise. Actually, you weren't capable of drinking a great deal. I think your bloodstream went into revolt.' Lillian picked up a pencil from the bedside table and lightly checked the menu.

'You smell terrific,' he said after several moments of looking up at her, remembering the sightlines from her lap and the touches of angels over his chest.

'So do you, lamb,' she replied, smiling, removing her glasses, and gazing down at Sam. 'Do you know, you have a very acceptable body?'

'It has its points.'

'I mean you have a fundamentally sound physique, moderately well proportioned and coordinated. It's really a pity you've let it disintegrate.' She tapped her glasses against her chin like a doctor studying postoperative conditions.

'Well, I wouldn't go so far as to say disintegrate. I played lacrosse once. I was pretty good.'

'I'm sure you were, well over a decade ago. Now look here—' Lilly put down her glasses and peeled the blankets away from Devereaux's chest. 'See here. And *here* and here and *here*! Absolutely no tone whatsoever. Muscle pockets that've had no discernible use for years! And *here*.'

'Ouch!'

'Your latissimi dorsi are positively non-*existent*. When was the last time you exercised?'

'Last night. In the shower.'

'That aspect of your condition cannot be debated. But it's a minor part of the whole being—'

'Not to me it isn't!'

'—relative to the muscular network. Your body is a temple; don't let it crumble and decay with misuse and neglect. Spruce it up! Give it a chance to stretch and breathe and be useful; that's what it's meant for. Look at MacKenzie—'

'I object! I don't want to look at MacKenzie!'

'I'm speaking clinically.'

'I knew it,' mumbled Devereaux in defeat. 'I can't escape him. I'm possessed.'

'Do you realize that Mac is well over *fifty*? And take his body. It's taut. It's a coiled spring toned to perfection . . .'

Lilly's eyes drifted up – at nothing. As Anne's had done at the Savoy. She was remembering, as Anne had remembered – and those memories were not cold.

'Well, for God's sake,' said Sam. 'Hawkins spent his whole life in the army. Running and jumping and killing and torturing. He had to stay in shape so he could stay alive. He had no choice.'

'You're wrong. Mac understands the meaning of full capacity, experiencing the total potential. He once said to me – well, never mind, it's unimportant.' The girl removed her hand from Devereaux's chest and reached for her glasses.

'No, please.' The bedroom in the Kempinsky might have been a bedroom in the Savoy. But the wives were not interchangeable; they were very individual. 'I'd like to hear what Mac said.'

Lilly held her glasses in both hands, fingering the stems pensively. '"Your body should be a realistic extension of your mind, pushed to its limit but not abused."'

'I liked the "change the outside, mix up the inside" better—'

'What?'

'Something else he said. Maybe I don't understand; the intellectual and the physical are poles apart. I might imagine I could fly off the Eiffel Tower, but I'd better not try it.'

'Because that wouldn't be realistic; it would be abusive. But you might train yourself to scale down it in record time. *That* would be the realistic, *physical* extension of your imagination. And it's important to attempt it.'

'Scale down the Eiffel Tower?'

'If flying off is a serious consideration.'

'It's not. If I follow this pseudoscholastic doggerel, you're saying that if you think about doing something you should actually translate it as much as possible into physical terms.'

'Yes. The main thing is not to remain inert.' Lilly waved her arms in emphasis; the sheet plummeted down.

Unbearably lovely, thought Devereaux. But at the moment untouchable; the girl was in debate.

'This is either far more complicated or much simpler than it sounds,' he said.

'It's more complicated, believe me,' she answered. 'The subtlety is in the obviousness.'

'You believe in this challenge concept, don't you?' Sam said. 'I mean it's fundamentally the necessary satisfaction of meeting the challenge, isn't it?'

'Yes, I suppose it is. For its own sake; to try to reach out for what you can imagine. To test your potential.'

'And you believe that.' There was no question implied.

'Yes, I do. Why?'

'Because at this moment my imagination is working so hard I can't stand it. I feel the necessity of physical expression; to test my potential. Within reasonable limits, of course.' He rose from his base camp until he sat facing her, their eyes level. He reached out and took her glasses, folded them, and dropped them over the side of the bed. He held out his hand and she gave him the menu.

Lillian's eyes were bright, her lips parted in a half smile. 'I was wondering when you were going to ask.'

And then the Nazi telephone rang.

The voice on the other end of the line belonged to a man brought up in his formative years watching all those war movies from Warner Brothers. Every syllable dripped evil.

'Ve do not – vill not – cannot shpeak on der telephone.'

'Go across the street and open a window. We'll shout,' replied Devereaux irritably.

'Der time ist der essence! You vill go down to der lobby, to der fart chair in front of der vindow, on der richt of der hentrance! Under der arm carry a folded copy of *Der Spiegel*. Und you vill be crossing der legs every twenty seconds.'

'I'm sitting down?'

'You vould look foolish crossing der legs standing up, mein Herr.'

'Suppose someone's sitting in the chair?'

The pause conveyed both anger and confusion. There followed a short, strange sound that gave rise to the image of a small pig squealing in frustration. 'Remove him!' was the reply that followed the squeal.

'That's silly.'

'You vill do as I say! Dere is no time to argue! You vill be contacted. Fifteen minutes.'

'Hey, wait a minute! I just got up. I haven't had breakfast; I've got to shave—'

'Fourteen minutes, mein Herr!'

'I'm hungry!'

The connection was broken by a loud click on the line. 'To hell with him,' said Devereaux, turning back in anticipation to the extraordinary Lillian.

But Lillian was not where she should have been. Instead, she was standing on the other side of the bed in Sam's bathrobe.

'To coin a phrase, my darling, we were saved by the bell. You have things to do, and I really must get ready for class.'

'*Class?*'

'*Die erstklassige Strudelschule,*' said Lilly. 'Less expert but probably more fun than the Cordon Bleu in Paris. It starts at noon. We're over in the Leipziger Strasse; that's past Unter den Linden. I really should hurry.'

'What about – *us?* And breakfast and – don't you shower in the morning?'

Lilian laughed; it was a nice, genuine laugh. '*Die Schule* day is finished by three-thirty. I'll meet you back here.'

'What's your room number?'

'Five eleven.'

'I'm five nine.'

'I know. Isn't that marvellous?'

'Or something . . .'

The confusion in the Kempinsky lobby was absurd. 'Der fart chair in front of der vindow' *was* occupied by an elderly gentleman whose close-cropped, bejowled head kept nodding down into the folds of neck flesh as he dozed. On his lap, unfortunately, was a folded copy of *Der Spiegel*.

The elderly man was, at first, annoyed, then furious at the two men who flanked his chair and told him in no uncertain terms to get up and come with them. Twice Sam tried to intercede, explaining as best he could that he, too, had a folded copy of *Der Spiegel*. It did no good; the troopers were interested only in the gentleman sitting in the huge armchair. Finally, Devereaux stood directly in front of the two contacts and every twenty seconds, crossed and uncrossed his legs.

At which point the bell captain came up to Sam and in perfectly good, loud English gave him the directions to the men's room.

Whereupon a large woman with a striking resemblance to Dick Butkus approached the trio around the armchair and began hitting the two Gestapo men with both a hatbox and an extremely large, black leather handbag.

There was only one thing for it, thought Devereaux. He grabbed one of the contacts around the neck and pulled him away from the fire zone.

'You crazy son of a bitch! *I'm* the one! You're from Koenig, aren't you?'

Thirty seconds later Devereaux was propelled out of the Kempinsky entrance and into a nearby alley.

Halfway down the alley, taking up most of the space between the buildings, was an enormous open truck with a canvas tarpaulin stretched across the rear rigging poles. Under the tarpaulin, from deck to canvas, were hundreds of crates piled on top of one another, filled with thousands (it seemed like thousands) of screeching chickens.

There was a narrow corridor in the centre of the van between the crates. It led to the rear window of the cab. In front of the window were two tiny stools.

'Hey, come on! This is ridiculous! It's – goddamn it, it's unsanitary!'

His escorts nodded Germanically and smiled Germanically, and Germanically heaved Sam up into the tiny corridor and shoved him down the eighteen-inch passageway towards the stools.

All around him sharp beaks pecked at his person. The noonday sun was completely blanketed out by the heavy canvas tarpaulin above. The odour of chickenshit was unbearable.

They drove for nearly an hour into the countryside, stopping every now and then to be looked over by cooperative East German soldiers who waved them on, pocketing *Deutschmarks* as they did so.

They entered a large farming complex. Cattle were grazing in the fields, silos and barns could be seen, barely, through the opening of the tiny passageway between the crates and the flying feathers at the rear of the truck.

Finally they stopped. Escort number one grinned his Germanic grin and led Sam into the sunlight.

He was marched into a large barn that reeked of cattle urine and fresh manure. He was led – Germanically – down a crisscross series of turns through the stinking building until they came to an empty stall. A row of blue ribbons denoted the residence of a prize steer.

Inside, sitting on a milking stool, surrounded by piles of bullshit, was the heavyset man Sam knew was Heinrich Koenig.

He did not get up; he sat there and stared at Devereaux. In his tiny eyes, surrounded by folds of blemished flesh, were thunderbolts.

'So . . .' Koenig remained immobile, drawing out the word disdainfully, waving the escorts away.

'So?' replied Sam, his voice cracking slightly, aware of the wet chicken droppings on his back.

'You are the representative from this monster, General Hawkins?' Koenig pronounced the word 'general' with a hard Germanic *G*.

'I'd like to clear that up, if I may,' said Devereaux with

146

false laughter. 'Actually, I'm just a slight acquaintance, barely know the man. I'm a low-profile attorney from Boston; actually not much more than a law clerk. I work for a little Jewish man named Pinkus. You wouldn't like him. My mother lives in Quincy and through the strangest coincidence—'

'Enough!' A very loud fart could be heard in the vicinity of the milking stool. 'You are the contact, the intermediary, with this devil from hell!'

'Well, as to that, I would have to debate the legal association; said association subject to the clarification of intent with regard to foreknowledge. I don't believe—'

'You are a jackal, a hyena! But such dogs bark loudly if the meat is sufficient. Tell me. This Hawkins. He is a Gehlen operation, *nein*?'

'A who?'

'*Gehlen!*'

Devereaux remembered. Gehlen was the master spy of the Third Reich who bought and sold for all factions after the war. It would not do for Koenig to think there was any connection between Hawkins and Gehlen; for it would mean there was a link to one Sam Devereaux, who was way out of his league.

'Oh, I'm sure not. I don't think General Hawkins ever heard of what's-his-name. I know *I* haven't.' The chicken-shit was melting under Sam's shirt, all over his fevered back.

Koenig rose slowly from the milking stool, a second flatus loudly proclaiming his ascent. He spoke with quiet, intense hostility.

'The general has my reluctant respect. He has sent me a babbling idiot. Give me the papers, fool.'

'The papers—' Sam reached into his jacket pocket for another Xerox copy of the Shepherd Company's limited partnership agreement.

The German fingered the papers silently, squeezing each one as he flipped it. His audible reactions were blunt: a combination of farts and grunts.

'This is outrageous! A great injustice! Political enemies

everywhere! All wishing only to destroy me!' Beads of saliva formed at the corners of Koenig's mouth.

'I agree wholeheartedly,' said Devereaux, eagerly nodding his head. 'I'd throw it away if I were you.'

'You would like that? All of you. You are all out to get me! My great contributions that kept peace in the world, enemies in constant touch, that opened hot lines and red lines and blue lines between the great powers – these are forgotten. Now you whisper behind my back. You tell lies about non-existent bank accounts, even my humble places of residence. You never concede that I earned every *Deutschmark* I possess! When I retired, none of you could tolerate it; you did not have me to kick around any longer! And now this! The injustice!'

'Oh, I understand.'

'You understand nothing! Give me something to write with, you idiot.'

He farted and signed.

CHAPTER FOURTEEN

The bells of the Angelus pealed in solemn, vibrant splendour. They echoed throughout St Peter's Square, floated above Bernini's marble guardians, and were heard in quiet celebration beyond the dome, deep in the Vatican gardens. Seated on a bench of white stone, looking up at the orange rays of the descending sun, was a corpulent man with a face best described as having weathered seven decades good-naturedly, if not always peacefully. The face was full; but the peasant quality of the bone structure under the folds of flesh would tend to deny that the face was pampered. The man's eyes were wide and large and brown and soft; they held nearly equal parts of strength, perception, resignation, and amusement.

He was dressed in the splendid white robes of his office. The highest office of the Holy Apostolic Catholic Church, the descendant of Peter himself, the Bishop of Rome, the spiritual commander of 400 million souls throughout the earth.

Pope Francesco I, the Vicar of Christ.

Born Giovanni Bombalini in a small village north of Padua in the first years of the century. It was a birth that was recorded sketchily, at best, for the Bombalinis were not affluent. Giovanni was delivered by a midwife who, as often as not, forgot to report the fruits of her labours (and her patient's labours) to the village clerk, secure in the knowledge that the church would do *something*; christenings made money. Actually Giovanni Bombalini's emergence into this world might never have been legally recorded at all except

149

that his father had a wager with his cousin Frescobaldi, three villages to the north, that his second child would be a male. Bombalini Senior wanted to take no chances that his cousin Frescobaldi would renege on the bet, so he went to the village hall himself to report the birth of a male child.

As it happened, part of the wager was that Frescobaldi's wife – who was expecting in the same month – would *not* give birth to a boy. But of course she did, and the bet was cancelled. This child, Guido Frescobaldi, was born – according to the sketchy records – two days after *his* cousin, Giovanni.

Early in his life Giovanni showed signs of being different from the other children of the village. To begin with he did not care to learn his catechism by verbal repetition; he wanted to *read* it, *then* memorize it. This upset the village priest for it smacked of precociousness and somehow was an affront to authority, but the child would not be denied.

The ways of Giovanni Bombalini were indeed extraordinary. Although he never shirked his labours in the fields, he was rarely too tired to stay up half the night reading whatever he could get his hands on. When he was twelve he discovered the *biblioteca* in Padua, which was hardly the library in Milan, nor Venice, nor certainly Rome, but it was said by those who knew Giovanni that he read every book in Padua, then Milan, then Venice. By which time his priest recommended him to the holy fathers in Rome.

The church was Giovanni's answer to a prayer. And as long as he prayed a great deal – which was easier, though no less time-consuming than labouring in the fields – he was allowed to read more than he ever thought would be allowed him.

By the age of twenty-two, Giovanni Bombalini was an ordained priest. Some said the best-read priest in Rome, an *erudito fantastico*. But Giovanni did not possess the properly stern visage of a proper Vatican *erudito*; nor did he assume the proper attitudes of certainty with regard to everyday truths. He was forever finding exceptions and flexibilities in liturgical history, pointing out (some said mischievously) that the writings of the church found their strength in honest contradictions.

At twenty-six Giovanni Bombalini was a sharp pain in the large Vatican ass. Aggravated further by his matured appearance, which was the antithesis of the gaunt, academic image so desired by Rome's *eruditi*. He was, if anything, the caricature of a field peasant from the northern districts. Short of stature, stocky, and wide of girth, he looked like a farmhand more at home in the goat stables than in the marble halls of the various Vatican *collegia*. No amount of theological erudition, or good nature, or, indeed, deep belief in his church could counteract the combined aggravation of his mind and appearance. So posts were found for him in such unlikely locations as the Gold Coast, Sierra Leone, Malta, and, through an error, Monte Carlo. An exhausted Vatican dispatcher misread the name Montes Claros and inserted Monte Carlo – no doubt because he had never *heard* of Brazil's Montes Claros – and the fortunes of Giovanni Bombalini turned.

For into the cauldron of high stakes and high emotions wandered the simple-looking priest with the bemused eyes, gentle humour, and a head packed with more knowledge than any twelve international financiers put together. He'd had little to do in the Gold Coast, Sierra Leone, and Malta, so he had occupied his time, when not praying or teaching the natives, by subscribing to scores of reading services and adding to his already extraordinary memory bank.

It is common knowledge that people who live with constant motion, and high risk, and a great deal of alcohol, occasionally need spiritual consolation. So Father Bombalini began to comfort a few stray lambs. And to the amazement of these first few strays, they found not so much a simple priest who outlined penance, but a most amusing fellow who could discourse at length on almost any subject: economic conditions of world markets, historical precedents for anticipated geopolitical events, and, particularly, food. (Here he favoured the more basic sauces, eschewing the artifices of the often inappropriate *haute cuisine*.)

Before too many months had passed, Father Bombalini was a regular guest at many of the larger hotel suites and great houses of the Côte d'Azur. This rather odd-looking, rotund prelate was a marvellous raconteur, and it always made everyone feel better to have him around before going out to covet – successfully – his neighbour's wife.

And a number of excessively large contributions to the church were made in Father Giovanni's name. With increasing frequency.

Rome could no longer overlook Bombalini. The exchequers of the Vatican treasury said so.

The war found Monsignor Bombalini in various Allied capitals and occasionally attached to various Allied armies. This was brought about for two reasons. The first was his adamant deposition to his superiors that he could not remain neutral in light of the known Hitlerian objectives. He catalogued his thesis with sixteen pages of historical, theological, and liturgical precedents; none but the Jesuits could understand it, and they were on his side. So Rome shut its eyes and hoped for the best. The second reason for his wartime travels was that the international rich of Monte Carlo in the thirties were now colonels and generals and diplomats and ambassadorial liaisons. They *all* wanted him. There were so many intra-Allied requests for his services that in Washington, J. Edgar Hoover marked Bombalini's file: *Highly Suspect. May be a fairy.*

The postwar years were a time of rapid acceleration up the Vatican ladder for Cardinal Bombalini. Much of his success was due to his close friendship with Angelo Roncalli, with whom he shared a number of unorthodox views, as well as a penchant for decent, but not necessarily exclusive, wine and a good game of cards after the evening prayers.

As he sat on the white stone bench in the Vatican gardens, Giovanni Bombalini – Pope Francesco – reflected that he missed Roncalli. They had accomplished much together; it had been good. And the similarities of their respective ascendencies to the chair of St Peter never ceased to amuse him. Roncalli, John, would have been amused, too; no doubt was, of course.

They were both compromises offered by the stern, orthodox constituencies of the Curia to quiet the fires of discontent within the global flock. Neither compromise expected to reign very long. But Roncalli had it easy; he had only theological arguments and undeveloped social reformers to contend with. He didn't have damn fool young priests who wanted to marry and have children and, when of other persuasions, run homosexual parishes! Not that any of these personally bothered Giovanni; there was absolutely *nothing* in theological law or dogma that actually prohibited marriage and offspring; and, as far as the other, if love of fellowman did not surmount biblical ambiguities, what had they learned? But, Mother of God, the fuss that was made!

There was so much to do – and the doctors had made it clear that his time was limited. It was the only thing they *were* clear about; they could isolate no specific illness, no particular malady. They just conferred and confirmed that his 'vital signs' were slowing down at an alarming rate. He had demanded openness from them; Mother of God, he had no fear of death! He welcomed the rest. He and Roncalli could plough the heavenly vineyards together and take up their baccarat again. At last count Roncalli owed him something over six hundred million lire.

He had told the doctors that they looked too long in their microscopes and too little at the obvious. The machine was wearing out; it was as simple as that. Whereupon they nodded pontifically and uttered sombrely: 'Three months, four at the most, Holy Father.'

Doctors. *Basta!* Veterinarians with *cugini* in the Curia! Their bills were outrageous! The goatherders of Padua knew more about medicine; they had to.

Francesco heard the footsteps behind him and turned. Walking up the garden path was a young papal aide whose name escaped him. The youthful priest carried a clipboard in his hand. There was a painted crucifix on the underside; it looked silly.

'Your Holiness asked that we resolve some minor matters before the vesper hour.'

'By all means, Father. What are they?'

The aide rattled off a series of inconsequential functions, ceremonial in nature, and Giovanni flattered the young prelate by requesting his opinion on most of them.

'Then there is a request from an American periodical, *Viva Gourmet*. I would not mention it to the Holy Father except that the inquiry was accompanied by a strong recommendation from the United States Armed Forces Information Service.'

'That is a most unusual combination, is it not, Father?'

'Yes, Your Holiness. Quite incomprehensible.'

'What was the request?'

'They had the effrontery to ask the Holy Father to submit to an interview with a lady journalist regarding the pontiff's favourite dishes.'

'Why is that an effrontery?'

The young prelate paused; he seemed momentarily perplexed. Then he continued with confidence. 'Because Cardinal Quartze said it was, Holy Father.'

'Did the learned cardinal give his reasons? Or, as usual, did he commune with God all by himself and simply deliver the divine edict?' Francesco tried not to overdo his perfectly natural reaction to Ignatio Quartze. The cardinal was a loathsome fellow in just about every department. He was an *erudito aristocratico* from a powerful Italian-Swiss family, who had the compassion of a disturbed cobra. Looked like one, too, thought Giovanni.

'He did, Holy Father,' replied the priest. And the instant he spoke, the aide was struck by a sudden embarrassment. 'He – he—'

'May I suggest, Father,' said the pontiff with graceful understanding, 'that our splendidly berobed cardinal offered the opinion that the pope's favourite dishes were less than impressive?'

'I – I—'

'I see he did. Well, Father, it is true that I subscribe to

simpler cooking than does our cardinal with the unfortunate nasal drip, but it is not due to lack of knowledge. Merely lack of, perhaps, ostentation; not that our cardinal, who is afflicted with that unfortunate eye that strays to the right as he talks, is ostentatious. I don't believe it ever crossed his mind.'

'No, of course not, Holy Father.'

'But I think that during these days of high prices and widespread unemployment, it might be a fine idea for your pontiff to outline a number of inexpensive, though I assure you, quite excellent dishes. Who is the journalist? A lady, you say? Don't ever tell anyone I said it, Father, but they are not the best cooks.'

'No, surely not, Your Holiness. The nuns of Rome are strenuous—'

'Galvanizing, Father. Positively galvanizing! Who is the journalist from this gourmet periodical?'

'Her name is Lillian von Schnabe. She is American, from the state of California, married to an older man, a German immigrant who fled Hitler. As coincidence would have it, she is currently in Berlin.'

'I merely asked who she was, Father. Not her biography. How do you know all this?'

'It was in the recommendation from the United States Army Information Service. The military think highly of her, apparently.'

'More than apparently. So, her husband fled Hitler? One does not turn away from such compassionate women. Coupled with the state of food prices – a number of inexpensive papal dishes is called for. Set up an appointment, Father. You may tell our resplendent cardinal, who suffers from the unfortunate affliction of a high-decibelled wheeze, that we truly hope our decision is not an affront to him. *Viva Gourmet.* The Lord God has been good to me; it is a mark of recognition. I wonder why its correspondent is in Berlin? There's a monsignor in Bonn who makes an excellent *Sauerbraten.*'

*

'I swear, you've got feathers in your teeth!' said Lillian as Sam walked into the room.

'It's better than chickenshit.'

'What?'

'My business contact had a strange method of transportation.'

'What are you talking about?'

'I want to take a shower.'

'Not with *me*, honey!'

'I've never been so hungry in my life. They wouldn't even stop for a – what the hell is it? A strudel. Everything was *ein, zwei, drei*! *Mach schnell!* Christ, I'm starved! They really think they won the war!'

Lillian backed away from him. 'You are the filthiest, most foul-smelling man I've ever seen. I'm surprised they let you in the lobby.'

'I think we goose-stepped.' Sam noticed a large white business envelope on the bureau. 'What's that?'

'The front desk sent it up. They said it was urgent and they weren't sure you'd stop for messages.'

'I can only conclude your ex, the fruitcake, has been busy.' Devereaux picked up the envelope. Inside were airline tickets and a note. He didn't really have to read the note; the airline tickets said it all.

Algiers.

Then he read the note.

'*No!* Goddamn it, *no*! That's less than an hour from now!'

'What is?' asked Lillian. 'The plane?'

'What plane? How the hell do *you* know there's a plane?'

'Because MacKenzie called. From Washington. You can imagine his shock when I answered—'

'Spare me your inventive details!' roared Devereaux as he raced to the telephone. 'I've got several things to say to that devious son of a bitch! Even convicts get a day off! At least time for a meal and a shower!'

'You can't reach him now,' said Lillian quickly. 'That was one of the reasons he called. He'll be out for the rest of the day.'

156

Sam turned menacingly. Then he stopped. This girl could probably cut him in two. 'And I suppose he offered a suggestion as to why I should be on that plane. Once he got over the shock of hearing your lovely voice, of course.'

Lillian looked puzzled. It crossed Devereaux's mind that the puzzlement was not entirely genuine. 'Mac mentioned something about a German named Koenig. How anxious this Koenig was for you to leave Berlin – one way or the other.'

'The less controversial method being Air France to Paris and from Paris to Algiers?'

'Yes, he did say that. Although not in those exact words. He's terribly fond of you, Sam. He speaks of you as a son. The son he never had.'

'If there's a Jacob, I'm Esau. Otherwise, I'm fucked as Absalom.'

'Vulgarity isn't called for—'

'It's the only thing that *is* called for! What the hell is in Algiers?'

'A sheik named Azaz-Varak,' answered Lillian Hawkins von Schnabe.

Hawkins left the Watergate in a hurry. He had no desire to talk to Sam; he had absolute faith in Lillian, in all the girls, actually. They were doing their jobs splendidly! Besides, he was to meet with an Israeli major who, with any luck, could put the final pieces of the puzzle together for him. The puzzle being Sheik Azaz-Varak. By the time Devereaux reached Algiers a telephone call would have to be made. The Hawk could not make it without that final item which would ensure the last of the Shepherd Company's capitalization.

That Azaz-Varak was a thief on a global scale was nothing new. During the Second World War he sold oil at outrageous prices to the Allies and the Axis simultaneously, favouring only those who paid instantly in cash. This did not make him enemies, however; instead, his policies engendered respect, from Detroit to Essen.

But the war was ancient history. That war. It was Azaz-

Varak's behaviour in a far more recent conflagration that interested Hawkins: the Mideast crisis.

Azaz-Varak was nowhere to be found.

While oaths were hurled across the lands of the Middle East, and the world watched armies clash against armies, and crisis-laden conferences took place, and outrageous profits were made, the greediest sheik of them all claimed to have a case of shingles and went to the Virgin Islands.

Goddamn! It didn't make sense! So MacKenzie went back into Azaz-Varak's raw files and studied them with the eye of a professional. He began to find the pattern in the years between 1946 and 1948. Sheik Azaz-Varak had apparently spent a considerable amount of time in Tel Aviv!

According to the reports, his first few trips were made quite openly. It was supposed that Azaz-Varak sought Israeli women for his harem. Thereafter, however, Azaz-Varak continued to fly into Tel Aviv, but not openly, landing at night in outlying airfields that could accommodate his most modern and expensive private planes.

More women? Hawkins had researched exhaustively and was unable to unearth the name of a single Israeli female who ever went back to the sheikdom of Azaz-Kuwait.

Then, what had Azaz-Varak been doing in the state of Israel? And why had he travelled there so frequently?

MacKenzie's breakthrough came, strangely enough, from information supplied by naval intelligence on the island of St Thomas, where Azaz-Varak had fled during the Mideast war. There, he tried to buy up more property than anyone wished to sell. Rebuffed, he became furious.

The islanders had enough trouble. They did not need Arabs with harems and slaves. Jesus! *Slaves!* The very idea sent the bureau of tourism into apoplexy; visions of all that kitchen help in revolt were positively nauseating. Azaz-Varak was systematically prevented from buying two buckets of sand. When it was suspected he was trying to negotiate through second and third parties, covenants were included that would have made Palm Beach green with envy and the

ACLU purple with rage. Simply put: no fucking Arabs could own, lease, sublease, visit, or trespass.

So in his frustration, the acquisitive sheik angrily, and hastily, brought in an American holding company called the Buffalo Corporation and tried to negotiate through it. There *were* laws and St Thomas was a United States possession. And it did not take much research on Hawkins's part to uncover the fact that the Buffalo Corporation – address: Albany Street, Buffalo, New York; telephone: unlisted – was a subsidiary of an unknown company called Pan-Friendship, main office: Beirut; telephone: also unlisted.

Subsequent overseas calls to several Israeli clearing houses made stunningly clear what Azaz-Varak had been doing during all those visits to the Jewish homeland. He owned half the real estate in Tel Aviv, much of it in the poorer sections of town. The sheik was a Tel Aviv slumlord.

The Buffalo Corporation collected rents from all over the city. And if the Israeli major – who was in ordnance and supply – confirmed a report the Hawk had received from some old Cambodian buddies in the CIA, the Buffalo Corporation was also in another business. One that held most unfortunate implications for the owner of said Buffalo Corporation, insofar as he was the very Arab who scared hell out of the realtors in St Thomas.

The report was simple; all MacKenzie needed was one military official to corroborate it. For the CIA boys learned that a major expeditor of petro-chemicals and fuel for the army of Israel during the Mideast war was a little-known American company called the Buffalo Corporation.

Sheik Azaz-Varak not only owned half the real estate in Tel-Aviv, but at the height of the conflict, he fed the Israeli war machine so the maniacs in Cairo wouldn't damage his investments.

It was the sort of information that simply demanded a long-distance call, thought MacKenzie Hawkins. To the sheikdom of Azaz-Kuwait.

Devereaux appreciated the sympathy from the Air France

stewardess, but he would have appreciated food more. There were no supplies in the galley of the 727, a condition that would be corrected in Paris. Apparently – and there was no way to be sure he understood correctly – the Boche catering trucks that serviced Air France had been tied up in a Russian-induced traffic jam on the autobahn, and what had been left in the galley had been stolen by the Czechoslovakian ground crew in Prague. And besides, the food was better in Paris.

So Sam smoked cigarettes, caught himself chewing bits of tobacco, and tried to concentrate on the doings of MacKenzie Hawkins. His seatmate was some kind of Eastern religious, perhaps a Sikh, with brown skin tinged with grey, a very small black beard, a purple turban, and darting eyes that were as close as a human's could be to those of a rat. It made thinking about MacKenzie easier; there would be little conversation on the trip to Paris.

Hawkins had raised his third ten million. And now there was an Arabian sheik who was the fourth and final mark. Whatever it was that MacKenzie had culled from the raw files had the effect of thermonuclear blackmail. Christ! *Forty million!*

What was he going to *do* with it? What kind of 'equipment and support personnel' (whatever the hell *they* were) could possibly cost so much?

Granted one did not kidnap a pope with a dollar and a quarter in one's pocket, but was it necessary to cover the Italian national debt to do it?

One thing was certain. The Hawk's plan for the kidnapping included the exchange of extraordinary sums of money. And whoever accepted such sums were *ipso facto* accessories to the most outrageous abduction in history! It was another avenue he, Sam, could explore. And a pretty good one at that. If he could obtain the names of even a few of Mac's suppliers, he could scare them right out of the picture. Certainly the Hawk was not going to say to someone: *Yes, I'll buy that railroad train because I'm going to kidnap this pope fellow and it'll be a big help.* No, that was hardly the way of an experienced general officer who had drugged half the pouch

160

couriers in Southeast Asia. But if he, Sam, reached that same someone and said: *You know that train you're selling to that bearded idiot? It's going to be used to kidnap the pope. Have a good night's sleep* – well, that was something else again. The train would not be sold. And if he could prevent a train from being sold, perhaps he could prevent other supplies from reaching the Hawk. MacKenzie was army; lines of supply were paramount to any operation. Without them whole strategies were altered, even abandoned. It was military holy writ.

Yes, reflected Devereaux, gazing out into the German twilight from the foodless Air France plane, it was a very decent avenue to explore. Coupled with his first consideration – finding out how the Hawk intended to pull off the kidnapping, and the second consideration – finding out what specific blackmailing material MacKenzie held over his investors, the suppliers were a third, powerful ingredient. In preventive medicine.

Sam closed his eyes, conjuring up visions of long ago. He was in the basement of his home in Quincy, Massachusetts. On the huge table in the centre of his room was his set of Lionel trains, going around and around, weaving in and out of the miniature shrubbery and over the tiny bridges and through the toy tunnels. But there was something strange about the sight. Except for the engine and the caboose, all the other vehicles were marked identically: 'Refrigerator Car. Food.'

At Orly Airport, the passengers to Algiers were told to remain on the plane. For Devereaux nothing mattered once he saw the white truck pull up alongside the aircraft and men in white coats transferring immaculate steel containers into the galley. He even smiled at Rat Eyes beside him, noticing as he did so that his seatmate's purple turban had slipped somewhat over his brown forehead. Sam might have said something – he'd learned long ago that even strangers appreciated it when you told them their zippers were open – but since several other turbaned acquaintances who'd boarded at Orly had come up to pay their respects and had said nothing, Devereaux felt it wasn't his place. Besides most of the other purple turbans seemed a touch lopsided. Perhaps it was a custom indigenous to the particular religious sect.

Regardless, all Sam could think about were the immaculate steel trays, now securely in the Air France galley broilers, sending out deliriously inviting wafts of *escalope de veau*, *tournedos*, *sauce Béarnaise*, and, if he was not mistaken, steak *au poivre*. God was in his heaven and on Air France as well. Good Lord! Devereaux vaguely calculated the hours since he'd eaten: it was nearing thirty-six.

Unintelligible words droned over the cabin loudspeakers; the 727 taxied out on to the field. Two minutes later they were airborne and the stewardesses went about the business of distributing the most meaningful literature Sam could think of: menus.

His order took up more time than anyone else in the cabin. This was partially due to the fact that he salivated and had to swallow as he spoke. There followed an agonizing hour. Normally it was not agonizing to Sam, for it was taken up with cocktails. But today he could not drink. His stomach was too empty.

At length, dinner approached. The stewardess went down the aisle spreading the miniature tablecloths, placing the napkin-enclosed silverware, and reconfirming the choice of dinner wines. Sam could not help himself; he kept craning his neck over the edge of the seat. The scents from the galley were driving him crazy. Every odour was a banquet to his nostrils; the juices ran down his throat at each recognizable smell.

And naturally it had to happen.

The weird-looking Sikh beside him lunged from his seat and unravelled his purple turban. Out of the cloth fell a large, lethal revolver. It crashed to the deck of the aircraft; Rat Eyes lunged down, retrieved it, and screamed.

'*Aiyee! Aiyee! Aiyee! Al Fatah! Al Fatah! Aiyee!*'

It was the signal; a screeching symphony of 'Aiyees' and 'Fatahs' could be heard behind first class, throughout the tube of the long fuselage. From somewhere in his trousers. Rat Eyes pulled out an extremely long, murderous-looking scimitar.

Sam stared numbly. In complete defeat.

So the man wasn't a Sikh. He was an Arab. A goddamn fucking Palestinian Arab.

What else?

The stewardess now faced the murderous blade; the barrel of the huge pistol was jammed between her breasts. She did her best, but the terror could not be concealed.

'On the wires! On the wires to your captain!' screeched the Palestinian. 'This aircraft will proceed to Algeria. This is the wishes of Al Fatah! To Algiers! Only Algiers! Or you will all die. *Die! Die!*'

'*Mais oui, monsieur,*' screamed the stewardess. 'The aircraft *is* proceeding to Algiers! *That* is our destination, monsieur!'

The Arab was crestfallen. His wild, piercing eyes became temporary pools of dull mud, the frustration conveyed by the tiny dots of questioning chaos in the centre of the mud.

Then the eyes sprang back once more to the vivid, cruel, violent exuberance.

He slashed the air with the huge scimitar and waved the pistol maniacally.

His demonic, defiant screams were worthy of shattering the high-altitude glass, but fortunately did not.

'*Aiyee! Aiyee! Arafat!* Hear the word of Arafat! Jewish dogs and Christian pigs! There will be no food or water until we *land! That is the word of Arafat!*'

Deep within the recesses of Sam's subconscious a small voice whispered: *You're fucked, babe.*

CHAPTER FIFTEEN

The stage manager winced; two violins and three horns went sour during the crescendo of 'Musetta's Waltz'. The act's finale was ruined. Again.

He made a note for the conductor who he could see was smiling blissfully, unaware of the grating dissonance. It was understandable: the man's hearing wasn't so good anymore.

As the stage manager looked out, he saw that the spotlight operator had dozed off again; or had gone to the toilet. The shaft of light was angled down, immobile, into the pit – on a confused flautist – instead of on Mimi.

He made a note.

On the stage itself was another problem. Two problems. The swinging gates into the café had been hung upside down, the pointed tops inverted so that they vee'd up from the floor, providing the audience a clear view behind the scenery where numerous bare feet were being rubbed and not a few extras scratched themselves in boredom. The second problem was the step unit on stage left; it had become unhinged so that Rodolfo's leg plummeted down into the open space causing his tights to rip up to his crotch.

The stage manager sighed and made two more notes.

Puccini's *La Bohème* was being given its usual performance by the company. *Mannaggia!*

As he finished putting three exclamation points after his twenty-sixth note of the evening, the assistant box-office manager approached his lectern and handed him a message.

It was for Guido Frescobaldi, and because any distraction

was preferable to watching the remainder of the act, the stage manager unfolded the paper and read it.

Instantly, involuntarily, he caught his breath. Old Frescobaldi would have a fit – if it was possible for Guido to *have* a fit. There was a newspaper reporter in the audience who wanted to meet with Frescobaldi after the performance.

The stage manager shook his head sadly, recalling vividly Guido's tears and protestations when the last (and only) newspaper reporter interviewed him. There were two reporters actually: a man from Rome and a silent Chinese colleague. Both Communists.

It was not the interview that had upset Frescobaldi, it was the article that came out of it.

Impoverished Opera Artist Struggles for People's Culture as Cousin, the Pope, Lives in Indolent Luxury off the Honest Sweat of Oppressed Workers!

That had been for openers. The front page headlined the story in the Communist newspaper, *Il Popolo*. The article had gone on to say that diligent investigative reporting on the part of *Il Popolo's* journalists – ever alert to the inequities of capitalism's unholy alliance with savage organized religion – had uncovered the crass injustice done to this look-alike relative of the world's most powerful and despotic religious leader. How one Guido Frescobaldi sacrificed for his art while his cousin, Pope Francesco, stole everyone blind. How Guido contributed his great talent for the good of the masses, never seeking material rewards, satisfied only that his contributions uplifted the spirit of the people. So different from his cousin, the pontiff, who contributed nothing but new methods to extract money from the frightened poor. Guido Frescobaldi was the earthly saint; his cousin the subterranean villain, no doubt with orgies in the catacombs, surrounded by treasures.

The stage manager did not know a great deal about Guido's cousin, or what he did in the catacombs, but he did know Frescobaldi. And *Il Popolo's* reporter had etched a portrait that was somewhat at variance to the Guido they all knew. But it was *this* Guido the world outside of Milan read about. *Il Popolo* stated in an editorial that the shocking story was to be reprinted in all the Socialist countries, including China.

Oh, how Frescobaldi had screamed! His roars had been the protestations of a thoroughly embarrassed man. The stage manager hoped that he could catch Guido during the act change and give him the message, but it was not always easy to find Guido during an act change. And it was useless to put the note in the dressing room for he would never see it.

For the role of Alcindoro was Guido Frescobaldi's moment in the operatic sun. It was his single triumph in a lifetime devoted to his beloved *musica*. It was proof that tenacity really did overshadow talent.

Guido was usually so moved by the events on stage – as well as his own performance – that he waddled in a trance behind the scenery until the confusion of an act change was over, his eyes invariably moist, his head held high in the knowledge that he had given his all for the audience of La Scala Minuscola, the fifth-string company of the world-renowned opera house. It was both a training ground and a musical cemetery, allowing the inexperienced to flutter their vocal wings and the over-the-hill to stay occupied until the Great Conductor summoned them to that glorious festival in the sky.

The stage manager reread the note to Guido. In the audience that night was a lady journalist named Signora Greenberg who wished to chat with Frescobaldi. He had been recommended to her by no less a distinguished source than the United States Army *Informazione Servizio*. And the stage manager knew why this Signora Greenberg included the recommendation in her note. Ever since the Communists wrote that terrible article, Guido refused to talk to anyone from the newspapers. He had even grown a huge walrus moustache and beard to lessen the likeness between himself and the pontiff.

The Communists were stupid. *Il Popolo*, through habit, was always picking a fight with the Vatican, but they soon learned what everyone else knew: Pope Francesco was not a man to vilify. He was simply too nice a fellow.

Guido Frescobaldi was a nice fellow, too, thought the stage manager. Many a late night they had divided bottles of wine together; a middle-aged signaller of cues and the elder character actor who had given his life for music.

What a drama was in the *real* story of Frescobaldi! It was worthy of Puccini himself!

To begin with, he lived only for his beloved opera; all else was inconsequential, necessary solely to keep body and musical soul together. He had been married years ago. And six years later his wife had left him, taking their six children with her back to her native village near Padua and the security of her father's not immodest farm. Though Frescobaldi's circumstances, which by tradition meant the circumstances of his family, had not been destitute. And if his own income was currently less than adequate for *him*, it was by choice, not necessity. The Frescobaldis were actually quite well off; their cousins, the Bombalinis, had been sufficiently wealthy to allow their third son, Giovanni, to enter the church, and God knew that took a little money.

But Guido turned his back on all things clerical, mercantile, and agricultural. He wanted only his music, his opera. He badgered his father and mother to send him to the academy in Rome, where it was soon discovered that Guido's passion far outdistanced his talents.

Frescobaldi had the Latin fire and the soul, perhaps, but he also possessed a rotten musical ear. And Papa Frescobaldi was getting nervous; so many Guido associated with were *non stabili* – they wore funny clothes.

So at the age of twenty-two, Papa told Guido to come home to the village north of Padua. He had been studying in Rome for eight years; no noticeable progress had been made. No jobs – at least in music – had been offered, no musical future seemed to hold promise.

Guido did not care, however. It was the total immersion in things musical that counted. Papa could not understand. But Papa would no longer pay, so Guido came home.

The elder Frescobaldi told his son to marry his nice village cousin, Rosa Bombalini, who was having a little trouble finding a husband, and Papa would give Guido a *fonografo* for a wedding present. Then he could listen to all the music he wished. Also, if he did not marry Cousin Rosa, Papa would break his ass.

So for six years, while his cousin and brother-in-law, Father Giovanni Bombalini, studied in the Vatican and was sent to strange places, Guido Frescobaldi endured a forced marriage to the three hundred-pound bundle of self-indulgent hysteria named Rosa.

On the morning of his seventh anniversary, he gave up. He awoke screaming; he smashed windows, broke furniture, threw pots of linguini against the walls, and told Rosa that she and her six children were the most repulsive human beings he had ever met.

Basta!

Enough was enough!

Rosa gathered the children together and fled to the village farm; and Guido walked downtown to his father's pasta shop, picked up a bowl of tomato sauce, heaved it in Papa's face and left Padua for ever. For Milan.

If the world would not let him be a great operatic tenor, he at least would be near great singers, great music.

He would clean toilets, sweep stages, sew costumes, carry spears. Anything.

He would make his life at La Scala!

And so it had been for over forty years with Frescobaldi. He had risen slowly but happily from toilets to brooms, from stitching to spears. Finally he was awarded those first few words on stage – *Not so much to sing, Guido! More like talk, you see?* – and the sheer openness of his emotion made him an instant favourite of less discriminating operagoers. Of La Scala Minuscula. Where the ticket scale was lower.

In his way Frescobaldi became a beloved fixture as well as a devoted participant. He was always available to help in rehearsals, to cue, to stand in, to recite, and his knowledge was formidable.

Only once in all the years did Guido cause any trouble for anyone, and it wasn't really his fault. That, of course, was the *Popolo* attempt to embarrass his cousin, the pope. Luckily, the Communist writer had not discovered Frescobaldi's early marriage to the pontiff's sister. It would have been difficult for him, however, because Rosa Bombalini had died of overeating three decades earlier.

Hurriedly, the stage manager made his way to Frescobaldi's dressing room. He was too late. The lady speaking to Guido surely was the Signora Greenberg. She was very American and, indeed, very well endowed. Her Italian was a little strange, however. Her words were drawn out like yawns, but the lady did not appear sleepy.

'You see, Signor Frescobaldi, the purpose will be to counteract those nasty things the Communists wrote.'

'Oh, yes, *please!*' cried Guido imploringly. 'They were infamous! There is no finer man in the world than my dear cousin, *Il Papa*. I weep for the embarrassment I caused!'

'I'm sure he doesn't feel that way. He speaks so well of you.'

'Yes – yes, he would,' replied Frescobaldi, the moisture clouding his blinking eyes. 'As children we would play in the fields together, when our families visited. Giovanni – excuse me, Pope Francesco – was the best of all the brothers and cousins. He was a good *man* even as a *boy*. Does that make sense? And brains!'

'He'll be happy to see you again,' said the Signora. 'We haven't scheduled the exact time yet, but he hopes you'll meet with him for the photographs.'

Guido Frescobaldi could not help himself. Although he lost not a dram of dignity, he wept – quietly, without a sound or a gesture. 'He is such a kind man. Did you know that when that terrible magazine came out he sent me a note, in his own hand. He wrote to me: "Guido, my cousin and dear friend: Why have you hidden yourself all these years? When you come to Rome, please call on me. We will play some bocce. I put a course in the garden. Always, my blessing, *Giovanni*."' Frescobaldi dabbed his eyes with the edge of the makeup towel. 'Not a hint of anger or even displeasure. But of course I would never disturb so great a personage. Who am I?'

'He knew it wasn't your fault. You understand that your cousin would rather not have it known that we're planning this anti-Communist story. With politics the way they are—'

'Not a *word*!' interrupted Guido. 'I say *nothing*. I wait only to hear from you and I shall come to Rome. If need be – and I am scheduled to perform – I shall allow my understudy to take my place. The audiences may throw vegetables, but for Francesco, *anything*!'

'He'll be touched.'

'Did you know,' said Frescobaldi, leaning forward in the chair, lowering his voice, 'that under this moustache of mine, the face is very like my exalted cousin's?'

'You mean you *really look alike*?'

'It was ever so since we were children.'

'It never would have crossed my mind. But now that you mention it, I do see a resemblance.'

The stage manager closed the door silently. It had been partially open; they had not seen him and there was no point in interrupting. Guido might be embarrassed; the dressing room was small. So Frescobaldi was going to see his cousin, the pope. *Buonissimo!* Perhaps he might beseech the pontiff to allocate some funds to La Scala Minuscola. They could use the money.

The singing was really terrible.

'Aiyee! Al Fatah! Arafat!'

The screaming Palestinian revolutionaries dashed through the exit doors and down the steps to the concrete of Dar el Beida airport. They hugged and kissed each other and slashed at the night air with their blades. One unfortunate had his finger sliced off in the rejoicing, but it did not cause much concern. Under the leadership of Rat Eyes the group made a dash for the fence that surrounded the field.

No one tried to stop them. Indeed, the searchlights were swung in their direction to help them see their way over the fence. The authorities understood that it was desirable for the idiots to leave the field this way. If they walked into the terminal and out through the doors, a large degree of face would be lost. Besides, the quicker they left the better. They were doing nothing for the tourist trade.

The instant the final Palestinian raced out of the aircraft, Sam had lurched into the Air France galley. To no avail. In the midst of crisis, Air France had kept its head, and its financial acumen. The gleaming metal trays were in place for the next contingent of passengers.

'I paid for some goddamned food!' yelled Sam.

'I'm sorry,' said the stewardess, smiling blankly. 'Regulations prohibit the serving of food after landing.'

'For God's sake, we were hijacked!'

'Your ticket reads Algiers. We are in Algiers. On the ground. After landing. There can be no food.'

'That's inhuman!'

'That is Air France, monsieur.'

Devereaux staggered through the Algerian customs. He held four American five-dollar bills in his hand, separated as though they were playing cards. Each of the four Algerian inspectors down the line took one, smiled, and passed him on to the next man. No luggage was opened; Sam grabbed his suitcase off the conveyor and looked frantically for the airport restaurant.

It was closed. For a religious holiday.

The taxi ride from the airport to the Aletti Hotel on Rue de l'Enur El Khettabi did nothing to calm his nerves or soothe his agonizingly empty stomach. The vehicle was ancient, the driver more so, and the road down into the city steep and filled with winding curves and hairpin turns.

'We're terribly sorry, Monsieur Devereaux,' said the dark-skinned desk clerk in overly precise English. 'All of Algiers is in a state of fasting until the sun rises in the morning. It is the will of Mohammed.'

Sam leaned over the marble counter and lowered his voice to a whisper. 'Look, I respect everyone's right to worship in his own way, but I haven't eaten and I've got a little money—'

'Monsieur!' The clerk's eyes widened in Algerian shock as he interrupted and drew himself up to his full height of roughly five feet. 'The will of Mohammed! The way of Allah!'

'Good Lord! I don't believe my *eyes*!' The shout came from across the Aletti lobby. The light was dim, the ceiling high. The figure was obscured in shadows. The only thing Sam knew was that the voice was deep and feminine. And deeply feminine. Perhaps he had heard it before, he could not be sure. How could he be sure of anything – at that moment – in such an unlikely spot as an Algerian hotel lobby during an Algerian religious holiday – in the last stages of starvation. All was beyond sureness.

And then the figure walked through the hazy pools of light, led by two enormous breasts that cleaved the air in majestic splendour.

Full and Round. Naturally; why did he even bother to act surprised? Ten million – thirty million, forty million dollars no longer shocked him. Why should the sight of Mrs MacKenzie Hawkins, number two?

She pressed the cool, wet towel on his forehead; he lay back on the bed. Six hours ago she had taken off his shoes and socks and shirt and told him to lie back and stop shaking. In truth, she'd *ordered* him to stop shaking. And while he was at it, to stop babbling incoherently about crazy things like Nazis and chicken droppings and wild-eyed Arabs who wanted to blow up airplanes because they flew where they were supposed to fly. Such talk!

But that had been six hours ago. And during the interim she had taken his mind off food, and MacKenzie Hawkins, and some sheik named Azaz-Varak, and – oh my God! – the *kidnapping of the pope*!

She had reduced the dimensions of the whole insanity to the simpler proportions of a terrifying nightmare.

Her name was Madge; he had remembered that. And she

had sat next to him on the bean bag in Regina Greenberg's living room; and she had reached over to touch him every time she emphasized a point. He remembered that distinctly because each time she had leaned toward him, Full and Round seemed to burst out of her peasant blouse, as they seemed now about to burst out of the silk shirt she wore.

'Just a bit longer,' she said in her deep, somewhat breathless voice. 'The desk clerk promised you'd be the first tray out of the kitchen. Now just relax.'

'Tell me again.'

'About the food?'

'No. About how come you're here in Algiers. It'll take my mind off the food.'

'Then you'll just start babbling again. You simply won't believe me.'

'Maybe I missed something—'

'You're teasing me,' said Madge, leaning over danger-ously, adjusting the towel. 'All right. Short and to the point. My late husband was the leading West Coast importer of African art. His gallery was the largest in California. When he died he had over $100,000 tied up in seventeenth-century Musso-Grossai statuary. What the hell am I going to do with five hundred statues of naked pigmies? I mean *really*! You'd do just what I'm doing. Try to stop the shipment and get your money back! Algiers is the clearing house for Musso-Grossai – Now, damn it! There you *go* again!'

Devereaux could not help himself. Tears of laughter rolled down his cheeks. 'I'm sorry. It's just that it's so much more *inventive* than a sudden London vacation from a philandering husband. Or a gourmet school in Berlin. My God, it's beautiful! Five hundred naked pigmies! Did you think it up, or did Mac?'

'You're too suspicious.' Madge smiled gently, knowingly, and lifted the towel from his forehead. 'That's no way to live. Here, I'll soak this with some cool water. Breakfast should be here in fifteen or twenty minutes.' She rose from the bed and looked over at the window in silent thought.

The orange rays of the new day were streaming through the window. 'The sun's up.'

Devereaux watched her; the dawn's light washed over her striking features, heightening the sheen of her auburn hair and adding a soft, deep glow to her face. It was not a young face but it had something better than youth. An openness that accepted the years and could laugh gracefully at them. There was a directness that touched Sam.

'You're a terrific looking person,' he said.

'So are you.' She replied quietly. 'You've got what an old friend of mine used to call a face you'd like to know. Your eyes level. My friend used to say "watch the eyes, especially in a crowd; see if they listen". Actually, Mac said it. A long time ago. I suppose that sounds silly, eyes listening.'

'It doesn't sound silly at all. Eyes do listen. I had a friend who used to go to Washington cocktail parties, and he'd repeat the word "hamburger" over and over again – just "hamburger", nothing else. He swore that ninety per cent of the time the people around him would say things like, "Very interesting. I'll check the statistics on that"; or "Have you mentioned it to the undersecretary?" He always knew who'd say those things because their eyes were moving so fast; you see, he wasn't very important.'

Madge laughed softly; their eyes locked and she smiled. 'He sounds very important to me.'

'You're a *nice* person, too.'

'Yes, I try to be.' She looked over at the window again. 'MacKenzie also said that too many people run from their perfectly natural inclination to be concerned human beings. As if concern was a sign of weakness. He said: "Goddamn, Midgey, *I'm* concerned and no son of a bitch better call *me* weak!" And no one ever did.'

'I suppose being concerned is another way of being nice,' added Devereaux, mulling over the latest homily.

'There's no better way,' said Madge, carrying the towel into the bathroom. 'I'll be out in a minute.'

She closed the door. Sam repeated the words to himself: *Too many people run from their perfectly natural inclination to be concerned human beings*. MacKenzie was a man of more complications than Devereaux cared to think about. At least, until breakfast arrived.

The bathroom door opened. Madge stood in the door frame and smiled deliberately, a sense of marvellous fun in her eyes, very much aware of the picture she presented. She no longer wore her skirt. Instead her breasts were now lovingly encased in an ivory-coloured brassiere made of webbed lace. Below, her short slip accentuated the curve of her hips and bore witness to the soft white flesh that touched – and wanted to be touched – between her upper thighs.

She walked around to the side of the bed and took his immobile hand. She sat down gracefully and leaned over, her incredible spheres touching him, sending electricity through him, causing him to suddenly inhale very short breaths. She kissed him on the lips. She pulled back and undid his belt and with the swift, graceful movements of a dancer, pulled down his trousers.

'Why Major, you have been thinking nice thoughts—'

And the Algerian terrorist telephone rang.

The galaxy went out of whack again. Sanity vanished in a sudden rush of hysteria. Sweet reason and laced brassieres and soft flesh were no more. Instead, screams in Arabic, commands that threatened unbelievable violence should they be disobeyed.

'If you'll stop yelling about pigs and dogs and vultures for a second, maybe I can figure out what you're trying to say,' said Sam, holding the phone away from his ear. 'All *I* said was that I couldn't come down right now.'

'I am the emissary from Sheik *Azaz-Var*ak!'

'What the hell is that?'

'Dog!'

'It's a dog? You mean a puppy dog?'

'Silence! Azaz-Varak is the god of all khans! The possessor of the desert winds, the eyes of the falcon, the courage of all the lions of Judea, the prince of thunder!'

'Then what does he need me for?' ventured Sam hesitantly, reluctantly recognizing the name of the Hawk's fourth mark. The final ten million. Jesus! He thought about it now with no more emphasis than ten boxes of Pop Tarts!

'Silence, dog! Or both your ears will be cut from your head and placed with hot irons up your unspeakable.'

'Now, goddamn it, that's not friendly! You talk nicer or I'm going to hang up; there's a lady here.'

'Please, Mr Deveroo,' said the Arabic voice, suddenly quite gentle with a trace of a whine. 'In the name of Allah – for the love of Allah, do not be difficult. It will be *my* ears in unspeakable places if you are difficult. We must leave for Tizi Ouzou immediately.'

'Tizi – who?'

'Ouzou, Mr Deveroo.'

'Ouzou? Did you say Ouzoo?'

Suddenly, without any warning whatsoever, the most unexpected thing Sam could imagine happened. Madge grabbed the telephone from him.

'Give me that!' she ordered. 'I know Tizi Ouzou; my husband and I stayed there once. It's a dreadful place! – Listen here, whoever you are, you'd better have a damn good reason to ask my friend to go to Tizi Ouzou. It's the godforsaken end of nowhere! Without a decent hotel *or* restaurant, to say nothing about toilet facilities!'

The girl held the phone to her ear, nodding briefly every three or four seconds. The whine on the line became very audible.

'Really, Madge, I can handle—'

'Be quiet. This son of a bitch isn't even Algerian . . . Yes. Yes . . . All right. Then we'll *both* be down! . . . Take it or leave it, you desert gnat, that's the only way it's going to be . . . They're *your ears*, sweetie . . . And one other thing. The minute we get there, I want a huge meal waiting for my friend here, do you understand? . . . And no biscuits of camel dung, either! All right. Five minutes.'

She hung up and smiled at Devereaux, who was mostly naked and completely pale.

'That was very generous of you, but it's not necessary—'

'Don't be silly. You don't know these people; I do. You

have to be firm, they're quite harmless, despite those goddamned knives. Besides, do you think I'd let you out of my sight for a minute? After I've seen what nice thoughts you've been thinking? And in your condition.' She leaned over and kissed him again. 'It's really very touching.'

Devereaux realized that in his weakened condition he might be subject to hallucinations; but he was not prepared for the two robed Arabs that met them in the Aletti lobby.

Peter Lorre and Boris Karloff. Quite a bit younger than the more recent photographs Sam remembered, but otherwise unmistakable.

The next twenty minutes were a blur. Yet he *had* to be able to think clearly. Azaz-Varak (*whoever* and *wherever* he was) signified the last of the investors. He had to begin putting together the pieces of his counterstrategy.

Peter Lorre sat in the front seat next to Boris, who drove. The car sped through the streets and careened dangerously around the corners of early morning Algiers. They were halfway up a winding, steep hill when Devereaux realized they were heading for Dar el Beida airport.

'We going on a plane?' asked Sam apprehensively.

Madge answered beside him. 'Oh, sure, sweetie. Tizi Ouzou's like two hundred miles east. You wouldn't want to drive. Remember, I've *been* there.'

Devereaux looked at her. He wondered, and whispered. 'I remember. What I can't understand is why you're here. Do you know what you're involved with? Do you know what you're *doing*?'

'I'm trying to be helpful.'

'So was Rose Mary Woods.'

The interior of the helicopter was only slightly smaller than the main level of Pennsylvania Station. Pillows were everywhere and beside each seat was an elaborate water pipe attached to the wall with a kind of Bunsen burner underneath it. An open galley was at the rear.

And after three minutes in the air, Sam was given the first sustenance he could recall. A small cup of acrid, black liquid that vaguely smelled of coffee, but more of bitter liquorice mixed with stale sardines.

He drank it in one swallow, grimaced, and looked at the tiny person wrapped in sheets who had poured it for him. The tiny person manipulated several wheels around the water pipe in the wall and held a match to the burner beneath. A long rubber tube with a mouthpiece was reeled from somewhere and held out for Sam.

He took it and wondered. It probably would not do him any good, but on the other hand it was something to put in his mouth, and nothing of that nature at this point could be any worse than the numbed agony he was experiencing. He inserted the mouthpiece between his teeth and drew on it.

It wasn't smoke exactly; it was more a vapour. Sweet and pungent at the same time. Really very pleasant. Actually quite delightful. Rather diverting in its way.

He drew more heavily; and then more rapidly; he looked across at Madge, sitting opposite him in a bank of pillows. 'Would you mind, my dear?' he heard himself saying calmly. 'Please remove all your clothes.'

'I'd go easy on that,' replied the girl in her most provocative, breathless whisper.

Was she whispering? Her voice seemed to arrive at his ears on different levels of sound.

'Your blouse first, if you please.' Again he was not quite positive he had said what he heard himself saying. 'Then perhaps if you would remove your skirt while performing a small, undulating dance. That would be very accommodating.'

'Put that damn thing down.'

'It's up?' He could actually smell her perfume. And the pains were gone from his stomach. Instead he could feel a surging force of great strength pulsating throughout his body. He was capable of giant deeds; he was – what was it? – the possessor of the desert winds. A prince of thunder, a hurler of lightning. With the courage of all the lions of Judea.

'That's not a Lucky Strike you're pulling on. It's pure hashish.'

'Who . . . ?' The information reached that small section of his brain that was functioning. *What the hell was he doing?* He spat out the mouthpiece and tried to stabilize the aircraft; it had to be the helicopter because *something* was suddenly going around and around. The lion of Judea was shrinking; a mangy pussycat was taking its place.

And then he heard the whining words of Peter Lorre, who had walked back from the pilot's area. 'We are on a heading south-south-east of Tizi Ouzou.'

'How come?' Madge was upset and did not bother to conceal it. 'You said Tizi, not someplace else. I've got friends on Rue Joucif, you fly! My late husband did a lot of favours for the Algerian government!'

'A thousand nights of blissful pardons, lady of Deveroo, but my government is Azaz-Kuwait. My sheik is the sheik of all sheiks, the god of all khans, the eyes of the falcon, the courage—'

'*When you're calling mee, calling meee, calling meeee!*' Sam suddenly found himself bursting forth in song; at least, it sounded like him. It *was* a song.

'Shut up, Major!' shouted Madge.

'*Alone - alonnnnne on this night that was meant for—*'

'Will you be quiet!' yelled the girl.

'It seemed appropriate,' mumbled Sam.

'Where are we going?' asked Madge of the whining Arab, who was looking at Devereaux as though the American should be watched closely.

'Seventy miles south-east of Tizi Ouzou is a stretch of desert that is traversed only by Bedouin tribes. It is very remote and lends itself to confidential rendezvous. An eagle's tent has been spread for the sheik of all sheiks, the god of all khans. Azaz-Varak, the magnificent, is flying in from his holiest of kingdoms to meet with the unspeakable dog named Deveroo.'

'*When I'm calling yoooo – Deverooo – only yooooo—*'

'Will you shut up!'

CHAPTER SIXTEEN

There were maps everywhere, covering the Watergate bed, spilling over the coffee table, scattered about the floor, propped up against the bureau mirror, and draped over the hotel sofa. There were gasoline road maps, railroad maps, elevation charts, geological and vegetation carto-analyses; even aerial photographs from sequential altitudes of 500, 1,500, 5,000, and finally 20,000 feet.

These plus 363 ground-level photographs of every inch of the terrain under study.

Nothing could be left to chance.

Five minutes ago he had made his final decision. The real estate broker from the highly confidential, international firm of Les Châteaux Suisses des Grands Siècles would be arriving imminently. Naturally, secretly; the first law of Les Châteaux Suisses was absolute secrecy.

Mac had selected a remote château in the canton of Valais, south of Zermatt, in the countryside near Champoluc. The surrounding lands – two hundred acres – were in the cartographical shadow of the Matterhorn and were virtually inaccessible.

What was uppermost in his mind were two factors. The first was terrain. It would have to come as close as possible to duplicating Ground Zero, as Hawkins had decided to name it. Every turn and curve and rise of the road; each slope and hill that might play a part in the approach to or the escape from Ground Zero would have to be simulated as precisely as possible. Manoeuvres were useless if the training grounds did not reflect the combat zone.

The second factor was the inaccessibility. His base of operations, as Mac had come to think of the leased property, had to be completely concealed from the outlying country roads as well as from the air. The area had to be one where huge pieces of equipment could be hidden in seconds; where a complement of at least a dozen men could live and train for a minimum of eight weeks.

The château in question possessed these specifics. And it was not that far from Zürich. The Shepherd Company's capital would be transferred to Zürich. Devereaux would have to see to this centralization of finances. As well as the vetting of the château's lease.

There was a discreet knock at the hotel door. MacKenzie stepped carefully over the maps and photographs on the floor and went to it. He stood close to the panel and spoke.

'Monsieur D'Artagnan?' Les Châteaux Suisses used pseudonyms all the time.

'*Oui, mon général,*' was the quiet reply from the corridor.

Hawkins opened the door and a middle-aged, nondescript, portly man entered. Even his slightly waxed moustache was nondescript, thought MacKenzie. He'd be a tough fellow to spot in a crowd; there was absolutely nothing outstanding about him.

'I see you have pursued the information we sent you,' said Monsieur D'Artagnan in an accent formed west of Alsace-Lorraine. He was obviously a man who wasted no time on the amenities, and the Hawk was grateful for that.

'Yes, I have. I've made my decision.'

'Which property?'

'Château Machenfeld.'

'Ahh, *Le Machenfeld! Magnifique extraordinaire!* What history has been played on its rolling fields; what battles won and lost in front of its towering parapets of granite! And the indoor plumbing has been kept most functioningly modern. An exquisite choice. I congratulate you. You and your coterie of religious brothers will be very happy.' D'Artagnan removed the fattest envelope Hawkins had ever seen from his inner jacket pocket. The highly secretive firm did not carry briefcases, Mac remembered; so much confidential information crammed into one repository was too dangerous. The brokers carried only those papers of immediate concern.

'Are those the leasing arrangements?'

'*Oui, mon général.* All completed and ready for your chosen and agreed-upon mark. And the six months' deposit, of course.'

'Well, before we get to that, let me go over the conditions—'

'There are *new* ones, monsieur?'

'No. I just want to make sure you understand the old ones.'

'But, my *général*, everything *was* understood,' said D'Artagnan, smiling. 'You dictated the specifications; I transcribed them myself, as is our policy, and you approved the transcript. Here. See for yourself.' He handed Hawkins the papers. 'I think you know we would never alter our clients' demands. We have only to fill in the specific château and cross-check to make sure the demands are not in conflict with the owner's conditions of lease. I have done so with all potential locations; there are no conflicts.'

MacKenzie took the papers and picked his way between the maps and photographs to the sofa. With one hand he removed two huge elevation charts and sat down.

'I want to be positive that what I'm reading is what I heard.'

'Ask any questions you wish. As is the policy of Les Châteaux Suisses des Grands Siècles, each broker is completely familiar with all conditions. And when our business is concluded, the papers are microfilmed and placed in the company vaults in Geneva. We suggest you make similar arrangements with your copies. Untraceable.'

Hawkins read aloud. 'Whereas the party of the first part, hereafter known as the lessee, takes possession *in-nomen-incognitum . . .*' Mac's eyes skimmed downward. 'In the absence of . . . *communicatum-directorum* between the party

182

of . . . and the party of . . . Goddamn! You boys got your training in clandestine operations.'

D'Artagnan smiled; the waxed moustache stretched a little. 'Ask your questions, monsieur.'

And so it began.

Les Châteaux Suisses des Grands Siècles was nothing if not thorough and specific – in the language of a lease that would never from that moment on see the light of day.

To begin with all identities were held sacrosanct, never to be divulged to any individual, organization, court, or government. No law, national or international, superseded the agreement; *it* was the only law. Payments were made to the firm either in cash or treasurer's cheques; in the case of the Shepherd Company, from a Cayman Island depository.

Whenever explanations of 'source' were desirable, they would be expedited where necessary and in the interests of controlling outside curiosity. In the case of the Shepherd Company, the sole explanation of 'source' was a loose federation of international philanthropists interested in the study and promulgation of an historic religiosity.

All supplies, equipment, transportation, and services would be expedited in complete confidentiality by Les Châteaux Suisses des Grands Siècles and consigned to branch offices in Zermatt, Interlaken, Chamonix, or Grenoble. Any and all deliveries of consequence to Le Château Machenfeld would be made between the hours of midnight and 4 a.m. Drivers, technicians, and labourers, where possible, would be from the ranks of the Shepherd Company's brotherhood, who would be sent down from Le Machenfeld to the branch offices. In the absence thereof, only employees of Les Châteaux Suisses who had no less than ten years' acceptable service with the firm would be assigned the deliveries.

All payments were to be made in advance, based on book retail value, with a surcharge of 40 per cent for the confidential services of Les Châteaux Suisses.

'That's a lot of per cent,' said MacKenzie.

'It's a very wide boulevard,' replied D'Artagnan. 'We

don't avail ourselves to those who drive in narrow streets. We think our consultation fee is ample proof of this.'

It was, thought the Hawk. The 'consultation fee' – applied against whatever lease was arrived at, *if* a lease *was* signed – was $500,000.

'You do mighty fine work, Mr D'Artagnan,' said Hawkins, taking up a fountain pen.

'You're in good hands. In a few days you will, as it were, vanish from the earth.'

'Don't worry. Everybody I know – that's *everybody* – will be extremely grateful never to hear from me again. Seems I generate complications.' The Hawk laughed quietly to himself. He signed his name: *George Washington Rappaport.*

D'Artagnan left with MacKenzie's treasurer's cheque drawn on the Cayman Island's Admiralty Bank. The amount was for $1,495,000.

The Hawk picked up a handful of photographs and walked back to the hotel sofa. As he sat down, however, he knew he could not dwell on the majesty of Machenfeld. There were other immediate considerations. Machenfeld would be worthless without the personnel to train within its borders. But former Lieutenant General MacKenzie Hawkins, twice winner of the Congressional Medal of Honour, knew where he was going and how to get there. Ground Zero was several months away. But the journey had begun.

He wondered how Sam and Midgey were doing. Goddamn, that boy was getting around!

The helicopter descended, dropping straight down and causing torrential clouds of sand to blast up in increasingly furious layers from the desert floor. So thick was the enveloping storm that the only way Sam knew they had landed was the jarring thud of the undercarriage as it met and was swallowed by the dunes.

They had been in the air somewhat longer than had been anticipated. There had been a minor navigational problem: the pilot was lost. It had to be the pilot since it was unthinkable to admit the possibility that the eagle's tent of

Azaz-Varak was in the wrong place. But at last, they saw the complex of canvas below.

The sand settled and Peter Lorre opened the hatch. The desert sun was blinding. Sam held Madge's arm as they stepped out of the aircraft; if the sun was blinding, the sand was boiling. 'Where the hell are we?'

'*Aiyee!*' '*Aiyee!*' '*Aiyee!*' '*Aiyee!*'

The screams were everywhere, and from everywhere there was rushing movement. Turbaned Arabs, their sheets flying in the wind like a hundred white sails, raced out of the various tents towards them. Peter Lorre and Boris Karloff flanked Sam, gripping his arms as if displaying an animal carcass. Madge stood in front, somewhat protectively, thought Devereaux uncomfortably, as though she were about to give instructions to a slaughterhouse butcher. The racing battalion of sheets and turbans formed two single lines that created a corridor leading slightly uphill in the sand to the largest of the tents, about fifty yards away.

Peter Lorre's nasal shriek filled the air. '*Aiyee!* The eye of the falcon! The hurler of lightning! The god of all khans and the sheik of all sheiks!' He turned to Sam and screamed even louder. '*Kneel! Unworthy white hyena!*'

'*What?*' Devereaux wasn't arguing; he just thought the sand would melt his trousers.

'It is better to kneel,' said the deep-throated Boris Karloff, 'than to find yourself standing on stumps.'

The sand was, indeed, uncomfortable. And Sam, in an instant of real human concern, wondered what Madge was going to do; she wore a very short skirt above her desert boots. He squinted and looked at her.

He need not have indulged in human concern, he thought. Madge was not kneeling at all. Instead she had moved slightly to the side and was standing erect. She was spectacular.

'Bitch,' he whispered.

'Keep your head,' she answered quietly. 'That's meant figuratively – I think.'

'*Aiyee!* Behold the prince of thunder and lightning!' shrieked Peter Lorre.

There was movement at the tent at the end of the corridor of abus and turbans. Two minions swept back the front flap and prostrated themselves on the ground, their faces in the sand. From the shadowed recesses emerged a man who was a major disappointment, a walking anticlimax, to the dramatic preparations for his entrance.

The prince of thunder and lightning was a spindly little Arab; peering out from the shrouds was about the ugliest face Devereaux had ever seen. Below the outsized, narrow, hooked nose, Azaz-Varak's lips were curled – actually curled – so that his thin black moustache seemed fused to his nostrils. The pallor of his skin (what could be seen) was a sickly beige, which served to emphasize the dark, deep circles under his heavy-lidded eyes.

Azaz-Varak approached, lips pressing, nostrils sniffing, head bobbing. He looked only at Madge. When he spoke there was a certain authority in his whine.

'The wives of the lion's lair, the royal harem – none understand the awesome responsibilities that befall my generous person. Would you like a camel, lady?'

Madge shook her head with a certain authority of her own. Azaz-Varak continued to stare.

'Two camels? The aeroplane?'

'I'm in mourning,' said Madge respectfully but firmly. 'My wealthy sheik passed away just after the last crescent moon. You know the rules.'

The heavy-lidded eyes of Azaz-Varak were filled with disappointment; his curled-up lips smacked twice as he replied. 'Ahh, it is the awesome burdens of our faith. You have two crescents of the calendar to survive. May your sheik rest with Allah. Perhaps you will visit my palaces when your time has passed.'

'We'll see. Right now, my escort is hungry. Allah wants him to protect me; he can't do that if he faints.'

Azaz-Varak looked at Sam as though studying the preslaughtered carcass. 'He has two functions, then. One worthy, one despicable. Come, dog. To the eagle's tent.'

'That's where the food is, isn't it?' Devereaux smiled his best, most ingratiating smile as he scrambled to his feet.

'You will partake of my table when our business is concluded. Pray to Allah that it is finished before the northern snows come to the desert. Did you bring the unmentionable agreement?'

Devereaux nodded. 'Did you bring any hot corned beef?'

'*Silence!*' shrieked Peter Lorre.

'Lady,' said Azaz-Varak, addressing Madge, 'my servants will see to your every wish. My palaces are lovely; you would like them.'

'It's tempting. We'll see where I am in a month or so.' She winked at Azaz-Varak. His lips went through a series of wet pressings before he snapped his fingers and proceeded towards the eagle's tent.

The minutes stretched into quarter hours, those to the inevitable hour, and then two more of them. Devereaux honestly believed he had reached the end. A promising legal career was being snuffed out, starved out, in the middle of some godforsaken stretch of desert, seventy miles south of a ridiculously named place called Tizi Ouzou in North Africa.

What made the ending so ludicrous was the sight of Azaz-Varak poring over each sentence of the Shepherd Company's limited partnership papers, with eight to ten screeching Arabs looking over his shoulder, arguing vehemently among themselves. Every page was treated as though it were the only page; every convoluted – and unnecessary – legalism torn apart for a meaning that was not there. Sam saw clearly the terrible irony: the esoteric, legalistic nonsense that was the essence of every lawyer's livelihood was keeping him from his own survival.

An insane thought went through his pained brain: if all legal documents were written to be understood between meals – all meals postponed until said understanding was clear – the state of justice would be on a much higher plane. And most lawyers of his acquaintance out of work.

Every now and then one of Azaz-Varak's ministers would carry over a page and point to a particular paragraph, asking him in excellent English what it meant. Invariably Devereaux would explain that it was a standard clause – which invariably it was – and not important.

If it was not important, why was the language so confusing? Only significant items were in confusing words; otherwise there was no need for the confusion.

And, too, good things were stated clearly; unworthy things were often obscured. Did standard mean unworthy?

And so it went. Until at one point Sam screamed.

Nothing else; he simply screamed.

Azaz-Varak and his gaggle of ministers looked over at him. They nodded as if to say, 'Your point is well taken.' And then went back to screaming at each other.

At the instant the darkness started to cloud his vision, his last look at living things, thought Sam, he heard the words, whined by the sheik of sheiks.

'The northern snows have reached the desert, unspeakable one. These foul papers are like camels' prints in storms of sand: they are without meaning. Not any meaning that would bring the wrath of Allah, or certain international authorities. My generous, all-knowing person has signed them. Not that I subscribe to the despicable suggestion made to my ear, but only to help unite the world in love, you hated dog.'

Azaz-Varak rose from the mountain of pillows beneath him. He was escorted to a screened-off section of the enormous tent by several hunched-over ministers and disappeared beyond the silks.

Peter Lorre came up to Sam, the limited partnership agreement in his hands. He gave it to Devereaux and whispered, 'Put this in your pocket. It is better that the eye of the falcon not fall on it again.'

'Is falcon edible?'

Perplexed, the tiny Arab looked at Sam. 'Your eyeballs are swimming in their sockets, Abdul Deveroo. Have the faith of the Koran, first paragraph, book four.'

'What the hell is that?' Sam could hardly speak.

'"The feasts were brought among the unbelieving infidels and no longer were they unbelieving."'

'Does that mean we eat?'

'It does. The god of all khans has ordered his favourite: boiled testicle of camel braised with the stomach of desert rat.'

'*Aiyeeeeee!*' Devereaux blanched and leaped up from the floor of the eagle's tent. The spring had been sprung; there was nothing left but self-annihilation. The end was at hand; the forces of destruction called for his finish in an explosion of violence.

So be it. He would meet it swiftly. Surely. Without thought, only blinding fury. He ran around the pillows and over the rugs and out on to the sand. It was sundown; his end would come with the orange sun descending over the desert horizon.

Boiled testicles! Stomach of rat!

'Madge! *Madge!*'

If he could only reach her! She could bring back news of his demise to his mother and Aaron Pinkus. Let them know he died bravely.

'*Madge!* Where are you?!'

When the words came he felt stirrings of bewilderment that were contradictory to the last thoughts of those who were about to perish.

'Hi, sweetie! Come on over. Look what I've got *here*. It's a *gas!*'

Sam turned, his ankles deep in sand, his caked lips trembling. Fifty yards away a group of Arabs were gathered around the front of the helicopter, all peering into the pilot's cabin.

In a trance of confusion, Devereaux staggered towards the bewildering sight. The Arabs squealed and grumbled but let him through. He gripped the ledge of the window and peered inside. It was easy; the aircraft had sunk into the dune upon landing.

It was not his eyes, however, that were assaulted. It was his ears.

There was a continuous, deafening crackle of static from the helicopter's panel that filled the small enclosure like jack hammers in a wind tunnel. Madge was in the co-pilot's seat, her blouse neckline lowered another several buttons.

Then he heard the words riding through the static and Sam froze, his hunger and exhaustion replaced momentarily by a kind of hypnotic terror.

'Midgey! Midgey, girl! You still there?'

'Yes, Mac, still here. It's just Sam. He's finished with what's-his-name.'

'*Goddamn!* How is he?'

'Hungry. He's a very hungry boy,' said Madge, expertly manipulating switches and dials on the radio panel.

'There'll be plenty of time for rations later. An army travels on its stomach, but first it's got to evacuate the fire zone! Before it gets its ass shot off! Does he have the papers?'

'They're sticking out of his pocket—'

'He's a fine young attorney, that boy! He'll go far! Now, get out of there, Midgey. Get him to Dar el Beida and on that plane for Zermatt. Confirm, and over and out!'

'Roger confirm, Mac. Out.' Midge whipped through several dozen switches as though she were a computer programmer. She turned her face to Devereaux and beamed. 'You're going to have a nice rest, Sam. Mac says you really deserve a vacation.'

'Who? Where . . . ?'

'Zermatt, sweetie. It's in Switzerland.'

PART THREE

The smooth-running corporation is largely dependent on its executive personnel, whose backgrounds and allegiances are compatible with the overall objectives of the structure and whose identities can be submerged to the corporate image.

Shepherd's Laws of Economics:
Book CXIV, Chapter 92

CHAPTER SEVENTEEN

Cardinal Ignatio Quartze, his thin, aristocratic features bespeaking generations of *noblesse oblige*, stormed across the rugs of his Vatican office to the large balconied window overlooking St Peter's Square. He spoke in fury, his lips compressed in anger, his nasal voice searing like the screech of a bullet.

'The Bombalini peasant goes too far! I tell you he is a disgrace to the college which – God help us all – elevated him!'

The cardinal's audience was a plump, boyish-looking priest who sat, as languorously as his habit allowed, in a purple velvet chair in the centre of the room. His pink cheeks and pursed, thick lips bespoke, perhaps, a less aristocratic background than his superior but no less a love of luxury. His speech was more a purr than a voice.

'He was and remains only a compromise, Cardinal. You were assured his health would not permit an extended reign.'

'Every *day* is an extension beyond endurance!'

'He has certain ... humilities that serve us. He has quieted much hostile press. The people look upon him warmly; our worldwide contributions are nearly as high as they were with Roncalli.'

'Please! Not that name! What good is a treasury that expands and contracts like a thousand concertinas because the Holy See subsidizes everything he can put his fat peasant hands on! And we don't need a friendly press. Division is far better to solidify our own! Nobody understands.'

'Oh, but I do, Cardinal. I really do—'

'Did you see him today?' continued Quartze as if the priest had not spoken. 'He openly humiliated me! In audience! He questioned my African allocations.'

'A patently obvious ploy to appease that terrible black man. He's forever complaining.'

'And afterwards he tells jokes – *jokes*, mind you – to the Vatican guard! And waddles into the museum crowds and eats an ice – *eats* an *ice*, mind you – offered by some Sicilian brood mare! Next he'll drop lire in the men's room and all the toilet seats will be stolen! Such indignities! What he does to the bones of St Peter! They will turn to dust!'

'It cannot be very long, my dear Cardinal.'

'Long enough! He'll deplete the treasury and fill the Curia with wild-eyed radicals!'

'You are the next pontiff. The negative reactions of the broad middle hierarchy support you. They are silent, but resentments run deep.'

The cardinal paused; his mouth curved slightly downward as he stared out into the square, his jaw jutted forward below the dark hollows of his deep-set eyes. 'I do believe we have the delegates. Ronaldo, get me the plans for my villa at San Vincente. It calms my nerves to study them.'

'Of course,' said the priest, rising from the purple chair. 'You must remain calm. And when summer comes you will be rid of the Bombalini peasant. He will stay at Castel Gandolfo for at least six weeks.'

'The *plans*, Ronaldo! I'm very upset. Yet in the midst of chaos, I remain the most controlled man in the Vatican—. The plans, you transvestite!' screamed the cardinal.

The moment the papal aide with the ever present clipboard left the room, Pope Francesco I got out of the elevated, high-backed, white velvet chair (a repository that would have frightened Saint Sebastian) and sat next to the lady from *Viva Gourmet* on the couch. He was struck immediately by the beauty of her voice; it was warm and lilting. Very lovely. It befitted such a healthy looking woman.

The aide had suggested that the interview be limited to

twenty minutes; the pontiff had suggested that it should end when concluded. The lady journalist had reddened slightly with embarrassment, so Giovanni put her at ease by switching to English and asking her if she thought there was a market for clipboards with crucifixes painted on the underside. She had laughed while the aide, who did not understand English, stood by the door, his clipboard clutched to his breast like a plastic stigmata.

The aide would have to be replaced, thought the pope. He was another young prelate seduced by the pretensions of Ignatio Quartze. The cardinal was too obvious; he was moving his charges into the papal apartments before the papal funeral was arranged. But Francesco had made up his mind: the Church was not going to be left in the pontifical hands of Ignatio Quartze. To begin with, they held the chalice at Mass as though wringing the neck of a chicken.

The interview with *Viva Gourmet*'s Lillian von Schnabe was productive and pleasant. Giovanni expounded on two of his favourite subjects: that good, substantial meals could be created from inexpensive stock and flavoured with simple, spiced sauces; and that in these difficult days of high prices it was a mark of distinction – to say nothing of Christian brotherhood – to share one's table with one's neighbour.

Mrs von Schnabe saw immediately what he was trying to communicate. 'Is this a form of "the loaves and the fishes", Your Holiness?'

'Let us say He was not preaching to the wealthier sections of Nazareth. A number of His miracles were based in sound psychological principles, my dear. I open my basket of fruit, you open your basket of pasta; we have fruit *and* pasta. The simple addition alone gives variety. Variety we rightly equate with more rather than less.'

'And the diet's improved,' agreed Lillian, nodding.

'*Perfetto*. You see? Two *principii*: reduce the cost and share the supply.'

'That sounds almost socialistic, though, doesn't it?'

'When stomachs are empty and prices are high, labels are foolish. In the *Borsa Valori* – the stock exchange, you call it –

they are not prone to open baskets; they sell them. It is fitting that they do so, considering the nature of their labours. But I do not address such people. They eat at the Grand Hotel, on each other's expense accounts. I believe that, too, is a derivative of the "loaves and fishes" principle.'

They discussed numerous recipes based on the village dishes from the pope's past. Giovanni could see that the nice lady with the lovely voice was impressed. He had done his nutritional homework; carbohydrates, proteins, starch, calories, iron, and all kinds of vitamins were to be found in his recipes.

Lillian filled half a notebook, writing as rapidly as the pope spoke, stopping him occasionally to clarify a word or phrase. After nearly an hour had passed, she paused and asked a question Giovanni did not understand.

'What about your own *personal* requirements, Your Holiness? Are there any restrictions or specific necessities called for in the meals brought to you?'

'*Che cosa?* What do you mean?'

'We are what we eat, you know.'

'I sincerely hope not. I am in my seventh decade, my dear. An excess of onion or olive or pimento ... But such information is not needed for your article. People my age quite naturally gravitate to and regulate their personal needs in this area.'

Lillian put her pencil down. 'I didn't mean to pry, but you're so fascinating a man – and I *am* considered one of the best nutritional experts in America. I suppose I just wanted to approve of the way your kitchen treats you.'

Ahh, thought Giovanni Bombalini, *how many years it had been since a lovely person of the opposite gender had been concerned about him! He could not remember, it was so long ago! Pinched-faced nuns and officious nurses, yes. But so attractive a lady, with such a lovely voice ...*

'Well, my dear, these outrageous doctors *do* insist on certain foods ...'

Lillian picked up her pencil.

And they talked for another fifteen minutes.

At the end of which time there was a knock on the door of the papal apartment. Francesco rose from the couch and returned to the elevated, high-backed, white velvet chair that belonged in one of those Cinecittà biblical spectaculars.

An agitated Cardinal Ignatio Quartze stood in the doorway, a handkerchief dabbing his aquiline nose, noises emerging from his throat. 'I am sorry to interrupt, Holy Father,' he said in both Italian and high dudgeon, giving the word 'holy' a rather profane but eminently courteous connotation, 'but I've just been informed that Your Holiness has seen fit to disagree with my instructions regarding the convocation of the Bankers for Christ.'

'"Disagree" is too strong a term. I merely suggested that the convocation committee reconsider. To occupy the Sistine Chapel for two days at the height of the spring tourist season seems unwarranted.'

'If you will forgive my contrary observation, the Sistine is the most favoured *and* frequented site we possess. All convocations of merit convene there.'

'Thus denying thousands every year of its beauty. I'm not sure there's merit in that.'

'We are *not* an amusement park, Pope Francesco.' Strange noises continued to come from the area of the cardinal's throat; he blew his nose with aristocratic vigour.

'I sometimes wonder,' replied Giovanni. 'We sell such a diversity of baubles everywhere. Did you know there's a stand featuring rhinestone rosary beads?'

'*Please*, Your Holiness. The Bankers for Christ. They *expect* the Sistine. We are finalizing extremely important matters.'

'Yes, my dear Cardinal, I received the memorandum. "Accruals for Jesus" is somewhat laboured, I think, but I suppose there are certain tax advantages.' Giovanni's attention was suddenly drawn to Lillian. She had closed her notebook politely but firmly; she was anxious to leave. *Ahh*, it had been such a pleasant interlude! And Quartze was not going to spoil it; he could wait. He addressed the attractive lady with the lovely voice. In English, of course; a language only barely understood by Quartze. 'How rude we are. Do forgive us. The agitated cardinal with the propellers in his nasal passages has once again found my judgements lacking.'

'Then I would have to say *his* judgement left much to be desired,' said Lillian, rising from the couch and placing her notebook in her purse. She looked into Giovanni's eyes and spoke softly with feeling. 'I suppose this isn't a proper thing to say but since I'm not Catholic, I'll say it anyway. You're one of the most attractive men I've ever met. I hope you're not offended.'

Giovanni Bombalini, Pope Francesco, Vicar of Christ felt the stirrings of memories of fifty years ago. And they were good. In a profoundly sacred sense – for which he was grateful. 'And you, my dear, possess an honesty – however erroneous your present opinion – that walks in the warm light of God.'

'If I do, it's because I was taught by someone quite like you, I think. Although few would recognize the similarity.'

'I am flattered. This – someone, give him the blessings of a farmhand-priest.'

Lillian smiled. She started for the door, where Quartze's handkerchief fluttered a tattoo in front of his agitated face and the sounds of mucus still could be heard beyond his aquiline nose and very thin lips. The prelate sidestepped to let her pass, doing his best to ignore her. So Lillian paused briefly, forcing him to look at her. When he did so, she winked.

As she closed the door the words from Pope Francesco were clear and firm. For in his anger, the pontiff raised his voice, in English.

'Talk to me not of the Sistine, Ignatio! Instead, discuss these plans I requested for your waterfront home at San Vincente! What are "security arrangements"? They include a *steam bath*?'

Hawkins had reserved both seats in the first-class section of the Lufthansa 747. Since he needed elbow room, there was no point in inconveniencing a fellow passenger. This way, he was able to place the folders beside him for quick referrals.

He had specifically chosen the night flight to Zürich. The travellers, by and large, would be diplomats, bankers, or corporate executives used to transatlantic flights; they would use the night for sleep, not socializing. He would have a minimum of interruptions.

For selections would have to be made, offers of recruitment dispatched immediately from Zürich.

MacKenzie's briefcase contained assorted personnel profiles from which he would choose his troops. They were the last of the files he had Xeroxed at the G-2 archives. Those fortunate enough to be chosen would be his brigade; his personal army that would be privileged to engage in the most unusual manoeuvre in modern military history.

And each soldier would return from the engagement one of the richest men in his part of the world.

For, where possible, they would be from separate parts of the world. For the inviolate condition of recruitment was that none would ever acknowledge the existence of the others once the engagement was completed. It would be better if they came from different places.

The dossiers in the Hawk's briefcase were those of the most accomplished double and triple agents in the US Army data banks. And there was a common denominator running through each file: all were in forced retirement.

The state of double and triple agenting was at a low ebb. The experts described in the dossiers had not had really gainful employment for some time, and for such men inactivity was anathema. It meant not only a loss of prestige within the community of international criminals, but also a reduced scale of living.

The prospects of $500,000 per man would not be lightly dismissed. And each potential recruit was worth it. Each was the best at his speciality.

It was all a question of logistics. Think – then *out*-think. Every function handled by an expert, every move timed to the split second.

And that required a commander who demanded flawless precision from his troops. Who trained them to perform at peak efficiency levels. Who did not stint when it came to equipment and simulation; who would duplicate as far as technically possible the *exact conditions* projected for the assault. In essence, a general officer of the first rank. Himself. *Goddamn!*

Once the brigade was selected and assembled, Mac would outline the basic strategy. Then he would allow his officers to offer suggestions and refinements. A good commander always listened to his subordinate officers but, of course, reserved final judgement for himself.

The weeks of training would show where the strengths and weaknesses lay; the objective was merely to eliminate all weakness.

The fewer troops the better, but not so few as to impair the efficiency of the mission. Which was why there was only one payment for each soldier: $500,000. There would be no rewards if they were caught. At least, not the kind they were after. There *would* be certain family allotments in the case of capture. It was the sort of thing all armies had learned to take for granted. Men performed better under combat conditions if their minds were free of concern about their families. It was a good thing, too. It was another proof of separation between the species.

The Shepherd Company would bank funds for dependants in advance of Ground Zero; to be deducted, of course, from all final payments upon the successful completion of the operation.

Goddamn! He was not only pro, he was a very thorough pro at that! If those idiots in the Pentagon had turned over the whole US Army to him, they would not be having all that trouble with volunteer enlistments. The Pentagon pricky-shits did not really understand 'the book'. If a soldier took the book for what it was and didn't try to bend it politically, or find ambiguities to hide behind – well, it was a goddamned good book. Flawed but workable.

He had no time to think about pricky-shits. He had about

refined his brigade. The required areas of expertise were seven: camouflage, demolition, sedative medicines, native orientation, aircraft technology, escape cartography, and electronics.

Seven experts. He had narrowed the dossiers down to twelve. Before he reached Zürich he knew he would have the seven. It was just a question of reading and rereading. He would send out his offers from Zürich, not from the Château Machenfeld; nothing could be traced to Machenfeld.

He even had to be careful in Zürich. Not with regard to traces, however; he could handle that problem. But he had to make damn sure he didn't run into Sam Devereaux. Sam was due within hours of his own arrival; he wasn't ready for Sam's kind of panic. He could handle *that* problem better within the confines of Machenfeld.

But then, thought the Hawk, he didn't really have anything to worry about. Devereaux was the girls' problem and they had – each and every one – carried out their assignments with real know-how.

Goddamn! They were splendid! A man had to count himself fortunate, indeed, to have such a quartet of fine women behind him. 'Behind *every* great man . . .' they said. Behind *him* there wasn't *one* fine lass, there were *four*.

And a grander, more upstanding group of girls there never was! Sam was a lucky fellow and he didn't know it. Hawkins made a mental note to tell him when he saw Sam at Machenfeld.

Tomorrow, if the schedule held.

Devereaux walked down the station platform looking for the correctly numbered railway car. The task was made difficult because he could not stop belching. He had eaten his way from Tizi-whatever-the-hell-it-was, through Algiers, past Rome, into Zürich. Madge had seen him off at Dar el Beida airport admitting no more in their good-byes than she had saying hello in the Aletti Hotel room.

But Sam had made up his mind not to speculate any

further about the girls. Whatever propelled them to do what they did for the Hawk could be left to Krafft-Ebing; he had other things to concentrate on.

The capitalization of forty million dollars was committed. Hawkins now had his marbles (no, he did not have his marbles, but that was another question), and he would start playing the game. The Hawk would begin his final arrangements, make his purchases, recruit his – what was it? – 'support personnel'.

Jesus! Support personnel!

So he could kidnap the pope!

Oh, my God! The whole world was an enormous fruitcake!

There was only one thing to bear in mind, one objective to keep in focus: how to stop MacKenzie Hawkins.

Two objectives: stay out of jail himself. And out of the homicidal clutches of the Mafia, the Peerage, the Nazis, and particularly those Arabs who wanted to stuff his unmentionables into unspeakables.

He found his compartment, the sort made famous by Rex Harrison and Margaret Lockwood. Shadows and black velvet collars and the incessant *therumping* of the metal wheels against the metal tracks below signifying the inevitable approach of terror. And large windows on the sliding doors, with curtains suddenly drawn back revealing the faces of evil.

Night Train, Orient Express – with slow dissolves to hands inching into folds of dark overcoats, ever so slowly withdrawing the black steel of murderous pistols. The train started.

'Well, ah declare! Ah said to myself, Ah simply *don't beleeeeve it*! It's the *mayjor*! Right here in *l'll ole Zürich*!'

There was no reason to be the least astonished. After all, *Titanics* was on schedule.

Regina Sommerville Hawkins Clark Madison Greenberg stood in the corridor outside the railroad compartment and spoke through the wood-framed window. She slid the door open and filled the small enclosure with remembrances of magnolia blossoms. Sam sat down calmly by the window, amazed at his own casualness. 'Your timing's nothing short of brilliant. The train rolls and so do you. If I tried to get off at Lucerne I have an idea you'd start screaming "rape"!'

'Why, what a peculiar thing to say. I hope you haven't forgotten the Beverly Hills Hotel; I never will.'

'My memories have no beginnings, no middles, no ends. The world fornicates in a thousand broken mirrors; we abuse ourselves in the reflections of Sodom and Gomorrah . . .

'Now, tell me why you just *happen* to be in Zürich. At the Hauptbahnhof, on this particular train, in this particular car.'

'Oh, that's easy. Manny's shooting a picture in Geneva. For UA. I think it's so porn they had to make it outside the States.'

'That's Geneva; this is Zürich. You can do better than that. Let's have it for Hawkins's Harem. A little imagination, please.'

'Honestly! Now you're downright offensive!' Regina swept her vicuña back and placed her hands defiantly on her hips. Two cannons had Devereaux in their sights. 'I don't think you've got a damn thing to complain about. We root ourselves up out of *very* comfortable circumstances, traipse *all* over the world, subject ourselves to every kind of inconvenience – *rush, rush, rush* – check on everything – look after you, body *and* soul – make sure no one hurts you – see to your every comfort—. Oh, Lawdy, what more could we do?! And for what? Abuse! Just plain, big ole abuse!'

Regina dropped her defiant pose and began to cry. She opened her purse, withdrew a Kleenex, and sat down opposite Sam, dabbing her eyes.

A lost, hurt little girl.

'Hey, come on. That's not fair.'

As are most men, Sam was helpless before a tearful woman.

Regina sobbed; her chest throbbed. Devereaux got out of

his seat and knelt in front of her. 'It's okay. It's all right. Don't cry, please.'

Between subsiding gasps, the girl looked at him gratefully. 'Then you don't hate me? Say you don't hate me.'

'How could I hate you? You're lovely – and sweet – and for Christ's sake, please stop crying.'

She put her face next to his and her lips against his ear. 'I'm sorry. It's just that I'm exhausted. The pressure's been simply God-awful. I've stayed by the telephone night and day, always worryin' – and, of course, wonderin'. I really missed you.'

Ginny's coat was like a warm, comforting blanket between them. The huge, soft lapels came close to enveloping Devereaux's arms. She took both his hands and guided them between the folds of thick fabric and placed them on the softer, warmer, more comforting swells of loveliness that were beneath the silk of her blouse.

'That's better. Stop crying now.' It was all he could think to say, so he said it softly.

She whispered into his ear, causing all kinds of things to happen to his metabolism. 'Do you remember those marvellous old English movies that took place on trains like this?'

'Sure. Rex Harrison saving Margaret Lockwood from the evil Conrad Veidt—'

'I think you can slide the door closed and lock it. And there are curtains . . .'

Devereaux rose from the floor. He locked the door, closed the curtains, then turned back to Regina. She had removed her vicuña coat and spread it invitingly over the soft seat of the railroad compartment.

Beneath them the *therumping* sounds of the metal against metal signified the inexorable journey, the beat somehow sensual. Outside, the lovely countryside of Switzerland whipped by, bathed in a Swiss twilight.

'How much time do we have before we reach Zermatt?' he asked.

'Enough,' she replied, smiling. She began unbuttoning her silk blouse. 'And we'll know. It's the last stop.'

CHAPTER EIGHTEEN

Hawkins registered at Zürich's Hotel D'Accord with a counterfeit passport. He'd purchased it in Washington from a CIA agent who realized the courts would not let him write a book when he retired; the man also offered a selection of wigs and hidden cameras but MacKenzie demurred. On settling into the room, his first act was to go right down to the lobby again and negotiate with the head switchboard operator: cash for cooperation. Since the cash was one hundred dollars, it was agreed that all his calls and cablegrams would be routed through her board.

He returned to the room and spread the seven dossiers (his final selections) over the coffee table. He was immensely pleased. These men were the most devious, experienced *provocateurs* in their fields. It was now merely a question of enlisting them. And MacKenzie knew he was an exceptionally qualified recruiter.

Four he knew he could reach by phone. Three by cable. Admittedly, the telephone contacts would be difficult, for in no case would one call find the expert in. But he would reach them by using various codes from the past. One call would be made to a Basque fishing village on the Bay of Biscay; another to a similar coastal town in Crete. A third would be placed to Stockholm, to the sister of the espionage expert who was currently living as a minister of the Scandinavian Baptist Church. The fourth call would be to Marseilles where the man sought was employed as a tugboat pilot.

And the geographical diversity! In addition to those he could reach by telephone (Biscay, Crete, Stockholm and

Marseilles), there were the cablegrams: to Athens, Rome, and Beirut. What a spread! It was an intelligence director's dream!

MacKenzie took off his jacket, threw it on the bed, and withdrew a fresh cigar from his shirt pocket. He chewed the end to its proper consistency and lighted up. It was just nine-fifteen; the afternoon train to Zermatt was at four-fifteen.

Seven hours. Now that was a good omen if ever one existed! Seven hours and seven subordinate officers to recruit.

He carried the three dossiers to the desk and arranged the files in front of the telephone. The cablegrams would be sent first.

At precisely twenty-two minutes to four the Hawk replaced the telephone and made a red check mark on the dossier titled *Marseilles*. It was the last of the phone contacts; he needed only two replies – to the cables to Athens and Beirut. Rome had responded two hours ago. Rome had been out of work longer than the others.

The calls had gone smoothly. In each case the initial conversations with the middlemen – and women – had been reserved, polite, general, almost abstract. And with each MacKenzie employed just the right words, quietly, confidentially. Each expert he had wanted to reach called him back.

There had been no hitches with anyone. His proposals were couched in the same universally understood language; the term *yellow mountain* the springboard. It was the highest score an agent could make for himself. The *yellow mountain* figure was a 'five hundred key' with advance funds banked against contingencies. The *security controls* included 'inaccessible clearing houses' that maintained no connections with international regulatory agencies. The *time factor* was between six and eight weeks, depending on the 'technological refinements called for in the sophisticated engineering process'. And finally, as leader, his own background encompassed wholesale service to entire governments in most of Southeast Asia, proof of which could be confirmed by several accounts in Geneva.

He had done his research well. To a man, they all needed to mine the *yellow mountain*.

Hawkins got up from the desk and stretched. It had been a long day and it wasn't over yet. In twenty minutes he would have to leave for the railroad station. Between now and then he would speak with the switchboard operator and give her instructions for those callers who might try to reach him. The instructions would be simple: he had reserved the room for a week; he would return to Zürich in three days. The callers could contact him there, or leave numbers where they could be reached. MacKenzie did not want to return to Zürich, but Athens and Beirut were exceptional recruits.

The telephone rang. It was Athens.

Six minutes later Athens was in.

One more to go.

The Hawk moved his untouched luggage to the door and repacked his briefcase, leaving Beirut's dossier in a separate, easily accessible spot. He looked at his watch: three minutes to four. There was no point in procrastinating any longer. He had to leave for the station. Returning to the desk he dialled the switchboard operator and told her he wanted to leave a few simple instructions—

The operator interrupted politely.

'Yes, of course, mein Herr. But may I take them later? I was about to ring your room. An overseas call has just come in for you. From Beirut.'

Goddamn!

Sam opened his eyes. The sun was streaming through the huge French doors: the breeze billowed the drapes of blue silk. He looked around the room. The ceiling was at least twelve feet high, the fluted columns in the corners and the intricately carved mouldings of dark wood everywhere spoke the word 'château'. It all came into focus. He was in a place called Chateau Machenfeld, somewhere south of Zermatt. Outside the thick, sculptured door of his room was a wide hallway with Persian prayer rugs scattered over a glistening dark floor, and muted candelabra on the walls. The hallway led to an enormous winding staircase and a proliferation of crystal chandeliers above a great hall the size of a respectable ballroom. There, among priceless antiques and Renaisssance portraits, was the entrance – gigantic double doors of oak opening on a set of marble steps that led to a circular drive large enough to handle a funeral for the chairman of General Motors.

What had Hawkins *done*? How did he do it? My God, why? What was he going to use such a place for?

Devereaux looked at the sleeping Regina, her dark brown hair lying in waves over the pillow, her California-tanned face half buried under the eiderdown quilt. If she had any answers, she wouldn't tell him. Of all the girls, Ginny was the most outrageously manipulative; she had orchestrated him down to the moment of sleep. Partially, granted only partially, because he was fascinated by her. There was a will of steel beneath the soft magnolia exterior; she was a natural leader who, as all natural leaders, took delight in her leadership. She used her gifts, mental and physical, with imagination and boldness, and a considerable dash of humour. She could be the strong and moral proselytizer one moment, and the lost little girl in the middle of burning Atlanta the next. She was the laughing, provocative siren in the plantation moonlight, and with the flick of a switch, a conspiratorial, whispering Mata Hari giving orders to a suspicious looking chauffeur in the shadows of the Zermatt railroad station.

'Mack Feldmann's ass is in the bitter seltzer!'

To the best of Sam's recollection those had been the words Ginny had whispered to the strange man in the black beret, with the gold front tooth, whose catlike eyes riveted themselves to the front of her blouse.

'Mack's in felt!' had been the whispered reply. *'His sight's in an auto bomb's flower pot!'*

With that less-than-articulate rejoinder, Ginny had nodded, grabbed Devereaux's arm, and propelled him into the Zermatt street.

'Carry your suitcase in your left hand and whistle

something. He'll turn into an alley and we'll wait at the corner for him to bring out the car.'

'Why all the nonsense? The left hand. The whistling—'

'Others are checking. To make sure we're not being followed.'

The *Orient Express* syndrome was being somewhat overdone, Sam had thought at the time, but nonetheless he'd switched the suitcase to his left hand and started whistling.

'Not *that*, you ninny!'

'What's the matter? It's some kind of hymn—'

'Over here it's called "Deutschland Über Alles".'

He'd switched to 'Rock of Ages' as another man, this one in a real Conrad Veidt overcoat complete with velvet lapels, came up to Regina and spoke softly.

'Your warts are in the wagon.'

'Mack Feldmann's ass surely has sweet shekels,' she had answered quietly, rapidly. And within seconds a long black automobile raced out of the dark alley and they had climbed in.

That was how the tortuous, two-hour drive had begun. Miles of winding, uphill roads cut out of the Swiss mountains and forests, intermittently illuminated by the eerie wash of moonlight. Until they reached some kind of massive gate that wasn't a gate; it was an honest-to-god *portcullis*. In front of a *moat*.

A real moat! With heavy planks and the sounds of water below. Then another winding, uphill road that ended in the enormous circular drive in front of the largest country house Sam had seen since he toured Fontainebleau with the Quincy Boy Scouts. And even Fontainebleau didn't have parapets. This place did, certainly high and definitely stone, with the sort of cutout patterns one associated with *Ivanhoe*.

Quite a place, Château Machenfeld. And he had only seen it at night. He wasn't sure he wanted to see it in daylight. There was something frightening about the mere thought of such a massive edifice when related to one MacKenzie Hawkins.

But where did the château fit in? What was it for? If it was going to be the son of a bitch's command post, why didn't he just rent Fenway Park and be done with it? It had to take an army of minions to keep the place running; minions talked. Ask anyone at Nuremberg or in Sirica's courtroom.

But Regina wouldn't talk. (Of course, she wasn't a minion; in no way did the word fit.) Yet he had tried. All the way down from Zürich – well, perhaps not every moment – and half the night in Machenfeld – perhaps less than half – he had done his best to get her to tell him what she knew.

They had sparred verbally, each talking obliquely, neither coming to grips with any positive statements that could lead to any real conclusions. She admitted – she had no choice – that all the girls had agreed to turn up in the right places at the right times so that he, Sam, would have company and not be led into temptations that could be debilitating on such a long business trip. And have someone trustworthy to take messages for him. And watch out for him. And where goddamned cotton-pickin' hell was the harm in *that*? Where was he going to find such a concerned group of ladies who had his best interests at heart? And kept him on schedule?

Did she know what the *business trip* was about?

Lawdy, no! She never asked. None of the girls asked.

Why not?

Landsakes, honey! The Hawk had told them not to.

Couldn't any of them draw . . . certain inferences? I mean, my God, his itinerary wasn't exactly that of a New England shoe salesman.

Honeychile! When they were married to the Hawk – individually, of course – he was always involved with top-secret army things they all knew they shouldn't ask questions about.

He wasn't *in* the army now!

Well-live-and-die-in-Dixie! That's the *army's* fault!

And so it went.

And then he began to understand. Regina was no patsy. None of the girls was. *Fall guy* was not in their collective vocabulary. If Ginny, or Lillian, or Madge, or Anne knew anything concrete they weren't about to say so. If they perceived a lack of complete integrity, each put on blinkers, and her own particular activity remained unrelated to any larger action. None certainly would discuss anything with *him*.

There was another problem in the midst of the Hawk's insanity: Sam genuinely liked the girls. Whatever the whack-a-doo furies were that drove them to do MacKenzie's bidding, each was her person, each an individual, each – God help him – had an honesty he found refreshing. So, if he did spell out what he knew, the instant he did so they were accessories. To a *conspiracy*. It didn't take a lawyer to know that. What was he thinking about; he *was* a lawyer.

As of this . . . point in time . . . each girl was clean. Maybe not like a hound's tooth; maybe not even like a wino's bridgework, but legally it could be argued that each had operated in a vacuum. There was no conspiracy under the circumstances.

Thank you, Mr Defence Attorney. The bench suggests that you reclaim your tuition from law school.

Sam got out of the ridiculously oversized, canopied bed as quietly as possible. He saw his shorts halfway across the room towards the French doors, which was where he was heading, anyway, and briefly wondered why they were so far from the bed. Then he remembered, and he smiled.

But this was morning, a new day, and things were going to be different. Ginny had given him one specific to hang on to: Hawkins would arrive by late afternoon or early evening. He would use the time until then to learn whatever he could about Château Machenfeld. Or more precisely, what the Hawk was planning for Château Machenfeld as it related to one Pope Francesco, Vicar of Christ.

It was time for him to mount his own counterstrategy. Hawkins was good, no question about it. But he, Sam Devereaux from the Eastern Establishment's Quincy-Boston axis, wasn't so bad, either. Confidence! Mac had it; so did he.

As he put on his shorts, the obvious first move in his counterstrategy came into focus. It wasn't just obvious, it was blatant; bells rang! Such an extraordinary place (mansion, estate, compound, small country) as Machenfeld would demand an unending series of supplies to keep it functioning. And suppliers were like minions, they could see, and hear, and bear witness. The Hawk's proclivity for massiveness could be the most vulnerable aspect of his plans. Sam had considered disrupting Mac's supply lines as *one* of his options, from a military point of view, but he had no idea how positively logical it was. It might be all he needed.

He'd circulate rumours as massively dangerous, as gigantically outrageous, as the sight of Machenfeld itself. He'd start with the servants, then the suppliers, then everyone else who came near the château, until a state of isolation was brought about and he could come to grips with a deserted Hawkins, and – *what the hell was that noise?*

He walked rapidly to the French doors and through them to the small balcony beyond. It overlooked the rear of Château Machenfeld. He assumed it was the rear; there was no circular drive below. Instead, there were gardens in spring bloom, with gravelled paths and latticed arbours and scores of small fishponds carved out of rock. Beyond the gardens were green fields that merged into greener, darker forests, and in the distance were the majestic Alps.

The noise continued, spoiling the view. He could not, at first, determine where it came from, and so he squinted in the sunlight. And instantly wished to hell he hadn't. Because he could now see what was making the noise.

One, two, three . . . five, six . . . eight, nine! Nine assorted – *insanely* assorted – vehicles were slowly going down a dirt road that bordered the fields, progressing south towards the surrounding forests.

There were two long black limousines, a huge earthmoving bulldozer, an outsized tractor with pronged forks in front, and five – goddamn it, yes, five motorcycles!

It didn't take a lot of imagination to get the picture. The Hawk was about to enter manoeuvres! He had bought himself his own personal *papal motorcade*! Plus equipment that could shove the ground around into any design he liked: The route of said papal motorcade!

But he hadn't even arrived at Machenfeld! How the hell was he able to – and what the hell was *that*?

In his anger and confusion, Devereaux gripped the balcony, shaking his head in frustrated bewilderment. His eyes were arrested by an extraordinary sight fifty yards away.

Within a kind of patio, outside a pair of open doors that looked like the entrance to some sort of enormous kitchen, stood a large man wearing a chef's hat, who was in the process of checking off items from a thick sheaf of papers in his hand. In front of the man was a mountain of crates and cartons and boxes that must have reached the height of fifteen feet!

Lines of supply, *shit*!

There wasn't anything left in Europe for Hawkins to buy. There was enough food down there to eliminate half the famine on the Ganges! The son of a bitch had requisitioned enough rations for an army, goddamn it, an army setting out on a two-year bivouac!

Limousines, motorcycles, bulldozers, tractors, food for the entire Lost Battalion! Sam's counterstrategy move number one was shot to hell by a parade of nine idiotically assorted vehicles and some gasping eccentric in a chef's hat.

The only state of isolation in the foreseeable future was from any and all lines of supply. They were totally unnecessary.

That left the minions. The dozen or so servants that had to be around to keep Machenfeld afloat. Kitchens, gardens, fields (that probably meant barns, maybe livestock), and at least thirty to forty rooms with cleaning and waxing and polishing and dusting. Christ! There *had* to be a staff of twenty!

He'd begin right away. Perhaps with the drivers of the nine vehicles; convince them to get the damn things off the château's grounds before it was too late. Then he'd rapidly go from one group of servants to another. Let them know in ominous terms, which meant legal terms, that if they knew what was good for them they'd get the hell out of Machenfeld before all the agents of Interpol descended.

All the food in Switzerland wouldn't do the Hawk any good if there was no one on the premises. To *run* the premises. And a few well-chosen words to those manning the vehicles, words like 'International violations', 'personal accountability', and 'life imprisonment', would surely cause that stream of motorcycles and limousines and trucks to barrel-ass back over the moat into safer territory.

Sam was so preoccupied with his new strategy that he wasn't really aware that his undershorts kept sagging, causing him to hold them up with a free hand. He was forced to be aware of it now because as he gripped the railing his shorts had plummeted down to his ankles. Swiftly, he retrieved his modesty, noting with a degree of self-satisfaction that the games with Ginny Greenberg must have been pretty damned exciting indeed. But it was no time for pleasant reminiscence; there was work to do. His watch read nearly eleven; he hadn't realized he'd slept so long – the games were not only exciting, but exhausting. He had barely five or six hours to get everybody out. Such a large staff of servants probably had lots of personal belongings. That would mean transportation, perhaps more complicated than he had considered. But one thing had to be clear: when the minions left the grounds of Machenfeld, they were *not to return*. For *any* reason. Anything less would weaken his basic premise: Machenfeld was a threat to everyone who remained, therefore no one was to do so.

Evacuation!

The château was to be deserted!

Then what the hell was MacKenzie going to do?

Stew in his cigar juice, *that's* what he was going to do!

It was merely a question of logistics and execution.

Goddamn! Logistics and execution! He was beginning to *think* like the Hawk! And have the confidence of the Hawk! Be bold! Be outrageous! Take fate by the balls and . . .

Shit! Before anything could happen, he had to get dressed. He raced through the French doors into the room. Ginny stirred and moaned a little and then buried her head farther into the eiderdown quilt. He stepped out of the torn underwear, and crossed quietly to his suitcase which was on an overstuffed armchair against the velour-covered wall.

It was empty.

There wasn't a goddamned thing in his suitcase.

He looked around for the closet.

Closets. There were four.

Empty. Except for Ginny's dresses.

Shit!

He ran as quietly as possible to the sculptured door and opened it.

Sitting across the wide hallway was the black beret with the gold front tooth and catlike eyes which were now focused on Sam's lower extremities. In the confusion that, perhaps, was understandable. The sneer was not.

'Where are my clothes?' whispered Devereaux, partially closing the door, leaning against it.

'In the *launtree*, mein Herr,' replied the black beret in an accent formed in some Swiss canton run by Hermann Göring.

'Everything?'

'Courtesy of Château Machenfeld. All was dirty.'

'That's ridiculous!' Sam tried to keep his voice low. He did not want to wake Ginny. 'Nobody asked me—'

'You were asleep, mein Herr,' interrupted the black beret, grinning suggestively, his gold tooth gleaming. 'You were very tired.'

'Well, now I'm very angry! I want my clothes back. Right away!'

'I cannot do that.'

'Why not?'

'It is the *launtree's* day off.'

'What? Then why did you take them?'

'I told you, mein Herr. They were dirty.'

Sam stared at the catlike eyes across the hallway. They had narrowed ominously; and the gold tooth was no longer seen because the grin had disappeared, replaced by an adamant mouth. Sam closed the door. He had to think. Quickly. As Mac would say, he had to weigh his options. And he had to get out.

He did not consider himself a brawler, yet he was not a physical coward. He was a pretty big fellow, and regardless of what Lillian said in Berlin, he was in fair shape. Still, all things considered it was a good guess that the black-bereted maniac across the hall could beat the shit out of him. Even naked, he could not leave by the stairs.

Option One considered and rejected.

That left the windows, more specifically the small balcony beyond the French doors. He grabbed his shorts off the floor, put them on, held them up, and walked silently outside. The room was three storeys off the ground, but directly below was another balcony. With sheets, or drapes, tied together he could make it with reasonable safety.

Option Two was feasible.

He went back inside and studied the drapes. As his mother in Quincy would say, they were spring drapes. Silk, billowy, not strong. Option Two was fading. Then he looked at the bed sheets, ignoring the inviting sight of Regina who was now more outside the eiderdown quilt than under. If the sheets were combined *with* the drapes, this would probably hold him. Option Two was re-emerging.

Battle dress.

That was a problem. There was nothing *but* dresses.

So, assuming Option Two succeeded and he reached the ground, he had Options Three and Four to consider. And as he considered them there was a sinking feeling in his stomach. He could race around Machenfeld in underwear that kept falling down to his ankles or he could put on one of Ginny's Balenciaga prints and hope the zipper held.

A man running around spreading alarms in dishevelled underwear, *or* a Paris original, was not likely to be taken too seriously. There might even be Options Five and Six to contend with: be locked up, or raped.

Shit!

He had to keep his head; he had to get hold of himself and

think things out. Slowly. He could not allow a minor item like clothing to stand in the way of evacuation. What would the Hawk do? What was that goddamned term he used so frequently?

Support personnel! That was it!

Sam raced back out on the balcony. The man in the chef's hat was still checking off items on his list. It'd probably take him a week.

'*Psssst! Psssst!*' Devereaux leaned over the railing, remembering at the last instant not to let go of the underwear. 'Hey, *you!*' he whispered loudly.

The man looked up, startled at first, then smiled broadly. '*Ahh! Bonjour, monsieur! Ça va?*' he shouted.

Sam held his finger to his lips. 'Shhh!' He gestured for the chef to come closer.

He did so, carrying his papers, making a last notation as he walked. '*Oui, monsieur?*'

'I'm being held prisoner!' whispered Devereaux with solemn urgency and much authority. 'They've taken my clothes. I need *clothes*. And when I get down I want you to get everyone who works here into the kitchen. I've got some very important things to say. I'm a lawyer. *Avocat.*'

The man in the chef's hat cocked his head. '*Je ne comprends pas, monsieur. Désirez-vous le petit déjeuner?*'

'Who? – No. I want clothes. *See?* All I've got is this, *these.*' Sam stretched his torn undershorts so they could be seen between the rails; then he pointed to his legs. 'I need pants, *trousers*! Right away. *Please!*'

The expression on the man's face changed from bewilderment to suspicion. Perhaps even distaste mingled with hostility. '*Vos sous-vêtements sont très jolis,*' he said, shaking his head, turning back towards the patio and the crates of food.

'Wait! Wait a minute!'

'The chef is French, mein Herr, but not *that* French.' The voice came from below, from the balcony directly underneath. The speaker was an immense, bald man with shoulders nearly as wide as the depth of the railing. 'He thinks you are making a most peculiar offer. I can assure you he's not interested.'

'Who the hell are *you*?'

'My name is unimportant. I leave the château when the new master of Machenfeld arrives. Until then his every instruction is my command. His instructions do not include your clothing.'

Devereaux had an overpowering urge to let his shorts fall and copy Hawkins's action on the roof of the diplomatic mission in Peking, but he controlled himself. The man on the balcony below was huge. And obviously couldn't take a joke. So instead he leaned over and whispered the words conspiratorially.

'Heil Hitler, you fucker!'

The man's arm shot forward; his heel clicked like the bolt of a rifle. '*Jawohl! Sieg heil!*'

'Oh, shit!' Sam turned and walked back into the room. In exasperation, he kicked off his shorts. Then he absently studied them as they lay on the floor. Perhaps it was the angle of the fabric, he was not sure. But suddenly they looked strange.

He bent down and picked them up.

Christ! What games?

The elastic waist had been cut deliberately in three places! The incisions were *incisions*, not tears. There were no loose threads or stretched cloth. Someone had taken a sharp instrument and sliced the goddamn things! On purpose. Immobilizing him by the simplest method possible!

'Lawdy! What's all that shoutin' about?' Regina Greenberg yawned and stretched, modestly pulling the eiderdown quilt over her enormous breasts.

'You bitch,' said Devereaux in quiet anger. 'You devious bitch!'

'What's the matter, honeychile?'

'Don't "honeychile" me, you Southern retardant! I can't get *out* of here!'

Ginny blinked and yawned again. She spoke with calm

authority. 'You know, Mac once said something that's been a comfort to me all through the years. He said, when the mortars are falling all around you and things look terrible – and, believe me, there were times when the world looked pretty terrible to me – he said, think of the good things you've done, the accomplishments, the contributions. Don't ponder your mistakes or your sorrows; that only puts you in a depressed state of mind. And a depressed state of mind is not equipped to take advantage of that one moment that could arise and save your ass. It's all a question of mental attitudes.'

'What the hell has that bullshit got to do with the fact that I don't have any clothes?'

'Not an awful lot, I guess. It's just that you sounded so depressed. That's no way to face the Hawk.'

Devereaux started to answer blindly, angrily. Then he stopped, looked at the sincerity in Ginny's eyes and began again. 'Wait a minute. "Face the Hawk." You mean you want me to fight him? *Stop* him?'

'That's your decision, Sam. I only want what's best for everyone.'

'Will you help me?'

Ginny was pensive for a moment, then replied firmly. 'No, I won't do that. Not in the way you're thinking. I owe MacKenzie too much.'

'Lady!' burst out Devereaux. 'Do you have *any idea* what that lunatic is up to?'

Mrs Hawkins number one looked at him with an expression of suddenly imposed innocence. 'A lieutenant doesn't question a general officer, Major. He can't be expected to understand the intricacies of command—'

'Then what the hell are we talking about?'

'You're a smart fellow. The Hawk wouldn't have promoted you if you weren't. I just want him to have the finest advice he can get. So he can do whatever it is he wants to do the best way possible.' Ginny rolled over under the eiderdown quilt. 'I'm really very sleepy.'

And Devereaux saw them on the bedside table next to her head.

A pair of scissors.

CHAPTER NINETEEN

'Sorry about the clothes,' said the Hawk in the huge drawing room. Sam glared and retied the curtain sash he used as a belt around the eiderdown quilt. 'You'd think the laundry would have more than one key, wouldn't you? These big fancy places don't trust anyone; shows the kind of house guests they must be used to, I suppose.'

'Oh, shut up,' mumbled Devereaux, who found it necessary to double-loop the sash because the silk kept slipping. 'The laundress will be here in the morning, I presume.'

'I'm sure of it. She's one of the few who go home at night. To the village. That'll change, of course; there'll be a lot of changes.'

'Just tell me there'll be *one* change and I'll go back and have dinner with Azaz-Varak.'

'Come on now, Sam, you've got a one-track mind. Let's get on to other things. You sure you don't want a shirt and a pair of trousers? Just take me a minute to go upstairs . . .' Hawkins made a gesture past a dozen or so overstuffed, antimacassared armchairs towards the great hall.

'No! I don't want anything from you! – I take that back. I *do* want something. I want you to call off this crazy business and let me go home!'

MacKenzie bit off the chewed end of his cigar, spitting it between the feet of a suit of armour. 'You will go home, I promise you that. The minute you centralize the company finances and make a few deposits that can be tapped under certain conditions, I'll drive you to the airport myself. That's the word of a general officer.'

'It's the reasoning of a brain soaked in linseed oil! Do you have any idea what you're asking me to do? That's not chopped liver you're talking about, it's *forty million dollars*. I'm marked for life! They'll have a record sheet on me in every Interpol headquarters and police station in the civilized world! You don't put your name on forty million dollars' worth of bank transfers and expect to go back to a normal law practice. Word gets out.'

'That's not so, and you know it. All that Swiss banking stuff is confidential.'

Devereaux looked around to make sure no one else was within hearing. 'Even if it's supposed to be, it's not going to be once a . . . certain attempt is made to snatch a . . . certain person in Rome! And that's *all* it will be! An attempt! You'll have your ass in a net, and every contact you've made since China will be put under a microscope and my name will surface and so will forty fucking million dollars in Zürich and that's the *ballgame*!'

'Now, goddamn, boy, we've been over that! Your job's finished now. Or will be soon's you take care of the money. You don't have to be involved anymore. And you're *clean*, son. You're a hundred per cent Clorox!'

'I'm not.' Devereaux choked as he whispered and clutched the eiderdown quilt. 'I just *told* you: the minute *you're* nailed, *I'm* nailed!'

'For what? Say you happened to be right – which I don't for a second consider remotely possible – what can they nail you for? Banking funds for an old soldier who told you he was raising money to support an organization dedicated to spreading religious brotherhood? Let me ask you a question, Mr Attorney. Could you, under oath, testify to any wrongdoing?'

'You're *insane*!' broke in Sam, stumbling slightly as he stepped forward. 'You *told* me! You're going to kidnap—' Devereaux stopped and made charade-like gestures that included hauling a body over his shoulder and the sign of the cross.

'Well, *hell*, boy, there are *oaths* and there are *oaths*! Be reasonable. Anyway, that's hearsay. Not admissible.'

Sam closed his eyes; he began to understand what martyrdom was all about. He continued, his whisper strained but controlled. 'I walked out of those archives with that fucking briefcase chained to my wrist!'

'Outside of that,' mumbled MacKenzie. 'Anyhow, that's army stuff; neither of us has much use for the army. Anything else?'

Devereaux thought. 'Circumstantially, it's the mother-loving end. There hasn't been a single above-board trans-action.'

'That's objective,' said Hawkins, shaking his head, confirming his own judgement. 'There's been no violence; no one's lied. No theft, no collusion. Everything voluntary. And if the particular methods *seem* unusual, that's the prerogative of every individual investor, as long as he doesn't infringe on the rights of others.' Mac paused and held Sam's eyes. 'There's something else, too. You said yourself that a lawyer's first responsibility was to his client, not abstract moral dilemmas.'

'I said that?'

'You surely did.'

'That's not bad—'

'It's goddamned eloquent, that's what it is. You've got a silver tongue in your head, young man.'

Sam stared back at the Hawk, trying to see beneath his guile. But it wasn't guile; he meant what he said. And since personal sincerity was the momentary leveller, Devereaux decided to be personally sincere.

'Listen to me,' he said quietly. 'Say you go through with this – this insanity, because that's what it is, you know. Say you really do it. You actually kidnap the pope and get away with it. Even for a few days. Do you know what might happen? What you could trigger?'

'Surely do. Four hundred million green samolians from four hundred million howling mackerel snappers. No offence intended, just a harmless phrase.'

'*No*, you gung-ho son of a bitch! There'd be international *revulsion*! And *recrimination*. And then mainly *accusations*! Governments would point their fingers at other governments! Presidents and chairmen and prime ministers would use blue lines and red lines and then very *hot* lines. And before you know it, some asshole recites a code from a tiny black box in a briefcase because he didn't like what some other asshole said. Jesus, Mac! You could start World War Three!'

'*Goddamn!* Is that what you've been thinking about?'

'It's what I've tried *not* to think about.'

Hawkins threw his cigar into the cavern that was the Machenfeld fireplace and stood arms akimbo, a flame dying in his eyes. 'Sam, boy, you couldn't be farther from the truth. You know, son, war isn't what it used to be. Hasn't any spirit to it anymore. Bugles and drums, and men caring for men, and hating an enemy because he can hurt the things you love. That's all gone now. Now it's buttons and shifty-eyed policitians who blink a lot and wave their hands without meaning very much. I hate war. I never thought I'd hear myself say it, but I'm saying it and learning it now. I'd never allow a war.'

Devereaux bored into the Hawk's eyes; he would not let MacKenzie look away. 'Why should I believe that? Everything you've done reeks of con. Immense con. Why should a war stop you?'

'Because, young man,' replied Hawkins quietly, returning Sam's stare in full measure, 'I just told you the truth.'

'All right. Suppose you provoke one without meaning to?'

'*Goddamn!* Now you're pushing me too far!' MacKenzie strode from the fireplace to a second suit of armour to the right of the mantel. The face piece was open so he slammed it shut. 'I put in damned near forty years and got fucked by the plastic men! *Your* words, boy! Now, I don't feel sorry for myself because I knew what I was doing, and was accountable for my actions! But, goddamn, don't ask me to feel sorry for *them* or be accountable for their *stupidity*!'

So much for personal sincerity, thought Devereaux. Like

Options One, Two, Three, and Four in the morning, it was shot to hell. This time in a burst of self-righteousness. There was nothing for it but to find another way. One would present itself, Sam was convinced of that. The Hawk had a way to go before the pontiff of the Catholic Church blessed the edelweiss at Machenfeld. Something would turn up; and Option Seven – Options Five and Six happily avoided – was coming into focus. For the moment he had to calm MacKenzie down and under no circumstances lose his confidence. And then Mac did have a point. A legal point.

He, Sam, was clean. Legally clean. In every other way the mud was an inch thick, but in evidentiary considerations, he was not a good case for any prosecutor.

'Okay, Mac, I'm not going to fight you. You were screwed and I did say it, and I believe you. You hate war. Maybe that's good enough. I don't know anymore. Personally, I just want to go back home to Quincy, and if I read about you in the papers, I'll remember the words of a scarred but honest warrior spoken in this room.'

'A tongue of silver, boy! I admire that.'

'As long as it's not a head of lead, I'll accept that. Do you have the papers for the Zürich bank?'

'Don't you want to hear the amount I've . . . accrued for your participation? How do you like that "accrued"? I'm a corporate president, you know; we don't fuck around with second-rate vocabularies.'

'I'm impressed. What's the entry figure?'

'The what?'

'The accrual; that's the noun root of the verb "to accrue".'

'Smartass shavetail. What do you say to a half a million dollars?'

Sam could not say anything. He was numb. He saw his hand move in astonishment, and he watched it with a certain fascination, not sure if the appendage belonged to him. It must have; when he thought about jiggling the fingers, they jiggled.

A half a million dollars.

What was there to think about? It was as insane as everything else. Including the fact that he was not indictable.

It was Monopoly time. Let's buy *Boardwalk* and *Park Place.*

Stop. *Go To Jail.*

Why worry?

It didn't do any good anyway.

'That's reasonable – severance pay,' Sam said.

'That's all you've got to *say*? With what I banked for you in New York, you can hire that Jewish fella and he'll be happy to take the job.' MacKenzie was the injured party. He obviously expected Devereaux to practise a little bit of his well-advertised overreaction.

'Let's say I'll erupt with enthusiasm when I'm looking at those figures – in a bank book – in Boston – with my mother sitting across the room complaining about the new management at the Copley Plaza. Okay?'

'Do you know something?' said Hawkins, his eyes squinting. 'You're kind of weird.'

'*I'm* kind of . . .' Devereaux did not finish the sentence. There was no point.

There was the abrupt, episodic clicking of high heels. Regina Greenberg walked through the cathedral arch into the drawing room. She was dressed in a beige pants suit, the rather severe jacket buttoned over Titanics. She looked, well, rather efficient, thought Sam. She smiled briefly and addressed Hawkins.

'I've met with the staff. Five will stay. Three couldn't; they'd have to live in the village and I explained that wasn't acceptable.'

'I hope they weren't hurt.'

Ginny laughed confidently. 'Hardly. I spoke to each individually, and gave all three two months' wages.'

'The rest understand the conditions?' MacKenzie reached into his pocket for a fresh cigar.

'And their bonuses,' said Ginny. 'Minimum three months. All with families to explain that they've been hired for resident staff work in France for the duration. No questions are to be asked.'

'No different from overseas duty,' commented the Hawk, nodding his head. 'And the money's a hell of a lot better than combat pay – without a weapon in sight.'

'The logistics are in your favour, too,' continued Ginny. 'Only two of the five are married. Not too happily, I gather. They won't miss, or be missed.'

'We'll have to get women, though,' countered MacKenzie, 'for R and R. I'll scout the grounds later; spec out tent arrangements – far enough away from the manouevres, of course. And the counsellor here is going into Zürich to take care of several financial items for me. What do you think, Sam? How long do you figure it will be before you're finished?'

Devereaux had to force himself to consider the Hawk's question. He was stunned by the obvious control MacKenzie wielded over Ginny. According to the data banks, she had divorced MacKenzie over twenty years ago; yet here she was deferring to him like a schoolgirl with a crush on her teacher.

'What did you say?' Sam knew the question but wanted a few seconds to evaluate.

'How long will Zürich take?'

'A day. Maybe a day and a half, with no hitches. A lot will depend on the account clearances. I think the transfers are coded through Geneva, but I may be wrong about that.'

'Can "hitches" be eliminated with a little honey in the pot?'

'Probably. Relinquishing-of-interest could apply. The time period's minor but the sums aren't. The depositories would pick up several thousand – on paper. That might act as a general incentive.'

'Goddamn, son, you hear yourself? You hear how *good* you are?'

'Elementary bookkeeping. A trial lawyer figures litigation with banks is prime meat. They've got more ways to lie to themselves – and everybody else – than anyone since tribes started to barter. A decent attorney simply picks the lie he knows will suit him best.'

'You hear that, Ginny? Isn't that boy something?!'

'You're mighty impressive, Sam; I've got to admit it. And, Mac, since the mayjor here's got everything under control, maybe I could go up to Zürich with him and kind of keep him company.'

'Why, that's a splendid idea! Don't know why I didn't think of it.'

'I can't imagine how it escaped you,' said Devereaux quietly. 'You're all heart.'

From all points of the compass the Hawk's subordinate officers arrived. They were met at the Zermatt railroad station by the bereted, gold-toothed, cat-eyed chauffeur whose name was Rudolph. And Rudolph had a hectic two days.

Crete showed up first, without incident. That is, he managed to cross international boundaries under the scrutiny of very professional authorities without incident (but with a forged passport) and got as far as the Zermatt station, where his troubles erupted. For Rudolph refused to acknowledge Crete to be Crete in spite of the proper identity markings on his clothing, and consequently would not let him into his Italian taxi.

Because, for reasons that escaped Hawkins, none of the G-2 data bank entries on Crete had established the fact that he was Black. Yet there it was. Crete was a brilliant aeronautical engineer, a Soviet sympathizer as long as the Ruskies paid him, a defected espionage agent complete with a doctor's degree and very black skin. Rudolph was totally bewildered, so MacKenzie had to use some very harsh language over the telephone with Rudolph, and finally the bereted maniac let the *Schwarzer* in the back seat of his car.

Marseilles and Stockholm were next. They flew in together out of Paris because they met each other on the previous night at Les Calavados on the Boulevard Georges Cinque and renewed an old acquaintanceship that went back to the days when both were making money from the Allies and the Axis. They were delighted to discover that they were both on a trip to the same yellow mountain in Zermatt. Rudolph had no trouble with Stockholm and Marseilles because they spotted him before he spotted them and they criticized him for his stupidity at being obvious.

Beirut did not take the train from Zürich; he hired an ambulance, instead. He had his reasons; they went back to several contraband run-ins with the Zürich police. So he flew in to Geneva, drove a rented car in the name of a socially elite transvestite, dropped it in Lausanne, contacted l'Hôpital des Deux Enfants in Montreux and leased the ambulance, ordering it to transport him as a coronary wishing to spend his last days in Zermatt. He timed everything to the Zürich train however and all would have gone smoothly except for Rudolph. Unfortunately, Rudolph had a flat tyre on the back roads of Machenfeld, and in his subsequent haste to reach the Bahnhof on time he had a minor collision in the railroad station's parking lot. With the ambulance.

Therefore it was difficult for Rudolph to identify the highly agitated coronary patient, who climbed out of the rear door yelling about imbeciles, with the figure whose markings identified him as Beirut.

But Rudolph was beginning to shrug more and more. The master of Machenfeld, he was beginning to suspect, was not all there in the head. And neither were the people he was sent up to Zermatt to meet.

And the lovely lady of his late-night dreams, the beautifully breasted Fräulein, had left the château for several days. Things were not the same.

Rome and Rudolph got along splendidly. Rome lost his luggage on the train. The combined chaos of finding his three suitcases and his contact from the château proved a strain nearly too much for Rome. Rudolph sympathized and allowed him to sit in the front seat on the trip to the château.

Biscay was extremely secretive. Once he displayed the coded identification (a pair of white gloves with black roses stitched on the back) Biscay excused himself to go to the men's room and disappeared through a window. After an hour, Rudolph's impatience turned to curiosity and the curiosity, in turn, became panic when he discovered the men's room empty. He tried to remain inconspicuous as he looked in nooks and crannies and luggage bins. Biscay followed him discreetly. And it was only after Rudolph called Machenfeld in panic that Biscay, listening from an adjacent booth, decided that his contact was authentic.

Biscay sat in the back seat, and Rudolph did not say a single word all the way to Machenfeld.

The last to arrive was Athens. If Biscay was suspicious, Athens was paranoid. To begin with, he pulled the emergency cord on the train, stopping it in the freight yards just outside the station. Conductors and engineers ran through the cars looking for the emergency, while Athens jumped off and raced over the tracks to the platform, where he concealed himself behind a concrete pillar. It was not difficult for Athens to spot Rudolph.

The train finally proceeded into the station. Rudolph examined all the disembarking passengers; Athens could see his anxiety. When there was no one left on the platform but railroad personnel, Athens approached Rudolph from the rear and tapped him on the shoulder. As he did so, he displayed his identification (a red kerchief) and gestured for Rudolph to follow him.

At which point, Athens raced back to the end of the platform, jumped down on to the tracks and started running towards the freight yard. He soon outdistanced Rudolph and started a series of *I-See-You*'s between the immobile cars.

Five minutes later a distraught Rudolph was being comforted by the energetic Athens as they walked out of the freight yards towards the taxi.

And as MacKenzie Hawkins watched the car approach from the ramparts of Machenfeld, he congratulated himself once more on his professionalism. Seventy-two hours had passed since he had begun making his coded contacts from the D'Accord; and in that seventy-two hours every one of his subordinate officers was physically on the premises.

Goddamn!

Based on the accepted principle that larceny goes a long way in the banking business, Sam's trip to Zürich – more specifically his trip to the Staats Bank to centralize the Shepherd Company's capital – was so successful so rapidly that he would be able to catch the early afternoon train back to Zermatt. And since Regina Greenberg was out shopping, he left a message for her at the Hotel D'Accord: *Have gone bowling. Will be home late.*

He wanted those hours on the train by himself; to think, to refine. For Option Seven was becoming more sharply defined as the hours passed. Due mainly to the papers he carried out of the bank given him by a perspiring trust officer who was considerably richer than he was before he'd met Sam.

Among the fourteen documents, four pertained to the account transfers from Geneva, the Cayman Islands, Berlin, and Algiers – minus accrued interest, of course; one listed the total assets of the Shepherd Company, with its bond of confidentiality, its codes of release and the account number; one was in the name of the family Devereaux (Sam did not explain it and the banker had asked no questions, treating the item as though it did not exist); and eight separate documents defined eight separate trusts.

One of these accounts was larger than the others and within it were four individual sets of figures ... obviously meant for four individuals. It did not take much reflection on Devereaux's part to identify them: Mrs Hawkinses one, two, three, and four.

That left seven trusts, each with an identical maximum figure.

Seven.

The Hawk's *support personnel.*

MacKenzie had recruited seven men to kidnap the pope. (Sam couldn't imagine that any were women; the Hawk's four ex-wives were capable of *anything* calling for feminine skills.) These seven were his – what was it? – subordinate officers. MacKenzie had allowed that his subordinate officers would be arriving at Machenfeld shortly.

'What do you mean "subordinate officers"?' Devereaux had asked.

'The troops, son, the troops!' The Hawk had replied, the flame reignited in his eyes.

'What do you mean "shortly"?'

'We're on blue alert, boy. That means all posts are manned, contact expected from here on in.'

'Like in a few days?'

'Maybe sooner, depending on enemy counterpersonnel blockades. Our troops will have to cross hostile territory on their way to base camp.'

'What the fuck are you talking about?'

'Nothing you have to be concerned with. Just bring back that money stuff from Zürich. Before I give my first briefing on the mission, I want my subordinate officers to see for themselves just how thoroughly command centre has taken care of their interests. It'll give 'em a real sense of purpose, of comradeship; it emanates from the top, you know. It always has.'

That was the other reason why Option Seven was coming into focus. *Bring back that money stuff . . . before I give my first briefing . . . command centre has taken care of their interests.*

The Hawk's troops had been recruited without knowing precisely what the war was all about. Militarily speaking there was nothing unusual in that, but considering the enormity of the projected enemy's resources – namely, the whole world – a few well-chosen words like, *'Do you realize what this maniac intends to do? Kidnap the pope!'* and *'You're dealing with a certified mental case!'* and *'Your commander is a fruitcake!'* and *'This lunatic shot the jade balls off a Chinese monument.'* – things like that could very well make the support personnel look to other fields of endeavour.

It was a question of timing. And psychology. If Sam read him correctly, Hawkins was going to hit his subordinate officers with a double-barrelled salvo: a highly technical, strategically 'feasible' description of the abduction, *and* bona fide documents from the Staats Bank du Zürich that guaranteed each man a fortune, *regardless of outcome*! It would be a tough act to cripple, but that's what Option Seven was all about.

Sam would reach the subordinate officers *first*. He would shoot off canons of doubt regarding the Hawk's fundamental sanity. There was nothing more frightening to criminal underlings than the possibility that their employers were unbalanced. Lack of balance meant lack of judgement, no matter how well disguised. And lack of judgement could spell ten-to-twenty-to-life; in this case, probably a long rope and a blindfold.

Even the criminal element in Europe had to have heard of the paranoid general who was thrown out of China. It wasn't that long ago. And when he had finished this part of his oral summation, Sam would place his high card on the table.

High? There were none higher. It was irresistible.

For on the train to Zermatt he would go through the documents from the Staats Bank du Zürich, specifically the trust accounts, and write out all the numbers and the sequential codes of release, and put them on seven pieces of paper.

He would give each man a card with the information written on it. Each could leave Château Machenfeld without so much as sitting through a meal, head for Zürich – *and claim his money*.

Each subordinate officer would make a fortune! For doing absolutely nothing. Irresistible!

Giovanni Bombalini, the Vicar of Christ, walked out into his beloved garden to be alone. He did not wish to see anyone, or talk with anyone. He was angry with the world, *his* world, and when one was angry it was always best to meditate.

He sighed. If he was to be truthful with himself, he had to admit he was angry with God. It was so senseless! He raised his eyes to the afternoon sky and a single word emerged plaintively from his lips.

'Why?'

He lowered his head and continued down the path. The sprays of lilies were in spring bloom, greeting life.

As he was about to leave it.

The doctors had just delivered their collective report. His vital signs were diminishing with increased acceleration. He had no more than six or seven weeks.

Death itself was easy. Good heavens, it was a relief! *Life* was the struggle. But struggle or no, he had not consolidated the necessary forces to carry on his and Roncalli's work. He needed more time; he needed the authority of the office to bring divergent factions closer together. Why could not God understand that?

Eh, my beloved Lord? Why? Just a little more time? I promise not to lose my temper. Nor will I insult the nasal-toned – pardon, most Holy Father – the cardinal or his band of antediluvian thieves. Six months would do nicely. Then I shall rest in the arms of Christ with grateful devotion. Five months, perhaps? Much could be accomplished in five months . . .

Giovanni tried with all his heart to perceive a heavenly response. If there was one, it was too weak to get through his vital signs.

Perhaps, dear Father, if you would speak to the Holy Virgin? She might find more eloquent words to convey my supplication. It is said that women are more persuasive in these matters . . .

Still nothing. Just a minor pain in his knees which meant the weight was hard on his old bones and he should sit for a while. What was it that lovely *giornalista* had said? There were certain exercises—

Basta! All he needed was to collapse doing push-pulls. Ignatio Quartze would roll his body under the bed and they would not find him for a week. In the meantime, Quartze would pack the Curia.

The pontiff reached his favourite white bench and lowered himself on to the cool stone. A breeze came from the garden walls, fluttering the leaves of the tree above him.

Was it a sign? It *was* refreshing. Then the breeze stopped; the still air returned and the fluttering of leaves was replaced by footsteps clattering over the path.

It was the new papal aide. A young Black priest from the diocese of New York City, a brilliant student who had done much good work in the Harlem districts. Francesco had sought out just such a deserving young prelate – over considerable opposition. It was a small part of a large design.

'Your Holiness?'

'Yes, my son. You look agitated. What's the matter?'

'I think I did something quite wrong. I was bewildered and you weren't in your rooms and there didn't seem to be anything else to do. I'm very sorry.'

'Well, now, we don't know the extent of this calamity until you describe it. You didn't, by any chance, find Cardinal Quartze in my closet and call the guards?'

The Black priest smiled. Ignatio had made clear his disapproval of the aide's appointment. Francesco took every opportunity to lessen the insult.

'No, Your Holiness. I heard your private telephone ringing. The one in the drawer of your bedside table; it just kept ringing.'

'It would, my son,' interrupted the pontiff. 'It is not connected to the Vatican switchboard. A minor indulgence. So you answered it. Who was calling? Only a few old friends and an associate or two of long standing have the number. There is no great harm in what you did. Who was it?'

'A monsignor in Washington, Holy Father. He was very upset—'

'Ahh, Monsignor Patrick Dennis O'Gilligan! Yes, he calls frequently. We play chess together long distance.'

'He was very excited – and he thought I was *you*. He didn't give me a chance to speak. He rattled on so fast I couldn't stop him.'

'Yes, that sounds like Paddy; he's had his problems. The Berrigans again? Those two keep busy—'

'No, Holy Father. Much worse. The *President* called him.

Something about the confidence of the confessional, and whether it was *admissible*. He wants to *convert*, Holy Father!'

'*Che cosa? Madre di Dio!*'

'It gets worse, Your Holiness. Sixteen White House aides want to find Jesus right away. Under certain conditions of Vatican privilege and something called Christian immunity.'

Giovanni sighed. There was *so much* to do.

Four months, oh Lord?

CHAPTER TWENTY

The unfamiliar faces had one thing in common, thought Sam. Very muscular bodies. As though each enjoyed the outdoors, kept in trim by moving rocks under the eyes of the penitentiary guards. And speaking of eyes, that was another thing in common. All their eyes seemed a little sleepy at first, the lids half closed. But it was only appearance. On closer examination the eyes could be seen spinning in their sockets like pinballs caught between magnets; very little went unobserved.

There was a tall, blond man who looked like he had jumped out of a television commercial for Scandinavian cigars; a Black who nodded silently a great deal and spoke an English refined in university lecture rooms; another dark-skinned fellow with distinctly sharp, northern features whose accent was like all those people in formal clothes at the Savoy; two Frenchmen who had something to do with boats; a long-haired man in very tight trousers who strutted when he walked like a tango dancer, aware of his ass – unmistakably Italian; and finally, a rather wild-eyed Greek who wore a red kerchief and kept telling jokes no one quite understood.

There was a soft-spoken politeness among them that was positively unctuous, complemented by manners that seemed born of breeding and wealth, were it not for the shifty eyes. They certainly were very much at home in the huge drawing room of Château Machenfeld, where the Hawk had everyone gather before the late dinner.

Gathered, but in the interests of international security, not introduced. No names were used.

Sam had returned to the château at seven. It would have been an hour earlier but he had to walk the last three miles because no taxi out of Zermatt was allowed to travel beyond certain zones and Rudolph was nowhere to be found. When Sam called information for Machenfeld's telephone number, he discovered there was no such place.

It all might have taken the heart out of him, but Option Seven kept him going. He knew when a case was won.

MacKenzie had greeted him with mixed feelings. The Hawk was pleased that he had brought back the financial papers so promptly, but felt that his treatment of Regina was most ungentlemanly. She was a fine girl, and now Sam could not properly say good-bye to her.

Why not?

Because her luggage had been sent to the airport. Ginny was on her way back to California, with a stop in Rome to look at the museums.

So much for Ginny, thought Devereaux. He was a little sad, but there was Option Seven to think about. And he began to think the timing was perfect.

MacKenzie told him that there would be no business discussed the first evening. Just social chitchat and strolls through the gardens and cocktails and dinner and brandy. Why? Because the troops would like a chance, he believed, to size each other up, check their rooms for bugs, oil their weapons, and generally assure themselves that Machenfeld was no Interpol trap. Sam could expect to hear noises during the night; most of the men would carry out their own surveillance, and that was good because they would undoubtedly run into one another and realize further that everything was on the up-and-up.

In the morning, when all were refreshed, the Hawk would hold his first briefing. Before he did that, however, he would certainly take the time to say good-bye to Sam. He was going to miss his young friend, no question about it. But the word of a general officer was his bond; it was the glue that held his battalions together.

Devereaux's work was finished. Rudolph would drive him

into Zermatt, where he'd take the morning train to Zürich and the late-afternoon flight to New York.

There was one thing Sam should be aware of, however, just in case he became nervous or was afflicted with hypertension. For the next month or so, several associates of the Shepherd Company's first investor, Mr Dellacroce, would stay in close touch with him. Their names were Fingers and Meat, Hawkins believed; it was just a temporary arrangement, no offence intended.

Yes. Sam understood. There was no point in MacKenzie being redundant.

Devereaux had terminated the conversation, saying he would shave and shower the sweat of three mountain miles off him, and return for cocktails.

In his room, Sam found the scissors Ginny had used on his underwear and cut out seven strips of paper five inches long, one inch wide. He wrote out the identical message on each.

Vitally important you meet with me in my room – third floor, rear of house, last door in the north hallway on the right. 2.00 a.m. sharp. Your life depends on it. I am a friend. Remember two o'clock this morning!

He folded the strips of paper neatly so they fitted into the palm of his hand and put them in his jacket pocket. He then removed the seven index cards from his briefcase, the ones with the account numbers and sequential codes-of-release written on them and put them in his trousers pocket. They were his high cards. Irresistible!

He returned to the drawing room downstairs and put to use all the social graces a fine Boston upbringing provided. He shook hands with the men.

And passed each his message.

By one-thirty in the morning he was ready. The Italian came first, his hands encased in sheer, skintight black gloves, his feet laced in balletlike slippers with ridged rubber soles. And then, one by one, the rest showed up in apparel not much different. There was a proliferation of gloves, and soft shoes or sneakers, and black sweaters, and narrow trousers with thick belts holding thicker knives, and small holsters with single straps across small pistols, and in several cases coils of wire.

Altogether a very professional group of psychopaths, thought Sam, as he told them with quiet, not completely heartfelt authority to relax and get comfortable, and smoke if they wished.

Since they all *were* relaxed, and most smoking already, he wasn't sure it was a good opening. But the best summations were those that built from quiet, even awkward, beginnings.

So he began. Softly, at first. Starting with man as a tribal being, looking to the heavens for meaning beyond his daily battle for survival, finding solace in that which he could not really comprehend, because there was comfort in primitive faith. There was structure, an organization to natural phenomena, and that meant there had to be a force, a mind, a profound all-knowing intelligence that conceived the whole. Yet could never be truly understood.

There was beauty in that lack of understanding, for men strove beyond themselves for the all-seeing, all-knowing force that created the earth, created *them*, knew *them* – loved *them*.

Without this search, man was an animal. With it he reached out, and compassion became a part of him.

Sam explained that symbols and titles were not important in themselves, for correlations could be drawn between all religions. The essence was the differentiation between good and evil. But symbols and titles held mystical meaning, and profound comfort, for millions everywhere. Faith. The poor and the oppressed prayed to them, held them in reverence and hope. And for millions these symbols were the warm light in their unceasing winters of darkness.

Devereaux paused. It was the moment for a crescendo.

'Gentlemen, facing you is a crime of such monstrous proportions, a crime of such profound evil – a crime which *cannot possibly succeed* and can only lead each of you to your death, or to a life endured, not lived, in a brutal prison cell. For within the walls of this château is a man who would rob you of your most priceless possessions! Your *freedom*! Your *very lives*! For he conceives the *impossible*. In his unbalanced – woefully unbalanced – mind he is convinced he can overcome the swift and terrible reaction, the vengeance, of the entire world! He expects to lead you into the gaping jaws of oblivion. He intends to kidnap the pontiff of the Catholic Church! He is, in a word, *insane*!'

Sam stopped. He bored his eyes into the face of each man. Cigarettes were suspended in midair, mouths were open in disbelief, eyelids were stretched stares conveying a paralysis born of shock.

He had them! The jury was in the palm of his hand! The phrases had come out like thunder!

It was time for his high cards. Those irresistible figures and sequential code words that would make each man in the room rich. Very, very rich. For doing nothing but avoiding the risk of oblivion.

'Gentlemen, I realize the state of shock you're in and it pains me to see it. It pains me to have caused it. As that great Roman, Marcus Aurelius, observed: We must all do what we have to do, at the moment fate demands that we do it. But as the Indian prophet, Baga Nishyad, also observed: Buckets filled with tears can be spread over grain and the rice will grow like jewels. I do not have jewels, gentlemen, but I do have riches for each of you. Deserved rewards. Sums of money that will lessen your pain, and send you back to the lands of your choice, to live in freedom, freedom from fear, from oblivion. And from want. Here. I pass among you these small index cards. Each is a passport to your personal nirvanas. Let me explain.'

And Sam did.

And the seven subordinate officers studied the cards, glancing at one another as they did so.

'Do you speak French?' asked one of the Frenchmen.

Devereaux laughed – a touch too gaily he felt. 'Not really.'

'Thank you,' said the Frenchman, turning to the others. *'Vous parlez tous français?'*

241

To a man they nodded affirmatively.

So they all began speaking French.

Quietly. Rapidly. Until seven heads nodded once again affirmatively. Sam was touched; he knew they were trying to find a way to thank him.

Which was why he was bewildered when two of the men suddenly approached and grabbed him, spun him around, and began wrapping his wrists in wire.

'What the hell are you doing?' he yelled. 'What are you doing to my hands? And what the hell is that?'

He gestured his head at the red kerchief the Greek had whipped from his neck and was now twirling.

'And what the hell are they?!'

He referred to a number of metallic cracks that sounded strangely like weapons being inspected.

'We have that compassion you spoke of, monsieur,' said the Frenchman. 'We offer the choice of a blindfold before we execute him.'

'*What!?*'

'Be brave, signore,' said the Italian. 'We all know this business. We accept the odds or we do not play.'

'Ya,' added the Viking. 'It is a game. Some vin. Some lose. You lost.'

'*Whaaat?!*'

'Take him down to the patio,' said the second Frenchman. 'We'll tell the staff it's target practice.'

'*Mac! Maac! Maaac!*' He was led down the hallway. Several pairs of hands clapped themselves over his mouth; he bit them. '*For Christ's sake! Hawkins! Where the fuck are you?!*'

Again the hands clamped over his face. The cordon marched with precision down the hallway towards the magnificent winding staircase. Devereaux again forced his mouth open and bit furiously at the flesh around his teeth; hands and arms whipped back momentarily. It was enough for Sam to kick out behind him and for an instant free himself.

He raced and plunged bodily down the curving steps, tumbling over and over as he fell.

'*Hawkins! You son of a bitch, get out here! These maniacs want to shoot me!*'

He bounced over the treads, careened against the wall, and plummeted shoulders over backside down into the last straightaway. His shouts were progressively blurred, but the overall meaning was unmistakable.

'*Blindfolds – ouch! Pistols! Goddamn – you – oh – ohh –. Hawkins! Uhu! Jesus – my head!*'

He reached the bottom of the staircase, a dishevelled heap. The Hawk strode through the cathedral arch from the drawing room, a cigar clenched between his teeth, several folded maps in his hand. He looked at Sam on the floor and then up at the band of subordinate officers.

'*Goddamn, boy! This changes everything!*'

Once again his clothes were taken. Only now there weren't even any dresses in the closet. His meals were brought up by Rudolph.

The Hawk explained that it had taken a command counterdecision to save his life; and the troops did not like it one bit.

'For a fact, I nearly had a mutiny on my hands before the brigade set its colours,' Hawkins had told him the next morning.

'Set its what? Never mind, don't tell me.'

'I mean it, son. I had to take stern measures and let them know right off that in matters of extreme prejudice, no authority – regardless of consensus – exceeded that of a field general. It was touch and go for a while, but I've handled the roughest in my day. Those pups, good as they are, weren't any match. It's in the eyes, boy. Always the eyes.'

'I don't understand,' Devereaux had moaned sincerely. 'I spelled everything out beautifully. I unravelled the whole ball of wax. The background, the motive. Jesus! Even the money! I had them!'

'You had nothing,' the Hawk replied concisely. 'You made two big mistakes. To begin with, you assumed that such a group of men, such a fine contingent of officers, would accept money surreptitiously, without earning it—'

'Get off it!' Devereaux had roared his interruption. 'You can't sell the honour-among-thieves bullshit because I won't buy it!'

'I think you're misjudging, boy, but if that's the way you see it, there's your second mistake to consider.'

'What mistake?'

'One of the oldest traps in Interpol is to set up a hot bank account and send someone after it. I'm surprised you didn't know that. You set up seven all at once.'

Sam had retreated under the eiderdown quilt and pulled it over his head. Unfortunately, he could not block out MacKenzie's words.

'You know, Sam, life is a series of compartments, some related to each other, most separate. But every once in a while these parallel compartments, as I call them, have to acknowledge one another's existence. Now, you saved my life in Peking. You brought to bear your skills and your experience and kept me from that oblivion I hear you talked about. And last night, here in Switzerland, I saved *your* life. Using what skills and experience *I* have. We're even. Our compartments in this area aren't parallel anymore. So don't fuck up, son. I can't be responsible. And that's the word of a general officer.'

By the end of two weeks, Sam was sure he'd lose what was left of his sanity. The mere thought of clothes drove him mad. Throughout his life clothes were an accepted part of living – sometimes pleasant, even ego-fulfilling – but they had not been a subject he ever dwelled on for any length of time.

That's a nice jacket; the price is okay. Get it. Shirts? His mother said he should get shirts. What's wrong with Filene's? So I'm a lawyer. Okay, J. Press. Shirts and grey flannels. Socks? His bureau drawer somehow always had socks in it. And shorts and handkerchiefs. A suit was a pretty big occasion, the few times in his adult life when he went out and bought one. Still, he'd never been tempted to have one tailor-made. And in the goddamned army, his civilian jackets and trousers were on hand only because they meant a change from the goddamned uniform. No. Clothes had never been a major factor in his life.

They were now.

But necessity – part of which was not losing one's sanity – was the mother of invention. And truer words were never said. So Sam began to invent, and the thesis of his invention was that he was undergoing a sincere change of position.

It had to be gradual, based on available alternatives. Since he was so completely, intrinsically, *legally* enmeshed in the Shepherd Company's operations and since all avenues of separation had been blocked, what was the point of fighting any longer? Life *was* compartmentalized; and he was locked into a big vault named MacKenzie Hawkins – which also held some forty million dollars, which was a lot of chopped liver.

Maybe, just maybe, his negative approach was self-defeating, all things considered. Perhaps, just perhaps, he should be putting his energies into productive channels; find areas where he could contribute. After all, there was one indelible bottom line. If the Shepherd Company got blown up, a hell of a lot of shrapnel would find its way into the hide of the second and only other corporate officer of record.

These were the conjectures he began to put into words – haltingly, without much conviction at first – during MacKenzie's daily visits at the start of the third week. But he realized that simply saying them was not very persuasive. The Hawk had to see his mind working, observe the transformation.

By Wednesday he had built up to the following:

'Mac, have you considered the legal aspects after – you know, after—'

'Ground Zero's good enough. What legal aspects? Seems to me you've obliged nicely in that department.'

'I'm not so sure. I've been involved in a fair amount of plea bargaining. From Boston to Peking.'

'What are you talking about?'

'Nothing. I was just – oh, nothing.'

By Thursday, this: 'There could be consequences after . . . this Ground Zero . . . that you haven't thought out. A cancer could be growing on the presidency of the Shepherd Company that ultimately may cripple the office.'

'Spell it out, boy.'

'Well . . . No, never mind. It's conjecture. What was all that noise this afternoon? It sounded very exciting.'

The Hawk squint-eyed him before being pulled into the question. 'Goddamn, it was exciting,' he answered after several seconds. 'Nothing like the evolvement of precision in manoeuvres! It fires up a man's heart! What the hell were you talking about? This cancer stuff.'

'Oh forget it. The old legal brain was just wandering. Are the manoeuvres really all that . . . top drawer?'

'Yeah . . .' Hawkins rolled the cigar from one side of his mouth to the other. 'They're all right, I guess.'

On Friday: 'How was the practice today? Sounded great.'

'Practice? Goddamn, it's not practice, it's manoeuvres!'

'Sorry. How were they?'

'A little sloppy; we've got some minor difficulties.'

'Sorry, again. But I've confidence in you. You'll straighten things out.'

'Yeah . . .' The Hawk paced at the foot of the bed, his cigar a mashed pulp. 'I may have to pick up a few diversion troops. Two or three, that's all. I wasn't concentrating. And, goddamn, Sam, I would have been on-the-barrel-sight except for the trouble you've caused!'

'I told you. I really regret all that. *I* wasn't concentrating—'

MacKenzie stopped and blurted out the words. 'Do you mean that?'

'Yes,' replied Devereaux slowly, with conviction. 'The first thing a lawyer learns is to deal with facts, hard evidence. All of it, not just the bits and pieces. I isolated. I'm truly sorry.'

'I won't pretend to understand that bullshit, but if you feel the way I think you're saying, what the hell were you talking about yesterday? And, damn it, the day before. Those "consequences" after Ground Zero.'

Bingo! as they said in Boston, thought Devereaux to himself. But he showed no emotion; he was the calm, probing attorney with his client's best interests at heart. 'All right. I'll spell it out. I know those trust accounts, Mac. Excluding the one major trust, which I gather is yours, your seven men can draw (or have their consigners draw) up to three hundred thousand on the basis of the first code releases. The second code releases are on a printout sheet in one of the other documents. The printout requires your countersignature and I assume you'll send it to Zurich just before you leave for Ground Zero. Am I right so far?'

'I really skull-sessioned that trust business. What's wrong?'

'Nothing. Yet. With the second release each man has a total of five hundred thousand, correct? That's his fee, right? A half a million for Ground Zero. Everybody the same.'

'Not bad for six weeks' work.'

'There are other things to consider. Plea bargaining on a large scale can include more than immunity. And not just through writing a book, although I understand a lot of cash is funnelled through publishers these days.'

'What are you talking about?' The Hawk squashed his cigar out on the bedpost.

'What's to prevent any or all of your subordinate officers from going straight to the authorities – through intermediaries, of course – and making separate deals? After the fact. They have your money; they avoid prosecution because they cooperate. Remember, we're talking about one of the biggest scores in history. They could make a few thousand on top of what they've got.'

MacKenzie's squinting eyes suddenly widened in relief. And self-satisfaction. There was definitely a sense of triumph in his grin. 'Is that what you've troubled yourself over, boy?'

'Don't make light of it—'

'Hell, no, I won't. And I didn't. None of my men would do anything like that. Because they're going to want to disappear like jackrabbits running from a brush fire. They won't surface anywhere for fear of colliding with *each other*.'

'Now *I* don't understand,' said Sam dejectedly.

The Hawk sat on the bed. 'I've covered all that, son. Sort of in the same way I lashed you to the loaded howitzer. You gave me the idea. I intend to say good-bye to each officer separately. And with each I'm going to hand him an open-faced bearer bond worth an additional half million. And tell him *he's* the *only* one getting it. Because like a good general officer I've kept my combat logs, and in rereading them I realized the mission could not have been successful without his particular strategic contributions. They're hung. Both ways. A man won't inform on a crime that couldn't have been committed without *his expertise* – especially when it's worth an additional half million – and he sure as shit doesn't want his fellow conspirators to know he got preferential treatment to the tune of half a million.'

'My God!' Sam could not stop the admiration from creeping into his voice.

'Clausewitz makes it clear that you don't engage the Berber in the same way you do battle with the king's dragoons. It's a question of applicable tactics.'

Devereaux, once again, was struck by the Hawk's sheer boldness. He spoke softly, barely above a whisper, 'You're talking about – Jesus! – three and a half million dollars!'

'That's correct; you add real quick. And a million apiece for the girls, that's four more million. Plus the original compensation for the officers, another three and a half. And for your information, though I should probably reconsider, I've got another bearer bond for you. That's a million on your paysheet.'

'*What?*'

'I kind of suspected you never understood the forty-mill capitalization. I didn't just come up with a figure, you know. That sum was arrived at after very careful deliberation. I got a booklet from the Securities and Exchange Commission which told what to look for in sound corporate financing. You see, before the company even *markets* its services, we

248

have a preoperation salary outlay of close to fifteen million; then there was the capitalization expenses, including travel and front money and finder's fees – I kinda screwed you on that, son, but I knew you had good things coming – and the corporate real estate and the equipment indigenous to the marketing sources . . .'

Involuntarily, Sam's ears distorted the sound waves. Isolated phrases such as 'aircraft purchases estimated at five million', and 'shortwave communication relays coming in at a million-two', and 'refurbishing, and supplies', and 'additional company offices' – all these came through with sufficient clarity to make Sam wonder where he was. Stark naked under an eiderdown quilt somewhere in Switzerland, or fully clothed in a boardroom somewhere in the Chrysler Building. Unfortunately for the state of his stomach, everything came together with the Hawk's brief summation.

'This SEC booklet was very specific about liquid assets available for reserve capital. It recommended a point spread of twenty to thirty per cent. Then I checked out the custom-of-the-trade practices with limited partnership agreements and found that the overcalls were generally ten to fifteen per cent, which struck me as inadequate. So I skulled a bit and decided on twenty-five per cent. And that's what we've got. The budget projections prior to marketing come to just about thirty million. Taking that as the base figure, you add ten for contingency. That makes forty million and that's what I raised. Damned sound economics, I'd say.'

Devereaux was temporarily speechless. His mind was racing but no words came. MacKenzie the military fruitcake was suddenly Hawkins the conglomerate financier. And that was more frightening than anything he had previously considered. Military principles (or lack thereof) when combined with industrial principles (of which there was a lack thereof) did a military-industrial complex make. The Hawk was a walking military-industrial complex!

If there was strident urgency in Sam's stopping MacKenzie before, it was tripled now.

'You're invincible,' said Sam finally. 'I rescind all my previous reservations. Let me join you, really join you. Let me earn my silly million.'

CHAPTER TWENTY-ONE

Each officer had been assigned a colour, in French. Not only was French spoken by everyone, but the sounds of the colour words were more distinctive in French than in any other language.

The American Negro from Crete was *Noir*, of course. The Viking from Stockholm, *Gris*; the Frenchman from Biscay was *Bleu*; while his countryman from Marseilles was *Vert*; the dark-skinned non-Black from Beirut was *Brun*; Rome was *Orange*; and finally, Athens was *Rouge*, in honour of his ever present kerchief. To instil a sense of discipline and identity among the men, the Hawk further insisted that the word 'Captain' precede each colour.

This aspect of authority and identity was desirable because MacKenzie's second command by necessity stripped his men of their specific individualities. For Ground Zero's assault was to be made in stocking masks. Head and face hair were to be at a minimum; skins powdered or bleached to medium Caucasian hues, and all ambulation which, no doubt, had been studiously disguised, drastically changed.

The men accepted the order without question. Razors and scissors and bleaching agents went to work; none had any desire to stand out any more distinctly from his fellow officers than basic nature dictated. There was security in anonymity, and they knew it.

The manoeuvres progressed into the fourth week. The forest road bordering the Machenfeld field had been shaped to conform as accurately as possible to the site of Ground Zero; boulders had been moved, trees uprooted, whole areas of bush transplanted. A second location had been selected and cosmeticized: a winding, narrow, back road that descended a relatively steep hill in the woods.

In redesigning both these sites the men worked from enlarged photographs – 123 photographs, to be exact – sent by an agreeable tourist in Rome by the name of Lillian von Schnabe. However, Mrs von Schnabe did not take credit for her films. As a matter of fact, the rolls were sent undeveloped by two relays of couriers unknown to each other and delivered to a bewildered Rudolph in Zermatt. In several cases of tampons. Rudolph put the strange cargo in the trunk of his Italian taxi, underneath the tools. A man had his dignity to consider.

On the third day of the fourth week the Hawk scheduled the first complete run-through of the assault. By necessity it was a start-stop hold-to-position exercise as the men switched around, assuming the pivotal roles of the adversary. Motorcycles raced, limousines sped, figures in stocking masks leaped from their stations to perform the tasks assigned. Using a stopwatch, MacKenzie clocked each phase of the manoeuvre; he had developed eight basic phases for the entirety, from incursion to escape. And goddamn, his officers were progressing beautifully! They knew that the overall success of Ground Zero depended on the complete success of each individual assignment within each specific phase. The concept of failure was not attractive.

Which was why the captains objected unanimously to the Hawk's prime tactical innovation: total absence of hand weapons. A well-placed knife or a rapidly exercised garrotte had served them all in past skirmishes, more often than not being the difference between survival and capture. But MacKenzie was adamant: it would be both guarantee and proof that no harm would come to the pope until the ransom was paid. Therefore, all pistols, knives, coils, foot studs, knee cleats, finger points – even pig-iron knuckles – were eliminated. Forbidden, too, were any forms of hand-to-hand above the level of basic jukato.

Eventually, they accepted the limitations. 'In Sweden

there is a saying,' intoned Captain Gris in his Nordic lilt. 'One Volvo in the garage is worth a lifetime of passes on the Scandinavian railroad. I shall accommodate the commander.'

'Oui,' agreed Captain Bleu, the Frenchman from Biscay. 'For the recompense involved, I shall sing them to sleep with Gascon lullabies, if it is required.'

But lullabies were not required. Instead, sleep was to be induced by half-inch hypodermic needles dispensing solutions of sodium pentothal. Each officer would be outfitted with a thin bandolier across his chest, which carried tiny hypodermic needles in small rubber receptacles – where once had been bullets. They were easy to extract swiftly. If administered properly, within a three-inch diameter on the lower right area of the neck, the anaesthetic would take effect in seconds. The problem was merely to immobilize the victims for those brief moments until the drug caused collapse. It was not a difficult problem and since there'd be considerable noise from the vehicles, even a partial scream or two might go unnoticed.

So the officers, heeding the words of wisdom from Gris and Bleu, re-evaluated their objections to the Hawk's order. In a way it was a challenge; and none were interested in lifetime passes on the Scandinavian railroad. Not when he could own a fleet of Volvos.

Each captain's expertise was called on. Captains Gris and Bleu were masters of camouflage and escape cartography. Captain Rouge was an expert in demolition; he had personally blown up six piers in the Corinth strait when it was rumoured the American fleet was sailing in. Sedative medicines were a speciality of the Englishman, Captain Brun, who had darkened his skin for a life in Beirut; most narcotics held interest for him. Aircraft technology and electronics were covered brilliantly. The first, of course, was the bailiwick of Captain Noir, whose exploits in Houston – and Moscow – were legend. The second was the province of Captain Vert, who found it necessary in Marseilles to devise an extraordinary variety of radio communications. It was such a busy port; and Interpol was always underfoot.

Lastly, native orientation was left to Captain Orange, who knew Rome like the back of his constantly gesturing hand. He would write out full descriptions of eight innocuous-looking sets of clothing that blended into the current dress, and further, he would provide a minimum of four separate methods of transportation, using public conveyances where feasible, to the site of Ground Zero. For during the final days of the fourth week, each captain was to travel to Rome and personally survey the assault area.

The airfield at Zaragolo would be no problem; they agreed to that. And neither would the helicopter at Ground Zero. It could be flown in the night before the assault. Gris and Bleu assured them the camouflage would be undetectable.

Goddamn, thought MacKenzie as he snapped the stopwatch at the end of the manoeuvre's Phase Eight. Twenty-one minutes! In another day or so it would get to the optimum eighteen. He felt a surge of pride in his once bemedalled chest. His machine was emerging as one of the finest ministrike forces in the military books.

Even the three privates (the diversionary troops) were splendid. They had but two functions: scream and lie still. But as was proper for the lowest enlisted ranks, they knew nothing. They had been recruited by Captain Brun from the poppy fields high in the Turkish hills, to which they would return the instant Ground Zero was terminated. They'd been hired to perform at a fixed price, did not care to know anything and, naturally, were housed by themselves in enlisted quarters and did not eat at the officers' mess.

They were called simply: Privates One, Two, and Three.

The run-through completed, the officers gathered around the Hawk beside the huge blackboard he'd set up on an A-frame in the field. Sweat was pouring through their stocking masks. Those in priestly habits took them off carefully, studying them for repairs that might be needed; and the inevitable cigarettes and matches came out of pockets. No lighters; fingerprints could be lifted from lighters.

The three privates, naturally, went off by themselves. In sight but not within hearing. Enlisted personnel were not privy to tactical analyses; it was not proper.

The analyses began. Although immensely pleased Hawkins did not dwell on the positive; he told them their mistakes, marking up the blackboard with his criticisms with such sharp authority that the officers cowered like rebuked children.

'Precision, gentlemen! Precision is everything! You must never allow your concentration to lapse, even for a second! Captain Noir, you're cutting your time too close between Phase One and your station in Phase Six. Captain Gris, you had trouble with your cassock over the uniform. Practise it, man! Captains Rouge and Brun, your execution of Phase Five was just plain sloppy! Take out that radio equipment! Go over your moves! Captain Orange! Yours was the most serious lapse of all!'

'*Che cosa?* I make *no* mistakes!'

'Phase Seven, Captain! Without the proper execution of Phase Seven, the whole mission goes up in mortar smoke! That's the *exchange*, soldier! You're the one who speaks Italian best. I put this Frescobaldi in the pope's car and take the pope. Where the hell were *you?*'

'In position, *Generale!*'

'You were on the wrong side of the road! And Captain Bleu, for an expert at camouflage, you stuck out like a plucked duck in your Phase Four station! *Cover*, man! Use the foliage for cover!

'Now, as to this latrine rumour that some of you are unhappy over Phase Eight, the escape routes to Zaragolo; that a few of you figure we should have two copters at Ground Zero. Well, let me tell you, there's no contingency for radar, gentlemen. One small bird with Italian air force markings, flying low, can get through. Two choppers would be picked up on a scanner. I don't think any of you cotton to having your asses a thousand feet in the air, surrounded by the whole guinea air force. No offence, Captain Orange.'

The captains looked at each other. They'd obviously discussed Phase Eight among themselves, and since the small helicopter at target centre was lifting out only the Hawk, the pope, and the two pilots, they had grumbled. But the commander painted a convincing picture. The escape routes on the ground had been exhaustively analysed by Gris and Bleu, who were not only the best in the business, but who would be using them as well. It was conceivable that the ground was safer.

'We withdraw our objections,' said Captain Vert.

'Good,' said MacKenzie. 'Now let's concentrate on—'

It was as far as he got. For in the distance, across the south field, running through the grass was the figure of Sam Devereaux in sweat pants, shouting at the top of his lungs.

'One, two, three, four! What do we like to *jog* for? *Good* health, *good* health! Five, six, seven, eight! Get the weight! Out of the freight! Four, three, *two*, *one*! Jogging is a lot of fun!'

'*Mon Dieu!*' cried Captain Bleu. 'The soft-headed one never stops! He has carried on so for five days now!'

'Before we rise in the morning!' added Gris. 'During rest periods, whenever there is a peaceful moment he is below the window, shouting.'

The other captains joined in a chorus of agreement. They had accepted the general's decision not to shoot the idiot, even grudgingly allowed that there was no harm in letting the fool out of the room to exercise – as long as two guards from the Machenfeld staff were assigned to him. The jackass wasn't going anywhere; not in sweat pants, with no top, over a high barbed-wire fence that led only to impenetrable Swiss mountain forests. But they had drawn the line regarding the clown's participation in Ground Zero.

So here he was, trying to impress them with his training. A pathetically poor athlete who cannot make the team, but will not stop trying.

'All right. All right,' said the Hawk, suppressing a laugh.

'I'll talk to him again, make him quiet down. He's just doing it for your benefit, you know. He really wants to join the big fellas.'

He was driving them all crazy, and he knew it. Of course there were times when he thought he might collapse from exhaustion, but the knowledge that his grotesqueries were having their desired effect kept him going. Everyone avoided him, some actually ran at the sight of him. His insane behaviour had become an irritating, aggravating joke. Already three dogs which had appeared out of nowhere to guard him were taken from the corridor outside his room to the staff quarters below because of their incessant barking. And he made it a point to run by the staff area repeatedly. The hounds, themselves weary of being screamed at for their perfectly natural reaction, now merely raised their heads and stared with hatred at him from behind the gates as he passed by.

As did the staff – and MacKenzie's officers. Sam was a loud nuisance, a joke that had worn thin. What was happening, of course, was that he was being taken for granted. And in a few days he would take advantage of that scorn.

Although he was not allowed to eat with Mac and his band of psychopaths, the Hawk was considerate enough to continue visiting him every day in the late afternoon when Sam was brought back to his room and the sweat pants removed. Devereaux understood. Hawkins needed a sounding board for his enthusiasms. And, bragging, he dropped the information that he and his men would be away for a day or two to execute a surveillance check of Ground Zero. They would then return for any last-minute alterations of strategy.

But Sam shouldn't be concerned. He would not be lonely at Machenfeld. What with the guards, and the dogs, and the staff.

Sam smiled. For when the Hawk and his freaks left the château, it was his own personal Ground Zero. He had begun to prime his guards, the wild-eyed Rudolph and some obvious killer with no name. He had convinced Rudolph and No Name on several occasions to sit in the middle of a field as he ran around it. It was not difficult; they were grateful to be stationary. They simply sat in the grass with two ominous looking pistols trained on him as he jogged and intermittently stopped to perform callisthenics. On each occasion he had gradually widened the distance between him and his guards so that this afternoon he was nearly 250 yards away from them.

The army had taught him *something* about small weapons; he knew that there was no handgun that was any damned good beyond thirty yards. Not in terms of accuracy; scatter shot was something else, but he had to take *some* chances. Stopping the Hawk was the kind of objective that in war made heroes of unheroic soldiers. What had MacKenzie said? 'It's commitment. Nothing takes its place. All the ammo in the world can't be a substitute . . .'

Sam was committed. The prospects of World War III loomed larger every day.

His plan was simple, and relatively safe. He had been tempted to give it an option number, but his options had not been noticeably successful so he decided against it. He would jog here in the south field, as he was doing now, where the bordering forest was thickest and the grass higher than in the other pastures. He would widen the distance between himself and the guards as he had done this afternoon and institute intermittent callisthenics. Among them pushups. Which naturally brought him close to the ground, below the level of the grass.

At the proper moment, he would crawl away as fast as he could towards the forest, then race to the fence. However, when he reached the fence, he would *not* climb it. Instead, he would remove the sweat pants – properly torn – and throw them over. And then, if all went as it should, if Rudolph and No Name were racing in several directions at once, he would scream as though severely hurt and get the hell out of the area. Into the thickest woods.

Rudolph and No Name would naturally run to the spot at the fence, see the sweat pants on the other side, and undoubtedly take the appropriate actions: one would go over the fence, while the other raced back to the château for the dogs.

At which point Sam would wait until he heard the barking. Then he would return to Machenfeld, go in through the door, steal clothes and a weapon. From that point to an automobile in the circular drive, and a pistol to threaten the gatekeeper, had to be clear sailing.

It had to be!

What could go wrong?

The Hawk wasn't the only one capable of strategies. He'd learn not to mess with a Boston lawyer who worked for Aaron Pinkus!

The shouts interrupted his thoughts. He was within sight of the manoeuvre area; he could see the strange-looking road signs and the vehicles. Rudolph and No Name were yelling at him to come back. Naturally, he would oblige; he was not permitted to observe manoeuvres.

'*Sorry fellas!*' he yelled breathlessly as he reversed direction, his legs pounding the soft earth. 'Let's head down to the gate and back and call it a day!'

Rudolph and No Name grimaced and got up from the grass. Rudolph gave him a finger; No Name a thumb to the teeth.

Sam made it a point every afternoon to end his jogging with a run down to the main gate. It was a good idea to study the premises as thoroughly as possible in anticipation of his escape. It was conceivable that he might have to operate the mechanism himself, depending upon the state of panic at the moment. If it was maximum (as MacKenzie would say) the gate might even be left open.

He contemplated this possibility as his feet clattered over the boards of the moat, when suddenly his musings were replaced by a feeling of discomfort. For down at the gate a long, black limousine was being admitted with much bowing and obsequious grinning on the part of the gatekeeper. And when he heard the words shouted from the driver's seat as the automobile was expertly whipped out of the gate towards him, he froze and instantly considered drowning himself in the Machenfeld moat.

'I don't believe it!' yelled Lillian Hawkins von Schnabe at the wheel. 'Sam Devereaux in *sweat pants*! God almighty, you took my advice. You're toning up that wreck of a vessel you live in!'

And if he considered drowning himself at Lillian's words, the next voice he heard drove him to the railing.

'You surely look better than you did in London!' shouted Anne from Santa Monica, Mrs Hawkins number four – Sloping yet Argumentative. 'Your little trip must have done you a world of good!'

CHAPTER TWENTY-TWO

Devereaux's escape plan did not become unglued as had Options One to Four. Neither was it bypassed as Options Five and Six had been. Nor had it exploded in a torrent of abuse as was the fate of Option Seven. It was, however, postponed.

He suddenly had two additional guards to contend with, one of whom was as much a shock to the Hawk as both were to Sam. MacKenzie admitted it. Casually, without letting it upset his schedule; merely using the reality to bolster his overall strength – turning a liability into an asset.

'Annie's got a problem, counsellor,' the Hawk said back in Devereaux's room. 'I think you might give it some legal thought. Do something about it when this is over.'

'All problems pale into insignificance—'

'Not hers. You see, Annie's family – the whole goddamn family – spent more time *in* prison than *out* of it. Mother, father, brothers – she was the only girl – they had record sheets that took up most of the precinct files in Detroit.'

'I never came across any of that. It's not in the data banks.' Devereaux was momentarily sidetracked from his own concerns. MacKenzie wasn't trying to con him now. There was no fire in the eyes, only sadness. Truth. But there *hadn't* been any mention of a criminal record in Anne's dossier. If he remembered correctly, she'd been listed as the only daughter of two obscure Michigan school teachers who wrote poetry in medieval French. Parents deceased.

'Course not,' said the Hawk. 'I changed all that for the

army. And everybody else, mainly her. It was a big hangup for the girl; it was holding her back.' MacKenzie lowered his voice, as if the words were painful, but nevertheless a reality that could not be brushed aside. 'Annie was a hooker. She fell into poor ways – very artificial ways for her – when she was growing up. She worked the streets. She didn't know any better then. She had no home life, most of the time no home. When she wasn't hooking she'd spend her time in libraries, looking at all the pretty magazines, imagining what it would be like to live decent. She was constantly trying to improve herself, you know. She never stops reading, even now, always after bettering herself. Because underneath there's a very fine person. There always was.'

Sam's memory went back to the Savoy. Anne in bed with a huge, glossy paperback of *The Wives of Henry VIII* on her lap. Then later, the words spoken with such conviction in the foyer doorway as she was about to get dressed. Words that meant a great deal to her. Devereaux looked up at the Hawk and repeated them quietly. '"Don't change the outside too much or you'll mess up the inside." She said you told her that.'

MacKenzie seemed embarrassed. It was obvious he had not forgotten. 'She had problems. Like I just said, underneath there was a very fine person she didn't recognize. Hell, *I* did. Anybody would.'

'What's her legal problem?' Sam asked.

'This goddamned gigolo-waiter husband of hers. She's stuck with that fucker for six years; helped him go from a hot-pants beach boy to owning a couple of restaurants. She *built* those restaurants. She's damned proud of them! And she likes the life. Overlooking the water, all those boats, nice people. She lives decent now, and *she did it*.'

'So?'

'He wants her out. He's got himself another woman and he doesn't want any lip from Annie. A quiet divorce and just get the hell out.'

'She doesn't want the divorce?'

'That's immaterial. She doesn't want to lose the restaurants! It's principle, Sam. They represent everything she's worked for.'

'He can't simply take them. There's the property settlement to consider, and California laws are rough as hell.'

'So's he. He went back to Detroit and dug up her police record.'

Sam paused. 'That's a legal problem,' he said.

'You'll work on it?'

'There's not much I can do here. It's a confrontation problem, big attack variety. Fire for fire, dig up counter-accusations.' Devereaux snapped both his fingers – the legal *Wunderkind* making a brilliant decision. 'Tell you what. Let me out of here and I'll fly straight to California! I'll hire out one of the best LA private detectives – like on television – and really go after this prick!'

'Good thinking, boy,' replied the Hawk, clucking his tongue in respect. 'I like that aggressive tone; you bear it in mind for later. Say, in a month or two.'

'Why not *now*? I could—'

'I'm afraid you can't. That's out of the question. You're here for the duration. Talk with Annie, though. Learn what you can. Maybe Lillian can help; she's a resourceful filly.'

With these words MacKenzie dispensed with his liability and gained an asset: Sam now had two additional people to keep an eye on him. He might outwit Rudolph and No Name; the girls were something else again.

Within hours after their arrival, however, it was apparent to Sam that Lillian would have very little time to pay attention to him. In her usual forthright manner she plunged into furious activity, commandeering two of the Machenfeld staff to help her. The work began first thing in the morning when the brigade went out for manoeuvres.

Upstairs. In the top floor rooms and on the ramparts of the château.

There was the banging of hammers and the whirring of saws and the cracking of plaster. Furniture was carried up and down the long winding staircase; those pieces too large or too awkward were raised and lowered by pulleys and ropes over the outside walls. Scores of potted plants and bushes and small trees were placed around the battlements – seen from the ground by Sam for he was not permitted above the third floor. Paints and brushes and panels of wood were transported daily by Lillian and her two helpers and when Sam could no longer politely ignore her labours, he asked her what she was doing.

'A little arranging, that's all,' she replied.

Finally, crates of crushed stone and washed gravel were hoisted up the wall, accompanied by several concrete benches and (if Sam was not mistaken, and being from Boston he was not) a marble *prayer stall*.

It was suddenly very clear to Devereaux exactly what Lillian was doing. She was turning the top floor and the ramparts of Château Machenfeld into a full-fledged papal residence! Complete with apartments and gardens and prayer stalls!

Oh, my God! A papal residence!

Anne, on the other hand, spent most of her time with Sam. Since MacKenzie had deemed it improper for the girls to eat at the officers' mess – it was diversionary for women to break bread with a strike force prior to combat – Anne and Lillian were assigned their meals in Devereaux's room, Sam under the eiderdown quilt, of course. But Lillian was rarely there; she spent most of her time upstairs – arranging.

So Sam and Anne were thrown together. On a surprisingly platonic basis. True, he had made no pass, but she made no offer either. It was as though both understood the insanity whirling around them, neither wanting the other to be involved, each, in a very real sense, protecting the other. And the more they talked together, the more Sam began to understand what MacKenzie meant about Anne. She was the most genuine, guileless person he had ever met in his life. All the girls were devoid of artifice, but there was something different about Annie. Whereas the others had reached certain plateaux, conscious of their worth, Anne was not satisfied. There was about her a delightfully irreverent sense of purpose that proclaimed for all the world to hear that she *could* expand, *could* experience – but *good heavens*! one did not have to be *gloomy* about it.

Devereaux recognized his imminent danger; he could get really sidetracked. He began to think that he had been looking for this girl for about fifteen years.

And he *couldn't* think about that. Another plan had come into focus. One he knew would work.

The very day Hawkins and his brigade of banana captains took off for Ground Zero!

The last sweet and sour strains of the orchestra filled the theatre. Guido Frescobaldi took his curtain calls, wiping a tear from his eyes. He had to shed his art and think of things plenipotentiary now. He had to hurry to his dressing room and lock up his makeup box.

The call had come! He was going to Rome! He was going to be embraced by his beloved cousin, the most beloved of all popes, Giovanni Bombalini, Francesco, Vicar of Christ! Ohh! Such blessings had come to him! To be reunited after all these years!

But he could say nothing. Absolutely *nothing*. That was part of the arrangements. It was the way Bombalini – *Madre di Cristo* – Pope Francesco wished it, and one did not question the ways of so munificent a pontiff. But Guido did wonder just a little bit. Why did Giovanni insist that he tell the management that small lie that he was going to visit family in Padua, not Rome? Even his friend, the stage manager, had winked when he told him.

'Perhaps you might ask your *family* to pray to Saint Peter for a little sacred lire, Guido. The box office has not been good this season.'

What did the stage manager know? And when did he know it?

It was not like the Giovanni of old to be secretive. And yet who was he, Frescobaldi, to doubt the wisdom of his beloved cousin, the pope.

Guido reached his small dressing room and began to take

off his costume. As he did so his eyes fell on his Sunday church suit, pressed and hanging neatly in the centre of the wall. He was going to wear it on the train to Rome. And he suddenly felt ungrateful and ashamed of himself.

Giovanni was being so *good* to him. How could he even *think* a compromising thought?

The lady journalist who was bringing them together had asked for all his measurements. Every last one. When he asked why, she told him. And he had wept.

Giovanni was buying him a new suit.

The Hawk and his subordinate officers returned from Rome. The final check of Ground Zero had gone off without a hitch; no alterations were required.

Further, all intelligence data had been gathered and processed. Using basic surveillance techniques employed in hostile territories, Hawkins had donned an enemy uniform (in this case a black suit and a clerical collar) and obtained a Vatican pass, and identification that certified him to be a Jesuit doing an efficiency study for the treasury. He had free access to all calendars and personnel schedules. From apartments to barracks.

They all confirmed the Hawk's projections.

The pope would leave for Castel Gandolfo on the same day he had chosen for the past two years. He was an organized man; time was to be allocated properly with regard to needs and functions. Castel Gandolfo expected him, and he would be there.

The pope would use the same modest motorcade he had employed previously. He was not a wasteful or pretentious man. One motorcycle point with two front and rear flanks. Basic. The limousines were restricted to two: his own, in which his most personal aides accompanied him; and a second, for secretaries and lesser prelates, who carried his current working papers.

The route of the motorcade was the scenic road he had spoken of with feeling whenever he mentioned Gandolfo:

the beautiful Via Appia Antica, with its rolling hills and remnants of ancient Rome along the way.

Via Appia Antica. Ground Zero.

The two Lear jets had been delivered to Zaragolo. It was an airfield for the rich. The small Fiat sedan, which was the diversion equipment for the Turk privates, had been purchased by Captain Noir, in the name of the Ethiopian embassy. It was parked in an all-night garage next to a police station, where the crime rate was at a minimum.

Guido Frescobaldi was on his way to Rome. Regina would handle him. She'd put him up at a *pensione* she rented called The Doge, on the Via Due Macelli, right near the Spanish Steps, and take good care of the old man until the morning of the assault. And first thing that morning she'd load him up with a thiopental solution that would keep him on a harmless high for damn near twelve hours.

The Hawk planned to pick Guido up in the Fiat on his way to Ground Zero. Of course, Regina would have him properly dressed by then, with a very large overcoat that covered his fancy clothes. Skirts, really.

There was only one last item to take care of. The two limousines used in manoeuvres had to be driven to a place called Valtournanche, several miles northwest of the Alpine town of Champoluc. To a little-used private airfield frequented by the jetsetters heading for their ski chalets. The limousines were a natural. They were registered to nonexistent Greeks, and the Swiss *never* bothered Greeks who could afford such automobiles.

Lillian could take care of the transfer. Oversee it, actually. She could use the two men who had helped her shape up the pope's BOQ. Once the cars were in position they could vanish along with Lillian. Mac, of course, would give them bonuses.

He'd get rid of Rudolph, too, and that psycho, what's-his-name, the minute they were back from Ground Zero and the pope was safely – secretly – in his quarters. The chef had to stay; what the hell, even if he did find out who he was cooking for, he was a French Huguenot wanted by the police in sixteen countries.

That left Anne. And Sam, of course.

He could handle Sam. Sam was so lashed to that loaded howitzer he was part of the casing. But he couldn't figure out Annie. What was the girl up to? Why wouldn't she leave? Why had she used his own oath against him?

'You gave your solemn word that if ever any of us came to you in need, you'd never abandon us. You'd never allow an injustice to be done if you could prevent it. I'm here. I'm in need, and an injustice has been done. I've nowhere else to go. Please let me stay.'

Well, of course, he had to. After all, it was the word of a general officer.

But *why*? Could it be Sam?

Goddamn!

So he would die in Gandolfo. It could be worse, thought Giovanni Bombalini, gazing out the windows of his study. A half-century ago all he had to look forward to was a gravesite in the Gold Coast, preceded by a long, drawn-out Last Rites ceremony delivered half in Latin, half in Kwa with swarms of flies circling his head. Gandolfo certainly held advantages over that exit.

He would be able to work better, too, at Gandolfo; use the weeks left to straighten out his own affairs, which were minimum, and do his best to set a course for the immediate future of the Church. He would bring with him several hundred analyses of the most powerful dioceses throughout the world and issue scores of promotions; balancing, but balancing in favour of younger, more vigorous perspectives. Which often had nothing to do with youth.

He had to keep reminding himself that the intractable old guard was not to be scorned, and should not be. The old war-horses had gone through ecclesiastical battles unknown to the vast majority of those who screamed for reform and change. It was not easy to alter the philosophies of a lifetime. But the *fine* old war-horses knew when to step aside and graze in the pastures, ready with an affectionate eye to offer advice when asked, compassion regardless. The others – the Ignatio Quartzes of the world – needed a push.

Pope Francesco decided that among his last acts would be a little pushing. It would take the form of a Last Rites Dissertation to be read to the Curia after his death, and then made public. It was a bit presumptuous, he supposed, but if God did not want him to complete it, He could always summon him at His will.

He had begun the dissertation, dictating to the young Black priest. And he had sent a papal memorandum to every office in the Vatican appointing his young aide as executor of his personal effects in the event he was called to the arms of Christ.

Giovanni was told that Ignatio Quartze threw up for nearly an hour after receiving the papal instruction. It must have wreaked havoc with the cardinal's nasal passages.

'Your Holiness?' The young Black aide came through the door of the bedroom carrying a suitcase. 'I can't find the miniature chessboard. It's not in the drawer with the telephone.'

Giovanni thought for a moment, then coughed an embarrassed laugh. 'I'm afraid it's in the bathroom, Father. Since Monsignor O'Gilligan solved his conversion problems by explaining penance, he's been an absolute terror in his moves. Concentration was required.'

'Yes, sir.' The young priest smiled as he put down the suitcase. 'I'll put it in the vestment trunk.'

'Are we about packed? I say "we", but you've done the work.'

'Almost, Holy Father. The pills and the tonics will stay in my briefcase.'

'A little fine brandy could do just as well.'

'I have that, too, Your Holiness.'

'You are truly a man of God, my son.'

CHAPTER TWENTY-THREE

RIGIRATI! COSTRUZIONE!

The large metal sign was secured to the centre of the wooden barrier that stretched across the width of the back country road.

It looked very official, right down to the last tiny red reflector, and the imposing insignia of Rome's municipal government. It also officially closed off a section of the Via Appia Antica to all approaching vehicles, offering instead a detour cut out of the forest down the Appian hill. And since this particular stretch of the Appian road was the narrowest on the entire route, there was no feasible alternative to the detour if the vehicles in question were larger than the smallest Fiat. Not even the size of the Fiat sedan which the Hawk had driven out of the garage next to the police station and which now lay overturned at the bottom of the hill.

Any larger automobile would not have room to turn around. To reverse direction a driver would have to steer his car backward for the better part of a mile, over countless potholes and around numerous blind curves. Of course the same driver might opt for negotiating the wide expanses of fields that regularly interrupted the Appian forests, but they were filled with rocks and mounds and intermittent stone walls, some built in ancient times. The fields were not only treacherous, but it was against the law to drive on them.

These thoughts went through Captain Noir's head, his black face powdered under the stocking mask, as he lay motionless in the bushes off the side of the road beyond the barrier. He had heard the sounds of the motorcycles in the distance.

All was ready.

Ground Zero had arrived.

The location was perfect. Only trees and fields and hills; the general had planned well. The abduction could probably be carried out on this isolated stretch of road without the detour but in some ways the detour was the most important aspect of Ground Zero. The vehicles *could* turn around by inches – but they wouldn't. They would use the detour.

Still, in case they didn't, Captain Noir held in his hand a piercing, high-frequency whistle. Its use meant that Plan Able, Phase One, Positions One to Three were aborted, instantly implementing Plan Baker, Phase Double Zero, Positions One Hundred and One to One Hundred and Ten: abduction farther up Appia.

Down the road beyond the barrier, the blue helmet with the white cross enamelled on the steel stood out like an enormous jewel in the Italian sunlight. It was on the head of the motorcycle patrolman in front of the papal column; the Vatican point, as the general termed him. The uniformed officer was travelling at medium speed; any faster on the old road would be uncomfortable for those in the limousines.

The patrolman spotted the barrier with the large official sign and drove up to it. Captain Noir held his breath. The officer jumped off his motorcycle, kicked out the stand, and walked up to the obstruction. He raised his eyebrows in bewilderment, looked beyond the barricade for signs of construction and grumbled unintelligibly.

He turned and held up his hands. The lead automobile had reached a point approximately a hundred feet from the barrier.

The patrolman returned to his idling bike, mounted, swung the bars, drove swiftly to the lead limousine, and spoke excitedly to those inside.

The rear door opened; a priest in a black cassock got out. He and the patrolman walked back towards the barrier, their attention on the sloping road down the Appian hill.

There was rapid, indistinguishable chatter between them; and then a series of gestures that conveyed only indecision. The priest turned, picked up the cloth of his cassock, and trotted back past the lead car to the papal limousine.

Captain Noir could not see too well, but the slight Appian breeze carried the sounds of more excited chatter. Noir swallowed and gripped the high-frequency whistle in his hand.

Then to his great relief he heard laughter. And the priest returned to the lead car, nodded his head, gesturing to the left at the patrolman, and climbed back into the limousine.

An adventurous decision had just been made; the general knew his enemy.

The motorcade turned left down the hill, led by the patrolman. All the vehicles entered cautiously, at very slow speeds, and when the two rear motorcycles reached the first curve on the slope, Noir got out of the grass and raced to the barrier, pulling it across the opening of the detour. He ripped off the top sign revealing the second:

DINAMITE! FERMA! PERICOLO!

He had done it! By God, he'd done it! He had escaped from Machenfeld and was on his way to Rome, and if everything held firm, no one would know he was gone until morning! Then it would be too late! The Hawk would be on his way to Ground Zero!

There was no way they could know he was gone. Unless they broke down the door to his room, which was highly unlikely under the circumstances. Anne wasn't talking to him; she'd stamped off to her room in the south wing. He had provoked an argument that could be heard on the peaks of the Matterhorn, eliciting language from her she must have learned from her felonious family.

Rudolph and No Name wanted absolutely nothing to do with him. Especially proximity. After the battle with Anne he had proceeded to complain to his guards of sudden, agonizing pains in his groin. He had doubled up and screamed.

'Oh, Jesus! It's Kuwaiti encephalitis! I saw it in the Algerian desert five weeks ago! Oh, my God! I caught it! The testicles swell

like basketballs, but heavier! I've got to have a doctor! Get me a doctor!'

'No doctor. No outside communications until the master of Machenfeld returns.' Rudolph was stern.

'Then you better watch it!' Sam continued. 'It's highly contagious!'

Whereupon he had fainted, clutching himself through the sweat pants. Panicked, No Name and Rudolph moved back swiftly against the wall in the drawing room. Revived but in agony, Sam crawled out of the room and up the staircase. To meet his Maker in peace, and with enormous testicles.

Rudolph and No Name stayed well behind until Sam reached his room and closed the door. When he opened the door for one last time – he saw that his guards were far down the hallway with double handkerchiefs tied around their faces, aerosol cans of disinfectant billowing clouds of spray around them.

The coast was clear! For a beautiful, foolproof exit from Machenfeld.

Lillian and two of the staff were driving the limousines to an airfield somewhere south. He'd overheard the Hawk explaining the route to Mrs Hawkins number three; the trip was four hours long and it was vital that she position the vehicles on a road by the west highway of the airfield.

An airfield!

That meant aeroplanes! And aeroplanes flew to Rome! And even if they didn't – or wouldn't – there were telephones! And radios!

His new plan had jelled instantly. He would be inside the trunk of the second limousine, the one being driven by a member of the château staff. It had been a simple matter to jam the lock of the vehicle's trunk while he had been saying goodbye to Lillian, helping her with the suitcases.

As soon as his guards disappeared in the cloud of disinfectant, Sam tied three blankets together, scaled down to the ground from the balcony, raced to the limousine in the drive, and crawled into the trunk.

Once inside, he wrapped the blankets around his upper body, grateful he still had his sweat pants, and waited. He was counting on nature to provide him with a shortcut to his objective and he was not disappointed.

The limousines sped through the gate and the trip had begun. After three and a half hours of bouncing, plunging, climbing, and racing through the Swiss mountains, Sam heard the rapid blasts of the limousine's horn. Within seconds there'd been a corresponding reply in the distance, from the lead automobile, and the car slowed down and stopped. The driver got out quickly. Devereaux could hear the footsteps outside the trunk. And then he'd heard the unmistakable muted splashing.

He opened the trunk, climbed silently out, and hit the urinating Swiss with a jack handle.

Before a half minute had passed, Devereaux had removed the man's trousers, jacket, shirt, and shoes. Pulling on the trousers and the jacket – enough to obscure him in the night darkness – he had raced around to the door and leaped into the driver's seat, tapping the horn twice as a signal to resume the trip.

Lillian honked back, and started off immediately.

The airfield at Valtournanche (that's what the sign had said) did present a minor problem, but it was more than compensated for by the extraordinary sum of money Sam found in the jacket he had taken from the Swiss. Five thousand dollars, American! The Hawk must have given the staff member a bonus!

It automatically gave birth to another, incredible plan! A magnificent finale!

He could stop the Hawk without the police! Without the authorities! Stop him cold, dismantle Ground Zero and disperse the brigade all at the same time! With no firing squads or hangmen or life imprisonment in the offing! It was perfect. Beyond error.

There was a curve in the road on the west border of the airfield. Sam slowed his limousine, and the instant Lillian's vehicle rounded the turn, he stopped the car, turned off the ignition, grabbed the shirt and the shoes, jumped out, and raced into the woods.

He waited in the darkness for the inevitable. Lillian's automobile could be heard in reverse gear. She and her escort got out and ran back to the abandoned second car.

'Isn't that the limit!' Lillian was angry. 'The ungrateful worm chickened at the last moment! And after Mac gave him all that money. Well, it doesn't surprise me. His neck muscles had no tone; it's always a sign of weakness. Come on! Get in! We're almost there.'

An hour later Devereaux, dressed in a leather jacket and baggy trousers oddly too large for his frame, was counting out $2,500 to a stunned pilot in a Valtournanche hangar, the fee for a rushed, unscheduled flight to Rome. Sam had chosen a man quite a bit smaller than himself, with no apparent muscle tone whatsoever. Pilots who took this kind of employment were not generally considered to be of the highest moral character. He didn't care to be rolled and dropped off into an Alpine mountain pass.

But he had made it! They were airborne! They'd reach Rome well before dawn. And then he, Sam Devereaux, the finest young attorney in Boston, would deliver the best summation of his career.

Captains Gris and Bleu, dressed in tight-fitting police uniforms, stood erect and motionless behind the trunks of two Appian maples on opposite sides of the winding road – motionless except for their right hands, which they flexed at their sides, thumbs caressing the short hollow needles that protruded from the inverted rings.

As the commander had predicted, the two motorcycles at either side of the papal limousine had dropped back and now rode parallel in front of the bikes flanking the rear. And again, as the commander had projected, the noise was deafening.

One by one the vehicles passed. As the final two patrolmen came between the two maple trees, Gris and Bleu leaped out, hammerlocked both men with their left arms, and each plunged a small needle into his man's neck.

Within seconds the patrolmen were limp.

Gris and Bleu lowered the motorcycles between their legs and dragged each body off into the underbrush. Together they entered the woods and raced diagonally downhill through the tangled foliage to position themselves for their next assignment. Secreted in these positions were the cassocks they would slip over their uniforms.

Captains Orange and Vert lay on their stomachs across from one another hidden by the tall weeds. Their posts were at the start of the second curve on the descending side road. Through the dense reeds they saw – and smiled as they did so – that the two final motorcycles failed to appear. Their other team of patrolmen struggled to keep their bikes upright, riding behind the second limousine.

Captain Orange crossed himself as the pontiff's vehicle passed.

Captain Vert spat. It was long past time for the Church to install a *French* pope; the Italians were pigs about that.

The papal car turned into the final downhill curve. Orange and Vert sprang up and out and executed the practised manoeuvres with lightning-swift dispatch against the motorcycle escorts.

The patrolmen collapsed; the papal limousine was entering the turn at the base of the Appian hill. There were only seconds remaining before the detonations of Phase Four, the smoke bombs from the overturned Fiat. Orange and Vert ran to their next assignment – the most prestigious of all: Phase Seven. Phases Five and Six, the destruction of the communications equipment and the sedation of the papal entourage, would be occurring any second.

Phase Seven was the zenith of Ground Zero: the exchange of the popes. Guido Frescobaldi for Giovanni Bombalini.

The explosions from the Fiat were positively frightening; the screams of the hysterical Turks terrifying. The Hawk grinned in appreciation. *Goddamn!* What a beautiful sight! All that smoke and noise and – well, the screams were overdone.

The motorcade stopped in shock, agitated voices swelling. One motorcycle and two limousines in an isolated back country road bordered by a steep hill on the south side and a tall, thick forest on the north.

Optimum, observed the Hawk, holding a weaving Guido Frescobaldi in the bushes.

Captain Noir reached his post and signalled Captains Rouge and Brun; they were strung out at ten-yard intervals, prepared for the moment to implement Phase Five: the destruction of all communications equipment.

It came.

The single Vatican policeman jumped off his motorcycle and ran towards the smoking Fiat with the trapped, screaming passengers. Every door of both limousines was swung open. The drivers and the priests screamed and waved their hands and shouted orders at everyone and no one, then ran towards the overturned car.

Now!

Dressed as priests, Noir, Rouge, and Brun dashed from their hidden recesses. Brun and Rouge plunged into the front seat of the first limousine, ripping out every wire in sight. Noir raced to the second automobile, the papal car, and dived through the open door towards the equipment.

Suddenly a hand lashed out over the seat, followed by an arm extending from a white cassock. But the hand and the arm were not white. They were *black*!

And the grip that held Noir's neck – accompanied by the swift, hard rabbit punches that hammered his head – was a street tactic Noir knew well. It was indigenous to a plot of turf called Harlem!

Noir wrenched his aching, pounding head and was suddenly, astoundingly, face to face with a brother!

A *brother* in the honkey white robes of the Church!

It went against Noir's grain to coldcock a brother, but there was nothing for it. The Catholic kid was good, but he hadn't taken advanced training above 138th Street and Amsterdam. Noir twisted his thumb and forefinger into the sensitive flesh; the Black priest screamed and released Noir's head as Noir yanked him halfway over the seat. He sighed as he chopped the Catholic kid at the base of the skull. He immediately went about his business, ripping wires and smashing dials. The fat old honkey in white robes – the *man*, himself, figured Noir – leaned forward and pulled the kid into the back seat, cradling the kid's head as if the kid was really hurt.

'He'll be okay, pops. I don't know how you boys do it. I *swear* I don't! The Baptists got his turf tide up in ribbons. They've got *rhythm*! Course, you've got the cops . . .'

Son of a bitch! What the hell else could go wrong? What other delays were concealed in the blinding sunlight of Rome's Leonardo da Vinci Airport? It was a nightmare being played out in the bright morning without benefit of sleep!

The goddamned, dwarf son of a bitch of a pilot from Valtournanche insisted that his aircraft be cleared by the narcotic inspectors! Nobody gave a damn if a plane flew in six vaults of stolen gold, or undeclared diamonds, or eyes-only defence plans for all of NATO, as long as there wasn't a joint on board! No amount of protesting on Sam's part made any difference whatsoever – Well, yes it did. It caused him to be stripped and searched.

'Per favore, signore. Where is your underwear? Where did you leave it? – Search the plane again!'

'That's crazy!' screamed Devereaux. 'How could a pair of shorts—'

'Che cosa?' inquired the capitano suspiciously.

'Shorts!' Sam outlined a pair of briefs. 'Where could I hide . . .'

'Ah haaa,' interrupted the capitano.' The mountain Swiss wear long underwear. With pockets. And flaps. And many buttons. Buttons are hollow.'

'I'm not Swiss! I'm American!'

The capitano's eyebrows shot up as he lowered his voice. 'Ah haa – Mafia, signore?'

And so it went until Sam had dispensed ten one-hundred-dollar American bills, which happened to coincide with the end of the capitano's shift, whereupon Sam was released.

'Where can I get a taxi?'

'Have your money exchanged first, signore. No taxi has change for American one-hundred-dollar bills.'

'I don't have any hundreds left. Only five hundreds.'

'Then they will call the police. For certainly such money cannot possibly be authentic. You will need lire.'

Oh, my God, the police! thought Sam. The police and hysterical taxi drivers were the last thing he wanted. They definitely were not part of his grand finale to thwart the Hawk.

And so he spent the better part of an hour in the exchange line only to be told by the lady with a moustache that bills of such denominations had to be examined by spectographs.

'Thank you, signore,' said the face of fur finally. 'We have processed these under four different machines. They are very nice. Here is your lire. Do you have an empty suitcase?'

It was 9.45. Still time! A taxi into Rome took about an hour when one considered the traffic, and then perhaps a half hour to get to the southern outskirts where he could pick up the Via Appia.

The ride down the Appia couldn't be more than twenty minutes or so. He would recognize the signs he had seen during manoeuvres, he was sure of that. He'd reach Ground Zero with at least a half hour to spare!

He'd stop the Hawk, prevent World War III, eliminate the spectre of life imprisonment, and go home to Boston with a real Swiss bank account!

Goddamn! If he had two cigars, he'd smoke them both at the same time!

He ran across the terminal to the door under the signs that read Taxi in three languages. He raced breathlessly on to the concrete.

Up and down the whole area were hundreds of immobile dollies filled with luggage. Groups of men were gathered in the street, close to riot.

Sam approached a tourist. 'What's going on?'

'Goldanged guinea bastards called a cab strike!' Sam backed away. He had several hundred thousand lire stuffed in his pockets like football pads. There had to be somebody in one of the parking lots with an automobile.

He found him. At twenty minutes past eleven. And offered money. The faster he drove the more thousands of lire he would get. The man agreed.

11.32! He would make it!

He had to!

It was the summation of his life!
Why was he kidding himself? It was his life.

Gris and Bleu pulled at the clerical ropes around their cassocks. They were on their knees, concealed by the dense underbrush and cascading branches at the base of the hill by the edge of the old road. Both were prepared to spring through the foliage to execute Phase Six, the immobilization of the motorcade. The overturned Fiat was directly in front of them, the smoke billowing everywhere, the five papal aides, the two chauffeurs and the remaining patrolman all making genuine attempts to reach the screaming Turks.

The numbers presented no problem. Once Gris and Bleu joined the smoke-engulfed mêlée, they would work swiftly, their church habits adding to the confusion. It would be a simple matter to incapacitate one adversary, then another. Rouge would join them on the west flank, intercepting anyone who might discover the conspiracy prematurely, and make a dash for the limousines.

Now!

Gris and Bleu lunged out of the brush into the confusion of smoke, screams, and flailing arms, their wide cassocks billowing, rings at the ready.

One by one the members of the papal entourage collapsed to the ground, beatific smiles on their peaceful faces.

'Tie them! Give me some cord!' yelled Gris to the Turks as the three 'victims' crawled out of the windows and from under the car.

'Not tight, you maniacs!' added Bleu harshly. 'Remember what the commander said!'

'*Mon Dieu!*' roared Bleu suddenly, grabbing Gris's shoulder, pointing to the ground beyond the rising smoke. '*Qu'est-ce que c'est que ça?*'

In the middle of the road, halfway to the limousines, lay Rouge flat on his back, one arm raised, the wrist bent, as though frozen in mid-pirouette. The stocking mask could not disguise the expression of Olympian repose underneath.

In the confusion, he had tripped over his cassock, plunging his needle into his stomach.

'Quick!' yelled Gris. 'The antidote! The general thinks of everything!'

'He has to,' said Bleu.

'*Now!*' ordered the Hawk, holding Guido Frescobaldi, who had suddenly raised his voice in song.

Across the dirt road, Mac could see Orange crossing himself as he leaped out of the bushes towards the papal limousine. It was wasted motion, he thought; the pope was not going to attempt any escape. He had helped his aide down on the seat and was getting out of the car, his face wrathful.

The Hawk took Frescobaldi by the hand, and led him towards the limousine.

'I bid you good day, sir,' said the Hawk to the pope. It was a proper military salutation for a surrender.

'*Animale!*' roared the pontiff in a roll of thunder that reverberated throughout the Appian forests and hills. '*Uccisore! Assassino!*'

'What's that?'

'*Basta!*' The thunder cracked again. And the lightning was in Francesco's eyes; the eyes of a giant in the body of a mortal. 'Take my life! You kill my beloved children! The children of God! You slay the *innocenti*! Send me to Jesus! Kill me, too! And may God have mercy on your soul!'

'Oh, for Chri – for heaven's sake, shut up! Nobody's going to kill anybody.'

'I see what I see! The children of God are slain!'

'That's plain horseshit! Nobody's hurt, and nobody's going to get hurt.'

'They are all *morto*,' said Francesco, with less conviction, his eyes darting everywhere in bewilderment.

'No more than you are. We wouldn't be tying them up if they were, would we? Orange! Over here!'

'*Si, Generale.*' Orange came around the hood of the limousine, crossing himself repeatedly.

'Get that coloured boy out of the car. Must be a house guest of the pope here.'

'That man is a *priest*. My personal aide!'

'You don't say? Must be a fine lad with the choirs. Easy, Orange,' said MacKenzie as the Italian pulled the unconscious Black prelate from the automobile. 'Put him in the brush and loosen that big robe. It's too damn hot for ponchos.'

'You mean,' asked Giovanni incredulously, 'they're all alive?'

'Certainly they're alive,' replied MacKenzie, signalling Vert to prepare Frescobaldi for the exchange; the pope's double sat serene.

'I don't believe you! You've murdered them!' roared the pope suddenly.

'Will you keep quiet!' The Hawk did not ask a question. 'Listen to me. I don't know how you handle your command, but I assume you can tell if a soldier's alive or not.'

'*Che cosa? . . .*'

'Captain Gris!' yelled MacKenzie to the masked Scandinavian tying up a priest by the hubcaps of the first limousine. 'Lift that man up and bring him here, please.'

Gris complied. MacKenzie took the pontiff's right hand.

'Here! Put your fingers on the side of the throat next to the collar bone. Now, see? Do you get a pulse?'

The pope's eyes narrowed, his concentration on the touch. 'The heart – Yes. You speak the truth. The others? They are the same? The hearts beat?'

'I gave you my word,' said the Hawk sternly. 'I must reprimand you, sir. Opposing commands do not lie when capture is secure. We're not animals, sir. But we haven't much time.' The Hawk gestured for Vert to bring over the narcotized Frescobaldi. 'I'm afraid we'll have to change some of your clothes. I'll have to—'

MacKenzie stopped. Pope Francesco was staring at Frescobaldi. It was the first moment he had taken cognizance of the singer who was clean shaven and now, without his moustache, looked more like Giovanni Bombalini than did Bombalini himself.

'Guido! It is Guido Frescobaldi!' The pontiff's voice could have been heard in the Bay of Naples, so loud was his roar. 'Guido, my own flesh! My blood! It is Guido! *Madre di Dio!* You are a part of this – this heresy?!'

Signor Guido Frescobaldi smiled.

'*Che gelida ... manina ... a rigido esanine ... ah, la-la ... la-laaa ...*'

'It's him, all right, but he's been a little out of things since this morning. And will be for a while longer. Come on, now. We've got to get some of that hardware off you and on him. Captain Orange? Captain Vert? Give Mr Francesco a hand.'

'*There!*' The Hawk spoke in the tones of a victorious general officer. He held the grinning Guido Frescobaldi by the shoulders, admiring the final result. 'He looks real fine, doesn't he?'

Francesco, transfixed, could not help himself. '*Jesus et Spiritus Sanctus*. The ugly Frescobaldi is myself. It is a miracle of God.'

'Two like-spits in the gunnery pool, Mr Pope!'

The pontiff was barely audible. 'You put ... Frescobaldi ... in the *chair* of *St Peter*?'

'For about two hours with luck – by my calculations.'

'But *why*?'

'Nothing personal. I understand you're a very nice fellow.'

'But why? In the name of God, *why*! That is no answer.'

'Didn't expect it to be,' replied the Hawk. 'I just don't want you screaming your head off. You've got a mighty loud voice.'

'Then I shall be – screaming my head out – if you do not tell me ... *Aiyeeeee!* ...'

'All right! All *right*! We're kidnapping you. Holding you for ransom. You'll be fine; no harm will come to you and that's the word of a general officer.'

The conference was interrupted by Captains Gris and Bleu, who raced up and snapped to attention.

'The area is secured, General,' barked Gris.

'All sedations are completed,' added Bleu. 'We are prepared to move.'

'Good! Let's move then. *Troops!* Evacuate the area! Prepare to execute escape procedures! By your numbers! *Move!*'

As if on cue, the sounds of the revving helicopter could be heard from the camouflaged area fifty yards away from the centre of Ground Zero.

And then there was another sound. From the road at the top of the Appian hill: a car screeching to a halt.

'*Stop!*' came a plaintive wail from the woods. 'For Christ's sake, *stop!*'

'*What?*'

'*Mon Dieu!*'

'*Che cosa?!*'

'*I say!*'

'*Tokig!*'

'*Bakasi!*'

'*Shit!*'

Sam stumbled down the old dirt road on the hill. He came racing around the last curve and fell to one knee.

Giovanni Bombalini watched in astonishment; automatically he gave the kneeling figure his rather confused benediction, '*Deus et filius—*'

'Will you shut up!' MacKenzie glared at Francesco. '*Goddamn*, Sam! What the hell are you doing here? You're supposed to be sick as a *dog—*'

'*Listen* to me, everybody!' broke in Sam. 'Everyone gather around!' He struggled to his feet; the captains stood where they were, their faces betraying a certain insensitivity. 'Escape! Run for your lives! Leave this man alone! It's a trap! Machenfeld has fallen! It happened last night! Hundreds of Interpol police are swarming . . .' Sam's jaw was suddenly a gaping orifice as he stared at the Hawk. '*What did you say?*'

'You're a real pistol, son. I respect your moxie, like I said before. But I can't say you have much respect for my know-how.' MacKenzie snapped one of the straps that crisscrossed his chest over his field jacket. It was attached to a large leather case that was lashed over his hip. 'No assault operation ever stays out of contact with its command centre. Not since 1971, anyway. Hell, I used to patch relays from Ly Sol in Cambodia right straight down to the Mekong units.'

'*What?*'

'Tri-arced, high-frequency radio contact, boy. Set a schedule and receive-send simultaneously. You're *dated*, Sam! As of an hour ago the only thing swarming around Machenfeld were butterflies. I don't know how you did it, but you're mighty lucky you got here alone ... Come to think of it, you'd be a damned fool to get here any other way. – All right, men! Resume Phase Eight! – Come on, Sam. You're going for a ride. And I tell you this now, boy. Any more trouble and I'm going to open a door at two thousand feet and you can fly by yourself!'

'Mac, you can't! Think of World War *Three!*'

'Think of a nice free-fall – without a parachute – straight into a plate of spaghetti!'

And then there was another sound. A frightening one. From the top of the hill. From the road again.

The captains and the Turks froze.

The Hawk whipped his head around – and up – towards the Via Appia.

The pontiff said one word.

'*Carabinieri.*'

The whining, jarring, two-note scream of the Italian state police sirens could be heard in the distance. Drawing nearer.

'*Goddamn! How?!* What the hell *happened?* Sam, you *didn't!*'

'My God, *no!* I didn't! I *wouldn't!*'

'I think there is a – miscalculation, signore,' said Pope Francesco softly.

'*What?* What mother – what miscalculation?'

'The motorcade was to stop at the small village – well, not so *much* a village – of Tuscabondo. It is a mile or so past the *deviazione,* your detour.'

'Jesus!'

'He can be merciful, Signor Generale.'

'Those bastards will be swarming the hills, the fields. Goddamn!'

'And the air, Generale,' said Captain Orange excitedly, breaking out in a sweat under his mask. 'The *carabinieri* have fleets of *elicotteri*. They are the *pazzi* of the sky!'

'Jesus H. Christ!'

'*Figlio di Santa Maria – Figlio di Dio* – He is the way, *Generale*.'

'I told you to shut up. *Men!* Check your maps! Quickly! Gris and Bleu, evaluate escape routes E-Eight and E-Twelve. Our previous routes were faster but more exposed. Deliver your decision in one minute! Orange and Vert. Give me Frescobaldi! Join the others! Sam, you stay here!'

The screams of the sirens were nearer, almost at the intercept point of the Appia. Frescobaldi, weaving in MacKenzie's grip, sang louder.

'Signore.' Giovanni Bombalini took a step towards Mac-Kenzie. 'You speak the word of a general. You have great sincerity when you say it.'

'What? Yes, of course. You're not much different, I suspect. Command's a big responsibility.'

'Indeed it is. And truth is responsibility's right arm.' The pope looked once more at the unconscious figures of his motorcade, each body comfortably stretched out, none harmed. 'And compassion, naturally.'

The Hawk was barely listening. He was holding Frescobaldi, keeping an alert eye on a stunned Sam Devereaux, and watching Captains Gris and Bleu make their final evaluations over the maps. 'What are you talking about?'

'You say you have no wish to inflict harm on my person.'

'Of course not. Wouldn't get much ransom for a corpse. Well, maybe with *your* people—'

'And Frescobaldi is as strong as an ox,' said the pope, as much to himself as to MacKenzie, while studying the half-conscious Guido. 'He always was. Signor Generale, if I said I would go with you without interference, perhaps even in the spirit of cooperation, would you grant me a small request? As one commander to another?'

The Hawk squinted at the pontiff.

'What is it?'

'A brief note, only several words – in English – to be left with my aide. I would want you to read it, of course.'

MacKenzie took out a combat pad from his field jacket, ripped off a page, unclipped the waterproof pencil and handed both to Francesco. 'You've got fifteen seconds.'

The pope put the paper against the limousine and wrote swiftly. He gave the page back to the Hawk.

I am safe. With God's blessing I shall reach you as the chess-playing O'Gilligan reaches me.

Honkey.

'If it's a code, it's pretty piss-poor. Go ahead, put it in the coloured fella's pocket. I like that part that says you're safe.'

Giovanni ran to the figure of his papal aide, stuffed the note under his cassock and returned to the Hawk. 'Now, Signor Generale, you waste time.'

'What?'

'Put Frescobaldi in the limousine! Hurry! Inside is a briefcase. With my pills. Get it, please.'

'*What?*'

'You would last five minutes in the Curia! Where is the *elicottero?*'

'The copter?'

'Yes.'

'Over there. In a clearing.'

Captains Gris and Bleu had completed their swift conference. Gris called out. 'We have briefed the men, General. We go! We meet at Zaragolo!'

'*Zaragolo!*' said the pontiff. 'The airport at Monti Prenestini?'

'Yes,' answered the Hawk, staring with sudden concentration on Pope Francesco. 'What about it?'

'Tell them to stay north of Rocca Priora! There are battalions of police in Rocca Priora.'

'That's east of Frascati—'

'Yes!'

'You heard him, Captains! Outflank Rocca Priora! *Now, scramble!*' roared the Hawk.

'*No!*' screamed Sam, backing away on the road, looking up at the hill. 'Everybody's crazy! You're out of your minds! I'm going to stop you. All of you!'

'Young man!' Giovanni stood erect and addressed Sam pontifically. 'Will you please be quiet and do as the general says?!'

Noir emerged from the clearing. 'The bird's ready, General! We've got a clean lift-off area.'

'We've also got an extra passenger. Get the counsellor, Captain. You might show him a needle, if you can manage it.'

'With real pleasure,' said Noir.

'One dosage, Captain!'

'Shit!'

And so Giovanni Bombalini, the Holy Father of the Catholic Church, and MacKenzie Hawkins, two-time winner of the Congressional Medal of Honour, put Guido Frescobaldi into the papal limousine and ran like hell through the Appian forest to the helicopter.

It was difficult for Francesco. The pontiff swore mildly at Sebastian, the patron saint of athletes, and finally in desperation pulled up the skirts of his habit, displaying rather thick peasant legs, and damn near beat MacKenzie to the aircraft.

The Lear jet soared above Zaragolo's cloud cover, Captain Noir at the controls, Captain Rouge in the co-pilot's seat. The Hawk and the pope sat in the forward section, across from one another, each by a window.

Bewildered, MacKenzie glanced over at Francesco. He knew from long years of experience that when command was stymied, the best thing to do was to do nothing, unless the combat at hand required immediate counter-strike.

Such was not the case now. The problem was that Francesco did not behave like any enemy the Hawk had ever fought.

Goddamn!

There he sat, his heavy robes unbuttoned down to his undershirt, his shoes off, and his hands folded casually across his wide girth, looking out of the Lear's window like some kind of happy delicatessen proprietor on his first aeroplane ride. It was amazing. And confusing.

Goddamn!

Why?

MacKenzie realized that there was no point in wearing his stocking mask any longer. The others had to, for their own protection, but for him it made no difference.

He removed it with a grateful sigh. Francesco looked over at him, not unpleasantly. The pope nodded his head, as if to say, Nice to meet you face to face.

Goddamn!

MacKenzie reached into his pocket for a cigar. He lifted one out, bit off the end, and pulled out a book of matches.

'*Per favore?*' Francesco was leaning towards him.

'What?'

'A cigar, Signor Generale. For me. Do you mind?'

'Oh, no, not at all. Here you are.' Hawkins extracted a second cigar from the pack and handed it to the pontiff. And then, as an afterthought, reached into his other pocket for the clipper.

But it was too late.

Francesco had bitten off the end, spat it out – somehow without offence – taken the matches from Mac's hand, and struck one.

Pope Francesco, the Vicar of Christ, lighted up. And as the circles of aromatic smoke rose above his head, the pontiff sat back in the seat, crossed his legs under his habit, and enjoyed the scenery below.

'*Grazie,*' Francesco said.

'*Prego,*' replied MacKenzie.

PART FOUR

The ultimate success of any corporation is
dependent upon its major product or service.
It is imperative that the projected consumer
be convinced through aggressive public relations techniques that the product, or service,
is essential – to his very existence, if possible.

Shepherd's Laws of Economics:
Book CCCXXI, Chapter 173

CHAPTER TWENTY-FOUR

Sam · sat in the cushioned, wrought-iron chair at the northwest corner of the Machenfeld gardens. Anne had picked the spot after careful deliberation; it was the area of the gardens that provided the best view of the Matterhorn whose peak could be seen in the distance.

It had been three weeks now since the awful thing: Ground Zero.

The captains and the Turks had departed – for unknown parts of the world, never to be heard from again. The staff had been reduced to one cook, who helped Anne and Sam with the housecleaning and the gardens. MacKenzie was not very good at either chore, but he did take turns driving into the village for the newspapers. Too, he checked daily with the high-priced doctor he had flown in from New York, just in case. The doctor, a specialist in internal medicine, had no idea why he was being paid such extraordinary sums of money to do absolutely nothing but live lavishly in a lakeside residence, and so in the spirit of the AMA he accepted the unreported cash and did not complain.

Francesco (Sam could not bring himself to say pope) had settled comfortably into the sealed-off top-floor apartments and could be seen daily walking on the ramparts through his rooftop gardens.

MacKenzie had really done it! He had won the biggest military objective of his career.

And he was currently, through a convoluted series of extraordinarily complex, untraceable conduits, making his ransom demands of the Vatican. Ultrahigh-frequency radio codes arcing from the Alps to Beirut to Algiers; relayed by desert and ocean towers from Marseilles, to Paris, to Milan, and so on to Rome.

According to the schedules he had imposed, the Vatican reply was to be radioed out of Rome and relayed from Beirut by 5 p.m.

MacKenzie had left Machenfeld to drive to the isolated transmission centre – a lone cabin high in the upper Alps, in which was installed the finest, most sophisticated radio equipment obtainable. It had been delivered to Machenfeld by Les Châteaux Suisses but put into operation by the Hawk himself. No one but MacKenzie knew the location of the mountain retreat.

Oh, my God! Five o'clock this afternoon! Sam forced his thoughts away from the awful thing.

There was movement up at the château. Anne had walked out the terrace door carrying the usual large, glossy picture book under her arm and a silver tray with glasses on it in her hands. She started across the lawn to the gardens. Her walk was firm, feminine; a graceful, natural dancer oblivious to the subtle rhythms inherent in her grace. Her light brown hair fell casually, framing the clear pink skin of her lovely face. Her wide, bright blue eyes reflected whatever light they faced.

He had learned something from all the girls, thought Devereaux. Something different and individually their own – gifts to him. And if a normal life was ever to return, he would be grateful for their gifts.

But perhaps he had learned the most important thing from Anne: try for improvement – but don't deny what's past.

There was laughter on the lawn. Anne was looking up at the ramparts where Francesco, dressed in a colourful ski sweater, was leaning over the parapet.

It had become their private game, Anne's and Francesco's. Whenever the Hawk was out of sight they held conversations. And Sam was sure – because Anne would not deny it – that she had made numerous trips up to his private apartments bringing him glasses of chianti, which was specifically forbidden from his diet. Anne and Francesco had become good friends.

Several minutes later that judgement was confirmed. Anne placed the silver tray with the drinks on the table next to Sam. Her eyes were smiling.

'Did you know, Sam, that Jesus was a very practical, down-to-earth person. When he washed Mary Magdalene's feet, he was letting everybody know she was a human being. Maybe a very fine one, in spite of what she used to do. And that people shouldn't throw rocks at her because maybe their feet weren't so clean, either.'

MacKenzie climbed the final precipice by means of an Alpine hook. The last two hundred yards of the spiralling summit road were too deep with mountain snow for the motorcycle, so it was faster to make the final ascent directly. It was eleven minutes to five, Zürich time.

The signals would commence in eleven minutes. From Beirut. They would be repeated after an interval of five minutes, to double-check for decoding errors. At the end of the second series he would confirm reception by transmitting the air-clearance code to the relay in Beirut: four dashes, repeated twice.

Once inside, the Hawk started the generators and watched with satisfaction as the myriad wheels spun with a smooth whirring sound within the casing, and the dials began registering *output*.

When the two green lights went on, signifying maximum performance, he plugged in the single electric heater, feeling the warmth of the glowing coils. He reached over to the powerful shortwave equipment, flipped on the receiving switches and turned the amplifier spools to high volume. Three minutes to go.

He walked to the wall. Slowly he began to turn a handle, hearing the gears mesh. Outside, beyond the iron grillework of the tiny window, he could see a webbed disc swing out and up on its track.

He returned to the radio receiving panel and revolved the parallel megacycle and tetracycle dials with delicate precision. The voices of a dozen languages emerged from the amplifiers. When the needles were in the exact parallel cycle points there was a silence. One minute to go.

MacKenzie took out a cigar from his pocket and lighted up. He inhaled with real contentment and blew out the smoke in ring after ring.

Suddenly the signals were there. Four short, high-pitched dashes; repeated once. The channel was cleared.

He picked up a pencil, his hand poised above a page of notepaper, prepared to write out the code as it was beamed from Beirut.

The message terminated, the Hawk had five minutes to decode. To convert the signals into numbers, then transfer the numbers into letters and the letters into words.

When he had finished, he stared in disbelief at the Vatican reply.

It was impossible!

Obviously, he had made several errors in receiving the Beirut transmission.

The signals began again.

The Hawk started writing on a fresh page of notepaper. Carefully.

Precisely.

The transmission ended as it began: four dashes, repeated once.

MacKenzie put the decoding schedule in front of him. He believed he had memorized it thoroughly, but this was no time to make a mistake. He cross-checked every dot, every dash.

Every word.

There were no errors.

The unbelievable had happened.

Relative to the insane request regarding the contribution of four hundred million American dollars, by assessing worldwide dioceses on the basis of one dollar per communicant, the treasury of the Holy See is in no position to consider such a request. Or any request at all for this particular charity. The Holy Father is in excellent health and sends his blessings in the name of the Father, the Son, and the Holy Spirit.

Ignatio Quartze,
Cardinal Omnipitum,
Keeper of the Vatican Treasury

The Shepherd Company suspended operations.

Mackenzie Hawkins walked the grounds of Château Machenfeld, smoking his cigars, staring blankly at the infinite beauty of the Alps.

Sam made an accounting of the corporation's monetary assets, exclusive of the properties and equipment. Of the original capitalization of $40,000,000, there remained $12,810,431.02.

Plus a contingency expense fund of $150,000, which had not been touched.

Not bad at all. Especially since the investors, to a panicked vulture, refused reimbursement. They wanted nothing whatsoever to do with the Shepherd Company or any of its management personnel. None would even bother to file for tax losses as long as Shepherd's corporate executives promised – on the Bible, *Burke's Peerage*, *Mein Kampf*, and the Koran – never to get in touch with him again.

And Francesco, now sporting a Tyrolean hat along with his favourite ski sweater, was allowed out of the top-floor apartments. For the sake of everybody's sanity, it was agreed to refer to him as Zio Francesco, somebody's uncle.

Since he showed no inclination to go anywhere or do anything other than enjoy the company, Zio Francesco roamed freely. There was someone always nearby, but not to prevent escape; for assistance. He was, after all, in his seventies.

The cook was especially taken with him, for he spent long

periods in the kitchen, helping with the sauces, and every once in a while asking permission to fix a particular dish.

He made one request of the Hawk. The Hawk refused it.

No! Absolutely no! Zio could not telephone his apartment in the Vatican! It made no difference whatsoever that his telephone was private or unlisted *or* concealed in the drawer of his bedside table! Telephone calls could be traced.

Not if they were radioed, insisted Francesco. The Hawk had impressed them all, frequently, by telling them about his complicated methods of communicating with Rome. Of course, a simple telephone call would not have to be nearly so complex. One little relay, perhaps.

No! All that spaghetti had gone to Zio's head. His brain was soft.

The Hawk's was softer, perhaps, suggested Francesco. What progress was the general making? Were not matters at a stalemate? Had not Cardinal Quartze outflanked him?

How could a telephone call change that?

How could it make things any worse? persisted Francesco. The Hawk could be at the radio, his hand on a switch, prepared to break the connection should Zio say anything improper. Was it not more advantageous to the general for at least two people to know he was alive? That the deception was *truly* a deception? There certainly was nothing to lose, for the Hawk had already lost. And possibly there was something to gain. Perhaps four hundred million American dollars.

Besides, Guido needed help. This was no criticism of his cousin, who was not only strong as a bull but a most gentle and thoughtful person. But he was new at the job and would certainly listen to his cousin Giovanni Bombalini. Helped, of course, by Giovanni's personal aide, the young American priest from Harlem.

The situation might *not* be remedied overnight – for there were matters of health and logistics to be considered. But when all was said and done, what alternative did the Hawk *have*?

He obviously had none. And so MacKenzie came down

from the Alpine cabin one afternoon carrying three canvas-wrapped cartons of radio equipment and proceeded to install the instruments in a Machenfeld bedroom.

When all was completed, the Hawk issued an irrevocable command. Only he and Zio Francesco were allowed inside during radio transmissions.

That was fine with Anne and Sam. They had no desire to be there. The cook thought everybody was crazy and went back to the kitchen.

And at least twice a week from then on – very late at night – the huge disc antenna was wheeled out and raised above the battlements. Neither Sam nor Anne knew what was being said or whether anything was being accomplished, but often when they sat in the gardens to talk and look at the glorious Swiss moon, they heard great peals of laughter from the upstairs room. The Hawk and the pope were like small boys thoroughly enjoying a new game.

A secret game, played in their personal clubhouse.

Sam sat in the garden absently looking at his copy of *The Times*. Life at Château Machenfeld had become routinized. For instance, every morning one of them would drive into the village to pick up the newspapers. Coffee in the gardens with the newspapers was a wonderful way to start the day. The world was such an unholy mess; life was so peaceful at Machenfeld.

The Hawk, having discovered the existence of riding trails on the property, purchased several fine horses and rode frequently, sometimes for hours at a time. He'd found something he'd been looking for, thought Sam.

Francesco discovered oil painting. He would trek over the fields in his Tyrolean hat with Anne or the cook, set up his easel and paints, and render for posterity his impressions of the Alpine splendours. That is, when he wasn't in the kitchen, or teaching Anne to play chess, or debating – always pleasantly – with Sam over points of law.

There was one thing about Francesco that nobody talked about, but all knew had something to do with his attitude.

Francesco had not been a well man when he was taken out of the Appian hills. Not well at all. It was the reason Mac had insisted on the availability of the New York specialist.

But as the weeks went by, Francesco seemed to improve in the Alpine air.

Would it have been the same, otherwise?

No one, of course, would speculate, but Francesco had said something at dinner one evening that registered on them all.

'Those doctors. I shall outlive every one of them! They would have had me buried a month ago.'

The Hawk responded with a coughing fit.

And Sam? What of him?

Whatever it was, he knew that it included Anne.

He looked at her now in the late morning sun, sitting in the chair reading the newspaper, the ever present book on the table beside her. *A Pictorial History of Switzerland* was the title today.

She was so lovely, so gloriously – herself. She'd help him become a better lawyer, by making the law seem not so important.

Now he began to think of other things.

Like reading quietly. Understanding. Evaluating.

Like – Judge Devereaux.

Oh, Boston was going to like Anne! His mother would like her, too. And Aaron Pinkus. Aaron would approve wholeheartedly.

If Judge Devereaux ever got back to Boston.

He'd think about that – tomorrow.

'Sam?' said Anne, looking over at him.

'What?'

'Did you read this article in the *Tribune*?'

'What article? I haven't seen the *Tribune*.'

'Here.' She pointed but did not give him the paper. She was engrossed. 'It's about the Catholic Church. All kinds of things. The pope has called a Fifth Ecumenical Council. And there's an announcement that a hundred and sixty-three opera companies are being subsidized, to elevate the spirit of creativity. And a famous cardinal – my God, Sam – it's that Ignatio Quartze! The one Mac yells about.'

'What about him?'

'It seems he's retiring to some villa called San Vincente. Something to do with papal disputes over Vatican allocations. Isn't that strange?'

Devereaux was silent for several moments before he replied. 'I think our friends have been very busy up on the ramparts.'

In the distance were the sounds of galloping hooves. Seconds later MacKenzie Hawkins emerged on the dirt road from beyond the trees and the fields where only weeks ago manoeuvres were held. He reined in his horse and trotted up to the northwest corner of the gardens.

'Goddamn! Isn't it a glorious day? You can see the peak of the Matterhorn!'

There was the music of a triangle coming from the other direction. MacKenzie waved; Devereaux and Anne turned and saw Francesco on the terrace outside the kitchen door, the triangle and the silver bar in his hands. He was dressed in a large apron, the Tyrolean hat firmly on his head.

Zio Francesco called out.

'Lunch, everybody! The *speciale di giorno* is *fantastico*!'

'I'm hungry as a horse!' roared back the Hawk as he patted his mount. 'What've you got, Zio?'

Francesco raised his voice to the Alpine hills. And there was music in his words.

'My dear friends. It's *Linguini Bombalini*!'

EPILOGUE

MacKenzie Hawkins, pleasantly surfeited with Zio's linguini and the splendid *chianti classico* Francesco had his cousin, Frescobaldi, ship to the railroad station in Zermatt, the Hawk wandered across the Alpine pasture to the edge of the field, its glorious view of the majestic mountains as always moving him. It was another ritual that had become part of his day. A few minutes alone, really alone, without even his horse beneath him, or the sound of human voices, only the rustle of the tall grass caressed by the gentle Alpine breezes. He needed these moments, for a man had to face both his accomplishments and his failures by himself, accepting the results without regret as long as he knew he had done his best with what was in him.

Regarding Zio, he had both lost and he had won. He had hardly reached the four hundred million dollars he envisioned, but what was left of the forty million capitalization wasn't exactly C-rations. Yet he had won something else, something far more important, a restored, healthy, *vital* Pope Francesco the First, the pontiff who wanted more than anything else to finish the job started by John the Twenty-Third. To blow the cobwebs out of the Catacombs and bring his church into the twenty-first century. Zio would have to go back, they both had agreed to that without telling the others – sometime soon, somehow. They could work it out. Somehow.

Well, that was just goddamned *fine* for Uncle Zio, but what about *him*, what about the Hawk? What the hell was *he* supposed to do? Sit on his ass in Edelweiss and let the world pass as he *vegetated?*

'Find another cause, Mac, perhaps a somewhat more earthly one,' had suggested Francesco. 'The world abounds with them, and you have extraordinary talents, my son—'

'Cut the "my son" crap, Zio.'

'Sorry, it goes with the office. If I had so many "sons", I'd make an extraordinary mockery of celibacy – which I intend to bring up one day. It's really so unnatural, so foolish, and nothing explicit in the Scriptures.'

'Maybe I should just keep you here before they hang you in St Peter's Square.'

'No, no, I must go back ... But what about you, my friend. What *will* you do?'

The Hawk had not replied, for he had no answer then. He thought about it now, gazing at the breath-taking skyline of the snow-capped Alps, when suddenly, an eagle swooped down from some unseen high altitude perch in search of ground-bound prey that would sustain it.

An *eagle*. A lone eagle, soaring in splendour and splendid freedom, the master of the air and the earth, its wingspread incredible and mesmerizing. The magnificent bird circled in the winds, descending lower and lower, then abruptly dove with marvellous speed into a field below ... Something *happened*! The eagle's massive wings were flapping furiously – it was caught, something had snared it, binding it to the ground! Then, in agonizing moments, the bird broke free, its movements frantic until it found the unencumbered air and soared aloft.

MacKenzie stared across at the would-be killing field, wondering what had caused the near tragic occurrence. The answer came in seconds: two men were racing out of a nearby cluster of brush, obviously annoyed that their decoyed trap had malfunctioned. They picked up the lethal animal-covered instrument, one throwing it into the grass in disgust.

The incident brought back memories to the Hawk, images from long ago when he was a young officer posted to a Ranger training base somewhere in the hills of Nebraska or Iowa, or was it Kansas? – no, it was Nebraska. The eagle itself was not the sole prodder of these memories, but the great bird was a large part of it because of what it somehow historically stood for in pictures and symbols, even in name. Full headdresses crowning the heads of once powerful chiefs, the single, double and triple feathers earned by deeds of bravery by the young tribal males.

The American Indian.

There had been an Indian reservation perhaps twenty miles from the secret training base, certainly no secret to the Indians who pathetically came to beg whatever they could from the strapping, well-fed troops. So pathetic were these pilgrimages, that many of the young Rangers, the Hawk among them, trekked over to the reservation to get a clearer understanding. It was a *disgrace*! These original inhabitants, the *owners* of the land, lived in abject poverty, scandalously shafted by the white invader! Naturally the Rangers stole the Quartermaster bare and until the soldiers left for scaling cliffs on D-Day, the Indians lived better than any of them could remember.

The *American Indian* – screwed by the same kind of pricky-shits who threw General MacKenzie Hawkins out of the army! That noble savage would be his *cause*! It might take months, even years, but *goddamn*, it was a quest worth serving.

The Hawk turned and raced back across the field, the tall grass whipped by his gathering speed. He saw Francesco by the vegetable garden, watering his precious herbs. 'Zio, Zio, I've *got* it!'

'What have you got, my son – forgive me, I mean Mac?'

'I'm going to free our American Indians, I mean *really* set them *free*!'

'They are in *chains*?' asked the bewildered Francesco, his watering-can drenching his Lederhosen.

'Worse, they're in economic bondage, shafted by the white pricky-shits!'

'Sometimes you can be obtuse, MacKenzie—'

304

'Don't you see, Zio? It's my grail, my quest, my *cause*! Hell, it might take me a long time, maybe even a few years, but the right *shaftees* are there, I know it, I *feel* it!'

'May this humble country priest bless in advance those you would free from this bondage? ... In the name of the Father, the Son, and the Holy Ghost, pray to your Maker, my children. The Hawk is on your horizon.'

THE ROAD TO OMAHA

For Henry Sutton

Godfather, wonderful actor,
superb friend and a great
human being

PREFACE

A number of years ago, the undersigned wrote a novel entitled *The Road to Gandolfo*. It was based on a staggering premise, an earthshaking concept that should have possessed the thunder of the ages . . . and you don't hardly come upon them things no more. It was to be a tale told by demons, the legions of Satan marching out of hell to commit a heinous crime that would outrage the world, a mortal blow to all men and women of faith regardless of their specific religion, for it would show how vulnerable are the great spiritual leaders of our times. Stripped to its essentials, the story dealt with the kidnapping of Rome's Pontiff, the beloved *compagnuolo*, a true man of God and of ordinary people everywhere, Pope Francesco the First.

Are you with me? I mean it's really *heavy*, isn't it? It should have been, but it wasn't . . . Something happened. Poor Fool, the novelist, peeked around the edges, glimpsed the flip side of the coin, and to his eternal condemnation he began to giggle. That's *no* way to treat a staggering premise, a magnificent obsession! (Not too shabby a title, by the way.) Unfortunately, Poor Fool could not help himself; he began to think, which is always dangerous for a storyteller. The *what-if* syndrome came into play.

What if the instigator of this horrible crime wasn't actually a bad fellow, but, in fiction's reality, a genuine military legend whom the politicians crippled because he vociferously objected to their hypocrisies . . . and what if the beloved Pope wasn't actually averse to being kidnapped, as long as his look-alike cousin, a none too bright extra from the La Scala Opera, took his place and the true Pontiff could run the immense responsibilities of the Holy See by remote, without the debilitating agenda of Vatican politics and the endless procession of blessings administered to supplicants expecting to buy their way into Heaven by way of the collection plate. Now *there* was another story.

I can hear you, I can *hear* you! *He sold himself down his own river of betrayal.* (I've frequently wondered what river the bromide refers to. The Styx, the Nile, the Amazon? Certainly not the Colorado; you'd get hung up on the white-water rocks.)

Well, maybe I did and maybe I didn't. I only know that during the intervening years since *Gandolfo*, a number of readers have asked me by letter, telephone, and outright threats of bodily harm, '*Whatever happened to those clowns?*' (The perpetrators, not the willing victim.)

In all honesty, those 'clowns' were waiting for another staggering premise. And late one night a year ago, the squirrelliest of my insignificant muses shrieked, '*By Jove, you've got it!*' (I'm quite sure she stole the line.)

At any rate, whereas Poor Fool took certain liberties in the areas of religion and economics in *The Road to Gandolfo*, he hereby freely admits having taken similar liberties in this current scholarly tome with respect to the laws and the courts of the land.

Then again, who doesn't? Of course, not *my* attorney or *your* attorney but certainly everybody else's!

The accurate novelization of authentic undocumented history of questionable origin demands that the muse must forgo certain ingrained disciplines in the search for improbable truths. And definitely where Blackstone is concerned.

Yet never fear, the moral is here:

Stay out of a courtroom unless you can buy the judge. *Or*, if in the unlikely event you could hire *my* lawyer, which you can't because he's all tied up keeping me out of jail.

So, to my many friends who are attorneys (they're either attorneys, actors, or homicidal killers – is there a running connection?), skip over the finer points of law that are neither fine nor very pointed. However, they may well be inaccurately accurate.

Robert Ludlum

DRAMATIS PERSONAE

MacKenzie Lochinvar Hawkins – Former general of the army, former by request of the White House, the Pentagon, the State Department, and most of Washington. Twice decorated with the Congressional Medal of Honor. Aka Madman Mac the Hawk.

Samuel Lansing Devereaux – Brilliant young attorney, Harvard Law School, US Army (reluctantly), lawyer for the Hawk in China (disastrously).

Sunrise Jennifer Redwing – Also an attorney, also brilliant, outrageously gorgeous, and a fiercely loyal daughter of the Wopotami Indian nation.

Aaron Pinkus – Soft-spoken giant of Boston law circles, the consummate attorney-statesman who happens to be Sam Devereaux's employer (unfortunately).

Desi Arnaz I – An impoverished miscreant from Puerto Rico who falls under the Hawk's spell, and who one day may be the director of the Central Intelligence Agency.

Desi Arnaz II – See above. Less of a leader but a mechanical genius, such as in hotwiring cars, picking locks, fixing ski lifts, and turning pesto sauce into an anaesthetic.

Vincent Mangecavallo – The *real* director of the CIA, courtesy of the Mafia dons from Palermo to Brooklyn. Any administration's secret weapon.

Warren Pease – Secretary of State. Every administration's malfunctioning weapon, but a former prep school 'roomie' of the President.

Cyrus M – A black mercenary with a doctorate in chemistry.

Screwed by Washington, and a gradual convert to the Hawk's sense of justice.

Roman Z – A Serbo-Croation Gypsy who was a cell mate of the above. In chaos he finds total delight, as long as he has an unfair advantage.

Sir Henry Irving Sutton – One of the theatre's finest character actors, and, by happenstance, a hero of World War II's North African campaign, because 'there were no lousy directors to warp my performance.'

Hyman Goldfarb – The greatest linebacker ever to have graced the football fields of the NFL. In his postprofessional days, he was calamitously recruited by the Hawk.

'Suicidal Six'

Duke	*Professional actors who have*
Dustin	*joined the army and are*
Marlon	*considered the finest*
Sir Larry	*antiterrorist unit ever produced*
Sly	*by the military. They have*
Telly	*never fired a shot.*

Fawning Hill Country Club Members

Bricky	*Fine fellows from the right*
Doozie	*schools and the right clubs*
Froggie	*who passionately support the*
Moose	*interests of the country – as*
Smythie	*long as theirs come first, way first.*

Johnny Calfnose – Information officer of the Wopotami tribe; he picks up a phone and usually lies. He also still owes Sunrise Jennifer bail money. What more can be said?

Arnold Subagaloo – White House Chief of Staff. He flies off the handle (free on government aircraft) whenever anyone mentions that he's not the President. What more can *anyone* say?

The rest of the *personae* may be of lesser importance, but it is vital to remember that there are no small parts, only small players, and none of ours is in that ignominious category. Each carries forth in the grand tradition of Thespis, giving his and her all for the play, no matter how inconsequential the offering. 'The play's the thing wherein we'll catch the conscience of the king!' Or maybe somebody.

PROLOGUE

The flames roared up into the night sky creating massive shadows pulsating across the painted faces of the Indians around the bonfire. And then the chief of the tribe, bedecked in the ceremonial garments of his office, his feathered headdress swooping down from his immensely tall frame to the ground below, raised his voice in regal majesty.

'I come before you to tell you that the sins of the white man have brought him nothing but confrontation with the evil spirits! They will devour him and send him into the fires of eternal damnation! Believe me, my brothers, sons, sisters, and daughters, the day of reckoning is before us and we will emerge *triumphant*!'

The only problem for many in the chief's audience was that the chief was a white man.

'What cookie jar did he jump out of?' whispered an elderly member of the Wopotami tribe to the squaw next to him.

'*Shhh!*' said the woman, 'he's brought us a truckload of souvenirs from China and Japan. Don't louse up a good thing, Eagle Eyes!'

CHAPTER ONE

The small distressed office on the top floor of the government building was from another era, which was to say nobody but the present occupant had used it in sixty-four years and eight months. It was not that there were dark secrets in its walls or malevolent ghosts from the past hovering below the shabby ceiling; quite simply, nobody *wanted* to use it. And another point should be made clear. It was not actually on the top floor, it was *above* the top floor, reached by a narrow wooden staircase, the kind the wives of New Bedford whalers climbed to prowl the balconies, hoping – most of the time – for familiar ships that signalled the return of their own particular Ahabs from the angry ocean.

In summer months the office was suffocating, as there was only one small window. During the winter it was freezing, as its wooden shell had no insulation and the window rattled incessantly, impervious to caulking, permitting the cold winds to whip inside as though invited. In essence, this room, this antiquated upper chamber with its sparse furniture purchased around the turn of the century, was the Siberia of the government agency in which it was housed. The last formal employee who toiled there was a discredited American Indian who had the temerity to learn to read English and suggested to his superiors, who could barely read English, that certain restrictions placed on a reservation of the Navajo nation were too severe. It is said the man died in that upper office in the cold January of 1927 and was not discovered until the following May when the weather was warm and the air suddenly scented. The government agency was, of course, the United States Bureau of Indian Affairs.

For the current occupant, however, the foregoing was not a deterrent but rather an incentive. The lone figure in the nondescript grey suit huddled over the rolltop desk, which wasn't much of a desk as all its little drawers had been removed and the rolling top was stuck at half mast, was General MacKenzie Hawkins, military legend, hero in three wars and twice winner of the Congressional Medal of Honor. This giant of a man, his lean muscular figure belying his elderly years, his steely eyes and tanned leather-lined face, perhaps confirming a number of them, had once again gone into combat. However, for the first time in his life, he was not at war with the enemies of his beloved United States of America but with the government of the United States itself. Over something that took place a hundred and twelve years ago.

It didn't much matter when, he thought as he squeaked around in his ancient swivel chair and propelled himself to an adjacent table piled high with old leather-bound ledgers and maps. They were the *same* pricky-shits who had screwed *him*, stripped him of his uniform, and put him out to military pasture! They were all the goddamned same, whether in their frilly frock coats of a hundred years ago or their piss-elegant, tight-assed pinstripes of today. They were *all* pricky-shits. Time did not matter, nailing them did!

The general pulled down the chain of a green-shaded, goosenecked lamp – circa early twenties – and studied a map, in his right hand a large magnifying glass. He then spun around to his dilapidated desk and re-read the paragraph he had underlined in the ledger whose binding had split with age. His perpetually squinting eyes suddenly were wide and bright with excitement. He reached for the only instrument of communication he had at his disposal, since the installation of a telephone might reveal his more than scholarly presence at the Bureau. It was a small cone attached to a tube; he blew into it twice, the signal of emergency. He waited for a reply; it came over the primitive instrument thirty-eight seconds later.

4

'*Mac?*' said the rasping voice over the antediluvian connection.

'Heseltine, I've *got* it!'

'For Christ's sake, blow into this thing a little easier, will you? My secretary was here and I think she thought my dentures were whistling.'

'She's out?'

'She's out,' confirmed Heseltine Brokemichael, director of the Bureau of Indian Affairs. 'What is it?'

'I just told you, I've *got* it!'

'Got what?'

'The biggest con job the pricky-shits ever *pulled*, the same pricky-shits who made us wear civvies, old buddy!'

'Oh, I'd love to get those bastards. Where did it happen and when?'

'In Nebraska. A hundred and twelve years ago.'

Silence. Then:

'*Mac*, we weren't around then! Not even you!'

'It doesn't matter, Heseltine. It's the same horseshit. The same bastards who did it to *them*, did it to you and me a hundred years later.'

'Who's "them"?'

'An offshoot of the Mohawks called the Wopotami tribe. They migrated to the Nebraska territories in the middle eighteen hundreds.'

'*So?*'

'It's time for the sealed archives, General Brokemichael.'

'Don't *say* that! Nobody can *do* that!'

'You can, General. I need final confirmation, just a few loose ends to clear up.'

'For *what*? *Why?*'

'Because the Wopotamis may still legally own all the land and air rights in and around Omaha, Nebraska.'

'You're *crazy*, Mac! That's the Strategic Air Command!'

'Only a couple of missing items, buried fragments, and the facts are there . . . I'll meet you in the cellars, at the vault to the archives, General Brokemichael . . . Or should I call you co-chairman of the Joint Chiefs of Staff, along with me, Heseltine? If I'm right, and I know damn well I am, we've got the White House-Pentagon axis in such a bind, their collective tails won't be able to evacuate until we tell 'em to.'

Silence. Then:

'I'll let you in, Mac, but then I fade until you tell me I've got my uniform back.'

'Fair enough. Incidentally, I'm packing everything I've got here and taking it back to my place in Arlington. That poor son of a bitch who died up in this rat's nest and wasn't found until the perfume drifted down didn't die in vain!'

The two generals stalked through the metal shelves of the musty sealed archives, the dull, webbed lights so dim they relied on their flashlights. In the seventh aisle, MacKenzie Hawkins stopped, his beam on an ancient volume, its leather binding cracked. 'I think this is it, Heseltine.'

'Good, and you can't take it out of here!'

'I understand that, General, so I'll merely take a few photographs and return it.' Hawkins removed a tiny spy camera with 110 film from his grey suit.

'How many rolls have you got?' asked former General Heseltine Brokemichael as MacKenzie carried the huge book to a steel table at the end of the aisle.

'Eight,' replied Hawkins, opening the ancient yellow-paged volume to the pages he needed.

'I have a couple of others, if you need them,' said Heseltine. 'Not that I'm so all fired-up by what you think you may have found, but if there's any way to get back at Ethelred, I'll *take* it!'

'I thought you two had made up,' broke in MacKenzie, while turning pages and snapping pictures.

'*Never!*'

'It wasn't Ethelred's fault, it was that rotten lawyer in the Inspector General's office, a half-assed kid from Harvard named Devereaux, Sam Devereaux. He made the mistake, not

Brokey the Deuce. Two Brokemichaels; he got 'em mixed up, that's all.'

'Horseshit! Brokey-Two put the finger on *me*!'

'I think you're wrong, but that's not what I'm here for and neither are you . . . Brokey, I need the volume next to or near this one. It should say CXII on the binding. Get it for me, will you?' As the head of Indian Affairs walked back into the metal stacks, the Hawk took a single-edged razor out of his pocket and sliced out fifteen successive pages of the archival ledger. Without folding the precious papers, he slipped them under his suit coat.

'I can't find it,' said Brokemichael.

'Never mind, I've got what I need.'

'What now, Mac?'

'A long time, Heseltine, maybe a long, long time, perhaps a year or so, but I've got to make it right – so right there's no holes, no holes at all.'

'In what?'

'In a suit I'm going to file against the government of the United States,' replied Hawkins, pulling a mutilated cigar out of his pocket and lighting it with a World War II Zippo. 'You wait, Brokey-One, and you watch.'

'Good *God*, for *what*? . . . Don't smoke! You're not supposed to *smoke* in here!'

'Oh, Brokey, you and your cousin, Ethelred, always went too much by the book, and when the book didn't match the action, you looked for more books. It's not *in* the books, Heseltine, not the ones you can read. It's in your stomach, in your gut. Some things are right and some things are wrong, it's as simple as that. The gut tells you.'

'What the *hell* are you talking about?'

'Your gut tells you to look for books you're *not* supposed to read. In places where they keep secrets, like right in here.'

'Mac, you're not making sense!'

'Give me a year, maybe two, Brokey, and then you'll understand. I've got to do it right. Real right.' General MacKenzie Hawkins strode out between the metal racks of the archives to the exit. '*Goddamn*,' he said to himself. 'Now I really go to work. Get *ready* for me, you magnificent Wopotamis. I'm *yours*!'

Twenty-one months passed and *nobody* was ready for Thunder Head, chief of the Wopotamis.

CHAPTER TWO

The President of the United States, his jaw firm, his angry eyes steady and penetrating, accelerated his pace along the steel-grey corridor in the underground complex of the White House. In seconds, he had outdistanced his entourage, his tall lean frame angled forward as if bucking a torrential wind, an impatient figure wanting only to reach the storm-tossed battlements and survey the bloody costs of war so as to devise a strategy and repel the invading hordes assaulting his realm. He was John of Arc, his racing mind building a counterattack at Orleans, a Harry Five who knew the decisive Agincourt was in the immediate picture.

At the moment, however, his immediate objective was the anxiety-prone Situation Room buried in the lowest levels of the White House. He reached a door, yanked it open, and strode inside as his subordinates, now trotting and breathless, followed in unison.

'All right, fellas!' he roared. 'Let's *skull*!'

A brief silence ensued, broken by the tremulous, high-pitched voice of a female aide. 'I don't think in here, Mr President.'

'What? *Why?*'

'This is the men's room, sir.'

'Oh? . . . What are *you* doing here?'

'Following you, sir.'

'Golly gee. Wrong turn. Sorry about that. Let's go! *Out!*'

The large round table in the Situation Room glistened under the wash of the indirect lighting, reflecting the shadows of the bodies seated around it. These blocks of shadows on the polished wood, like the bodies themselves, remained immobile as the stunned faces attached to those bodies stared in astonishment at the gaunt, bespectacled man who stood behind the President in front of a portable blackboard on which he had drawn numerous diagrams using four different colours of chalk. The visual aids were somewhat less than effective as two of the crisis management team were colour blind. The bewildered expression on the youthful Vice-President's face was nothing new and therefore dismissible, but the growing agitation on the part of the chairman of the Joint Chiefs of Staff was not so easily dismissed.

'*Goddamn* it, Washbum, I don't –'

'That's Washburn, General.'

'That's nice. I don't follow the legal line.'

'It's the orange one, sir.'

'Which one is that?'

'I just explained, the *orange* chalk.'

'Point it out.'

Heads turned; the President spoke. 'Gee whiz, Zack, can't you tell?'

'It's dark in here, Mr President.'

'Not that dark, Zack. *I* can see it clearly.'

'Well, I've got a minor visual problem,' said the general, abruptly lowering his voice, '. . . distinguishing certain colours.'

'What, Zack?'

'*I* heard him,' exclaimed the tow-headed Vice-President, seated next to the JC chairman. 'He's *colour* blind.'

'Golly, Zack, but you're a soldier!'

'Came on late, Mr President.'

'It came on *early* with me,' continued the excitable heir to the Oval Office. 'Actually, it's what kept me out of the *real* army. I would have given *anything* to correct the problem!'

'Close it up, gumball,' said the swarthy-skinned director of the Central Intelligence Agency, his voice low but his half-lidded dark eyes ominous. 'The friggin' campaign's over.'

'Now, really, Vincent, there's no cause for that language,' intruded the President. 'There's a lady present.'

'That judgement's up for grabs, Prez. The lady in question is not unfamiliar with the lingua franca, as it were.' The DCI smiled grimly at the glaring female aide and returned to the man named Washburn at the portable blackboard. 'You, our legal expert here, what kind of . . . creek are we up?'

'*That's* better, Vinnie,' added the President. 'I appreciate it.'

'You're welcome . . . Go on, Mr Lawyer. What kind of deep ca-ca are we really into?'

'Very nice, Vinnie.'

'Please, Big Man, we're all a little stressed here.' The director leaned forward, his apprehensive eyes on the White House legal aide. 'You,' he continued, 'put away the chalk and let's have the news. And do me a favour, don't spend a week getting there, okay?'

'As you wish, Mr Mangecavallo,' said the White House attorney, placing the coloured chalk on the blackboard's ledge. 'I was merely trying to diagram the historical precedents relative to the altered laws where the Indian nations were concerned.'

'What *nations*?' asked the Vice-President, in his voice a trace of arrogance. 'They're tribes, not countries.'

'Go on,' interrupted the director. 'He's not here.'

'Well, I'm sure you all recall the information our mole at the Supreme Court gave us about an obscure, impoverished Indian *tribe* petitioning the Court over a supposed treaty with the federal government that was supposedly lost or stolen by federal agents. A treaty that if ever found would restore their rights to certain territories currently housing vital military installations.'

'Oh, yes,' said the President. 'We had quite a laugh over that. They even sent an extremely long brief to the Court that nobody wanted to read.'

'Some poor people will do anything but get a job!' joined in the veep. 'That *is* a laugh.'

'Our lawyer isn't laughing,' observed the director.

'No, I'm not, sir. Our mole sends word that there've been some quiet rumours which may mean absolutely nothing, of course, but apparently five or six justices of the Court were so impressed by the brief that they've actually debated its merits in chambers. Several feel that the lost Treaty of 1878, negotiated with the Wopotami tribe and the fourteenth Congress, may ultimately be legally binding upon the government of the United States.'

'You gotta be outta your *lemon* tree!' roared Mangecavallo. 'They can't *do* that!'

'Totally unacceptable,' snapped the pin-striped, acerbic Secretary of State. 'Those judicial fruitcakes will never survive the polls!'

'I don't think they have to, Warren.' The President shook his head slowly. 'But I see what you mean. As the great communicator frequently told me, "Those mothers couldn't get parts as extras in *Ben-Hur*, not even in the Colosseum scenes."'

'Profound,' said the Vice-President, nodding his head. 'That really says it. Who's Benjamin Hurr?'

'Forget it,' replied the balding, portly attorney general, still breathing heavily from the swift journey through the underground corridors. 'The point is they don't need outside employment. They're set for life, and there's nothing we can *do* about it!'

'Unless they're all impeached,' offered the nasal-toned Secretary of State, Warren Pease, his thin-lipped smile devoid of bonhomie.

'Forget that, too,' rebutted the attorney general. 'They're pristine white and immaculate black, even the skirt. I checked the whole spectrum when those pointy-heads shoved that negative poll tax decision down our throats.'

'That was simply *grotesque*!' cried the Vice-President, his wide eyes searching for approval. 'What's five hundred dollars for the right to *vote*?'

'Too true,' agreed the occupant of the Oval Office. 'The good people could have written it off on their capital gains. For instance, there was an article by a fine economist, an alumnus of ours as a matter of fact, in *The Bank Street Journal*, explaining that by converting one's assets in sub-section C to the line item projected losses in –'

'Prez, *please*?' interrupted the director of the Central Intelligence Agency gently. 'That bum's doing time, six to ten years for fraud, actually ... A lid, please, Big Man, okay?'

'Certainly, Vincent ... Is he really?'

'Just remember, none of us remember him,' replied the DCI, barely above a whisper. 'You forgot his line item procedures when we had him at Treasury? He put half of Defense into Education, but nobody got no schools.'

'It was *great* PR –'

'Stow it, gumball –'

'"Stow it," Vincent? Were you in the Navy? "Stow it"s a navy term.'

'Let's say I've been on a lot of small fast boats, Prez. Caribbean theatre of operations, okay?'

'*Ships*, Vincent. They're always "ships." Were you by way of Annapolis?'

'There was a Greek runner from the Aegean who could *smell* a patrol boat in pitch dark.'

'Ship, Vincent. *Ship* ... Or maybe not when applied to patrols –'

'Please, Big Man.' Director Mangecavallo stared at the attorney general. 'Maybe you didn't look good enough into that dirt bag character spectrum of yours, huh? On those judicial fruitcakes, as our high-toned Secretary of State called 'em. Maybe there were omissions, right?'

'I used the entire resources of the Federal Bureau,' replied the obese attorney general, adjusting his bulk in the inadequate chair while wiping his forehead with a soiled handkerchief. 'We couldn't hang a jaywalking ticket on any of them. They've all been in Sunday school since the day they were born.'

'What do those FBI yo-yos know, huh? They cleared *me*, right? I was the holiest saint in town, *right*?'

'And both the House and the Senate confirmed you with rather decent majorities, Vincent. That says something about our constitutional checks and balances, doesn't it?'

'More about cheques made out to "cash" than balances, Prez, but we'll let it slide, okay? ... Owl Eyes here says that five or six of the big robes may be leaning the wrong way, right?'

'It could simply be minor speculation,' added the man named Washburn. 'And completely in camera.'

'So who's takin' pictures?'

'You misunderstand, sir. I mean the debates remain secret, not a word of them leaked to the press or the public. The blackout was actually self-imposed on the grounds of national security, *in extremis*.'

'In who?'

'Good heavens!' cried Washburn. 'This wonderful country, the nation we love, could be placed in the most vulnerable military position in our history if five of those damn fools vote their consciences. We could be *obliterated*!'

'Okay, okay, cool it,' said Mangecavallo, staring at the others around the table, quickly passing by the eyes of the President and his heir apparent. 'So we got us some room by this top-secret status. And we also got five or six judicial fruitcakes to work on, right? . . . So, as the intelligence expert at this table, I say we should make sure two or three of those zucchinis stay in the vegetable patch, *right*! And since this sort of thing is in my personal realm of expertise, I'll go to work, *capisce*?'

'You'll have to work quickly, Mr Director,' said the bespectacled Washburn. 'Our mole tells us that the chief justice himself told him he was going to lift the debate blackout in forty-eight hours. In his own words, Chief Justice Reebock said . . . "They're not the only half-assed ball game in town" – that's a direct quote, Mr President. I personally do not use such language.'

'Very commendable, Washbum –'

'That's *Washburn*, sir.'

'Him, too. Let's *skull*, men – and you, too, Miss . . . Miss . . . '

'Trueheart, Mr President. Teresa Trueheart.'

'What do you do?'

'I'm your Chief of Staff's personal secretary, sir.'

'And then some,' mumbled the DCI.

'*Stow* it, Vinnie.'

'My Chief of Staff . . . ? Gosh 'n crackers, where *is* Arnold? I mean this is a *crisis*, a real zing doozer!'

'He has his massage every afternoon at this hour, sir,' replied Miss Trueheart brightly.

'Well, I don't mean to criticize, but –'

'You have every *right* to criticize, Mr President,' interrupted the wide-eyed heir apparent.

'On the other hand, Subagaloo's been under a great deal of stress lately. The press corps calls him names and he's quite sensitive.'

'And there's nothing that relieves stress more than a massage,' added the Vice-President. 'Believe me, I know!'

'So where do we stand, gentlemen? Let's get a fix on the compass and tighten the halyards.'

'Aye, *aye*, sir!'

'Mr Vice-President, give us a break, huh? . . . The compass we're locked into, Big Man, should better be fixed on a full moon, 'cause that's where we're at – looney-tune time, but nobody's laughin'.'

'Speaking as your Secretary of Defense, *Mr President*,' broke in an extremely short man whose pinched face barely projected above the table and whose eyes glared disapprovingly at the CIA director, 'the situation's utterly preposterous. Those idiots on the Court can't be allowed to even consider devastating the security of the country over an obscure, long-forgotten, so-called treaty with an Indian tribe nobody's ever *heard* of!'

'Oh, I've heard of the Wopotamis,' again interrupted the Vice-President. 'Of course, American history wasn't my best subject, but I remember I thought it was a funny name, like the Choppywaws. I thought they were slaughtered or died of starvation or some dumb thing.'

The brief silence was ended with Director Vincent Mangecavallo's strained whisper as he stared at the young man who was a heartbeat away from being the nation's Commander-in-Chief. 'You say one more word, butter skull, and you're gonna be in a cement bathrobe at the bottom of the Potomac, do I make myself clear?'

'*Really*, Vincent!'

'Listen, Prez, I'm your head honcho for the whole country's security, right? Well, let me tell you, that kid's got the loosest mouth in the beltway. I could have him terminated with extreme prejudice for saying and doing what he didn't even know he said or did. The hit off the record, naturally.'

'That's not fair!'

'It's not a fair world, son,' observed the perspiring attorney general, turning his attention to the White House lawyer at the blackboard. 'All right, Blackburn—'

'*Wash*burn—'

'If you say so . . . Let's zero in on this fiasco, and I mean zero to the max! For starters, just who the hell is the bastard, the *traitor*, who's behind this totally unpatriotic, un-American appeal to the Court?'

'He calls himself Chief Thunder Head, native American,' answered Washburn. 'And the brief his attorney submitted is considered one of the most brilliant ever received by the judiciary, our informer tells us. They say – confidentially – that it will go down in the annals of jurisprudence as a model of legal analysis.'

'Annals, my ass!' exploded the attorney general, once more working his soiled handkerchief across his brow. 'I'll have that legal banana peeled to his bare bones! He's finished, eliminated. By the time the department's through with him, he won't get a job selling insurance in Beirut, *forget* the law! No firm'll touch him and he won't find a client in the meat box at Leavenworth. What's the son of a bitch's name?'

'*Well*,' began Washburn hesitantly, his voice squeaking briefly into a falsetto, ' . . . there we have a temporary glitch, as it were.'

'Glitch – *what* glitch?' The nasal-toned Warren Pease, whose left eye had the unfortunate affliction of straying to the side when he was excited, pecked his head forward like a violated chicken. 'Just give us the name, you idiot!'

'There isn't any to give,' choked Washburn.

16

'Thank God this moron doesn't work for the Pentagon,' snarled the diminutive Secretary of Defense. 'We'd never find half our missiles.'

'I think they're in Teheran, Oliver,' offered the President. 'Aren't they?'

'My suggestion was *rhetorical*, sir.' The pinch-faced head of the Pentagon, seen barely above the surface of the table, shook back and forth in short lateral jabs. 'Besides, that was a long time ago and *you* weren't there and *I* wasn't there. Remember, *sir*?'

'Yes, yes, of course I don't.'

'Goddamn it, Blackboard, why *isn't* there a name?'

'Legal precedent, sir, and my name is . . . never mind –'

'What do you mean "never mind," you wart? I want the *name*!'

'That's not what I meant –'

'What the hell *do* you mean?'

'*Non nomen amicus curiae*,' mumbled the bespectacled White House attorney barely above a whisper.

'What are you doin', a Hail Mary?' asked the DCI softly, his dark Mediterranean eyes bulging in disbelief.

'It goes back to eighteen twenty-six when the Court permitted a brief to be filed anonymously by a "friend of the Court" on behalf of a plaintiff.'

'I'll kill him,' mumbled the obese attorney general, an audible flatus emerging from the seat of his chair.

'*Hold* it!' yelled the Secretary of State, his left eye swinging back and forth unchecked. 'Are you telling us that this brief for the Wopotami tribe was filed by an *unnamed* attorney or attorneys?'

'Yes, sir. Chief Thunder Head sent his representative, a young brave who recently passed the state's bar, to appear before the Justices in camera and act as temporary counsel anticipating the necessity of the original anonymous counsel should the brief be held inadequate . . . It wasn't. The majority of the Court deemed it sufficient under the guidelines of *non nomen amicus curiae*.'

'So we don't know *who* the *hell* prepared the goddamned

thing?' shouted the attorney general, his attacks of duodenal gas unrelenting.

'My wife and I call those "bottom burps,"' snickered the Vice-President quietly to his single superior.

'*We* used to call them "caboose whistles,"' replied the President, grinning conspiratorially.

'For Christ's *sake*!' roared the attorney general. 'No, no, not *you*, sir, or the kid here – I'm referring to Mr Backwash –'

'That's . . . never mind.'

'You mean to tell us we're not allowed to know who *wrote* this garbage, this swill that may convince five air-headed judges on the Court to affirm it as law – and, not incidentally – *destroy* the operational core of our national defence!'

'Chief Thunder Head has informed the Court that in due time, after the decision has been rendered and made public and his people set free, he will make known the legal mind behind his tribe's appeal.'

'That's nice,' said the chairman of the Joint Chiefs. 'Then we'll put the son of a bitch on the reservation with his redskin buddies and nuke the whole bunch of them off the god-damned map.'

'To do that, General, you'd have to wipe out all of Omaha, Nebraska.'

The emergency meeting in the Situation Room was over; only the President and his Secretary of State remained at the table.

'Golly, Warren,' said the chief executive. 'I wanted you to stay because sometimes I don't understand those people.'

'Well, they certainly never went to *our* school, old roomie.'

'Gosh, I guess they didn't, but that's not what I mean. They all got so excited, shouting and cursing and everything.'

'The ill-born are prone to emotional outbursts, we both know that. They have no ingrained restraint. Do you remember when the headmaster's wife got drunk and began singing "One-Ball Reilly" at the back of the chapel? Only the scholarship boys turned around.'

'Not exactly,' said the President sheepishly. 'I did, too.'

'*No*, I can't believe it!'

'Well, I sort of peeked. I think I had the hots for her; it started in dancing class, the foxtrot, actually.'

'She did that to all of us, the bitch. It's how she got her kicks.'

'I suppose so, but back to this meeting. You don't think anything could come of that Indian stuff, do you?'

'Of course not! Chief Justice Reebock is just up to his old tricks, trying to get you mad because he thinks you black-balled him for our Honorary Alumni Society.'

'Gee, I swear I didn't!'

'I know you didn't, I did. His politics are quite acceptable but he's a very unattractive man and wears terrible clothes. He looks positively ludicrous in a tuxedo. Also, I think he drools – not for us, old roomie. You heard what that Washboard said . . . he said Reebock told our mole that we "weren't the only half-assed ball game in town." What more do you need?'

'Still, everybody got so angry, especially Vincent Manja . . . Manju . . . Mango whatever.'

'It's the Italian in him. It goes with the bloodlines.'

'Maybe, Warren. Still he bothers me. I'm sure Vincent was a fine naval officer but he could also be a loose cannon . . . like you-know-who.'

'*Please*, Mr President, don't give either of us nightmares!'

'I'm just trying to prevent 'em, old roomie. Look, Warren, Vincent doesn't get along too well with our attorney general or the Joint Chiefs, and definitely not with the whole defence department, so I want you to sort of cultivate him, stay in close touch with him on this problem – be his confidential friend.'

'With a *Mangecavallo*?'

'Your office calls for it, Warty old boy. State's got to be involved in something like this.'

'But *nothing* will *come* of it!'

'I'm sure it won't, but think of the reactions worldwide when the Court's arguments become public. We're a nation of laws, not whims, and the Supreme Court doesn't suffer nuisance suits. You have some international spin-control in front of you, roomie.'

'But why *me*?'

'Golly gosh and zing darn, I just *told* you, Warty!'

'Why not the Vice-President? He can relay all the news to me.'

'Who?'

'The Vice-President!'

'What *is* his name, anyway?'

CHAPTER THREE

It was a bright midsummer's afternoon and Aaron Pinkus, arguably the finest attorney in Boston, Massachusetts, and certainly one of the kindest and most gentle of powerful men, climbed out of his limousine in the fashionable suburb of Weston and smiled at the uniformed chauffeur who held the door. 'I told Shirley this huge car was ostentatious enough, Paddy, but that silly cap with the shiny visor on your head comes perilously close to the sin of false pride.'

'Not in old Southie, Mr Pinkus, and we got more sins than they got votive candles in a wax factory,' said the large middle-aged driver whose partially greying hair bespoke a once full crown of bright red. 'Besides, you've been saying that for years now and it doesn't do much good. Mrs Pinkus is a very insistent woman.'

'Mrs Pinkus's brain has been refried too often under a beauty shop hair dryer ... I never said that, Paddy.'

'Of course not, sir.'

'I don't know how long I'll be, so drive down the block, perhaps around the corner out of sight –'

'And stay in touch with you over the beeper,' completed the Irishman, grinning, obviously enjoying the subterfuge. 'If I spot Mr Devereaux's car, I signal you, and you can get out through the back door.'

'You know, Paddy, if our words were part of a transcript, any transcript, we'd lose the case, whatever it was.'

'Not with your office defending us, sir.'

'False pride again, my old friend. Also, criminal law is but a small part of the firm and not really outstanding.'

'Hey, *you* ain't doing nothin' criminal!'

'Then let's lose the transcript . . . Do I look presentable for the grande dame, Paddy?'

'Let me straighten your tie, sir, it slipped a touch down.'

'Thank you,' said Pinkus as the driver adjusted his tie. His eyes strayed to the imposing blue-grey Victorian house, fronted by a white picket fence and profuse with gleaming white trim around the windows and below the high gables. Inside was the matron of this landmark residence, the formidable Mrs Lansing Devereaux III, mother of Samuel Devereaux, potential attorney-extraordinary and currently an enigma to his employer, one Aaron Pinkus.

'There you are, sir.' The chauffeur stepped back and nodded approvingly. 'You're a grand and splendid sight for one of the opposite sex.'

'Please, Paddy, this is not an assignation, it's a mission of compassionate inquiry.'

'Yeah, I know, boss. Sam's been kind of off the wall every now and again.'

'You've noticed then?'

'Hell, you've had me pick him up at Logan Airport a dozen times or more this year. As I say, every now and again he seemed a little squirrelly, and it wasn't just the boyo booze. He's troubled, Mr Pinkus. The lad's got a trouble in his head.'

'And that head contains a brilliant legal mind, Paddy. Let's see if we can find out what the trouble is.'

'Good luck, sir. I'll be out of sight but *in* sight, if you know what I mean. And when you hear my beep, get the hell out of there.'

'Why do I feel like a bony, overage Jewish Casanova who couldn't scale a trellis if a horde of pit bulls were snapping at my rear end?' Pinkus understood that he asked the question of himself, as his driver had raced around the hood of the limousine so as to climb inside and vanish – in sight but out of sight.

Aaron had met Eleanor Devereaux only twice over the years since he had known her son. The first time was the day Samuel came to work for the firm several weeks after his graduation from Harvard Law School, and then, suspected Aaron, it was because his mother wanted to look over her son's workaday environs as she might inspect the counsellors and the facilities of a summer camp. The second and only other time was at the welcoming home party the Pinkuses gave for Sam upon his return from the Army, said homecoming one of the strangest in the chronicles of military separation. It took place over five months past the day that Lieutenant Devereaux was to arrive in Boston as an honourably discharged civilian. Five months unaccounted for.

Five months, mused Aaron as he started toward the gate in the white picket fence, nearly half a year that Sam would not talk about — would not discuss except to say he was not permitted to discuss it, implying some type of top-secret government operation. Well, had thought Pinkus at the time, he certainly could not ask *Lieutenant* Devereaux to violate a sworn oath, but he was curious, both personally as a friend and professionally in terms of international legal negotiations, and he did have a few connections in Washington.

So he telephoned the President on the private White House line that rang in the upstairs living quarters and explained his conundrum to the chief executive.

'You think he may have been involved in a covert operation, Aaron?' the President had asked.

'Speaking frankly, I wouldn't think he's at all the type.'

'Sometimes they go for that, Pinky. You know, rotten casting turns out the best casting. Also speaking frankly, a lot of these lousy long-haired, dirty-minded directors stink up the big screen with that kind of thing. I hear they wanted Myrna to use the *S* word a couple of years ago, can you *believe* it?'

'It's difficult, Mr President. But I know you're busy –'

'Heck no, Pinky. Mommy and I are just watching *Wheel of Fortune*. You know, she beats me a lot, but I don't care. I'm President and she's not.'

'Very understanding. Could you just possibly make a few inquiries for me on this matter?'

'Oh, sure. I wrote it down. Devereaux – D-e-v-a-r-o, right?'

'That will do, sir.'

Twenty minutes later the President had called him back. 'Oh, wow, Pinky! I think you stepped into it!'

'Into what, Mr President?'

'My people tell me that "outside of China" – those were the words – whatever this Devereaux did had "absolutely nothing to do with the United States government" – those, too, were the exact words, I wrote them down. Then when I pressed them, they told me I didn't *want to know* –'

'Yes, of course, the exact words. It's called deniability, Mr President.'

'There's a lot of that going around, isn't there?'

Aaron paused on the path and looked up at the grand old house thinking about Sam Devereaux and the rather odd, even touching way he had grown up in this gracefully restored relic from a far more graceful era. In truth, considered the attorney, the sparkling restoration had not always been in evidence; for years there had been more the aura of neat but shabby gentility about the place rather than the current façade of spanking new paint and a manicured front lawn. These days, care was lavished continuously, no expense spared – spared, that was, ever since Sam had returned to civilian life after a five-month disappearing act. As a matter of course, with every potential employee of his firm, Pinkus always studied the personal and academic histories of each so as to avoid heartbreak or a mistake. Young Devereaux's résumé had caught his eye as well as his curiosity, and he had frequently driven by the old house in Weston, wondering what secrets were held within its Victorian walls.

The father, Lansing Devereaux III, had been a scion of the Boston Brahmin élite on a par with the Cabots and the Lodges, but with one glaring aberration. He was a bold risktaker in the world of high finance, far more capable of losing money than hoarding it. He had been a good man, if somewhat wild and tempestuous, a hard worker who had opened doors of opportunity for many, but for himself saw too few initiatives come to fruition. While watching a stock market report on television, he had died of a stroke when Sam

24

was a boy of nine, leaving his widow and his son a fine name, a grand residence, and insufficient insurance to maintain the life-style to which they were accustomed and the appearance of which Eleanor refused to abandon.

As a result, Samuel Lansing Devereaux became that contradiction among the wealthy, a scholarship boy who waited on tables at Phillips Andover. While his classmates attended proms, he tended a snack bar at those proms; and when his increasingly distant acquaintances in the social set entered regattas on the Cape, he worked on the roads they travelled leading to Dennis and Hyannis. He also worked on his studies like a young man possessed, fully understanding that academia was the only route back to the affluent world of the ancestral Devereauxes. Besides, he was sick of being merely an observer of the good life instead of a participant.

More generous scholarships followed at Harvard and its Law School, his expense monies supplemented quite nicely by a heavy schedule of tutoring his brother and sister classmates, the preponderance of whom were the latter as there were frequently bonuses having nothing to do with finance. There followed an auspicious beginning at Aaron Pinkus Associates, menacingly interrupted by the United States Army, which in the era of massive Pentagon expansion desperately needed all the lawyers it could dredge up to forestall wholesale indictments of its procurement personnel on bases here and abroad. The fascist military computers unearthed a long-forgotten deferment granted one Samuel Lansing Devereaux, and the armed services gained a handsome, if pathetic, soldier, but one with a superb legal brain, which they used and obviously abused.

What had happened to him? questioned Pinkus in the silence of his mind. *What horrible events had taken place years ago that had come back to haunt him now? To warp and, at times, to short-circuit that extraordinary mind, a mind that cut through legalistic abstractions and made common sense out of the most abstruse constitutional interpretations so that judges and juries alike were in awe of his erudition and his deeply penetrating analyses.*

Something had happened, concluded Aaron, approaching

the huge front door replete with antique bevelled panes of glass in the upper panel. Also, where did Sam ever get the money to restore the damn house to begin with? Pinkus was, indeed, generous with his outstanding and, in truth, his favourite employee but not to the extent that he could pour a minimum of a hundred thousand dollars into the renovation of the family residence. Where had the cash come from? Drugs? Laundering money? Insider trading? Selling illegal armaments abroad? None made sense where Sam Devereaux was concerned. He'd be a total bust at any of those endeavours; he was a *klutz* where subterfuge was concerned. He was – God in heaven be praised – a truly honest man in a world of worms. This judgement, however, did not explain the apparently inexplicable – the *money*. Several years ago when Aaron had casually mentioned the fine improvements made on the house which he drove by frequently on his way home, Samuel had, with equal casualness, offered that a well-to-do Devereaux relative had passed away and left his mother a very decent bequest.

Pinkus had pored over the probate rolls and the taxable inheritance records only to discover that there was no such relative and no such bequest. And he knew deep in his religious heart that whatever was plaguing Sam now had something to do with his unexplained affluence. What *was* it? Perhaps the answer was hidden inside this grand old house. He rang the bell – bass-toned chimes, naturally.

A full minute passed before the door was opened by a plumpish, middle-aged maid in a starched green and white uniform. 'Sir?' she said, somewhat more coldly than was necessary, thought Aaron.

'Mrs Devereaux,' replied Pinkus. 'I believe she's expecting me.'

'Oh, *you're* the one,' responded the maid, perhaps even more icily, considered Aaron. 'Well, I hope you like the damn camomile tea, buster, it sure isn't my taste. Come on in.'

'Thank you.' The celebrated, but less than physically imposing, attorney walked into the foyer of Norwegian rose marble, his mental computer estimating its extravagant cost.

'And what variety do you prefer, my dear?' he asked pointlessly.

'A cup laced with rye!' exclaimed the woman, laughing raucously and jabbing her elbow into Pinkus's frail shoulder.

'I'll remember that when we have high tea at the Ritz some afternoon.'

'*That'll* be the Jesus-lovin' day, won't it, little fella?'

'I beg your pardon?'

'Go on through those double doors over there,' continued the maid, gesturing to her left. 'The hoity-toity's waiting for you. Me, I got work to do.' With that command cum explanation the woman turned and walked without precision across the expensive floor, disappearing beyond the elegantly balustraded winding staircase.

Aaron approached the closed double doors, opened the right panel, and peered inside. At the far end of the ornate Victorian room sat Eleanor Devereaux on a brocaded white couch, a glistening silver tea service on the coffee table in front of her. She was as he remembered her, an erect fine-boned woman with an ageing face that must have launched a thousand yachts in its prime, and with large blue eyes that said far more than she would ever reveal.

'Mrs Devereaux, how good to see you again.'

'Mr Pinkus, how good to see *you*. Please come and sit down.'

'Thank you.' Aaron walked inside, conscious of the huge, priceless Oriental rug beneath his feet. He lowered himself into the white-brocaded armchair to the right of the sofa, the spot indicated by a nod of Mrs Devereaux's aristocratic head.

'From the rather frantic laughter I heard in the hallway,' said the grand lady, 'I gather you've met cousin Cora, our maid.'

'Your cousin . . . ?'

'If she weren't, do you think she'd last five minutes in this house? In a family sense, being more fortunate imposes certain obligations, doesn't it?'

'*Noblesse oblige*, madam. And very nicely said.'

'Yes, I suppose so, but I wish to hell nobody ever had to say

27

it. One day she'll choke on the whisky she steals and the obligation will be over, won't it?'

'A logical conclusion.'

'But you're not here to discuss Cora, are you? ... Tea, Mr Pinkus? Cream or lemon, sugar or no?'

'Forgive me, Mrs Devereaux, but I must resist. An old man's aversion to tannic acid.'

'Good! An old woman's, too. This fourth little dear I fill myself.' Eleanor picked up a Limoges teapot to the left of the silver service. 'A fine thirty-year-old brandy, Mr Pinkus, and *its* kind of acid couldn't hurt anybody. I also wash the damn thing myself so Cora doesn't get ideas.'

'My very favourite, Mrs Devereaux,' said Aaron. 'And I shan't tell my doctor so *he* won't get any ideas.'

'*L'chaim*, Mr Pinkus,' toasted Eleanor Devereaux, pouring them each a good dram and then raising her teacup.

'*A votre santé*, Mrs Devereaux,' said Aaron.

'No, no, Mr Pinkus. The Devereaux name may be French, but my husband's ancestors migrated to England in the fifteenth century – actually they were captured during the battle of Crécy but stayed long enough to raise their own armies and be knighted by the crown. We're High Anglican.'

'So what should I say?'

'How about "Up your banners"?'

'That's religious?'

'If you're convinced He's on your side, I imagine it is.' They both sipped and replaced their cups in the delicate saucers. 'That's a good beginning, Mr Pinkus. And now shall we plunge right into the puzzling issue at hand – namely, my son?'

'I believe it would be prudent,' nodded Aaron, glancing at his watch. 'Right now he's about to go into a conference entailing an extremely complex litigation that should take the better part of several hours. However, as we both agreed over the telephone, these past months he's frequently displayed erratic behaviour; he might very well leave the conference in midsentence and drive home.'

'Or go to a museum or a movie or, God forbid, to the

airport and take a plane to heaven knows where,' interrupted Eleanor Devereaux. 'I'm all too aware of Sam's impetuous proclivities. Only two Sundays ago I returned from church and discovered a note that he'd left for me on the kitchen table. In it he wrote that he was out and would call me later. He did so during dinner. From Switzerland.'

'Our experiences are too painfully similar, so I will not take up our time recounting my and my firm's variations.'

'Is my son in danger of losing his position, Mr Pinkus?'

'Not if *I* can help it, Mrs Devereaux. I've looked too long and too hard for a successor to give up so easily. But I'd be less than honest if I told you that the status quo was acceptable. It isn't. It's not fair to Sam or to the firm.'

'I'm in total agreement. What can we do – what can *I* do?'

'At the risk of presuming on the privilege of privacy, and I do so only out of affection and professional concern of the highest regard, what can you tell me about your son that might shed light on his increasingly enigmatic behaviour? I assure you that whatever is said between us will remain in the strictest confidence – as it were, a lawyer-client relationship, although I would never presume to be your attorney of choice.'

'Dear Mr Pinkus, a number of years ago I could never presume to approach you to be my attorney of choice. Had I felt that I was capable of paying your fee, I might have salvaged large sums of money owed my husband's estate after his death.'

'Oh . . . ?'

'Lansing Devereaux steered a great many of his colleagues into immensely lucrative situations with the understanding of reasonable participation after their venture capital was recouped. Once he died, only a few honoured those agreements, a precious few.'

'Agreements? *Written* agreements?'

'Lansing was not the most precise person when it came to specifics. However, there were minutes of meetings, synopses of business conversations, that sort of thing.'

'You have copies of these?'

'Of course. I was told they were worthless.'

'Your son, Samuel, confirmed that judgment?'

'I've never showed him those papers and I never will . . . He had a rather painful adolescence in some regards, no doubt character building, but why open healed wounds?'

'One day we may go back to those "worthless" papers, Mrs Devereaux, but at the moment let's return – to the moment. What happened to your son in the army? Have you any idea?'

'He had a "rather good show," as the British say. He was a legal officer both here and overseas and, I'm told, did outstanding work in the Far East. When he was discharged, he was an adjutant in the office of the Inspector General with the temporary rank of major. You don't do much better than that.'

'The Far East?' said Aaron, his antennae picking up a nuance. 'What did he do in the Far East?'

'China, of course. You probably wouldn't remember because his contribution was "played down," as they say politically, but he negotiated the release of that crazy American general in Beijing, the one who shot the . . . private parts . . . off a venerated statue in the Forbidden City.'

'"Madman" *MacKenzie Hawkins?*'

'Yes, I believe that was his name.'

'The most certifiable lunatic of the lunatic *fringe?* The gorilla's guerrilla who almost plunged the entire planet into World War *Three?* Sam represented *him?*'

'Yes. In China. Apparently he did a fine job.'

Aaron swallowed several times before he found his voice again. 'Your son never mentioned any of this to me,' he said, barely audibly.

'Well, Mr Pinkus, you know the military. So much is hush-hush, as I understand it.'

'Hush-hush, mush-mush,' mumbled Boston's celebrated attorney, in his voice a Talmudic prayer. 'Tell me, Mrs Devereaux, did Sammy –'

'Sam or Samuel, Mr Pinkus.'

'Yes, of course . . . Did Sam ever mention this General Hawkins to you after his separation from the army?'

'Not with that title or that name, and never when he was entirely sober ... I should explain that before he was discharged and came back to Boston, somewhat later than we expected, I should add –'

'Don't add to me, Mrs Devereaux. Explain to the deli that supplied fifty pounds of lox why he never showed up.'

'I beg your pardon?'

'It's insignificant. What were you saying?'

'Well, a colonel in the Inspector General's office phoned me and told me that Sam had been put through "pressure-point-max" in China. When I asked him what that meant, he became rather abusive and said that as a "decent army wife" I should understand. And when I explained that I wasn't Sam's wife but his mother, that very abusive man said something to the effect that he "figured the clown was a little weird," and told me that I should expect a couple of months of mood swings and conceivably some heavy drinking.'

'What did you say to that?'

'I wasn't married to Lansing Devereaux without learning a few things, Mr Pinkus. I know damned well that when a man gets broiled because the pressures become too much, it's a reasonable petcock to let off steam. Those Janie-come-lately liberated females should give a little in that department. The man still has to keep the lion from invading the cave; that hasn't changed, and biologically it shouldn't. He's the poor fool who has to take the heat – physically, morally and legally.'

'I'm beginning to see where Sam gets his acumen.'

'Then you'd be wrong, Aaron – may I call you Aaron?'

'With the greatest of my pleasure ... Eleanor.'

'You see, "acumen" or perception or whatever you want to call it, can only be useful if there's imagination first. That's what my Lansing had, only the macho times restricted my supplying a stronger balance, the supplemental caution, if you like.'

'You're a remarkable woman ... Eleanor.'

'Another brandy, Aaron?'

'Why not? I'm a student in the presence of a teacher of

things I have never really considered. I may go home to my wife and fall on my knees.'

'Don't overplay it. We like to believe we're manipulators.'

'Back to your son,' said Pinkus, sipping his brandy in two swallows rather than one. 'You say he didn't refer to General Hawkins by name or by title, but you implied that he *did* allude to him ... when not necessarily sober, which is perfectly understandable. What did he say?'

'He'd ramble on about "the Hawk," that's what he called him,' mused Eleanor softly, her head arched back against the brocaded sofa. 'Sam said he was a legitimate hero, a military genius abandoned by the very people who once praised him as their spokesman, their idol, but who fled from him the moment he became an embarrassment. An embarrassment despite the fact that in his actions he was fulfilling their fantasies, their dreams. But he was doing it for real, and that terrified them, because, again, they knew that their fantasies, if acted upon, might lead to disaster. Like most fanatics who've never been in a real fight, they find embarrassment and death unattractive.'

'And *Sam?*'

'He claimed he never agreed with the Hawk, never wanted to be associated with him, but was somehow forced to – how I don't know. Sometimes when he just wanted to talk, he'd make up incredible stories, pure nonsense, like meeting hired killers at night on a golf course – he actually named a country club on Long Island.'

'Long Island, as in New York?'

'Yes. And how he negotiated contracts worth a great deal of money with British traitors in London's Belgrave Square and with former Nazis on chicken farms in Germany ... even Arab sheiks in the desert who were actually slumlords in Tel Aviv and wouldn't permit Egypt's army to shell their properties during the Yom Kippur war. *Insane* stories, Aaron, I tell you they were – *are* – totally mad.'

'Totally mad,' repeated Pinkus quietly, weakly, a knot forming in his stomach. 'You say "are"? He still tells these crazy stories?'

'Not as much as he used to, but yes, when he's terribly distressed or has had that extra martini he didn't need, and wanders down from his lair.'

'His lair, like in cave, perhaps?'

'That's what he calls it, his "château's lair."'

'"Château," like in a very big house or a castle?'

'Yes, he even speaks now and then of a great château in Zermatt, Switzerland, and of his "Lady Anne," and "Uncle Zio" – pure unadulterated fantasies! I believe the word is "nuts."'

'I sincerely hope so,' mumbled Pinkus.

'I beg your pardon?'

'Oh, nothing. Does Samuel spend much time in his "lair," Eleanor?'

'He never leaves it except for an occasional dinner with me. It's actually the east wing of the house, shut off from the rest of us with its own entrance and facilities – two bedrooms, office, kitchen – the usual amenities. Even his own cleaning service – oddly enough, they're Muslims.'

'His own apartment, really.'

'Yes, and he thinks he has the only keys –'

'But he doesn't?' asked Aaron quickly.

'Good heavens, no. The insurance people insisted that Cora and I should have access. Cora stole his key ring one morning and had duplicates made ... Aaron *Pinkus!* Eleanor Devereaux looked into the attorney's deep-set eyes and saw the message in them. 'Do you really think we might learn something by ... by going through the château's lair? Isn't that illegal?'

'You're his mother, my dear lady, and you're justifiably concerned about his current state of mind. That's a calling beyond any law. However, before you make that decision, one or two more questions ... This house, this grand old house, has had many splendid things done to it over the past years. From the outside alone, I judged the expenditure to be in the neighbourhood of a hundred thousand dollars. Now seeing the inside, I'd have to place the figure many times that. Where did the money come from? Did Sam tell you?'

'Well, not in so many words, that is not precisely . . . He said that while he was in Europe on this very secret mission after his discharge, he invested in some works of art, newly discovered religious artefacts actually, and in a matter of months the market exploded and he did enormously well.'

'I see,' said Pinkus, the knot in his stomach tightening, but nothing clear, only the rumbling of distant thunder in his mind. 'Religious artefacts . . . And this "Lady Anne" you say he talked about. What *did* he say?'

'It was all pure rubbish. In my son's delusions, or deliriums, if you will, this Lady Anne, this fantasy of his that he calls the perpetual love of his existence on earth, left him and ran away with a pope.'

'Oh, dear God of Abraham,' whispered Pinkus, reaching for his teacup.

'We of the High Church of England can't really accept that connection, Aaron. Henry the Eighth aside, the apostasy of any pontiff's infallibility simply doesn't wash. He's a reasonable, if somewhat pretentious, symbol, but not a scratch more.'

'I think it's time you made your decision, dear Eleanor,' said Pinkus, swallowing the rest of his brandy, wishing the spreading pain in his stomach would go away. 'To glance over the château's lair, I mean.'

'You really think it might help us?'

'I'm not sure what I think, but I *am* sure that we'd better.'

'Come along then.' The Lady Devereaux rose from the couch, a touch unsteadily, and gestured towards the double doors. 'The keys are in a flower pot in the foyer. "Flower pot in the foyer," that's a hell of a mouthful, isn't it? Try it backwards, Aaron.'

'Foyer, flowerflot, flowernot, floyer,' attempted Pinkus, getting to his feet, not entirely sure where they were.

They approached the thick heavy door of Samuel Lansing Devereaux's château's lair, and Sam's mother inserted the key with the gentle assistance of the man who was now her attorney of choice. They entered the sanctum sanctorum, walking down a narrow corridor that opened on to a wider hallway, the rays of the afternoon sun streaming through an imposing, seemingly impenetrable, glass-panelled door on the left, which was the apartment's separate entrance. They turned right, and the first open door they came to revealed a darkened room; the venetian blinds were securely down and closed.

'What's in here?' asked Aaron.

'I believe it's his office,' replied Eleanor, blinking. 'I haven't been up here since I can't remember when – probably when the construction was finished and Sam showed me through.'

'Let's take a look. Do you know where the lights are?'

'The switch is usually on the wall.' It was, and three floor lamps lit up the three visible walls of a large pine-panelled office. The walls themselves, however, could barely be seen as they were covered with framed photographs and, contrarily, Scotch-taped newspaper articles, many askew as if hastily, perhaps angrily, stuck to the surfaces between the profusion of photographs. 'This place is a bloody mess!' exclaimed the mother of the inhabitant. 'I'll insist he clean it up!'

'I wouldn't even consider it,' remarked Pinkus, approaching the nearest newspaper clippings on the left wall. In the main, they depicted a white-habited nun dispensing food and clothing to indigent people – white, black, and Hispanic – in various parts of the world. *Sister Anne the Benevolent Carries Her Message to All Points of the Globe*, cried one headline over a photograph of a slum in Rio de Janeiro, the mountain crucifix seen clearly in the upper distance of that jet-set city. The other clippings were a variation of the same theme – photos of a markedly attractive nun in Africa, Asia, Central America and the leper islands in the Pacific. *Sister Anne, Sister of Charity, Sister of Hope*, and finally, *Anne the Benevolent, a Candidate for Sainthood?*

Aaron, putting on his steel-rimmed glasses, studied the photographs. They were all taken at some extravagant retreat reeking of edelweiss, the Alps generally in the background, the subjects in the photographs happy and carefree, the enjoyment of life lighting up their faces. Several were instantly recognizable: a somewhat younger Sam Devereaux;

35

the tall aggressive figure of the maniac general, 'Madman' MacKenzie Hawkins; an ash-blonde woman in shorts and a halter – voluptuous, indeed, and unmistakeably Anne-the-Benevolent; and a fourth figure, a stout, smiling, jovial fellow in a short chef's apron that barely concealed his lederhosen. Who *was* he? The face was familiar but – no, *no, NO!*

'The God of Abraham has deserted us,' whispered Aaron Pinkus, trembling.

'What in the name of the Celtics are you talking about?' asked Eleanor Devereaux.

'You probably wouldn't remember for it meant nothing to you,' answered Aaron rapidly, unsteadily, a distinct quiver in his soft voice. 'But a number of years ago the Vatican was in disarray – financial disarray. Monies were flowing out of its treasury in . . . in megabuckets, supporting causes so unlikely as third-rate opera companies and carnivals and houses throughout Europe to rehabilitate prostitutes, all manner of *insanities*. The people thought the Pope had gone *crazy*, that he was, as they say, *pazzo!* Then, just before the Eternal City's complete collapse, which would have resulted in panic throughout the investment world, everything suddenly returned to normal. The Pontiff was back in control, his old self! The media everywhere said it was as if he had been *two people* – one a *pazzo*, the other the fine good man they all knew and loved.'

'My dear Mr Pinkus, you're not making the slightest bit of sense.'

'Look, *look!*' cried Aaron, pointing at a smiling, fleshed-out face in one of the photographs. 'That's *him!*'

'Who?'

'The Pope! That's where the money came from. The ransom! The press was right, they *were* two people! General Hawkins and your son *kidnapped* the *Pope!* . . . Eleanor, *Eleanor?*' Aaron turned from the wall.

The Lady Devereaux had collapsed to the floor unconscious.

CHAPTER FOUR

'*Nobody's* that clean,' said Director Mangecavallo quietly, his voice laced with incredulity as he addressed the two dark-suited men seated across the table in the DCI's dimly lit kitchen in McLean, Virginia. 'It's not natural, you know what I mean? Maybe you didn't scrounge around hard enough, huh, Fingers?'

'I tell you, Vinnie, I was shocked,' replied the short obese man who answered to the name of Fingers as he touched the knot of his white silk tie that fell over his black shirt. 'Like you say, it ain't natural – it ain't even *human*. What kind of world do these high-type judges live in? One with no germs, maybe?'

'You didn't answer my question,' interrupted Vincent softly, arching his brows and quickly shifting his penetrating gaze to his second visitor. 'What do you say, Meat? You boys aren't getting sloppy, are you?'

'Hey, *Vin*,' protested the large, barrel-chested guest, his heavy hands spread out in front of him, partially obscuring the red tie above his pink shirt. 'A first class – *world* class – job we did, what can I tell ya? The high-types called for it, right? We even brought in Hymie Goldfarb's boys in Atlanta, and who better to get the goods on a saint, am I right or not?'

'Yeah, Hymie's boys know the tunnels, no question,' agreed the CIA director, pouring himself another glass of Chianti and removing a Monte Cristo cigar from his shirt pocket. 'A lot better than all the Feds in Hooverville. They dug us up garbage on a hundred and thirty-seven congressmen and twenty-six senators that guaranteed my confirmation, along with a little largesse spread around, of course.'

'Largest what, Vinnie?' asked Fingers.

'*Largesse* – forget it . . . I just can't figure it. Every *one* of these six squirrelly judges got *nuthin'* we can tap into? That's extraterrestrial!' Mangecavallo got up from the table and lit his cigar. He paced back and forth in front of a darkened wall upon which hung alternating prints of saints, popes, and vegetables until he suddenly stopped, a cloud of smoke ringing his skull like a halo from way down under. 'Let's go back to the basics,' he said, standing motionless. 'Let's really *look*.'

'At what, Vinnie?'

'These four or five maybe liberal clowns who can't think straight. What's with them that Goldfarb's people couldn't find? . . . What about the big black cat? Maybe he ran numbers as a kid, did anyone think of that? Maybe no one went back far enough. That could be the mistake!'

'He was an acolyte and a choirboy, Vin. Right down the pike, a real angel, plus a big, big brain.'

'How about the lady judge? She's a big cannoli, right? That means her husband has to shut up and pretend he *likes* her being the big cannoli – which he can't nohow because he's a *man*. Maybe she doesn't feed him and he's mad like hell but can't say anything. People keep stuff like that quiet.'

'It's also a wash, Vin,' said Meat, shaking his head sadly. 'He sends her flowers every day at the office and tells everybody how proud he is of her. It could be legit on accounta he's a big avvocato himself and he ain't gonna make no enemy on that court, even his own wife.'

'*Shit!* . . . Hey, that Irish drink of water, maybe he has a couple too many like a lot of Micks do after their big parade. How about *that?* We could build a little file – top secret, national security, that sort of thing. We buy a couple a dozen witnesses who state they've seen him fried and gurgling in his suds after he leaves the office. It could *work*. Also, with his name we could add a few girlies. It's a *natural!*'

'It's snake eyes, Vin,' countered Meat, sighing and again

38

shaking his head. 'The Irish guy's so Clorox he makes the sheets squeak. He's never been known to have more than a glass of white wine and girlies aren't even in his ballpark.'

'Something *there*, maybe?'

'You're reaching, Vin. He's Boy Scout time.'

'Double shit . . . All right, all *right*. We don't touch the two WASPs because our people are making nice inroads with the banking boys in the better part of town. There should be no offence to the country club set, that's the word. I don't like it, but I accept it . . . So we come to our own *paisan*.'

'A bad person, Vinnie!' interrupted Fingers angrily. 'He's been very rough on a lot of our boys – like he didn't even *know* us, you know what I mean?'

'Well, maybe we'll let him know *we* know who *he* is, how about that?'

'Okay, Vin, but how about what?'

'How the hell do *I* know? Goldfarb's boys should have come up with something, *anything*!. Like maybe he slugged a couple of nuns in parochial school, or he skimmed the collection plates at Mass so he could buy a Harley and join a motorcycle gang, whatever! I gotta think of *everything*? He's got a weakness, he has to. All fat *paisans* do!'

'Meat's kinda fat –'

'A lid, Fingers, a bean pole you're not.'

'You can't touch that *paisan*, Vin,' interjected the pink-shirted Meat. 'He's a real *erudito*, a man with so many big words he confuses the biggest brains and he's as clean as the bleached Mick, no action at all except maybe he irritates people by singing opera a lot in not too good a voice. Goldfarb's boys went after him first because, like most yarmulkes, they call themselves liberals and the heavy boy's not. They were like politically motivated, you know?'

'What the *hell* has politics got to do with *any* of this? We got a problem, the biggest problem this country has ever faced and we're chewing ass over *politics*?'

'Hey, Vinnie,' pleaded Fingers, 'you were the one who wanted the mud on these big judges, right?'

'Okay, *okay*!' said Mangecavallo, puffing on his cigar

erratically and returning to his chair at the kitchen table. 'I know when the bam-bams won't work, all *right*? So where are we? We gotta protect the country we love because without the country we love, we are out of *business*!. Do I make my case?'

'Oh, yeah,' said Fingers. 'I don't wanna live nowhere else.'

'I couldn't,' added Meat. 'What with Angelina and the seven kids, where could I go? Palermo's too hot, and I sweat, you know? Angie's even worse than me – *boy*, does she sweat! She can really stink up a room.'

'That's disgusting,' said Mangecavallo softly, his dark eyes levelled on his huge, pink-shirted associate. 'I mean really disgusting. How can you talk about the mother of your children like that?'

'It's not her fault, Vin. It's her *glands*.'

'You take the whole mozzarella, you know that, Meat? . . . *Basta*, this ain't gettin' us nowhere.' The CIA director again rose from the chair and paced angrily about the kitchen, puffing on his cigar and pausing long enough to briefly lift the lid of a steaming pot on the stove, only to drop it because of the scorching metal. 'What the hell is she cooking now? Looks like monkey brains.' He shook his hand in pain.

'Your maid, Vinnie?'

'Maid? *What* maid? You mean the *contessa* who sits around with Rosa knitting and talking, talking and knitting, like two old Sicilian broads trying to remember who humped who in Messina forty years ago! She don't cook – she don't cook and she don't do windows or the cans and together she and Rosa waddle around the supermarkets buying crap I wouldn't feed the cats.'

'Get rid of her, Vin.'

'Oh, funny *scungilli*, you! Rosa says she's like one of her sisters, only nicer and not so ugly . . . No, they can eat that *escremento* themselves, *we're* goin' out. National security emergency, you get my drift?'

'Got it, Vinnie,' affirmed Fingers, nodding his large head with the slightly irregular nose. 'Like when they say the "natives are restless," right?'

'*Jeez*, what the hell have natives got to do with – hold it . . . *hold it!* Natives. "Native American." That's *it*! . . . Maybe, like.'

'Like maybe what, Vin?'

'We can't scrounge out the judges, right?'

'Right, Vinnie.'

'So the Supreme Court could maybe dump us all in the toilet, right?'

'Right, Vin.'

'Not necessarily . . . Suppose, just *suppose*, this meatball Indian chief who could just maybe cause our biggest national security crisis in history is a very bad man, a screwed-up individual with no love in his heart, only evil intentions, you see what I mean? Suppose he don't care crapolla about his Wild West Indian brothers but just wants a motherlode for himself with all the publicity that goes with it? We knock his faked-up good character off, we knock his case off. It's done all the time!'

'I dunno, Vin,' countered Meat haltingly. 'You yourself told me that when you questioned that White House legal brain – the one with the coloured chalk – he said that five or six of those judges admitted crying their eyes out when they read this Sitting Bull's case. How there was a whole litany – you said "litany," Vin, I had to look it up – of deceit and dishonesty, even killing and starving whole tribes in the original US of A. Now, you, me, and Fingers here – you bein' the smartest, naturally, and me maybe pretty far behind and Fingers not actually in the running – but do any of us figure a crumb phony could flatten out the brains of these high-type big judges with pure bullshit? It don't make sense.'

'We're not looking for sense, *amico*, we're looking for a way out of a possible national emergency, get that through your skull. And right now its name is this Thunder Head. Send Goldfarb's boys out to Nebraska!'

'Nebraska . . . *Nebraska* . . . Nebraska,' intoned Hyman Goldfarb into the telephone, as if the state were incorporated into an Old Testament psalm. Seated behind his elegant desk in his elegant office on Atlanta's very elegant Phipps Plaza, he rolled his eyes upward and brought them down to gaze fondly at the slender, well-dressed, middle-aged couple sitting in front of him – middle-aged being mid-forties, only several years younger than the muscular, tanned Goldfarb, who was himself attired in a tight-fitting white linen suit that framed his still awesome athlete's body. 'I should once again send my best people out to this – to say the least – this out-of-the-way Nebraska so they can chase after a fog, a mist . . . a cloud of vapour who calls himself Thunder Head, chief of the Wopotamis? Is that what you're saying? Because if it is, I should have been a rabbi which I studied for instead of a football player which entailed very little knowledge.' Hyman Goldfarb paused, listening, and every now and then removing the phone from his ear and sighing, then finally, obviously, interrupting the caller.

'Please pay attention to me and let me save you some money, will you do that? . . . Thank you, just listen. If there *is* a Chief Thunder Head, he's nowhere to be found. My people cannot say he *doesn't* exist, for whenever they mentioned the name among what's left of the Wopotamis on their pathetic reservation, they were met with silence, interspersed with incomprehensible whispers in the Wopotami language. They tell me that suddenly you think you're in a cathedral cut out of a scrawny forest primeval where there's far too much available alcohol, and you begin to believe that this Thunder Head is more of a myth than a reality. An icon, perhaps, a tribal god sculpted on a totem pole to which his believers make obeisance, but not a human being. In plain words, I do not believe such a person exists . . . What *do* I think, is that your question – and it's not necessary to shout? Quite frankly, my excitable friend, I believe Chief Thunder Head is a symbolic amalgam of – no that is *not* a reference to sexual preference – of narrowly defined special interests, no doubt benevolent, and centred about our government's generally unfortunate treatment of the American Indian. Perhaps a small group of legal scholars from Berkeley or NYU who've unearthed sufficient precedents to embarrass the lower courts. A scam, my friend, pure and simple a scam, but a very *brilliant* scam.'

Once more Goldfarb pulled the telephone away from his ear and briefly closed his eyes as the voice over the line metallically filled the elegant office. '*What kind of talk is that?*' roared the caller. '*This great country could be in a big national crisis, and you got nothin' to offer but "presents" that don't make no sense? Well, lemme tell ya', Mister Big Linebacker, the man in Langley, Virginia, who you can't talk to nohow, says you better come up with somethin' on this Thunder Head and come up quick! I mean none of us want to live in Palermo, you know what I mean?*'

'Redundancy aside, "*Per cento anno*, signore,"' said Goldfarb. 'We'll be in touch.' The CIA consultant replaced the telephone, leaned back in his swivel chair and sighed audibly as he addressed the attractive couple in front of his desk. 'Why me, oh Lord, why me?' he asked, shaking his head. 'You're positive you're right?'

'I wouldn't put it so strongly, Hyman,' replied the woman in a clipped British accent that bespoke several generations of expensive breeding. 'No, we're not *positive*, I don't think anybody could be, but if there *is* a Thunder Head, he's simply nowhere to be found, as you so clearly explained to the gentleman on the phone.'

'I used your words, of course,' added Goldfarb. 'And I question the title of "gentleman."'

'With good reason, I suspect,' said the woman's male companion, also obviously British. 'We employed Plan *C*. We were Cambridge-based anthropologists studying a great if diminished tribe whose ancestors were brought over to the Crown by Walter Raleigh in the early seventeenth century. If there really *is* a Thunder Head, by all logic he should have rushed forth to claim the Crown's recognition, as well as the long-buried remittance, which at the time was no doubt minor, but by any standard an enormous sum today. He didn't; therefore, our conclusion: he doesn't exist.'

'But the brief to the Supreme Court *does*,' insisted the consultant. 'It's *crazy*.'

'Simply incredible,' agreed the Englishman. 'Where do we

go from here, Hyman? I gather you're "under the gun," as we used to say in Her Majesty's Secret Service, although I always thought it was a rather banal expression conveying more melodrama than was necessary.'

'It both is and it isn't,' said Goldfarb. 'We're dealing with an off-the-wall megillah, but it's still an extremely dangerous situation . . . What are those judges *thinking* of?'

'Justice and the law, I dare say,' offered the woman. 'At a cost we all recognize as beyond the extraordinary. Regardless, dear Hy, and forgive me for saying it, but the man on the phone you say is no gentleman is basically correct. Whoever's hiding behind the mantle of this Thunder Head – or whoever *they* are – that's the key.'

'But Daphne, by your own admission, you can't *find* him.'

'Then perhaps we didn't look hard enough, Hyman. Eh, Reggie?'

'Dear girl! We trekked all over that blasted backwater bog with horrible lodgings and *no* civilized facilities, I remind you, and got absolutely nowhere. No one made any sense at all!'

'Yes, I know, dear, but there was *one* who didn't *want* to make sense, do you recall my mentioning it?'

'Oh, him,' replied the Englishman, his tone dismissing the memory. 'Nasty young fellow, quite sullen, really.'

'*Who?*' Goldfarb instantly sat forward.

'Not sullen, Reggie, simply uncommunicative, incoherent, actually, but he understood everything we were saying. It was in his eyes.'

'Who *was* he?' pressed the CIA consultant.

'An Indian brave – that's the word, I think – in his early twenties, I'd judge. He claimed not to understand English very well and just shrugged and shook his head when we asked him several questions. I didn't think much about it at the time – the young are so hostile these days, aren't they?'

'He was indecently dressed, if I do say,' interrupted Reginald. 'Hardly more than a loin cloth, really. Rather disgusting. And when he leaped up on that horse, I can tell you he betrayed a definite lack of equestrian skill.'

'What *are* you talking about?' asked a bewildered Goldfarb.

'He fell off,' answered Daphne. 'Dressage is hardly his strong suit.'

'Wait a minute, *wait* a minute!' Goldfarb's broad chest was halfway across the desk. 'You say you didn't think much about this, this young Indian at the time, but you're thinking about him now. Why?'

'Well, in light of the circumstances, dear Hy, I'm trying to think of *everything*.'

'What you mean is he may know something he didn't want to tell you?'

'It's only a possibility –'

'Do you think you could find him again?'

'Oh, yes. I saw which tepee he came out of, which one belonged to him.'

'Tepee? They live in *tepees*?'

'Well, naturally, Hyman,' replied Reginald. 'They're Indians, chap. Redskins, as you say in your cinema.'

'There's also a rotten whitefish somewhere,' said Goldfarb, picking up the telephone and dialling. '*Tepees!* Nobody sleeps in tepees any more! ... Don't unpack,' he added to the couple, instantly shifting his attention back to the phone. 'Manny? ... Reach "The Shovel" and get over to the field. You're taking the Lear out to the state of Nebraska.'

The young Indian brave, naked but for an odd-looking short leather skirt, stood outside the large decorated tepee and shouted. 'I want my clothes back, *Mac*! You can't *do* this. I'm sick of it – we're *all* sick of it! We *don't* sleep on dirt in these dumb tents and we *don't* burn our hands trying to cook over camp fires and we *do* use toilets, not the goddamn woods! And while I'm at it, you can take that miserable, distempered nag and ship him back to Geronimo! I *hate* horses and I don't ride – none of us do, for God's sake. We drive Chevys and Fords and a couple of old Cadillacs, but *not horses*! ... Mac, are you *listening* to me? Come on, Mac, *answer* me! ... Look, we appreciate the money and your good intentions – even the nutty clothes from that costume factory in Hollywood, but it's all gone too far, can't you *see* that?'

45

'Did *you* ever see the movie they made about me?' came the bellowing roar from within the closed tepee. 'The son of a bitch playing me had the biggest lisp I ever heard! Embarrassing, *real* embarrassing!'

'Mac, that's what I'm talking about. This crazy *charade* you're putting us through is embarrassing to *us*. We're going to get shot down and be the laughing stock of all the reservations!'

'Not yet you're not – *we're* not! Although the term "shot down" is kinda interesting.'

'No, it isn't, you lotus brain! It's been over three months now and we haven't heard a *word*. Three months of insanity, running around half naked or in costumes with beads that scratch our asses like hell, and burning our fingers and getting poison ivy in places *also* embarrassing whenever we have to run into the woods –'

'Slit trenches have always been an acceptable part of military life, boy. And you can't argue with the separation of the sexes – the army wouldn't have it any other way.'

'This *isn't* the army and I'm *not* a soldier and I want my *clothes* back –'

'Any day now, son!' interrupted the harsh, gravelled voice inside the tepee. '*You'll* see!'

'No, you lunatic, not any *day* or any month or any *year*! Those old farts on the Supreme Court are probably sitting around in chambers laughing their heads off and I won't be able to practise in the loosest court in American Samoa . . . Come on *Mac*! Admit it, it's over – it was a hell of an idea and I've got to say there was maybe a grain, a *grain*, maybe, of substance, but now it's become ridiculous.'

'Our good people have suffered for a hundred and twelve years, boy. Suffered at the hands of the brutal, avaricious white man, and we shall be justly recompensed and *set free*! . . . What's a few more days?'

'Mac, you're not remotely related!'

'In this old soldier's heart we're *bonded*, son, and I won't let you down.'

'*Let* us down, *please*? Let *me* down, and give me my clothes back and tell those two idiots who follow me around to leave me alone!'

'You're too impatient, young fella, and I can't let you turn on our tribal brothers –'

'*Our . . . ?* Mac, you're certifiable, so let me lay one on you, brother *brave*. It's a little matter of a pro forma judicial statute of which you may not be aware, but you damn well should be. Four months ago when this whole whack-a-doo war dance started, you asked me if I'd passed my bar exam, and I told you that I was sure I had. Well, I'm still sure I passed the damn thing, but if you asked me to provide you with certification, I couldn't do it. You see, I haven't received formal notification from the Nebraska bar, and I may not for another two months, which is perfectly normal for the bar and perfectly impermissible where your legal *powwow* is concerned with the Supreme Court.'

'*What . . . ?*' came the prolonged disembowelling roar from behind the closed front flap of the tepee.

'That joint's a busy place, *brother*, and except under extraordinary circumstances which must be spelled out and approved, no unaccredited attorney may petition the Supreme Court, even as temporary counsel. I *told* you that. You're dead by default even if you were awarded a positive decision, which is about as likely as this Indian brave learning to ride a goddamned horse!'

The harrowing scream from within the cone of painted ersatz animal skins was longer than before and infinitely more heartrending. 'How could you *do* this?'

'*I* didn't do it, Mac, *you* did! I told you to officially list your attorney-of-record, but you said you couldn't because he was dead and you'd figure something out later, and in the meantime we'd use the *non-nomen* precedent from 1826.'

'*You* dug that one up!' cried the faceless roar.

'Yes, I did and you were grateful, and now I suggest you dig up your late attorney of research-and-record.'

'I can't.' The roar suddenly became the whimper of a bewildered kitten.

'Why not?'

'He won't talk to me.'

'I would hope to hell not! Christ, I don't mean his corpse, I mean his papers, his findings, interrogatories – his *research*. They're all acceptable.'

'He wouldn't like that.' The kitten was now a piping mouse.

'He wouldn't *know*! . . . Mac, listen to me. Sooner or later one of those judges' law clerks in DC will learn that I'm a kid barely out of law school with hardly six months of clerking myself, and he'll blow a shrill whistle. Even if you had a prayer, the lord god of the Court, Chief Justice Reebock, would throw a lightning bolt into it for defrauding his holy institution. Worse, for making fools of them, if even one or two corkscrews were leaning in your favour, which, as I say, is totally impossible. *Forget* it, Mac! It's *over*. Give me my clothes back, *okay*, and let me get out of here –'

'Where would you go, son?' The unseen piping mouse was getting out of the vocal cellar and climbing back up to a crescendo. 'I mean *where*, boy?'

'Maybe American Samoa with a forwarded certification from the Nebraska bar, who the hell knows?'

'I never thought I'd *say* this, son,' cried the faceless once more shouting voice from the tepee, 'because I really thought you had the right stuff, but I can see now that I can't bring you up to snuff!'

'Thanks for the rhyme, Mac. Now, how about my clothes?'

'You *got* 'em, you yellow-skinned coyote!' The fake animal skin flap opened and an assortment of Ivy League garments was hurled out of the dark space.

'That's redskin, Mac. Not yellow-skinned, remember?' The young loinclothed brave lurched for the flying shorts, shirt, grey flannel trousers and navy blue blazer. 'Thank you, Mac, I really *thank* you.'

'Not yet, boy, but you *will*. A good officer never forgets the grunts, no matter how unworthy they might appear in the heat of battle . . . You were a help, I'll say that, in the GHQ strategy sessions. Leave your forwarding address with that drunken flake you call Eagle Ass!'

'Eagle *Eyes*,' corrected the brave, discarding his loincloth and putting on his shorts. He reached for his Oxford blue shirt. 'And *you* gave him the booze – you gave everyone *cases* of booze – I never allowed so much.'

'Beware the sanctimonious Indian who turns on his tribe!' yelled the unseen manipulator of the Wopotamis.

'Fuck off, Mac!' cried the brave, shoving his feet into his Bally loafers and his striped tie into his pocket, and getting into his blazer. 'Where the hell's my Camaro?'

'Camouflaged beyond the east pasture, sixty running deer strides to the right of the August owl's tall pine.'

'Sixty *what? What* goddamned owl?'

'You never were too sharp in the field; Eagle Ass told me that himself.'

'Eagle *Eyes*, and he's my uncle and he hasn't inhaled a sober breath or seen straight since you got here! . . . East pasture? Where is it?'

'Check the sun, boy. It's the compass that never fails you, but make damn sure you ash up your weapons so the glares don't give you away.'

'*Certifiable!*' screamed the young brave of the Wopotamis as he fled due west.

At that moment, accompanied by a primordial roar of defiance, a tall figure strode out of the tepee, the flap whipping up and sticking to the exterior wall of animal hides. This giant of a man, gloriously resplendent in full flowing Indian headdress and beaded buckskins, all signifying his highest tribal office, squinted in the sunlight as he shoved a mutilated cigar into his mouth and began chewing on it furiously. His bronzed, leather-lined face and narrowed eyes betrayed an expression of consummate frustration – also perhaps a degree of fear.

'*Goddamn!*' swore MacKenzie Hawkins to himself. 'I never thought I'd ever have to do this.' The Hawk reached inside his painted buckskin doublet with the beaded yellow bolts of lightning across the chest and pulled out a cellular telephone. 'Boston area information? I want the number of the Devereaux residence, first name Sam –'

CHAPTER FIVE

Samuel Lansing Devereaux drove cautiously on the Waltham-Weston road at the height of the Friday evening rush hour exodus from Boston. As usual, he drove carefully, as though he were manoeuvring a tricycle through a battlefield of opposing tanks closing in for their thunderous kills, but tonight was worse than usual. It was not the traffic; that was maddeningly standard. It was the pulsating pain in his eyes along with the pounding in his chest and the moveable vacuum in his stomach, all the result of an acute seizure of depression. He found it almost impossible to keep his mind on the erratic rhythms of the surrounding vehicles, but forced himself to concentrate on those nearest him, hoping to heaven he stopped short of a collision. He kept the window open, his hand waving continuously, until a truck swerved so close that he touched its side view mirror; he shrieked and instinctively grabbed it, thinking for a moment he was watching his arm disappear over his hood.

There was nothing else for it, or, as the great French playwright phrased it – he could not actually remember the man's name or the exact phrase in French, but he knew the words said it all. Oh, *Christ*, he had to get home to his lair and let the music swell and the memories revive until the crisis passed! ... *Anouilh*, that was the goddamned playwright's name – and the phrase ... *Il n'y a rien* – hell, it sounded better in English than in the lousy French he could not recall: *There was nothing left but to scream*, that was it! Actually, it was pretty stupid, thought Sam. So he screamed and turned north into the Weston exit, only minimally aware of those drivers and passengers nearest his car who stared at him through their windows as if watching an act of sodomy between man and beast. The prolonged scream had to go; it was replaced by a wide grin worthy of Alfred E. Neuman as Devereaux pressed the accelerator and three cars crashed behind him.

It had all started within minutes after he left the office following an afternoon conference with a gaggle of related corporate executives whose single-family company was in deep shit if they did not take his advice. The problem was not in their criminality, it was in their stupidity that could not be prised away from their stubbornness until Sam had made it clear that if they did not follow his instructions, they could all look for different representation and he would visit each of them in the prison of his and her destination, but only on a social basis. Although somewhat obscure, the law *did* make it clear that grandfathers and grandmothers could not place their grandchildren – especially those between the ages of six months and twelve years – on the company's board of directors at salaries exceeding seven figures. He had weathered the onslaught of Irish indignation, accepted the eventuality of eternal damnation for shorting the bloodlines of the clan of Dongallen, and fled to his favourite bar two blocks from the firm of Aaron Pinkus Associates.

'Ahh, Sammy boyo,' had said the owner-barkeep as Devereaux slumped on the stool farthest from the entrance. 'It's been a rough day, it has, I can see it. I always know when one or two liquid remedies may lead to a couple more – you sit down at this end of the bar.'

'Do me a favour, O'Toole, and soften the brogue. I've spent damn near three hours with your crowd.'

'Oh, they're the worst, Sam, let me tell you! Especially the two-toilet variety, who are the only ones who can afford you fellas. Here, it's early, so let me pour you the usual and turn on the television and you take your mind off business ... There's no Sox game this afternoon, so I'll turn on the all-day news.'

'Thanks, Tooley.' Devereaux had accepted his drink with a grateful nod as the solicitous owner turned on the cable news network, which was apparently in the middle of a human interest segment, in this case depicting the good works of a supposedly obscure individual.

' ... *a woman whose selfless charity and kindness keeps her forever young, a face the angels kiss with the gift of youth and clear-eyed perseverance,*' proclaimed the sonorous announcer as the camera zoomed in on a white-habited nun dispensing gifts in a children's hospital located in some war-torn Third World country. '*Sister Anne the Benevolent, they call her,*' continued the vowel-rolling narrator, '*but that's all the world knows about her ... or will ever know from her own lips, we are told. What her true name is or where·she came from remains a mystery, a mystery wrapped in an enigma perhaps filled with unendurable pain and sacrifice –*'

'Mystery, my *ass*!' had screamed Samuel Lansing Devereaux, both leaping and falling off the barstool as he roared at the television screen. 'And the only unendurable pain is *mine*, you bitch!'

'Sammy, *Sammy!*' yelled Gavin O'Toole, racing down the length of the mahogany, waving both arms in a sincere effort to quiet his friend and customer. 'Shut the fuck up! The woman's a goddamned saint and my goddamned clientele ain't exactly all Protestant, do you get my goddamned message?' O'Toole had lowered his voice while pulling Devereaux over the bar – then he glanced around. '*Jesus*, a few of my daytime regulars are takin' exception to your words, Sammy! Don't worry, Hogan can handle them. Sit down and *shut up!*'

'Tooley, you don't *understand!*' cried the fine Boston lawyer, close to weeping. 'She's the enduring love of my life on earth –'

'That's better, that's much better,' whispered O'Toole. 'Keep it up.'

'You see, she was a *hooker* and I *saved* her!'

'Don't keep it up.'

'She ran off with Uncle Zio! *Our* Uncle Zio – he *corrupted* her!'

'Uncle *who*? What the hell are you talkin' about, boyo?'

'Actually, he was the *Pope*, and he messed up her head and he took her back to Rome, to the Vatican –'

'*Hogan!* Get over the wood and hold back the bastards! . . . Come on, Sammy, you're leavin' through the kitchen, the front door you'd never make!'

That innocent episode had brought on his acute depression, thought Devereaux as he sped north on the less travelled road to Weston. Couldn't the unknowing '*world*' understand that the '*mystery*' was not unknown to one lovesick, adoring Sam-the-lawyer-type, who had nurtured Anne-the-many-married-hooker from Detroit back into self-respect, but it was she who had slammed the gates shut on their marriage only to follow in the steps of crazy Zio? . . . Well, Uncle Zio hadn't actually been crazy, he was only misguided where the life of Samuel-my-son-the-fine-attorney was concerned. He was also Pope Francesco I, the most beloved Pope of the twentieth century who had permitted his own kidnapping on Rome's Via Appia Antica because he had been told he was dying, and it was better that his identical cousin, one Guido Frescobaldi from LaScala Minuscolo, be put on St Peter's throne and take radio instructions from the true pontiff somewhere in the Alps. It all had worked! For a while. Mac Hawkins and Zio for weeks on end would go up to the ramparts of Zermatt's Château Machenfeld and over the shortwave radio explain to the less than bright, tone-deaf Frescobaldi what next to do in the cause of the Holy See.

Then everything fell apart – with a thud that had to sonically rival the first creation of planet earth. The Alpine air restored Uncle Zio – Pope Francesco, of course – to his former healthy self, and conversely, Guido Frescobaldi accidentally fell on the private shortwave radio, his bulk smashing it to smithereens, and the Vatican went into an economic tailspin. The remedy was painful but obvious; however, far more painful to Sam Devereaux – far, *far* more painful – was the loss of his one true love, Anne-the-Rehabilitated, who had listened to all that crap Uncle Zio kept spewing quietly into her ear as they played chequers every morning. Instead of marrying one Samuel Lansing Devereaux, she opted for 'marrying' one Jesus Christ, whose credentials, Sam had to admit, were considerably more impressive than his own, although the earthly perks somewhat less so – immensely less so when one took into account the life that the glorious Anne-the-Rehabilitated had chosen. My *God*, Boston at its worst was better than leper colonies! Well, certainly most of the time.

Life marches on, Sam. It's combat all the way so don't let yourself be boondoggled if you lose a skirmish or two. Get your ass up and charge ahead!

Words from the lowliest lowlife in the universe, the ultimate, incontestable argument for sexual abstinence or stringent birth control. General MacKenzie Hawkins, Madman Mac the Hawk, scourge of sanity and destroyer of all things good and decent. Those fatuous words, that clichéd military psychobabble, were all the slugworm could offer during Sam's moments of desperate anguish.

She's leaving me, Mac. She's actually going with him!

Zio's a damn good man, son. He's a fine commander of his legions, and we who know the loneliness of command respect one another.

But, Mac, he's a priest, the big enchilada of priests, the Pope! They won't be able to dance, or cuddle, or have kids or any of those things!

Well, you're probably right about the last two, but Zio does a hell of a tarantella, or have you forgotten?

Nobody touches in tarantellas. They whirl around and kick up their legs but they don't come near each other!

Must be the garlic. Or maybe the legs.

You're not listening to me. This is the mistake of her life – you should know that! For God's sake, you were married to her, which hasn't made me entirely comfortable these past weeks.

Pull back your caissons, boy. I was married to all the girls and none of them came out the worst for it. Annie was the toughest – and considering her background, maybe it was to be expected – but she caught on to what I was trying to tell her.

What the hell was that, Mac?

That she could be better than herself, but still be herself.

Slugworm! Devereaux swung the wheel to the left so as to avoid an intruding guardrail on the right. *All the girls*, God, how did he *do* it? Four of the most entrancing and endowed women on earth had married the maniacal military delinquent and after each marriage had been – not amicably, but lovingly – terminated, the four divorcees had wilfully, enthusiastically banded together to form their own unique club which they called 'Hawkins's Harem.' At the press of the Hawk's button, they all rallied around to support their former husband, whatever the time, and wherever it was in the world. Jealousies? None whatsoever, for Mac had set them free, free from the ugly chains that had bound them before he came into their lives. Sam could accept all that, for throughout the events that led up to Château Machenfeld, each former wife had succoured him in his moments of hysterical crisis. Each had been not only compassionately – even passionately – warm in her efforts to extricate him from the impossible situations the Hawk had placed him in, but expert in the ways that led to his escape.

All had left their indelible marks on both his body and his mind, all were extraordinary memories, but the most glorious of all was the ash-blonde, statuesque Anne whose large blue eyes held an innocence far more real than the reality of her past. Her never-ending stream of hesitant questions on just about any topic imaginable was as startling as her voracious appetite for reading materials, so much of which she could not possibly understand but understand she eventually would if it took her a month on five pages. She was truly a lady making up for the lost years but never with a hint of pity for herself and always giving despite that which had been taken from her so brutally in the past. And, oh *God*, could she laugh, her eyes lighting up with mischievous humour, yet never mean, never at the expense of another's hurt. He *loved* her so!

And the crazy bitch had opted for Uncle Zio and those goddamned leper colonies instead of a wonderful life as the wife of Sam Devereaux, attorney-at-law, eventually, inevitably, Judge Samuel Lansing Devereaux who could enter any lousy regatta he wanted to on Cape Cod. She was bananas!

Hurry! Hurry home and get to the lair and find solace in the memories of unrequited love. *'Tis better to have loved and lost than never to have loved at all.* Who *was* that asshole?

He sped down the street in Weston and swerved around the corner into his block. Only minutes now, and then with aid of the grape and the swelling sounds of The Alpine Yodelers' one and only recording, he would retreat into the cave of his dreams, his lost dreams.

Holy shit! Up ahead, in front of his house . . . was that – *was* it . . . ? Jesus, it *was*! Aaron Pinkus's limousine! Had something happened to his mother that he knew nothing about? Had an emergency occurred while he had been screaming at O'Toole's television set? He'd never *forgive* himself!

Screeching to a stop behind Aaron's outsized vehicle, Sam leaped out of his car and ran forward as Pinkus's chauffeur appeared from around the hood of the limousine. 'Paddy, what *happened*?' yelled Devereaux. 'Is anything wrong with my mother?'

'Not that I could tell, Sammy, except maybe the language, some of which I haven't heard since Omaha Beach.'

'What?'

'I'd get in there if I were you, boyo.'

Devereaux sped to the gate, leaped over it, and raced up to the door, fumbling in his pocket for his key ring. It wasn't necessary as the door was opened by cousin Cora, who wasn't necessarily altogether there. 'What's *happened*?' repeated Sam.

'Hoity-toity and the little fella are either stinkin' drunk or under the curse of a full moon while the sun's still in the sky.' Cora hiccuped once, then belched.

'What the hell are you talking about? Where *are* they?'

'Up in your place, buster boy.'

'*My* place? You mean . . . ?'

'That's what I mean, big fella.'

'*Nobody* goes into the lair! We all *agreed* –'

'Somebody lied, I guess.'

'Oh, my *God*!' screamed Samuel Lansing Devereaux as he

ran across the huge foyer of Norwegian rose marble and raced up the winding staircase to the east wing of the house.

'Reduce power for final approach,' said the pilot calmly, looking out the side left window, wondering briefly if his wife had made the roast beef hash she had promised him for dinner. 'Prepare full flaps, please.'

'Colonel *Gibson*?' The radio operator sharply intruded on his thoughts.

'Hoot's on the toot, Sergeant. What is it?'

'You're not plugged into the tower, sir!'

'Oh, sorry, I just switched them off. Anyway, it's a beautiful sunset and we've got our instructions and I have every confidence in my first officer and in you, you great communicator.'

'Switch *over*, Hoot! . . . I mean, Colonel.'

The pilot snapped his head over at his co-pilot, astonished to see his subordinate's open mouth and bulging eyes.

'They can't *do* this!' cried the first officer under his breath.

'Do *what*, for Christ's sake?' Gibson instantly flipped on the tower frequency. 'Repeat the information, please. The flight deck was in the middle of a crap game.'

'Funny man, Colonel, and you can tell that gentleman sky-jock on your right that we *can* do it because it's a direct order from Rec-Wing command, *sir*.'

'I repeat, please repeat. The gentleman-jock's in shock.'

'So are we, Hoot!' came a second familiar voice from the tower, a fellow officer of Gibson's rank. 'We'll fill you in when we can, but right now follow the sergeant's instructions to your refuelling coordinates.'

'*Refuelling* . . . ? What the hell are you *talking* about? We've done our eight hours! We scanned up the Aleuts and into the Bering so close to the Mother we could smell her borscht. It's time for dinner, for roast beef hash, to be exact!'

'Sorry, I can't say any more. We'll bring you back as soon as we can.'

'An *alert*?'

'Not Mother Borscht, I can tell you that much.'

'That much isn't enough, *especially* that much. Are the little lucite people on their way from Quasar Tinkerbell?'

'We're operating direct on CINCSAC with SCD controls, is that enough for you, Hoot?'

'It's enough to louse up my roast beef hash,' replied a subdued Gibson. 'Call my wife, will you?'

'Sure. All spouses and/or live-in relations will be apprised of the change in orders.'

'Hey, Colonel!' interrupted the first flight officer. 'There's a little place in downtown Omaha, on Farnam Street, called Doogies. Around eight o'clock there'll be a redhead at the bar – dimensions roughly thirty-eight, twenty-eight, thirty-four, and she answers to the name of Scarlet O. Would you mind sending –'

'That'll be *enough*, Captain, you're out of order! ... Did you say Doogies?'

The mammoth EC-135 jet, known as 'Looking Glass' for the Strategic Air Command's never-ending search of the skies, angled upward, accelerating airspeed to an initial altitude of eighteen thousand feet, where it banked northeast across the Missouri River, leaving Nebraska and entering the state of Iowa. On the ground, the tower at Offutt Air Force Base, the control centre for the entire worldwide Strategic Air Command, instructed Colonel Gibson to switch to a coded northwest heading and rendezvous in the still bright western sky with its refuelling cargo aircraft.

There could be no argument. The 55th Strategic Reconnaissance Wing was the host unit at Offutt and conducted global-scale observation missions, but host or not, it, too, like its brother 544th Strategic Intelligence Wing, was subject to the needs of the Cray X-MP supercomputer which was conveniently placed under the ostensible control of AFGWC, otherwise known as the Air Force Global Weather Control, and also which few sophisticated students of SAC believed had anything to do with meteorology.

'What's going on down there?' asked Colonel Gibson, mostly of himself but including his first flight officer.

'What the hell *will* be going on at Doogies, that's what *I'd* like to know,' said the young angry captain. '*Shit!*'

At the Pentagon, in the beflagged office of the omnipotent Secretary of Defense, a tiny man with a pinched face and a slightly askew toupee sat on three cushions behind an enormous desk and virtually spat into his telephone.

'I'll *screw* 'em! By God, I'll *ream* those ungrateful savages until they beg for poison and I won't even let them have *that*! Nobody's going to mess around with me ... I'm keeping those 135s in the air in *force* if I have to keep refuelling night and day!'

'I'm on your side, Felix,' said the somewhat bewildered chairman of the Joint Chiefs of Staff, 'but then I'm not Air Force. Don't we have to let them come down every now and then? You'll have four 135s in the air by tomorrow afternoon, all out of Offutt, and that's the cutoff time. Couldn't we share the load with the other SAC bases?'

'*No* way, Corky. Omaha's the control centre and we're not giving it up! Haven't you ever seen the Duke's movies? Once you let those bloodthirsty redskin scum have an inch, they'll sneak up behind you and take your scalp!'

'But what about the aircraft, the crews?'

'You don't know anything, Corky! Haven't you ever heard of "Beam me up, Scotty," and "Beam me down, Scotty"?'

'Maybe I was in Nam.'

'Get *with* it, Corky!' The Secretary of Defense slammed down the telephone.

Brigadier General Owen Richards, supreme commandant of the Strategic Air Command, stared silently at the two men from Washington, both dressed in black trench coats and dark sunglasses under dark brown hats which they had not removed even in the presence of the female Air Force major who had escorted them into his office. That discourtesy Richards had ascribed to a nonsexist military, which he had never really accepted; he usually opened a door for his secretary and she was only a sergeant, but she was also a woman and some things were just natural. No, it was not the lack of courtesy on the Washingtonians' part, it was the fact that they were lunatics, which probably accounted for their wearing their heavy trench coats and their dark hats on a warm summer's day, and not removing their smoked sunglasses in the decidedly dim light of the general's office; all the venetian blinds were closed to block out the blinding rays of the setting sun. No, thought Owen, they were just crazy. *Nuts!*

'Gentlemen,' he began calmly, in spite of his apprehensions which had caused him to quietly open a lower drawer where there was a weapon. 'Your credentials got you in here, but perhaps you'd better give them to me for personal verification . . . *Don't* reach under your coats or I'll blow you both *away!*' roared Richards suddenly, yanking his GI issue .45 out of the drawer.

'You asked for our IDs,' said the man on the left.

'How do you expect us to show them to you?' asked the man on the right.

'*Two* fingers!' ordered the general. 'If I see a full hand, you're both splattered into the wall.'

'Your combat background makes you inordinately suspicious.'

'You've got *that* right, I spent two years in Washington . . . Put 'em on the desk.' Both did so. 'Goddamn it, these aren't IDs. They're handwritten notes!'

'With a signature you must certainly recognize,' said the agent on the left. 'And a telephone number – which you certainly know – should you care to embarrass yourself with verification.'

'With what you just ordered me to do, I'd check the President's stool before I complied.' Richards picked up his private Red Line, punched four buttons, and moments later winced as he heard the voice of the Secretary of Defense. 'Yes, sir, *yes*, sir. Orders received, sir.' The general hung up the phone, his eyes glazed, and looked at the two intruders. 'All Washington's gone *crazy*,' he whispered.

'No, Richards, not *all* Washington, only a very *few* people in Washington,' said the agent on the right, keeping his voice low. 'And everything must be kept max-classified – to the ultimate max. Your orders are to pretend to stand down as of eighteen hundred hours tomorrow – SAC's command centre is for all intents and purposes *shut down*.'

'For Christ's sake, *why*?'

'In real phony deference to a debate over a decision that could make a new law we can't permit,' replied the agent on the left, his eyes mysteriously invisible behind the sunglasses.

'*What* law?' shouted the general.

'Probably Commie-oriented,' answered the other emissary from the nation's capital. 'They've got moles in the Supreme Court.'

'*Commie . . . ?* What the hell are you talking about? It's *glasnost, perestroika*, and the goddamned Court is as far right as the communicator and his understudy could make it!'

'Wishful thinking, soldier boy. Just get one thing through your GI brain. We're *not* giving up this base! It's our nerve centre!'

'Give it up to *whom*?'

'I'll tell you this much. Code name WOPTACK, that's all you have to know. Keep it under your sombrero.'

'Wop . . . *attack?* The Italian *army* is invading *Omaha*?'

'I didn't say that. We don't indulge in ethnic slurs.'

'Then what the hell *did* you say?'

'Maximum-classified, General. You can understand that.'

'Maybe I can and maybe I can't, but what about my four aircraft that'll be upstairs?'

'"Beam 'em down, Scotty," then "Beam 'em up."'

'*What?*' screamed Owen Richards, lunging up from his chair.

'We listen to our superiors, General, and so should you.'

Eleanor Devereaux and Aaron Pinkus, their faces devoid of colour, their mouths gaping and their eyes four stationary glass orbs, sat next to each other on Sam Devereaux's two-seater leather couch in the private off-limits office he had built for himself in the restored Victorian house in Weston,

Massachusetts. Neither spoke, for neither was capable of speech; the babbling, moaning, incoherent gurgles that had emanated from Sam's throat had, in essence, formed contiguous affirmatives to the initial questions both had posed. It did not help matters that Samuel Lansing Devereaux, paralysed by the assault on his château's lair, had pinned himself against the wall, both arms outstretched, palms spread, covering as many of the incriminating photographs and newspaper articles as he could manage.

'Samuel, my son,' began the elderly Pinkus, finding his voice, but only to the extent of a hoarse whisper.

'Please don't *say* that!' protested Devereaux. '*He* used to say that.'

'Who said who?' mumbled the barely cognizant Eleanor.

'Uncle Zio –'

'You don't have an uncle named See Oh, unless you mean Seymour Devereaux, who married a Cuban and had to move to Miami.'

'I don't believe that's who he means, dear Eleanor. If an old man's memory doesn't fail him, especially during certain negotiations in Milan, "*zio*" is "uncle," and there were more "*zios*" than this attorney could handle in Milan. Your son is saying, literally, "Uncle Uncle," do you comprehend?'

'Not for a minute –'

'He is referring to –'

'Don't *say* it!' shrieked the Lady Devereaux, covering her aristocratic ears.

'Pope Francesco the First,' trailed off the foremost attorney of Boston, Massachusetts, his face now the pallor of a six-week-old corpse without refrigeration. '*Sammy* . . . Samuel . . . Sam. How *could* you?'

'It's difficult, Aaron –'

'It's *incredible*!' thundered Pinkus, now in full if uncontrollable volume. 'You exist in another *world*!'

'You might say that,' agreed Devereaux, pulling his arms down from the wall and falling to his knees, then knee by knee inching his way to the small oval table in front of the miniature couch. 'But you see, I had no *choice*. I had to do whatever that slugworm *told* me to do –'

'Including the kidnapping of the *Pope*!' squeaked Aaron Pinkus, unable once again to find his voice.

'*Stop* it!' roared Eleanor Devereaux. 'I'll hear no *more*!'

'I think we'd better, dear Eleanor, and if you'll pardon my untenable language, please be quiet. Go on, Sammy. I don't wish to hear it, either, but I think, by the god of Abraham, who controls the universe and who may now have some explaining to do, how did it *happen*? And it's all so obvious that it *did* happen! The press was right, the media *everywhere* were right! There *were* two people – it's there on your walls! There were *two* popes and you kidnapped the *original*!'

'Not exactly,' pleaded Devereaux, each inhaled breath more difficult than the last. 'You see, Zio figured it was okay –'

'*Okay?*' Aaron's chin came perilously close to the top of the coffee table.

'Well, yes. He wasn't well and . . . well, that's another part of the story, but Zio was smarter than any of us. I mean he was really *with* it.'

'How did it *happen*, Sam? It was because of this lunatic General MacKenzie Hawkins, wasn't it? He's in all these photographs. *He* was the one who made you become the most unknown notorious kidnapper in the history of the *world*! Am I even reasonably accurate?'

'You might say that. Then again you might not.'

'How, Sam? *How?*' pleaded the elderly attorney as he picked up a copy of *Penthouse* from the coffee table and began waving it in front of the comatose face of Eleanor Devereaux.

'There are some excellent articles in that magazine . . . very academic.'

'Sammy, I beg you, do not *do* this to me, or to your lovely mother here, who bore you in pain, and at this moment may be in need of ministration beyond our capabilities. In the name of the Lord God of Hosts, to whom I shall vigorously protest in temple on tomorrow's Sabbath, what *possessed* you to be a part of this monstrous act?'

'Well, actually, Aaron, "possessed" is a fairly accurate

description of the alleged – I restate, the *alleged* – criminal enterprise to which you refer.'

'I don't have to "refer," Sam, I simply point to these very specific articles of evidence on your walls!'

'Yes, well, actually, Aaron, they're not entirely conclusive –'

'You want I should subpoena the *Pope*?'

'Vatican executive privilege wouldn't permit it.'

'These photographs *alone* would obviate the rules of evidentiary procedure! I've taught you *nothing*?'

'Pick Mother's head up, please.'

'It's better she's out, Sam. What was this "possessed"?'

'Yes, well, actually, Aaron, without any intent on my part, I walked out of the army intelligence G-two computer banks with copies of maximum-classified files chained to my wrist twenty-four hours before my discharge from the Army.'

'*So?*'

'Well, you see, Aaron, as MacKenzie Hawkins's attorney-of-record, I had to accompany him to his final Six-Thirty-Five resolution of all the classified intelligence reports relative to his military career, from World War Two through Southeast Asia.'

'*So?*'

'Well, you see, Aaron, that's when Mac's friends in the army intruded on the procedure. I'd made a minor mistake in the Golden Triangle and instituted charges against a certain General Ethelred Brokemichael for dealing in drugs, when it actually was his cousin Heseltine Brokemichael, and Ethelred's supporters were mad as hell and since they were all friends of Mac Hawkins, they rallied around the Hawk and played his game.'

'What *game*? Heseltine ... Ethelred! Drugs, Golden Triangle! So you made a mistake, you withdraw the indictment. So?'

'It was too late. The military's worse than Congress. Ethelred didn't get his three stars and his buddies blamed it on me and helped Mac.'

'*So?*'

'One of those bastards chained a briefcase on my wrist,

slapped a max-security label on it, and I signed out with two thousand six hundred forty-one copies of top-secret files on my person, the majority of which had nothing to do with Mac Hawkins, who stood innocently at my side.'

Aaron Pinkus closed his eyes and sank back on the small settee, his shoulder touching the totally dazed Eleanor Devereaux. 'So you were his for the immediate future – roughly five months.' Aaron cautiously opened his eyes.

'Either that or have my discharge postponed indefinitely ... or I'd spend twenty years in Leavenworth.'

'Then the money came from the ransom –'

'What money?' interrupted Sam.

'The money you spent so lavishly on this house ... hundreds of thousands of dollars! It was your share of the ransom, wasn't it?'

'What ransom?'

'For Pope Francesco, naturally. When you released him.'

'We didn't get any ransom. Cardinal Ignatio Quartz refused to pay.'

'Cardinal *who*?'

'It's another story. Quartz was happy with Guido.'

'*Guido?*' asked the apoplectic Pinkus.

'You're shouting, Aaron,' murmured Eleanor.

'Frescobaldi,' answered Devereaux. 'Zio's look-alike cousin; he was an extra in La Scala's third opera company and sometimes got to play small parts.'

'*Enough!*' The celebrated attorney took several deep breaths, doing his best to find some self-control. Lowering his voice, he spoke as calmly as possible. 'Sam, you returned home with a great deal of money that did not come from a deceased wealthy Devereaux. Where did it come from, Sam?'

'Well, actually, Aaron, as a general partner, it was my pro rata share of the remaining capitalization initially raised for the corporation.'

'What corporation?' asked Pinkus, his quiet voice floating and barely audible.

'The Shepherd Company.'

'The Shepherd ... ?'

'Like in the Good Shepherd.'

'Like in the Good Shepherd,' repeated Aaron, as if in a trance. 'Money was raised for this corporation –'

'Actually, in increments of ten million dollars per investor, said investors restricted to four and forming a limited partnership with the general partners, their individual risks naturally limited to the capital ventured and based on projections anticipating a ten to one return on their investments . . . Actually, none of the four investors cared to be legally acknowledged and preferred to consider their investments as charitable contributions in exchange for anonymity.'

'Anonymity . . . ? Forty million dollars worth of *anonymity*?'

'Actually, that was pretty much guaranteed. I mean, where could I possibly file the papers of incorporation, Aaron?'

'*You?* You were *counsel* for this travesty of a business enterprise?'

'Not by choice,' protested Devereaux. '*Never* by choice.'

'Oh, yes, those two thousand-plus intelligence files you walked out with. No discharge. Leavenworth.'

'Or worse, Aaron. Mac said there were ways less public than a firing squad if the Pentagon public relations ruled out an execution.'

'Yes, yes, I understand . . . Sam, your dear mother here, who mercifully is in a state of shock, mentioned that you told her your money came from religious artefacts –'

'Actually, as was clearly stated in the bylaws of the limited partnership, the primary function of the corporation was the "brokering of *acquired* religious artefacts." I covered it rather nicely, I thought.'

'Dear *God*,' exclaimed Pinkus, swallowing. 'And naturally the "acquired" religious artefact in question was the person of Pope Francesco the First whom you *kidnapped*.'

'Well, actually, Aaron, that's not really legally sound, much less conclusive. The allegation itself might even be considered libellous.'

'What are you *saying*? Look at your walls, the *photographs*!'

'Actually, I might suggest that you – you, Aaron – look at them again. Legally speaking, kidnapping is defined as abduction by force or coercion and holding a person or personages against their will, their being freed subject to the payment of funds. Although as I've acknowledged, a preliminary strategy had been meticulously financed and was in place to implement such an objective, the strategy failed and would have been aborted but for the voluntary – I might say enthusiastic – cooperation of the subject. And those photographs hardly depict the subject in question to be under any constraints whatsoever. In fact, he appears to be content and in excellent spirits.'

'*Sam*, you belong in a room made of thick sponge rubber! Hasn't the enormity of what you did made even a dent in your moral armour?'

'The crosses I bear are heavy indeed, Aaron.'

'That's not the most appropriate allusion you could employ ... I don't really want to know, but how did you ever get – *him* – back to Rome?'

'Mac and Zio worked it out. The Hawk called it a "very back channel" mission and Zio began singing opera.'

'I'm exhausted,' whispered Pinkus. 'I could only wish this day never happened, that I had not heard a word uttered in this room and that my sight had deserted me.'

'How do you think I feel every day of my life? The eternal love of my life is gone, but I've learned something, Aaron. Life *must* go on!'

'How uniquely phrased.'

'I mean it, it's *over*. It's all in the past, and in a way, I'm glad today *did* happen. Somehow, it's freed me. Now I have to get off my ass and charge ahead, knowing that slugworm son of a bitch can never touch me again!'

And, of course, the telephone rang.

'If that's the office, I'm in temple,' said Pinkus. 'I'm not prepared for the outside world.'

'I'll get it,' said Sam, rising and heading for the desk as the phone rang again. 'Mother's up here – sort of – and it's better Cora doesn't answer. You know, Aaron, now that it's all out in the open I really feel better. With your support I *know* I can charge ahead and face new challenges, find new horizons –'

'Answer the damn thing, Sammy. My head is splitting.'

'Oh, yes, of course, sorry.' Devereaux picked up the phone, greeted whoever was on the line, paused for a reply, and then proceeded to scream hysterically, with such uncontrollable frenzy that his mother bolted up from the settee, shot over the oval coffee table, and ended up splayed out on the floor.

CHAPTER SIX

'*Sammy!*' shouted Aaron Pinkus, dashing back and forth between the unconscious Eleanor and her son, who was now, in an outburst of panic, ripping down every framed photograph he could reach on the walls and smashing them down on the floor. 'Sam, get *hold* of yourself!'

'*Slugworm!*' screamed Devereaux. 'Maggot of the universe, the most despicable human being on the face of the *earth*! He has no *right* –'

'Your *mother*, Sammy. She may be *dead*!'

'Forget it, she wouldn't know how,' replied Devereaux, racing to the wall behind the desk and continuing his assault on the myriad photos and newspaper clippings. 'He's sick, sick, *sick*!'

'I didn't say sick, Sam, I said *dead*,' continued Aaron, kneeling painfully and holding the mother's quivering head firmly, hoping his ruse might have an effect on the son. 'You really should show some concern.'

'*Concern?* Has he ever showed *me* any concern? He tears my life apart then steps on the pieces, grinding them into the dirt! He rips my heart out and blows it up into a balloon –'

'I didn't say *he*, Sam, I said *she*! Your *mother*.'

'Hello, Mother, I'm busy.'

Pinkus withdrew the beeper from his pocket and held his finger down on the signal button; then he kept pressing it in continual bursts. His driver, Paddy Lafferty, would somehow get the message of *emergency*. He *had* to.

He did. In moments, Paddy could be heard crashing through the east wing entrance, ordering cousin Cora in his most commanding sergeant's roar to get out of his way or he'd throw her to a bunch of war-weary drunken infantrymen looking for a little feminine amusement.

'It's no threat, Mick!'

Sam Devereaux was tied to the chair behind his desk, his arms and legs bound with sheets torn from his bed and ripped with abandon by the once and former Sergeant Patrick Lafferty of Omaha Beach, World War II. Ripped, that was, after he had cold-cocked Sam and found the bedroom. Devereaux shook his head while blinking and attempted a semblance of his voice. 'Five drug addicts attacked me,' he offered.

'Not exactly, Sam boyo,' said Paddy, holding a glass of water to the lawyer's lips. 'Unless you consider a touch of Bushmills in that category, which I don't advise you to do in old Southie or even in O'Toole's saloon.'

'*You* did this to me?'

'I had no choice, Sam. When a man goes over the edge of combat fatigue, you bring him back however you can. It's no disgrace, boyo.'

'You were in the army? In *combat* ... ? You were with MacKenzie *Hawkins*?'

'You know that *name*, Sam?'

'*Were* you?'

'I never had the privilege of meetin' the great general personally, but I seen him! For ten days in France he took over our division, and I tell you this, laddie, Mac the Hawk was the finest commanding officer the army ever had. He made Patton look like a ballet dancer, and frankly I kinda liked old George, but he just wasn't in the Hawk's league.'

'I'm *screwed*!' screamed Devereaux, straining at the binding sheet strips. 'Where's my mother ... where's *Aaron*?' he asked suddenly, glancing around the empty room.

'With your mother, boyo. I carried her to her bedroom. Mr Pinkus is administering a little brandy to help her sleep.'

'Aaron and my *mother*?'

'Be a touch flexible, lad. You've met Shirley with the concrete hairdo .... Here, now, drink a little water – I'd give you some whisky but I don't believe you could handle it. Your eyes don't convey much human, more like a cat's that's heard a loud noise.'

'*Stop* it! My whole world is coming apart!'

'Don't unravel, Sam, Mr Pinkus'll stitch it back together. A grander man in that department there never was . . . . *There*, he's comin' back now. I hear what's left of the door.'

The exhausted, frail figure of Aaron Pinkus trudged into the off-limits office as if he had just returned from an assault on the Matterhorn. 'We have to talk, Samuel,' he said, sinking breathlessly into a chair in front of the desk. 'Would you please leave us, Paddy? Cousin Cora suggested that you might enjoy a char-grilled porterhouse in the kitchen.'

'A *porter*?'

'With Irish ale, Paddy.'

'Well . . . you understand that first impressions are not always written in stone, am I correct, Mr Pinkus?'

'That, too, is written in stone, my old friend.'

'What about *me*?' yelled Devereaux. 'Will somebody cut me *loose*?'

'You will remain exactly where you are and how you are until our conversation's over, Samuel.'

'You always call me "Samuel" when you're mad at me.'

'Mad? Why should I be mad? You've only involved me and the firm in the most heinously insidious crime in the history of civilization since the Middle Empire of Egypt four thousand years ago. *Mad*? No, Sammy, I'm merely hysterical.'

'I think I'd better leave, boss.'

'I'll beep you later, Paddy. And enjoy your porterhouse as if you were having my last meal in this life.'

'Oh, you carry on so, Mr Pinkus.'

'Then carry me out to the temple if I do not signal you within the hour.' Lafferty made a rapid exit, signified by the screeching sound of the shattered outside door being pulled shut. Hands folded in front of him, Aaron spoke. 'I must assume,' he began calmly, 'that the person who contacted you on the telephone was none other than General MacKenzie Hawkins, am I correct?'

'You know damn well you're correct and that sewer rat can't *do* this to me!'

'What precisely has he done?'

'He *talked* to me.'

'There's a law prohibiting communication?'

'Between the two of us, there certainly is. He swore on the Manual of Army Regulations never to speak to me again for the rest of his miserable, misbegotten life!'

'Yet he saw fit to violate this solemn oath, which means he felt he had something of great import to tell you. What was it?'

'Who *listened*?' yelled Devereaux, again straining against the constricting white strips pinning him to the chair. 'All I heard him say was that he was flying into Boston to see me and everything went crazy.'

'You went crazy, Sam .... When is he to make this journey?'

'How do *I* know?'

'That's right. You turned off your ears and turned on your precordial anxiety .... However, based on the assumption that he had something vital to tell you, or he would not have broken his agreement never to contact you, we can assume that his flight to Boston is imminent.'

'So's my departure for Tasmania,' said Devereaux emphatically.

'That is the one thing you must not do,' interjected Pinkus with equal firmness. 'You cannot run away nor can you avoid him –'

'One *reason*!' broke in Sam, shouting. 'Give me *one* reason short of murdering the son of a bitch why I *shouldn't* avoid him? He's a walking distress signal from the Titanic!'

'Because he will continue to hold over your head – and by extension mine as your only employer since law school – your participation in this crime of the ages.'

'*You* didn't walk out of the data banks with over two thousand top-secret intelligence files, *I* did.'

'That seemingly ominous act sinks to the level of complete insignificance compared to the evidence you've been trying to tear off your walls . . . But since you mention it, was there any point to the theft of those files?'

'Forty million points,' answered Devereaux. 'How do you think that diabolic general from the River Styx raised his capitalization?'

'Blackmail . . . ?'

'From the Cosa Nostra to some Brits who weren't exactly in line for the Victoria Cross; from former Nazis whose respectability was up to their thighs in chickenshit, to Arab sheiks who made money by protecting their Israeli investments. He refined the whole sticky ball of wax and made me go after them.'

'Good God, your mother said those were all your delusions! Killers on a golf course, Germans in chicken farms . . . Arabs in the desert. They were *real*.'

'Sometimes, not often, I have a martini I shouldn't have.'

'She also mentioned that . . . And Hawkins unearthed these scoundrels from the intelligence files and forced them to capitulate to his demands?'

'How low can you get –'

'How *ingenious* can a man *be*?'

'Where's your moral armour, Aaron?'

'Certainly not for the benefit of scoundrels, Sam.'

'Then in support of the evidence you've seen on my walls?'

'*Definitely* not!'

'So where do you stand?'

'One has nothing to do with the *other*. There's no linkage.'

'Not if you were me, Counsellor.'

Aaron Pinkus took several deep breaths in silence while placing his ten fingers across his forehead, his head bowed. 'For every impossible problem there must be an eventual solution, either in this life or in the hereafter.'

'I prefer the former, if you don't mind, Aaron.'

'I tend to agree,' agreed the elderly attorney. 'Therefore, we will, as you expressed in your own singular vernacular, "get off our asses and charge ahead."'

'To what?'

'To our mutual confrontation with General MacKenzie Hawkins.'

'You'd *do* that?'

'I have a vested interest, Sammy. You might even say a potentially disastrous one. Furthermore, I should like to bring to your attention a truism of our profession, true because of its validity . . . A lawyer who represents himself has a fool for a client. Your General Hawkins may possess an extraordinary military mind with all its brilliant eccentricities, but, I modestly submit, he has not matched his skills against those of Aaron Pinkus.'

The befeathered Chief Thunder Head of the Wopotamis spat out his mutilated cigar and returned to the interior of his huge tepee, where, in addition to the expected American Indian artefacts, such as ersatz scalps lining the walls, he had installed a waterbed and various electronic equipment that would make the Pentagon proud – *had* made the Pentagon proud, before it was stolen. Sighing audibly in both sadness and anger, Thunder Head carefully removed his awesome tribal head-dress, dropping it on the dirt floor. He reached into a buckskin satchel and pulled out a fresh cigar of indeterminate make and limited quality; he shoved it into his mouth and proceeded to mangle a good two inches of the end until his teeth were stained. He crossed to the waterbed, lowered himself down on its instantly rolling swells and immediately lost his balance, falling backward, as the cellular telephone inside his beaded tribal tunic erupted. The ringing persisted as he thrashed about, trying to calm the rough waters beneath him, finally succeeding by pushing himself forward and planting his boots firmly on the dirt. Angrily he yanked out the phone and spoke harshly. 'What is it? I'm in powwow!'

'Come on, Chief, the only powwows around here are when the kids hear their dogs bark.'

'You never know who's calling, son.'

'I didn't know anyone else had the number.'

'Always operate on the assumption that the enemy can scan and lock into a frequency.'

'What . . . ?'

'Just stay alert, boy. Now, what is it?'

'You know that English couple who were here yesterday asking for you, the ones we played dumb Injun for?'

'What about 'em?'

'They're back, but with a couple of associates. One looks like his keeper doesn't know he's missing from his cage, the other sniffs a lot – he's either got a bad cold or a couple of very inflamed nostrils.'

'They must have smelled something.'

'Not with his honker –'

'I don't mean the support troops, I mean the English types. That legal idiot of yours, Charlie Redwing, must have tipped them off to something.'

'Hey, come on, T.H., except for falling off that lousy horse, he was terrific. They didn't learn bean one about you, and that fancy lady kept looking at his jockstrap –'

'*Loin*cloth, son, loincloth. Maybe it was the horse.'

'Maybe it was the loincloth,' suggested the caller as Thunder Head, caught in a rolling vinyl wave, was thrown back on the waterbed.

'*Augh!*'

'Hey, our legal eagle may really *have* something, huh? I guess you agree.'

'I agreed to nothing! My BOQ accoutrements here are loused up –'

'You designed them, T.H.'

'And I'd advise you to cut the familiarity, *boy*! You're a low-life enlisted man and you will address me as *Chief*!'

'Fine, chiefy-baby, then you can drive into town and get your own rotten cigars –'

'I didn't redress you that severely, son, I just want to maintain a logical order of command. All I'm saying is that support troops are not called up for such R and R as "loincloths," do I make myself clear?'

'Maybe . . . So what do you figure? What they smelled, I mean.'

'Not what *they* smelled, young man, but what someone *else*

75

smelled that called for auxiliary support. Those Brits didn't re-assault by themselves, they were ordered back by a combat officer who wanted a reassessment. It's as clear as Porkchop Hill.'

'Porkchops . . . ?'

'Where are they now, boy?'

'At the souvenir lean-to. They're buying up a load of stuff and being very friendly, even the ox. Incidentally, the girls – excuse me, the *squaws* – are happy as hell. We just got in a new supply from Taiwan.'

Thunder Head frowned, lit his cigar, and spoke. 'Stay on the line, I've got to think.' Several quarts of smoke fogged the tepee when, finally, the Hawk resumed speaking. 'Pretty soon the Brits will bring up my name.'

'I guess they will.'

'So, have one of our downtrodden brethren tell them my tepee is roughly two hundred running antelope strides above the north pasture, past the buffalo mating ground by the great oaks where the eagles lay their precious eggs. It's an isolated place so I can commune with the gods of the forest and contemplate. Got it?'

'I can't understand a word you just said. We've got a few cows but no buffalo, and I've never seen an eagle except in the Omaha zoo.'

'You'll admit there's a forest.'

'Well, woods, maybe, but I don't remember any great big trees.'

'Damn it, son, just get 'em up into those woods, okay?'

'Which of the paths? They're all clear but some are better than others. It's been a lousy tourist season –'

'Good thinking, boy!' exclaimed Thunder Head. 'Fine tactics. Tell 'em they'll find me quicker if they separate. The one who reaches me can call the others; they're not that far away from one another.'

'Considering the fact that you're not anywhere near those woods, it's not "fine tactics," it's dumb. They'll get lost.'

'Hopefully, son, hopefully.'

'What?'

'In light of the nature of this engagement, the enemy's using unorthodox strategy. Nothing wrong with unorthodoxy – hell, I've employed it most of my career – but it doesn't make any sense if it retards your progress. In this situation a frontal assault is our adversary's most productive course – his only course, really – but instead he's going around our flanks firing mortars filled with horseshit.'

'Lost me again, Chief,' said the caller.

'Anthropologists looking for the remnants of a great tribe?' scoffed Thunder Head. 'A tribe from the Shenandoahs, savages brought over to the English court by Walter Raleigh, you *believed* all that crap?'

'Well, I suppose it's possible. The Wopotamis came from someplace in the East.'

'From the Hudson Valley, *not* the Shenandoahs. For a fact, they were run off by the Mohawks 'cause they couldn't farm and they couldn't raise cattle and wouldn't get out of their tepees if it snowed. They weren't a great tribe, they were losers from day one until they reached the Missouri River, in the middle eighteen hundreds, where they found their true calling. They first hornswoggled, then corrupted the white settlers!'

'You know all that?'

'There's very little about your tribe's history I don't know . . . No, son, someone's behind this covert operation and I'm going to find out who it is. Get to work now. Send 'em up to the woods!'

Twenty-three minutes passed and one by one the members of Hyman Goldfarb's scouting patrol entered the four paths in the short dense forest. They had decided to separate insofar as the precise instructions they had received at the souvenir lean-to were totally imprecise and contradictory, the crowd of yelling squaws in a raucous debate over which path actually led to the great Thunder Head's tepee, a residence obviously equated with some holy shrine.

Forty-six minutes later, one by one, each member had been ambushed and bound – arms and legs – to a sizeable tree trunk, their mouths gagged with ersatz beaver pelts, all assured that rescue was imminent as long as they did not somehow find a way to remove the gags and scream. Should that happen, the wrath of a downtrodden, exploited people would descend on their heads, specifically their scalps which would be no longer attached to their heads. And each, of course, was accorded treatment commensurate with his and her station and sex. The English lady was much tougher than her like-talking male associate who attempted some complicated Oriental defence, only to wrench his left arm out of its elbow socket. The shorter, sniffing American tried to make a deal while slowly removing a short-barrelled Charter Arms automatic from his belt and therefore had to be visited with several cracked ribs. The most strenuously difficult, however, Chief Thunder Head – né MacKenzie Lochinvar Hawkins (his middle name having been stricken from all records) – he saved for the last. The Hawk always felt it was proper to permit his harshest challenge to have the honour of being the final barrier. You didn't take out a Rommel with the first wave against the *Afrika Corps* – it just wasn't, well, proper.

The challenge in question was outsized in bulk but not too sizeable in the brain department. Following a damn good workout with a man no more than half his age, the Hawk prevailed by ducking twice in rapid succession and sending rigid, pointed fingers into the middle of the enemy scout's stomach; he knew it would work by smelling the hostile's breath. Up came an excess of Indian food from the scout's throat; a hammerlock forcing the huge enemy head down toward his embarrassing accident did the rest.

'Your name, rank, and serial number, *soldier!*'

'Wadda ya talkin'?' belched the hostile referred to as the Ox by Thunder Head's security.

'I'll settle for your name and who you work for. *Now!*'

'I got no name and I don't work for nobody.'

'*Down* you go.'

'Holy shit, have a heart!'

'Why? You tried to rip it out of my chest. Into the mess you go, soldier.'

'It smells so *bad!*'

'Not as bad as what I smell around all four of you clowns. Give me what I want, prisoner!'

'It's *wet*! ... Okay, *okay*, they call me the Shovel.'

'I'll accept a nom de guerre. Who's your commander?'

'Wadda ya *talkin'*?'

'Who do you work for?'

'Wadda ya now, *nuts*?'

'All right, soldier, lose the rest of your stomach! You like our grub? Have it again, you old redskin lover!'

'*Jeez*, you got it *yourself*! I didn't have to say nothin'. Redskins!'

'Come again, grunt?'

'He played for 'em! The *Redskins* ... Lemme up, for Christ's sake!'

'*Played* for ... ? I need more, you latrine-cleaner! What kind of hot air are you trying to peddle?'

'You're *closer*, real close! They couldn't put nuthin' in the air while he was around. He didn't need no defence hulks, he just broke right through and nailed the quarters from Namath on down! The Hebrew Hercules, maybe ... ?'

'Quarters –? Namath? *Redskins*? ... Christ on a surfboard, football! And Hercules? ... There was only one linebacker like that in NFL history. Hymie the Hurricane!'

'I didn't say *nuthin'*! *You* said it.'

'You haven't the vaguest idea what I said, soldier.' The Hawk spoke softly, rapidly, as he released the bull of a man while swiftly manipulating the ropes that secured him to the tree. 'The Golden Goldfarb,' he continued hoarsely under his breath. 'I *recruited* the son of a bitch when I was posted at the Pentagon!'

'You *what*?'

'You never heard that, Shovel – *believe* me, you never heard it! ... I've got to get out of here, pronto. I'll send someone back for you idiots, but *you*, you never told me *anything*, you understand?'

'I didn't! But I'm also happy to oblige, Mr Big Indian Chief.'

'That's a small accomplishment, son, we're on to bigger

things. We just struck the gusher by rattling the biggest exposed nerve in Dizzy City! ... The Golden Goldfarb, wadda ya know? Right now, I need a goddamned attorney-of-record fast and I know exactly where that ungrateful asshole *is*!'

Vincent Mangecavallo, director of the Central Intelligence Agency, stared at the secure telephone in his outstretched hand as though the instrument were the inanimate embodiment of a communicable disease. When the hysterical voice on the line paused for breath, the DCI yanked the phone to his ear and mouth and spoke quietly but grimly. 'You listen to me, you pinstriped baked apple. I'm doing the best I can with talent your crowd only *pays* for but wouldn't know how to talk to, much less let into your la-di-da country clubs. You wanna take *over*? Be my guest, and I'll laugh like a goosed fruit when you get drowned in a vat of minestrone ... You wanna know something else, you lock-jawed cannoli?' Mangecavallo suddenly, briefly stopped, then resumed speaking in a much softer, more friendly voice. 'Who's kidding who? We all may be drowning in that barrel of soup. So far, all we got is zilch. That Court's as clean as my mother's thoughts – and no cracks from the whiffenpoof group, thank you very much.'

'Sorry I blew up, old fellow,' said the nasal-toned Secretary of State on the other end of the line. 'But surely you can understand the extraordinary disadvantages we face in the upcoming summit. My *God*, think of the embarrassment! How can the President negotiate from a position of strength, with the full authority of his office, if the Court even thinks of permitting a totally unknown *tiny* tribe of Indians to cripple our first line of defence? The sky's where it's at, you know, old boy!'

'Yeah, I figured, *bambino vecchio*.'

'I beg your pardon?'

'It's guinea-speak for something I never could understand with your types. How can a little kid be old?'

'Well, the tie, you see. The old schools, old bonds, the

symbols, I suppose. Therefore, the "old boys." Quite simple, really.'

'Maybe like *famiglia antica maledizione*, huh?'

'Well, I got the "familiar" part, and I imagine in broad sense there's a correlation. It's a rather lovely foreign phrase.'

'We don't think so. You get killed for it.'

'I beg your pardon –'

'No matter, I just wanted a couple of moments to think.'

'*I* do that all the time. Tangential intrusions.'

'Yeah, sure, so let's intrude on this summit problem. Number one, can the Big Man call it off because he's got the flu – or maybe shingles – hey, *they're* rough, how about it?'

'Terrible image, Vincent. No way.'

'His wife has a stroke? I can arrange it.'

'Again, no, old sport. He'd have to rise above personal tragedy and perform heroically – that's *bible*.'

'Then we're in the minestrone ... Whoa, *whoa*, I think I got it! If the Court's debate goes public, suppose the Big Fella says he *supports* the right of what do you call it – petition?'

'You're bonkers!'

'Who?'

'Insane! On what possible basis could he endorse such a position? This isn't merely pro choice or against it, it's *real*. You can't tab votes on this, you have to take a stand – and the only stand he can take pits him against the constitutional balances of power. He's embroiled in a battle between the Executive and the Judicial. Everybody loses!'

'*Boy*, you got a lot of big words, baked apple. I don't mean he "endorses," I mean he "supports" the public debate in the sense that he looks after the little people – like the Commies used to do but never did – and, anyway, he knows he's got twenty-two other SAC bases in the country, and eleven or twelve outside. So what's his problem?'

'Roughly *seventy billion* dollars' worth of equipment in Omaha he can't move out!'

'So who knows that?'

'The General Accounting Office!'

'Now we're getting down to the marbles. We can shut those guys up. I can arrange it.'

'You're relatively new in this town, Vincent. By the time your enforcers are in place, the leaks will have begun, the seventy billion instantly escalated to well over a hundred and any attempt to suppress even the rumours, those figures will reach nine hundred billion, making the savings and loan fiasco petty cash. By that time, since there's obviously a healthy grain of validity in that malodorous brief, we'd all be prosecuted under the laws of Congress for covering up something we had absolutely nothing to do with over a hundred years ago for the sake of political advantage. Furthermore, despite the fact that this is the most intelligent course of action we professionals could take, we'd not only be facing fines and imprisonment but they'd also take away our limousines.'

'*Basta!*' yelled Mangecavallo, switching the phone to his other less-abused ear. 'This is *nuthouse* time!'

'Welcome to the real world of Washington, Vincent ... Are you absolutely certain there's nothing, shall we say, "convincing," on any of those six idiots on the Court? What about the black fellow? He's always struck me as quite uppity.'

'He would and you would, but he's probably the cleanest and the brightest.'

'You don't say?'

'And the *paisan*'s right behind him, if he's your next in line for heavy objective thinking.'

'Actually, he was – nothing personal, you understand, I love opera.'

'Nothing personal and opera loves you, especially Signor Pagliacci.'

'Ah, yes, all those Vikings.'

'Yeah, Vikings ... And speaking of thunder –'

'Were we?'

'You were ... We're still waiting for word on that Chief Crazy Ass who calls himself Thunder Head. Once we got him, he could be our way out of this whole mess.'

'Really? How?'

'Because as the principal, what do you call it, the plaintiff, he has to show up in the big Court with his attorneys for all arguments. That's mandatory.'

'Well, of course he does, but how would that change anything?'

'Suppose – just *suppose* – this big scungilli shows up like a total psychiatric outpatient screaming that the whole scam is a *joke*? That he doctored all those historical records to make some kind of radical statement. How about that, *huh*?'

'It's absolutely brilliant, Vincent! ... But how can you possibly *do* that?'

'I can arrange it. I got a few medical types on a special payroll. Like with chemicals not exactly approved by the FDA, okay?'

'*Magnificent!* Why are you holding back?'

'I got to *find* the son of a bitch! ... *Hold* it, baked apple, I'll call you back. My other subterranean line is blinking.'

'Please do so, old boy.'

'*Basta* with the old bambino crap!' The honourable director of the Central Intelligence Agency broke off one line and admitted the second call with a touch of two buttons. 'Yeah, what is it?'

'I realize that I should not call you directly, but I felt that in light of the information, you would not accept it from anyone but myself.'

'Who *is* this?'

'Goldfarb.'

'Hymie the *Hurricane*? Lemme tell you, pal, you were the *greatest* –'

'Stop it, silly boy, I'm in a different business.'

'Sure, *sure*, but do you remember the Super Bowl of seventy-three when *you* –'

'I was there, *pal*, so naturally I remember. However, right now we have a situation that you should be apprised of before you make any moves ... Thunder Head got out of our net.'

'What?'

'I've spoken to each member of my *very* expensive unit, for which you will be billed via the sleazy motel in Virginia

Beach, and their unanimous conclusion may appear difficult to accept, but from everything I've heard, it's as good as any.'

'What are you *talkin*'?'

'This Thunder Head is, in actuality, the living person of Big Foot, the supposedly mythical creature that roams the Canadian forests, but who is very much a human being.'

'*What?*'

'The only other explanation is that he's the *yeti*, the Abominable Snowman of the Himalayas who has crossed continents to put a curse on the government of the United States . . . Have a nice day.'

CHAPTER SEVEN

General MacKenzie Hawkins, his shoulders stooped, and dressed in a rumpled, nondescript grey gabardine suit, walked through Boston's Logan Airport looking for a men's room. Finding one, he rushed inside with his oversized flight bag, placed it on the floor, and checked his appearance in the long mirror running the length of the sinks where two uniformed airline personnel washed their hands at each end. Not bad, he thought, except for the colour of the wig; it was a mite too red and a touch too long in the back. The thin steel-rimmed glasses, however, were splendid; sloping downward over his aquiline nose, they gave him the appearance of a distracted academic, a pointy-headed thinker who could never find a latrine in a crowded airport with the cool efficiency of a trained military man. And 'military,' or specifically the lack of same, was the linchpin of the Hawk's current strategy. All traces of his background had to be buried; the city of Boston was pointy-head territory, everyone knew that, and he had to meld in for the next twelve hours or so, enough time to reconnoitre and study Sam Devereaux in his own environment.

Sam seemed to have some minor objections over their getting together, and as much as it pained Mac, it was entirely possible that he might have to take Devereaux by force. Time itself was of the essence now and the Hawk needed Sam's legal credentials just as soon as possible; no hour could be wasted although several might be used up convincing the attorney to join forces in a holy cause ... Strike the word

85

'holy,' thought the general; it could revive memories best left forgotten.

Mac washed his hands, then proceeded to remove his glasses and dab water on his face, careful not to disturb the reddish wig, which was also a touch loose. He had a tube of scalp adhesive in his flight bag and when he checked into a hotel . . .

All thoughts of the inadequate wig instantly vanished as the Hawk felt the presence of a nearby body. He rose from the sink to find a uniformed man standing beside him, his ugly grin revealing that several of his teeth were missing. A short glance to his right revealed a second man in uniform shoving a couple of rubber doorstoppers under the door of the men's room. Further swift appraisal of both men disclosed the obvious: the only airline they could possibly be associated with had neither aircraft nor passengers, only getaway cars and mugging marks.

'You got yourself a liddle *agua* refreshment, hey man?' said the first grinning hostile in a pronounced Hispanic accent, confidently smoothing his dark hair, which flared from the sides of the visor of his officer's hat. 'You know, is good for you to splash a liddle *agua* on the face after a long flight, h'ain't it?'

'Oh, yeah, man!' cried the second hostile, approaching, his officer's hat improperly askew. 'Is better than shoving your head into a toilet, right, man?'

'Is there a point to these remarks?' asked the former general of the Army, alternately staring at both men, appalled at the sloppy open collars of their shirts beneath their tunics of authority.

'Well, is not such a good idea to put your head in a toilet, h'okay?'

'I must agree with you there,' replied the Hawk, suddenly considering that which he actually considered impossible. 'You're not by any chance advance combat intelligence, are you?'

'We got enough brains – and kindness – not to let you put

your head in a toilet, which would not be so intelligent, right?'

'I didn't think so. The man who's expecting me wouldn't consider recruiting battle scouts like you. I taught him better than that.'

'Hey, *man*!' said the second improperly dressed impersonator of an officer as he edged himself to the Hawk's opposite flank. 'You trying to insult us? Maybe you don' like the way we talk – we're not good enough for you?'

'Get this straight, *soldados estúpidos*! Never in all my years have I ever let a man's race, religion, or the colour of his flesh have a goddamned thing to do with my appraisal of his qualifications. I've promoted more Coloureds and Chinks and Spanish-speaking personnel to the officer corps than most anyone in my position – not *because* they were Coloureds or Chinks or Spics, but because they were *better* than their competition! Is that *clear*? . . . You're just not in their ranks. You're pissants.'

'I think that's enough conversation, man,' interrupted the first hostile, his grin disappearing as he withdrew a long-bladed knife from under his jacket. 'Pop guns make too much noise – just hand over your wallet, your watch, and anything else us Spanish-speaking Spics might consider valuable.'

'You've got balls, I'll say that for you,' said MacKenzie Hawkins. 'But tell me, why should I?'

'*This*!' yelled the grinless man, snapping the knife up in front of the Hawk's face.

'You've got to be *kidding*?' With that expression of bewilderment, the Hawk spun in place, gripping the wrist holding the knife and wrenching it counterclockwise with such force the weapon was instantly dropped while he crashed his left elbow up into the throat of the man behind him, rendering him sufficiently dazed to administer a *chi sai* chop to his forehead. He then immediately returned to the thug with missing teeth who was on the floor holding his painfully injured hand. 'All right, you jackasses, that's a short lesson in counterinsurgency.'

'What . . . man?' mumbled the conscious hostile on the

floor, trying to reach for the hunting knife, which Hawkins pinned to the tiles with a stomping foot. 'H'okay, I got no leverage,' admitted the perpetrator. 'So I go back to a cell, what else is new, huh, man?'

'Just hold it, *amigo zonzo*,' said the Hawk, squinting and thinking rapidly, 'maybe you can be *better* than that. For a fact, your tactics weren't bad, just poorly executed. I liked the uniforms and the doorstoppers, that showed imagination under these flexible rules of engagement. What you didn't have was your follow-up strategy – the what-ifs in the event the enemy counters with a sidewinder you hadn't considered. You simply didn't project your analysis properly, son! . . . And for another fact, I'm going to need support adjutants who've faced fire. Maybe with a little discipline I can use you. You got a vehicle?'

'A what?'

'A car, an automobile, a means of conveyance that isn't necessarily registered to a person living or dead who could be traced by a licence plate.'

'Well, we got a chopped-up h'Oldsmobile from the Midwest that's still registered to a big shot who don't know he's got a *duplicado* with a very old Mazda engine.'

'Perfect. We ride, *caballeros*! And with thirty minutes' worth of training and a couple of haircuts, you've got yourselves temporary, respectable employment that pays handsomely . . . I *do* like the uniforms – very imaginative and extremely useful.'

'You're one *loco hombre*, mister.'

'Not at all, son, not at all. I've always believed in doing my best for the disenfranchised – which is at the heart of my current pursuits . . . Come along now, fall to, and stand up straight, boy, I want perfect posture from both of you! Help me get your comrade off the floor and let's roll!'

Devereaux's head slowly emerged from the right panel of the heavy glistening double doors that led to the exclusive penthouse offices of Aaron Pinkus Associates. Furtively, he peered first to his right, then to his left, repeated the exercise, and nodded. Instantly, two heavyset men in brown suits walked out into the corridor and faced the elevators at the end of the hallway, sufficiently apart to allow Sam to walk between them.

'I promised Cora I'd pick up some scrod on my way home,' said the attorney without expression to his guards as they proceeded down the corridor.

'*We* get scrod,' said the man on Sam's left, looking straight ahead, in his voice a mild complaint.

'She feeds Paddy Lafferty porterhouses,' added the guard on the right, more than a mild complaint in his voice. 'Chargrilled.'

'All right, all right, we'll also stop and get a couple of steaks, okay?'

'Better get four,' suggested the left guard in a quiet monotone. 'We're relieved at eight o'clock and those gorillas will smell the porters.'

'It's the rim of fat,' opined the right guard, his focus rigidly forward. 'It lingers so good for a long time.'

'So be it,' agreed Devereaux. 'Four steaks and the scrod.'

'What about potatoes?' asked the left guard. 'Cora's not too big with potatoes and everybody likes potatoes.'

'After six o'clock Cora don't cook potatoes so good,' said the RG, permitting himself a slit of a smile on his impassive face. 'Sometimes it's a little rough finding the oven.'

'*I'll* bake 'em,' said LG.

'My Polish associate can't live without his "cartoffables."'

'That's *kartofla*, you *dupa*. My Swedish associate shoulda stayed in Norway, right Mr D?'

'Whatever.'

The elevator doors parted and the threesome walked inside where they were startled to find two uniformed men who had obviously ridden to the penthouse by mistake, since they made no attempt to get off. Sam nodded politely, turned to face the closing panels, and then blanched, his eyes widening in astonishment. Unless his practised lawyer's vision had deceived him, both uniformed officers at the rear of the elevator had small *swastikas* attached to their shirt collars!

Pretending to have an itch at the back of his neck, Devereaux turned casually to scratch, his eyes taking in their necks. The small black emblems *were* swastikas! He briefly locked eyes with the man in the corner who smiled, the friendly grin somewhat diminished by the absence of several teeth. Sam quickly turned his head back to the front, his confusion mounting – then suddenly the explanation was clear. In New York's Broadway parlance, Boston was a 'tryout town.' Obviously, there was a World War II play, probably at the Shubert or the Wilbur, presenting its wares in Bean Town before assaulting the Big Apple. Still, these actors should know better than to appear off the stage and on the streets in such costumes. On the other hand, he had always heard that actors were a breed apart; some *lived* their roles twenty-four hours a day. Wasn't there an English Othello who actually tried to kill his Desdemona in a Jewish delicatessen one night on Forty-seventh Street over a pastrami sandwich?

The doors opened on the crowded lobby and Devereaux stepped out; he stood in place, glancing around, as his guards flanked him. The threesome proceeded rapidly toward the building's entrance, dodging bodies and a plethora of attaché cases, finally emerging on the wide pavement where Aaron Pinkus's limousine awaited them at the kerb.

'You'd think we were in Belfast, coverin' our asses from all those bomb-throwin' lunatics,' said Paddy Lafferty behind the wheel as the three passengers plummeted into the rear seat, Devereaux viced between his two barrel-chested protectors. 'Straight home, Sam?' continued the chauffeur as he swung the huge car into the flow of traffic.

'Two stops, Paddy,' replied Devereaux. 'Scrod and steaks.'

'Cora's doin' her thing, eh, boyo? She cooks a mean porter as long as you remind her to get it off the fire quick enough. Otherwise you've got nuked gristle and floatin' in bourbon, it is. But you better make it three porters, Sam. My orders are to stay and bring you back into town by eight-thirty.'

'That's five porters,' said the Polish praetorian.

'Thanks, Stosh, but I'm not so hungry –'

'Not you, the relief.'

'Oh, yeah, they'll smell 'em. You know why, don't you? It's the border of fat that sizzles and hangs around –'

'All *right*,' cried Devereaux, trying to find a pause in the conversation to ask what he felt was a fairly vital question. 'Scrod, five porters, rims of sizzling fat and the goddamned relief's olfactory senses – it's all settled! Now *why* is Aaron bringing me back into town at eight-thirty?'

'Hey, boyo, it was *your* idea, Sammy, and I tell you, Mrs Pinkus thinks you're the darlin' of the day.'

'What for?'

'You got that fancy invite to the art gallery *soirée* – how do you like that? I heard her say *soirée*, which means you get pickled at night after work and nobody cares.'

'Art gallery . . . ?'

'Remember, lad, you told me it was that fancy dan client who thinks his wife has the hots for you, which is fine by him, and then you told Mr Pinkus that you didn't want to go and he told Mrs Pinkus, who read that the senator was going to be there, so now you're all going.'

'That crowd's a bunch of leeching fund-raisers and political vultures.'

'They're top society, Sammy.'

'Same thing.'

'Then we go back with you, Paddy?' asked the guard on Devereaux's right.

'No, Knute, there won't be time. You take Mr D's car here. Your relief can follow us in their own.'

'What's with the time?' Stosh objected. 'Just drop us off downtown. Mr D's car is very shaky in the turns.'

'You didn't get it fixed, Sam?'

'I forgot.'

'You'll have to live with it, Stosh. Nothing suits the boss better than driving his little Buick like he's doing now from the office, but not Mrs Boss. This is her chariot, especially with the licence plate he happens to hate, and especially for a wing-ding like tonight.'

'Leeches and politicians,' muttered Sam.

'Same thing, huh?' said Knute.

MacKenzie Hawkins squinted through the windshield of the stolen Oldsmobile at the limousine's licence plate directly in front of him. The raised white letters across the green background spelled out the name *PINKUS* as though the announcement should strike fear in the hearts of observers. It would help if the name were somewhat more threatening, thought Mac, nevertheless glad that he had spotted it in front of Devereaux's place of employment, the name itself one the Hawk would never forget. For weeks during the young lawyer's initial work on behalf of their former corporation, Sam kept yelling *What would Aaron Pinkus think?* until Mac could not stand it any longer and confined the hysterical attorney to quarters just to get some peace. This afternoon, however, a brief telephone call to the law office confirmed the fact that Sam had come home and somehow – God knew how – made peace with one Aaron Pinkus, whose name was an anathema to the Hawk.

From there it was a simple matter to show his newly trained and newly sheared aides-de-camp a six-year-old photograph of Devereaux and order them to stay riding on the single elevator that went up to the penthouse floor until the subject appeared and subsequently to follow him at a discreet distance wherever he walked, keeping in touch with their commanding officer over the walkie-talkies he supplied them from his flight bag. *Don't get any ideas, caballeros, because stealing government property is a thirty-year offence, and I've got your stolen car with your fingerprints all over it.*

Frankly, Mac thought that Sam would head to a friendly bar after work, not that his former legal liaison was a heavy drinker – he was barely a decent one – but he did like a nip or two after a hard day in the field. Well, *goddamn*, had thought the Hawk when he saw Sam emerge from the building under protective escort. How suspicious and how ungrateful could a man *be*? Of all the unmitigated, detestable strategies to employ – *convoys!* And to ring in his employer, the obviously equally detestable Aaron Pinkus, was downright treasonous, definitely *un-American*! The Hawk was not sure his newly acquired aides-de-camp were up to a new strategy. On the other hand, a good combat officer always brought out the best in his troops, no matter how raw they were. So he glanced at them, scrunched beside him in the front seat – he certainly could not permit a potential adversary to sit behind him in a foxhole.

They definitely looked better with regulation haircuts and clean-shaven faces, even though both were bobbing their heads up and down to the Latin beat emanating from the radio. 'Okay, men, '*tenhut!*' cried the Hawk, snapping off the radio while holding the wheel.

'Wot, *loco* man?' asked the astonished aide with less than all his teeth, sitting next to the window.

'That means "attention." You're to pay *attention* to what I say.'

'Maybe better, man, *you* pay us some cash, huh?' said the aide sitting next to Mac.

'All in good time, Corporal – I've decided to make you each a corporal because I'm forced to place additional responsibilities on your basic assignments. Naturally, that calls for an upgrade in pay ... Incidentally, for identification purposes, what're your names?'

'I'm Desi Arnaz,' replied the aide by the window.

'So am I,' said his associate.

'Fair enough. D-One and D-Two, in that order. Now, listen up.'

'Up where?'

'Just *listen*. We've encountered complications from the enemy that will require some aggressive initiative on both your parts. You may have to separate so as to draw hostile personnel away from their posts, thus allowing the objective to be taken –'

'So far,' interrupted D-One, 'I got the "required" 'cause it's used a lot in courtrooms, like "remanded." The rest, I'm not so sure.'

So the Hawk shifted to fluent Spanish, which he had learned as a young guerrilla leader in the Philippines fighting the Japanese. '*Comprende?*' he asked when he had finished.

'*Absolutamente!*' cried D-Two. 'We cut up the chicken and spread around the pieces so we catch the big lousy fox!'

'Very *good*, Corporal. You learn that from one of your latino revolutions?'

'No, señor. My mama used to read the *noosurry* stories when I was a liddle kid.'

'Wherever it comes from, grunt, *use* it . . . Now, this is what we're going to do – *Christ* on a *pogo* stick! What the hell are you wearing on your *collar*?'

'What, man?' asked D-One, shaken by the Hawk's sudden vocal explosion.

'You, *too!*' cried Hawkins, his head swivelling back and forth. 'Your shirts – the collars on your *shirts* . . . I didn't see them before!'

'We didn't have no ties on before, neither,' explained D-Two. 'Chu give us dinero and tol' us to buy two black ties before we go into the big building with d'fancy elevator . . . Also, *loco* man, these h'ain't our own shirts. A couple of bad gringos on motorcycles were very unfriendly to us outside a restaurant on the highway . . . We sold the motorcycles but we kept the shirts. Nice, huh?'

'You idiots! Those insignias are *swastikas!*'

'Waz that?'

'Pretty liddle things,' observed D-Two, fingering the black emblem of the Third Reich. 'We got big fancy ones on the back –'

'Rip 'em off your collars, Corporals, and keep your goddamn tunics on.'

'Toon hocks?' D-One asked, bewildered.

'The jackets, your coats, your *uniforms* – keep them on.' The Hawk stopped in mid-statement as up ahead the Pinkus limousine slowed down and turned right into a side street; Mac did the same. 'If Sam lives in this neighbourhood, the boy's sweeping floors, not filing briefs.' The neighbourhood referred to was a short dark block lined with small shops sandwiched between entrances to time-worn apartments above, bringing to mind those turn-of-the-century sections of large cities teeming with immigrants. All that was missing were pushcarts and pedlars and the sounds of foreign tongues in abrasive counterpoint. The limousine glided into the kerb fronting a fish market; Mac could not do the same as there was no available parking space until the end of the block, at least a hundred feet away and barely seen. 'I don't like it,' said the Hawk.

'You no like what?' asked D-One.

'It could be an evasion manoeuvre.'

'*Invasion*?' cried D-Two, his eyes wide. 'Hey, *loco* man, we no fight in no war, no *revolucion*! We are peaceful malefactors, dat's all.'

'Malefactors . . . ?'

'They also use that lots a' times in court,' clarified the uniform by the window. 'Like "required" and "remanded," you know?'

'No war and no revolution, son, just a cowardly, ungrateful *malefactor* whose escorts may have spotted us . . . You, D-One, I'm going to stop for a moment; you get out and look around that fish store – pretend you're shopping for dinner – and stay in touch. There may be a back door, but it isn't likely; they may even change clothes but our target would swim in his convoy's duds. Still, we can't take chances. He's in the hands of pros now, men, and we've got to show our calibres!'

'Does all dat *tonteria* mean I should watch the tall guy in the picture?'

'That's it, Corporal, and it's not proper to question your superior's direct orders with improper invective.'

'Dat's beautifool!'

'*Move!*' yelled the Hawk, braking the car as D-One opened the door and got out, slamming it shut behind him. 'You, D-Two,' continued Mac, shooting forward, 'as soon as I park, I want you to cross the street and walk halfway back to that big vehicle and keep your eyes on it *and* the store. If anybody comes out in a hurry and gets into the limo *or* any car near it, let me know.'

'Isn't dat what Desi-One is doin', man?' asked D-Two, taking the walkie-talkie out of his pocket.

'He could be ambushed if the eye-corps is sharp enough,

but I sort of doubt it. I generally stayed two vehicles behind the target-moveable so I don't think they reconnoitred positive.'

'You talk funny, you know dat?'

'Into position!' ordered the Hawk, swerving into the parking space near the corner and instantly switching off the ignition. D-Two leaped out of the car, rounded the hood, and raced across the street with the alacrity of a seasoned point. 'Not bad, *caballero*,' said Mac to himself, reaching into his shirt pocket for a cigar. 'You've both got definite possibilities. Real noncom stature.'

And then there was a gentle tapping on the windshield. A policeman stood on the kerbside, gesturing with his club. Momentarily confused, the Hawk looked across the street at the opposing empty space. Just before it was a sign. *No Parking Here to Corner*.

Sam selected the slabs of scrod, thanked the Greek owner with his customary, if mispronounced, '*Aph-háristo*,' and was welcomed by a courteous '*Paracalla, Mr Deveroo*,' as he paid the bill. The two guards, their interest in fish minimal, were bored, and so they looked at the enlarged, faded, framed photographs of various Aegean islands on the wall with no interest whatsoever. Several other customers, seated at two white Formica tables and all speaking Greek, seemed more intent on conversing with one another than buying anything. They greeted two newcomers to the store, but not a third, a man in an oddly unidentifiable uniform who proceeded to walk to the rear counter, which was empty except for chopped ice, and kept peering over the top. Then, under the scrutiny of his unseen observers, the uniformed man pulled a hand-held radio out of his pocket, raised it to his lips and began to speak.

'*Fascisti!*' screamed an elderly bearded Zorba from the table nearest the rear counter. '*Look!* He signals the *Germans!*'

As one, the former over-age partisans from Salonika stumbled forward to attack and capture the hated enemy of fifty years ago as Sam's two guards rushed to his side, their weapons drawn. The object of the aged Greek warriors' assault slashed his arms and kicked his feet out at his attackers, parting them with a certain professional expertise, and raced to the door, stopping just briefly enough to reach into a fishtank by the entrance.

'I *know* that man!' yelled Devereaux, breaking away from the grips of his protectors. 'He wore a *swastika* on his collar! I saw it when we were in the elevator!'

'*What* elevator?' asked the Scandinavian cohort.

'The one we rode down on from the office!'

'I didn't see no coloured swastikas in the elevator,' proclaimed the Polish contingent.

'I didn't say *colour*, I said on his *collar*!'

'You talk funny, you know?'

'You *hear* funny, have you ever considered *that*? ... He's closing in, I can feel it!'

'Feel what?' asked Knute.

'The Titanic. He's on his disaster course – for me – I *know* it! He's the most devious son of a bitch that hell ever created. Let's get *out* of here!'

'Sure, Mr D. We'll pick up the porterhouses at that meat market on Boylston and head right to your place.'

'*Hold* it!' cried Devereaux. 'No, we won't ... Give your coats to a couple of those fellows over at the tables and pass out a few hundred dollars to convince them to get into Aaron's limo and be driven around the harbour ... You go out first, Knute, and tell Paddy to drop them off at some gin mill on the way to the Pinkus house and I'll meet him there. Stosh, you call for a cab, and we'll coordinate the whole thing.'

'This all sounds *crazy*, Mr D!' said Stosh, taken aback at Sam's sudden tone of authority. 'I mean, sir, it doesn't sound like yourself ... sir.'

'I'm going back in time, Stanley, and I was taught by a master. He *is* closing in. I really *do* know it. But he made a mistake.'

'What was that ... sir?' asked Knute.

'He used a real US Army man to do his dirty work. The

uniform was plucked like a chicken, but did you notice the posture, the clipped hair on the back of his neck – that bastard was government issue!'

'*Loco man, where are you?*'

'*Around the block, stuck in the goddamned traffic! Which one are you?*'

'*Desi-Dos. Desi-Uno is wid me.*'

'*Hello, loco man. You are crazier than a bunch of coo-coo parrots.*'

'*What's the on-scene evaluation?*'

'*Cut the crap, man, I got almost killed!*'

'*A firefight?*'

'*Wid fish? Don't be dumb . . . wid crazy old men wid beards who don't speak no h'English.*'

'*You're not making sense, D-One.*'

'*There h'ain't a lot of that goin' around. Specially wid the tall skinny gringo you got a bad thing for.*'

'*Be clearer, Corporal!*'

'*He sent some old men away in the big black car wearing silly clothes – he thinks we don' catch on. He's one dumb gringo!*'

'*Catch on to what?*'

'*He's waidin' for annuder car. One of his amigos is standing in front, lookin' around.*'

'*Goddamn, I'll never get back there in time. We're going to lose him!*'

'*Not to worry, loco man –*'

'*Not worry? Every hour counts!*'

'*Hey, man, how far do these liddle radios go for talkin'?*'

'*They're military-cellular megahertz frequencied. Up to a hundred and fifty miles over land, twice that over water.*'

'*We h'ain't goin' swimmin' in no cars, so everything's h'okay.*'

'*What the hell are you talking about?*'

'*We're gonna follow the gringo and his amigos.*'

'*Follow . . . ? For the love of Caesar's legions, in what?*'

'*Desi-Dos already hot wired a nice Cheffy. Not to worry, we'll stay in touch wid chu.*'

'*You're stealing a car?*'

'Hey, we don' steal nudding. It's like you say – good estrategia. Right, loco man?'

Paddy Lafferty was definitely not amused by the three bearded, elderly Greeks in the back of the Pinkus limousine. One, they smelled like a combination of dead fish and baklava; two, they kept turning on every switch they could find like mental cases in a Video World; three, they looked ridiculous in the ill-fitting jackets belonging to Sam, Stosh and Knute – especially with their beards half covering the lapels; four, there was a distinct possibility that one of them had blown his nose – twice – on the velour window drapes; five – oh, *hell*, what was the *point*? He'd have to do a complete detail job on the car before Mrs Pinkus stepped into it.

It wasn't that Paddy objected to what Sam was doing; actually, it was kind of exciting and surely broke up the monotony of his daily driving schedule, but nothing was really clear to Lafferty. In truth, the whole truth was known only to the Devereaux boyo and Mr Pinkus. Apparently, Sammy had been mixed up in some terrible shenanigans a few years ago and now someone was coming after him to settle a score or two. That, of course, was enough for Paddy; he was very fond of Devereaux, even though the hotshot lawyer could be a little squirrelly at times, and anybody who knew the name of one of the army's great men, namely General MacKenzie Hawkins, was someone sort of special in Lafferty's eyes. Too few people these days, especially the young yuppie types, paid the respect due the great old soldiers, so it was nice to know that among Sam's qualities was a regard for the country's true heroes.

All this was on the plus side for Mr Pinkus and his favoured employee, but what wasn't so plus was the information Paddy felt they all should be given. For instance, who was after Sam and why and what did they look like? Surely the answers to these simple questions were vital to Devereaux's protection. Well, not necessarily the *why* because that could be a legal thing, but the *who* and what the hell they looked like were pretty damned important. Instead, all they were told was that Sam would know, Sam would raise an alarm the instant he recognized the bastard or bastards coming after him. Well, Lafferty had never been an officer, but even a combat sergeant knew a short proper response to that kind of reasoning. As that great soldier, Mac the Hawk, might have said: 'You don't make a primary target one of your forward scouts.'

Suddenly, the limo's telephone rang, abruptly shattering the chauffeur's hero-oriented thoughts about a man he surely worshipped from ten glorious days in France when that great soldier led their battalion. 'Lafferty here,' he said, the phone out of its recess and next to his ear.

'Paddy, it's Sam Devereaux!' yelled the voice over the line.

'Somehow I can tell that, boyo. What is it, Sammy?'

'Are you being followed?'

'I was hopin' to be but I'm afraid not and I've kept one eye on the mirrors –'

'We *are*!'

'That don't make sense, lad. Are you *sure*?'

'Definitely! I'm calling from a pay phone on the Waltham road – at a place called Nanny's Naughty Follies Et Cetera.'

'Hey, boyo, get out of there. You shouldn't be seen on those premises. Mr Pinkus wouldn't like it.'

'What? Why?'

'Are you callin' from the phone about ten feet from the jukebox?'

'Yes, I guess so, I see a jukebox.'

'Look over to your left, at that big circular bar below a long, raised platform.'

'Yes, yes, I will . . . There's just a bunch of dancers – oh, my God, they're all *naked*! Women and men!'

'That's the *et cetera*, boyo. Now, if I were you, I'd take fleet feet and beat it.'

'I can't! Knute and Stosh went out after the Chevy that was following our cab and stopped when *we* stopped. I mean, they're really professionals, Paddy. They spotted the "tag" – they called it a "tag" – and got rid of the taxi, and now they're closing in.'

'I'll be there in less than ten minutes, Sammy! I'm droppin' these Greek archbishops off at the next gas station and swingin' north. I know a short cut. Ten minutes, boyo!'

'Loco man, are you wid us?'

'If your trail markers are accurate, no more than five minutes, D-One. I just passed the Chicken Shot Café, the one with the red neon rooster sign.'

'Maybe you gringos don' know dee difference. Maybe you eat chicken McRooster, no? . . . It don't take you even five minutes from that place.'

'What's the status – what's happening?'

'We good corporales. We got a liddle surprise for you, loco man.'

'Ten-four!'

'Ees not six o'clock –'

'Rolling!'

The stolen Oldsmobile from somewhere in the Midwest careened into Nanny's parking lot in less than three minutes, MacKenzie Hawkins chewing the stub of his cigar and peering out the windshield for his aides-de-camp. Instantly, he saw D-Two at the far end of the asphalt, waving what looked like a large, torn dark blanket. As he raced toward his mechanically talented adjutant, he saw that the signal flag was not a blanket but, instead, a pair of trousers. The Hawk leaped out of the car and approached D-Two, taking a moment to straighten his too long, too red, and, definitely still, too loose wig.

'What's your report, Corporal?' asked Mac anxiously. 'And what the hell are *those?*' he added, nodding at the trousers.

'Dere pants, loco man, what you think?'

'I can see they're pants, but what are you doing with them?'

'Ees better I got 'em than the bad *amigo* who usually wears dem, no? As long as I have deze and Desi-Uno has the odders, the two dumb *amigos* stay where dey are.'

'The two – the escorts, the convoys? *Where are they* . . . and where's the *target?*'

'Come wid me.' D-Two led the Hawk down the deserted far side of the building that was obviously used for deliveries and garbage pick-ups. Parked next to a large trash dumpster, parked so close that the door could not possibly be opened, was a Chevrolet coupé, its opposite door equally secured by a long, discarded tablecloth knotted to the handle and tied to the rear bumper. Inside, one in front, the other in the narrow rear seat, were Devereaux's two guards, their apoplectic faces pressed against the glass of the windows. Closer inspection disclosed the fact that both wore only undershorts, and further surveillance revealed two pairs of shoes and socks placed neatly by the exposed rear tyre. 'De odder windows we open a liddle bit so they got h'air, you know?' explained D-Two.

'Good thinking,' said Mac. 'The Geneva Convention calls for humane treatment for prisoners of war ... Where the hell's *D-One*?'

'Right here, *loco* man,' answered Desi the First, coming around the trunk of the Chevrolet while counting a roll of bills. 'Deze *amigos* should find better yobs or better women. If it wasn't for your man in de photograph, they h'ain't worth the trouble.'

'We don't strip prisoners of nonhostile personal possessions,' said the Hawk firmly. 'Put it back in their wallets.'

'Hey, man,' protested D-One, 'what's personal about dinero? I buy somet'ing from you, I pay. You buy somet'ing from me, you pay. A personal possession is somet'ing you keep, right? No one keeps dinero, so it's not personal.'

'They didn't buy anything from you.'

'What about deze?' said D-One, holding up a pair of trousers. 'And doze,' he continued quickly, pointing at the shoes.

'You stole 'em all!'

'Dat's life, *loco* man. Or, as you say, dat's "strategy," right?'

'We're wasting time, but I'll say this now. You've both shown exemplary initiative, one might even say extraordinary inventiveness under fire. You're a credit to this outfit and I'll recommend you for commendation.'

'Dat's beautifool!'

'Is dat more dinero, huh?'

'We'll get to that later; the objective comes first. Where's the target?'

'De skinny man in d'photograph?'

'Right on, soldier.'

'He's inside, and *dat* is a joint my mama and my priest would spit on me for ever goin' into!' exclaimed D-Two, blessing himself. 'H'oh *boy!*'

'Bad whisky, eh, son?'

'Bad *entretenimiento*. Like you say here, *repugnancia!*'

'I don't think we say that, boy. You mean disgusting?'

'Well . . . one half, not the other half.'

'I don't follow you, Corporal.'

'Everything jiggles. Top and bottom.'

'Top and . . . ? Holy hordes of Genghis Khan! You *mean* –'

'Daz wot I mean, *loco* man! I sneaked in to find the gringo you don' like . . . he was hangin' up the *teléfono* and went to dee big round bar where all these crazy people were dancin' – *desnudo*, señor!'

'*And?*'

'He's h'okay. He watched the *mujeres* not the *hombres*.'

'*Christ* spinning a yo-yo! We don't just have to take the son of a bitch, we have to *rescue* him. *Roll*, troops!'

Suddenly, without warning, a small green Buick sped out of the line of cars in the Nanny's Et Cetera parking lot, screeching to a stop only yards in front of the Hawk and his advancing aides-de-camp. A frail figure emerged, his gaunt face impassive, but his dark eyes alive with electricity. 'I think this is as far as you should go,' he said.

'Who the hell are *you*, little man?' cried MacKenzie Hawkins.

'Little in stature, but not necessarily in stature, if you can follow a dual application of terms.'

'I break the liddle old gringo in half, but I don' hurt him too bad, h'okay, *loco* man,' said D-One, walking forward.

'I come to you in peace, not violence,' said the driver of the Buick rapidly. 'Simply to confer on a civilized basis.'

'*Hold it!*' ordered the Hawk, stopping D-One. 'I repeat, who are you and what's the nature of this conference?'

'My name is Aaron Pinkus –'

'*You're* Pinkus?'

'One and the same, sir, and I assume that under that rather foolish looking wig, you're the celebrated General MacKenzie Hawkins?'

'One and the same, sir,' replied Mac, dramatically ripping the inadequate toupee away from his bristled, grey military brushcut and standing erect, the very breadth of his shoulders threatening. 'What have we to say to each other, sir?'

'I'd estimate a great deal, General. I'd like to think of myself, with your permission, General, as your counterpart, the commander of the opposition for this small skirmish we find ourselves in. Is that acceptable?'

'I'll say this for you, Commander Pinkus. I thought I had superb support adjutants but you outflanked 'em, I'll not deny it.'

'Then you must reevaluate that judgement, General. I didn't outflank *them*, I outflanked *you*. You see, you remained on that busy street for over an hour, so I had my Buick brought down and stayed behind you when you followed Shirley's limousine.'

'I beg your pardon, *sir*?'

'Your two men were brilliant, positively *brilliant*. In fact, I would happily employ either of them. The business in the fish market, the reconvening in the shadows of the doorways across the street – and, *wondrously*, without a car key, but by simply raising the hood of this car in front of us, turning on the *engine*! All my purported wisdom deserts me. How did they *do* it?'

'Ee's simple, *Comandante*,' said a bright-eyed D-Two. 'You see, there are three wires that have to be pried loose and den you cross –'

'*Halt!*' yelled the Hawk, staring at Aaron Pinkus. 'You said you outflanked *me*, you old bastard –'

'I suspect we're the same age,' interrupted the renowned Boston attorney.

'Not where *I* come from!'

'Nor perhaps myself, except for the shrapnel in my spine from Normandy,' said Pinkus quietly.

'*You* were –'

'Third Army, General. But let's not get off the track. I *did* outflank you because I've recently become familiar with your military record, your unorthodox but marvellously successful tactics. I had to be for Sam's sake.'

'*Sam? Sam's* the man I've got to see!'

'You will do that, General. And I shall be in attendance for every word you say.'

Again, without warning or even a hint of sound until it swung off the highway and into the parking lot, the thunderous engine of the Pinkus limousine announced the vehicle's Wagnerian presence in the area. Obviously spotting his employer's Buick, Paddy Lafferty swerved to the left and sped across the pavement, tyres howling as he skidded to a stop ten feet in front of the small gathering at the side of the building. The chauffeur leaped out of the car, his sixty-three-year-old bulk prepared for all manner of brutal assaults.

'Stand *aside*, Mr Pinkus!' he roared. 'I don't know what you're doin' here, sir, but these scum won't touch you!'

'Your concern is very gratifying, Paddy, but no show of force is required. Our conference proceeds peacefully.'

'Conference . . . ?'

'A council of commanders, you could say . . . Mr Lafferty, may I introduce you to the great General MacKenzie Hawkins, of whom you may have heard.'

'Jesus, Mary, and *Joseph*,' whispered the chauffeur, dumbstruck with awe.

'Dee *loco* man is really a h'enerale *grande*?' said Desi-One, equally impressed.

'*El soldado magnifico*!' added Desi-Two softly, staring in wonder at the Hawk.

'You won't believe this,' choked Paddy, finding a small part of his voice. 'I was thinkin' about you only moments ago, sir, your great name having passed the lips of a reverent former young soldier.' Suddenly the chauffeur stood at attention, whipping his right arm up in a snapping salute. 'Gunnery

Sergeant Patrick Lafferty at your service and your command, sir! . . . This is a privilege beyond me wildest dreams –'

Then the screaming began, muted at first by the distant highway traffic, but growing louder by the moment as the racing feet approached them. 'Paddy, *Paddy!* I saw the *limo!* Where *are* you, Paddy? . . . For Christ's sake, Lafferty, *answer* me!'

'Over *here*, Sam. Quick march, *soldier*!'

'What?' Devereaux raced around the corner of the building gasping for breath. Before he could adjust his eyes to the shadows, Patrick Lafferty barked his authoritative sergeant's bark. *"Tenhut*, boyo! I present you to one of the great men of our time, General MacKenzie Hawkins!'

'Hi, Sam.'

Devereaux was momentarily paralysed, capable only of deep-throated moans that emerged from his gaping mouth, the bulging eyes above wild in panic. Abruptly, with the speed of a terrified egret, the frantic attorney whipped around and started racing across the parking lot, waving his arms helter-skelter and raging at the descending sun.

'After him, adjutants!'

'For God's sake, stop him, Paddy!'

The Hawk's aides-de-camp were swifter of feet than Aaron Pinkus's older chauffeur. Desi the First tackled Sam perilously close to the lowered tailgate of a pickup truck, while Desi the Second held Devereaux's head and, ripping off his tie, stuffed it into Sam's mouth.

'*Boyo*,' shouted the revisited Gunnery Sergeant Patrick Lafferty, 'it's a *disgrace*, you are! Is that any way to show respect to one of the finest men who ever wore the uniform?'

'*Mmmfff!*' protested Samuel Lansing Devereaux, pinching his eyes shut in defeat.

CHAPTER EIGHT

'Nice quarters, Commander Pinkus, *very* nice, indeed,' announced MacKenzie Hawkins, striding out of a bedroom in the hotel suite to where the conference had repaired. The former general's nondescript grey gabardine suit had been replaced by his Indian buckskins and his beaded Wopotami jacket – without, however, his tribal head-dress. 'It's obvious you're high strategy staff.'

'I keep the place for business purposes and also because Shirley likes the address,' said Aaron absently, his concentration on the voluminous pages scattered over the desk in front of him, his eyes behind his thick glasses wide with anticipation. 'This is *incredible!*' he added quietly.

'Well, sir, having been with Winston at Chequers,' interjected the Hawk, 'I wouldn't go *that* far. I simply said it was very *nice*. The ceilings aren't nearly so high, and the historical prints on the walls are definitely third rate and actually clash with the decor, as well as with accuracy.'

'We in Boston do our best to introduce the tourists to our past, General,' mumbled Pinkus, his concentration on the papers uninterrupted. 'Accuracy has little to do with environmental authenticity.'

'Dante crossing the river –'

'Try Boston Harbor,' broke in Aaron, turning over a page. 'Where did you *get* this?' he suddenly cried, taking off his glasses and staring at MacKenzie. 'What extraordinary scholar of both law and history put it all together? Who's responsible?'

'Him,' replied the Hawk, pointing at the abruptly shell-shocked Devereaux, sitting on the couch ten feet away, squashed between his two guards, Stosh and Knute, his arms and legs free to move but not his mouth which was bound with three-inch wide adhesive tape. Of course, General Hawkins had insisted that Sam's lips be layered with Vaseline so as not to violate the Geneva accords for prisoners of war. In truth, no one could stand to listen to Devereaux's diatribes any longer, including the general's aides-de-camp, Desi-One and Desi-Two, who stood behind the couch, their postures erect and their arms militarily akimbo.

'*Samuel* did this?' asked Aaron Pinkus in disbelief.

'Well, not actually himself, but he certainly was the spirit behind it, so you could say that in a very real sense he's responsible.'

'*Mmmfff!*' came the muted but still howling protest from the couch as Devereaux lunged forward, tripping over his feet and landing face down on the floor. Grimacing in fury at the Hawk, he scrambled up as the general gave his command.

'*Adjutants*, assault positions!' As a trained commando unit, Desis One and Two leaped over the couch, the former using the rim of the sofa, the latter the head of Knute to vault over the couch and instantly close the distance between themselves and Sam. Pinning him back on the floor, they looked up at the Hawk for instructions.

'Well done, gentlemen.'

'No wonder you recruited from your own personnel, General,' said Pinkus admiringly, standing up behind the desk. 'Are they Rangers?'

'In a manner of speaking,' replied MacKenzie. 'They're specialists in airport security . . . Let him up, men. Put him in the chair in front of the desk and flank him.'

'You two,' said Aaron, looking over at Sam's bewildered Boston guards and speaking gently but not without a mild rebuke. 'I don't mean to criticize, yet it appears to me that you might benefit from some of this military instruction, as it obviously pertains to your work. These soldiers are inordinately quick to perceive the necessity for action, and their nonviolent tactics – such as stripping you of your trousers – is most impressive.'

'Hey, *Comandante*!' offered D-Two, grinning widely. 'You rip off a gringo and take his pants, he h'ain't goin' run into d'street yellin' his head off, h'okay?'

'That'll do, Corporal. Barracks humour doesn't carry well with passive combatants.'

'Beautifool!' cried D-One.

'General,' said Pinkus, 'if you think it's feasible, I believe it's time we now restrict this conference to you, Samuel and me.'

'I quite agree, sir,' agreed the Hawk. 'The sequestered discussions between us should be opened up to include the young fellow.'

'Perhaps you might consider tying him – loosely, to be sure – to the chair, as Mr Lafferty – excuse me, *Sergeant* Lafferty did previously.'

'Then you must have dismissed the gunny when you talked to Sam.'

'The gunny? . . . Oh, yes, the gunnery sergeant – yes, I did.'

'No need for that, now. I'm here . . . Adjutants, stand to! You're dismissed for mess call.'

'Hey, *loco* man, we're real pretty.'

'*Grub*, Corporal. Get some food in your bellies and report back here in one hour.' MacKenzie reached into his buckskin pocket and withdrew his money clip, peeling off several bills and handing them to D-One. 'I'm adding this to your per diem due to your outstanding efficiency.'

'Ee's our dinero?' said D-Two, scowling at the money.

'Supplemental pay, Corporal. It's in *addition* to your dinero which will come later. Take the word of a general officer.'

'H'okay, *grande* h'enerale,' responded D-One. 'We take a lot but when do you *give*?'

'Let's have no hint of insubordination, young fella. Despite the fact that our close association on this mission permits a degree of camaraderie, others might not understand.'

'Beautifool! I don't understand, neither.'

'Get something to eat and come back in an hour. *Dismissed!*'

Desis One and Two shrugged and went to the door, the former checking the time on the three watches strapped to his left wrist as they let themselves out. The Hawk then nodded to Aaron Pinkus. 'As my captive and somewhat contrary to tradition, also my host, you may address your troops, Commander.'

'Your what and I'm who? . . . Oh, yes, I understand.' Pinkus turned to the perplexed Stosh and Knute on the couch. 'Gentlemen,' he began hesitantly, searching for the appropriate words, 'you are relieved of your current duties, and if you would be so kind as to come to our office tomorrow – at your convenience, of course – you will be reimbursed by our accounts department, naturally including the rest of the evening.'

'*I'd* put'em in the *stockade*!' shouted the Hawk, shoving his cigar into his mouth. 'They're assholes! Dereliction, incompetence, and freezing under fire – damn near court martial material.'

'We do things differently in civilian life, General. Dereliction and incompetence are necessary components in the lower ranks of the work force. Otherwise, their superiors, who are frequently less competent but speak better, could never justify their salaries . . . Off you go, gentlemen, and I'm quite sincere in my suggestion that you seek the training so well inculcated in your counterparts on the general's staff.' Stosh and Knute, their sad expressions conveying their genuinely hurt feelings, left quickly. 'There, General,' said Aaron. 'We're alone.'

'*Mmmfff!*' cried Devereaux.

'I included you, Samuel. As much as I might prefer to overlook you, it's not very easy to do so.'

'*Mmmfff?*'

'Cut your whining, son,' ordered the Hawk. 'As long as you don't shout your goddamned head off, your hands are free and you can remove the security strip : . . No sweat, your mouth will still be there, I'm sincerely sorry to say.' Slowly at first, then in a burst of machismo, Sam yanked the tape off, instantly yelped, then proceeded to purse his lips about in

110

various contortions as if to make sure they were functional. 'You look like a skinny piglet in heat,' added MacKenzie.

'*You* look like a cigar store Indian who just escaped from a quarantined wigwam!' yelled Devereaux, leaping up from the chair. 'What the hell are you supposed to be, Tonto with a *lobotomy*? . . . And what the hell do you mean – *I'm* responsible for whatever that crap is on Aaron's desk? I haven't seen you or heard from you in years, you low-life worm of worms!'

'You still have a tendency to get a mite excitable under pressure, don't you, boy?'

'In his defence, General,' interrupted Pinkus, 'in the courtroom he's ice-cold, a veritable laid-back James Stewart, the stutter itself pure calculation.'

'In a *courtroom*,' exploded Sam, 'I know what the hell I'm doing! When I'm around this subterranean son of a bitch, I *never* knew because he either didn't tell me, or the gung ho maggot *lied* to me!'

'Wrong terminology, young fella. It's called disinformation for your own protection –'

'It's called *bullshit*, ensuring my own self-destruction! Now answer my question: Why am I responsible – no, wait a minute – *What* am I responsible for? How can I be responsible for whatever dumb thing you've done when we haven't spoken to each other in years?'

'Again, in fairness,' Pinkus broke in, gently but firmly, 'General Hawkins stated that you were responsible only in the sense that you were the spirit behind the project, said spiritual influence subject to the widest possible interpretation or misinterpretation thus limiting or conceivably eliminating any liability or even association with the endeavour.'

'Stop playing lawyer with this overgrown mutant, Aaron. The only law he knows makes jungle justice look like high tea in an English rose garden. He's pure savage without one iota of redeeming morality!'

'You ought to have your blood pressure checked, son.'

'You ought to have your head checked into a taxidermy shop! Now what the hell have you *done* and why *me*?'

'Please,' Pinkus intruded once again, shrugging apologetically at the Hawk, his brows now arched. 'Permit me to attempt an explanation, General. As one attorney might to another, is that acceptable?'

'We of command know best how to handle our own personnel, sir,' replied MacKenzie. 'Truthfully speaking, I cousined the hope that you might clear your flanks and march to my drummer in that direction. Frankly, it's why I showed you the core of the operation – not the tactics or my rules of engagement, naturally, but the down range objective, as it were. Such basic intelligence is rarely a secret between such men as ourselves.'

'Excellent initial strategy, General. I commend you.'

'*Commend* him?' shouted the still shell-shocked Devereaux. 'What the hell is he doing, marching on *Rome*?'

'We did that, Sam,' said the Hawk quietly. 'Remember, son?'

'That is *one* topic you will never refer to in my presence, General Hawkins,' insisted Aaron coldly.

'I figured you knew –'

'You think Samuel would tell me?'

'Hell, no. You could order him to a kamikaze squadron and he'd short out the spark plugs. No stomach.'

'Then how?'

'The Irish gunny described your covert surgical strike into Sam's quarters. Gunnies usually try to impress command with their contributions.'

'So?'

'Well, you mentioned that the sergeant had tied the boy up and that told me you had dismissed the gunny before talking to Sam, which you admitted.'

'*And?*'

'Why tie him up unless he was hysterical like he is now? And why would such a cool officer of the court – a side of Sam I haven't seen a whole hell of a lot of – be hysterical unless this incursion of yours produced something about him that he never wanted anyone, especially you, to know about?'

'Based on certain obvious premises, your deductive reasoning is acute.'

'That and the fact that when Sam slammed the phone down on me, he missed. I heard another voice over the line – one that didn't have much more control than Sambo's – and when we met in the parking lot, I knew it was you, Commander Pinkus. You yelled a fair amount yourself that afternoon. Especially about a certain operation of ours that concerned the Vatican.'

'So much for a priori deduction,' said Aaron, now shrugging in defeat.

'So much for *lizardshit!*' roared Devereaux. 'I'm here! I exist! If you prick me, do I not bleed –'

'Hardly appropriate, Samuel.'

'What's *inappropriate?* I'm listening to a couple of refugees from a Prussian time warp! My future, my career, my life itself – all are about to shatter into a thousand pieces of broken mirrors –'

'Very nice, son,' broke in the Hawk. 'Like the imagery.'

'He stole it from a French playwright named Anouilh,' added the venerated Boston lawyer. 'Samuel's full of surprises, General.'

'Stop it!' screamed Devereaux. 'I *demand* to be heard!'

'Hell, boy, they can hear you down in Washington, right to the Army G-two data banks, where they keep all those intelligence files.'

'I have the right to remain silent,' mumbled Sam, barely audible and collapsing back into the chair, pouting.

'Then perhaps I may be allowed to break the silence since you've restricted it to yourself?' asked Pinkus.

'*Mmmfff,*' came the tight-lipped reply.

'Thank you ... The point of your question, Samuel, focused on the material provided me by General Hawkins. Granted, there hasn't been time to read it thoroughly, but from what I can glean with a fairly practised eye that's been perusing such documents for nearly fifty years, it's incredible. Rarely have I ever read a more convincing brief. The legal historian who compiled this had the patience and imagination to perceive suspended or broken lines of legislative debate knowing that somewhere there had to be buried additional records that formed contiguous data spelling out the missing pieces. If this all stands up, the conclusions would appear to be *indisputable*, supported by copies of the original, authentic papers! Where did your source ever find them, General?'

'It's only rumour, of course,' answered the Hawk, frowning quizzically, 'but I've heard that they could only have been unearthed from the sealed historical archives at the Bureau of Indian Affairs.'

'The sealed archives . . . ?' Aaron Pinkus looked harshly at the general, then sat down quickly in the chair and picked up several pages, bringing each close to his eyes, studying them not for content but for something else. 'Dear Abraham,' he whispered, 'I know these watermarks . . . they were picked up by an extremely sensitive copier, a state-of-the-art machine.'

'Only the best, Commander.' Hawkins abruptly stopped; it was instantly apparent that he regretted the statement. He glanced over at Sam who was staring at him, then cleared his throat. 'I guess those pointy-heads – those *scholarly* types – get the best equipment.'

'Almost never,' uttered Devereaux in a low, accusing monotone.

'Regardless, General,' continued the excited Pinkus. 'A number of these papers – I refer to the ones concerning the historical documents – are actually reproductions of the original photostats – photographs of *photographs*!'

'I beg your pardon?' The Hawk began mutilating the cigar in his mouth.

'In the days before copiers, when you couldn't simply flatten out aged or rotted parchment, or piece fragments together, and run a beam of light over the whole for an accurate facsimile, photographs, then later photostats, were made to be entered into the archives replacing the disintegrating originals.'

'Commander, I'm not really interested in that technical crap –'

'You should be, General,' interrupted Aaron. 'Your

unnamed legal source may well have come upon a decades-old conspiracy, but his discovery may conceivably be based on stolen evidence long since consigned to the sealed vaults of the government's archives for reasons of the gravest national concern.'

'What?' mumbled Hawkins numbly, aware that Sam Devereaux was now glaring at him.

'The watermarks on these archival photostats indicate a rare, steel filamentous paper designed to withstand the ravages of time and the environmental conditions of the vaults. Actually, I believe Thomas Edison invented it around the turn of the century, and it was ordered into limited archival use in nineteen ten or eleven.'

'*Limited* use . . . ?' asked Devereaux hesitantly, his teeth clenched as he continued to stare at the Hawk.

'Everything's relative, Samuel. In those days deficit spending, when it existed, was restricted to no more than several hundred thousand dollars, and even those figures could freeze the Potomac. The steel-threaded pages in these photographs were enormously expensive and to convert thousands upon thousands of historical documents into them would have broken the treasury. Therefore, only a limited number were chosen.'

'Limited to what, Aaron?'

Pinkus turned to General MacKenzie Hawkins, his demeanour perilously close to that of a judge pronouncing sentence. 'To those documents determined by the government to remain beyond scrutiny for a minimum of a hundred and fifty years.'

'Well, *goddamn!*' The Hawk whistled softly, and further mangled his cigar, as he slapped his beaded buckskins. 'Pay dirt!' he added, looking benevolently at Sam. 'Aren't you proud, son, to have been the "spiritual influence," as the fine commander here put it, behind this grand project?'

'*What* fucking project?' choked Devereaux. 'And *what* goddamned spiritual influence?'

'Well, Sam, you know how you always used to talk about the downtrodden people on this earth and how so little was done to help them? Some might have called all that spewing and mewing horseshit left-wing garbage, but I never did. I mean, I really respected your point of view, son, I really did.'

'You never respected anything or anybody that couldn't blow you away into a grave!'

'Now that's not true, boy, and you know it,' admonished MacKenzie, shaking his index finger at Devereaux. 'Remember all those discussions you had with the girls? Each one of those dear ladies would call me and express her genuine respect and affection for you and your philosophical expressions of compassion. Especially Annie, who –'

'*Don't ever mention that name to me!*' roared Sam, clapping his hands over his ears.

'I don't know why not, son. I talk with her frequently, especially when she gets herself in some of those hairy situations she's prone to, and let me tell you, Sam, she really cares for you.'

'How *could* she?' yelled Devereaux, trembling with rage. 'She married Jesus, not *me!*'

'Dear Abraham,' intoned Pinkus. 'I'm not a party to this colloquy.'

'That's a different calibre of weapon, son, if you'll forgive the comparison . . . But hear me out, boy. I searched for the downtrodden, a people who got screwed by the system, and put all my efforts in setting things right. Somehow I thought you'd be proud of me – God knows, I tried.' The Hawk lowered his chin down into the open collar of his beaded Wopotami jacket, his gaze forlornly on the carpeted floor of the hotel suite.

'Cut that crap *out*, Mac! I don't know what the hell you did or tried to do, I only know I don't *want* to know!'

'Maybe you should, Sam.'

'Just . . . one minute,' Pinkus interrupted, his eyes on the contrite Hawk. 'I think it's time I should reach into my exaggerated bag of legal expertise and pull out a specific, if rarely used, statute. The penalty for unauthorized invasion of sealed government archives carries a sentence of thirty years' imprisonment.'

'You don't say?' said the general, his gaze roaming the carpet as if trying to find a pattern on the all-blue covering.

'Yes, I do say, General. And since this information has no discernible effect on you, I must happily presume that your counsel had full authorization to study the documents referred to in this brief.'

'*Wrongo!*' shouted Sam. 'He *stole* them – it's the G-two mess all *over* again! This lousy excuse for a human being, this unmitigated military mistake, this legend of larceny did it *again*! I know it because I know *him* – I know that dirty little boy look, the rotten kid who wets his bed and tells you it was raining under the covers. *He's* the one who did it!'

'Judgements made in the white heat of emotional reactions are rarely sound, Samuel,' said Pinkus, shaking his head critically.

'Judgements made in the cold light of objective observation over a long and agonizing period of time are generally irrefutable,' rejoined Devereaux. 'If the cookies are made of molasses and the son of a bitch has his hand in the jar with his fingers stuck together, you can be goddamned sure you found the perpetrator! Recidivism is a term the criminal courts have lived with for years.'

'Well, General,' continued Aaron, peering at the Hawk over the rim of his glasses. 'The prosecution seems to have raised a valid point since he relates the current circumstances to a previous act you yourself have confirmed regarding the stolen intelligence files. Behavioural patterns are limited but acceptable evidence.'

'Now, Commander Pinkus,' began MacKenzie, squinting and pursing his lips in bewilderment. 'All this legal verbiage has my head spinning. To tell you the truth, I can't follow half of what you say.'

'*Liar!*' cried Sam, suddenly breaking into a loud sing-song chant as a child might taunting another. 'It's raining under the cov-*verrs*, it's raining under the cov-*verrs* . . . !'

'Samuel, be *quiet*,' admonished the elderly lawyer, his voice ringing with authority as he turned back to the Hawk. 'I believe we can settle this expeditiously, General. Professional courtesy has restrained me from insisting on the name of your incredibly gifted counsel, but now I'm afraid that I must. As an officer of the court, he can refute my young associate's allegation and clear up the matter.'

'It's hardly proper, sir,' said Hawkins, standing erect, his expression stoic, 'for one commanding officer to ask another to betray a confidence. That sort of thing is for the lower echelons where honour's not so prevalent and spines are less than steel.'

'Now come, really, General, where is the harm? Surely this brief, as brilliantly persuasive as it appears to be from what I've read, still has not been tested. Heaven knows, without attorney attribution and in the absence of government challenge, it certainly hasn't been submitted to any court.' Aaron paused, laughing softly. 'If it had been, we'd all know about it as our entire judicial system, as well as the Department of Defense, would come to a stop, all the participants screaming in frenzy. So you see, General Hawkins, there's nothing to be lost or gained . . . ' Pinkus's genial countenance suddenly froze on his face. Slowly, involuntarily, it faded as his eyes grew wide and the pallor of his pale face became ashlike. 'Dear Abraham, please don't desert me,' he whispered, staring at MacKenzie Hawkins's totally blank expression. 'My *God*, it *was* submitted!'

'In a manner of speaking, it found its way to the place where it was intended.'

'It surely couldn't have been a legitimate court of *law*.'

'Again, Commander, you might find allies in that assessment.'

'*Was* it?'

'Some say it is.'

'But there's been nothing in the *media*, and, believe me, they'd all be colliding with one another to get such extraordinary news out. It's catastrophic!'

'There could be a reason for that.'

'What reason?'

'Hyman Goldfarb.'

'Hyman who?'

'Goldfarb.'

'It strikes a bell, but I really haven't the *vaguest* –'

'He used to be a football player.'

In the flash of several seconds, Aaron Pinkus's face lost twenty years. 'You mean *Hymie the Hurricane*? The Hebrew *Hercules* ... ? Do you really *know* him, Mac – I mean ... General, of course.'

'*Know* him? I recruited that yarmulke yo-yo.'

'You *did*? ... Not only was he the greatest linebacker in the NFL, but he broke the stereotype of – shall we say, the overly cautious Jewish male. He was a lion of Judea, the terror of the defence – on a par with Moshe Dayan on the American football field!'

'He was also a crook –'

'*Spare* me! He was my hero of the hour, a symbol for all of us – the highly intelligent muscular giant who made us proud ... What do you mean, he was a *crook*?'

'Well, he's never actually been indicted – close, but no arraignments – but then there are reasons for that, too.'

'Indictments, *reasons*? What are you talking about?'

'He does a lot of work – not exactly officially – for the government. For a fact, I kinda started him off in that department, for the Army, actually.'

'Will you please make sense, General?'

'In a short shell casing, we had some fat loose lips regarding certain weapons specifications that we couldn't uncover even though we knew where the leaks were coming from. I ran across Goldfarb, who was setting up a consulting business on security measures – hell, a picture of him in an undershirt would scare the shit out of Godzilla – and told him to get to work on the problem. You might say that he and his troops go where the Inspector General's office wouldn't get near.'

'*General*, what has Hyman Goldfarb got to do with the silence that has followed your incredible brief when there should be pandemonium?'

'Well, as these things happen in Dizzy City, one thing led to another for the Hurricane. I mean his reputation spread like a brush fire started with flamethrowers, and before you could sit Shiva, everybody in town wanted his services – especially against one another. His list of government agency clients reads like the who's who and what's what around the Potomac. He's got a lot of powerful friends who wouldn't admit they ever heard of him if you plucked their short hairs with a pair of pliers. Squashing indictments are his for raising an eyebrow . . . You see, that's when I really knew we might be close to pay dirt.'

'Pay dirt . . . ?' Aaron shook his head back and forth as though trying to stop the clanging cymbals inside his skull. 'May I ask for clarification?' he pleaded.

'His people came after me, Commander Pinkus. It was an ambush, the objective capture and silence – I read 'em like a book.'

'Capture . . . silence, a book? They came after you . . . ?'

'*After* the Wopotami brief was filed – *long* after! Which has to mean the brief's being taken seriously but the news is being kept under the ponchos because the beltway's about to spiral up to the moon. So what do they do in the meantime? They hire Hymie the Hurricane to solve their problem. Search, capture and destroy! Read 'em like a book.'

'But, General, the lower judiciary, with its caseloads and backlogs and . . . ' Once again, Aaron Pinkus's expression froze as his words trailed off into audible vapour. 'Oh, dear God, it wasn't . . . ? It *wasn't*.'

'You know the rules, Commander. A plaintiff suing the State has direct access, dependent only on the validity of argument.'

'No . . . no, you *couldn't* have!'

'I'm afraid I did. A little outside persuasion on a couple of sensitive law clerks and we went right up to the big legal bathtub.'

'What *bathtub*?' shouted a totally confounded Devereaux. 'What kind of crap is this moral degenerate trying to *sell*?'

'I fear he may have sold it to someone else,' said Aaron, his voice faint. 'He's taken this brilliantly evolved brief – based on materials stolen from the sealed archives – directly to the Supreme Court.'

'You've got to be *kidding*!'

'For everyone's sake, I wish I were.' Pinkus abruptly found his voice and his posture. 'But now, however, we can plumb the depths of this insanity. Who's the attorney-of-record for the plaintiffs, General? A simple phone call will reveal the name.'

'I'm not sure it will, Commander.'

'What?'

'It just got there this morning.'

'This morning . . . ?'

'Well, you see, there was this Indian brave who fed me misinformation, which is different from disinformation, regarding a little matter of a bar exam –'

'Just answer my *question*, General! The attorney-of-record, if you please!'

'Him,' replied the Hawk, pointing at Sam Devereaux.

CHAPTER NINE

Vincent Francis Assisi Mangecavallo, known in certain select circles as Vinnie the Bam Bam, and also as code Ragu, director of the Central Intelligence Agency, paced his office in Langley, Virginia, a perplexed, frustrated man. He had heard nothing! What could have gone wrong? The plan was so simple, so flawless, so airtight. A equals B equals C, therefore A equals C, but somewhere within that simple equation Hyman Goldfarb and his people had lost their marbles and Vincent's own man, the best and most innocuous shadow in the business, had only managed to get lost! *Big Foot! The Abominable Snowman!* What the hell was wrong with the Hurricane? Who had chewed up his well-advertised brains? And where was that miserable slime Vincent had rescued from a not-so-small debt in Vegas and put on a respectable government payroll, telling the casino boys to lose the slime's markers in the interests of national security? *Gone,* that's where he was! But *why*?

Little Joey the Shroud had been overjoyed to hear from his big shot friend from the old days when they all used Little Joey to tail the deadbeats from the Brooklyn docks to the fancy clubs in Manhattan – and Joey was good! He could stand alone by himself in the middle of Yankee Stadium and no one would notice him even if every seat in the place was sold out. Nobody *ever* noticed Little Joey the Shroud; he just faded into the wallpaper as fast as he did in a crowd on the subway. It was a talent he had, like total insignificance – even his face was sort of grey and nondescript . . . So where the hell was he? He had to know he was better off with his old friend

Vincent than *without* his big Washington connection – after all, the markers could be reinstated and the casino Tuxedoes would come after him again. It didn't make sense – nothing made sense!

So the telephone rang, the telephone hidden in the lower right-hand drawer of the director's desk. Mangecavallo ran to it; he had installed that line himself, at night, and with professionals far more experienced than the so-called experts in the Agency's department of clandestine communications. In fact, no one in the government had the number; it was limited to really important people who got things done. 'Yes?' barked the DCI.

'It's Little Joey, Bam-Bam,' said the piping voice on the telephone.

'Where the fuck have you *been?* Thirty-six hours, maybe a day and a half, I don't hear from you!'

'Because for every minute of that time I been spinning my head and racing my ass from one fuckin' place to another keeping up with a *testa zuccone!*'

'What are you talkin'?'

'Also you told me not to call you at home, which number I ain't got, and definitely not through the big spy joint's switchboard, right?'

'Yeah, right. So?'

'So between airplanes and hustling airline clerks and paying off taxi drivers ready to spit in my face, and bribing a retired cop who once put a collar on me to do a little checking with his old buddies in the black-and-whites to find a certain stretch limo with a funny licence plate, I ain't had a hell of a lot of free time!'

'Okay, okay. Tell me what happened. Did you get anything I can use?'

'If you can't, *I* can. This jigsaw's got more crazy pieces than a pasta salad, definitely worth more than those markers in Vegas.'

'Hey, Joey, those markers were over twelve thousand!'

'What I got's worth double, Bam-Bam.'

'Don't use that name, huh?' said Mangecavallo defensively. 'It don't fit with this high class office.'

'*Hoo-hay*, Vinnie. Maybe the dons shouldn't have sent you to school. You lose your humility, you don't get no respect.'

'Knock it off, Joey. I'll take care of you, on my father's grave.'

'Your poppa's *alive*, Vinnie, I saw him the other week at Caesars. He's rolling high in Vegas, only not with your momma.'

'*Basta* . . . He's not in Lauderdale?'

'You want a room number? If a bimbo answers, don't hang up.'

'That's enough, Joey. Stick to business or those markers will reach fifty big ones with the vigorish and I cut you loose, *capisce*? Now, what *happened*?'

'Awright, awright, just testing the water, okay, Vinnie? . . . What happened – *jeez*, what *didn't* happen?' Little Joey the Shroud took a deep breath and began. 'Like you figured, Goldfarb sent a crew out to that Indian reservation – I knew right away when I recognized the Shovel walking through the big fake stockade gate past the nut Welcome Wigwam and head straight to the food counter. Boy, can that huge *fazool* eat! Right behind him is this scrawny gibrone who blows his nose a lot, but the bulge in his hip pocket ain't Kleenex. Then I mingled and heard two other friends of the Shovel who talked funny English asking about this Thunder Head you're interested in, and let me tell you they were hot for his warm body . . . So I wait from a big distance and the four cannolis – one of which is a broad – run out of the souvenir joint and race like hell up a dirt road where each of them goes into a different path –'

'A path?' interrupted the bewildered Mangecavallo. 'Like more dirt?'

'S'help me, Bam-Bam – excuse me, Vincenzo – dirt and bushes and trees, a regular forest, you know what I mean?'

'What the hell, it's a reservation, I guess –'

'So I waited and waited and waited,' continued Little Joey rapidly.

'So am I, Joey!' broke in the director.

'Okay, okay. Finally, this big shot Indian comes running out of the woods – I mean, he's got to be your big shot Thunder Head 'cause he's got a clothesline full of feathers from his head to his ass – and barrels down the dirt road, then hangs a right till he reaches a big funny-looking tent and goes inside. Then I saw what I tell ya', Vinnie, I couldn't believe with my own eyes! This big shot Indian comes out a few minutes later, only he's *not* the same *guy*.'

'What are you smokin', Little Joey?'

'No, I mean it, Vin. He's the same *gumbar* but he don't *look* like the same *gumbar*! Instead, he looks like a four-eyed accountant in a regular suit, wearing glasses and some dumb fuckin' wig that don't fit, and carrying a big cloth suitcase . . . Well, naturally, the suitcase tells me he's breaking out of the reservation, and the way he looks tells me he don't wanna be an Indian no more.'

'Is this gonna be a long story, Little Joey?' asked Mange-cavallo plaintively. 'Get to the goddamned point.'

'You want your markers' worth and I wanna prove what I got's worth more, okay? . . . But I'll cut to the airport in Omaha where I followed him and where he got a ticket on the next plane to Boston, which I also did the same. However – and this is important, Bam-Bam – while I'm at the counter I show the little girlie one of my phony federal badges and tell her the government's interested in the big fella with the stupid lookin' wig. I think the wig did it, 'cause the broad was so helpful I had to explain to her that everything was on the quiet and she shouldn't call nobody. Anyway, I got the name from the big *gumbar's* credit card –'

'Give it to me, Joey!' exclaimed the DCI, picking up a pencil.

'Sure, Vin. It's *M*, small *a*, small *c*, capital *K*, *Hawkins*, *G-e-n* with a period, then *U.S.A.* followed by a big *R*, then *e* and a *t*. I wrote it down but I don't know what it all means.'

'It means his name is somebody Hawkins and he's a retired army general . . . Holy shit, a *general*!'

'There's more, Vinnie, and you better hear it –'

'I've *got* to hear it! Go on.'

'So I resume the tail in Boston and everything goes crazy, I mean *pazzo*. At the airport he runs into a men's room where he meets a couple of Spics wearing uniforms I never seen before, and they go out to the parking area and get into an Oldsmobile with an Ohio or Indiana licence plate and drive away. Quick, I lay a fast fifty on an off-duty taxi and tell him to stay with the Olds when things go even *more* crazy! . . . This now accountant type Indian chief takes his two refried beans to a fuckin' barber shop, then s'help me God, Bam-Bam, they drive to some park by the river where the big lasagna makes his two enchiladas march around the grass like a couple of *marionetti* while he keeps yellin' at 'em. I tell ya, it was weird!'

'Maybe this retired general is a Section Eight, it could happen, you know.'

'Like he got bounced for mixing up tanks for dirigibles and saluted the trucks?'

'You read about it all the time. Like some of our dons, sometimes the bigger the guns the flakier they get. Remember Fat Salerno in Brooklyn?'

'Hoo-hay, do I remember! He wanted to make oregano the flower of New York State. He walked right into the Albany legislature yellin' his head off about discrimination.'

'That's just what I was thinking about, Little Joey. Because if this M-small-a-small-c Hawkins, retired General Fruit-of-the-Loom, is Chief Thunder Head like I agree with you, we got ourselves another Fat Salerno yelling his head off in Washington also about discrimination.'

'He's *Italian*, Vinnie?'

'No Joey, he's not even an Indian. So then what happened?'

'So then the big lasagna and his two enchiladas got back in the Olds – that's when I had to slip my off-duty creep another fifty – they drove to a busy downtown street and just stayed there. Not the two refrieds; they get out, and after they stop at a men's store, they go into a big building, but the nut-Indian-chief-now-four-eyed accountant just keeps sitting in the car. That's when I had to hand over *two* fifties to the lousy off-duty thief 'cause he says his wife's gonna hit him with a hot frying pan if he don't come home, and he had a point . . . It was over an hour before a big stretch limo pulls up in front of the big building and three gumbars get in, followed by the two enchiladas who go right to the Olds which follows the limo. Then I lost both of them.'

'You *lost* . . . ? What are you telling me, Joey?'

'Not to worry, Bam-Bam –'

'*Please!*'

'Sorry. Vincent Francis Assisi –'

'Forget *that*, too!'

'Awright, awright, I apologize with all my heart –'

'Your heart's gonna stop unless you tell me why I shouldn't worry!'

'I lost the *zuccones* in the traffic, but not before I got the licence of the big dark-blue stretch, and at the same time, would you believe, I remembered the name of the Boston police-prick who collared me twenty years ago and who, I figured, had to be in his late sixties, and who, Christ willing, might still be alive like I was, since we were both pretty much the same age.'

'I *hate* long stories, Little Joey!'

'Okay, okay. So I went to his house, which wasn't much after his long years of public service, and we raised a glass or two of good cheer to the old days.'

'*Joey*, you're driving me *nuts!*'

'Awright, awright. I implored him to maybe put his downtown connections to work, along with ten C notes for himself, to find out who owned the limo with the funny licence plate, and maybe also where it went when it was followed by the Olds and maybe even where it was at the present time . . . Would you believe he answered the first question without so much as a break between whiskies?'

'*Joey*, I can't *stand* you!'

'*Calma, calma*, Bam-Bam. Right away he tells me the limo belongs to one of the biggest lawyers in Boston, Massachusetts. He's a yarmulke named Pinkus, Aaron Pinkus, who is considered a very upright guy and very respected by the lowest and the highest of the fish, both legit and not so legit. He's immaculate – God forgive me – but it's true, Vinnie.'

'He's a fuckin' slime, that's what he is! What else did the shamus tell you?'

'That as of twenty minutes ago the stretch is parked outside the Four Seasons Hotel on Boylston Street.'

'What about the Olds and the big phony Indian chief? Where the fuck is *he*?'

'We don't know where the Olds is, Vinnie, but my shamus got the word on the Midwest licence plate and you ain't gonna believe it – I mean it's *unreal*!'

'So try me.'

'It belongs to the Vice-President!'

'*Magdalene?*' yelled the Vice-President of the United States, slamming down the telephone in his study. 'Where's that darn *Oldsmobile* of ours?'

'Back home, honeybunch,' replied the lilting voice of the Second Lady from the living room.

'Are you sure, lovey-dove?'

'Of course, lamb chop. Just the other day the maid called to say the gardener's assistant had trouble driving it on the highway. It simply stopped and wouldn't start again.'

'My God, did he *leave* it there?'

'Heavens no, dimplekins. The cook called the garage and they towed it in. Why?'

'That awful man from the CIA, the one with the name I can't pronounce, just phoned to tell me it was seen in Boston being driven by vicious criminals and when did I lend it to them. We may have image problems –'

'You've got to be *shitting* me!' screamed the Second Lady, bursting into the room, her hair rolled up in pink curlers.

'Some son-of-a-bitch bastard must have stolen the fucking thing!' yelled the Vice-President.

'You sure you *didn't* lend it to one of your crumb bum buddies, you asshole?'

'Christ no! Only *your* scumball friends would ask to borrow it, you bitch!'

'Hysterical recriminations will get us nowhere,' stated an emphatic but shaken Aaron Pinkus, as MacKenzie Hawkins straddled Sam Devereaux, the general's knees pinning the lawyer's shoulders to the floor while occasional cigar ash fell on Sam's contorted face. 'I suggest we all cool it, as the young people say, and try to understand the position each of us finds himself in.'

'How about a firing squad right after my disbarment proceedings?' choked Devereaux.

'Come on, Sam,' said the Hawk reassuringly. 'They don't do that any more. The goddamned television loused it up.'

'Oh, I forgot! You explained it once before – public relations, I remember now. You made it clear that there were other ways, such as shark fishing trips for three and only two come back, or duck hunting in a blind where suddenly a dozen water moccasins show up when nobody knew there were any snakes around. Thanks a bunch, you psychotic maggot!'

'I was only trying to keep you in line for your own benefit, son, because I cared for you. Like Annie still does to this day.'

'I *told* you! Never mention that *name* to me!'

'You really lack understanding, boy.'

'If I may, General,' interrupted Pinkus from behind the desk, 'what he lacks at the moment is a clarification of the circumstances, and he's entitled to that.'

'Do you think he can handle it, Commander?'

'I believe he'd better try. Will you try, Samuel, or shall I call Shirley and explain that we are not at that art show because you appropriated her limousine, packed it with exuberant elderly Greeks, and forced me, as your employer, to attend to your personal difficulties – which, by extension, are not legally inseparable from my own?'

'I'd rather face a firing squad, Aaron.'

'A wise decision. So would I. I understand that Paddy has to send the velour curtains to the cleaners ... Let him up, General, and allow him to take my chair here.'

'Behave now, Sam,' said Hawkins, cautiously getting to his feet. 'There's nothing to be gained by violence.'

'That's a fundamental contradiction to your entire existence, Mr Exterminator.' Devereaux rose from the floor and proceeded to hobble around the desk as Pinkus gestured at his chair. Sam sat down with a resounding thump, his eyes on his employer. 'What am I looking at and for, Aaron?' he asked.

'I'll give you an overview,' answered Pinkus, walking across the room to the mirrored bar recessed in the hotel suite's wall. 'I will also bring you a decent thirty-year-old brandy, a luxury your lovely mother and I have in common, for you will need the effects of a mild depressant as, indeed, we did prior to our examination of your "château's lair." I may even give you a very generous portion because it could not possibly alter the sobriety your attorney's mind will be shocked into by what you read.' Aaron filled a crystal goblet with a richly dark brown cognac, brought it to the desk, and placed it in front of his employee. 'You are about to read the incredible and after doing so, you're going to have to make the most important decision of your life. And may the God of Abraham – said Abraham who I sincerely believe has royally screwed up – forgive me, but I, too, shall have to make a momentous decision.'

'Cut the metaphysical stuff, Aaron. What am I looking for? What's your overview?'

'In a matzo ball, my young friend, the United States government stole the lands of the Wopotamis through a series of conspiracies in which promises were spelled out in treaties, said treaties subsequently determined never to have existed, yet actually buried in the sealed archives of the Bureau of Indian Affairs in Washington.'

'Who the *hell* are the *Wopotamis*?'

'An Indian tribe whose territories extended north along the Missouri River to Fort Calhoun, west following the Platte to Cedar Bluffs, south to Weeping Water, and east to Red Oak city in Iowa.'

'So what's the big deal? Historical real estate was compensated by the coin-of-the-era as spelled out by the Supreme Court in – I think in nineteen twelve or thirteen.'

'Your photographic memory is, as usual, extraordinary, Sam, but you're permitting a gap, a lapse, as it were.'

'I never do that! I'm *perfect* – legally, that is.'

'You're referring to treaties that were part of the record.'

'What other kind *were* there?'

'Those that were buried, Sam . . . That's what's in front of you now. Read them, my young friend, and render me your astute legal opinion in an hour or so. In the meantime, drink the brandy sparingly – your instinct may be to swill, but don't, just sip . . . There are pads and pencils in the upper-right drawer and the brief starts with the stack on your left, marked alphabetically in succeeding sheaves across the desk. You'll want to make notes, I'm certain of that.' Aaron turned to the Hawk. 'General, I think it would be a good idea if we left Sam alone. Every time he looks at you I sense that his concentration goes astray.'

'Must be the tribal outfit.'

'I'm sure there's a connection. And regarding your appearance, what do you say we have Paddy – Sergeant Lafferty – drive us to a small restaurant I often frequent when I don't care to run into inquisitive acquaintances.'

'Hold it, Commander Pinkus. What about Sam here? He's had a rough day in the field and an army travels on its stomach, you know.'

'Our young friend is extremely adept where room service is concerned, General. His expense vouchers confirm his expertise . . . However, at the moment he appears impervious to hunger.'

Sam was. Mouth gaped and eyes wide, Devereaux leaned forward over the initial pages of the brief, a pencil gripped in his hand, poised over a yellow legal pad. He dropped the pencil, and as it clattered on the desk, he whispered, 'None of us will survive. They can't afford to let us live.'

Over three thousand miles due west and slightly north of Boston, Massachusetts, is the venerable city of San Francisco, California, and it is no surprise to learn that statistics indicate that the majority of East Coast migrants to the Bay City are former residents of Boston. Some demographers claim it is the glorious harbour, so reminiscent of the home of the Tall Ships, that has drawn these refugees from New England; others say it is the highly charged academic atmosphere represented by the numerous university campuses and the proliferation of debate-prone cafés so indigenous to the Massachusetts capital; still others insist the magnet lies in the progressive and often obsessive tolerance of differing lifestyles that appeals to the contrariness of the Boston mentality, for with what delightful frequency have the voters of Boston gone against the national tide? Regardless – or perhaps via the dicta of numerous television and radio talk-show hosts, one should say *irregardless* – this statistic has little to do with our story except that the individual we are about to meet, as one Samuel Lansing Devereaux was a graduate of the Harvard Law School.

Actually, she might have met Devereaux a number of years ago, as the firm of Aaron Pinkus Associates was intensely interested in her and actively sought her interest in them. Fortunately or unfortunately, she sought other environs, as she was thoroughly fed up with her status as a member of a minority that basically bewildered the Boston professionals and academic poseurs alike. She was neither black nor Jewish, neither Oriental nor Hispanic, had neither roots in the Mediterranean nor forebears in lands of the Bengal or the Arabian Sea – and these presumably comprised the legitimate minorities within Boston's American melting pot. There were no clubs, no societies, no panels founded to espouse the cause of her particular minority because ... well, nobody actually *thought* about them as a group concerned with upward mobility, which was, of course, the key to public expression. They were just there, doing their thing, whatever it was.

She was an American Indian.

Her name was Jennifer Redwing, the 'Jennifer' having supplanted 'Sunrise,' which, according to her uncle, Chief Eagle Eyes, was given to her as she emerged from her mother's womb with the first rays of the morning sun at

Omaha's Midlands Community Hospital. During her formative years, it became apparent that she, and then later her younger brother, were among the Wopotami tribe's more gifted offspring, so the Council of Elders raised the necessary funds to ensure educational opportunities. And once she had taken advantage of those gifts to the fullest extent of her talents, she could not wait to head back west – as far west as possible – to where people did not expect *Indians* to wear saris and have little red dots on their foreheads.

However, her migration to San Francisco was more of an accident than a plan. She had returned to Omaha, passed the Nebraska bar, and was employed by a prestigious law firm when the accident happened. A client of the firm who was a noted wildlife photographer had been commissioned by *National Geographic* to roam a modern Indian reservation and do a photographic essay on its contemporary fauna. His pictures would be juxtaposed with prints of the past, the obvious point being to show the decimation of the life-sustaining animal kingdom once known by the country's original inhabitants. The photographer was a seasoned if somewhat libidinous professional, and he knew a downer assignment when it was presented to him; who the hell wanted to look at a dying world of wildlife next to romanticized etchings of fertile plains and forests, a hunter's paradise? On the other hand, perhaps with a little imagination, things could be turned around – say with an authentic Indian guide in all the pictures ... say with a *zaftig* female guide in various casual shots, bending this way and that ... Say with 'Red' Redwing, that stunner of a lawyer who had the office next to his own attorney, and for whom the photographer had a definite letch.

'Say, Red,' began the lensman one morning, poking his head into the lady-lawyer's office and using the nickname her coworkers used, derived naturally from her surname and not her shining dark hair. 'How'd you like to pick up a couple of hundred bucks?'

'If you're suggesting what I think, I suggest you go down to Doogies,' was the ice-cold reply.

'Hey, momma, you've got me wrong.'

'Not from the circumstantial hearsay that abounds around this office.'

'On my honour –'

'Strike one.'

'No, honest, it's a legit assignment from the *Geographic*.'

'They show naked Africans but I don't recall seeing any naked white women, and I've had regular medical and dental checkups so I'm familiar with the publication.'

'You're off-base, lady. I'm merely looking for a pictorial guide in an essay that zeros in on some pretty rough circumstances about reservations. A Harvard-trained lawyer who just happens to be a member of an Indian tribe could make the difference between attention being paid and flipping over the pages.'

'*Oh?*'

So the shoot was done and despite the fact that Red Redwing was an extremely promising young attorney, she was also extremely naive in the world of professional photography. In her fervent desire to help her people, she acceded to the photographer's selection of clothes, refusing only to pose in a bikini while holding up a dwarfed river trout, and not thinking to get initialled approval of the photographs aimed for publication. There was one other 'only': she caught the lensman snapping pictures of her bending over the carcass of an electrocuted squirrel, a photograph that surely would show more of her generous breasts beneath the loose peasant's blouse than a proper attorney should permit, and threw a hefty punch into the man's mouth. What followed unnerved her to the point that she declared the session over. Lips bleeding, the photographer fell to his knees screaming. 'It's over, babe, but please, *please* do that again!'

The article appeared and the subscription department of the *National Geographic* was swamped with a burst of new activity. It also came under the scrutiny of one Daniel Springtree, a part Navajo senior partner of Springtree, Basl and Karpas, a law firm to be reckoned with in San Francisco. He placed a call to Jennifer 'Red' Redwing in Omaha and pleaded his case, a case based in his guilt at not having done enough for his father's side of the family. The firm's Rockwell jet was sent to Omaha to bring Redwing to San Francisco for an interview, and the moment Red saw that Springtree was seventy-four years old and still in love with his wife of fifty years, she knew it was time to leave Nebraska. The firm in Omaha was distraught but powerless; since the appearance of the *National Geographic* article, its client list had tripled.

On this particular morning, junior partner Redwing of Springtree, Basl and Karpas, soon many believed to become Basl, Karpas and Redwing, had legal matters on her mind light years away from tribal concerns. That was until her intercom buzzed and her secretary announced, 'Your brother's on the line.'

'*Charlie?*'

'That's who. He says it's urgent and I believe him. He didn't even take the time to tell me that he knew I was beautiful by the sound of my voice.'

'Good Lord, I haven't heard from him in weeks –'

'Months, Miss Red. I like his calls. Level with me, boss. Is he as handsome as you are gorgeous? I mean, is it a family thing?'

'Take an extra half hour for lunch and let me talk to my brother.' Redwing touched the lighted button on the telephone line. 'Charlie, darling, how *are* you? I haven't heard from you in . . . in months.'

'I've been busy.'

'The clerking? How's it going?'

'It's over. Finished.'

'That's good.'

'Actually, I've been spending some time in Washington.'

'That's even better,' exclaimed the sister.

'No, it's not. It's worse – *the* worst.'

'Why, Charlie? A good DC firm would be terrific for you . . . I know I shouldn't tell you this but you'll find out in a day or so. I had a call from an old friend on the Nebraska bar and you not only passed the exam, little brother, you were in the highest percentile! How about that, you genius you?'

'It doesn't matter, sis, nothing matters any more. When I said it was over and finished, I meant me and all thoughts I ever had of a legal career. I'm destroyed.'

'What are you *talking* about? . . . Oh, is it money?'

'No.'

'A girl?'

'No, a guy. A man.'

'*Charlie*, I never even *suspected*!'

'Oh, for God's sake, not that.'

'Then *what*?'

'We'd better have lunch, sis.'

'In *Washington*?'

'No, here. I'm downstairs in the lobby. I didn't want to come up – the less you have to do with me in public, the better it is for you . . . I'll get to Hawaii first, then work on the ships and maybe reach American Samoa, where, with any luck, they don't get much news –'

'You stay right where you are, *feather head*! Big sister's on her way down and I might just beat the *crap* out of you!'

A stunned Jennifer Redwing stared at her brother across the table; she was speechless, so Charlie struggled to break the silence. 'Nice weather you have in San Francisco.'

'It's pouring, you idiot . . . *Charlie*, why didn't you *call* me before you got mixed up with this lunatic?'

'I thought about it, Jenny, honest, but I know how busy you are, and in the beginning it seemed like one big joke and we were all having a lot of fun and the joker was spending money and no one was getting hurt – a little broiled now and then but not hurt – then all of a sudden it wasn't a joke any more and I was in Washington.'

'A litigant before the Supreme Court under false represen- tation, *that's* all!' interrupted the older sister.

'It was only for show, Jenny, I didn't actually *do* anything . . . except meet two of the justices – on a very informal basis.'

'You *met* with –'

'*Very* casually, sis, they'd never remember me.'

'How and why not?'

'Hawkins told me to hang around the lobby every once in a while in a tribal jacket and buckskins – I tell you, I felt like a goddamned fool – and one day the big black judge came out and shook my hand and said, "I know where you're coming from, young man," and a week later the Italian fellow met me in a hallway and put his arm around my shoulder and said kind of sadly, "Those of us who came from across the sea were frequently treated no better than you."'

'Oh my *God* . . . !' mumbled Red Redwing.

'It was very crowded, sis,' added her brother quickly. 'Lots of tourists and lawyers – whole crowds.'

'*Charlie*, I'm an experienced attorney; I've argued before the Court, you know that! Why didn't you pick up a phone and *call* me?'

'I guess part of the reason was that I knew you'd get all upset and ream me out, but the real reason was that I figured I could talk Mac the Clown out of the whole mess. I explained to him that it was a lost cause made total because of my situation, which would annihilate any conceivable leanings in the brief's favour, a prospect as improbable as my entering a rodeo. My idea was to immediately file a writ of default based on subsequent discoveries, wiping the slate clean . . . I learned this much while wandering those hallowed halls like Minnie Ha Ha's brain-damaged kid. They'll drop a case quicker than Uncle Eagle Eyes can belt down a shot on the slightest pretext.'

'What did this Hawkins say to your suggestion?'

'That's the problem, I never got a chance to spell it out in full. He wouldn't listen; he only shouted, and when he finally gave me my clothes back, the clothes you sent me the money for while clerking –'

'Your *clothes*?'

'It's another story. Anyway, I was so grateful to get 'em and so pissed off, I just ran. Again, I figured I'd call him later, like in the morning and try to reason with him.'

'Did you?'

'He was gone. *Split*. Johnny Calfnose – you remember Johnny . . . ?'

'He still owes me bail money.'

'Well, Johnny was sort of Mac's special adjutant for security matters, and he told me that Hawkins left for Boston but made it clear that if there were any calls or mail from Washington, Johnny was to reach him immediately at a number in Weston, Massachusetts – that's outside of Boston.'

'I know where it is. I spent a few years in Cambridge, remember? So did you call him?'

'I tried to. Four times, in fact, and each time all I got were minor variations of the same woman's hysterical scream along with incoherent accusations that I think somehow concerned the Pope or *a* pope.'

'That's not unusual. Boston's predominantly Catholic, and in times of stress its communicants seek solace from their Church. Wasn't there anything else?'

'No. After the last call, whenever I tried again, all I got was a busy signal which I took to mean that crazy lady took the phone off the hook.'

'It also means that Hawkins is in Boston . . . Do you have the number?'

'I know it by heart.' He recited it and sighed. 'I'm sunk.'

'Not yet, Charlie,' said Sunrise Jennifer 'Red' Redwing, glaring at her sibling. 'I have a not-so-minor vested interest in your predicament. I *am* your sister and I *am* an attorney and regardless of what the law states, there's a hell of a lot of guilt by association in this business. Also, you're a pretty nice kid and, God help me, I love you.' The sister signalled a waiter who came over immediately. 'Bring me a phone, will you please, Mario?'

'Certainly, Miss Redwing. I'll get the one from the next booth.'

'You won't see me again for years,' began the brother. 'Once I get to Honolulu or Fiji, I'll find work on the ships and –'

'Oh, shut up, Charlie,' said the sister as Mario the waiter plugged in the telephone and handed it to her. She dialled, and seconds later spoke. 'Peggy, it's me and you can have two hours for lunch if you'll take care of a couple of things for me.

First, find out the name and address of the person who has this phone; it's in Weston, Massachusetts.' She recited the number as Charlie wrote it out on a napkin. 'Then book me on a late afternoon flight to Boston – yes, I said Boston and no, I won't be in tomorrow, and to anticipate your next question, I will not send my brother in to take my place because you'd corrupt him ... Oh, and Peg, get me a hotel reservation. Try the Four Seasons, I think it's on Boylston Street – we had our Law Review party there.'

'Jenny, what are you *doing*?' cried Charlie Redwing as his sister hung up the phone.

'I think it's pretty obvious. I'm flying to Boston and you're not going anywhere but to my apartment where you will behave and stay by the telephone. Your only other option is for me to have you arrested for fraud and nonpayment of outstanding debts – or possibly I could call up a close friend and client who could watch over you. Frankly, I think jail's preferable; my friend plays offensive guard for the Forty-niners.'

'I refuse to dignify terrorist threats, and I repeat: What the *hell* do you think you're doing?'

'I'm going to find this lunatic Hawkins and stop him. Oh, not just for you, Charlie, and parenthetically for me, but for our people.'

'I know. We'd be the laughing stock of the reservations, I told Mac that.'

'Far worse, little brother, *far* worse. Everything you've told me boils down to one irreducible catastrophe. SAC – Offutt Air Force Base, the global headquarters of the Strategic Air Command, which is smack-dab in the centre of this lunatic general's grand design. No matter how insane it sounds and unquestionably is, do you think those goliaths in Washington will sit still for a minute with even the hint of any interference with SAC?'

What can they do except laugh it out of court or pay no attention at all and fry me on the side for false representation? I mean, what *can* they do?'

'Make new laws, Charlie, laws effectively destroying the

tribe. They could start by condemning the land we do have and dispersing the inhabitants thereon. Hell, it's been done for highways – even country roads and backwater bridges by politicians owing a few debts. What are they compared with SAC's limitless payrolls?'

'Disperse . . . ?' asked the brother softly.

'Sending our people hither and yon to ratty houses and dinky apartments as far away from one another as possible,' replied his older sister, nodding. 'What we – or they – have now is no Garden of Eden, but it's *theirs*. Many of them have lived there all their lives and most of those lives span seventy and eighty years. They're the human stories behind the cold government statistics that supposedly justify national interests.'

'Could Washington *do* that?'

'At the blink of an eye on a campaign contribution; it's legend. Country roads and backwater bridges are only a spit in the taxpayers' ocean, but the government's largesse where SAC's concerned is Lake Superior.'

'Again, sis, what can you really *do* in Boston?'

'Break a retired general's ass, little brother, and everyone else's around him.'

'*How?*'

'I'll know better when I find them, but I suspect it'll be something as outrageous as the lunacy in their own ballpark . . . Say a conspiracy mounted by the enemies of democracy to bring the honourable giant to its knees and destroy our beloved America's first-strike capabilities worldwide. Then tie in legal terrorism with racist undercurrents by trumped-up depositions tracing the cabal to fanatical Arabs and resentful Israelis in concert with the hard-liners in Beijing along with the Reverends Moon, Farrakhan and Fallwell, joined by the Hari Krishnas, Fidel Castro, the peaceniks on Sesame Street – and God knows what else. This planet abounds with rotten fish and perceived rotten fish that provoke instantaneous and passionate reactions. We'll guarantee in pretrial examinations to throw the whole spectrum at them.'

'*Pretrial . . . ?*'

'You heard me.'

'This is all positively *nuts*, Jenny!'

'I know that, Charlie, but so are *they*. Anyone can sue anybody in a free society, that's both the insanity and the glory. It's not the litigation that's important, it's the threat of public exposure ... Good Lord, I can't wait to get to Boston!'

CHAPTER TEN

Desi the First knocked sharply on the hotel door for the third time, shrugging as he did so at his comrade in arms, Desi the Second, who shrugged back in reply. 'Maybe our *loco* man, the great h'enerale, has taken a poof-powder, no?'

'Wa' for?'

'He owes us dinero, yes?'

'I don' think he' do dat – I don' *wanna think* he'd do it.'

'Neither do I, man, but he tol' us to come back in an hour, no?'

'Maybe he dead. Maybe that even more *loco* gringo who yells all the time put him and the liddle old man away.'

'Then maybe we break the door down.'

'And make so much noise the gringo police come after us and we eat the lousy gringo food again for a long time? You make good plans, amigo, but chu got no mechanical abilities, y'know wad I mean to say?'

'What *mecánico*?'

'Hey, man, we promise each odder, we speak h'English, no?' replied Desi-Two, removing a small many-bladed contraption from his pocket, a penknife-type instrument that defied description. 'So better we can "h'assimilate," waddever that means.' The jump-starter of Chevrolet automobiles approached the door, briefly glancing up and down the deserted corridor. 'We don' gotta break down no door. Dese liddle *plástico* locks no problem – dey got a liddle white *plástico* release.'

'How chu know so much about hotel doors, man?'

'I work lotsa times as a waiter in Miami, man. The gringos

142

call for room service and by d' time you got the tray there, they too drunk to find d' door an' if you bring the tray back, you get yelled at in the kitchen. Ees better to know how to open doors, no?'

'Ees good school you go to.'

'Before that I worked in d' parking lots. *María Madre*, they are *universidades!*' Desi the Second, his grin ebullient, twisted a white plastic blade in the vertical lock space and slowly opened the door. '*Señor!*' he exclaimed at the figure inside. 'You *b'okay*, man?'

Sam Devereaux sat trancelike behind the desk, his glazed eyes fixed on the pages in front of him. 'Nice to see you again,' he said quietly, the words in no way connected to his concentration.

'We almos' knock the door down, man!' cried Desi the First. 'What's *wrong* wid chu?'

'Please don't knock *me* down again,' came the all but monotonic reply. 'I possess the weight of the legal world on my person – I don't need you.'

'Hey, come on, gringo,' continued D-One, approaching the desk. 'What we done was nudding like personal, man. We jus' follow orders from the *grande* h'enerale, y'know?'

'The *grande* h'enerale has haemorrhoids in his mouth.'

'That h'ain't nice to say,' rebutted D-Two, joining his companion as he closed the door and put his indescribable break-and-entry tool back into his pocket. 'Where's the h'enerale and the líddle fella?'

'What . . . who? Oh, they went to dinner. Why don't you join them?'

''Cause he tol' us to be back here in one hour and we are good *soldados!*'

'Oh . . . yes, well, I can't comment on that because my office was not the instrument of instruction.'

'Wad chu saying?' asked D-One squinting, looking at the attorney as one might a deformed paramecium under a microscope.

'What? . . . Hey, look, guys, I'm kind of involved here and

you're right, I don't take anything that's happened personally. Believe me, I've been where you're at.'

'Wad does dat mean?' D-One said.

'Well, Mac's a pretty strong person; he can be very convincing.'

'Wad's a "mac"? A piece of meat can talk?'

'No, that's his name. MacKenzie – I call him Mac, for short.'

'He not short, man,' said Desi-Two. 'He's one big gringo.'

'That's part of it, I guess.' Sam blinked several times and leaned back in the swivel chair, arching his neck as if to briefly relieve the pressure he felt. 'Big, tough, rough and all powerful – and he makes men like you and me march to his cymbals when we should know better ... You two, you're street smart, and me, I'm law smart, and still he beats us down.'

'He don't beat *nobody!*' said D-One emphatically.

'I didn't mean literally –'

'I don' give a shit how you mean it, man, he makes me and my amigo here *feel* better, so wadda you say about *that?*'

'I can't think of a thing.'

'We talked while we ate the rotten tacos made by some blond-haired gringo down the street,' added D-Two, 'and we both say the same thing. The *loco* man's h'okay!'

'Yes, I know,' said Devereaux wearily, focusing his eyes back on the pages in front of him. 'You really like him, that's fine.'

'Where does he come from, man?' asked Desi the First.

'Come from? ... How the hell do *I* know? The army, where else?'

Desis One and Two exchanged glances. The former spoke, addressing his companion. 'Like we saw in the window with the pretty pictures, right, man?'

'Get the name spelled out good,' said D-Two.

'H'okay.' Desi the First turned back to the preoccupied attorney. 'You, Señor Sam, do like my fren' says.'

'Do what?'

'Write out the *grande* h'enerale's name.'

'What for?'

''Cause if you don', man, your fingers h'ain't gonna work so good.'

'Delighted to oblige,' said Devereaux quickly, picking up a pencil and tearing off a page from his legal pad. 'There you are,' he added, writing down Hawkins' name and rank. 'I'm afraid I don't have an address or a telephone number, but later on you might check the penal institutions.'

'You talkin' dirty about the *grande* h'enerale?' asked Desi the Second suspiciously. 'Why you don' like him? Why you run h'away and yell at him and try to fight him, huh?'

'Because I was a bad person, a *terrible* person,' cried Sam plaintively, his hands outstretched in supplication. 'He was so good to me – you *saw* how nice he talks to me – and I was so *selfish*! I'll never forgive myself, but I've seen the error of my ways and I'm trying to make it up to him by doing this work he wants me to do – *needs* me to do . . . I'm going to church tomorrow morning to ask God to forgive me for being so awful to a great man.'

'Hey, Señor Sam,' said Desi-Two, in his voice God's forgiveness. 'Nobody's all a' time perfect, you know? Jesus, He unnerstand dat, right?'

'You can bet your beads on it,' replied Devereaux under his breath. 'There's a nun I know who's got to stretch even His compassion.'

'Wad chu say, man?'

'I said the well-known compassion of nuns beads in on what you say – that's an American expression meaning you're right.'

'Dat's cool,' interrupted Desi the First, 'but me and Desi-Two got some heavy t'inking to do, so we gonna *vamos* an' accept the word of a religious man that the *grande* h'enerale is h'okay like we say.'

'I'm afraid I don't understand.'

'The *grande* h'enerale owes us dinero –'

'Money, you mean?'

'Dat's wad I mean, gringo, an' we *wanna* trust him, but we

145

gotta be *positivo*, you know? So you tell the *grande* h'enerale dat we'll be back here tomorrow for our dinero, h'okay?'

'Okay, but why don't you wait for him – outside, of course?'

''Cause, like I say, we gotta t'ink and talk . . . an' also we gotta know we can trust him.'

'To be perfectly frank, I don't understand you.'

'You don' have to. Just' tell him what I say, h'okay?'

'Sure.'

'Come on, amigo,' said Desi-One, extending his left wrist beyond his sleeve, revealing the three wristwatches. 'I tell ya', ya' can' trust *nobody* no more! Dis lousy Rolex is a phony!'

With these cryptic words, Desi the First and Desi the Second left the suite, both waving cordially to Sam as they closed the door. Devereaux shook his head, sipped his brandy, and returned to the sheaves of papers on the desk.

Dawn broke over the eastern skyline of Boston, Massachusetts, to the extreme annoyance of Jennifer Redwing, who had forgotten to pull the window drapes. The harsh rays of the early sun penetrated her eyelids and woke her up . . . Forgotten, hell, she had been too damned tired to think of them when she staggered in from the airport at two in the morning. Four hours of sleep was not enough even with her energy, but circumstances precluded staying in bed. She got up, partially closed the drapes, turned on the bedside lamp and scanned the room-service menu, finding what she hoped she would find: twenty-four-hour availability. She picked up the phone, ordered a Continental breakfast and thought about the day ahead.

Everything came down to short-circuiting a son-of-a-bitch former general, MacKenzie Hawkins, and whoever the scum were behind him. And she *would* short-circuit them, *blast* them into the electrified legal grids, no matter what it took, no matter the avenues of legal deceit she had always abhorred. Today was different. Although forever grateful to her tribe and her people – that gratitude acknowledged by her overseeing their investments and contributing a third of her income to their accounts – she was furious that outsiders would attempt to take advantage of the tribe's admittedly chequered history and naiveté solely for profit. Her little brother, Charlie, was right, although he misinterpreted her anger. She wouldn't merely 'ream' him out, she was going to ream *all* of them out – right out of their unconscionably corrupt ballpark!

Breakfast arrived, and with it a degree of calm. She had to concentrate. All she had was a telephone number and an address in Weston. It wasn't much, but it was a beginning. Why didn't the hours pass faster? *Damn*, she wanted to get started!

It was five-thirty in the morning and Sam Devereaux, his eyes close to bleeding, had finished the Wopotami brief along with thirty-seven pages of notes on his legal pad.

Oh, *God*, he had to rest, if only to find some sense of perspective, if there was any in the whole insane mess! His head was bursting with hundreds of relevant and irrelevant facts, definitions, conclusions and contradictions. Only a period of calm would restore his oft-praised faculties of reason and analysis, which at the moment were so diminished he doubted he could handle kindergarten recess, much less talk Sanford somebody-or-other out of beating him up when they were both six years old during one of those periods in the playground. He wondered whatever happened to that out-sized bully; he undoubtedly ended up a general in the army, or a terrorist. Not unlike 'Madman' Mac Hawkins, who was currently asleep in the hotel suite's guest bedroom and who was responsible for bringing two hundred-odd pages of unmitigated disaster to the attention of Aaron Pinkus and Samuel Lansing Devereaux, who now conceded that he would never wear the judicial robes – except perhaps as a last wish before being shot in the cellars of the Pentagon by the combined orders of the President, the Department of Defense, the CIA, the DIA, and the Daughters of the American Revolution. And Aaron – poor Aaron! He not only had to face Shirley with-the-freeze-dried-bouffant over a little matter of a missed art show, but he, too, had read Mac's brief, in itself a veritable invitation to oblivion.

Christ Almighty, the *Strategic Air Command*! If the toons on the Court gave even partial credence to the appeal – and it was an appeal to conscience as well as legality – whole segments, if not *all* of SAC, would be the property of some minuscule, indigent Indian tribe with the half-assed name of Wopotami! The law was specific: All subsequent structures and materials found on usurped or stolen real estate belonged to the injured party or parties. Holy *shit*!

Rest – maybe even sleep, if he could manage it. Aaron had been right when he and Mac had returned around midnight and Sam had bombarded Hawkins with what he had to admit were relatively hysterical questions and accusations.

'Finish it, my boy, then get some sleep and we'll talk tomorrow. Nothing's accomplished when the strings are too taut to find the proper notes; and to be perfectly honest with you, gentlemen, I face a discordant coda for the evening when I see my darling Shirley . . . Why, oh why, Sam, did you ever mention that infernal art show to me?'

'I figured you'd be mad at me when you found out I didn't go to it with one of our richest clients because his wife keeps trying to feel me up. Also, *I* didn't tell Shirley.'

'I know, I know,' had said Aaron in defeat. 'Would you believe I told her because I thought it was amusing as well as pointing up an honourable aspect of your character? A minimum of five hundred attorneys I know would be in intimate contact with the lady at the slightest provocation.'

'Sam's *better* than that, Commander Pinkus,' MacKenzie Hawkins had insisted. 'The lad's got principles, although they're not always so apparent.'

'General, may I suggest once again that you remove yourself from Samuel's presence for the reasons we discussed at dinner? You'll find the guest bedroom most accommodating.'

'Has it got television? I like to find those war movies, that's what it's all about, you know.'

'You don't even have to get out of bed. Just aim the remote and shoot from a comfortable foxhole.'

Jesus, he was exhausted! thought Devereaux as he got out of the chair and ambled his way into the master bedroom, only vaguely aware that Aaron had had the courtesy to turn on the bedside lamp. He closed the door – firmly – and concentrated on his shoes – which should he take off first, and how? The conundrum was solved when he reached the bed and fell down on it, his shoes intact, his eyes closed. Sleep was immediate.

Then, from distant halls of complete vacuum, a jarring, incessant alarm reached him, growing in volume until his personal galaxy was shocked into successive explosions. He reached for the telephone, noting that the crystal bedside clock read eight-forty. 'Yes?' he mumbled.

'This is *Scratch Your Assets*, you lucky, *lucky* person you!' shrieked the voice over the line. 'This morning we're calling hotels picked at random from our revolving bowl by a member of our *great* audience, and then a room number from the second bowl picked by the most recent grandmother from our great, *great* audience, and you're *it*, you lucky person! All you have to do is tell me what tall bearded president gave the Gettysburg Address and you win a Watashitti clothes dryer from the Mitashovitzu Company, who just happens to own this *great* station! What's your answer, you *terrific* person?'

'Fuck off,' replied Sam, blinking at the sunlight that streamed through the windows.

'Cut the *tape*! Somebody get the juggling dwarfs and go out to the audience –'

Devereaux replaced the phone and groaned; he had to get up and read his notes and the prospect was not appealing. Nothing at all was appealing in his foreseeable future, which was filled with black holes that would swallow him up and endlessly deep crevices through which he would fall, spinning in agony for an eternity. *Goddamn* Hawkins! Why did the manic military son of a bitch have to come back in his life? . . . Where *was* Hawkins? It was not like the drill-happy war-horse to greet the morning with less than a full-throated battle cry. Maybe he had died in his sleep – no, some things were too good to be hoped for realistically. Mac would go on forever, terrifying succeeding generations of peaceful innocents. Still, silence and MacKenzie Hawkins were a dangerous combination; nothing good ever came from a quiet predator. So Sam rose from the bed, surprised but hardly astonished that his shoes were still on his feet, and walked unsteadily to the door. Cautiously he opened it, only to see Von Maniac seated behind Aaron's desk in a bathrobe, looking for all the world like a kindly old grandfather, peering through metal-framed glasses at that ill-begotten, nefarious brief.

'Your morning reading material, Mac?' asked Devereaux sarcastically, walking into the suite's sitting room.

'Well, hello there, Sam,' said the Hawk warmly, removing his glasses as though he were a retired elderly academic of gentle disposition. 'Have a good sleep? I didn't hear you get up.'

'Don't give me that little old winemaker routine, you conniving python. Outside of the telephone, you probably heard every breath I took, and if there were trees in here and it was dark, I'd have a garrotte around my throat.'

'Now, son, you really do misjudge me, and let me tell you it pains me sorely.'

'Only a megalomaniac could make such an appeal referring to himself three times in one sentence.'

'We all change, boy.'

'The leopard has spots when he's born and he has spots when he dies. You are a leopard.'

'I guess it's better than a python, eh? . . . There's juice and coffee over on the table, also a couple of Danish. Have some; it keeps the morning blood sugar up – damned important, you know.'

'Are you into geriatric medicine now?' asked Devereaux, going to the room-service table and pouring himself black coffee. 'Selling tonic to natives?'

'I'm not getting any younger, Sam,' answered Hawkins, a note of sadness in his voice.

'I was just thinking about that in a roundabout way, and you know what I decided? I decided that you were going to live forever, an eternal threat to the planet.'

'That's an impressive evaluation, son. There are good threats and bad threats, and I thank you for the status you afford me.'

'Christ, you're impossible!' mumbled Devereaux, carrying his coffee to the chair in front of the desk and sitting down. 'Mac, where did you *get* all that stuff? *How* did you get it? *Who* put it together?'

'Oh, didn't I mention that?'

'If you did, my state of shock precluded my hearing it ... Let's start with the sealed archive materials. *How?*'

'Well, Sam, you've got to understand the psychological manifestations of those of us who toil in the vineyards of our government, both civilian and military. Try to comprehend the paradox in which we generally find ourselves after long years of service –'

'Cut the preamble horseshit, Mac,' broke in Devereaux harshly. 'Spell it out.'

'We're screwed.'

'That spells it out.'

'We make half, if that, of what we could make in the private sector, most of us believing that we're making something else as equally important as financial gain. It's called "contribution," Sam, real honest-to-God contributions to a system we believe in –'

'*Stop* it, Mac. I've heard all of this before. You also have damn good pensions and retirement perks like buying at PXs at half price, and generous insurance, and it's damned hard to fire you if you're no good at your jobs.'

'That's a particularly narrow point of view, Sam, and applicable to the few, not the overwhelming many.'

'All right,' said Devereaux, sipping his coffee and looking hard at the Hawk. 'I'll concede that. I just got up from three hours' sleep, I feel rotten, and you're an easy target. Now, how did you get the archival stuff?'

'Remember "Brokey" Brokemichael, not Ethelred but Heseltine, the one you hung that bum drug rap on?'

'If I live to be four hundred and ten, I'll carry those preposterous names to my grave . . . If *you* remember, they, or *he* started me on my road to hell with General Lucifer by having me walk out of the data banks with a couple of thousand top-secret files.'

'Yeah, well there's sort of a connection in a way. You see, when the Army wouldn't give Brokey his third star – because of you, young fella, and the confusion over the names – he mounted his high horse and said "I quit!" . . . Well, even the army has a conscience, as well as connections. You can't cut loose a goddamned military legend and just let him fade away like that rich fruitcake MacArthur opined to Congress. I mean, Brokey didn't sell his expertise to a foreign government like Manila and have a bundle in reserve. So the boys over at Defense scouted around for a job for old Brokey, something not too tough in the brain scan department, but the kind of title that warrants a fair sum so Brokey could augment his retirement pay, both of which he so richly deserves.'

'Don't tell me,' interrupted Sam. 'The Bureau of Indian Affairs. The *big* office.'

'I always said you were the brightest lieutenant I ever met, boy.'

'I was a *major*!'

'Temporary and reduced in rank by Heseltine's friends. Didn't you read your discharge?'

'Only my name and the date of separation . . . So we have déjà vu; you and the insidious Brokemichael are really back in my life . . . Obviously, *Brokey* – honour-bound by comrades bonded in battle – saw fit to let some air into a few musty archive depositories and rummage through a number of sealed files.'

'Oh, nothing so random as that, Sam,' protested the Hawk. 'A lot of research went into this investigation before that action was deemed necessary. Of course, the fact that Brokey was where he was had a kind of stimulating effect at the beginning, and I can't deny that having access to all that centralized Indian history wasn't a help, but months of research were required to uncover some mighty peculiar shenanigans that called for aggressive decisions.'

'Decisions like illegally breaking into the sealed archives without judicial appeals or warrants which are available to any legitimate party with probable cause?'

'Now, son, certain operations are best carried out away from the floodlights, if you know what I mean.'

'Such as holding up a bank or breaking out of prison.'

'That's harsh, Sam. Those are criminal activities; this is rectifying a great crime.'

'Who put it all together?'

'What do you mean?'

'Who wrote it? The structure, the verbiage, the arguments and appraisals . . . the concrete refutations of the status quo?'

'Oh, that wasn't hard, just time-consuming.'

'*What?*'

'Hell, there are all kinds of forms to follow in the law books, and fancy language that complicates simple meanings to the point where you can go nuts trying to follow the nonsense, but it reads very official-like.'

'*You* did this?'

'Sure. I just worked backwards, from the simple to the obscure, with a little heartfelt indignation thrown in.'

'Jesus *Christ!*'

'You're spilling your coffee, Sam.'

'It's a casebook brief!'

'Well, I don't know about that, but thanks, son. I just took it one sentence at a time, cross-checking with all those law-school textbooks. Hell, anybody could do it if they've got twenty-one free months to write it in and their brains don't blow out with all that mumbo-jumbo horseshit. You know, sometimes it took me a whole week just to get down half a page so it sounded right . . . Now you went and spilled the rest of your coffee, boy.'

'I may also throw up,' said Devereaux with a quiver in his voice as he rose from the chair, his trousers stained throughout the pelvic area. 'I am vapour, I don't exist. I am merely an aspect of some undiscovered dimension where eyes and ears float indiscriminately in spirals, seeing and hearing but with no knowledge of form or matter, reality itself an abstraction.'

'Sounds fine, Sam. Now if you'll throw in "whereas" a couple of times, and a few "parties of the first and second parts," you could take it into court ... You all right, boy?'

'No, I am not all right,' replied Devereaux in what could only be described as a soft ethereal cadence. 'However, I must heal myself and find my karma so as to struggle through another day and find the shadows in the light.'

'The shadows *where* ... ? You got funny cigarettes stashed away in that bedroom?'

'Speak not of things beyond your understanding, Sir Neanderthal. I am a wounded eagle soaring up into the sky for my final release from earth.'

'Hey, Sam, that's *good*. I mean it's real *Indian* talk!'

'Oh, shit.'

'Now you broke the spell, son. The tribal elders don't countenance that kind of language.'

'Well, hear *this*, you Anglo-Saxon savage!' yelled Sam suddenly, close to losing control but abruptly pulling back to the vocal strains of his previous search for karma. 'I remember Aaron's words precisely. " ... we'll talk tomorrow," that's what he said, and "tomorrow" in itself does not define a specific time. Therefore, as party of the second part whose opinions were solicited, I prefer to construe "tomorrow" as having a wide latitude of hours since the word fundamentally implies "toward morning" but without prior restrictions regarding the rest of the day until darkness descends.'

'Sam, can I get you an ice bag, an aspirin – maybe a drink of that fine brandy?'

'No, you may not, you diseased plaguer-of-the-planet. You will listen to my determination.'

'*Termination* ... ? That's my lingo, boy!'

'Be quiet,' continued Devereaux, walking to the hotel door and turning, the unfortunate coffee stain on his light-coloured trousers having spread maliciously. 'I hereby determine that the hour of our conference will take place post meridian, the specific time to be mutually agreed upon with later communication by telephone.'

'Where are you going, son?'

'To where I can find solitude in isolation and collect my thoughts. I have a great deal to think about, Mr Monster. I'm going home to my lair, shower in steam for an hour or so, and then sit in my favourite chair and ponder. *Au revoir, mon ennemi du coeur*, for so it must be.'

'*What?*'

'See you later, General Asshole.' Devereaux went out into the hotel corridor, closed the door, and walked to the nearby bank of elevators on the right. Having used his limited French on the Hawk, his thoughts briefly returned to Anouilh, and the conclusion the playwright reached when he wrote that there were times when there was nothing left but to scream. This was one of those times, but Sam refused to give in to the temptation. He pressed the descending button, his entire being on hold.

The elevator door opened and Devereaux walked inside, nodding briefly, unconsciously, at the only other passenger, a woman. And then he looked at her. Suddenly *lightning* flashed before his eyes and *thunder* crashed into his ears as life and blood instantly returned to the walking corpse he had been only seconds before. She was *glorious*! A bronzed Aphrodite with glowing dark hair and incandescent eyes of a light, bewildering colour; with a face and body sculpted by Bernini! She responded to his stare with a modest glance until her gaze obviously strayed to the large wet circle of cloth that saturated the crotch of his trousers. Oblivious to anything but her beauty, yet conscious of the weakness in his knees, Devereaux spoke.

'Will you marry me?' Sam said.

CHAPTER ELEVEN

'You take one step toward me and you won't see for a *month*!' With the speed of a vice squad decoy, the striking bronze-skinned woman ripped open her purse and whipped out a small metal cylinder. Arm outstretched, she held it in front of her, the tube of Mace upright and aimed at Devereaux's face barely three feet away.

'*Hold* it!' cried Sam, his hands above his head in abject surrender. 'I'm sorry – *please* – I apologize! I don't know what made me say that . . . it was an involuntary slip, a result of stress and exhaustion – a mental accident.'

'It seems you've had a physical one as well,' said the woman, her tone ice cold as her eyes dropped briefly down to Devereaux's trousers.

'What?' Sam saw exactly what she meant. 'Oh, my God, the coffee – it was *coffee* . . . *is* coffee! You see, I've been working all night and there's this crazy client – you probably won't believe this, but I'm an attorney – and he drives me up the wall, and I was having coffee when I just couldn't *stand* it any longer, *him* any longer, and I spilled the coffee. I just wanted to get out of there – see, I was in such a hurry I forgot my jacket!' Devereaux suddenly stopped, remembering that he didn't have his jacket; some bearded Greek had it. 'Actually . . . never mind, it's all too grotesque.'

'That thought occurred to me,' said the woman, studying Sam and, satisfied, putting the cylinder of Mace back in her purse. 'If you're really an attorney, I suggest you get some help before the court insists on it.'

'I'm considered a rather superior attorney,' offered Devereaux defensively, drawing himself up to his full height, the image somewhat vitiated by roaming hands trying to cover his soiled trousers. 'I really am.'

'Where? In American Samoa?'

'I beg your pardon?'

'Forget it. You remind me of someone.'

'Well,' began Sam, a touch relaxed and genuinely embarrassed. 'I'm sure he was never the idiot I look like.'

'I wouldn't cover that bet with a great deal of money.' The descending elevator slowed to a stop. 'I wouldn't cover it with a dime,' the woman added quietly as the door opened.

'I *am* sorry,' repeated Devereaux as they walked out into the hotel lobby.

'It's okay. To tell you the truth, it was a real mallet. I've never been hit with that one before.'

'Then the men of Boston have lost their eyesight,' said Sam brightly, but innocently, no leer in his statement.

'You *do* remind me of him.'

'I hope the resemblance isn't too unpleasant.'

'At the moment, *mezzo-metz* ... If you're going into an early conference, change your trousers.'

'*Oh*, no. This stressed-out legal beagle is taking a taxi home to get unwound before the next dog race.'

'I'm getting a taxi, too.'

'At least let me tip the doorman, my apology thus backed up with a couple of bucks.'

'Very lawyerlike. Maybe you *are* good.'

'Not bad. I wish you needed legal advice.'

'Sorry, Clarence Darrow, it's in oversupply.'

Out on the pavement and the doorman attended to, Devereaux held the door of the taxi as she climbed inside. 'In light of my asinine behaviour, I don't suppose you'd care to meet me again.'

'It's not your behaviour, Counsellor,' answered the siren of his morning dreams as she once again opened her purse, this time removing a piece of paper – to Sam's relief, 'but I'm only here for a day or two and my court calendar is jammed.'

'Sorry about that,' said Devereaux, perplexed. And then his lady of the morning sunlight turned to the driver and gave him the address of her destination. 'Christ *Almighty*!' whispered Sam in shock as he involuntarily closed the door.

Conference ... Clarence Darrow ... Counsellor – court calendar! The address the bitch gave was his own *house*!

Sitting anxiously forward in his chair in the Oval Office, the President of the United States was annoyed, *really* annoyed, as he gripped the telephone in his hand. 'Now, come *on*, Reebock, give a little, you ca-ca son of a doggie girl! The Court has to take *some* responsibility if there's even an outside possibility that we all get our tailgates blown away by those aggressor islands in the Caribbean, say nothing of the superpowers in Central America!'

'Mr President,' intoned the Chief Justice of the Supreme Court, his sombre vocal presence marred by a recurrent nasal twang. 'Our system of the rule of law in an open society requires expeditious adjudication of legal redress, the relief from injury swift and adequately compensatory. Therefore the Wopotami hearings must be made public. To coin a phrase, "justice delayed is justice denied."'

'I've heard that before, Reebock, you didn't make it up.'

'Really? No doubt I was the inspiration. I'm known for that sort of thing, I'm told.'

'Yes, well along those lines, Mr Chief Justice –'

'Inspiring people, you mean?' interrupted the leader of the Supreme Court. 'Do tell.'

'No, regarding things you're known for,' corrected the President. 'I've just had a call from Vincent Mangee ... Mangaa – that fellow over at the CIA.'

'In my early days as a young prosecutor, Mr President, he was known as Vinnie the Bam-Bam.'

'No kidding?'

'One does not kid about such sobriquets, sir.'

'I guess not. Gosh, it sounds like it could sort of deflate his degree from Oxford.'

'From *where?*'

'It's not important, Reebock, but it's a real coincidence that you should mention your early days as a prosecutor –'

'A very *young* prosecutor, Mr President,' broke in the Chief Justice apprehensively.

'Yes, Vincent understands that. He even said there's probably no relevance now – today, so many years later – but still we've all got to cover our backsides because this Wopotami thing is going to set off a national debate, I mean a real zing doozer!'

'I'm afraid that's your problem, Mr President, or should I say the combined responsibilities of the Executive and the Legislative branches.' The Chief Justice paused, then added, stifling a giggle, 'It's in your lap, baby – *tee hee*.'

'Reebock, I heard that!'

'Terribly sorry, sir, an insect in my nose ... I'm merely trying to explain that we are not an activist Court. We do not make the laws, we *uphold* them in the grand tradition of strict constructionists. And as you know, several members of the Court feel strongly that the Wopotami case may be built on a firm foundation of constitutional law, although they certainly haven't rendered any final decisions, and they better not. However, to keep the hearings closed would be construed as *interpreting* that great document like those dirty liberals do, not reflecting its true intent.'

'Golly, I know that,' said the President, drawing out his words plaintively, 'and that's what's got Vincent upset. All your individual opinions will be studied by scholars, and newspaper editors and columnists and, well, darn it to doo-doo-ville, everybody! And you could be in trouble, Reebock.'

'*Me?* ... I don't support the goddamn thing! My correct-thinking colleagues and I will argue until we bury those sanctimonious idiots who keep throwing that garbage of "collective conscience" at us. We'll run them out of the Court before we give in and they know it. Good *Christ*, you think I'd give those arrow-happy aborigines a nickel's worth of mule-shit? They're no better than the *Neegros*!'

'That's what Vincent figured –'

'Figured what?'

'It seems that when you were a young assistant prosecutor there was a definite pattern in your indictments and the cases you tried –'

'With a record of convictions that was the envy of the office!'

'Almost all exclusively black and Hispanic,' completed the President.

'Hell, yes, and I got those mothers! They were the ones committing all the crimes, you know.'

'*All* of them?'

'Let's put it this way . . . the ones I wanted to go after for the good of the country. With felonies on their records, they couldn't vote!'

'Vincent figured that, too.'

'What are you driving at, Mr President?'

'Frankly, Vincent's trying to protect you, protect your place in history.'

'*What?*'

'Although you're the strictest of the strict constructionists, you're against the Wopotamis, yet I'm told you even refuse to read the brief. Is that because they're "no better than the *Neegros*"! Do you really want to go down in the books as the racist chief justice who's going to vote against the purported evidence because of the colour of the plaintiff's skin in a landmark decision?'

'Who could *think* that?' asked the flustered champion of constitutional law. 'My interrogations will be filled with compassion ultimately overridden by the practical realities, which I'm firmly convinced will be the Court's finding by at least three votes. The country will understand. The hearings must be open.'

'Would that mule ca-ca stand up against the published record of your excessive convictions of darker skinned minorities as an assistant prosecutor – especially if that record revealed that you frequently chose the public defenders, most of which had rarely tried a case?'

'Oh, my God . . . ! Those records could *surface?*'

'Not if you give Vincent time to expunge them. National security concerns, of course.'

'He could *do* that?'

'He says he can manage it.'

'The time? . . . I don't know what my colleagues would say if I delay the public hearings. I can't appear to be recalcitrant, it might look . . . heaven forbid . . . suspicious.'

'Vincent understands that, too. He knows that there are several members of the Court who can't stand your "apricots" – I believe it's a pejorative term, Reebock.'

'Christ, I'm being compromised for doing the right *thing!*'

'For the wrong reasons, Mr Chief Justice. Vincent counted on it. What shall I tell him?'

'How long does he think it would take to . . . shall we say, remove the misunderstood materials that could lead to erroneous conclusions?'

'To do a thorough job, he says a year –'

'The Court would *revolt!*'

'He'll settle for a week.'

'It's yours.'

'He'll manage it.'

Mangecavallo leaned back in his chair and relit his Monte Cristo cigar, a temporarily satisfied man. He had seen the light when everyone else including Hymie the Hurricane saw only the dark clouds of confusion. So the gumballs on the Supreme Court who were maybe leaning toward the vicious Wopotami savages were whistle clean, there had to be another way to buy some time to catch this Thunder Head phony and either blow him full of holes or mess his head up so bad he'd be happy to call the whole thing off, labelling it for what it was: a very major scam. So the suspicious five or six *frutti* got them nowhere, so why not look in the other direction, say with the big banana himself? That *facisti* couldn't possibly vote for the Wopotamis; it just wasn't in his heart. And since it wasn't, what kind of rotten heart was in his bigoted chest that made him immediately turn off his big brain? Maybe someone should inquire.

So now they had an extra week, which was about all they could hope for what with the big banana's popularity rating among his colleagues at zip-minus. And a week should be enough since Little Joey the Shroud had cornered the Section Eight General Lasagna with the Wopotami feathers hanging down to his ass in Boston, where, as everyone knew, accidents happened with alarming frequency. Maybe not in the New York-LA-Miami league, but it wasn't small time, either. Mangecavallo blew three perfect smoke rings and looked at his diamond-rimmed watch. The Shroud had two minutes left in the prescribed morning's timespan to call; the unseen telephone buzzed in the lower right-hand section of the director's desk. He reached down, opened the drawer and picked it up. 'Yes?'

'It's Little Joey, Vin.'

'You always gotta wait until the last second to call? I told you, I got a high-level conference at ten o'clock and you make me nervous. Suppose this phone rang when the guys in suits were here in the office?'

'So you tell 'em it's a wrong number.'

'*Pazzo*-head, they don't see the phone!'

'You hire blind spies, Vinnie?'

'*Basta*. What've you got? Quick!'

'Hoo-hay, a bundle, Bam-Bam –'

'I *told* you –'

'Sorry, Vincenzo . . . Anyway, quick, I gotta room at this fancy hotel like I mentioned before.'

'No long stories, Joey. I know you got a room last night down the hall from the yarmulke, so?'

'So much *activity*, Vin! The big General Indian Chief is here with the yarmulke, only they left for a couple of hours last night. Then the chief's soldiers came back and *they* left after talkin' to somebody *else* inside before the chief and the yarmulke came back. Then the old Jewish guy left, leavin' the chief with whoever it was inside, but before that there was a lot of yellin' – I mean real *stridore* – and *then* the yarmulke left and everything was *silenzio*.'

'You're tellin' me, Little Joey, that the nest of this terrible *cospirazione* is right down the hall from you, right?'

'*Right*, Bam-Bam! . . . Sorry, Vin, it comes natural, you know what I mean, from the old days?'

'*Basta di nuovo*. What else, although I think we got all we need? Can you find out who the crumb was inside – maybe just a broad, huh?'

'*Hoo-hay*, Vinnie, it was no broad and I *saw* him. He's a mental case, a real *vegetale*.'

'What are you talkin'?'

'Like always, I keep the door open an inch, maybe an inch and a half, maybe two inches –'

'*Joey!*'

'Okay, okay. I see the gumbar come out and he goes to the elevators, right?'

'That makes him a mental case . . . ?'

'No, Vin, his pants do.'

'*Huh?*'

'He's pissed all over 'em! Big wet circles down to his knees – on both sides. I mean, he's walkin' out in public with his pants filled with pee! If that don't make him a mental case, you tell me what does, huh, Bam-Bam?'

'He's all shook up, that's what he is,' concluded the astute director of the Central Intelligence Agency. 'Around this place they call it "operational burn-out," or sometimes "deep-cover bends," depending on the mission.' Mangecavallo's console hummed; it was his secretary's line. 'I only got a couple of seconds, Little Joey. Try to find out who this creep with the pissed-up trousers is, okay?'

'I *know*, Vinnie! I went to the front desk and made like a friend of a priest who was lookin' for him on account of some personal tragedy and described him, although I didn't make a big thing about the pants . . . I thought maybe I should get a religious collar, you know what I mean, but I figured it would take too long –'

'*Joey!*' roared Mangecavallo. '*Stop* already! Who *is* he?'

'His name is Devereaux, and I'd better spell it out for you. He's a sharp attorney in the big yarmulke's firm.'

'He's a ferocious un-American traitor, that's what he is,' pronounced the DCI, writing out the name as the Shroud spelled it. The director's visible phone rang again; his visitors were impatient. 'Stay put with your eyes open, Little Joey. I'll be in touch.' Mangecavallo hung up and placed his private telephone back into the drawer. He then buzzed his secretary twice, the signal to admit subordinates. As he did so, he picked up a pencil and wrote out in block letters another name below that of Devereaux. *BROOKLYN!* Enough was enough; it was time for solid professionals.

Colonel Bradley 'Hoot' Gibson, pilot of the still airborne EC-135, the 'Looking Glass' for the Strategic Air Command's global operations, shouted into his radio. 'Have you idiots gone to lunch on the last quasar beyond *Jupiter*? We've been up here for fifty-two hours, refuelled three times, and apologized in six languages, two of which weren't even in the fucking computers! Now, what the hell's going *on*?'

'We read you loud and clear, Colonel,' came the reply from Offutt's control tower, using its UTF radio band, otherwise known as Ultra Tropopausic Frequency, which unfortunately had a tendency to pick up cartoons from Mongolian television but otherwise had a clear range throughout the Pacific. 'We've handled the complaints on this end very effectively. It's a pretty good bet you won't be missiled down, how about that?'

'You get our maximum leader on the horn or I'm heading off your screens to Pago Pago and sending for my wife and kids! I've *had* it – *we've* had it!'

'Easy, Colonel, there are five other aircraft in roughly your same predicament. Think about them.'

'I'll *tell* you what I think about them. I think we'll rendezvous, head to the Australian outback, auction off these electronic tubes of spaghetti to the highest bidders and have enough cash to start our own country! . . . Now get that clown of a commander on the phone!'

'I've been on it, Colonel Gibson,' said a distinctly different voice over the radio. 'I've got a patch here to all airborne equipment.'

'Eavesdropping, General? Isn't that against the law?'

'Not in this outfit, fly-boy . . . Come on, Hoot, how do you think *I* feel?'

'I think you feel your ass in a cushioned chair inside a building on dry ground, that's what I think you feel, Owen.'

'I suppose you also think I issued those orders myself, don't you? Well, I'll let you in on a little national security secret: I'm not permitted to. They were issued to *me* – code Red *Plus*.'

'To repeat myself, what the *hell* is going on?'

'You wouldn't believe it if I told you, but then I couldn't because I didn't understand a word the trench coats said – well, I understood most of the specific words, but not what they meant when put together.'

'What *trench coats*?'

'Again, you wouldn't believe me. It's hot as hell down here, and they kept their coats and hats on, and they don't open doors for women.'

'Owen . . . *General* Richards,' said the pilot with firm gentleness. 'Have you been to the base hospital lately?'

In his office, the commandant of SAC sighed as he replied to the pilot 800 miles west and 40,000 feet above. 'Every goddamn time the red phone rings I want to turn myself in.' So, of course, the red telephone hummed as its red light flashed on and off. 'Holy shit, there it goes! . . . Hang on, Hoot, don't go anywhere.'

'I'm not cancelling the Australian outback, Owen.'

'Oh, shut up,' ordered the commandant of SAC as he picked up the red telephone. 'Rec-Wing Headquarters, General Richards,' he said with ill-felt authority.

'*Beam* 'em down, Scotty!' cried the half whining, half wheezing voice of the Secretary of Defense. 'Beam 'em *all* down!'

'I beg your pardon, Mr Secretary?'

'I said bring 'em back, soldier! We've got ourselves a little

165

breathing room, so stand down till I call you again and then be prepared to send up the whole *flotilla*!'

'Flotilla, sir?'

'You heard me, whatever your name is!'

'No, Mr Secretary,' said Richards, a calm suddenly spreading through him. 'You hear me, *sir*. You've just given your last order to whatever-my-name-is.'

'*What* did you say, *mister*?'

'You heard me, sir, and my title is "general" in contradistinction to the civilian "mister," not that either term would mean anything to you.'

'You being *insubordinate*?'

'To the fullest extent of my vocabulary, mister . . . Why we put up with you Washington sewer pipes is something I'll never understand, but I'm told it's spelled out somewhere by somebody who never ran into anyone like you and I'm not about to introduce you because all the rules would be changed – like opening doors for ladies – and I'm not sure that's such a good idea.'

'Are you *sick*, soldier boy?'

'Yes, I'm sick, you snivelling tiny rat with a rug on your tiny head, *sick* of you dumb politicians who think you know more about my business than I do after thirty years in this uniform! And you can bet your butt I'm beaming them all down, *Scotty*, and I would have done so whether you called or not!'

'You're *fired*, soldier!'

'Stick your head in a toilet, toupee and all, *civilian*. You *can't* fire me, isn't that nice? You can relieve me, and I hope to Christ you do, but you can't *fire* me. It's in my contract. Good-bye and have a rotten fucking day!' The general slammed down the red telephone and returned to the UTF radio connection. 'You still there, Hoot?'

'I'm here and I heard you, *Private* Richards. You ready for latrine duty?'

'Is that son of a bitch ready for my press conference?'

'Good point, Corporal . . . I gather we're coming back.'

'Everybody. We resume normal operations as of *now*.'

'Call my wife, will you?'

'No, I'll call your daughter; her head's on tighter. Your wife thinks you were shot down over Mongolia and she's enshrined a plate of roast beef hash.'

'You're right, talk to the kid. And tell her to wear longer skirts.'

'Over and out, Colonel.' General Owen Richards hung up the UTF receiver and pushed his chair back, pleased with himself. Career be damned, he should have done what he did a long time ago. Retirement wouldn't be so awful, although he had to admit it would not be all that easy to put his uniform in a cedar chest. He and his wife could live wherever they wanted – one of his pilots told him that American Samoa was a terrific place. Still, it was going to be rough sledding leaving the one thing he loved best outside of the wife and children. The Air Force was his *life* – to *hell* with it!

And, naturally, the red telephone erupted. Richards picked it up, his temper in flames. 'What is it, you fucking *skinhead*?'

'Golly, gosh, and gee whillikers, General, is that any way to answer a friendly telephone call?'

'*What?*' The voice was familiar but Richards couldn't place it. 'Who the hell *is* this?'

'I think I'm called your Commander-in-Chief, General.'

'The *President?*'

'You can bet your socks on it, sky jock.'

'*Sky jock?*'

'Different uniform but pretty much the same equipment, General, except for the high-tech jet stuff.'

'*Equipment?*'

'Ease off, pilot. I was there when you were in diapers.'

'My *God*, you are him!'

'"He" is better grammar, Owen. I only know that because my secretary tells me.'

'I'm sorry, *sir*!'

'Don't be, General. I'm the one who's apologizing. I just got off the horn with our Secretary of Defense –'

'I understand, sir. I'm relieved of my command.'

'No, Owen, *he* is. Well, not actually, but he's not making any more decisions where you're concerned without checking with me. He told me what you said and I couldn't have put it better with my best speechwriters. You have any more problems, you call me direct, got it?'

'Got it, Mr President . . . Hey, you're *okay*!'

'Let's just say I kicked a little ass – but for God's sake, don't quote me.'

Sam Devereaux paid ten dollars for the doorman to shriek his whistle at all points of the compass so as to find him a taxi. For three minutes none were to be had, although two swiftly passed a frustrated Sam in the middle of the street, the drivers' eyes focused on his trousers. He rejoined the doorman as a couple arrived at the Four Seasons' kerb, said couple somewhat flustered as Sam threw their luggage out of the trunk and ignored their objections, opting only to leap into the cab and scream the address of his own residence in Weston.

'What the hell are you *stopping* for?' yelled Devereaux after several blocks.

'Because if I don't, I'll hit the jerk in front of me,' replied the driver.

It was an early morning traffic jam in Boston, as always, extended by the insane one-way streets that forced unfamiliar drivers to travel eleven miles to reach an address fifty feet away. 'I know a shortcut to the Weston road,' said Sam, leaning far forward and embracing the rim of the front seat.

'So does everybody else in Massachusetts, buddy, and unless you got a gun, get the hell away from me.'

'No gun, no threat. I'm just a nice person in a terrible hurry.'

'I figured you took care of that "hurry" by what I seen of your pants. If you got another "hurry," get outta here!'

'No – *no*, that's coffee! I spilled a cup of *coffee*!'

'Who am I to argue? Would you mind sitting back in the seat – it's in our insurance?'

'Sure,' said Sam, moving back but still on the edge of the rear seat. 'Look, I'm just trying to impress upon you that this is an emergency, a *real* one! A lady whose name I don't know

168

is heading out to my house and I've got to get there before she does. She left a few minutes ago from the hotel in another cab.'

'Naturally,' said the driver with philosophical resignation. 'She got your address from your wallet during the night and now she figures she can pick up a little extra mattress money by dropping in on the Mrs. When will you fishtails learn? . . . Hey, we gotta break up ahead. I'll swing down Church Street and up to the Weston road.'

'That's the shortcut I was talking about.'

'With any luck not too many of the summer crowds know about it.'

'Just get me home as fast as you can.'

'Listen, mister, the law says that without indications of harmful intent or abusive language or unsanitary appearance, I gotta take you where you tell me. Now, you are close to the line on all three counts – over it on one, in my opinion – so don't push, okay? Nobody wants you home and out of this cab faster than me.'

'Of course it's the law,' rejoined a slightly bewildered Devereaux. 'You think I don't know that? I'm an attorney.'

'Yeah, and me, I'm a ballet dancer.'

Finally, at *last*, the cab swung into Devereaux's street. Checking the meter, Sam dropped the amount of the fare over the front seat along with a generous tip. He opened the door, leaped out on the pavement, and saw that there was no other taxi in sight.

He had *done* it and, boy, was that woman in for the surprise of her life! Just because a female using minimal language of the law was outrageously gorgeous, with a face and body created by a straight Botticelli, she had no right to give *his* address to a cabdriver and imply some vague legal threat without being properly introduced! No, sir, Samuel Lansing Devereaux, attorney of high regard, was made of sterner stuff . . . Maybe he *should* change his trousers. He started toward the path that led to his private entrance when the front door opened, revealing cousin Cora beckoning him rather wildly, even for her.

'What is it?' he asked, instantly vaulting over the white picket fence and rushing up to the steps with a slight inkling of impending doom.

'What *is* it?' repeated Cora in high dudgeon. 'Maybe you'd better tell *me* what it is you've done, other than the obvious,' she added, glancing at his trousers.

'Oh, oh.' It was all Sam could think to say.

'I guess that's a start –'

'What happened?' interrupted Devereaux.

'A little while ago, this long-legged sunburned dish who musta stepped out of one of them California beach commercials came to the door inquiring about a certain unmentionable person. Well, Sammy, I thought your mother was goin' to have a stroke, but the leggy lady with a face you could *kill* for calmed her down and now they're both inside the living room with the doors closed.'

'What the *hell* is all this?'

'I can only tell ya that the hoity-toity went into the pantry for her teapot but she didn't order no tea.'

'Son of a *bitch*!' cried Devereaux, racing across the marble hall and flinging open both French doors of the living room as he burst inside.

'*You!*' shouted Jennifer Redwing, lurching out of the brocaded chair.

'*You!*' yelled the furious son and attorney. 'How did you get here so quickly?'

'I used to live in Boston. I know several shortcuts.'

'Several . . . ?'

'*You!*' shrieked Eleanor Devereaux, rising from the brocaded couch, her mouth gaped as she stared at Sam. 'Your *trousers*, you terrible, incontinent boy!'

'It's coffee, Mother!'

'It's coffee,' said the bronzed Aphrodite. 'He says.'

CHAPTER TWELVE

'Now you've got the broad outlines of the Mac-and-Sam international blackmail carnival as it pertains to the general's ability to dig way down deep and come up with indictable dirt,' said Devereaux. They had moved to his château's lair, into his office now stripped of all photographs and newspaper articles and without his mother, who found it imperative to take to her bed with 'the vapours.' Sam sat at his desk, Jennifer Redwing in the chair in front of him which still had strips of torn sheets tied to the arms.

'It's only *incredible*, but you have to know that.' She slowly opened her purse, a bright lady in shock. 'Good *God*, forty million dollars!'

'No *Mace*!' cried Devereaux, pushing his swivel chair back into the wall.

'No Mace,' confirmed Redwing, withdrawing a pack of cigarettes. 'It's only a vice I give up every other week until something like this happens, but then nothing like *this* has *ever* happened ... At least, I cut down.'

'It's a crutch, you know. You should have stronger discipline.'

'All things considered, Counsellor, I don't think you're in a position to be holier-than-me. Do you have an ashtray or shall I set this expensive rug on fire?'

'Since you're adamant,' said Sam, opening a desk drawer and pulling out two ashtrays along with a pack of cigarettes. 'I guess I'll concede ... I see we both use low-tar.'

'Let's get back to the low blows, Mr Devereaux.' Both lawyers lighted their crutches and Miss Redwing continued.

'This brief to the Court is all nonsense, you also have to know that, too.'

'Redundancy, Counsellor. "Also" and "too" are redundant.'

'Not when used for emphasis in front of a jury by a competent attorney, Counsellor.'

'Agreed. Who's which?'

'We're both both,' said Redwing. 'Speaking as the latter on behalf of the Wopotamis, the tribe's interests are not served by this frivolous litigation which has gone entirely too far.'

'Speaking as an equal once disastrously associated with General Hawkins,' countered Sam, 'the litigation is not at all frivolous. Realistically, it doesn't have a chance but the tribe's case against the government is pretty damn convincing.'

'What?' Redwing locked eyes with Devereaux, her cigarette poised in front of her, the smoke suspended as if caught in a still photograph. 'You've got to be kidding.'

'I wish I were. Life would be a lot easier.'

'Come again?'

'The evidence unearthed in the sealed archives appears to be authentic. Territorial treaties executed in good faith were replaced by legislated relocations without regard to prior agreements – existing rights of land ownership.'

'"Legislated relocations"? Made to move?'

'That's it, and the government had no authority to abrogate the legally arrived at doctrine of ownership and force the Wopotamis off their lands. Certainly not without a federal court hearing with full tribal representation.'

'They *did* that? No court, no hearing for the tribe? How *could* they?'

'The government lied – specifically with regard to the Treaty of 1878, finalized between the Wopotamis and the fourteeth Congress.'

'But *how*?'

'The Department of the Interior, obviously with a little help from the Bureau of Indian Affairs, claimed that such a treaty never existed, that it was a fantasy dreamed up by swacked-out medicine men pouring zombie-water down their throats while prancing around campfires . . . The brief goes so far as to speculate on the origins of the fire that destroyed the First Bank of Omaha in 1912.'

'That strikes a bell,' said Redwing, frowning and crushing out her cigarette.

'It should. It's where the Wopotamis kept all their tribal records, none of which survived, of course.'

'What was the speculation?'

'That it was torched by federal agents acting on orders from Washington.'

'That's pretty heavy, Counsellor, even eighty years later. On what basis was the speculation?'

'The bank was supposedly broken into in the middle of the night, all the cash and valuables cleaned out, and the robbers escaped without a trace. Yet before they ran for it, they apparently decided to set fire to the bank, which was pretty stupid since they were making a clean getaway and a fire like that might just wake up a few citizens.'

'Stupid but not unheard of, Mr Devereaux. Pathological personalities aren't a recent phenomenon, and the hatred of banks has a long history.'

'Granted, but when the initial source of the conflagration was determined to be the bank's basement where the document files were located, said files overturned, scattered, and the rooms soaked with lamp oil, it makes you kind of wonder, doesn't it? If the whole structure didn't go up, those rooms certainly would . . . Also, it was the shortest abandoned manhunt in the annals of crime as the perpetrators were reported to be seen in South America. Of course, Cassidy and Sundance said they'd never been to Omaha, and they were the only American bank robbers ever known to have surfaced down there in those days . . . Naturally, I've just given you a quick overview, as my sainted employer would say – did say.'

'It's disastrously convincing.' The lovely Indian attorney suddenly shook her head back and forth in rapid stabs. 'It can't go forward, you *must* understand that.'

'I'm not sure it can be stopped,' said Sam.

'Of course it can! This general, this catastrophic trouble-maker Hawkins, can simply withdraw – take my word for it, the Court adores withdrawals, even my brother learned that while he was down there.'

'*He's* the one?'

'The one who?'

'The young brave of the tribe who worked with Mac but didn't pass the bar.'

'Didn't *pass*? I'll have you know my little bro – my *brother* – passed in the highest percentile!'

'So did I.'

'It figures,' said Redwing, no enthusiasm whatsoever in her concession. 'It seems you're cut from the same crazy quilt.'

'*He's* the one I remind you of? Is that what you meant before?'

'It means, Counsellor, that your goddamned General Hawkins found another Samuel Devereaux for his latest cataclysmic frolic.'

'Your brother was in the army?'

'No, he was on a *reservation* – the wrong one . . . Back to the mad general.'

'Actually, the "mad" was part of his military nickname.'

'Why do I find that not totally surprising?' Jennifer fumbled in her purse for another cigarette.

'Hey, Counsellor,' interrupted Devereaux as Redwing withdrew her pack. 'You were doing so well; you only had a couple of puffs and you put it out. I did, too, sort of to help you.'

'Get off my case, *Counsellor*! I don't want to talk about your brain surgery or my frailties, I want to talk about Hawkins and his appeal to the Supreme Court and how we can squash it!'

'Actually, in legal terms, it's not an appeal, for no decision was made in a court of law that requires overturning, like in appellate procedures –'

'Don't you *dare* quote law to me, *pee-pants*!'

'It was coffee and I changed my trousers and you agreed it was coffee.'

'It was also an appeal in the broader legal sense, an appeal to right a wrong,' said Redwing, a touch defensively.

'My trousers?'

'No, you idiot, the lousy brief!'

'Then you agree with Mac. If everything I've told you stands up to scrutiny, *your* scrutiny, a crime was committed against your people. Don't you think it should be "righted"?'

'Whose side are you *on*?' protested the native American beauty.

'At the moment, I'm a devil's advocate suppressing my natural inclinations. I want to know what you think.'

'Don't you understand? What *I* think doesn't matter! I care for my people and I don't want them hurt ... Come on, Devereaux, be realistic. A small Indian tribe against the majestic national power of SAC – how long would we survive? Even the spectre of such a possibility, whether it had a chance or not, could result in new laws passed, land condemned by eminent domain, our people scattered – all resulting in economic and racial genocide, and it wouldn't be the first time we've experienced it – them.'

'Isn't that worth fighting against?' asked Sam, his expression passive. 'Anywhere?'

'Theoretically, of course, and in the vast majority of instances, *actively*. But not here. Our people are not unhappy. They have the land they live on, with decent government subsidies – which *I'm* parlaying into investments with damn good returns – and to suddenly plunge them into a morass of legal violence – and that's what it would be, *violence* – I simply can't permit it.'

'Mac won't go along with you. He's an original and violence of any kind isn't a threat, it's a come-on ... Also, Miss Redwing, and now I've got to speak for my admittedly terrified self, and I suspect for the greatest attorney I've ever known, namely my employer, one Aaron Pinkus, I don't think we can go along with you, either. You see, when you come right down to it, we're officers of the court, and a great crime *was* committed, and to turn our faces away wouldn't be terribly appropriate. Not if we really believe what we think we are. That's what Aaron meant when he said to me that we both had to make the individual decisions of our lives. Do we turn away or do we uphold a truth that may destroy us professionally, but knowing in our souls that we're right?'

Jennifer Redwing, her eyes wide and staring at Sam, swallowed several times, then spoke haltingly. 'Will you marry me, Mr Devereaux? . . . *No!* I didn't *mean* that! It's like what you said to me in the elevator! A slip, a mental *slip!*'

'Hey, it's okay, Miss . . . Miss – do you have a first name? After all, I said it first – the dumb slip, I mean.'

'People call me Red.'

'Not for your hair – *Christ*, it's the most gorgeous, lustrous ebony I've ever seen in my life.'

'It's the genes,' said Redwing, getting slowly out of the chair. 'My people ate a great deal of red buffalo meat. I'm told it gives a sheen genetically.'

'I don't give a wigwam damn what does it,' said Devereaux, also rising slowly and walking around the desk. 'You're the most beautiful woman I've ever met in my life.'

'Looks are only surface, Sam – may I call you Sam?'

'It's a good substitute for "idiot,"' said Devereaux, his arms encircling her. 'You *are* glorious!'

'*Please*, Sam, that's so irrelevant. If I'm attracted to you – and I obviously am – it's not because of your handsome face and your tall lean body – which can't be discounted – but it's because of your basic integrity to and great love of the law.'

'Oh, yeah, I *got* it! I really got *that!*'

'Don't be frivolous, Sam. Please, *don't* be.'

'Never, *never!*' And naturally the goddamned telephone rang. Devereaux's hand crashed down on the desk, only glancing off the base of the instrument but causing the receiver to flip over onto the blotter; he picked it up angrily. 'This is a recording,' said Sam in a loud, flat monotone. 'You've reached the Lugosi Funeral Home but there's no one here who can get up and answer the phone –'

'*Cut* it out, boy,' interrupted the harsh, growling voice of MacKenzie Hawkins, 'just you listen up sharp. We're under attack and you're a target so I want you to take rapid cover.'

'Listen, fossil brain, I left you barely two hours ago and my

176

instructions were that I was not to be disturbed until post meridian! For your edification, that's after twelve *noon* –'

'No, Sam, you listen to *me*,' broke in the Hawk, his very calm sending the message of genuine concern. 'Get out of your house. Now.'

'Why the hell should I?'

'Because you don't have an unlisted number and that means your address is in the telephone book.'

'So are several million others –'

'But only two of them ever heard of the Wopotamis.'

'*What?*'

'I'll say this only once, son, because neither of us can waste time. I don't know how it happened – it isn't Hymie the Hurricane's modus operandi. Oh, hell, he'll send a goon or two but not an enforcer – and that's exactly what we got on our rear flank, a *hit* man.'

'It's a little early for you to get juiced, isn't it, Mac?'

'Hear *this*, Lieutenant,' said Hawkins, his voice now both calm and cold. 'My adjutant, Desi-One, who unbeknownst to me was temporarily employed in the New York area – specifically the Brooklyn barrio – spotted a man in the hotel lobby he'd seen before from a distance during his previous temporary employment. A very *bad* man, Lieutenant, and because the corporal is conscientious and dressed properly, he stood beside this *hombre vicioso*, as he called him, at the front desk and heard him distinctly ask about two gentlemen. The names were Pinkus and Devereaux.'

'*Holy . . . !*'

'Precisely, boy. This bad individual made a phone call, then returned to the desk where he got himself a room two floors below us . . . I don't like that phone call, Sam.'

'Neither do *I*.'

'I just spoke to Commander Pinkus and we agree. Take your mother and that whacko maid he said was a relative and get out of there. We can't allow hostages.'

'*Hostages?*' cried Devereaux, glancing at the glorious Red Redwing who watched him, her expression one of complete bewilderment. 'My God, you're right.'

'I'm rarely wrong under these conditions, son. Commander Pinkus orders you to head for that crummy joint where the two of us met in the parking lot, and he'll send the gunny sergeant for you as soon as he can locate him . . . Seems the Mrs took over the limo for shopping and isn't talking to the commander, except to yell about some dirty curtains and an odour in the backseat that smells like a combination of fish and Danish pastry.'

'We're on our way but I'll have to use Mother's Jaguar. Stosh hasn't returned my car so have Aaron tell Paddy to look for the Jag . . . What about *you*, Mac – not that I frankly give a damn – but that bad person is only two floors below?'

'I'm really touched by your concern, son, but I've got a little time to pick up the bivouac and remove all the papers.'

'How do you know that? I hate to tell you, but you're not actually invincible. That son of a bitch could be coming up after you right now!'

'No, not for a while, Sam. Desi-Two did a job on that son of a bitch's lock that jams it from both the outside *and* the inside. The only way he can get out is either through the fifth floor window or until the hotel takes the whole door down, which being steel plated under the fancy panelling means a blowtorch. *Goddamn*, can I pick personnel or can I pick *personnel*!'

'I'll reserve judgement on that, but I will tell you I had a very strange conversation with them last night.'

'Heard all about it, boy. Guess what? They're joining the *army*! I told 'em to hold off for a day or two and I'll have 'em sent directly to postbasic G-two training. Christ Almighty, they're already light years ahead of the assholes who've finished the course! Naturally, Desi-One's got to get his teeth fixed; it simply isn't proper for him to have that gap in his mouth, but I've still got my connections. The army'll take care of that –'

'We're getting *out* of here, Mac,' interrupted Devereaux sharply. 'As you said, we can't waste time.' With those words, Sam slammed down the phone and turned to Red Redwing. 'We've got a serious problem,' he said, his hands clasping her shoulders. 'Recalling the essence of our prior communication, will you trust me, *please*?'

'Emotionally or intellectually?' asked the suddenly doubting legal adversary.

'They're inseparable. We could get our asses blown away, maybe our heads. I'll explain later.'

'You mentioned something about getting out of here, so what are we *waiting* for?'

'We have to get Mother and cousin Cora.'

'In the parlance of Indian legend, let's run like the northern winds before the palefaces close in on us with their thunder sticks!'

'God, that's *magnificent*!'

'What is?'

'The "northern winds," the "thunder sticks"!'

'Not if you're born into a tribe, buster. Come on! You get cousin Cora and I'll get your mother.'

'Shouldn't it be the other way around?'

'Are you kidding? Your mother doesn't trust you for a second.'

'She has to, I'm her *son*.'

'She'll deny that, take my word for it.'

'But I love you – you love *me*. We agreed!'

'We were both carried away – you superficially; me, I was intellectually moved. We'll discuss it later.'

'That's the most hurtful thing I think I could ever hear you say.'

'Try me with a thunder stick pointed at my head in a calm northern wind, Counsellor. Let's go. The last time I saw Cora she was in the pantry checking out the teapots. You find *her*, and I'll bundle up your mother. We'll meet in the garage. Bring the keys to the Jag.'

'The garage . . . ?'

'You forget I'm an Indian. We circle an encampment before we strike. White man never learns.'

'Magnificent!'

'Oh, shut up. Let's *go*!'

Cora, however, refused to budge, and when Sam implied

that there was the possibility of a real physical threat to her life, his distant uncle's cousin opened a concealed, magnetically released drawer below the oven and pulled out not one, but two .357 magnums, both loaded, proclaiming that she was the true protector of the house. 'You think I'd count on those lousy alarms no one can figure out and go off whenever the technical bullcrap meets their fancy, nephew? No way, Sammy! I come from another branch of the family, one the hoity-toity and her smooth-talkin' husband didn't care too much about – but by God, I'll earn my keep!'

'I don't *believe* in guns, Cora!'

'So believe what you like, Sammy. This place is what yer hard-drinkin', faraway cousin is paid for lookin' after and you ain't goin' to take that away from me, you got that, *buster*?'

'Buster . . . ? I can't handle two "busters" within the space of five minutes.'

'You always talk funny, Sam-boy.'

'Did I ever tell you that I love you, Cora?'

'A couple of times, Sammy, when you were oiled up to your last cylinders. Now, you and the leggy unbelievable take the hoity-toity and get out of here . . . And may the good Protestant Lord have mercy on any bastards who try to get in. Just in case, however, I may give the police a ring; let 'em earn *their* keep for a change.'

The yellow Jaguar, with Redwing holding a semi-cognizant Eleanor in the backseat, sped out of the driveway and headed for the streets that led to the Boston road. At the second corner they passed a long black limousine that had all the earmarks of a vintage 1930s black *Maria*, including a face pressed against a window whose features were best described as having been caught in the lens of a zoological photographer. Despite disinclinations, Devereaux pressed forward, confident in the knowledge that Cora was more than a match for two gunsels who were stupid enough to look for the address of an unfamiliar house in a huge black automobile in broad daylight. Police aside, his ersatz cousin from the other branch of the family would blow them away with her magnums. Where did she ever *get* them?

'Sam, your mother has to go to the bathroom!' said Redwing twelve minutes later, cradling Eleanor Devereaux in her arms.

'My mother doesn't do that. That sort of thing's for other people. She never goes to the bathroom.'

'She says it runs in the family – witness your trousers.'

'Coffee!'

'You say.'

'We'll be at Nanny's in a couple of minutes. Tell her to hold on.'

'Nanny's Naughty Follies?' cried the lawyer-daughter of the Wopotamis. 'We're going *there*?'

'You know it?'

'Well, when I was at school we had a couple of legally oriented . . . orientations. A course in constitutional censorship, that sort of thing . . . You *can't* take her there! It's open twenty-four hours a day.'

'No choice, Counsellor. It's only two or three minutes from here.'

'She'll be mortified!'

'Then she can blame it on the family trait of incontinence.'

'You are a male child carrying the demon seed of the evil spirits below the earth.'

'What the f – f . . . what does *that* mean?'

'It means your birth was not acceptable to the benevolent gods and your carcass will be devoured by carrion after a painful death.'

'That's not very sociable, Red. I mean it doesn't sound in tune with our little talk in my office.'

'I told you, I was carried away. I heard words I haven't heard in a very long time – too long. The practice of law is frequently in conflict with a love for the law. I momentarily lost control of my perspective, and I do *not* enjoy losing control.'

'Wow, thanks a lot. A little soul-searching turns you on no matter who the "idiot" is who brings it up, is that it?'

'I think we could all do with a little soul-searching now and then in our profession.'

'Then you really *are* a lawyer.'

'I am.'

'What firm?'

'Springtree, Basl and Karpas, San Francisco.'

'Christ, they're *sharks*!'

'I'm glad you understand ... How far away are we? Your mother can barely whisper but she's terribly uncomfortable.'

'Less than a minute ... *Hey*, maybe we should take her to the hospital! I mean, if she's really –'

'Forget it, Counsellor. That would mortify her more than Nanny's. The teapot was empty.'

'Is that another twig from the tribal tree of wisdom? ... No, it couldn't be. Cora mentioned teapots – so did *you*.'

'Some things, Mr Devereaux, like childbirth, are distinctly feminine experiences.'

'Thanks again – for the *mister*,' said Sam, swinging into the parking lot of Nanny's Naughty Follies Et Cetera. 'Nobody has to make-my-day, *or* last night. Madman Mac and his two absurd "adjutants" who keep tackling me, bearded Greeks who've got my clothes, Aaron Pinkus calling me "Samuel," a brief that should be consigned to some legal hell, a bombed-out mother, the most beautiful woman I've ever met in my life falling in and out of love with me in the space of twenty minutes – and now a fucking *hit* man from Brooklyn after my *ass*! Maybe I should take myself to the hospital.'

'Maybe you should stop the *car*!' shouted Red Redwing as Devereaux passed by the canopied entrance of Nanny's emporium. 'Now, back up about thirty yards!'

'You people bury your captives up to their heads in killer anthills,' mumbled Sam.

'It's an option I'll take under consideration,' said Redwing, opening the door and gently urging Eleanor Devereaux out of the car. 'Will you get your *ass* outside and help me, or a hit man from Brooklyn will be the least of your worries!'

'All right, all *right*.' Sam did as he was told, finally holding his mother's right arm as the three of them walked to the imposing building where photographs of naked men and women were plastered all over the place, on the stucco walls and above the doorframe. 'Perhaps I shouldn't leave Mother's car,' Sam offered softly.

'*Good* thinking, Counsellor,' agreed Redwing, not without a note of sarcasm. 'It might not be here two minutes later ... I've got Eleanor, you just wait for that man Paddy or whatever his name is.'

'Eleanor?'

'We women more readily recognize kindred souls than men do. We're brighter ... Come along, Ellie, you'll be fine.'

'*Ellie?*' said the astonished Devereaux as the stunning Indian woman took his mother inside. 'Nobody calls her Ellie –'

'Hey, Fancy Dan!' intoned the coarse voice of a huge heavyset, middle-aged man, more apelike than human, who stood by the Jaguar and was obviously a guard-cum-bouncer. 'We ain't exactly got *vallatt* parking here. Move the fag Jag!'

'Right away, officer.' Sam trotted back to the car under the disapproving eye of Nanny's Special Force veteran.

'I ain't no cop,' said the older carnivore of a man as Devereaux got behind the wheel. 'Read that as no police restraints, mister.'

'Understood, sir.' Sam started the engine. 'You're obviously with the diplomatic corps,' he added, spinning the wheel and shooting across the lot in a circle where he stopped. The moment he saw Redwing and his mother come outside, he would rush back to the canopy, counting on the fact that even Nanny's elderly King Kong would reflect on Red's beauty and have a gentler disposition. Then the three of them could wait in the Jaguar for Paddy Lafferty to arrive with further instructions ... Jesus, an '*enforcer!*' And a black limousine right out of a funeral procession racing down the street to his *house*! What was happening? He could certainly understand Washington's desperation if there was any sympathy whatsoever for the Wopotami brief, but a hit man and a black Maria with a passenger who bore no resemblance to 'Penrod' was not the way for a civilized government to proceed. Negotiators were sent, not exterminators. Quiet meetings were held to seek civilized solutions, not death squads to impose them

. . . *Whoa*, thought Devereaux. On the other hand, if Washington had learned that former General MacKenzie Hawkins – Madman Mac the Hawk – was behind this potential if remote fiasco of national security proportions, exterminators and death squads *were* the only solutions. The Hawk gave no quarter where the lace-pants of Dizzy City were concerned. Those pricky-shits, as he termed them, had taken the army out of his life and nothing, absolutely *nothing*, was too putrid to shove down their throats, the higher placed the better.

Whoa . . . no, *double* whoa! considered Sam with a sudden mental jolt. If Washington was responding in kind to Mac's assault, it would include any and all persons *around* the Hawk. And the enforcer had used the names of Pinkus and Devereaux at the front desk! How the hell did *that* happen? Hawkins had arrived in Boston barely eighteen horrible hours ago, and by his own admission nobody in Washington had yet heard of one Sam Devereaux, much less Aaron Pinkus! How then? Even with today's instantaneous global communications one source had to have a fact or a name to transmit to a second source or the specific information could not be received – and the name of an innocent, insinuated Devereaux was *not* known and therefore neither was that of Pinkus. *How?* . . . Good God, there was only one answer – the Hawk was being followed! Right now, at this moment!

Where was Paddy? Christ, he had to get word to Mac! Somewhere close by, unseen by the Hawk, was a second person watching every move the old soldier made, and it took no criminal imagination to know that second unknown person was in touch with the enforcer two storeys below Mac . . . Paddy, where *are* you?

Sam glanced over at the canopy; there was no sign of Redwing or his mother – also Nanny's ageing King Kong had left. Perhaps, if he was quick about it, he could get inside to the pay phone against the wall that he had used last night and reach Hawkins at the hotel. He was about to start the engine when, to his surprise, the huge bouncer came walking out of the door, rushed to the kerb, and looked around, immediately centring his gaze on Devereaux and the yellow Jaguar. He gestured at Sam, instructing him to drive instantly to the entrance. *Oh, my God, something's happened to Mother!* Devereaux gunned the engine and screeched to a stop under the canopy in 2.4 seconds. 'What *is* it?' he cried to the now smiling simian with the straight grey hair.

'*Boyo*, why didn't y'tell me you were with Miss Redwing? She's a grand little girl, y'know, and I surely wouldn't't've been so impolite if I knew you were an acquaintance. Me apologies, bucko!'

'You *know* her?'

'Well, now, truth be told, I been at this lousy joint for more years than I care to count, since I got the pink slip from the force. Y'see, this rotten establishment is owned by m'widowed daughter-in-law – which had somethin' to do with my gettin' the pink slip, 'cause m'stupid son took the wrong bread to buy the place and got totalled in the crossfire – and Miss Redwing and her pals from *Haavadd* actually sued City Hall and got me a bigger pension. What d'ya think of *that*?'

'I have no thoughts, no comprehension of the events that swirl around me –'

'Yeah, the lovely Injun miss said you might sound a touch confused – and I wasn't to pay no attention to your trousers.'

'I *changed* them! She knows that!'

'And I don't care to know no details, boyo, but I tell ya this. You do dirt to that girl and you'll answer to me, bucko. Now, get out and join the ladies. I'll watch this fruit car of yours.'

'*Inside?*'

'They ain't in a yacht in Boston Harbor, lad.'

A completely bewildered Devereaux got out of the car, barely finding his balance on the pavement, when Aaron Pinkus's limousine came thundering down the entrance ramp into the parking lot and sped toward the yellow Jaguar by the canopy, coming to a crushing stop behind it. '*Sammy!*' yelled Paddy Lafferty from the open window. 'Oh, hello there, Billy Gilligan, how are ya'?'

'Survivin', Paddy,' replied Nanny's semi-benevolent King Kong. 'And you, kiddo?'

'Better now that I see you got my boyo in tow.'

'He's yours?'

'Me and my fine employer's, as it were.'

'Then take him, Paddy. He's a bit off in the head, y'know. I'll watch both the cars.'

'I thank you, Billy,' said Lafferty, leaping from the oversized automobile and running toward Sam and Tarzan's enlarged Cheeta of later years; he totally ignored Devereaux. 'Billy-boy, you won't believe what I've got to tell you, but I swear it on all the graves of County Kilgallen!'

'So, what is it, Paddy?'

'I not only met the man but he drove beside me in the front seat and we had a very meaningful conversation between us! Between just the *two* of us, Billy!'

'The *Pope*, Paddy? Your Jewish fella brought the Pope over?'

'Go one better, Billy!'

'Well, I couldn't now, really – except one, of course, but that's out of the question.'

'No, Billy, you *got* it, lad! *Himself*, it was! General MacKenzie *Hawkins*!'

'Don't say that, Paddy, m'heart will stop dead –'

'I mean it, Billy Gilligan! It was himself in the God-given flesh, and a grander, greater man there never was. Remember how we used to talk in France, crossin' through the woods in the Marne. "Give us Mad Mac and we'll break through the shit-kickin' Krauts!" And then for ten days he was there and we busted through, singin' and shootin' our hearts out with himself ahead of us, *ahead* of us, Billy, shoutin' his head off, tellin' us we could *do* it because we were better than the bastards who'd put us in chains! *Remember*, Billy?'

'The most glorious days of m'life, Paddy,' answered Gilligan, tears welling in his eyes. 'Outside of our Lord Jesus, he's maybe the greatest man God ever put on earth.'

'I think he's in trouble, Billy. Right here in Boston!'

'*Not* while we're about, Paddy. Not while the Pat O'Brien Commemorative Legion Post has a breathin' soldier in its membership . . . Hey, Paddy? What happened to your boyo? He's flat out on the cement.'

'He's fainted, Billy. Must run in the family.'

'*Mmmfff* . . . !' came the unconscious protest from Sam Devereaux's throat.

CHAPTER THIRTEEN

'Samuel Lansing Devereaux, get up at once and behave yourself!' cried the Lady Eleanor with admirable authority, considering the fact that she clutched Jennifer Redwing's arm under Nanny's canopy for stability.

'Come on, Sam boyo,' said Paddy. 'Grab my hand, lad.'

'He's lighter than me daughter-in-law, Lafferty,' added Billy Gilligan. 'We can just heave him into the Hebrew canoe.'

'Yer daughter-in-law should play for the Patriots, Billy, and I'll ask you not to refer to Mr Pinkus's fine stretcheroo in derogatory terms.'

'Guess where I got that derogatory term, Paddy?' asked Gilligan, chuckling as the two men carried Devereaux to the limousine and angled him into the back seat. 'Don't bother, I'll tell you. From old Pinkus himself, boyo. Remember when you and he come over and we –'

'That'll be *enough*, Billy, and I thank you for your assistance. The keys are in the Jaguar, and I'll thank you again if you'll stash it and lock it where you can keep your eye on it.'

'Oh, no, Lafferty!' objected Gilligan. 'I'm callin' my relief and headin' directly over to the Pat O'Brien Commemorative Post and rounding up the members. If the greatest general who ever kissed the sword of battle has troubles, he can count on us, by the graves of Donegal!'

'We can't *do* nothin', Billy, until the general and Mr Pinkus give us our orders. I'll stay in touch, my word as a gunny.'

'Oh, the glory of it! To meet the magnificent man himself – General of the United States Army, MacKenzie Hawkins!'

'Oh, that *dreadful* name!' exploded Eleanor Devereaux.

'You're seconded, Ellie,' agreed Redwing.

'*Mmmfff,*' came the muffled cry from the back seat of the limousine.

'Pay no attention, Gilligan, the girls aren't well . . . But, Billy, I didn't promise that you'd meet the great man himself, I only said I'd try.'

'And I didn't promise I wouldn't sell the Jaguar, neither, Paddy. I only said I'd try not to.'

'Come along, ladies,' Lafferty interrupted, with a scowl at Gilligan. 'I'm to take you to the Ritz-Carlton where Mr Pinkus has made private arrangements –'

'*Paddy!*' yelled a partially revived Sam Devereaux from the back seat. 'I've got to reach Mac . . . he doesn't know what's happening!' The attorney lurched unsteadily out of the limousine on the far side, slammed the door, and crawled to the automobile's cellular telephone.

'Ladies, *please?*' cajoled Lafferty, helping Jennifer to gently insert Eleanor into the back seat, and closing the door after them. Paddy then climbed behind the wheel, concerned that Sam was having difficulties with the switchboard at the Four Seasons Hotel.

'What do you *mean* all calls to the Pinkus suite are being transferred to another room?' shouted Devereaux.

'Calm down, boyo,' said Lafferty, climbing behind the wheel and starting the engine. 'You'll get more with honey than vinegar.'

Sam glowered at the chauffeur. '"MacKenzie Hawkins, Superstar,"' he muttered. 'Why don't you clowns write a new musical? . . . It's *what*, Operator? Busy? Never mind, I'll call back . . . I've got to reach Aaron,' said Devereaux, manipulating the buttons on the phone.

'That won't be easy right now,' offered Lafferty, speeding up the ramp and on to the highway. 'When he called me, he said he was leaving the office for an hour or so and he'd see you all at the Ritz.'

'You don't understand, Paddy! Mac could have been taken by now . . . or worse.'

'The *general*?'

'He's been followed ever since he got to Boston!'

'By *God*!' shouted Lafferty. 'Give me that phone and I'll call the Pat O'Brien boys at the Legion Post myself! I'll leave word for Billy Gilligan –'

'Let me try the hotel one more time.' Frantically, Sam dialled and glanced over his shoulder into the rear section of the limousine. The hard look in Redwing's luminous eyes told him that she understood the state of emergency; his mother blinked rapidly at nothing. 'The Pinkus suite, please, Operator, and I realize that all calls are transferred to another room.' Devereaux held his breath until a strange, half whining, high-pitched voice answered.

'This is Little Joey,' said the man/woman/hermaphrodite or dwarf. 'Whaddya want?'

'I believe I may have the wrong room,' replied Sam, doing his best to control his panic. 'I'm trying to locate General MacKenzie Hawkins, twice winner of the Congressional Medal of Honor, hero of the United States Army and close friend of the whole Joint Chiefs of Staff, as well as the President, who will immediately order an invasion of the hotel if the general's life is threatened in any way, shape, or manner!'

'I gotcha. You want the big pasta fazool . . . Hey, Mickey Ha Ha, it's for you.'

'You'll never rise in the ranks with that sort of insubordination, Little Joseph!' came the growling, approaching voice of the Hawk. 'Commander Pinkus, is that you?'

' . . . Little *Joseph*? Mac, what the hell are you *doing*? . . . Never mind, we don't have time – you're being *followed*! Someone's been *following* you ever since you got to Boston!'

'Why, Lieutenant Devereaux, you're shaping up. I mean you're really counting off the numbers like a master sergeant, no offence to your bars.'

'You *know*?'

'Well, it was pretty obvious after my adjutant reported what he overheard at the front desk.'

'But you said you *didn't* know how it happened, that it wasn't Hymie somebody-or-other's modus operandi!'

'I *didn't* know then and it wasn't the Hurricane's m.o. I *do* know now and it still isn't Hymie. This fella wasn't hard to find; his door was open exactly an inch and a half.'

'For Christ's sake, make sense!'

'I just did, and you've got to get off this line. We're expecting another call.'

'From *whom*?'

'I thought you would have figured that out by now.'

'How?'

'You heard me ask if you were him –'

'"He" –'

'What?'

'Never mind ... Who?'

'Commander Pinkus, of course.'

'He's on his way to the Ritz.'

'Not for a while, son. He and my adjutants are on a supply run.'

'Who the fuck is Little *Joseph*? ... Sorry, Mother.'

'He's kind of a sweet old guy,' answered the Hawk, lowering his voice to a near whisper, 'with the size and shape of a good night patrol point, especially in hill country, but I'm afraid his age and his temperament don't go with the job any longer ... I wouldn't care to tell him that, naturally. It could destroy his confidence, you can understand that, Lieutenant.'

'I don't understand a goddamned thing! *What* job?'

'Those pricky-shit lace pants in Dizzy City must really be crippled by the deficit,' continued the general rapidly and so quietly Devereaux could barely hear him. 'Son of a bitch, boy, that sort of thing never bothered any of *us*!'

'He's from *Washington*?'

'I know, I know,' said the Hawk with weary, if impatient, finality. 'Commander Pinkus explained that it was vital we leave him room for deniability.'

'*Deniability*?'

'Bye, Sam.' The line went dead.

'What is it?' asked Redwing intensely, leaning forward in

the back seat, her right hand firmly gripping Eleanor's shoulder.

'Is the grand and great general all right, boyo?' cried Lafferty, accelerating the limousine and weaving in and out of the traffic toward Boston. 'Shall I call Gilligan and the troops?'

'I don't know, Paddy, I really don't know. I don't think so.'

'Don't give me no crap, lad!'

'What *do* you know, Sam,' said Jennifer, her question posed calmly, warmly, the consummate attorney. 'Take your time and collect your thoughts.'

'Cut the friendly interrogation, please, because that's exactly what I'm doing. I'm trying to figure it out and it's not easy, it's just crazy.'

'Then get your act together, Counsellor.'

'That's better, Red . . . Mac's obviously in control and my guess is that he's found the man who's been following him – guess, hell, it's a given; he's too condescending for it to be anything else – and he's learned that the surveillance is from Washington.'

'Oh, good Lord . . . !'

'Exactly my sentiments, Miss Indian On-and-Off Love Call. Certain segments of Dizzy City are climbing the wall, and that's the worst news we could hear.'

'What segments, Counsellor?'

'From what I can glimmer, Counsellor, they're very unhealthy. Their emissaries to Boston carry guns.'

'They wouldn't *dare*!' cried Redwing.

'Shall we revisit Watergate or Iran-contra or to balance the agenda half the elections in Chicago since 1920? There's no "wouldn't dare" in those events. And even if there were, compare the bucks spread out to all of those historical connivances combined with one *month* of the Strategic Air Command. They're infinitesimal, Indian Lady, we're talking mega*billions*! You think our benevolent battalions of defence contractors along with their representatives from all over the country – suppliers from Long Island to Seattle – won't push their panic buttons at even the prospect of denting all those profit sheets? Jesus, if one tenth of one percent of the defence budget is cut, they're all howling for blood. This kind of thing could open up their vampire factories.'

'You're assuming that the Wopotami brief has been put on the Supreme Court's schedule for argument.'

'It doesn't have to be put on any schedule, just word leaked that it's even being considered, or worse, being held over for future *possible* argument.'

'That's always the bellwether for later serious consideration,' broke in Redwing.

'You've got it. Either way the money boys and their political hacks will mount a counter-attack.'

'Wait a minute, Sam,' pleaded Redwing, one hand on Eleanor's head, the other on Devereaux's shoulder. 'A counter-attack in congressional terms would mean spokesmen, or advocates, making their case in the House and the Senate, not hit men!'

'Granted, but Congress isn't in session, and I submit our current situation as Article A for evidence.'

'I see what you mean. The hit men are here. So one way or the other, word *has* been leaked . . . Oh, my God, they've got to silence all of us!'

Paddy Lafferty snapped out the cellular phone from its cradle, and with practised fingers punched the numbers with his thumb. 'The O'Brien Post, you are?' he shouted, and after less than a second, he spoke firmly. 'Is Billy Gilligan there? . . . All right, all *right*, I'm glad for the fact that our telephone relays are workin', now listen to me. When Billy G. gets there, have him lead a column of armed vehicles to the Four Asses Hotel on Boylston and pipe up every entrance! You got it, lad? It's the *great* man we're talkin' about, and I'll brook no mistakes. G'bye to ya, and get hoppin'!'

'Paddy, what have you *done*?'

'There are times, Sam boyo, when you charge ahead and look back afterwards. It's a lesson we learned during ten glorious days in France.'

'We're not *in* France and this *isn't* World War Two, and if there's any suggestion of immediate danger down at the hotel,

Aaron will call in the police. Everything's too murky, too unclear, but Mac and our very quick-thinking employer are in touch with each other ... I repeat, Aaron is not a gung-ho mutant nor is he indecisive. If he feels the police are necessary, they'll be there.'

'I dunno, boyo. The police have certain restraints placed upon them – ask Billy Gilligan, he'll tell you.'

'He's already *told* me, Paddy, but we don't know what Mac and Aaron are doing, and not knowing, we could be lousing them up. Now call off the hounds of Killarney!'

'He's right, Mr Lafferty,' interjected Jennifer from the back seat. 'Mind you, I'm not opposed to protection in any form, and I'd be grateful if your friends were, shall we say, available. However, Sam has a point; we're in the dark and perhaps we shouldn't do anything until we reach the Ritz-Carlton and talk to Mr Pinkus ... I believe you said pretty much the same thing to Mr Gilligan back at Nanny's.'

'Well, you put it better than the lad here –'

'I simply used your own words, your own wisdom, Mr Lafferty.'

'Cheap tactics,' mumbled Devereaux.

'All *right*,' said Paddy. 'I'll call 'em off,' he added, touching the car phone buttons. 'For a moment I guess I got too excited ... Hello, Post O'Brien? ... Who's this now? ... Rafferty, it's Lafferty, boyo. Is Gilligan there yet? ... He *what*? Holy Mary ... how bad was it? ... Small favours are still a blessing, Rafferty. Now, listen to me, lad – about the members headin' off to the Four Seasons on Boylston, I want you to tell 'em –' Suddenly, the limousine swerved dangerously – involuntarily – close to a huge truck on the highway. 'They *what*, Rafferty? What the hell are you *sayin'*, boyo? ... Jesus, Mary and Joseph!' Aaron Pinkus's chauffeur swallowed; in silence he replaced the phone.

'What's the matter, Paddy?' asked Sam, looking at Lafferty as though he did not care to hear the answer.

'The lads have just taken off for the hotel, Mr Devereaux. However, it's *not* a full column, which is usually four automobiles – only three – and maybe a couple of the boys are pissed to the eyeballs.'

'Oh, my God!'

'But the good news is that Billy Gilligan wasn't hurt too bad.'

'Hurt?'

'He got piled up on the highway, his car pretty much totalled. One of the police on the scene is a member of the Post and called to let the members know what hospital.'

'Hospital . . . ?'

'He's okay. He's yellin' and screamin' to get out of there and join the others.'

'For Christ's sake, let him! Maybe he can stop them!'

'Well, there's a formality or two –'

'If he can yell and he can scream, he can get *out* of there!' Furiously, Sam yanked the phone out of its receptacle. 'What *hospital?*' he demanded angrily.

'Won't do any good, boyo. There's a mite bit of confusion over the accident report. Y'see, it wasn't exactly *his* car on the highway. It was your mother's yellow Jaguar.'

'*Yellooow birrd* . . . ' came the lilting high-pitched words and music from the tremulous throat of Eleanor Devereaux in the back seat.

'Hey, *Comandante*, wadda chu tink?' asked Desi the Second, standing resplendently in cutaway tails and admiring himself in the mirror of a successful formal wear store Aaron Pinkus Associates had virtually put in business.

'Positively striking,' replied Aaron, sitting in a velvet padded chair he could not move due to the heavy tuft of the shiny black carpet. 'Where is your associate, the other Corporal Arnaz?'

'We are *sergeants* now, *Comandante!*'

'My deepest apologies, but where is he? We must move quickly.'

'Well, you see, the lady who measured his *pantalones* ees from *Puerrtoo Reekoh* an' I t'ink they got a –'

'We have no *time* –'

'Desi *Uno!*' yelled Sergeant D-Two. '*Venga! Vámonos! Ahorita!* Right away-like, man!'

Somewhat sheepishly, Desi the First emerged from a slatted dressing room door, followed by a generously endowed dark-haired girl who made it a point to stretch and check her measuring tape while adjusting her blouse. '*Comandante,*' said D-One, smiling broadly, his absent teeth all too apparent. 'The pants we had to stitch closer. My hips are like a *toreador's!* What can I say?' He, too, was in tails and there was no question about it, Desi the First also cut a striking figure.

'You look splendid, Sergeant Arnaz,' observed Pinkus. 'Now to my orthodontist who says he has forty or fifty plastic devices, one or two of which he claims he can glue into your mouth for an hour or so.'

'Dad's nice. Wad does he do for a living?'

'Joseph, I'm tired of your evasions, little fella,' said the Hawk, sitting in the hotel's desk chair as Joey the Shroud reclined on the bed, his arms above his head on the pillow. 'I could break your wrists one by one and force you to tell me who you are and where you come from, but I've always figured that sort of thing was barbaric, as well as against the Geneva conventions. But if push comes to shove, Joseph, you'll leave me no option, will you?'

'I seen you fazools all my life, Mickey Ha Ha,' answered Little Joey, unimpressed. 'I can tell who will and who won't ... Oh, you tough *soldatos* will smash heads like they were pizza pans in a Brooklyn riot, but one on one, if there ain't no big advantage, you don't want it on your soul.'

'*Goddamn!*' roared Hawkins, getting up from the chair menacingly. 'I don't *have* any soul like that!'

'If you didn't, I'd be scared shitless, and I'm not scared shitless ... You're like the *facisti* from Salerno up the boot into Rome itself. I was a punk kid then but I always knew the difference ... If they found me out, they'd scream *esecuzione!* then we'd talk and they'd say *non me ne importa un bel niente* – who cares – the war's over, and let me go. And some of those guys were the best donkeys in the Italian army.'

'The ... *army*? Soldiers? *Salerno*? *You* were –'

'Fourth Army, Mark Clark, fazool. I guess we're about the same age, except maybe you look better. As I say, I was punk private until they found out I could speak Italian better than the interpreters so they put me in civilian clothes, raised me to a temporary first lieutenant 'cause they figured I'd last a day and a half, and sent me north to radio back info on installations. No big deal. I had lotsa lira, all the broads and the vino I wanted, and only got caught three times – the like of which I already explained.'

'*Joseph!*' shouted the Hawk. 'We're *comrades!*'

'If you're a fuckin' homo, get away from me, Mickey!'

'No, Joseph, I'm a *general!*'

'I know that, fazool.'

'And you're a first lieutenant!'

'That don't count no more. When the brass found me in Rome, livin' a pretty good life a few miles north in the Villa d'Este, they busted me back to a private. I got no use for you shitheads.'

The hotel telephone rang. MacKenzie glared at it between repeated glances at Private Little Joseph, and then picked it up. 'Temporary headquarters!' he roared.

'I'd suggest a different, less strident announcement,' said Aaron Pinkus on the line. 'Your adjutants are prepared. Have you learned what we have to know?'

'I'm afraid not, Commander. He's one fine old soldier.'

'I will not presume to understand that statement. Shall we proceed then?'

'Proceed, sir!'

The three automobiles from the Pat O'Brien Commemorative Legion Post raced down Clarendon Street, careening around the corner into Boylston, and, as prearranged, sped to within a block of the Four Seasons Hotel, each vehicle parking in an available space. Swiftly, they rendezvoused at the car nearest the hotel's entrance, their *d'avant-guerre* conference somewhat held up by the Duffy brothers, who had not been reached by the phone relay insofar as they had been at the Legion Hall's bar since early morning due to a medium-sized dispute with their wives who happened to be sisters.

'I damn sure there's somethin' in the Church that says we shouldn't have done what we did, Petey!' cried a grey-haired Duffy brother as he was led to the rendezvous.

'But we did it thirty years ago, Bobby!'

'But they're sisters, Petey. And we're brothers —'

'They're not *our* sisters, Bobby —'

'Still, brothers and sisters — I'm sure there's somethin', boyo!'

'Will you two shut yer faces!' ordered a leather-lined Harry Milligan, put in charge of the small brigade by the injured Billy Gilligan. 'Yer too pissed for combat, so I'm orderin' you to stand watch.'

'What are we watchin'?' asked a weaving Bobby Duffy, running his hand through the imagined hair on his bald head. 'Where are the Krauts comin' from?'

'Not *Krauts*, Bobbo! The dirty bastards who want to shoot the heart out of the great general!'

'What do they look like, Harry boy?' inquired a wide red-eyed Peter Duffy, gripping the side-view mirror and quite by the accident of his bulk, bending it out of shape — downward.

'How the hell do *I* know, Petey?' replied the CO of the Milligan-Gilligan brigade. 'My guess is that they'll be runnin' like a Donegal wind out of there once we find 'em.'

'How will we do that, Harry boy?' asked Bobby Duffy, his words interspersed with one hiccup and two belches.

'Come to think of it, I'm not sure.' Milligan squinted, the leathered lines in his face like crevices on a rhino skin. 'Gilligan never actually told me.'

'You got it wrong, Harry,' protested the erratically unstable Peter Duffy. 'You yourself are Gilligan.'

'I'm not himself at all, you slotted asshole! I'm *Milligan*!'

'Very nice to make your acquaintance,' said Bobby Duffy, sinking down to the kerb like an overripe, overdone baked potato punctured by a fork.

'M' brother has been afflicted by the evil anti-Christ

demons!' cried Peter, falling down against the car door, his leg over his brother's face. 'It's the curse of the witch-sisters!'

'Good lad,' agreed Harry Milligan, kneeling and patting Petey's head. 'You stay here and ward off those terrible demons.' Harry rose to his feet and addressed the seven remaining troops of the Milligan-Gilligan brigade. 'Come on now, boyos, we know what we have to do!'

'What exactly is that, lad?' asked a gaunt septuagenarian wearing an ill-fitting World War II field jacket replete with a dozen patches representing duty in the European theatre of operations.

'Billy Gilligan gave me the two names – the first, of course, the great General Hawkins and, the second, his employer, a gentleman of the law of which we've all heard of not unkindly. The Jewish fella who's a big shillelagh in Boston and who has a number of fine Catholic lawyers in his firm.'

'Smart, they're always so *smart*,' intoned an elderly unidentified voice in the magnificent seven. '*They* hire Micks, but how many of *us* hire the skull caps? *Smart.*'

'So this is what we do, boyos. I myself will go to the front desk and make the inquiry. I'll be tellin' 'em I have to reach either the great general or his friend, the grand lawyer named Pinkus, because I got an urgent confidential message that concerns both of 'em, and the dear Lord knows I'm not lyin' about that! Now, with such highfalutin fellas they got no choice but to put me in touch with one or the other, right?'

A chorus of affirmatives followed, marred by the dissenting voice of the oldest combatant in the field jacket. 'I dunno, Gilligan –'

'I'm Milligan!'

'Wish you were Gilligan, he was on the force, y'know.'

'I'm *not* . . . so what don't you know, ya old fart?'

'Suppose you get a secretary on the telephone, what are you goin' to say? . . . "My apologies, lass, but somebody or other is about to blow away the great general and his friend, the Jewish shillelagh" . . . Somehow, lad, I think they'd call for the boys who drive those little white trucks with thick rubber walls and bars in the windows.'

'I don't hafta talk to *nobody*, you walkin' object of a wake! Paddy Lafferty has told us all about the grand *suit* his employer keeps at the Four Asses, only we don't know where it is. Now the clerks got to tell me on account of the urgent confidential message I'm carryin', *right?*'

Again there was a chorus of affirmatives, again marred by the septuagenarian legionnaire. 'Suppose they don't believe you? I wouldn't. You got shifty eyes when a person can see'em.'

There was now a brace of nodding heads as the combatants studied the flesh-encased eyes of Harry Milligan. 'Oh, *shut* up!' cried Harry, shocking his troops back to the issue at hand. 'They can believe me or not believe me, it don't make no difference. They still got to give me a room number to call – then we'll know where it is!'

'Then what?' asked the cautious disbeliever.

'Then we split up, and *you*, ya shrivelled-up cadaver, you stay by the front entrance and if we flush the bastards out and they run into getaway automobiles, you damn well get the licence plate numbers ... Thank Christ you weren't in *my* outfit, you'd be arguing with Ike himself!' Milligan pointed to three of the remaining unassigned six legionnaires. 'You lads cover whatever other exits there are to the street – Lafferty was clear about that –'

'Where are they, Harry?' said a short middle-aged man in a leather Air Corps jacket. 'I was a tail gunner, so I'm not too familiar with ground tactics.'

'You gotta *find* 'em, boyo! Paddy said to pipe 'em up.'

'What does that mean, Harry?'

'Well ... well, Paddy *wasn't* too clear about that, but I figure he meant not to let anybody out who shouldn't.'

'Like who?' asked a tall slender man in his late sixties, his dress code in conflict with the mission, as he wore a loud Hawaiian shirt profuse with orange passion flowers, but nevertheless topped by a blue legionnaire's cap.

'Harry awready told us!' cried an overweight member of medium height, a metal combat helmet framing his bubbled-out face. 'Any bastards who are runnin' outside to getaway cars.'

'Then we *shoot* 'em!' confirmed the slender gentleman in the Hawaiian shirt.

'In the *legs*, boyo!' clarified Harry Milligan. 'Like we used to do with the Kraut scouts. We gotta save 'em for interrogation!'

'Right on, Harry,' agreed the helmeted infantryman. '*Boy*, do I remember! We'd capture 'em and all they did was cover their balls! 'Course I never had to shoot, but they got the message.'

'Lads, I suggest you take off your headgear. Kinda obvious, you know what I mean?' Harry then addressed the last three combatants from Post O'Brien. 'You boys, you stay with me, properly behind and mixin' with the people in the lobby, but keep your *eyes* on me. When *I* move, you move with me, got it, boyos?'

Once more, and again now louder with determination, the chorus of consenting adults was heard. 'We'll go in first,' said the beefy ground soldier, clipping his helmet on to his combat belt beneath his bowling shirt, which proclaimed the virtues of O'Boyle's meats. 'Give us two minutes and we'll find the exits and get stationed.'

'Good thought, boyo. Off with you now for there's no time to waste!' Milligan checked his watch as the three-man advance unit dodged the Boylston traffic and ran as fast as their elderly legs could manage into the hotel. The sight of them did not exactly overwhelm the uniformed doorman with inspirational thoughts. Harry turned to the remaining three and issued his orders. 'When we get inside I'll go to the front desk, very casually, mind you, like I walk through the lobby every day of me life, and sort of lean over the counter like a very important man, maybe winkin' a couple of times to convey the fact that I got a confidential message for other important persons. Then I'll hit 'em with the one-two punch, namely the two illustrious names of Hawkins and Pinkass.'

'I think that's Pinkoos, Harry,' offered a florid-faced balding man in his late sixties who was obviously a bowling colleague of the infantryman; unfortunately the O'Boyle's Meat Market T-shirt was inside out.

'He's right, Milligan,' confirmed a short man sporting a large, bushy moustache usually associated with English sergeant-majors at the turn of the century. Contrarily, his present uniform consisted of soiled Levis held up by red braces over a yellow and black plaid shirt. 'I heard Paddy say Pinkoos lotsa times.'

'*Pinkuss* is closer,' corrected the third member of Harry's unit, an inordinately tall reed of a man wearing a dark green tank top that afforded a generous view of the tattoos on both his arms, especially an elongated hissing blue snake with the legend below it reading *Don't Thread On Me*.

'I'll just say "Pinkiss" real quick like, that'll cover it . . . All right, boyos of Post O'Brien, we *charge* and win this one for the General!'

Inside Aaron Pinkus's Buick coupé, the sartorially stunning Desis One and Two, the former's mouth somewhat enlarged by a plastic front denture, sat in the cramped back seat, each admiring himself and both constantly running their hands over the smooth dark fabric of their cutaways, especially the satin lapels.

'Remember now, Sergeants, pretend you don't understand a word of English,' said Aaron behind the wheel as they turned into Boylston Street. 'You're ambassadors to the United Nations from Spain and very important men.'

'Dad'sss nice,' interrupted Desi-One, lisping heavily due to the intrusion behind his lips, 'but we still don't know how we get the *vicioso* to be so mad at us.'

'You mistake him for someone else, Sergeant, we've gone *over* that. When you see him in the lobby, you rush over and point at him, yelling that he's a hunted criminal from Madrid.'

'Yeah, we gone over dat,' said Desi-Two. 'An' we don' like dat. The *vicioso*, like all *viciosos*, gotta gun, man, an' he gonna let us *know* dat!'

'He won't have a chance to do you any harm at all,' replied

Aaron to the implied protest. 'The general will be right behind him and will immediately interfere – "immobilize," I believe was the word he used. You trust the general, don't you?'

'Oh, yeah, we like him,' answered Desi-One. 'We really like that crazy *hombre*. He gonna get us into da army!'

'He also beat d' shit out of us at d' airport, amigo. Dad's why *I* trust him.' Desi-Two kept nodding his head as he fingered the crease on his cutaway trousers. 'Dad ole man got big *testículos*.'

'So what den, *Comandante?*' asked a bewildered Desi the First.

'The general, in his uniquely peculiar way, is quite correct,' replied Pinkus, hugging the kerb behind several taxis to the Four Seasons's entrance. 'No government dares offend an allied government over lapsed security, especially countries that are strategically important. They might shut down their embassies and sever relations!'

'Dad'sss wad we don' like,' broke in Desi-One. 'We don' want no embassy *Español* shut down, even tho' we never been to *España*, especially if we gotta get shot. Our relations won' like dat.'

'The general has given you his word.'

'Ees better be fooking good! . . . But den what?'

'Well, the best way to explain it to you is that whoever sent this terrible person to Boston after the general will be forced to reconsider his methods.'

'Don' understand.'

'He'll be frightened to the point of calling off such assaults, warning everyone in Washington who had anything to do with sending such a vicious criminal after the general to cease and desist or disappear. Hawkins is geopolitically accurate. Our bases in Spain – mainly those with planes – must be sustained.'

'*Olé, Comandante!*'

MacKenzie Hawkins gave his command. 'Blowtorch the door open *now*! I want it down in five minutes, got that, Captain?'

'You *got* it, General,' replied the voice of the hotel's engineer over the telephone. 'But you promised, *sir*. I get a picture of you and me together, *right*?'

'My pleasure, son, and I'll put my arm around your shoulders like we crossed the Rhine by ourselves.'

'Holy Christ, I'm in heaven before I lay down to die!'

'*Now*, Captain. It's imperative to the assault.'

'Four minutes and eight seconds, General!'

Hawkins punched the bar of the telephone and dialled the number of the cellular phone in Aaron Pinkus's Buick. 'Commander?'

'Yes, General?'

'I'll be down in five minutes. Where are you positioned?'

'Three cars from the entrance.'

'Good. Establish yourselves at the front desk and synchronize your watches. Zero option is between thirteen and seventeen minutes. *Read* me?'

'You're not entirely illegible, General. I understand.'

The Post O'Brien brigade was in place – tank top, tattoos, flight jacket, a bulging combat helmet, red braces, Hawaiian shirt, soiled Levis, and a squinty-eyed winking leader at the front desk.

'Yes, sir?' said the clerk, pulling a handkerchief from his breast pocket as if the sight of the man might produce an accompanying odour.

'I'll tell ya what I got, boyo, and you better move quick. Does the names Pinkiss and Hawkins strike a bell, lad?'

'Mr *Pinkus* maintains a suite here, if that's what you mean.'

'I'm not referrin' to his inner private life, boyo, and I don't give a damn how many sweeties he's got. I gotta get a message to him and the general. It's urgent *and* confidential. Now, how do you propose I do that, eh?'

'I suggest you telephone Mr Pinkus's . . . rooms. Extension five thousand five.'

'Five-zero-zero-five, right, lad?'

'That's correct.'

'That's his room number?'

'We do not have fifty floors, sir. No hotel in Boston has fifty floors. That is the telephone extension number.'

'It don't make no sense. In any *decent* hotel the room number is the phone number!'

'Not necessarily.'

'Why not? How can a person know where it is?'

'Good point,' agreed the clerk. 'You yourself might illustrate it.'

'Illustrate what, boyo?'

'The point, sir ... The house phones are over on that ledge.'

Bewildered, Harry Milligan turned and hurried toward the bank of telephones on a marble counter attached to the wall. He picked one up and dialled rapidly. The line was busy.

'This is your Washington surveillance,' said MacKenzie Hawkins into the phone, lowering his voice and speaking softly, urgently.

'My *what*?' asked the man in a hotel room two storeys below, his voice equally low but hardly soft.

'Just listen to me. The target's checking out – my informant tells me he called the bell captain to have his luggage taken downstairs.'

'Who the fuck are *you*?'

'Your liaison to DC and you should thank me, not curse me. Hurry up. Follow him.'

'I'm locked in!' shouted the would-be assassin furiously. 'The fuckin' door jammed; they're working on it now!'

'Out. We can't be involved any longer.'

'Holy *shit*! ... Wait a minute, the door's being pulled out!'

'Hurry.' The Hawk hung up the phone and looked down at Little Joey the Shroud sitting on the edge of the bed. 'Are you going to tell me you didn't know that man was in the hotel?'

'*What* man?' protested Joey. 'You are the fazool of fazools, Mickey Ha Ha. You need help, big fella, like maybe a nice place with green grass lawns and iron gates and lots of doctors.'

'You know, Little Joseph, I believe you,' said the general. 'It wouldn't be the first time command has kept certain aspects of an operation from the troops.' With these words the Hawk walked rapidly to the door and let himself out; he could be heard accelerating his pace down the corridor . . . And the telephone rang. Joey reached over and picked it up.

'Yeah?'

'Is this the grand and great general himself, *sir*?'

'So?' replied a squinting, curious Little Joey.

''Tis the privilege of me *life*, General! 'Tis Private First Class Harry Milligan and I'm here to tell ya that we got the place not only surrounded but *infiltrated*, sir! No harm'll come to ya, *sir*, on the word of the patriotic boyos of the Pat O'Brien Commemorative Legion Post!'

Quietly, slowly, Joey replaced the telephone and leaned back on the pillow. *Fazools*, he mused. The whole world was peopled with flakereenos, especially in Boston, Massachusetts, where the friggin' pilgrims were probably inbred to begin with. After all, what did they have to do but have a little fun on the long journey in that boat, the Maypot? . . . Well, thought Joey, he was going to order a nice, early room-service dinner and then call code Ragu in Washington. Vinnie the Bam-Bam was going to hear a long, very screwed-up story whether he liked it or not. *Fazools!*

Aaron Pinkus escorted his two diplomats in their cutaways to the front desk and proudly announced that his guests, the ambassadors from Spain, would be occupying his suite and whatever courtesies were extended would be greatly appreciated, not only by their host, but by the government of the United States of America.

The entire front desk converged to pay homage to the distinguished visitors, and when it was learned that neither spoke English, a Puerto Rican bellboy was summoned to act as interpreter. The bellboy, whose name was Raul, was overjoyed as his first communication with Desi the First consisted of the following – freely translated.

'*Hey, man, where'd you get that fancy uniform with the shiny buttons? You in the army?*'

'No, *man*, I carry suitcases. I'm assigned to you so I can make the *gringos* understand what you say.'

'Hey, that's cool! Where are you from?'

'PR.'

'So are we!'

'No, you're not, you're big-shot diplomats from Madrid! That's what the cat said.'

'That's for the *gringos*, man! Hey, maybe later we have a nice party, what do you say?'

'Hey, man, where you're staying, they got everything!'

'They got maybe girls? Nice girls, of course, because my associate is very religious.'

'I'll get him what he wants, and I'll get us what we want. Leave it to me, man.'

'What did they say, Pedro?' asked the head clerk.

'Raul, sir.'

'Terribly sorry. What did they say?'

'They are very appreciative of the fine manners and exemplary kindness displayed by all of you. They are especially gratified by the fact that you have assigned this modest Raul to be with them throughout their stay.'

'My word!' said an assistant manager. 'You speak extremely well for a sp ... for a newly arrived person to our shores.'

'Night school, sir. Boston University Extension Course for Immigrants.'

'Keep your eyes on this young man, gentlemen. He's different!'

'*He's the biggest asshole of them all. This is a good place; he won't last a month.*'

'*Tell us something we don't know*, Pedro!'

'Perhaps,' said Aaron Pinkus, interrupting, 'you'd like to look around this magnificent lobby. It's really very unique ... Would you translate, please, Raul.'

'With great pleasure, sir.'

Harry Milligan approached the tank top-cum-tattoos and whispered into his ear, only vaguely aware that a number of people in the lobby stared at them. 'The great general moves in wondrous and mysterious ways, lad. I explained our mission and he was kinda quietlike, but as the Lord is my witness, I could hear the wheels spinning in that fine brain of his ... Y'know, that grand man could be scalin' down the outside walls at this minute. I'm told he taught all the Rangers everythin' they ever learned!'

Suddenly, the intrusion startling, the septuagenarian in the patch-laden field jacket, his bowed legs a set of churning parentheses, rushed up to Milligan and Tank Top. 'I've *got* it, boyos! They're *terrorists!*'

'*Who*, for Christ's sake?'

'Them fancy-dans in the fish 'n chips!'

'What're ya talkin' about?'

'Those two dark-skinned, black-haired creeps leavin' the front desk! They're supposed to be big shots, *right*?'

'Well, I guess they are, boyo. Look at 'em.'

'Since when do big shots in big-shot threads get out of a lousy, small three-year-old Buick instead of a big limousine type automobile? I ask ya, Harry Milligan, does it make *sense*?'

'No, it don't, 'cause it ain't natural, not with highfalutin duds like that in a place like this. A three-year-old Buick just ain't fittin' transportation, yer right about that.' Harry squinted at the splendidly dressed visitors who looked for all the world like preening peacocks, foreigners from some sun-drenched country in the Mediterranean by the dark complexion of their faces ... *Arabs!* Arab *terrorists* who surely were not comfortable in the clothes they wore or they wouldn't be hitching up their shoulders and wiggling their asses in their tight-fitting trousers. No, sir, those boyos were used to desert robes like in the movies and long-curved knives under their belts, not fancy dan sashes around their waists. 'Holy Mary, mother of *God*,' whispered Milligan to Tank Top. 'This could be it, boyo! Get word to each of our lads – tell 'em to move in slowly, keepin' their eyes on those two Sahara rats. If *they* get into an elevator, *we* get in, too!'

'Harry, I didn't go to confession this week –'

'Oh, shut up, there are seven of us, for Christ's sake!'

'That's more than three on one, ain't it?'

'Now you're an accountant, lad? Hurry along now, and lastly, tell the boyos that if I give the lodge war cry, we rush 'em!'

Like a gracefully choreographed pavane with somewhat less than graceful dancers, the Milligan-Gilligan brigade began threading through the well-dressed guests in the hotel lobby. Bare arms with tattoos and T-shirts from O'Boyle's meats mingled with tropical worsteds and Christian Dior prints, while a swinging combat helmet kept crashing into the stomachs of Brooks Brothers blazers and Adolfo cocktail dresses, all to the growing concern of the entire front desk as well as the appalled victims in the lobby being assaulted by the offending intruders in their very strange costumes.

Suddenly, a heavyset man with fire in his eyes emerged from an elevator. He looked around and moved quickly to a vantage point near the front entrance where he could obviously survey the lobby. Unseen by him, a tall grey-haired figure in a buckskin Indian jacket came out of the shadows and sidestepped his way to within several feet of the agitated man.

'¡*Caramba!*'

'¡*Madre de Dios!*'

The screaming duet filled the lobby as the two men in cutaways roared at the top of their voices while pointing accusingly at the heavyset man near the entrance.

'¡*Homicido!*'

'¡*Asesino!*'

'¡*Criminal!*'

'¡*Demendare el policia!*'

The stunned, unfriendly-looking gentleman who was the object of the cutaways' shrieking accusations began to run but was instantly stopped by the tall man in an Indian costume who hammerlocked the man's neck and head while jamming his knee up into the base of the accused's spine.

'That's *him*, boyos!' came another roar that echoed off the walls and over the pandemonium of the crowds in the lobby. 'It's the great man *himself*! *Erin go bragh*, boyos! *Charge* in the memory of Saint William Patrick O'Brien!'

And, naturally, the Milligan-Gilligan brigade pummelled

through hysterical bodies and fell upon the two Arab terrorists in cutaways.

'Wa chu *doing*, ole man?' yelled Desi the First, fending off an assault by a fat stranger now wearing a combat helmet.

'Hey, *loco* jerk!' cried Desi the Second, his foot sending an O'Boyle Meats advocate into a lovely Queen Anne chair that collapsed under his bulk, and gripping the bare arm of Tank Top. 'Das a nice-lookin' snake, ole gringo, an' I don't wanna hurt it, but chu gotta leave me alone! I got no *disputa* wid chu!'

'*Sergeants!*' roared the Hawk, crashing through the collapsing figures around his two extremely adept adjutants. 'Commander Pinkus has ordered an evacuation!'

'As quickly as possible,' added Aaron by the door. 'The hotel security was filling out stolen property forms in the office, but they're out of there now and the police have been summoned. *Quickly!*'

'Wad about the *vicioso*, h'enerale?'

'When he wakes up he'll have a bad back for a month or two. I wonder if the Mafia has Medicare.'

'Will you three please *hurry!*'

'H'okay, *Comandante*,' said Desi-One, looking around at the mêlée in the lobby. 'Hey, *Raul!*'

'*Sí, Señor Embajador?* You freak!'

'We'll call you later, man! Maybe you wanna join the army wid us, no?'

'Maybe, amigo. It could be safer than this place. Adios!'

Aaron Pinkus's Buick coupé raced down Boylston Street and turned round the first corner that would lead them to Arlington and eventually the Ritz-Carlton hotel. 'I simply don't *understand!*' protested the vaunted attorney. 'Who *were* they?'

'They were lunatics – *old* lunatics, *senile* lunatics!' replied an angry MacKenzie Hawkins, glancing into the back seat. 'Did you two suffer any wounds?' he asked.

'You crazy, h'enerale? Dose ole men couldn't steal chickens.'

'What's *that?*' yelled the Hawk abruptly as he watched Desi the First place four wallets on the seat between himself and Desi-Two.

'Wad's wad?' asked D-One, innocently looking up at the general.

'Those are billfolds – wallets – four of them!'

'Ees a big crowd back there,' offered D-Two. 'My fren' don' work so hard today 'cause he can do lots better.'

'Good Lord,' said Pinkus behind the wheel, a sense of defeat again overwhelming him. 'The hotel security . . . those stolen property reports.'

'You can't *do* that, Sergeant!'

'*I'm* not so lousy, h'enerale. Ees only a sideline, as you gringos say.'

'Oh, dear Abraham,' pleaded Aaron softly, 'I really must calm myself, my blood pressure is stratospheric.'

'What's the matter, Commander Pinkus?'

'Let's just say this hasn't been a normal working day for me, General.'

'Do you want me to drive?'

'Oh, no, thank you. Driving actually takes my mind off things.' Aaron reached over to the radio and turned it on.

The strains of Vivaldi's Concerto in D for flute filled the small car causing Desis One and Two to look at each other in disapproval and Pinkus to breathe steadily, deeply, for a few moments of peace. However, it *was* only a few moments. Suddenly, the music stopped and the excited voice of an announcer replaced the soothing Vivaldi with a nerve-shattering news flash.

'*We interrupt this programme to bring you an exclusive bulletin. The Four Seasons Hotel on Boylston Street was only minutes ago the scene of an extraordinary incident. The circumstances have not been clarified, but apparently there was a riot in the hotel's lobby causing numerous guests to be jostled and thrown to the ground – fortunately with only minor injuries so far reported. We switch you now by telephone to our correspondent, at the scene, Chris Nichols, who was having a late lunch at the hotel –*' the announcer paused, involuntarily adding, '*Lunch at the Four Seasons? On our salaries . . . ?*'

211

'*Not lunch, you idiot!*' broke in a second voice, deep and resonant. '*My wife thinks I'm in Marblehead –*'

'*You're ON, Chris!*'

'*Just kidding, folks . . . but there was no humour in what took place here barely five minutes ago. The police are trying to unravel the facts and it's not an easy job. All we know at this moment is that the cast of characters might have come out of a Hitchcock film . . . A famous Boston lawyer, two Spanish ambassadors, Arab terrorists, a large elderly American Indian with the strength of a buffalo, an odd assortment of World War Two veterans in strange attire and even stranger hallucinations, and finally, a reputed Mafia executioner. Only the first and the last have been identified. They are the renowned attorney, Mr Aaron Pinkus, and one Caesar Boccegallupo, allegedly a capo primitivo in the Borgia family of Brooklyn, New York. The first named, Mr Aaron Pinkus, presumably escaped with the two Spanish ambassadors or was taken hostage by the Arab terrorists, depending on whose version one cares to accept. Mr Boccegallupo is in custody, and according to reports keeps shouting that he insists on speaking to his lawyer who he claims is the President of the United States. Well, regardless of political parties, we all know the President is not an attorney.*'

'*Thank you, Chris, thank you for this exclusive report, and good luck in Marblehead with that exciting yacht club regatta –*'

'*It's over, you stupid son of a –*' The Vivaldi returned but did nothing to lower Aaron Pinkus's blood pressure.

'Abraham has truly deserted me,' whispered the foremost lawyer of Boston, Massachusetts.

'I *heard* that, Commander!' shouted MacKenzie Hawkins. '*He* may have, but as sure as leopards have spots, *I* haven't! We'll face the fire together, turn it on 'em, and blow 'em away, old buddy!'

'Is it possible,' asked Aaron Pinkus softly, glancing at the Hawk, 'that I have been presented with the human form of my own personal dybbuk?'

CHAPTER FOURTEEN

Sunrise Jennifer Redwing quietly shut the bedroom door and walked to the writing desk in the sitting room of the Ritz-Carlton suite arranged by Aaron Pinkus. 'Your mother's asleep,' she said as she pulled the chair away and sat down facing Devereaux on the couch. 'At last,' she added, firmly crossing her legs and glaring at Sam.

'I don't suppose it would do any good to tell you that my mother isn't always tanked.'

'If I were a mother, Samuel Devereaux, and I had learned about my son what she's learned about you during the last several days, I wouldn't draw a sober breath for the next five years!'

'Isn't that a little severe, Counsellor?'

'Only if you chose to immolate yourself on the stage of the San Francisco Cow Palace, all proceeds going for the benefit of mothers driven to cuckooville by their offspring.'

'She told you quite a bit then,' said Sam, unsuccessfully trying to avoid the lovely lady's positively unfriendly gaze.

'Only bits and pieces at the house, but for the past half hour, I've listened to a compendium of horrors – that's when you may have heard me locking the door as she instructed me to do . . . Underworld killers on a golf course, English traitors, Nazis on chicken farms, Arabs roasting goats' testicles in the desert – and my *God*, kidnapping the Pope! You made allusions to this mad general scouring intelligence files to raise forty million dollars – but nothing like *this*! Jesus *Christ*, the *Pope*! I can't believe it . . . she must have got that wrong.'

'They're not actually one and the same, you know. Christ and the Pope, I mean. Remember, I'm Anglican, although I can't specifically recall when I last went to church. Early teens, I think –'

'I don't give a *damn* whether you're Anglican or a moon drop from a Tibetan zodiac, you are *certifiable*, Counsellor! You have no right walking the streets, much less – much, *much* less – being an officer of the court!'

'You're hostile,' observed Devereaux.

'I've gone completely out of my mind! You make my maximum-nut brother Charlie look like Oliver Wendell Holmes!'

'I'll bet we'd get along.'

'Oh, sure, I can see it now. Redwing and Devereaux –'

'*Devereaux* and Redwing,' interrupted Sam. 'I'm older and more experienced.'

' . . . the law firm that set all manner of jurisprudence back to the Stone Age!'

'Probably a lot clearer then,' said Sam, nodding. 'They couldn't chip out all those codicilic phrases on the rocks.'

'Be *serious*, you idiot!'

'An idiot I'm not, Red. A playwright once said that there comes a time when there's nothing left to do but scream. I'm simply substituting an ironic chuckle for a shriek.'

'You're referring to Anouilh, and he also said "bearer of life, give light," and *I* substitute "law" for "life" – which for a few moments in your house I thought you believed, too. We must give light, Sam.'

'*You* know about Anouilh? I thought I was the only person I knew who –'

'He was never a practising attorney in Paris,' interrupted Jennifer, 'but he loved the law – especially the language of the law – and he turned a great deal of it into poetry.'

'You scare me, Indian Lady.'

'I *hope* so. We've got a very scarifying problem on the docket, Counsellor.'

'I don't mean Mac's megamess, although you're right, it's

scary as hell. But somehow – don't ask me how – I think we'll muddle through, at least with our lives if not our sanities intact.'

'I'm glad you're so confident,' observed Redwing. 'I'm not, on either point.'

'"Confident" is the wrong word, Red. Let's say I'm fatalistic because the fates will probably be on our side if for no other reason than the combine of Aaron Pinkus and MacKenzie Hawkins, two of the most resourceful men I've ever known are running interference for us. And if I'm called off the bench, I'm not exactly inadequate myself.'

'Then you've lost me. What *were* you talking about?'

'You, lady ... In the space of a few hours, from a crazy moment in an elevator to this hotel suite, we've gone through quite a bit.'

'That may be the understatement of your professional career,' Redwing broke in quickly, quietly, her eyes still glaring.

'I know, I know, but something happened –'

'Has it *really*?'

'To me,' completed Sam. 'I've watched you in what the psychology boys would probably call moments of extreme stress, and I like what I saw, respect what I saw. You can learn an awful lot about a person under those kinds of circumstances ... You can discover wonderful things, beautiful things.'

'This is getting a little saccharine, Mr Devereaux,' said Jennifer, 'and I'm very sure it's not the time for it.'

'But it is the time, don't you see? If I don't say it now when I feel it so strongly, I might not say it later. It may just slip away and I don't want that to happen.'

'Why? Because the memory of – what was it your mother said? – oh, yes, the "eternal love of his life," some benevolent nun who ran away with the *Pope*, has come back to you? That's only another crooked house on a crooked mile in cuckooville!'

'That's part of what I'm saying,' insisted Sam. 'Because that memory's fading, I can feel it, sense it. Only last night I wanted to kill Mac for even mentioning her name, but now it doesn't matter, at least I don't think it does. I look at you and I can't see her face any more, and that tells me something pretty goddamned important.'

'Are you telling me there actually *was* such a person?'

'Yes.'

'Counsellor, I've got to be in the middle of a horror movie that has exhausted my popcorn, half of it sticking to a gum-laden floor.'

'Welcome to the world of MacKenzie Hawkins, Counsellor. And don't get up from your seat because if the greasy popcorn doesn't make you slip down on your ass, you'll lose your shoes to the gum ... Why do you think your brother beat feet? Why do you think I did everything within the power of the very powerful Aaron Pinkus to avoid getting mixed up with the mad Hawk again?'

'Because it *is* total madness,' answered the bronze-skinned Aphrodite, her eyes softening. 'Yet your brilliant Mr Pinkus – and I concede that brilliance for I know something about him – has *not* cut off the mad general. He's apparently in constant touch with him, *working* with him, when we both know he could sever the relationship with one call to Washington, exonerating himself from any association whatsoever by simply stating that he never sought it ... And *you*, I watched you on the phone in the car; you were beside yourself with anxiety, no matter your feeble disclaimers. *Why*, Counsellor? What hold does this creature have on you, on *both* of you?'

Sam lowered his head, his eyes roaming within an imaginary circle of his shoes. 'The truth, I guess,' he said simply.

'What *truth*? It's chaos!'

'Yeah, there's that, too, but underneath there's truth. Like with Pope Francisco. It started off as the biggest scam in the history of the world, as Aaron called it, but down below there was something else. That beautiful man was being hamstrung by self-righteous people around him, men more interested in power than in progress. Uncle Zio wanted to widen the doors opened by John the Twenty-third, and they wanted to shut them. That's why Zio and the Hawk became such friends in the Alps. Why they did what they did.'

'The *Alps*! What they *did*?'

'Easy, Counsellor. You asked and I'm answering with a limited response. The Alps aren't important, it could have been an apartment in Jersey City. What is important is the truth, and that's Mac's insidious trap. Through whatever circuitous routes his mind travels, he arrives somehow at a fundamental truth, always, I grant you, with a terrific scam . . . Your people were *raped*, lady, and he's produced what appears to be irrefutable evidence of that assault. Sure, there's millions to be made by bringing even that appearance to judicial light, and more millions spread around by those refuting the evidence, but there's no way we can deny his basic premise if his sources are authentic . . . I can't, Aaron can't, and finally, you can't.'

'But I *want* to deny it! I don't want my people put through this wringer! Many are quite old and many, many more are ill-equipped by lack of education to deal with these complexities. They'd only get confused, undoubtedly corrupted by special interests, and in the end, *hurt*. It's wrong!'

'Oh, I see,' said Sam, sitting back on the couch. 'Let's keep the happy darkies down on the plantation, singing their spirituals and driving the mules.'

'What are you saying? How *dare* you say that to me!'

'*You* just said it, Indian lady. You got out of there, and from your exalted professional perch in San Francisco you decree that the underlings are not fit to break the chains that keep them under.'

'I never said they weren't fit, I said they weren't *ready*! We're building another school, hiring the best teachers we can afford, appealing to the Peace Corps, and sending more and more children off the reservation for better educations. But it's not all done overnight. You can't change a disenfranchized people into a politically aware society in a month or two, it takes years.'

'You don't have years, Counsellor, you've got right now. If you let this chance, as slim as it is, to right a vindictive wrong slip away, it's not going to come around the bend again. Mac was right about that; it's why he's handled it the way he has – every weapon in place and concealed, the high command out of reach but still very much in control.'

'What does that gobbledygook mean?'

'I suppose the Hawk would call it something like Delta Strike Force, Zero Hour Shock.'

'Oh, of course. Now I understand completely!

'Surprise attack, Red. No prior notice, no newspaper or media coverage of any kind, no attorneys proclaiming their march to the Court – everything stiletto-quick and quiet.'

'Catching everyone off guard . . . ' concluded Jennifer, now beginning to understand.

'Exactly,' said Devereaux. 'Forget the odds, say they just get a single swing vote, there's no appeal to a Supreme Court decision, only a legislative correction by changing the rules, the laws.'

'And Congress, even galvanized, has the speed of a turtle,' completed the lady lawyer. 'Thus leaving your crazy Hawk in the catbird seat.'

'Thus leaving the Wopotamis in the same chair,' amended Devereaux. 'It's called write-your-ticket time.'

'It could also be called an express elevator to hell,' said Redwing, getting up and walking to the hotel window overlooking Boston's Public Garden. 'It can't happen, Sam,' she continued, shaking her head slowly. 'They couldn't handle it. The carpetbaggers in their limousines and Lear jets would descend on them like an army of pterodactyls, parading Bacchus and his Bacchae in numbers they couldn't walk away from . . . And I couldn't stop them, none of us could stop them.'

'*Us?*'.

'There's about a dozen of us, kids the Council of Elders decided were *ogottowa* – smarter than the others, is the easiest translation, although it goes deeper – and were given opportunities not available to the other children. We're all doing pretty well, and except for three or four who couldn't wait to assimilate and buy their BMWs, we get together and look after the tribe's interests. We do our best, but even we couldn't protect them from this kind of Olympian spoils of law.'

'We're very Greek today, aren't we?'

'I wasn't aware of it. Why?'

'I don't know. Some Greek is walking around in my best J. Press blazer. Sorry, I didn't mean to interrupt.'

'Yes, you did. You're trying to figure out how to answer me.'

'Quick, very quick, Counsellor . . . Yes, I am, and I think I can. Am I correct in assuming that you're the top gun of this specially chosen dozen?'

'I suppose so. I'm very committed and I'm in a position to advise legally.'

'Then use that expertise before the fact, *if* the fact ever becomes a reality.'

'In what way?'

'How many others in the tribal whiz kids can you trust?' answered Sam with another question.

'My brother Charlie, of course, when he's got his head straight . . . perhaps six or seven others who I don't think could be bought into Alice-in-penthouse-land.'

'Then form an irrevocable corporate trust, signed by each member of your Council of Elders, stating that no tribal business of an economic nature may be transacted or committed through any persons other than those constituting the executors of the aforesaid trust.'

'That opens us up to collusion prior to an anticipated legal action,' objected Redwing.

'What action? Have you been formally apprised of any legal action?'

'You're damned right I have. By my brother Charlie the nut, and my new acquaintance, Sam of the sotted trousers.'

'So lie a little. It's either that or an express elevator to hell.' Redwing walked back toward the desk; she paused, her hands on her hips, her head arched to the ceiling in thought. It was a provocative stance instantly provoking Devereaux. 'Do you have to do that?' he asked.

'Do what?' replied the Aphrodite of the Wopotamis, her eyes levelled at Sam.

'Stand like that.'

'Like what?'

'You may be a daunting lady, but you don't have an excess of testosterones.'

'What the hell are you talking about?'

'You're not a man.'

'You're damned right I'm not.' Redwing briefly surveyed her upright frontage. 'Oh, come on, Counsellor, get off it. Concentrate on your nun.'

'Do I detect a note of jealousy? It'd be the best sign I could hope for.' Sam instantly began an impoverished rendition of the song. '*Jell-loos-see, I hear you my jell-loos-see* . . . '

'For God's sake, shut up! . . . It's something Charlie could do.'

'I hope not.'

'What?'

'Never mind. What could Charlie do?'

'Form the corporate trust,' said Redwing, going to the desk and picking up the phone. 'He can use my secretary and fax everything out, have it all wrapped up in a day.'

'*Hey*,' shouted Devereaux, jumping up from the couch, 'you dial, but can I act like your secretary at *this* end?'

'Why?'

'I want to hear the voice of the poor son of a bitch who got suckered into the Hawk's larceny like I did. Call it perverse but I *did* overlook your proposal of marriage. How about it?'

'Be my guest,' said Jennifer, dialling.

'What's his full name?' asked Sam, standing beside the stunning Indian attorney. 'So he knows I'm authentic.'

'Charles . . . Sunset . . . Redwing.'

'You're *kidding*!'

'He was born during the last rays of the descending sun, and I don't care to listen to any fatuous comment from you.'

'I wouldn't dare.' Jennifer completed dialling and handed

the phone to Devereaux. After several moments, Sam replied to the quiet 'hello' at the other end of the line. 'Is this Charles *Sunset* Redwing?'

'You calling for Eagle Eyes?' said the brother. 'Is anything wrong back there?'

'Eagle Eyes?' Devereaux covered the phone with his hand and turned to Jennifer. 'He said "Eagle Eyes." What does that mean? Is it an Indian code?'

'He's our uncle. You used Charlie's middle name, which he doesn't exactly advertise. Let me talk to him.'

'He scares the *hell* out of me.'

'Charlie? Why? He's a nice kid.'

'He sounds like *me!*'

'Two points for the white man,' said Redwing, taking the telephone. 'Hello, you jackass, it's your big sister and you're going to do *precisely* what I tell you to do, and don't you dare make any moves on my secretary or I'll re-diaper you like I used to do but with a couple of missing parts. *Got* that, Charlie?'

Sam returned to the couch, then decided against sitting down, opting instead for the suite's mirrored bar built into the wall and stocked with all manner of spirits. As Red Redwing harangued her brother with instructions, he began producing a large glass pitcher of dry martinis. If there was nothing left to do but scream, he might as well yell half plastered.

'*There!*' said Jennifer, replacing the phone and turning, expecting to find Devereaux on the couch, instead shifting her eyes to the bar and the mixologist performing his ritual. 'What are you doing?'

'Making pain less painful, I guess,' answered Sam, poking a tiny fork into a jar of olives. 'Aaron should be here shortly, and sooner or later Mac also – if he ever gets out of the Four Seasons . . . It's not a conference I look forward to. Care for a belt?'

'No, thanks, because that's what it would be. A heavy belt landing me on the floor. I'm afraid that, too, is part of the genes, so I stay away.'

'Really? I thought that was just a dumb myth – Indians and firewater.'

'Do you think Pocahontas would have looked twice at that scrawny WASP John Smith if she wasn't tanked? Not with all those cute braves around.'

'I consider that a racist remark.'

'You bet your ass. Leave us something.'

The elegant manager of the exclusive Fawning Hill Country Club on the Eastern Shore of Maryland turned to his assistant as the heavyset man walked through the imposing front entrance and then past them, nodding his acceptance at having been greeted silently, no name mentioned. 'Roger, my boy,' said the tuxedoed manager, 'you have just witnessed at least twelve percent of the entire wealth of this country walk through those doors.'

'You're kidding,' said the younger, equally clean-cut subordinate, also in a tuxedo but without the white rose in his lapel.

'Not for an instant,' continued the manager. 'It's a private meeting in the Gold Room with the Secretary of State. No lunch, no drinks other than bottled water, nothing. Very serious. Two men from the State Department arrived an hour ago and swept the room with electronic devices to make sure there were no taps anywhere.'

'What do you figure it is, Maurice?'

'The movers and the shakers, Roger. Inside that room are the heads of Monarch-McDowell Aircraft, Petrotoxic Amalgamated, Zenith Ball Bearings Worldwide, and the Smythington-Fontini Industries, which stretch from Milan, Italy, to California.'

'*Wow!* Who's the fifth guy?'

'The king of international bankers. He's from Boston and holds more purse strings than the Treasury Department.'

'What do you think they're doing?'

'If I knew, I could probably get rich.'

'*Moose!*' cried Warren Pease, greeting the owner of Monarch-McDowell Aircraft at the door with a hearty handshake.

'Your left eye's in orbit, Warty,' said the bull of a man. 'Do we have problems?'

'Nothing we can't handle, sport,' replied the Secretary of State nervously. 'Say hello to the crowd.'

'Hi there, old buddies,' said Moose, walking around the table in his honorary green Fawning Hill golf jacket and shaking hands.

'Good to see you, chum,' said Doozie from Petrotoxic Amalgamated, his blue blazer encrested, not with the emblem of a club but with the escutcheon of his family.

'You're late, Moose,' said the blond-haired Froggie, owner and CEO of Zenith Ball Bearings Worldwide. 'And I'm in a hurry. They've developed a new alloy in Paris and it could make millions in our defence contracts.'

'Hell, I'm sorry, Frog-face, but I couldn't change the weather over St Louis. My pilot insisted on a detour ... Hello, Smythie, how are the ladies in Milan?'

'They still *pine* for you, Moose!' replied Smythington-Fontini. The half-British, half-Italian yachtsman wore his white flannels and his billowing yachtsman's blouse replete with the ribbons of his yachting triumphs.

'So, *Bricky*,' said Moose, grasping the extended hand of the Boston banker. 'How's the money pot? You made a bundle out of me last year.'

'Most of it tax deductible, old chum,' countered the New England banker, smiling. 'Would you have it any other way?'

'Hell, no, Brick! You sweeten my coffee every morning ... I sit here, right?'

'Right.'

'*Right!*' insisted Froggie. 'I'm in a hurry. Those new alloys in Paris could fall into the hands of German industry. Get with it, Warren.'

'All right, I shall,' said the Secretary of State, sitting down and furiously tapping his left temple to keep his wavering eye in place. 'I've informed you all by security phones that our good buddy and my old roomie, the President, has put me on top of the Italian problem at the CIA.'

'I suppose somebody has to,' observed Doozie of Petrotoxic. 'The man's become something of a menace, I understand. The stories of his so-called abusive tactics are practically legend.'

'Yet, since taking office,' said Moose, 'he's been effective. From the day he walked into Langley, our companies haven't had a serious union problem. Whenever there's a threat, former colleagues of his show up in limousines and the threats go away.'

'Nice touch, the limousines,' said Doozie of Petrotoxic, dusting a speck of lint off the family crest on his jacket. 'And I must say, he's been an inspiration the way he throws around his national security prohibitions at those scruffy environmentalists. Mummy and Daddy would have thought the world of him.'

'And although he's thoroughly unacceptable socially,' added the aristocrat of Boston merchant bankers, 'through his connections with certain offshore institutions, he's made possible extraordinary extensions of your corporate finances. We've all made millions by not paying millions in taxes.'

'Damn decent fellow,' admitted Moose of Monarch-McDowell Aircraft, his jowls jiggling as he nodded his head.

'No question,' concurred Doozie. 'He truly understands that the success of his betters can mean the betterment of himself. The real trickle-down theory, indisputably proven.'

'Also,' said the inheritor of the Smythington-Fontini multinational companies, 'where else could so many of us turn? He's an extremely patriotic American. He realizes that every defence project on every drawing board *must* be approved, no matter how questionable they may appear, for in the attempts, there's always valuable ... research, yes, *research*.'

'Hear, hear!'

'Hear, hear –'

'*Well*,' broke in Secretary of State Pease, holding up a trembling right hand that he instantly grabbed with his left and pulled back on the table. 'The splendid qualities that have made him such an asset may well be the very reasons why he could become an enormous liability.'

'What?'

'*Why?*'

'Because every one of you has had extensive dealings with him.'

'Buried, Warren,' said Froggie icily. 'Deep down.'

'Not for him.'

'What *happened*?' asked Boston Bricky, his already bleached face from the absence of sunlight in his vaults growing paler.

'It's directly related to the other difficulty we face which I'll bring up later.'

'Oh, my *God*,' whispered Doozie. 'The savages ... that Court with three left-wing senilities and one nerdy enigma still on it!'

'Yes,' confirmed Warren Pease, barely audible. 'In trying to short-circuit the whole stupid fiasco, Mangecavallo traced the crazy litigants to Boston, then called in his criminal hoods from New York. Real honest to P. and L. sheet killers. One was captured.'

'Oh, great green gobs of greasy, grimy gopher guts!' cried Bricky. '*Boston?*'

'I read about that,' said Moose. 'There was a riot at some hotel and the hood who was arrested said the President was his lawyer.'

'I didn't know your old roomie was a lawyer. Warty,' said Doozie.

'He's *not*. But if my old roomie's name can even be mentioned, how long before Mangecavallo surfaces, and as sure as there's plea bargaining, you'll all be next.'

'What did you expect, Mr Secretary?' remarked the blond Froggie, his voice in a deep freeze as he looked around the table at each member. 'You give a thug responsibility, you're responsible for thugs.'

The silence was the silence of the damned. Finally, Moose of Monarch-McDowell spoke.

'Good Lord, we'll miss him.'

'Then we're in agreement?' asked Warren Pease.

'Well, of *course*, old chum,' replied Doozie, his eyebrows arched in innocence. 'What other avenue can we possibly take?'

'All roads lead to my beautiful bank on Beacon Hill!' shouted Bricky. 'He's dead *monkey* meat!'

'He's too much for *any* of us!' cried Smythington-Fontini. 'A criminal warlord at the core of the intelligence service – especially one who knows *us*, could *name* us!'

'Who's going to *say* it?' demanded Moose. 'Goddamn it, somebody's got to *say* it!'

'I shall,' answered Froggie in a monotone. 'Vincent Mangecavallo must as soon as possible become the *late* Vincent Mangecavallo ... A terrible accident, of course, nothing *remotely* suspicious.'

'But *how*?' asked the Secretary of State.

'I, perhaps, can answer you,' said Smythington-Fontini, casually inhaling on his long cigarette holder. 'I am the sole owner of the Milano-Fontini Industries, and where but in Milan, Italy, are there always cadres of malcontents that my untraceable subordinates might appeal to with a few hundred million lira? Let's say ... I can arrange it.'

'Stout fellow!'

'Good man!'

'Damn fine show!'

'When it's all over,' exclaimed Warren Pease, his left eye reasonably in place, 'the President himself will award you a commendation medal! ... A quiet ceremony, of course.'

'How did he *ever* get through the hearings?' asked the pale-faced New Englander. 'I never expected it.'

'I, for one, have absolutely no desire to know,' replied the President's prep school roommate. 'However, as to the *nomination* of the silently generous Mr Mangecavallo, may I remind all of you that it was the result of the president-elect's Search Committee, the majority of whom are around this table. I'm sure you felt that he'd never survive the Senate, but he did, and there you have it ... Gentlemen, you yourselves are responsible for placing a Mafia godfather as director of the Central Intelligence Agency.'

'That's rather crudely put, old man,' observed the escutcheoned Doozie, jutting forth his chin as he fidgeted. 'After all, you and I, we did go to the same college together.'

'God knows it pains me, Bricky, old chum, but surely you understand. I've got to protect our *boy*; it's my job, honourbound and duty and all those other things.'

'*He* didn't go to college with us. He wasn't even pledged to our frat at the other place, the one for the grinds.'

'Life isn't fair to most of our crowd, Bricky,' said Froggie, gazing coldly, however, at the Secretary of State. 'But just how could you possibly protect our boy in the Oval Office by alluding to any responsibility on our parts regarding Mangecavallo, which we would promptly and vociferously deny?'

'Well,' fairly choked the Secretary, his left eye again a steel pinball shooting between two magnets, 'as it happens, we have the complete minutes of the Search Committee's meetings.'

'*How?*' exploded Bricky, the pallid New England banker. 'There were no secretaries and no minutes were *taken!*'

'You were taped, fellas,' answered the leader of the State Department, whispering.

'What?'

'I heard our loyal, fine-familied son of a bitch!' cried the Moose. 'He said we were *taped!*'

'With what, for God's sake?' demanded Doozie. 'I never saw any machines!'

'Voice-activated microphones,' said the Secretary, hardly louder than previously. 'Underneath the tables – wherever you met.'

'What was that? . . . Wherever we *met?*'

The faces around the table were frozen in angry astonishment; then one by one, as the realization hit them, the voices followed.

'My *house?*'

'My *lodge* on the lake?'

'My estate in *Palm Springs?*'

'The offices here in Washington?'

'Everywhere,' again whispered Warren Pease, his face white.

'How could you possibly *do* such a thing?' roared the angular Smythington-Fontini, his ascot askew and his cigarette holder a veritable sabre.

'Honour-bound and duty,' replied the blond Froggie. 'You unmitigated bastard, don't you ever expect to play at *my* club again.'

'And I suggest you cancel any plans you had for attending our class reunion, you despicable turncoat!' cried Doozie.

'As of this moment I accept your resignation from the Metropolitan Society!' stated Moose emphatically.

'I'm honorary chairman!'

'Not any longer, you're not. By this evening we'll have reports of your shocking behaviour at State. Say, sexual harassment, female *and* male. We can't tolerate that sort of thing! Not in our crowd!'

'And any thought you entertained about berthing your insignificant cabin cruiser at our yacht club is out of the question,' pronounced Smythie. 'Dirty pot sailor.'

'Moose, Froggie, Doozie – you, too, Smythie! How can you *do* this to me? You're talking about my *life*, all those things I hold dear!'

'You should have thought of that before –'

'But I had nothing to *do* with it. For God's sake, don't destroy the messenger because of the message he brings!'

'That has a familiar ring to it,' said Bricky. 'Commie-pinko propaganda, I think.'

'No, I think it's *Japanese*,' explained the green-jacketed Moose, 'and that's worse! They say our refrigerators are too big to sell and our cars too large for their streets. Why can't they build bigger houses and wider streets, the goddamned protectionist bigots.'

'It's none of those things, old fellows,' cried the Secretary of State. 'It's the truth!'

'*What's* the truth?' demanded Froggie.

'The message and the messenger. He bribed waiters and gardeners to install the equipment!'

'What the hell are you talking about, you Benedict Arnold?' shouted Petrotoxic's Doozie.

'That's it – that's *him*! Arnold!'

'Arnold who?'

'Arnold Subagaloo, the President's Chief of Staff!'

'Never could get his name straight. Certainly not one of us. What about him?'

'He's the one who sent the message – through me! What would *I* know about voice-activated tapes? Good heavens, I can't even work my damn VCR.'

'What did this Subaru do?' repeated the pale-faced New England banker.

'No, that's the automobile,' clarified the Secretary. 'It's Subagaloo.'

'Is that the refrigerator?' asked Moose of Monarch-McDowell. 'Sub-Igloo's a damn fine machine and should be in every lousy little Japanese household.'

'No, you're thinking of Subzero. This is *Subagaloo*, the Chief of Staff.'

'Oh, that bright fellow from Wall Street?' broke in Smythington-Fontini. 'He was very amusing on television a few years back. I thought they might give him his own show.'

'Sorry, Smythie, he's gone. That was before, with the other president.'

'Oh, yes,' agreed the yachtsman. 'The nice fellow from the cinema with the smile my wife went bonkers over – or was it my mistress, or the little chippee in Milan? Frankly, I never understood a word he said when he wasn't reading something.'

'I'm *talking* about Arnold Subagaloo, *this* President's Chief of Staff – '

'Certainly not one of us, not with that name.'

'*He* told me to tell you about the tapings of your meetings. *He* had them made!'

'Why would he do that?'

'Because he's against anyone or anything that could be a potential threat to the White House,' observed Froggie. 'Therefore, during the transition, he projected all manner of conceivable future problems and took appropriate protective measures –'

'In a damned ungentlemanly way!' interrupted Bricky.

'Forcing us to do exactly what we're doing,' completed the blond cynic, checking his gold Girard-Perregaux wristwatch. 'Eliminate Mangecavallo ourselves, thus removing the problem we, ourselves, created without touching the President . . . That Subagaloo is one devious son of a bitch!'

'Must be a whale of an executive,' concluded the crested Doozie of Petrotoxics. 'Probably sits on a dozen boards.'

'When his term's over,' added the green-jacketed Moose, 'I'd like his résumé. Anyone that devious is heaven-sent.'

'All right, Mr Secretary,' said the blond Froggie. 'My time is limited, and since Smythie's solved one vital problem, I suggest you address that other difficulty you mentioned before. I refer, naturally, to that insane *and* obscene brief to the Supreme Court that would turn Omaha over to the *Tacobunnies*, whoever the hell *they* are.'

'Wopotamis,' corrected the Secretary. 'I'm told they're a branch of the Hudson Mohawks, who disowned them because they wouldn't get out of their tepees when it snowed.'

'We don't give an Indian's fart *who* they are or *what* they did in their filthy igloos –'

'Tepees.'

'Are we back to the refrigerators . . . ?'

'No, he's the Chief of Staff –'

'I thought he played for Chicago –'

'The Japs are buying *Chicago* . . . ?'

'Where will they stop? They've already got New York and Los Angeles . . . !'

'They bought the *Dodgers* . . . ?'

'No, I heard it was the Raiders . . . '

'I thought I owned the Raiders . . . '

'No, Smythie, you own the Rams . . . '

'Will you all *shut up*?' shouted Froggie. 'I have a meeting in Paris in exactly seven hours . . . Now, Mr Secretary, what steps have you taken to kill this ridiculous brief and any public exposure of it? Any public airing would lead to a congressional inquiry and that could take months, every minority-prone freak spewing his intestines across the floors of the Senate and the House of Representatives. The prospect is intolerable! It could cost us *billions*!'

'Let me give you the bad news first,' replied the Secretary of State, now crashing the palm of his left hand against his head to control his swinging left eye. 'Believing we might buy ourselves guaranteed insurance, we employed the finest patriotic sleazeballs in the business to get something on those fruitcake judges who found some merit in that putrid brief. It all came to nothing. We even began to wonder how they managed to get through law school, no group of lawyers is that clean.'

'Did you try Goldfarb?' asked Doozie.

'The first, the *first*! He gave up.'

'He never gave up in the Superbowl. Of course, he's Jewish so I couldn't ask him to dinner at the Onion Club, but he was a damn fine linebacker ... *He* couldn't find any dirt?'

'Nothing. Mangecavallo, himself, told me that Hymie the Hurricane had lost – and I quote – "most of his marbles." He even told Vincent that this Chief Thunder Head was either the Canadian "Big Foot" or the Himalayan "Yeti," the Abominable Snowman!'

'The Golden Goldfarb is history,' said the crested CEO of Petrotoxic sadly. 'I'm going to sell my "Hurricane" bubble gum cards as soon as possible. Mummy and Daddy always told me to anticipate the market.'

'*Please!*' roared the blond-haired owner of Zenith World-wide, once more studying his gold wristwatch and glaring at the Secretary of State. 'What, if any, is the *good* news?'

'Put simply,' answered Pease, his left eye now somewhat in place. 'Our soon-to-be deceased director of the CIA has shown us the way. The appellants of the Wopotami brief – namely one Chief Thunder Head and his attorneys – must appear before the Supreme Court for oral interrogation prior to any Court decision.'

'*So?*'

'He'll never get there – *they'll* never get there.'

'What?'

'Who?'

'How?'

'Vinnie the Bam-Bam used his Mafia connections. We'll go one better.'

'What?'

'Who?'

'How?'

'We're going to unleash certain segments of our Special Forces – a number of whom are still in cages – and programme them to terminate this Thunder Head and his associates . . . You see, Mangecavallo – the soon-to-be the late Mangecavallo – was *right*. Eliminate the cause, you eliminate the result.'

'Hear, hear!'

'Good show!'

'Damn fine scenario!'

'And we know that son-of-a-bitch Thunder Head and his commie associates are in Boston. We just have to find him and his rotten, unpatriotic colleagues.'

'But can you *do* that?' asked the ice-cold, Paris-bound Froggie. 'You haven't done much else right.'

'It's practically done,' replied the Secretary, his left eye completely stable for once. 'That dreadful man they arrested in Boston, Caesar the Unpronounceable, is currently in a State Department sterile house clinic in Virginia, being – as they say – "shot to the moon" with a truth serum. Before the day is over, we'll know everything *he* knows. And Smythie, I think you should go to work immediately.'

'It . . . can be arranged.'

Algernon Smythington-Fontini got out of his limousine at a most unlikely place. It was a run-down gas station on the outskirts of Grasonville, Maryland, a relic of the days when local farmers would fill up their trucks in the early mornings and spend several hours grousing with one another about the weather, the falling market prices, and most of all, the invading agro industries that were their death knell. Smythie nodded at the owner-attendant, who sat in a distressed wicker chair by the front door. 'Good afternoon,' he said.

'Hi ya, fancy fella. Go right inside and use the phone . . . Leave your money on the counter as usual, and, as usual, I never saw you before in my life.'

'Diplomatic security, you understand, old man.'

'Tell your wife, not me, pal.'

'Impudence doesn't become your position.'

'Hey, I got no problem with that – any broad, any position –'

'*Really!*' Smythington-Fontini proceeded to go inside the small gas station. He walked to his left where there was a cracked Formica counter smudged with grease; there was also a decades-old black telephone. He picked it up and dialled. 'I trust the time is convenient,' he said.

'*Ah*, Signor Fontini!' replied the voice on the other end of the line. 'To what do I owe the honour? I trust everything goes well in Milano.'

'Exceedingly, as in California.'

'I'm happy we can be of service.'

'You won't be happy to learn what has been decreed. Among other ugliness, it's irrevocable.'

'Come now, what could be so serious for such words.'

'*Esecuzione.*'

'*Che cosa? Chi?*'

'*Tu.*'

'*Me* . . . Sons of *bitches!*' roared Vincent Mangecavallo. 'Slimeball tutti-frutti *bastards!*'

'We must discuss arrangements. I suggest a boat or a plane, leaving open a return.'

An apoplectic Vinnie the Bam-Bam furiously punched the buttons on his concealed telephone in the lower right-hand drawer of his desk. Twice he drew blood on his knuckles, as he misjudged the sharp wooden edges of the side panels. He barked the number of the hotel room he had to reach.

'*Yeah?*' said Little Joey the Shroud sleepily.

'Get off your fuckin' butt, Joey, the whole scenario got changed!'

'What are you talkin'? . . . Is this you, Bam-Bam?'

'You can bet the fuckin' graves of your ancestors in Palermo and Ragusa! The fuckin' fairies in their silk underwear just ordered my *esecuzione*! After all we *done* for 'em!'

'You gotta be *kiddin*'! Maybe it's a mistake. They talk in such polite language you can never tell when they want a shiv in your back or a pair of lips on your –'

'*Basta!*' yelled the director of the Central Intelligence Agency. 'I heard what I heard and it's *gold*!'

'Holy shit! Wadda we do?'

'Stay cool, Little Joey. I'm gonna disappear for a while, maybe a week, maybe two – we're working out the particulars – but right now, you got a new assignment. And you gotta do it *right*, Joey!'

'On my mother's grave –'

'Try someone else. Your momma did too much time.'

'I got a niece. A *nun* –'

'She got thrown out of the convent, remember? She and the fuckin' plumber!'

'Awright, *awright*! My aunt Angelina . . . she died after eating clams at Umberto's, and never was there a holier person. On *her* grave!'

'She was so fat she took up six plots –'

'But she was holy, Bam-Bam, really *holy*! The Rosary every hour of the day.'

'She didn't have nothin' else to do or do it with, but I accept your aunt Angelina. You ready to swear on that holy grave?'

'I swear on the threat of demonic possession, which is a big fuckin' thing with these gibrones in New York . . . Sometimes I think those Irish clowns don't have both oars in the water.'

'It's good enough,' pronounced Vincent Francis Assisi Mangecavallo. 'I accept your silence – your *omerta* – on what I am about to tell you.'

'And I will thank God for your guidance, Bam-Bam. Who do I cause to have his life cut short?'

'The *opposite*, Little Joey. You keep them alive! . . . I want you should set up a conference with this Thunder Head and his associates. I am suddenly very much a champion of their

cause. Such minorities have been trampled upon too much
and too often. It's intolerable.'

'You gotta be outta your fuckin' *mind*!'

'No, Little Joey, they are.'

CHAPTER FIFTEEN

The door of the Ritz-Carlton suite crashed open as Desis One and Two in their white ties and tails lurched into the room, prepared to do battle. Devereaux dropped his martini and Jennifer Redwing spun out of her chair, plummeting to the floor, genetically, perhaps, anticipating the worst from the white man.

'*Well* done, adjutants!' roared the buckskinned MacKenzie Hawkins, striding into the suite, followed by a perplexed Aaron Pinkus. 'There's no hostile action in evidence so you may stand to. *At* ease – casual positions are acceptable.' The Desis First and Second slouched. 'Not *that* casual, Sergeants!' Instantly, D-One and D-Two stood erect. 'That's better,' admonished the Hawk. '*Eyes* alert! Assault tactics at the ready!'

'Wad chu mean now?' asked Desi the First.

'Instant submission is the first sign of counterattack. Forget the tall skinny one; he's useless, but watch the female! They frequently carry grenades under their skirts.'

'You antediluvian son of a *bitch*!' yelled Redwing, getting to her feet and angrily smoothing her hair and her dress. 'You *barbarian*! You bellowing relic from a fifth-rate war movie, who the *hell* do you think you *are*?'

'Guerrilla tactics,' said Mac under his breath to his adjutants. 'The second phase after submission is loud verbal abuse – that's when they distract your concentration and pull the pins.'

'I'll pull *your* pin right out of its hairy recess, you walking junk bond! And how *dare* you wear those clothes? You look like a refugee from a Shriner's convention, you horse's-ass!'

'You see, y'see?' muttered the Hawk, mangling the cigar in his mouth. 'She's trying to distract me now – watch her hands, men. Those knockers she's got are probably plastic explosives.'

'I'll find out, h'enerale!' cried Desi the First, his eyes focused properly on the targets as his starched shirt whipped up out of place. 'Wad chu think?'

'You take one step toward me,' said Redwing, lowering her shoulders and grabbing the strap of her purse from the chair, then suddenly, snapping it open with her left hand and removing the cylinder of Mace with her right. ' . . . you'll be blinded for a month,' she completed, waving her weapon back and forth between the two formally clothed subordinates and their Wopotami-dressed superior. 'Try me and you won't merely make my day, you'll make my week.'

'This is where I came in,' interrupted Sam Devereaux, walking to the mirrored bar and the pitcher of martinis; he hop-skipped and soccer-kicked the fallen glass on the hotel rug.

'*Wait* a minute!' exclaimed Aaron, adjusting his steel-rimmed spectacles and studying the lovely bronze-skinned woman. 'I *know* you . . . Seven or eight years ago – Harvard, the Law Review, among the top of your class . . . an outstanding analysis of censorship within the framework of constitutional law.'

'Nanny's Naughty Follies, by God!' said Devereaux, laughing as he poured himself a drink.

'Be quiet, Samuel.'

'We're back to Samuel?'

'Shut up, Counsellor . . . Yes, Mr Pinkus, you interviewed me, and I was very grateful and flattered by your interest.'

'But you turned us down, my dear. Why was that? . . . You certainly don't have to answer me because it's none of my business, but I'm curious. I distinctly remember asking my associates what firm in Washington or New York you were heading for – frankly, I intended to call whomever it was and tell them how fortunate they were. Washington and New York are usually the goals of the best and the brightest, although I obviously disagree. However, I seem to recall that you went with a small, albeit fine firm in Omaha.'

'It's where I came from, sir. As you may have gathered, I'm a member of the Wopotami tribe.'

'I *half* gathered that, although my other half sincerely hoped you might refute the conclusion. Life would be less chaotic, if that were in the realm of possibility.'

'It's not, Mr Pinkus. My name is Jennifer Redwing and I'm a daughter of the Wopotamis. I'm also extremely proud of the fact.'

'But where in heaven's name did you ever meet' Samuel?'

'In an elevator – this morning – at the Four Seasons Hotel. He was extremely tired; he claimed he was exhausted and made several foolish remarks.'

'That was sufficient to cause you to be here with him now, Miss Redwing?'

'She went to my *house*,' interjected Devereaux. 'I apologized – I even tipped the doorman for her – and then I heard this crazy lady give my own address to the taxi driver! What would *you* have done, Aaron?'

'Obviously, followed her to your house.'

'I *did*.'

'I went to his house, Mr Pinkus, because it was the last address I traced down for that demented *creature* standing next to you!'

'Angry little filly, isn't she?' observed the Hawk.

'Yes, General Hawkins – for you couldn't possibly be anyone else – I *am* angry, and no, General, I am *not* a "little filly," as you will learn when I get through with you. In court or out of court, I'll chew your ass off!'

'Verbal abuse, Sergeants. Stay alert.'

'Oh, shut up, you lowest face on the dumbest totem. Incidentally, that beaded jacket you're wearing tells the story of an idiot buffalo who hasn't the brains to get out of a storm. Very appropriate.'

'Hey, Red,' broke in Sam, a martini at his lips. 'Cool it. Remember the corporate trust.'

'*Cool* it? Just looking at him makes me want to scream!'

'He has that effect on people,' mumbled Devereaux, drinking.

'A moment, please,' said Pinkus, gently holding up his hand. 'I believe I heard something that should be clarified.' The venerated attorney turned to Sam. '*What* "corporate trust"? What have you done *now?*'

Just a little *pro bono* advice, Aaron. You'd approve.'

'You and any approval on my part may well be mutually exclusive at this juncture ... Perhaps you will explain, Miss Redwing?'

'I'd be delighted to, Mr Pinkus. Especially for the benefit of your other guest, General Neanderthal. You may have to translate for him, but I suspect he'll eventually understand the bottom line, if only because he won't get anywhere near it.'

'That's succinct,' said Aaron, his expression not unlike that of Eisenhower's upon learning of MacArthur's dismissal.

'It's brilliant, and despite a profusion of faults too numerous to mention, the concept did originate with your employee, Mr Pinkus. I must grant him that.'

'The work of a fine attorney starts with a gracious attorney. Miss Redwing.'

'Really? I never thought of it that way ... Why? I'm merely asking, of course.'

'Because he – or she – has the confidence of his or her own abilities. There's no need to feed a tenuous ego by withholding praise from another. Hire that girl or that fellow; neither will distract themselves with real or imagined hostilities.'

'I think I just learned something –'

'It's hardly original, my dear. Without offence, I should point out that our general here said very much the same thing in military terms. Distraction through hostility – the weaker must pretend, the stronger merely watches. prepared to act.'

'Are you comparing that *ape* to *me* ... ?'

'Now, see here, you little Injun filly ... '

'*Please*, General! ... I said only in *military* terms. Miss

Redwing – troop strength, if you like. Say that handsome chest of yours actually did conceal plastic explosives – which I devoutly trust it does not – our general was only trying to instruct his associates to stay on the alert, and not to be distracted by your hostility. The equation is really quite simple.'

'Wad chu think about bein' distracted by wad *is* there, huh, man?'

'That's *enough* Sergeant –'

'I agree wid chu, Desi-Uno –'

'*Mairzy doats and dosie doats and little lambs eat ivy* . . . '

'Oh, shut up!'

'Samuel, stop it!'

'Son, you're spilling your drink –'

'What, my dear Miss Redwing, were you about to explain about this concept that was conceived in the brain of my presently not-altogether employee?'

'Quite simply, Mr Pinkus, as the Wopotami tribe is a registered incorporated entity, a trust at this moment is being set up and signed by the legally empowered Council of Elders, stating that all legal and fiduciary matters be negotiated solely through the offices of the executors of the trust, all parties referred to in prior documents having no authority whatsoever. In short words, the specifically named executors of the trust shall, in concert, hold sole collective power of attorney.'

'That sounds like mighty fine legalese, little lady,' said Hawkins. 'What's it mean?'

'It means, General,' replied Redwing, her eyes ice cold on the Hawk, 'that no one, repeat *no one*, other than the executors of the Wopotami trust can make any decisions, or enter into any agreements, involving the tribe's interests – or receive any benefits thereof.'

'Well, I must say that appears to be damn smart protection,' said Hawkins, removing the mutilated cigar, then suddenly cocking his head as if disturbed. 'But I suppose the next question is – are these here executors trustworthy, no pun intended, miss?'

'Beyond reproach, General. Among them are two attorneys, several doctors, a president of an international foundation, three vice-presidents of leading banks, a stockbroker or two, and a renowned psychiatrist whom you should definitely make an appointment to see. In addition, they are all true offspring of the Wopotamis, and, lastly, I am the chairperson of, as well as the spokeswoman for, the trust's executors. Any other questions?'

'Yes. just one. Is this what the Council of Elders wants?'

'It certainly is. They're guided by our advice and we are unwavering. So as you can plainly see, General Hawkins, even if your insane, utterly destructive scheme progresses an inch further, *we*, not you, will be in complete control so as to minimize the deleterious effects on an innocent people, of whom you've taken outrageous advantage. In brief, you're out, you maniac.'

The expression on the Hawk's face conveyed not only pain but deep personal hurt. It was as though a world he had nurtured with care and profound love had cast him aside, leaving a bereft, lonely old man, an abandoned champion who refused in dignity to give in to bitterness. 'I forgive you your unwarranted suspicions and your intemperate language,' he said softly, 'for you truly do not know what you're doing.'

'Oh, my *God*!'

'The reputed Son of God fits better,' suggested Devereaux, going back to the bar.

'Chu gettin' the shaft, h'enerale?' asked Desi the Second.

'Then maybe deze gringos go out for some air, huh, man?' said D-One. 'Through the windows, hokay?'

'No, gentlemen,' protested Hawkins, quietly, heroically, the sepulchral tones of a saint in his voice. 'This grand female has assumed the mantle of command, and the least I can do is to lessen that awesome responsibility –'

'Here it comes,' interrupted Sam, fingering his martini to catch an olive. 'Shovel time, fellas.'

'Son, you really do misjudge me –'

'You threw me that one before, Mac. Somehow I couldn't catch it.'

'Why not give me a chance, boy?'

'It's your bunny pulpit, Br'er Rabbit. Go ahead.'

'Miss Redwing.' The Hawk nodded his head once, a senior officer acknowledging another. 'I respect and understand your scepticism regarding my participation in the cause of the Wopotami. So now let me put it to rest. As an adopted son of the tribe, I accept all decisions of the wise Council of Elders. Benefits to my person are irrelevant, I only want to see justice done.'

Jennifer Redwing was stunned. The anticipated, vicious battle with a megalomaniacal giant had been reduced to her straightening out a sweet, injured puppy dog with a lot of legal claptrap. 'Well ... General ... I honestly don't know what to say.' Jennifer brushed her dark hair back defensively, for a moment ashamed to lock eyes with her wounded previous adversary. 'Please understand, sir,' she began, forcing her gaze on the old soldier who had given so much for his country – *their* country. 'I'm extremely protective, perhaps overly protective, of my people because our history *is* rife with injustices, as are the histories of American Indians everywhere. In your case, I was wrong. I apologize. Please accept that apology, it's meant.'

'He's *gotcha*!' cried Devereaux, swallowing the remainder of his martini. 'The raging lion is a wet pussycat and you buy it.'

'Samuel, that will be enough! Didn't you hear what the man *said*?'

'I've heard a hundred variations –'

'Shut up, Counsellor! He's a *great* man and he's just agreed to everything I wanted. Try to recall, if that gin-drenched brain will let you, your own words. An essential *truth*, remember?'

'You forgot the circuitous routes, Counsellor,' said Sam, heading back to the bar. 'There are bumpy roads ahead, fellas.'

And, naturally, the hotel telephone rang. Aaron Pinkus, shaking his head in equal parts irritation and anger, walked rapidly to the desk and picked up the intruding instrument. 'Yes?'

'To who is this am I presently speaking to?' asked the high-pitched voice on the line. 'The big Hebe lawyer or the big nuthouse general in the Geronimo beads?'

'This is Aaron Pinkus, and I'm an attorney, if that answers your question.'

'It's good enough, yarmulke. It's by your limo I found you.'

'I beg your pardon?'

'Well, it's a long story and I'd like to tell you, but the Bam-Bam don't like long stories, and to tell you the truth, you ain't got much time.'

'I don't understand a word you're saying.'

'Well, you see, years ago there was this half-assed shamus who put the collar on me, but now we got a truce, and on account of the fact that he's still got friends downtown, a lot of black-and-whites have been lookin' for your limo, *capisce?*'

'What are you *talking* about?'

'Maybe I should then talk to the wild man, right? Tell the asshole to take the fuckin' cigar out of his mouth and get on the Ameche.'

'I believe this is for you, General,' said Pinkus, turning and speaking slowly, hesitantly. 'A rather strange fellow who speaks like a chicken might speak – as I *imagine* a chicken might speak.'

'*Breakthrough!*' cried the Hawk, taking rapid strides to the desk and grabbing the phone, then instantly covering the mouthpiece and addressing the others. 'Old soldiers, even grunts, don't fade away. They remember the days, my friends, because they never end! ... is this *you*, Little Joseph?'

'We gotta talk, fazool. Everything's changed. By my side, you're not the bad guys any more, but the other bad guys are comin' after you.'

'Be a little clearer, Joseph.'

'There ain't *time*, fazool! The big man wants to set up a meet with you in a day or so, but he's got to play dead for a while, so I'm your connection.'

'Play *dead*, Joseph ... ?'

'On my aunt Angelina's grave. It's DC turf warfare and the big man temporarily lost ... He told me to tell you that the gumbar whose back you spiked but whose neck you didn't sufficiently break in the hotel lobby has spewed his guts out in some chemical factory in Virginia. By now they know you and your crowd are here in Boston and the silk underwear boys are unleashing – here, I wrote this down – the SFI's to go after you.'

'The *SFI's*? Hannibal in elephant shit! He said *SFI's*?'

'I couldn't make a mistake 'cause he repeated it maybe three times and I didn't know what it meant.'

'The animals of the world, Little Joseph. I taught 'em, so I should know. Special Forces – *Incorrigibles*. They're still in stockades, still trying to kill everyone but the cooks and the nurses.'

'Now it's you and your little group, fazool. It took me exactly thirty-one minutes to find you – how long will it take the fuckin' commandos once they've arrived in Boston, which they may have already? Get out of there and call me here at the room-service palazzo when you're out of the freak-heads' fire ... And don't use that fuckin' limo! It's a fuckin' landmark!' Joey the Shroud hung up and the Hawk turned to his troops.

'*Evacuate!*' he roared. 'Explanations will come later; there's no time for them now. *Adjutants*, hot wire two vehicles in the hotel's parking lot and meet us at the southeast corner. *Vamos!*' Mac looked harshly at Aaron Pinkus as Desis One and Two ran out the door, then forced his eyes on Sam Devereaux and finally Jennifer Redwing. 'You ask me why I fight the mendacities of those in power, why I take up the sword against the corruptors and the manipulators, whether a century ago or now. Let me make it clear, *goddamn it*! An unseen, unelected government *behind* our government has let loose a pack of psychopaths with only one mission, the success of which will set them free to roam the streets ... That mission is to kill us, *all* of us. *Why?* Because we raised the spectre of a crime against an innocent, *manipulated* people over a hundred years ago that to rectify will cost the manipulators *billions*!'

'*Goddamn* your essential truth!' said Devereaux, throwing his martini into the sink. 'Let's get out of here!'

'The *police*, General! I'm a respected man here in Boston. Surely they will protect us.'

'Commander Pinkus, in this out-of-sanction combat, civilian authorities are useless. How the hell do you think I blew up depots from Normandy to Kai Song?'

'I simply can't believe it,' said Redwing, trying to remain calm. 'I *won't* believe it!'

'*You* won't believe it, little Injun filly? Perhaps I should remind you of the Eastern companies who promised your people throughout the Midwest plains that they were being moved to far better lands where all you found was arid soil and your cattle froze. It's no different, young lady!'

'Oh, *Jesus*!' cried Jennifer, racing to the bedroom door.

'What are you *doing*?' yelled Devereaux.

'Your mother, you idiot!'

'Oh, yes, of course,' said Sam, blinking. 'Is there any coffee around?'

'No *time*, son!'

'Help Miss Redwing, Sammy.'

'At least we're out of Samuel –'

'I don't think there's a choice,' said Aaron Pinkus.

The five fugitives from the Ritz-Carlton stood side by side at the southeast corner of the hotel waiting for the arrival of Desis One and Two. They smiled inanely at several passersby, doing their best not to appear like a quintet of adult delinquents. The grand Eleanor was held up by Redwing as the former kept struggling with the words of the 'Indian Love Call.'

'Shut *up*, Mother!' whispered Sam.

'This is the daughter I've always wanted –'

'Put it on hold, Mom. She may be a better lawyer than me, and you *wouldn't* want that.'

'I don't think you're so hot. Half the time I can't understand you –'

'You're not supposed to, Mother. That's the law –'

'*Quiet!*' ordered the Hawk, nearest the edge of the building, Pinkus at his side. A Lincoln Town Car had swung in front of the canopied entrance of the hotel as, simultaneously, Desis One and Two plunged into the kerb with their two hot-wired cars from the parking lot. 'Everybody *hold* it!' continued Hawkins as he and Aaron watched four men in black raincoats climb out of the Lincoln, one from the front and three from the rear seat. The car instantly sped away and parked by the gates of the Public Gardens as the four black raincoats walked rapidly into the hotel. 'D-One, front and *centre!*' said the Hawk in a loud whisper. 'Repeat down the line!' he added.

'D-One, front and centre –'

'*Desi!* You with the crazy teeth and the curled-up shirt, get *out* here!' cried Devereaux. 'Go to Mac!'

'*Mizerloo, my Arab love who is my deseerloo* –'

'Shut up, Mother! You've got the wrong words and the wrong country anyway.'

'Don't talk to my friend, Eleanor, that way –'

'She's *my* mother! Suppose I refused to have her Jaguar fixed?'

'I'm sure I make a hell of a lot more money than you do, Counsellor. *I'll* take care of it!'

'Wad chu want, h'enerale?'

'See that car over there? The one in front of those gates.'

'Sure, I see. A gringo's sitting in the front.'

'I want him immobilized, the car incapacitated, do you understand what I'm saying?'

'Ees not so hard. He goes to sleep and I rip out the plugs – ees done every night in Brooklyn. Unless you want him dead, which, frankly, h'enerale, I do not do.'

'Hell, no! I want to send back a message. They want our asses blown up, boy, and I want 'em to know they can't *do* it!'

'Ees done, h'enerale. Den what?'

'Come back to the hotel, to Mr Pinkus's floor, but cover your flanks. Four men in dumb black raincoats went up to waste all of us . . . By the time you get there, I'll probably have removed at least three of the bastards, but you make sure of the fourth.'

'*Hey!* Why chu have all the fun? *I'll* take t'ree, *chu* take one!'

'I like your spirit, son.'

'Wad about Desi-Two?'

'I'm about to explain,' said Hawkins, turning to Aaron Pinkus. 'Tell me, Commander, have you got some place nobody knows about, like a hideaway where you take, say, underprivileged women who might enjoy your company?'

'Are you *crazy*? You don't know Shirley!'

'All right, I understand . . . But there must be someplace off the beaten track where we can stay for a day or two.'

'Well, the firm bought a ski lodge across the New Hampshire border because a very reliable client ran into terribly difficult times – the snow has been very irregular –'

'That's fine! We'll join you there.'

'But how will you know where it *is*?'

'*Das* simple, *Comandante*,' intruded Desi the First. 'D-Two wired only automobiles dat had *teléfonos* inside. We wrote down the *números* for both.' D-One pulled out a torn sheet of paper with two sets of numbers written across it. 'See? My amigo, he has the same as dis.'

'You two are really remarkable. I would very much like it if you'd call me –'

'No time for medals, Commander!' interrupted the Hawk firmly. 'Our mission's not finished. Take Sam, his mother, and the Indian girl up to your place in New Hampshire. Now, get *out* of here! My sergeant and I have work to do!'

The first two black raincoats never knew what happened. Each, to secure escape routes, stood by the exit doors and each in turn was taken from the staircase by the Hawk, rendered unconscious and stripped of all clothing, including his shorts. The third would-be assassin inched his way toward the Pinkus suite, only to be interrupted by a wavering, swivelling drunk who, once past the killer's body, swung around and delivered an immobilizing *chi sai* chop to the back of his neck. The fourth and last Hawkins left to his adjutant, Desi the First. It was, after all, the responsibility of command to instil confidence in his immediate support troops. Actually, it turned out to be a lesson in patience, the mark of a truly superior deep-cover intelligence field man, thought Mac. He waited in the shadows of the exit door, behind which lay the unconscious, naked first killer from SFI. D-One silently emerged from the elevator in his white tie and tails and walked, again silently, halfway down the hallway, then pressed his back against the wall across from the Pinkus suite. For what seemed like the better part of an hour, but in reality was barely eight minutes, Desi the First remained immobile, barely breathing, and then a door opened two doors to his left and a man in a black raincoat came out, an automatic in his hand.

'*Iguana, José!*' roared D-One, taking the would-be killer by such surprise that he never knew how the weapon was kicked out of his hand, nor would he ever know how he was rendered unconscious by a swift, hard fist in the middle of his forehead.

'Outstanding!' said the general, walking out of the shadows. 'I knew it was in you, son.'

'Why didn't chu do it, for Christ's sake?'

'On-scene evaluation, boy! It's how we all get ahead.'

'I coulda been *killed*!'

'I had every confidence in you, Sergeant. You're prime meat for Advance G-two.'

'Ees dat good?'

'We'll talk about it later. Right now we've got to strip this clown to his skin and get out of here. We're all between a rock and a hard place, adjutant. We've got to concentrate on our next moves, and for you and me it's joining the others somewhere up north.'

'No problem, h'enerale. Before I come back up here, I talked to my amigo on the car *teléfono*. Wherever dey go, Desi-Two will stay in the automobile so he can tell me where dey are.'

'Fine tactics, son –' The Hawk stopped at the sound of a door opening and then voices. A couple, obviously middle-aged guests of the hotel, walked out of their room. 'Quickly!' whispered Mac, reaching down for the unconscious body on the floor. 'Stand him up as if he just puked.'

'He came out dat door over there, h'enerale. Ees still open!'

'Let's go!' Together, Hawkins and his adjutant dragged the limp figure to the open door under the astonished stares of the hotel guests.

'Ees a *crazy* wedding downstairs, amigos!' shouted Desi the First, glancing behind him. 'You wanna join de party?'

'No . . . no, thank you,' said the middle-aged man, hurrying his wife toward the elevators.

The ski lodge in the hills of Hooksett, New Hampshire, was rustic and sturdy, deserted and dank, and in the best of times would never be awarded more than two stars in the least impressive travel guide. Still it was sanctuary and operational in terms of electricity, heat and telephone service. Also, as it was barely over an hour from Boston, Aaron Pinkus Associates found it to be a convenient out-of-the-city refuge for attorneys and teams of attorneys deliberating difficult cases. In fact, it had become so popular that Aaron had decided not to sell the property, opting instead for gradual and utilitarian remodelling.

'We really must return those two cars,' said Pinkus anxiously to the Hawk as they sat beside each other in deep leather chairs in the lodge's former lobby. 'There'll be police bulletins out everywhere.'

'Nothing to fear, Commander. My adjutants have 'em camouflaged in the back forty.'

'That's not the point, General. It's grand theft and Sam and I – officers of the court, I remind you – were willing accomplices. I really must insist.'

'Oh, hell, *details*! All right, I'll have the sergeants drive 'em back and park 'em down the street from the hotel. It's dark out now and even if they're picked up, those cops won't know how they landed up in the back seats of their patrol cars without their trousers. *Hah!*'

'Thank you very much, General.'

'Then they can wire up a couple of other vehicles –'

'*Please*, that won't be necessary! The firm has a standing arrangement with a car rental agency and my chauffeur,

Paddy, can drive one automobile out here and a friend of his can bring another.'

'They'll have to pick up my adjutants. I'm not ready to dismiss them yet.'

'Of course. Under the circumstances you've described, I'd feel much better if those two young men were around. Here, I'll write out the address of the rental agency; they can all meet there.' Pinkus reached into his pocket and withdrew a memo pad.

'Aaron, everything's taken care of!' said Devereaux, somewhat louder than necessary as he walked into the ersatz Alpine lobby with Jennifer Redwing at his side. 'The market in Hooksett is sending out a whole bunch of stuff and Red here says she can cook.'

'How do you want the split case of gin and bourbon?' asked Jennifer. 'Fried?'

'Industrial lubricant, young lady.'

'Also, quite possibly on your own expense sheet,' added Pinkus. 'How did you explain our presence?'

'I said our whole first team was up here busting our asses over a mess of probate problems.'

'Why probate?'

'They think it sounds sexy. Credibility, Aaron.'

'Mr Pinkus?' interrupted Redwing, for the sixtieth time in twelve hours, glaring at Sam. 'I'd like to use your phone to call San Francisco. I'll reverse the charges, of course.'

'My dear, you may turn down a lucrative career with my firm, but you may not embarrass me with such a ploy as reversing charges. You'll have quiet in what was the manager's office behind the counter over there – he wasn't much of a manager and it isn't much of an office, but you'll be alone and your privacy assured.'

'Thank you very much.' Jennifer turned and walked toward the former lodge's counter as Hawkins got out of his chair.

'Have you seen my sergeants, Sam?' he asked.

'Would you believe they're out back at the base of the hill about a hundred yards to the right trying to get that old rusted ski lift to work?'

'Very enterprising,' said Aaron.

'Very dumb,' said Devereaux. 'That damn cable never worked properly from the beginning. I once got stuck thirty feet in the air for almost an hour, my lady of the day twenty feet in front of me screaming her head off. We drove back to Boston the moment we were down and I never got to see the bedroom.'

'I suspect you've seen more than one after we assumed the mortgage.'

'Hey, come on, Aaron. You yourself once told me to get out of the office and come up here to cool off.'

'You were furious over losing a case you should have won,' said Pinkus, writing on his notepad, tearing off the page and handing it to the general. 'Because the judge was an ignorant political hack who couldn't follow your reasoning . . . Also, if that was your method of cooling off, there was an inversion of temperatures.'

'This legal stuff is way beyond me,' announced the Hawk. 'I'll go find my adjutants myself. I've decided to go into Boston with them. Little Joseph said he wanted a meeting so I believe I should surprise him prior to our formal conference . . . This is the car rental place?' Aaron nodded, and the Hawk walked to the door. 'I'll get back on my own. I want you to have two vehicles here.'

'Fine, General. And when Miss Redwing is finished, I'll reach Paddy Lafferty and set everything in motion.'

'Good thinking, Commander.'

'I'd get up and salute, General Hawkins, but I don't think I can manage it.'

Redwing closed the door of the minuscule office behind the counter, sat down at the desk and picked up the telephone. She dialled her apartment number in San Francisco, startled by the fact that before the first ring was over the excited voice of her brother was on the line.

'Yes?'

'Charlie, it's me –'

'Where the *hell* have you *been*? I've been trying to reach you for hours!'

'It's all too absurd, too incredible, and too insane to go into –'

'Try every *one* of those adjectives to what *I've* learned!' interrupted the younger brother. 'That nut son of a bitch outmanoeuvred me – *all* of us – we're *screwed!*'

'Charlie, calm down,' said Jennifer, contrarily feeling her blood pressure rise to uncontrollable limits. 'Calm down and speak slowly.'

'Both are impossible, sis!'

'*Try*, Charlie.'

'All right, all right.' In San Francisco, her brother took several audible deep breaths and did his best to be lucid. 'Without my knowing it, without anyone telling me, a number of weeks ago our Chief Thunder Head convened the Council of Elders with some scumhead sleaze of a lawyer from Chicago calling the legal shots, and had himself *legally* proclaimed temporary sole and absolute arbiter of the Wopotami tribe for a period of six months.'

'He can't *do* that!'

'He did, sis. Notarized, authorized, and recognized by the court.'

'He had to give something in *return*!'

'He did that, too. A million dollars to be divided by the five members of the Council, millions more to be given to the whole tribe within the six-month period.'

'*Corruption!*'

'Tell me something I don't know.'

'We'll fight it in the courts!'

'And, besides losing, make fools *and* heavy debtors out of our brothers and sisters?'

'What do you mean?'

'For starters, how about Uncle Eagle Eyes who bought a communal estate for the tribe's oldest in some desert in Arizona that won't have plumbing for a hundred years, if ever. And Aunt Doe Nose who invested in the name of our women in an oil rig on Forty-first Street and Lexington Avenue in

New York City, or Cousin Antelope Feet who took over controlling interest in a distillery in Saudi Arabia where they not only don't make booze, they don't drink it!'

'They're all over *eighty* years of age!'

'Certified as mentally competent, so covered by the scumhead attorney from Chicago and approved by the Omaha court.'

'I can't *believe* this, Charlie. I've been with Hawkins most of the afternoon, and after a bumpy start he came around. Only a couple of hours ago he was so contrite, so genine. He told me that our corporate trust was the right thing to do, that he'd go along with whatever the Council of Elders approved.'

'Why not? He *is* the Council of Elders.'

CHAPTER SIXTEEN

Jennifer did not walk out of the small office into the Alpine lobby, she burst into it, exploding the space in front of her. 'Where is he?' she said, in her voice the anger of nearby thunder, her eyes shooting out bolts of lightning. 'Where *is* that son of a *bitch*?'

'Obviously, you mean Sam,' answered Aaron Pinkus, leaning forward in the leather chair and pointing at the door leading to the kitchen. 'He said he remembered where he had concealed a bottle of gin, a place where his shorter colleagues couldn't reach it.'

'No, I'm not talking about *that* son of bitch, I mean the *other* one! The velvet-tongued idiot buffalo who's about to face the combined wrath of the Sioux and the Comanche, delivered by a furious daughter of the Wopotamis.'

'Our general?'

'You can bet your tuchis on it!'

'You speak Yiddish?'

'I'm a lawyer; it goes with the territory. Where *is* that *bastard*?'

'Well, I'm both apologetic, yet somewhat relieved, to tell you that he left for Boston with his two adjutants. He said something about meeting with a man named "Little Joseph," who apparently is the person who called him at the Ritz-Carlton. Our two stolen cars just raced down the drive only moments ago, thanks be to Abraham. With the blessings of God they will be returned without incident.'

'*Mister* Pinkus! Do you know what that horrible, *horrible* man has *done*?'

'Too many horrors to put into a medium-sized encyclopedia, I suspect. However, not the latest, which I gather you're about to tell me.'

'He *bought* our tribe!'

'How extraordinary! How could he possibly *do* that?' Redwing told the vaunted Boston attorney everything she had learned from her brother Charlie. 'May I ask you a question or two, perhaps three?'

'Of course,' said Jennifer, throwing herself into the leather armchair next to Pinkus. 'We're screwed,' she added quietly, discouragingly. 'We're really *screwed*!'

'Not necessarily, my dear. First, this Council of Elders. They may be wise and grand people, but have they been legally appointed as *guardian ad litem* for the Wopotami tribe?'

'Yes,' mumbled Red.

'I beg your pardon?'

'It was my idea,' said Jennifer, only slightly louder, her embarrassment showing. 'It gave them pride, which they sorely needed, and I never – *never* – thought that they'd ever convene in *any* major decision without consulting me, or in the event of my demise, the others of our group.'

'I see. Were there any codicils to the *ad litem* guardianships, say in the nature of the death or deaths of any or all of the appointees? Replacements, perhaps?'

'Voted upon by the remaining members of the Council.'

'Have there been any such replacements ... who might have been, shall we say, "reached" by General Hawkins?'

'None. They're all still alive. It's the history of rare buffalo meat in their diets, I think.'

'I see. And is there anywhere in the *ad litem* designation that makes mention of the selected children of the tribe who actually execute the fiduciary decisions of your people?'

'No, that would have been demeaning. As with the Orientals, "face" is terribly important to the Indian. We just *knew* – we assumed we knew – that should any problem arise, one of us would be called ... Frankly, myself.'

'You're speaking realistically, of course.'

'Of course.'

'But legally there's no proviso in the papers of incorporation that illuminates and clarifies the function of your group?'

'No ... Again pride, genuine pride. To include such a condition would mean there's a council *above* the elders, and tribal tradition could not accept that. Now do you see what I mean? That horrible man controls my people. He can say and do whatever he wants in their name.'

'I suppose you could always challenge him in the courts under the articles of conspiracy and possible fraud. However, in doing so, you'd have to tell your whole story and that could be extremely disadvantageous for obvious reasons. Also, your brother does have a point – you could lose.'

'Mr Pinkus, of the Council's five elders, three men and a woman are in their eighties, and the fifth is seventy-eight. None are equipped to deal with these legal complexities any more now than they were thirty years ago, which was zilch!'

'They don't have to be "equipped," Miss Redwing, they merely have to be sufficiently competent to understand the transaction and its benefits and liabilities. I submit they did, perhaps enthusiastically, even to the exclusion of yourself.'

'And I submit that's impossible!'

'Come now, my dear, a million dollars in solid cash with the promise of millions more to come within a short period of time? In exchange for what? The temporary holding of what they had to know was at best a ceremonial title? It must have been irresistible ... "Let the crazy white man have his few months of fun, where's the harm?"'

'There wasn't full disclosure,' insisted Jennifer.

'There doesn't have to be. If all business negotiations required full disclosure from all the parties involved, our economic system would collapse, you know that.'

'Not when it comes to fraud, Mr Pinkus.'

'Indeed not, but how can you prove fraud? As I understand it, he promised millions on the basis of turning the tribe's fortunes around, making them wealthy beyond their wildest dreams, then proceeded to back up his offer with an initial compensation of one million dollars, no strings attached, as they say.'

'They didn't understand! They didn't realize that he intended to make them litigants in the most inflammatory lawsuit against the federal government in the nation's history – my God, the *Strategic Air Command*!'

'Apparently, neither did they pursue with any degree of intense curiosity how he intended to make them extraordinarily wealthy. Instead, they joyfully took the million and spent it – rather injudiciously, I gather ... And forgive me, Miss Redwing, but I believe your brother was very much aware of the general's intentions. In fact, he was very much an accessory –'

'He thought it was all a big joke!' cried Redwing, lurching forward. 'A harmless *joke* that gave the tribe a lot of money, an influx of tourists, and a great deal of fun!'

'The Supreme Court is fun ... ?'

'He didn't think it would get to first base,' said Jennifer defensively. 'Besides, he had no idea about the million dollars or the deal Hawkins cut with the Council. He was appalled!'

'Lack of communication between friendly parties is not grounds for fraud *or* conspiracy, except perhaps between the parties themselves, which would then put them on an adversarial basis.'

'You're saying the Council *deliberately* withheld information from my brother.'

'I'm afraid I am. As he did from them to a large extent.'

'And if we, our group, suddenly insert ourselves –'

'Which you have no legal right to do,' interrupted Aaron gently.

' ... and tell the whole story,' continued Redwing, her eyes growing wide in astonishment, 'it will be interpreted as a self-serving action on our part to move into the money, stealing it from them if there ever is any! ... My God, it's all been turned around! It's *crazy*!'

'Yes, my dear, crazy – like a hawk. The general would have made a superb corporate attorney.'

Suddenly, from the open balcony of the Alpine lobby's

second floor, a figure emerged from a door and walked to the railing. It was Eleanor Devereaux, her hair groomed and her posture regal, very much the grande dame. 'I just had a horrible dream,' she announced, in full control of her voice and words. 'I dreamt that mad General Custer and all those savage Indians at the battle of Little Big Horn joined together and attacked a packed convention of the American Bar Association. The lawyers were all scalped.'

The tall, stooped, elderly gentleman in the long brown gabardine topcoat and wearing a black beret might have come from any of the various campuses in the Boston area, a professor, stern of face yet somewhat bewildered by the opulence of the Four Seasons Hotel lobby. He kept squinting behind his large tortoiseshell glasses, eventually gravitating to the bank of elevators after a brief, aimless stroll around the premises.

Of course, there was nothing aimless about the Hawk's surveillance and everything was contrived about his appearance. Previous reconnoitring had established every shadowed corner and each less obvious seating place, and he bore no resemblance whatsoever to the buckskinned giant who had severely disabled one Caesar Boccegallupo of Brooklyn, New York, five hours ago. An experienced soldier did not walk into enemy territory without checking the terrain. There were no surprises, so the general walked into an elevator and pressed the number of Little Joseph's floor.

'*Room* soivice,' said Hawkins, knocking at the door.

'I got awready!' cried the voice inside. ' . . . Oh, the apples and pears soaked in booze and set on fire? I thought they was comin' later!' The door opened and a stunned Joey the Shroud could only exclaim. '*You!* What the fuck are you doin' *here?*'

'All conferences between commanders are prefaced by preliminary meetings between their subordinates so the agendas are clear,' replied the Hawk, brushing Joey aside as he walked into the room. 'Since I consider my current adjutants unequal to the task – purely for linguistic reasons – I'm taking their place.'

'Fazool, you're the ass end of the trolley car!' cried the Shroud, slamming the door shut. 'I got enough on my mind, you I don't need.'

'But you need your apples and pears *flambé?*'

'Yeah, very tasty, a nice combination of burnt fruits, and the aroma is extremely full-bodied, like an old factory experience.'

'What?'

'It smells good. I read that on a menu in Vegas. Hoo-hay, my momma would shoot out of her grave if she thought I torched a pear, and my poppa would chase me right into Bed Sty! But what did they know, may they rest in eternal peace.' Joey blessed himself, then looked at the general and spoke harshly. 'Now, the fancy-shmancy talk aside, what *are* you doin' here?'

'I just explained. Before I formally confer with your superior officer, I'd like the landscape a great deal clearer. My rank requires it and I demand it.'

'You can require and demand all you like. General Fazool, but the big man ain't no fuckin' soldier boy. I mean, he's up there with the archangels of the government, y'know what I mean?'

'I've met a few in my day, Joseph, and for that very reason I want a G-two, one thousand one, or there'll be no conference.'

'What's that, a licence plate?'

'It's a full rundown of whom I'm *temporarily* scheduled to confer with.'

'Hoo-hay, on the grave of my aunt Angelina, it's for your own good!'

'I'll be the judge of that.'

'I can't tell you nothin' without permission, you gotta understand that.'

'Suppose I pluck your fingernails out, one by one, Little Joseph?'

'Hey, come on, Fazool, we been through this. Underneath your bullshit you may be a tough gibrone, but you ain't no screeching Nazi ... Here, *here* are my hands. You want I should call room service for a pair of pliers?'

'*Stop it*, Joseph ... This minor perspicacity on your part must never leave this room!'

'If what you mean is that you don't want no pliers, forget it. I tole that to a dozen *capitanos* in Mussolini's army – that fat lasagna!'

The telephone rang.

'That *has* to be your connection, Joseph. Sometimes the truth is the best avenue. Tell your superior I'm here – right *here* with you!'

'The time's right,' said the Shroud, looking at his watch. 'He's gotta be alone now.'

'Do as I say.'

'I got a choice? I can take the no-fingernails bit, but your outsized claw around my throat while you grab the Ameche is somethin' else.' Little Joey crossed to the bedside telephone and picked it up. 'It's me,' he said, 'and the big General Fazool is ten feet away as we speak, Bam-Bam. He wants words with you, only he don't know who he's talkin' to but I value my fingers, if y'know what I mean in Vegas terms, huh?'

'Put him on, Joey,' said the calm voice of Vincent Mangecavallo.

'*Here*,' cried the Shroud, holding out the phone for Hawkins, who walked rapidly over and grabbed it.

'Commander X, here,' said the Hawk into the mouthpiece. 'I assume I'm talking to Commander Y.'

'You are General MacKenzie Hawkins, serial number two-zero-one-five-seven. United States Army, twice recipient of the Congressional Medal of Honor, and the biggest pain in the ass the Pentagon has ever had to put up with. Am I correct?'

'Well, certain judgements are not necessarily absolutes ... Who the hell are you?'

'I am a man who barely a day ago wanted you in your grave – with full military honours, of course – but who now wants you to stay very much alive and above ground, do I make myself clear?'

'No, you don't, you DC pricky-shit. Why change sides?'

'Because the *zabagliones* who wanted your exit papers now want mine, and I find that determination not to my liking.'

'*Zabagliones?* . . . Little Joseph here . . . ? *You* were the clown who sent that asshole *Caesar* somebody-or-other to the Four Seasons?'

'To my disgrace and lack of respect, I did that. What can I say?'

'Easy, son, it wasn't your fault, it was his. He just wasn't very bright and I had two very street-smart adjutants.'

'*What?*'

'I don't want you to be too hard on yourself. Command has to expect the unexpected sidewinder, it's part of the options course in the War College.'

'What the *hell* are you talking about?'

'I guess you're just not officer material. What else can *I* say?'

'You can just listen to me, that's what . . . I'm very pissed off that certain people who I thought had great respect for me now want to see me in that grave we agreed was for you – only now they want me there *with* you, which I find to my distaste, *capisce?*'

'So what did you have in mind, Mr No Name?'

'I want you to stay alive and well so I can do unto those elegant respectable types exactly that which they would do unto me. Namely, bury the bastards.'

'Back up, Commander Y. If you're talking about termination-with-extreme-prejudice among civilian personnel, I'll need a direct order from the President, co-signed by the chairman of the Joint Chiefs and the DCI – that's the director of Central Intelligence.'

'No kidding?'

'I don't expect you to know how these things are done –'

'And I don't *want* done what you just said!' broke in Mangecavallo harshly. 'A few simple hits I don't need *you* for. A man buys the dirt, he's got peace; what I got in mind for these pearly white zucchinis is pure torment. I want them ruined, busted, broke – part of the homeless with a credit line of Hobo Pete!'

'"Hobo" who?'

'He used to clean urinals in the Brooklyn subways – *that's* what I want for those bastards! For the rest of their miserable lives, I want those scungilli to clean urinals in *Cairo*!'

'As a fact, Commander Y, as a young captain in the desert war against Rommel, I became quite friendly with the Egyptian officer corps –'

'*Basta*!' yelled Mangecavallo, instantly lowering his voice and oozing what charm there was in him. 'Forgive me, great, *great* general. I'm stressed out, if you know what I mean.'

'You can't let that happen,' admonished the Hawk. 'We've all been there, Commander, but you can't give in to it. Remember, your men look to you for the strength they may not have. Stand tall and *deliver* it!'

'I will treasure those words,' said a humbled Vinnie the Bam Bam. 'But right now I must warn you –'

'You mean the SFI's?' interrupted Hawkins. 'Little Joseph relayed your previous message and the current situation is under control. The hostile troops are immobilized.'

'*What*? They found you *already*?'

'More precisely, Commander, we spotted 'em first and took appropriate action. My forces are presently in safe shelter and will remain there out of combat range.'

'What *happened*? Where are the SF's?'

'SFI's,' corrected the Hawk. 'The *Incorrigibles*. Not those other brave *normal* men I trained and who gave so much. These are the psychopaths we never had a chance to weed out.'

'But where *are* they?'

'Well, by this time they're probably in jail, all on a morals rap, and if not, there are four stark-naked men running up and down the staircases of the Ritz-Carlton hotel doing their goddamnedest not to be seen ... Oh, the fifth member is no doubt still in a Lincoln that won't start, also naked, with a mobile cellular phone that's been ripped out and smashed in the gutter.'

'Holy *shit*!'

'I believe that message will ultimately be sent back to Washington . . . Now, let's get down to tactics, Commander. You obviously know what my agenda is, what's yours?'

'The same as yours, General. A rotten, terrible thing was done to a small, naive tribe of innocent original inhabitants of this great US of A, and a magnanimous wealthy nation must make restitution . . . How does that grab you so far?'

'Right in the gun sight, soldier!'

'Now what you don't know, General, is that several members of the Supreme Court found your attorney's brief kinda convincing. Not a firm majority by any means, but they're talking, like in private.'

'I *knew* it!' broke in the Hawk triumphantly. 'Otherwise they never would have reached the Golden Goldfarb – who I also kinda trained, goddamn it!'

'You *know* Hymie the Hurricane?'

'Damn good man, strong as an elephant and with the brains of a Rhodes scholar.'

'He *was* a Rhodes scholar.'

'What did I just tell you?'

'All right, all right,' smoothed Mangecavallo. 'But because of the SAC situation and for reasons of national security, the Court won't allow the brief to be made public for another eight days, and the day before it does, you and your attorney-of-record must appear in closed session to answer oral interrogation. That's for you to make final case.'

'I'm prepared for that, Commander Y. I've been prepared for it for damn near a year! I welcome the invitation. My case is pure.'

'Yeah, but the Pentagon, the Air Force, and most especially, the defence contractors aren't. They want your ass. General, a dead ass.'

'If the contingent they sent up to Boston this afternoon is an indication of their combat evaluation, I'll walk into that Court in full Wopotami regalia.'

'*Jesus!* I'm told they were like the most violent, the craziest, except for a unit they keep in the walled-up funny farm, where they like to play volleyball by throwing the guards over the net. They're called the Filthy Four – they'll come after you next!'

'In that case,' said the Hawk, squinting, 'and assuming you've got support personnel at your command, perhaps you might allocate a platoon for our assistance. To tell you the truth, Commander Y, I've only got two operative subordinates to defend our position, as it were.'

'That's the problem, General. Under normal circumstances, I could send up a whole crew of experienced hitters to protect you, but there's no time now – such secret protection takes a little time to put together, because it's got to be totally secret or we *all* lose.'

'That sounds to me like lace pants pricky-shit talk, Mr No Name.'

'It's not . . . on my aunt Angelina's grave –'

'That's Little Joseph's aunt.'

'It's a big family . . . Listen, I can collect two, maybe three, *very* close associates who can be counted on to keep the silence like holy monks, but any more than that could be a problem. They'd be missed, questions asked, bad rumours started like, "Who's he working for?" or "He looked fine yesterday, what do you mean he's in the hospital?" or maybe even, "I hear he spilled all our beans to the family in Hartford who wants our action – *that's* who he's working for!" . . . See what I mean, great General? Too many of those kind of questions would come up with large numbers protecting you, and with them my name might just surface, and that can't happen!'

'You in some kind of lizardshit, Commander Y?'

'I *told* you. I'm facing my own personal demise. I'm *finito*, *polvere*, my bones rock salt!'

'Feeling poorly, soldier . . . ? Hang in there, Commander, doctors don't know everything, fella.'

'*My* doctors do, 'cause they don't know a fucking thing about medicine!'

'I'd get a second, maybe a third, opinion –'

'General, *please*! It's what I explained before. Certain parties expect me to be cold chopped liver within a day or two, and that's the way it's got to be – maybe I should say that's the way it's got to *appear* – because while I'm dead I can operate on your behalf as well as my own.'

'I'm not much of a religious man,' concluded the Hawk pensively. 'Frankly, I've seen too much blood spilled by all those fanatics who say they'll kill everybody who doesn't believe the way they do. History's full of that shit and I don't go along with it. We all came from the same slime that crawled out of the water, or the same lightning bolt that put a primitive brain in our heads. So nobody's got a right to claim exclusivity.'

'Is this a long story, General? Because if it is, we don't have time.'

'Hell, no, it's short. If you're dead, Commander, you're sure as snow isn't pea-green going to operate from that grave of yours. Somehow I can't figure you to be a candidate for resurrection.'

'Jesus *Christ!*'

'Even if he was, you're not, soldier.'

'I won't *be* dead, General – I'm simply gonna disappear like I *was* dead, *capisce?*'

'Not entirely.'

'Like I said, we're working on it. It's vital that my enemies – *your* enemies – think I'm out of the scenario –'

'What scenario?'

'The one that's got your dead ass, and the dead asses of everybody that's involved in your Wopotami bullshit!'

'I take exception to that remark, sir.'

'Wrong word, I swear it on – oh, forget it! I mean your crusade for a wronged people, how does that grab you?'

'Clearer in the gun sight. Commander.'

'You see, while I'm supposedly dead and out of the scenario, I got my capo supremos working on Wall Street. They're gonna inflate those SAC stocks to the multibillion fuckin' zenith on the basis of sudden Pentagon reversals where Omaha's concerned, and then you walk into that

Supreme Court and they all crash – like a nuclear bomb on all their loans which are based on projections, and the country club boys, who can't pay their bills, are cleaning urinals in Cairo! You dig, General? We both get what we *want!*'

'I sense a certain hostility toward those people.'

'So you should, *Thunder Head!* They want us in dirt – *all* of us! . . . We'll coordinate through Little Joey. Stay in touch with him.'

'I should tell you, Commander, and I say this in front of Joseph, I really believe he's been abusing the per diem allocations. The only way you can reach him is when he's not calling room service, which is most of the time.'

'*Shithead!*' roared Joey the Shroud.

The Washington Post
DIRECTOR OF CIA FEARED
LOST AT SEA

Coast Guard Reveals Futile 18-Hour Search in Waters Off Florida Keys. Private Yacht Caught in Storm

Key West, Aug. 24 – Vincent F. A. Mangecavallo, director of the Central Intelligence Agency and guest aboard the yacht *Gotcha Baby*, is believed to have perished at sea along with the captain and crew of the 34-foot craft that left its Key West mooring at 6:00 a.m. yesterday on an ill-fated fishing trip. According to meteorologists, a sudden subtropical storm whipped out of the Muertos Cays at approximately 10:30 a.m. Eastern Daylight Time, veering almost instantly north, away from the coastline, but directly in the path of the yacht which had been heading due east toward the coral reef fishing grounds for nearly five hours. The search by Coast Guard aircraft and patrol boats will resume at daybreak, but there is little hope of survivors as the yacht is presumed to have crashed into the reefs and been destroyed.

Upon hearing the news, the President issued the following statement. 'Good old Vincent, a great patriot and a superb naval offer. If he had to go, I'm sure he'd welcome the briny deep as his final resting place. He's at one with the fishes.'

The Department of the Navy, however, has no record of Mr Mangecavallo having been a naval officer or even having served in the Navy. When apprised of this, the President had a curt remark. 'My old buddies should get their files in order. Vinnie served in the Caribbean theatre of operations with Greek partisans aboard patrol boats. Golly, gosh and zing darn, what's wrong with those new sailors?' The Navy Department had no response.

The Boston Globe
FIVE NUDE CULTISTS ARRESTED
AT RITZ-CARLTON

*Four Found Naked on Roof, Fifth Assaulted Jogger
in Public Gardens. All Claim Gov't. Immunity.
Washington Shocked.*

Boston, Aug. 24 – In a bizarre series of incidents during which numerous guests of the Ritz-Carlton hotel claimed to have seen naked figures racing through the corridors at various times, the Boston police cornered four nude unarmed men who had made their way to the roof of the building. Unaccountably, they pleaded for clothing without explaining their nakedness, but nevertheless claiming national security immunity for their efforts in rooting out enemies of the US. A fifth naked man was subdued by a Boston jogger, the professional wrestler known as 'Jaws' Hammerlocker, who told the police that the assailant tried to rip his sweat suit off him. Inquiries to Washington intelligence circles brought only consternation and swift denials of any involvement whatsoever. A highly placed unidentified source at the State Department, however, did suggest the similarity between the Boston five and a Southern California cult that commits crimes solely in the nude while singing 'Over the Rainbow' and brandishing small American flags. 'They're perverts,' said the unidentified spokesman, 'otherwise they wouldn't carry those flags. It's them all right and we don't even know who they are. So there!'

CHAPTER SEVENTEEN

It was night and the heavyset man of medium height, wearing dark glasses below an outsized red wig that fell over his ears, made his way down a narrow, dark, gas-lit street several blocks from the fishing piers in Key West, Florida. It was a street lined with small Victorian houses crowded close to one another, miniaturized versions of their sister mansions on the shore road. The man studied the numbers on the right side, peering in the semi-darkness until he found the address he wanted. Although similar in appearance to those flanking and opposing it, the house was decidedly different in one respect. Whereas the others had lights in the various first- and second-floor windows, quaintly subdued by fringed shades and venetian blinds, this home had only a single dim lamp glowing from a downstairs room obviously near the rear of the small structure. It was part of the visual code; *this* was the clandestine rendezvous.

The red-wigged stranger to the street walked up the narrow three steps to the porch and approached the door. He rapped on the wooden strips between the stained-glass panels, a prearranged signal that avoided the doorbell – a single knock, pause, four rapid ones, followed by another pause and two more quick taps. *Shave . . . and a haircut . . . two bits*, considered the man, wondering what covert operations genius had thought it up. The door opened and Vincent Mange-cavallo instantly had the answer. The huge *rinoceronte* standing in the tiny hallway was his sometime courier aptly nicknamed Meat, as usual wearing a white silk tie over a white shirt and a black suit.

'You the best we can do in this big fuckin' national emergency?'

'Hey, Vinnie – it *is* you, ain't it, Vinnie? . . . Sure, it's you, I can smell the garlic and the bay rum.'

'*Basta!*' said the veteran of the Caribbean theatre of operations, walking inside. 'Where's the *consigliere*? Him I want to see right away.'

'No *consiglieri*,' interrupted a tall, slender man emerging from a side door into the darkened vestibule. 'No dons, no Mafia lawyers, no Cosa Nostra guns, is that clear?'

'Who the hell are you?'

'I'm surprised you don't recognize my voice –'

'Oh . . . *you*?'

'Yes,' said the white-jacketed, yellow-ascoted Smythington-Fontini. 'We've talked several hundred times on the telephone,' continued the elegant Anglo-Italian, 'but we've never met, Vincenzo. My hand, sir – have you washed yours recently?'

'You got balls for a fruitcake, Fontini, I'll say that for you,' replied Mangecavallo, exercising the shortest handshake since George Patton met his first Russian general. 'How'd you find Meat?'

'Let's say he was the dimmest star in your constellation and I'm an expert in celestial navigation.'

'That doesn't answer my question.'

'Then let's say the dons from Palermo to Brooklyn, New York, want nothing to do with this enterprise. They give us their blessings and will gratefully accept whatever largesse may come their way, but basically, we're on our own. *They* selected your associate here.'

'There are some things I gotta do on the Big Street, a point of personal honour and self-respect considering what has been decided against my physical well-being. I trust that's understood – from Palermo to Brooklyn.'

'Most definitely, Vincenzo, a point of honour that must be answered, but *not* in like terms. I repeat, no guns, no graves, no *consigliere* leaning on the Boeskys in Wall Street. There can't be any involvement by your familial associates – which are not *my* associates, although I certainly expect to be apprised of your moves. After all, old boy, I paid for the damn yacht we blew up on the reefs, as well as the unknown non-English-speaking Venezuelan crew we flew back to Caracas.'

'*Meat*,' said Mangecavallo, turning to his sometimes lower-level colleague. 'Go make yourself a sandwich.'

'With *what*, Vinnie? All this guy's got in the kitchen is swelled-up crackers that break if you touch 'em and cheese that smells like stinky feet!'

'Just leave us, Meat.'

'Maybe I should call for a pizza –'

'No phones,' interrupted the cosmopolitan industrialist. 'Why not keep your eyes on the back courtyard? We wouldn't want any intruders and I'm told you're an expert at preventing such intrusions.'

'Hey, I guess you're right about that,' said the mollified Meat. 'And about the cheese, hell I don't even like Parmesan, you know what I mean?'

'Certainly.'

'And don't you worry about no intertrusions,' added the capo subordinato, heading for the kitchen. 'I got eyes like a bat; they never close.'

'Bat's eyes don't see so good, Meat.'

'No kiddin'?'

'No foolin'.'

'Where did you ever find him?' asked Smythington-Fontini as Meat walked into the kitchen. 'And why?'

'He gets certain things done for me, and most of the time he's not sure what he did. That's the best kind of street gorilla you can have . . . But I'm not here to talk about Meat. How's everything going?'

'Efficiently and on schedule. By early daybreak tomorrow the Coast Guard patrols will find debris, as well as several life jackets and various personal articles, including your floating waterproof cigar case with your initials on it. Naturally, the search will be called off, and you'll have the unique privilege of reading all those marvellous things people whose despise you say after you're dead.'

'Hey, you know some of those things could be very sincere, did you ever think of that? I mean, I gotta lot of respect in certain areas.'

'Not in our crowd, old boy.'

'Here we go with the "old boy" crap, huh? Well, lemme tell you, chum-chum, you're lucky you had an *aristocratica* mama who had more smarts than that dizzy title she picked up in Tea Town ever dreamed of. If it wasn't for her, the only football team you'd own would be a gang of scrawny hoods kicking a round ball in the streets of Liverlake or Liverpool, or whatever the fuck it is.'

'Without the Smythington banking connections, the Fontinis could never have gone international.'

'Oh, so that's why she kept the Fontini name permanently attached, so people would know who was picking up the markers, 'cause the foxtrot horsey boy couldn't.'

'This isn't getting us anywhere –'

'I just want you to know where you sit, *Smythie* – not *stand* but sit! The rest of your silk underwear crowd are going down the tube!'

'So I've been given to understand. Socially, it's a dreadful loss, of course.'

'*Naturalmente, pagliaccio* . . . So after this big Coast Guard search is over and I'm memorialized, what happens?'

'When the time is right, I foresee that you'll be found on one of the farthest out islands of the Dry Tortugas. Two of the Venezuelans will join you and swear while continually blessing God, themselves and you, that it was your courage and perseverance that saved all your lives. They'll be immediately flown back to Caracas and disappear.'

'Not bad, not bad at all. Maybe you're your mama's boy after all.'

'Conceptually and artistically. I believe you're right,' agreed the industrialist, smiling. 'Mother always said. "The blood of the Caesars will always be there, if only more of our southern cousins had blue eyes and blond hair like me."'

'A real queen, so filled with *tolleranza* . . . Now, what about

Thunder Ass? How do we keep him and his crazy Indian lovers above ground? They're no good to me in dirt.'

'That's where you come in. Apparently only you can make contact –'

'Correct,' broke in Mangecavallo. 'They're all in place and nobody knows where they are but me, and that's the way it's gonna stay.'

'If it stays completely that way, there'll be no protection. One cannot protect a quarry one cannot find.'

'I've got that worked out. You tell me what you've got in mind, and if I like it I reach the go-between and we set up the meet. What have you got in mind?'

'On the telephone before you flew down here, you said the general and his associates were in what you called "safe shelter," which, as a yachtsman, I assume is equivalent to "safe harbour," which basically means the ship is sheltered from a storm, usually in a deep leeward cove, *ergo* "safe shelter" –'

'You always torture yourself like this? . . . Yeah, I hope to hell that's what it means because the big soldier boy said it, and if it means something else we've got a really screwed-up army. What's your point?'

'Why not keep the status quo?'

'What status quo?'

'The safe shelter,' said Smythington-Fontini slowly, as if clarifying the obvious. 'Unless, as you suggest, we have a screwed-up military, which in the upper purchasing ranks of the Pentagon is entirely plausible. However, considering the general's recent accomplishments, we should take his word that the shelter *is* safe and well out of the weather.'

'The weather?'

'The term, as I employ it, connotes the negative. They're all in a deep leeward cove and protected from the elements. Why not have them stay where they are?'

'I don't know where the hell it is!'

'All the better . . . Does your go-between know?'

'He can find out if the reason's good enough to convince Thunder Ass.'

'You said on the telephone that he wanted – what was it? – oh, yes, "support troops." Would that be good enough?'

'I would hope to kiss a pig it would. That's what he needs . . . Who did you figure on?'

'Your associate with the unique name of Meat, to begin with –'

'Pass,' negated Mangecavallo. 'I got other work for him to do. Who else?'

'Well, we may have a problem then. As I mentioned, our *padrones* near and far are adamant that there be no traceable connection to any of the families such as might be construed by Mr Caesar Boccegallupo. I assume Meat is an exception because, as your batman of sorts, he's not enormously large in the brain department. I believe you said he's the penultimate "street gorilla."'

'*Penultimate?*'

'Well, the ultimate would be a real gorilla who understood English, wouldn't it?'

'What the hell does Batman have to do with my street-soldier Meat?'

'No, not *Bat*man, Vincenzo, but *batm'n*, someone who carries out various minor tasks for you.'

'You know, you frost my apricots, I mean, you are *weird*!'

'I'm doing my best,' said the industrialist, close to verbal exhaustion. 'I'm afraid we're on different wavelengths.'

'Well, get on mine, *Smythie*! You sound like that baked apple who runs the State Department, *chum-chum*!'

'That's why I'm valuable, don't you see? I understand him: he's marginally socially acceptable, but your solutions, as degrading as they may be, are infinitely more productive than *his* where my own interests are concerned. I may prefer his lemon daiquiris to your boilermakers, but I certainly know when to order a shot and a beer. Why do you think the industrial democracies are so blessedly tolerant? I may not care to break bread with you, but I'm more than happy to help you bake the loaf.'

'You know, Candy Balls, I think I hear your mama talking.

Underneath your bullshit, you're up front. So where do we go from here?'

'Since the normal avenues are closed to you, I suggest you recruit several men from an available pool of talent. Namely, mercenaries.'

'*Who?*'

'Professional soldiers for hire. They're generally the scum of the earth, but they fight solely for money and care not one whit for causes *other* than money. In the old days, they were ex-Wehrmacht hoodlums, or murderers on the run, or former disgraced military personnel no army would have in its ranks, and I suppose the last two categories remain the same since most of the fascists are either dead or too old to carry a drum or blow their damn bugles. Regardless, I believe it's the wisest course of action.'

'Where do I find these goody two-shoes Boy Scout types? I want protection up there as soon as possible.'

'I took the liberty of bringing you a dozen résumés from a Washington agency named Manpower Plus Plus. The messenger I sent over there, an executive of mine from Milan, actually, informs me that all the candidates are available within twenty-four hours with the possible exception of two who are expected to successfully break out of prison by tomorrow morning.'

'I like your style, Fontini,' said the temporarily deceased director of the Central Intelligence Agency. 'Where are these résumés?'

'In the kitchen. Come with me. You can tell Meat to watch the front porch.'

Ten minutes later, seated at a thick pine table, the file folders spread across the surface, Mangecavallo made his decision. 'These three,' he ordered.

'Vincenzo, you are indeed remarkable,' said Smythington-Fontini. 'I would have chosen two out of the three, except that I must tell you that those two are at this moment about to execute their escape from the Attica prison, so they'll be the most grateful for immediate employment. The third, however, is actually a certified lunatic, an American Nazi who keeps burning swastikas on the grounds of the United Nations.'

'He threw himself in front of a bus –'

'It wasn't a bus, Vincenzo, it was a patrol wagon carrying his friend, another lunatic who was arrested walking down Broadway wearing a Gestapo uniform.'

'Still, he went the whole nine yards to stop something from happening, and that's what I'm looking for.'

'Agreed, but it's debatable whether he really meant to take that action or was punched out by a rabbi on Forty-seventh Street.'

'I'll gamble . . . When can I get 'em to Boston?'

'Well, the first two we'll know about in the morning, after the prison roll call, and our Nazi is champing at the bit since he's drawing welfare on a stolen Social Security card of some loan shark he put in the East River.'

'I like him already – not his politics 'cause I don't go along with that lousy shit – but he can be useful. All those whacko nuts can be useful – like you say, all you gotta do is bang a drum and blow a bugle. And if the other two break out, they're the Holy Mary's gift to our cause to right a terrible wrong to a tribe of real losers who would drop fuckin' dead except for my benevolent intervention. The main thing is that we get this act together as fast as we can and shoot 'em up to Boston and that safe shelter place wherever the hell it is . . . You know, it's just possible that those zucchinis in Washington are zeroing in on the general at this moment.'

'I doubt that, old boy. If you don't know where he is, and your go-between doesn't know, how could Washington find him?'

'I just don't trust the silk underwears. They'll stop at nothing, those lowlifes.'

In a dimly lit booth at the rear of O'Toole's Bar and Grill barely two blocks west of Aaron Pinkus Associates, the young, elegantly dressed banker pressed his gentle assault against the middle-aged secretary by way of a third martini.

'Oh, I really shouldn't, Binky,' protested the woman,

giggling and running her hand nervously down the left side of her long, greying hair. 'It really isn't right.'

'What isn't *right*?' asked the walking advertisement for Brooks Brothers apparel, his mid-Atlantic accent somewhere between Park Avenue and Belgrave Square. 'I told you how I *feel*.'

'So many of our attorneys drop in here after work . . . and after all, I've only known you for an hour or so. People will talk.'

'Let them, dear heart! Who *cares*? I stated my case quite clearly and with abiding integrity. Those infantile idiots a man like me is expected to go out with simply don't *interest* me. I much prefer a mature woman, a woman of experience and insight . . . Here, cheers.' Both raised their glasses to their lips; however, only one swallowed and it was not the Ivy League banker. 'Oh, slight business, my love . . . When do you think our executive committee can meet with Mr Pinkus? We're talking several millions, of course, as his legal advice is very much sought after.'

'Binky, I told you . . . ' At this point, the suddenly perplexed secretary involuntarily crossed her eyes and hiccuped four times in succession. ' . . . Mr Plinkus hasn't been in touch with me all day.'

'Don't you know where he is, dear heart?'

'Not saxually – actually – but his chauffeur, Paddy Lafferty, called to have me clear the car rental agency for two automobiles.'

'*Really?* Two?'

'Something about the ski lodge in Hooksett. That's in Hew Nampshire, across the state border.'

'Oh, well, it's all irrelevant, just boring business . . . Will you excuse me for a mo', sweet thing. As they say, nature doth call.'

'You want me to go with you?'

'I'm not sure it's acceptable, you full-blown, *very* exciting lady, you.'

'*Eeyoo!*' squealed the secretary, attacking her martini.

Binky the banker got up from the table and walked rapidly

to O'Toole's pay telephone by the entrance. He inserted a coin and dialled; his call was instantly answered. 'Uncle Bricky?'

'Who else?' replied the owner of New England's largest lending institution.

'It's your nephew, Binky.'

'Trust you earned your keep, young fella. You're not good for much else.'

'Uncle Bricky. I was *really* good!'

'I'm not interested in your sexual exploits, Binky. What have you learned?'

'It's a ski lodge in Hooksett. That's across the border in New Hampshire.'

Binky the banker never returned to the table, and the understanding O'Toole put the inebriated secretary into a taxi, paying the fare to her residence, and waving good-bye to the confused face in the window with a single word. 'Lowlifes,' he said to himself.

'This is Bricky, old boy. It's a ski lodge in Hooksett, New Hampshire, roughly thirty miles north of the border on Route ninety-three. I'm told there are only a couple of such places in the area so it shouldn't be too difficult to find. There'll be two automobiles with the following licence plate numbers.' The ashen-faced New England banker gave the numbers and accepted the accolade accorded him by the Secretary of State.

'Well done, Bricky, it's like old times, isn't it, old chum?'

'I hope so, old boy, because if you mess this up, don't you dare show up for our reunion!'

'Don't you worry, old sport. They're called the Filthy Four and they're positively *animals*! They're flying into Logan Airport within the hour ... Do you think Smythie might reconsider mooring my yacht at his club?'

'I suspect that will depend on the results of your efforts, don't you think?'

'I have every faith in our foursome, old chum. They're really a *despicable* quartet. No mercy given, none taken, as it were. You honestly wouldn't care to get within a *mile* of them!'

'Good show, old boy. Keep me posted.'

It was past midnight on the outskirts of Hooksett, New Hampshire, when a black van without headlights coasted silently down the country road and came to a silent stop in front of the gravelled entrance to the former ski lodge. Inside, the driver, the blue outlines of an erupting volcano tattooed on his forehead and seen clearly in the summer moonlight, turned to his three associates in the rear of the vehicle. 'Hoods,' he said simply as the three reached into black knapsacks and pulled out black stocking masks which they promptly squeezed down over their heads. The driver-leader did the same in the front seat, all four adjusting the dark nylon fabric so their eyes peered menacingly out of the lined cut-out holes. 'Maximum weapons,' added the tattooed unit superior officer, his lips forming a grim smile beneath the cloth. 'I want dead, *all* dead! I want to see horror. I want to see pain; I want to see blood and grotesque faces, all those good things we were trained to do so well!'

'Like always, Major!' whispered a hulk of a man, his hands, as the others, robotically plunging into his knapsack and retrieving a MAC-10 automatic weapon along with five magazines of ammunition each containing eighty rounds, a total of sixteen hundred rapidly spewed-out bullets.

'Subordinate firepower!' continued the major, glancing around and satisfied that his second command had already been obeyed. Again, hands surged into knapsacks, and looped grenades were affixed to combat belts. '*Radios!*' came the final order and it was instantly executed. Miniaturized walkie-talkies were retrieved and shoved into pockets. 'Let's go! North, South, East and West, according to your numbers, have you got it?'

A unison of affirmatives followed as the four Maximum Incorrigibles slipped out of the van, lay on their stomachs, and then crawled off in their individual directions. Death was their mission and death was their salvation in all things. *Death before dishonour!*

'Do chu see what I see, amigo?' asked Desi-Two of Desi-One, both standing beneath a full maple tree and studying the descending landscape in the erratic moonlight. 'Ees crazy, no?'

'You chouldn't be so hard on dem, as the gringos say,' replied Desi the First. 'They never had to watch the chickens or the goats at night from bad neighbours.'

'I *know* dat, but why they so stupid? Black *cabezas* moving up the hill with the moon like big *cucarachas* ees plain dumb – like also the gringos say.'

'As the h'enerale says, we could teach dem better but not right now. Right now, we godda do what he wants us to do . . . An' also, it's been a *difficultoso* day for all our nice new friends, so we don't want to wake dem up. Dey need their sleep, no?'

'Dey ain't got no chickens or no goats, but only right now bad neighbours, is dat what you mean?'

'Dat's right. We do dis ourselves, h'okay?'

'Ees easy. I take the two over dere, chu get the two on the other side.'

'H'okay,' said Desi the First as both men crouched in the shadows. 'But chu remember, amigo, don'hurt nobody too bad. The h'enerale says we godda be civilized to prisoners of war.'

'Hey, man, we h'ain't no animals! Like the h'enerale also says, we go bide with the Genevil intentions. Maybe dese bad neighbours had lousy times when dey were liddle kids, like h'enerale Mac said *we* did. Dey probably need lotsa kindness and help.'

'Hey, *man*,' admonished D-One, whispering, don't let all those priests you like make you t'ink you're a saint! Chu give all dat kindness when dese black-headed *cucarachas* are laid out in de kitchen sink, h'okay?'

'Hey, man, my favourite *padre* used to tell me when I went into Old San Juan. "An eye for an eye, *niño*, but make sure you kick first – right in the *testiculos*."'

'Truly a man of God, amigo. Le's go!'

'Major Vulcan speaking,' said the black-hooded figure quietly into his radio as he crawled up the southernmost route leading to the former ski lodge. 'Come in by the numbers.'

'Two East reporting. Major. No activity, hostile or otherwise.'

'Number Three?'

'Three North, sir. A light's on in what appears to be a bedroom on the second floor. Can I blow it out?'

'Not yet, soldier, but when I tell you, take out everyone inside. Probably goddamned perverts watching as they exchange bodily fluids. They're *all* perverts, *savage* perverts. Keep your weapon and your grenades at the ready.

'Yes, *sir*! I want to blow 'em away first! Can I do that. Major?'

'Good attitude, soldier, but only when I give the word. Keep closing in.'

'What about *me*, sir?' interrupted Two East. 'Three North's a fucking idiot! Remember when the guards found him chewing the fence with his *teeth?* . . . *I* should have the first kill!'

'And you'll be *mine*!' broke in Three North. 'Don't forget. Major, Two East took all those strawberries that were meant for you at last Thursday's mess!'

'You've got a point. Number Three. I really wanted those strawberries.'

'I didn't *do* it. Major. It was Four West! . . . Own up, you son of a bitch!'

'Well. Four West?' said Vulcan. '*Did* you steal my strawberries?'

Silence.

'Come in. Four West!' continued the major. 'Is your lack of response an admission of guilt? *Answer* me, you prick. Did *you* steal my strawberries?'

Silence.

'Four West. Four West! *Reply!*'

Silence.

'His radio's out,' concluded Vulcan. 'Goddamned fairy Pentagon purchasing agents! These fucking "talkies" cost the high brass fourteen thousand apiece when you can buy the same goddamned things at Radio Shack for twenty-seven bucks! ... Four West, can you read me?' Silence. 'Okay, Three North, how close are you?'

Silence.

'Three North, come in!' A long silence. 'Goddamn it. Three North, *respond*!' Nothing. 'Son of a bitch, did any of you clowns check your *batteries*?' Again there was nothing. 'Two East! Give me your report *now*.'

Silence.

'What the fuck is going *on*?' fairly shouted Major Vulcan, momentarily forgetting the need for quiet communication. 'Will one of you bastards *answer* me?'

Silence, broken several seconds later by a friendly voice. 'Nice to meet chu.' said Desi the First, walking out of the shadows and into the moonlight above the black-hooded intruder. 'You are a prisoner of war, amigo sir, and you will be treated fairly.'

'*What?*' The major slapped his hand down for his weapon, but his movement was far too slow. The heel of D-One's boot crashed into Vulcan's forehead, right in the centre of the tattooed volcano.

'I didn't wan' to do dat, Mr Prisoner, but chu could'a hurt me an' dat h'ain't nice.'

Jennifer Redwing awoke with a start – something had happened; she could feel it, *hear* it! Of course, she could hear it, she considered. There were muted moans and throated cries from somewhere outside. Wounded dogs? Trapped animals? She lurched out of bed and ran to the window, totally disbelieving what she saw.

Sam Devereaux heard distant noises and pulled the second pillow over his damaged head. For roughly the five hundredth time he swore he would never have a drink after leaving O'Toole's Bar and Grill. However, the noises continued unabated, and after opening his less-than-white clear eyes, he understood that they had nothing to do with his physical condition. Unsteadily, he got out of bed and went to the window. *Holy shit!*

Aaron Pinkus was dreaming of Shirley, albeit an angry Shirley, whose head was coiled in eleven thousand pink curlers, all shrieking at him, each curler possessing its own mouth, incessantly opening and closing with the rapidity of machine gun fire. Was he back on Omaha Beach? . . . No, he was in his favourite bedroom at the old ski lodge. What was the racket? Slowly he rose from the comfortable bed and limped, as old legs do, to the window. *God of Abraham, what have You done?*

Eleanor Devereaux's sleep was maddeningly interrupted by the ruckus, and she naturally, instinctively, reached for her bedside telephone to instruct Cora to have the neighbours arrested, or whatever one did for such outrageous behaviour in Weston. Massachusetts. Unfortunately, there was no telephone. In high dudgeon she swung her feet from under the sheet, planted them on the floor, rose to her full height, and walked to the window. *Good heavens, how absolutely unique!*

MacKenzie Hawkins, opened his eyes, still mangling the cigar he had had in his mouth since the early hours of the morning. What the hell *was* it? *Nam? Korea?* Pigs squealing on some peasant's farm protected by Search and Destroy? *Jesus!* Where were his aides-de-camp? Why hadn't they alerted him to the enemy's *assault?* . . . No, he realized, as he felt the soft innards of the pillow surrounding his head – there *were* no pillows in combat bivouacs! So where *was* he? . . . Hannibal's legions, he was in Commander Pinkus's ski lodge! He sprang out of the comfortable civilian bed, hating himself for its lack of military rigidity, and ran in his skivvies to the window. *Genghis Khan forgive me, but even you wouldn't think of that, Big Fella!*

Like pedestrians intent on witnessing the horrible results of a major accident, the temporary residents of the former ski lodge descended from various staircases into the Alpine lobby. They were greeted by Desis One and Two, who flanked a long coffee table on which there were four MAC-10 machine pistols, twenty magazine clips, sixteen grenades, four miniaturized radios, two flamethrowers, four infrared binoculars, and a dismantled egg-shaped bomb that could blow up at least a quarter of the state of New Hampshire – the lesser southeastern part.

'We din' want to wake chu all up,' said Desi the First, 'but the h'enerale said we should protect the rights of prisoners of war ... We tried to do dat, but I t'ink they were very bad characters. Dese guns 'n t'ings will explain what I mean ... Now, great h'enerale, can Sergeant Desi-Two and me get some sleep?'

'*Goddamn*, boys, you're *lieutenants*! But what the hell is *out* there?'

'Please, *señores y señoras*, see for yourselves,' said Desi the Second, opening the front door. 'We did not t'ink it was too bad for de Genevil intentions, when we saw all dose guns 'n everyt'ing.'

Outside, on the repaired ski lift, halfway up the intermediate slope and at least fifteen feet in the air, were four jiggling bodies hanging upside down, their mouths taped, their feet wrapped in ropes.

'We bring dem back every hour and give dem water,' said Desi the First, smiling. 'Dat way we treat our prisoners of war real good.'

CHAPTER EIGHTEEN

'*What?*' shrieked the Secretary of State, his bellow causing his security pool stenographer to lurch out of her chair, propelling her shorthand pad directly into the head of her employer, who absently caught it in his left hand, which was in the process of pounding his skull to stop his maniacally pivoting left eye. 'They did *what? ... How?* I won't *have* it!' The Secretary began slamming the shorthand pad alternately against his temple and the edge of the desk until its pages flew hither and yon off their spiral.

'*Please!*' pleaded the stenographer, racing around and picking up the flying papers. 'These are top-secret notes, *sir!*'

'Well, there's no secret about *your* tops, is there?' cried the wide-eyed, swinging-eyed leader of State crazily. 'We live in a walnut world, miss! *You've* got coconuts, but *we're* all walnuts!'

Suddenly, the stenographer, standing rigid and staring down at her employer, said calmly but with great strength, 'Stop it, Warren. Calm down.'

'Warren? ... Who's Warren? I'm Mr Secretary – always *Mr Secretary!*'

'You are Warren Pease, and please cover the telephone, or I'll tell my sister and she'll tell Arnold Subagaloo that you've gone squirrelly.'

'Oh, God – *Arnold!*' Warren Pease, Secretary of State, instantly covered the mouthpiece. 'I forgot, Teresa, honestly, I just *forgot* for a moment!'

'I'm Regina Trueheart, my younger sister's Teresa, Subagaloo's assistant.'

'I'm terrible with names, but I never forget coconuts – I mean *faces*! Don't tell your sister.'

'*You* just tell whoever's on the line that you'll call back after you've had a chance to collect your thoughts.'

'I *can't*! He's on a pay telephone at the prisoners' compound in Quantico!'

'Order him to give you the number and to stay there until you call him back.'

'All right. Coconuts – Teresa – Regina – Madame Secretary!'

'*Stop* it, Warren. Do what I say!'

The Secretary of State did exactly as Regina Trueheart commanded, then fell forward on his desk, his head in his arms and, as they say, cried his eyes out. 'Somebody leaked and I got pissed on!' he gurgled. 'They got sent back to the compound in body bags!'

'*Who?*'

'The Filthy Four. It's horrible!'

'They're *dead* – whoever they are?'

'No, there were air holes in the canvas. It's worse than dead – they're *embarrassed*! We're *all* embarrassed!' Pease raised his tear-streaked face as if pleading for a swift execution.

'Warren, sweetie, knock it *off*. You have a job to do and people like me are here to see that you do it. Remember Fern of the North Mall, our patron saint and inspiration. *She* wouldn't permit any of her bosses to fall apart and neither will I.'

'She was a secretary, you're a security pool stenographer –'

'Far more, Warren, oh, far more,' interrupted Regina. 'I'm a roving butterfly with the sting of a bee, I flutter from one top-secret assignment to another, keeping my eyes on all of you, helping you through your days. That's the God-given assignment for all the Truehearts.'

'Can't you be *my* secretary?'

'And take that job from our dear, dedicated anti-Commie mother, Tyrania? Surely you jest.'

'The Tyrant's your *mother* . . . ?'

'Careful, Warren. Subagaloo, remember?'

'Oh, Christ. *Arnold.* I'm sorry, truly sorry – a great woman, awe-inspiring.'

'To the business at hand, Mr Secretary,' said the stenographer, sitting down, the notebook and the gathered pages securely held, her posture once again rigid, 'I have maximum clearance, as you know, so how can I help?'

'Well, maximum clearance isn't exactly the issue –'

'I see,' broke in Regina Trueheart. 'Body bags with air holes, corpses that weren't dead –'

'I tell you, the entire honour guard almost had mass cardiac arrest! Two are in the base hospital, three have demanded immediate discharges on psychiatric grounds, and four went AWOL by racing through the gates screaming their heads off about soldiers rising from the dead to curse the officers they never fragged ... Oh, my *God,* if this ever gets out – oh, *Jesus!*'

'I know, Mr Secretary.' Security Stenographer First Class Trueheart stood up. 'Embarrassment, sir, we've all been there ... All right, Warren, we're in this together. What do we start shredding?'

'*Shredding?*' Pease's left eye was now streaking back and forth with the speed of a laser.

'I understand,' said Regina, who promptly, without the slightest hint of sensuality, pulled her dress up to her waist. 'Documents to be removed, of course. As you can see, I'm fully prepared to carry out the mission.'

'Huh?' His left eye fixed, the Secretary of State was astonished at what he saw. Sewn into Ms Trueheart's panty hose, from knees to thigh, were light brown nylon pockets. 'How ... how incredible,' mumbled Pease.

'Naturally, we must remove all metal clips, and should we need more space, my brassiere has a zippered lining, and the back of my slip has an attached overlay of sheer silk that can accommodate the wider documents.'

'You don't understand,' said the Secretary, his chin impacting on the edge of the desk as the stenographer released her dress to its normal position. '*Ouch!*'

'Keep your mind on business, Warren. Now, what don't I

understand? The Trueheart girls are prepared for all emergencies.'

'Nothing was written *down*!' explained the panicked head of State.

'I see ... Unlogged, max-class, unsanctioned communications, is that it?'

'What? Were you with the CIA ... ?'

'No, that's my older sister, Clytemnestra. She's a very quiet girl ... So our problem goes back to leaks in the unsanctioned infrastructure; the unlogged word of mouth made a devious detour into forbidden ears.'

'It must have, but it *couldn't*! No one who knew could possibly have benefited from betraying the secret of our flying those lunatics up to Boston.'

'Without specific facts, Mr Secretary – which, of course, could be revealed by Pentothal but never, *never* in a confrontation with any subhuman congressional committee – please give me an abstract of the operation. Can you do that, Warren? ... If it would help you, I'll show you my pockets again.'

'It wouldn't hurt.' She did so, and Pease's left eye came slowly to a riveting stop. 'Well, you see,' he began, spittles of saliva emerging from his lips. 'Certain unpatriotic slimes, led by a maniac, want to cripple our first line of defence, namely our contractors and then a section of our Air Force that has international watchdog responsibilities.'

'*How*, sweetie?' Trueheart shifted her weight from one leg to the other, then back again.

'*Auugh.*'

'What, Warren? I asked how.'

'Oh, yes, of course ... Well, they claim that the land on which is located a huge and *very* vital Air Force base may just possibly belong to a group of people – savages, actually – because of some stupid treaty made over a hundred years ago, which never happened, of course! It's all *insane*!'

'I'm sure it is, but is it true, Mr Secretary?' Once more Regina's bared legs required a succession of shifting balances, five to be exact.

'Oh, *boy* . . . !'

'Sit *down*! Is it true?'

'The Supreme Court is thinking about it. The Chief Justice is keeping the Court arguments quiet for another five days, on national security grounds, until the slimes show up for oral interrogation the day before. We've got *four* days to find the bastards and send them to their happy hunting grounds, which have nothing to do with national security grounds. Goddamn savages!'

Regina Trueheart instantly released her dress. 'That will be enough of *that*!'

'Ouch! . . . *What?*'

'We Trueheart girls do not countenance obscene language, Mr Secretary. It simply reveals a lack of acceptable vocabulary and is offensive in the extreme to church-going people.'

'Aw, come on, Vergyna –'

'*Regina!*'

'I'm on your side . . . but don't you see, sometimes a little profanity says it. When you're stressed, it just comes out.'

'You sound like that horrible French writer, Anouilh, who would excuse everything.'

'Annie who?'

'Never mind . . . Was this secure circle of knowledgeable people restricted to only a few of our highest government officials and even fewer outside civilians?'

'The fewest of each!'

'And these all too alive and kicking body bags, were they covertly recruited to carry out their mission – which they obviously failed to do?'

'So covert they didn't even understand it! But then, they didn't have to – they're maniacs.'

'Stay here, Warren,' said Trueheart, placing the shorthand pad on the desk and straightening her dress. 'I'll be right back.'

'Where are you *going*?'

'To speak to your secretary, my mother. I'll be right back, and don't you *dare* get on the telephone!'

'Of course not, Pockets . . . I mean –'

'Oh, *shut* up! You appointees are very, *very* strange.' With these words the security pool stenographer walked out into the outer office and closed the door.

Warren Pease, Secretary of State and owner of a fishing yacht he longed dearly to berth at an acceptable club, was torn between slashing his wrists and calling his former brokerage firm and offering all manner of government insider information so as to reclaim his former partnership. Good *Lord*, why had he *ever* succumbed to his old roomie, the President's call to join the administration? Socially, of course, there were advantages, but there were disadvantages, too. One had to be polite to so many people one simply could not abide, and those dreadful dinner parties where he not only had to sit next to but have his picture taken with *Negroes*. Oh, no, it wasn't all peaches and cream! The sacrifices one had to make would test the patience of a saint . . . and now *this*! Body bags with *living maniacs*, and his own crowd wanting his scalp! How grotesque life had become! Of course, he had no razor blade and he dared not use the telephone, so he simply had to wait, perspiring profusely. In agonizing minutes, the wait was over. However, instead of Regina Trueheart, her mother, Tyrania, marched into the office, closing the door firmly behind her.

The matriarch of the Trueheart clan was the stuff of which legends are born. A striking woman with sharp Teutonic features and blazing light-blue eyes, she was just over six feet in height with an imposing body that stood tall and challenging, belying her fifty-eight years. As her mother before her, who had arrived with the legions of female government secretaries and clerks during World War II, Tyrania was a veteran of the Washington bureaucracy with awesome knowledge of its byways and back alleys, its follies and flagrant abuses. Again, like her mother, she had brought up her own daughters to serve the byzantine infrastructures of the government's myriad bureaus, departments and agencies. Tyrania believed it was the destiny of the family's women to guide the leaders and would-be leaders through Washington's minefields so they could exercise what generally feeble abilities they possessed. In her heart, the Trueheart maximum leader understood that it was women such as herself and her daughters who really ran the nation's government. Men truly were the weaker sex, so vulnerable to temptation and tomfoolery. This judgement no doubt accounted for the fact that no male child had been born into the family for three generations. It simply was not acceptable.

Tyrania studied the obviously distraught Secretary of State, in her long, silent gaze a mixture of pity and resignation. 'My daughter has relayed everything you told her, as well as describing your apparently overstimulated libido,' she said firmly but quietly, as if admonishing a small confused boy in the principal's office.

'I'm *sorry*, Mrs Trueheart! *Honestly*. It's been just a terrible day and I didn't mean to do anything wrong.'

'It's all right, Warren, don't cry. I'm here to help you, not to make you feel naughty.'

'*Thank* you, Mrs Trueheart!'

'But for me to help you, I must first ask you a very important question. Will you answer me honestly, Warren?'

'Oh, yes, yes I will!'

'Good ... Now tell me, among the very small circle of civilians – non-government people – who are aware of this counterstrike operation, do any of them profit from this conceivably threatened air base?'

'*All* of them, for God's sake!'

'Then look to *one* of them, Warren. He's selling out the others.'

'What ... ? *Why*?'

'Long range, I can't answer you until I have more facts – such as stock options and buy-outs – but short range the answer is obvious.'

'It *is*?'

'No one in the administration, with the exception of yourself, would enter into such a devious *solution* that employed incarcerated men, in military prison because of their violence-prone dispositions. The lessons of Watergate and Iran-scam have left their indelible marks, as repulsive and unpatriotic as they may be. Put simply, there were too many indictments.'

'But why am *I* the exception?'

'You're too new and too inexperienced in this town. You wouldn't know how to unite the President's advisers for this sort of clandestine operation. They'd all run to the hills at the suggestion – except, perhaps, the Vice-President, who probably wouldn't know what you're talking about.'

'You think it's one of the . . . *civilians*?'

'I'm rarely wrong, Warren . . . Well, I was once, but that was my husband. After we girls threw him out of the house, he ran down to the Caribbean and charters his run-down sailboat out of the Virgin Islands. A totally despicable human being.'

'Really? Why is that?'

'Because he claims to be a completely happy person, which we all know is unacceptable in our complex society.'

'No kidding . . . ?'

'*Mr* Secretary, may we concentrate on the immediate problem? I strongly suggest that you place the "body bags" in total isolation, squash whatever stories come out of Quantico as the result of drunkenness, and go underground and reach the Zero Zero Zero – dash – Zero Zero Six at Fort Benning.'

'What the hell is that?'

'Not what, but who,' replied Tyrania. 'They're called the Suicidal Six –'

'Like in the Filthy Four?' interrupted Pease, scowling.

'Light years beyond. They're actors.'

'Actors? What do I want with *actors*?'

'These are unique,' said Trueheart, leaning forward and lowering her voice. 'They'd kill for good reviews, which none has ever had in abundance.'

'How did they ever get to *Fort Benning*?'

'Nonpayment of rent.'

'*What*?'

'They haven't worked steadily in years, just went to classes and waited on tables.'

'I don't understand a word you're *saying*?'

'It's really quite simple, Warren. They joined the Army

together to start a repertory theatre and eat on a more regular basis. Naturally, a creatively thinking officer in G-two saw the possibilities and inaugurated a new programme for covert operations.'

'Because they were *actors*?'

'Well, according to the general in charge, they were – *are* – also in great physical shape. You know, all those Rambo movies where they got extra parts. Actors can be very vain where their appearances are concerned.'

'Mrs Trueheart!' exclaimed the Secretary of State. 'Will you please tell me where this conversation is leading us?'

'To a solution, Warren. I will only talk in abstract terms, so there's complete deniability, but I'm sure that your well-honed and well-brought-up intellect will understand.'

'Those are the first words that make sense to me.'

'The Suicidal Six can and will impersonate anybody and anything. They are masters of disguises and dialects, and can penetrate the impossible penetration.'

'That's *crazy*. They'd be penetrating *ourselves*!'

'Good point. That gives you an enviable overview.'

'Wait a minute.' Pease spun around in his swivel chair and stared at the crisscrossed flags of the US and the State Department, in his imagination seeing a portrait of Geronimo dressed in a general's uniform between them. 'That's *it*!' he cried. 'No indictments, no congressional hearings – it's perfect!'

'What is, Warren?'

'*Actors*.'

'Of course.'

'Actors can be anybody they want to be – convince other people they're not who they really are, right?'

'That's true. It's what they're trained to do.'

'No killers, no indictments, no goddamned hearings on the Hill.'

'Well, I wouldn't go that far without buying off a few senators, which our contingency funds allow for –'

'I can see it now,' interrupted Pease, spinning front, his left eye in place, both eyes wide with excitement. 'They arrive at

Kennedy Airport – red sashes, maybe beards and homburg hats – a *delegation*.'

'A what?'

'From *Sweden*! A delegation from the *Nobel* committee. They've studied the military history of the twentieth century and have come over to find General MacKenzie Hawkins to award him the Nobel peace prize for being the greatest soldier of our time!'

'Perhaps I should call a doctor, Warren.'

'Not at all, Mrs Trueheart, you *gave* it to me! Can't you understand? This banana's got an ego bigger than Mount Everest!'

'Who has?'

'Thunder Head.'

'*Who?*'

'MacKenzie Hawkins, that's who! He won the Congressional Medal of Honor – *twice*.'

'I think we should say a silent prayer to almighty God for having him an American and not a Commie –'

'*Bullshit!*' exploded the Secretary of State. 'He's the asshole of the millennium. He'll come running out from wherever he is to get that award ... Then it's Sweden and points north, *way* north! A lost plane – Lapland, Siberia, the tundra, who cares?'

'Despite your inane profanity, Warren, when you say north, it has the ring of brilliant truth, our truth ... *What* can I do, Mr Secretary?'

'To begin with, find out how we reach the officer running these dash-dash-zero-six actors, and then have my plane prepared to fly me down to Fort Benning ... *Perfect!*'

The two rental cars raced south on Route 93 toward Boston, Paddy Lafferty commandering the first, his wife, driving the second, approximately a mile behind. Aaron Pinkus sat in front with his chauffeur, while Sam Devereaux, his mother, and Jennifer Redwing were in the rear seat, the Indian attorney between Mother and son. The second vehicle carried General MacKenzie Hawkins in the front with Mrs Lafferty, as Desis One and Two were in the back, playing blackjack with a deck of cards appropriated from the former ski lodge.

'Now, you hear me good, little girl!' said the plumpish Erin Lafferty of fine Celtic features into the car telephone. 'I want the buster boy to have a full bowl of oatmeal with real milk – not that watered-down crap Grandpa drinks – and the tiny lass should have two slices of bread soaked in eggs and fried – two eggs, got that? . . . All right, girl, I'll get back to you later.'

'Your children?' asked the Hawk somewhat awkwardly as Mrs Lafferty replaced the phone.

'Have you got your brain anywheres near your head, man? Do I look like a woman who's got wee tots?'

'I merely overheard your conversation, madam –'

'That was my youngest, Bridget, who's lookin' after my older lad's – my second oldest lad's – kids, while them two-toilet suppositories are on a cruise . . . would you believe, a *cruise*?'

'Did your husband object?'

'How the hell *could* he? Dennis-boyo is a big accountant with all those letters after his name. He does our taxes.'

'I see.'

'May the devil fart perfume, you do! Never have kids who are brainier than you. There's hell to pay.' The car telephone buzzed and Mrs Lafferty picked it up. 'What is it, Bridgey? You can't find the refrigerator, girl? . . . Oh, it's you, Paddy, darlin', who I may just push your head into a barrel of used crank case oil.' Erin Lafferty held the phone out for Hawkins. 'Paddy says Mr Pinkus wants to talk to you.'

'Thank you, madam . . . Commander?'

'No, it's still Paddy, great General. I'll put the boss on in a second or two. I just wanted to tell you not to pay no attention to my woman. She's a good girl, sir, but she's not been in true combat, if you know what I'm drivin' at.'

'I understand, Gunny. But if I were you, I'd make damn sure "buster boy" gets his oatmeal with real milk and the "tiny lass" has her fried bread with two eggs.'

'Oh, she's been on the breakfast bit again, has she?

Grandmothers can be the end of the good life, General . . . Here's Mr Pinkus.'

'General?'

'Commander? What're the map coordinates, sir?'

'That what? . . . Oh, where we're going. Yes, well, I've just made arrangements for us all to stay at my brother-in-law's summer house in Swampscott. It's on the beach and rather delightful, and as he and Shirley's sister are in Europe, it's completely available.'

'Well done, Commander Pinkus. A comfortable bivouac under combat conditions is good for the troops' morale. Do you have an address? I have to relay it to Little Joseph in Boston because our support personnel will be arriving shortly.'

'It's known as the old Worthington estate on the Beach Road, now owned by Sidney Birnbaum. I'm not sure there are numbers, but the entire front wall is painted in royal blue, which very much appealed to Shirley's sister.'

'That's good enough, Commander Pinkus. Our support will undoubtedly be chosen from an élite corps and they'll find it. Anything else?'

'Simply tell Paddy's wife where we're going. If we get separated in the traffic, she knows the way.'

The Hawk relayed the information only to be greeted by Erin Lafferty's succinct reply. 'Oh, Jesus, Himself, be praised! I'll be dealin' with the kosher boys, and let me tell you, General, they *really* know where to get the best meat and the freshest vegetables!'

'You've been there before, I presume?'

'*Been* there! Don't ever tell my parish priest, but the grand Sidney and his dear wife, Sarah, made me the godmother of their boy, Joshua – Jewish style, you understand. Josh is like one of my own, and Paddy and I keep prayin' that he and Bridgey can get it together, if you know what I mean.'

'Would your parish priest?'

'What the hell does he know? He drinks all them French wines and bores us to death about their *bookays*. A loser.'

'The true, fine melting pot,' said the Hawk quietly.

'Have you ever thought of running for Pope?' asked MacKenzie, chuckling. 'I once knew one who thought like you.'

'Awe, gowann! A dumb Irish broad like me even thinkin' like that?'

'"The meek shall inherit the earth," for on their shoulders lie the morality of all mankind.'

'Hey, you! You tryin' to come *on* with me? Because if you are, my Paddy could break you in half!'

'I wouldn't dream of it, madam,' replied the Hawk, looking at Erin Lafferty's profile. 'And I'm sure he could,' added the soldier who was arguably the most proficient hand-to-hand combat officer ever to have served in the military. 'He would, of course, demolish me.'

'Well, he's gettin' on, but my boy still has it.'

'He has you, and that's far more important.'

'Where're you *at*, buster? I'm an old lady, for Christ's sake!'

'And I'm an older man and one thing has nothing to do with the other. I'm merely saying that it's a privilege to know you.'

'You *confuse* me, soldier man!'

'I don't mean to.'

Erin Lafferty pressed the accelerator to the floor and sped ahead.

Wolfgang Hitluh, born Billy-Bob Bayou, walked through the gate and followed the signs in the wide corridor to Logan airport's baggage claim area. As one third of the highly, if mysteriously, paid security unit recruited by Manpower Plus Plus, he was to meet his two *Kameraden* in the enclosed parking lot across from the taxi stand. As identification, he was to carry a folded *Wall Street Journal*, with various articles clearly circled in red ink, although he had stubbornly argued for a copy of *Mein Kampf*.

If he hadn't needed the employment so badly, he would have turned down the job on principle. The *Journal* was a well-known symbol of the decadent, money-grasping democracies and should be burned along with ninety-nine per cent of all of the country's newspapers and magazines starting with the despicable *Amsterdam News* and *Ebony*, which were published in and for Harlem, New York, a steaming hotbed of inferior black troublemakers, just as Wall Street was a treacherous armed camp of Jewish money! Unfortunately, however, Wolfgang did need the job as his welfare cheques had been cut off – by a suspicious *black* clerk at the unemployment office! – and so he had put his principles on a back burner and accepted the advance of two hundred dollars and an airline ticket.

All he knew was that he and his two *Kameraden* were to protect a group of seven people who were in hiding, and three of those were military themselves. That meant that there were six mercs watching over four civvies – a piece of strudel, which he had come to love from his two glorious months training in the Bavarian mountains with his Fourth Reich *Meisters*. Wolfgang Hitluh, the *Journal* in one hand, his carryon in the other, dodged the traffic and crossed the unroofed two lanes that led to the parking lot. He must *not* be conspicuous! he considered as he walked through the late afternoon sunlight toward the huge garage. Everything was so secret, according to Manpower Plus Plus, that he could not breathe a word of the job even to the Führer, if he was alive – always a possibility, *natürlich*! The assignment obviously entailed the protection of such high officials that the government could not trust the weak, non-Aryan types that had infiltrated the Secret Service ... Where were his *Kameraden*? he wondered.

'You, Wolfie?' asked an enormous black man, emerging from the shadows of a circular concrete pillar and approaching Hitluh.

'What? ... *Who? What* did you say?'

'You heard me, little fella. You've got the newspaper and we saw the red ink when you crossed those two streets out in the open.' The dark giant extended his hand and smiled. 'Nice to know you, Wolf – that's one hell of a name, by the way.'

'Yes, well ... I guess it is.' The Nazi accepted the hand as though it would infect him for life having touched the flesh.

'It seems like a good gig, brother.'

'*Brother?*'

'Here,' continued the huge man, gesturing behind him, 'let me introduce you to our partner, and don't be put off by his appearance. Once we broke out, he couldn't wait to get back into his usual threads. I tell you, Wolfie, you wouldn't believe the way those old fortune-tellers and their crazy moustachioed husbands talk!'

'Fortune-tellers . . . ?'

'Come on, Roman, get out here and meet Wolfie!'

A second figure came out from the shadows of the pillar, this a muscular man in a billowing orange blouse with a blue sash around his waist above skin-tight black trousers and circlets of dark hair on his forehead; he also wore a single gold earring. A *gypsy!* thought Wolfgang. The scourge of the Moldavians, worse than the Jews and the Negroes! *Deutschland über Alles*, a *gypsy!*

''*Allo*, Misstair Wolfowitz!' cried the earringed man, holding out his hand, his blinding white teeth below a dark moustache the antithesis of Wolfgang's vision of a *Kamerad*. 'I can tell by the shape of your eyes that you will have a long, long life with great financial assets! No money is required for this precious information – we work together, no?'

'Oh, great Führer, where the hell are ya?' whispered Hitluh, absently shaking hands.

'What's that, Wolfie?' asked the large black, clamping his huge, strong hand on Wolfgang's shoulder.

'Nothing, *nothing*! . . . You're sure there's no mistake? You're from Manpower Plus Plus?'

'Nowhere else, brother, and from what Roman and I can figure out, this is going to be like picking up bread in the street. By the way, my name's Cyrus – Cyrus M. My buddy's name is Roman Z, and you're Wolfie H. Naturally, we never ask what the letters of our last names stand for – which wouldn't make a hell of a lot of difference anyway because we got so many different ones, right, brother?'

'*Jawohl*.' Wolfgang nodded, then blanched. 'I mean you're absolutely correct . . . *brudder*.'

'What?'

'Brother,' added Hitluh instantly, apologetically. '*Brother*, I mean brother!'

'Hell, don't get upset, Wolfie, I understood you. I speak German, too.'

'You *do*?'

'Hell, yes. Why do you think I've been in prison?'

'Because you speak *German* . . . ?'

'Sort of, little fella,' said the dark-skinned giant. 'You see, I'm a government chemist, and I was loaned out to Bonn to work for a plant in Stuttgart to help out in a fertilizer project, only it wasn't.'

'Wasn't what?'

'Fertilizer . . . Oh, it was shit, but it wasn't fertilizer, just gas, very unhealthy gas. On its way to the Middle East.'

'*Mein Gott!* But perhaps there were reasons . . . ?'

'Sure, there were. Cash and the wasting of a lot of people the bosses didn't think were too important. Three of them found me one night analysing the final compounds. They called me a *Schwärzer Neger* and rushed me, two pulling guns on me. . . . That was that.'

'That was *what*?'

'I threw all three of those honkey Krauts into the vats – which sort of meant they couldn't show up in court to answer my plea of self-defence . . . So, in the interests of diplomatic relations, I drew five years in the can over *here* rather than fifty over *there*. I figured I owed three months, so Roman and I broke out last night.'

'But we're supposed to be *mercs*, not chemists!'

'A man can be different things, little fella. To put myself through two universities in seven years, I took a few months off now and then. Angola – both sides, incidentally – Oman, Karachi, Kuala Lumpur. I won't be a disappointment to you, Wolfie.'

'*Misstair* Wolfowitz,' interrupted Roman Z, expanding his orange-clothed chest, and planting his feet as though he were about to do a gypsy dervish. 'You see before you the greatest man with a blade, a *silent* blade, that you could ever hope to meet! . . . Slash, *slash*, parry, *thrust!*' The words were accompanied by wild gestures and rapid pivots as the blue sash whipped through the air and the orange blouse billowed. 'Ask anyone in the mountains of Serbo-Croatia!'

'But you were in prison over *here* –'

'I passed several hundred bad cheques, what can I tell you?' added Roman Z in a disconsolate voice, his hands extended in a plea. 'One immigrates, however the methods, he comes to nothing in a foreign land that does not understand him.'

'There, Wolfie,' said Cyrus M, in his voice a certain finality. 'You know about us now, what about you?'

'Well, fellas, you see *Ah'm* what some people call a rogue-like underground investigatah –'

'You're also a Southern boy – a Southern boy who speaks German,' interrupted Cyrus. 'Now that's a strange combination, isn't it?'

'You can tell?'

'I think it comes out when you're kind of excited, Wolfie. Why are you excited, little fella?'

'You're not readin' me, Cyrus. Ah'm just anxious to git started on this heah gig!'

'Oh, we'll get started on it right away, you can bet your uptight ass on that. It's just that we'd kinda like to know a little more about our partner. You see, we could be putting our lives in your hands, you can understand that, Wolfie, can't you? . . . Now, how did a good ole boy like you learn German? Was it part of that underground investigating you did?'

'You're right on!' answered Wolfgang, a flat petrified grin plastered on his lips. 'Y'see, Ah was trained to interfilterate all them German cities lak Berlin and Muniken lookin' for them dirty Commies, but y'know what Ah found out?'

'What did you find out, *mein Kleiner*?'

'Ah found out that our mewly-mouthed gov'mint looks the other way an' don't give a shit!'

'You mean like all those Communist bastards around the Brandenburg Gate and walking on Unter den Linden?'

'They sure was under rocks, I tell ya that!'

'*Sie sprechen nicht sehr gut Deutsch*.'

'Well, Ah never learned so much to catch it so quick, Cyrus, but I got yer drift.'

'Sure, I understand. Just certain key words and phrases . . . ' Without warning, the huge black suddenly shot out his right arm in an angled salute. '*Heil* Hitler!'

'*Sieg Heil!*' screamed Wolfgang with such a roar that a number of Logan Airport's arrivals spun their heads around, stared, and immediately fled from the scene.

'Wrong part of town, Wolfie, the Brandenburg's on the other side of the Wall before it came down. They were *all* Commies.' Cyrus M suddenly hauled the stunned Hitluh into the shadows of the pillar, and with one punch rendered the neo-Nazi unconscious.

'What ze hell did you do *that* for?' cried the bewildered blue-sashed gypsy, following his prison mate into the darkened area.

'I can smell these mothers a mile away,' replied the large black chemist, holding the immobilized figure of Wolfgang against the stone and yanking the Nazi's carryon out of his right hand. 'Open it up and dump the stuff on the ground.'

Roman Z did so and the blood-red cover of *Mein Kampf* stood out like a rubied diadem. 'Zeese is not a nice fellow,' said the gypsy, bending down and picking up the book. 'What do we do now, Cyrus?'

'I heard something on my cell radio yesterday and it kind of grabbed me. And would you believe, it happened right here in Boston.'

The Boston Globe

Nude American Nazi Found on Steps of Police Station.
Copy of 'Mein Kampf' Strapped to Chest.

Boston, Aug. 26 – In what appears to be a grotesque pattern of nude criminal activities, the writhing body of a naked man with wide-ribbed packaging tape around his mouth and over his chest, under which was a copy of Adolf

Hitler's *Mein Kampf*, was dumped by two men on the steps of the Cambridge Street Police Headquarters at 8:10 last evening. Seven witnesses, who were in the vicinity at the time and who refused to give their names, said that a taxi swung into the curb and two men, one flamboyantly dressed, the other a large black man, carried the body to the steps, returned to the taxi and raced away. The victim has been identified as Wolfgang A. Hitluh, a wanted American Nazi, born with the legal name of Billy-Bob Bayou in Serendipity Parish, Louisiana, and presumed to be violent. The authorities are both stunned and bewildered, for Mr Hitluh, as the four nude men found on the roof of the Ritz-Carlton hotel two days ago, is claiming government immunity from prosecution, as he was performing his duty as part of a deep-cover, top-secret operation. The information officer at the Federal Bureau of Investigation, while denying any involvement, had the following comment. 'We do not permit our agents to remove their clothing under any circumstances, preferably not even their neckties.' A spokesman for the Central Intelligence Agency, also denying any knowledge of Mr Hitluh's activities, issued the following statement. 'As is well known, the Charter of 1947 prohibits the Agency from operating domestically. In the few instances where our expertise is sought by national authorities, it can only be given at the sole discretion of the director in consultation with congressional oversight. If the late and patriotic Vincent Mangecavallo made any such arrangements, they have not surfaced in our files. Therefore, any inquiries should be directed at those (expletives [two] deleted) in Congress.'

The Boston Globe

(Page 72, Advertisements)

Aug. 26 – A taxi belonging to Abul Shirak of 3024 Center Avenue was briefly stolen early yesterday evening while he was having coffee at the Liberation Diner. He reported the theft to the police; then at 8:35 p.m. called back saying the vehicle had been returned. When initially questioned by the police, he could only recall having sat next to a man in an orange silk shirt and wearing a gold earring who engaged him in lively conversation, after which he discovered that his car keys were missing. No further investigation is anticipated as Mr Shirak said he was compensated.

'You gimme an *answer*, you fancy-talking English *cannoli*!' yelled the red-wigged Vinnie the Bam-Bam into a pay telephone on Collins Avenue in Miami Beach, Florida. 'What the fuck *happened*?'

'Vincenzo, *I* did not pick the lunatic, *you* did,' said the voice of Smythington-Fontini from his suite at New York's Carlyle Hotel. 'If you recall, I warned you against him.'

'He never got a chance to *do* anything! Those whackos can be programmed to put their bare asses in a muskrat hole, but he got short-circuited before he could find his ass!'

'What did you expect with a black man and a gypsy in concert with a fanatical Hitlerite? I believe I mentioned that.'

'You also mentioned that all those clowns didn't give doodly-squat about anything but *cash*, right?'

'On that point, I must refine my thinking. On the other hand, I should give you the good news. Our two first choices have made contact with the general and are at this moment in the new compound and have taken up their posts.'

'How the hell do you know that?'

'Because Manpower Plus Plus called and so informed me. Operative Cyrus M reached them from a telephone in some place called Swampscott and said everything was under control. He also mentioned that he did not care to be made a field colonel by the general. Are you now satisfied, Vincenzo?'

'Goddamn it, *no*! Did you read what those fuckers at the Agency said about me? They said I could have made all these *arrangements* by myself without telling anybody! What kind of crap is *that*?'

'Nothing new, Vincenzo. Who better than a dead man to put the blame on – if there is any blame down the road? And even if you rise from the dead in the out islands of the Dry Tortugas, some things haven't changed. You *did* do it.'

'Only through *you!*'

'I'm invisible ... Bam-Bam. From here on, if you care to leave the Dry Tortugas, you work only for me, *capisce*? You *sit*, Vincenzo, you do not stand.'

'I don't *believe* this!'

'Why not? You said it yourself. I am my mother's son ... Carry out your endeavours on Wall Street, my friend. I'll make a megakilling, and you'll make – well, we'll decide that later.'

'*Mamma mia!*'

'Well put, old sport.'

CHAPTER NINETEEN

The immense living room of the Birnbaum summer house looked out over the beach through a series of sliding glass doors that led to a large redwood deck running the length of the building. It was daybreak and the skies were overcast, the ocean below disturbed, churning in watery rebellion, the short intense waves lurching on to the sand with an anger of their own, reluctantly receding but with promise of return.

'It's going to be a rotten day, isn't it?' said Sam Devereaux, walking out of the door to the kitchen, carrying a mug of coffee.

'It doesn't look too promising,' replied the huge black man, introduced to all of them last evening as *Cyrus M.*

'Have you been up all night?'

'Habit, Counsellor. I know Roman Z, but I don't know the two Hispanic guys. *Desis* One and Two – come on, what kind of aliases are those?'

'What kind of name is Cyrus M?'

'Actually, it's Cyril and the M stands for my mom, who told me how I could get out of a backwater patch in the Mississippi Delta. Books were part of it, but I assure you the emphasis was on tough.'

'You could have played in the NFL, I'd think.'

'Or swung a bat, or boxed, or been the Black Behemoth of wrestling? . . . Get with it, Mr Lawyer, that's meat, and unless you're the best you end up with bruises and half a brain and nowhere to go. I can also assure you that I couldn't have been the best. My soul wasn't in it.'

'You sound like an educated man.'

'I'm schooled.'

'That's all you'll say?'

'Please get this straight, Counsellor. I'm hired to protect you, not to give you my life story,' said Cyrus pleasantly.

'Okay. Sorry ... What's your analysis of the current situation – since that's what we're paying you for?'

'I've checked out the grounds, from all points on the beach and up through the dunes on the bourn to the road. We're vulnerable, but by noon we won't be.'

'What do you mean?'

'I called my firm, the firm that hires me, and told them to shoot up six lithium battery-operated, trip-wire machines with waist-high antennae – they'll blend in with the high grass and cover the waterfront.'

'What the hell does *that* mean?'

'It means that any moving object over a density weight of fifty pounds crossing through those beams will set off alarms heard at least five miles away.'

'You know your business, Cyrus M.'

'I hope you know yours,' mumbled the guard, bringing a pair of binoculars to his eyes and scanning the grounds outside.

'That's an odd remark.'

'I think you mean impertinent.' Cyrus's grin could be seen below the field glasses.

'Yeah, I suppose you could say that, but it's still an odd remark. Would you mind explaining it?'

'I'm probably older than you think, Mr D, and I've got a pretty good memory.' Cyrus adjusted the focus in his binoculars and continued quietly, casually. 'When we were introduced last night – by our noms de guerre, of course – and given our instructions by the general, my mind went back a few years ... Having spent some time over there, newspaper stories about the Far East usually catch my attention ... Your general's the same one who got thrown out of China for desecrating some kind of national monument in Beijing, isn't he? As a matter of fact, I even remember the name – General MacKenzie Hawkins – which fits neatly with "Commander

H," except that all of you kept calling him "General," so the "commander's" rank was fairly obvious . . . He's the man all right, the same general who had Washington spinning yo-yos into their toilet bowls over his Chinese trial.'

'Without acknowledging a word of truth in your ludicrous and outrageous conjecture, what's your point?'

'Well, it's related to the method of my recruitment for this particular job.' Cyrus swung the binoculars slowly back and forth, his large head and shoulders moving like the animated upper torso of an impressive statue, no less menacing for its sculptured lines. 'You see, I've worked for this outfit off and on for a number of years, a lot more in the early days, frankly, but I know them and the rules don't change. On any normal job we're given a brief but in-depth rundown on the assignment –'

'What exactly does that mean?' asked the quick-thinking attorney that was Sam in his normal element.

'Names, backgrounds, quick verbal brush strokes describing the nature of job –'

'Why?' interrupted Devereaux.

'Hey, Counsellor,' said Cyrus softly, lowering the field glasses and looking at Sam. 'You're really playing lawyer now, aren't you?'

'Since you obviously know that I am one, what do you expect? . . . How *did* you know, by the way?'

'You cats are all alike,' replied the guard, chuckling. 'You couldn't hide it if you were mute – your hands would fly off your wrists arguing in sign language.'

'You *heard* me?'

'I heard the three of you – the old guy, the tan-skinned lady who doesn't need the sun to get that way, and you. If you remember, I was ordered by the general to walk around this place for a couple of hours last night checking every point of entry. The three of you stayed up after your mother – at least I think she's your mother – and "Commander H," who might actually be *Preparation H*, went to bed. Let's say I've been in and around the law a few times in my adult life so I know when I hear lawyers talking.'

'All right,' conceded Devereaux. 'To my first question: Why are you merely hired guards given rundowns on your jobs?'

'Because we're not merely guards, we're mercenaries –'

'You're *what*?' screamed Sam.

'Combat soldiers for hire, and *keep* your voice down.'

'Oh, my *God*!' Unfortunately, with that misdirected prayer, Devereaux spilled the mug of coffee all over the front of his slacks. '*Jesus*, it's *hot*!'

'Good coffee usually is.'

'Shut your face!' cried Sam, bending over and billowing his trousers in futility. '*Mercenaries?*'

'You heard me, and that should lead to the answer to your first question, namely, why are we given rundowns on our assignments. I'll tell you . . . The conventional wisdom is that mercenaries will accept any assignment for the almighty dollar, but it isn't true. I've swung on both sides when it didn't matter, but I won't when it does. I just won't take the job . . . I also won't take it if I don't feel comfortable with those who do – which is why you're lacking a third "guard."'

'There was supposed to be someone else?'

'He's not here so there's no point going into it.'

'Okay, *okay*!' Devereaux straightened up and continued with what dignity he could summon. 'Which leads me to my second question, which was – what the hell *was* it?'

'You didn't pose it, Counsellor, I left it open.'

'Clarify, if you please.'

'Why *weren't* we given a more complete rundown on this assignment? . . . And from long experience, I'll try to give you a reasonable answer.'

'Please do.'

'All we were told was that there were seven of you, three military, and that second fact was to sweeten the job. No circumstances, no description of potential enemies, not a shred of politics – politics in the broader sense, like in the legality or illegality of a cause – in essence, nothing except numbers which could be meaningless. Does that tell you anything?'

'The obvious,' replied Sam. 'The circumstances surrounding this assignment, as you call it, must remain secret.'

'That's acceptable government-speak, not merc-speak.'

'Merc?'

'Mercenary language. We accept high risk for high dollars, but we're not duty bound to operate in the dark on a, let's say, need-to-know basis. That's for career intelligence junkies who go deep cover into Cambodia or Tanganyika and are lucky if their families get their full pensions when they don't come home. Do you begin to see the difference?'

'So far it's not very difficult to grasp, but I don't know what you're driving at.'

'I'll spell it out for you. The absent pages of this scenario have one of two possibilities. The first is unsanctioned government intervention, which means nobody can know anything because anybody who does, official and otherwise, could end up in Leavenworth or in a lye pit ... and the second possibility is even less promising.'

'Do tell?' said Devereaux, his anxious eyes studying the impassive face of Cyrus M.

'A sting operation, Counsellor.'

'A *sting* ... ?'

'Yes, but not the lovable sort that trips up a crook who's mounting a con, or even one that catches nasty people taking bribes when they shouldn't, but a far more lethal one ... There's a term for it; it's called a "permanent sting."'

'"Permanent?"'

'As in no recovery.'

'You mean –?'

'*Dum-dum-tee-dum, dum-tee-dum-tee-dum-tee-dum,*' hummed the huge mercenary.

'*What?*' yelled Sam.

'Keep your voice down! ... I'm trying to explain the second possibility. A wall of protection is built to disguise the real intent. Execution.'

'Jesus *Christ*! ... Why are you *telling* me this?'

'Because I may pull Roman Z and me out.'

'*Why?*'

'I didn't like the third merc they sent and beyond that, now knowing who Commander H is, somebody's really after your general's ass, probably all of your asses since you're all in his sandbox. You may be lunatics, but from what I can see, you don't deserve this, especially the girl, and I don't want to be a part of it . . . I'll set up the lithium trips – if they ever get here – and then we'll think about it.'

'My *God*, Cyrus . . . !'

'I thought I heard voices, also a few shrieks,' said Jennifer Redwing, walking through the kitchen door carrying a cup of tea. '*Sam Devereaux!*' she roared, staring at the attorney's trousers. 'You did it *again*!'

The six men ranged in age from twenty-six to thirty-five, some with more hair rather than less and several taller or shorter than the others, but there were three constants that applied to all. Each face had a distinctive 'look,' whether sharp or broad featured, with piercing or neutral eyes, the face itself had a quality of immediacy, of . . . let's face it, theatricality. And each body was a trained body; the years studying acrobatics, swordsmanship, dance (modern and chorus), martial arts (stunt pay, according to the Screen Actors Guild), double takes and pratfalls (indigenous to high comedy and farce), and costume movement (very big in Shakespeare and those Greek playwrights), these were necessary. Lastly, each pair of vocal chords was capable of the widest range of octaval pitch, along with an even wider range of dialects (mandatory for voice-over commercials). All of the above were essential to their craft – nay, their art! – and naturally to their résumés, which had fallen with staccato regularity on the desks of unappreciative agents and producers. For they were *actors*, the most bled and most misunderstood human beings on the face of the earth – especially when unemployed. In a word, they were unique.

Their unit, too, was unique in the annals of covert operations. It was initially formed by an elderly G-two colonel in Fort Benning who was an addict where films, television and the stage were concerned. He was known to call off whole night training sessions if they interfered with a movie he wanted to see in Pittsfield, Phenix City, or Columbus; he also reputedly caged Air Force transportation to see certain plays in New York and Atlanta. But because of its accessibility, television was his personal narcotic. It was confirmed by his fourth wife in their divorce proceedings that he incessantly stayed up all night in front of the TV set watching, at times, two or three late films by switching the channels on his remote control. So, naturally, when six actors, real honest-to-Equity *actors*, showed up at Fort Benning, his imagination went into high gear – some fellow officers claimed the old boy let it fly right out of the gear box.

He monitored each man throughout basic training, marvelling at their individual physical capabilities as well as their collective proclivity for calling attention to themselves in a crowd, but always in a positive way. He stood in awe at the way each instinctively mixed so naturally with his immediate and changing surroundings, one minute using the vernacular of the streets with urban recruits, the next employing the down-home language of the country boys.

Colonel Ethelred Brokemichael – former *Brigadier General* Brokemichael, until that lousy Harvard lawyer in the Inspector General's office had wrongfully accused him of drug dealing in Southeast Asia! *Drugs?* He didn't know a coke from a cola! He had facilitated the transport of medical supplies, and when offered money, gave most of it to the orphanages, saving a minor amount for future theatre tickets. But with these actors he knew when he had found his way back to the rank he so richly deserved. (He often wondered why his cousin Heseltine had opted for resignation when *he* was the one who had been severely reprimanded and reduced in rank, not Heseltine, that whining debutant who always wanted the fanciest uniforms this side of some goddamned operetta.) Nevertheless, he had *found* it! A totally *original* concept for clandestine operations: a unit of trained, professional actors, like chameleons capable of altering appearances and attitudes commensurate with whatever targets they were to penetrate.

A living, breathing, repertory acting company of *agents provocateurs*! A winner!

So the demoted Colonel Ethelred Brokemichael, using a few well-placed Pentagon connections, had his small group of performers assigned solely to him, to upgrade as he wished, and to send into the field as covert projects required. He had thought of calling them 'The Z Team,' but the actors, in concert, rejected the name. They refused to accept the last letter of the alphabet, and since the first letter was undoubtedly copyrighted, they insisted on some other appellation, because if there was ever a television series, they wanted control of casting, scripts, residuals and subsidiary rights, in that order.

The name came with their third infiltration within a nine-month period when they penetrated a notorious band of the Brigate Rosse in Colonna, Italy, and freed an American diplomat who was being held hostage. They had done so by taking an ad out in the newspapers claiming they were the finest Communist caterers in the city, which no one had ever done, and were subsequently hired by the Brigate to cater a birthday party for its vicious terrorist chief at their hidden headquarters. The rest, as the bromide says, was *zuppa anitra*, duck soup. However, within covert operations, the legend was born. The *Suicidal Six* was a force to be reckoned with.

Subsequent operations in Beirut, the Gaza, Osaka, Singapore, and Basking Ridge, New Jersey, only added to the unit's reputation. They had managed to infiltrate and draw out many of the world's most savage criminals, from drug runners and arms merchants to contract killers and real estate developers, and throughout these hazardous missions they had suffered no casualties whatsoever.

They had also never fired a gun, or unleashed a knife, or thrown a grenade. However, only one man knew that – the reinstated Brigadier General Ethelred Brokemichael. It was such a *disgrace*! The famed Suicidal Six, that assumed paragon of those lethal death squads, had never wasted *anybody* – they had *talked* their way into and out of every potentially fatal assignment they were given. It was utterly *humiliating*!

So when Secretary of State Warren Pease arrived at Fort Benning and had driven in a two-man Jeep to the farthest point of the ninety-eight thousand acres that was the army preserve to deliver his top-secret instructions to Brokemichael, did Ethelred see the light at the end of his own personal tunnel, his own very private *revenge*! The conversation went as follows.

'I've cleared it with our people in Sweden,' said Pease. 'They'll tell the Nobel committee that it's a national crisis, and how much herring do we have to import anyhow? Then your boys fly up from Washington, *not* Stockholm, presumably having talked to the President, and the mayor of Boston greets them at the airport with a press conference and limousines and motorcycle escorts, the whole enchilada.'

'Why Boston?'

'Because it's the Athens of America, the seat of learning, the place where such a delegation should speak from.'

'Also maybe where Hawkins happens to be?'

'We think it's possible,' interrupted the Secretary of State. 'What's certain, however, is that he can't walk away from that award.'

'For God's sake, the Hawk would bust out of a compound in Hanoi and swim across the Pacific to get it! *Jesus*, the Soldier of the Century! Old Georgie Patton will be sending down lightning bolts.'

'And once he shows up, your boys take him and we're off across the Atlantic heading north, far north. Along with every one of the unpatriotic bastards who works for him.'

'Who might they be?' asked General Brokemichael, only mildly interested.

'Well, the first is a Boston attorney who defended Hawkins in Beijing, a lawyer named Devereaux –'

'*Aurragh!*' screamed the brigadier, his roar only to be compared to a nuclear blast on a desert. 'The Harvard *prick*?' he shrieked, the veins in his elderly throat so pronounced that the Secretary of State thought he might expire on the adjacent bush of wildflowers.

'Yes, I believe he went to Harvard.'

'He's dead, dead, *dead*!' yelled the general, suddenly punching the Georgia air with his fists and kicking up the dirt with his quite unnecessary paratrooper boots. 'He's *history*, I *promise* you! ... Brian Donlevy said that at Château Neuf in *Beau Geste*.'

Marlon, Dustin, Telly and The Duke sat facing one another in the four front swivel chairs of Air Force II while Sylvester and Sir Larry were at the small conference table in the centre of the plane. All kept going over their written lines as well as the 'improv' lead-ins that would result in spontaneous rambling conversations. As the official aircraft began its initial descent into the Boston area, the babble of six different voices was heard, all heavily laced with individual interpretations of a Swedish dialect as applied to the English language. Eight-by ten-inch mirrors were also held in front of each face as the warriors of Suicidal Six checked their make-up – three chin beards, two moustaches, and a toupee for Sir Larry.

'*Hi*, there!' yelled a youngish blond-haired man emerging from a closed cabin door at the rear of the plane. 'The pilot said I could come out now.'

The cacophony of voices subsided as the Vice-President of the United States walked, grinning, into the wide body of the aircraft. 'Isn't this fun?' he said brightly.

'Who's him?' asked Sylvester.

'He,' corrected Sir Larry, adjusting his toupee. 'Who's *he*, Sly.'

'Yeah, sure, but what is it?'

'This is my *plane*,' replied the heir-apparent to the Oval Office. 'Isn't it great?'

'Take a seat, Pilgrim,' said The Duke. 'If you want some grub or a bottle of rot gut, just press one of the buttons over there.'

'I know, I *know*. All these swell guys are my crew!'

'He – he – he – he's the – the – vice – vice – vice ... *you* know,' cried Dustin, shaking his head, but not back and forth, instead in circles. 'He was born at precisely – precisely – precisely eleven twenty-two in the morning in nineteen fifty-one – fifty-one – fifty-one, exactly six – six – six years, twelve days, seven hours – hours – hours and twenty-two – two – two minutes after the Japanese – Japanese – Japanese surrendered on the battleship – ship – ship Missouri.'

'*G'wan*, Dusty!' shouted Marlon, scratching his left armpit with his right hand. 'I'm sick of that bit – bit – bit, you got an understanding of wherefrom I'm coming from, *huh*, Dusty?'

'You and your streetcar – streetcar – *streetcar!*'

'Hey, come on, baby face, you wanna lollipop?' asked Telly, grinning at the Veep, but with eyes that were not smiling at all. 'You're okay, kid, but sit down and close the choppers, all right? We got work to do, you dig?'

'I was told you're *actors!*' said the Vice-President, lurching into an aisle seat across from the foursome, his expression alive with excitement. 'I've often thought I'd like to be an actor. You know, a lot of people think I look like that movie star –'

'*He* can't act!' pronounced Sir Larry in high British dudgeon from the table behind. 'It was all luck and pull and that stupid, implausible face of his, totally devoid of character.'

'A passable director – director – *director*,' offered Dustin.

'Wadda *you, crazy*?' belched Marlon. 'That was casting. The actors carried him!'

'Maybe he cast 'em,' suggested Sylvester. 'Y'know, it's possiblelike, man.'

'You listen to me, Pilgrims,' said The Duke, squinting, his eyes roving around the chairs. 'It's all that dirty business in those offices of them land grabbin', cattle rustlin' agents. It's what they call "pyramid deals." You get the star, you take all the crap beneath.'

'*Boy*, this is real *actor* talk!' exploded the Vice-President.

'It's shit, baby, and don't get your pretty face near it.'

'*Telly!*' cried Sir Larry angrily. 'How many *times* have I told you that some people can get away with obscenity, but *you* can't, dear heart! From you, it's offensive.'

'Hey, man,' interrupted Marlon, making facial contortions into his mirror. 'What the hell is he supposed to say? "Fie on you, great Caesar?" I tried that a couple of times and it din't work.'

'You don't speak so good, Marley,' said Sylvester, gluing on his chin beard. 'You gotta speak *real* good to make them stupid words make sense.'

'You should talk, you gutter person!'

'I also don't try too much of that Jake's beer, which for me is a dollar a pitcher!'

'*Hey*, very good, Sly!' shouted Marlon in his perfectly normal Midwest voice, devoid of slurs and slushes. 'Really terrific!'

'Fine retort, mi'boy,' said Telly, as if he were a cultured university professor of English.

'We can do *anything*,' added Dustin, smoothing his moustache.

'Well, we'd better be damn good down there at Logan Airport, gentlemen,' said The Duke, checking his slightly rouged nose and speaking in a voice properly belonging to a high-ranking corporate executive.

'Hog *damn*, we're great!' yelled Sir Larry, in tones reminiscent of the Okefenokee Swamp.

'Good *Lord*,' exclaimed Sylvester, the mid-Atlantic vowels of a Yale Drama School graduate coming through as he stared at the Vice-President. 'You really *are* him!'

'*He*, Sly!' again corrected Larry, briefly slipping back into aristocratic British. 'At least, I think so.'

'A naturally evolved vernacular legitimizes its usage,' retaliated Sylvester, still looking at the Vice-President. 'We appreciate the use of your aircraft, sir, but how come?'

'Secretary of State Pease thought it would make a nice impression on Boston, and since I wasn't doing anything – I mean, I do a lot, but I wasn't doing anything this *week* – so I said, "Sure, why not?"' The heir apparent leaned forward conspiratorially. 'I even signed the "finding."'

'The what?' asked Telly, taking his eyes off his face in the mirror.

'The intelligence finding for your operation.'

'We know what it is, young man,' said The Duke, his well-spoken voice reflecting his current role as somebody's chief executive officer. 'But I believe only the President can sign such a document.'

'Well, he was in the bathroom, and I was there, so I said, "Sure, why not?"'

'Fellow thespians,' pronounced Telly, returning to his mirror, his vibrato right out of that famed theatrical institution, The Players, in New York's Gramercy Park. 'If we don't pull it off, Congress will give this young man a testimonial dinner he'll never forget.'

'Actually, I've made some new friends over there –'

'With him on the spit – spit – spit,' completed Dustin, jerkily revolving his head as he reverted to type-casting, of course. 'For exactly – exactly – exactly four – four hours, twenty – twenty – *twenty* minutes and thirty-two – two – *two* seconds. His ass will be extremely well done.'

'Oh, a roast! I'd like that. It shows they really like you!'

'Are you going to introduce us at the airport press conference?' asked Marlon sceptically, his quiet, warm Midwest accent pronounced.

'Me? No, the mayor will meet you. Actually I'm not supposed to get off the plane for an hour or so, and then without any press whatsoever.'

'Then why get off the plane at all,' said the erudite Yalie who called himself Sylvester. 'We're using Air Force equipment to take us to –'

'Don't *tell* me!' shrieked the Vice-President, cupping his ears with his hands. 'I'm not supposed to know anything!'

'Not supposed to know anything?' questioned The Duke. 'You signed the finding, *sir*.'

'Well, sure, why not? But who the heck ever reads those dumb things?'

'*Pore Jud is daid, a candle lights his haid*,' sang Telly softly from his swivel chair, his bass-baritone perfectly acceptable for the touching Rodgers and Hammerstein song.

'I repeat,' repeated Sylvester. 'Why leave the plane?'

'I have to. You see, some son of a butterball stole my wife's car from back home – *her* car, not *mine* – and I have to identify it.'

'You're kidding!' said Dustin, no eccentricities in his delivery. 'It's here in *Boston*?'

'I'm told it was driven by some very unsavoury characters.'

'What are you going to do?' asked Marlon.

'Kick some fucker's ass to the eighteenth hole and back, *that's* what I'm going to do!'

Once more there was a brief silence as The Duke rose to his full height, surveying his comrades' quiet attention on the Vice-President, then spoke in the lingo of his namesake. 'You may be *rancho correcto* after all, Pilgrim. Maybe we could even help.'

'Well, of course, I never curse, at least hardly ever –'

'Curse, baby,' broke in Telly, reaching into his vest pocket and withdrawing a stringed piece of candy. 'Have a lollipop and don't back off. You just may have made a couple of friends here. I figure you can use 'em.'

'*Prepare for our final descent into Boston's Logan Airport*,' came the words over the loudspeaker from Air Force II's flight deck. '*Estimated arrival in eighteen minutes.*'

'There's still time for us to have a drink, *sir*,' said the soft-spoken Marlon, studying the young blond-haired politician. 'All you have to do is summon your steward.'

'Why the hell *not*?' The Vice-President of the United States rebelliously pressed the button, and within moments – perhaps too many moments – the Air Force steward appeared – perhaps not too enthusiastically.

'Wadd'ya want?' asked the corporal, insistently cowing the young Veep.

'*What* did you say, *Pilgrim*?' shouted The Duke, still standing.

'I beg your pardon ... ?'

'Do you know who this man *is*?'

'Yes, sir, of course, sir!'

'Then sit straight in yer saddle and canter, don't trot!'

In far fewer minutes than his arrival might indicate, the

corporal and a second crewman returned with drinks for everyone. And everyone smiled as they raised their glasses.

'To you, sir,' toasted Dustin in his clear, precise voice.

'I'll second that,' said Telly. 'And forget the lollipop, my friend.'

'Third ... !'

'Fourth ... !'

'Fifth ... !'

'Sixth!' finalized The Duke, nodding his head in the best tradition of corporate acknowledgment.

'Gosh, you guys are really great fellows!'

'It's our convenient and ubiquitous privilege to befriend the Vice-President of the United States,' said the gentle Marlon, glancing at the others as he drank.

'Gee, I don't know what to say. I feel like I'm one of you!'

'You are, Pilgrim, you are,' said The Duke, raising his glass for a second time. 'You've been crapped upon, too.'

Jennifer Redwing, with the enthusiastic assistance of Erin Lafferty, as well as the sous-chef labours of Desis One and Two, created a multinational barbecue on the redwood porch. Since the steel-constructed pit contained four broiling areas, each regulated by a separate dial, the tastes of everyone could be served. Paddy Lafferty's wife called the kosher boys in Marblehead and had them deliver the finest salmon and the freshest chickens, then she reached the boyos in Lynn to send up the best porterhouses they had in stock.

'I don't know what I can *do* about you, you outrageously beautiful lass,' cried Erin, looking wide-eyed at Jennifer in the kitchen. 'Should I try to get some buffalo meat?'

'No, dear Erin,' replied Jenny, laughing as she peeled the large Idaho potatoes they had found in the subcellar. 'I'll broil a few slices of the salmon.'

'Oh, like yer Indian fishes in them rushin'-like-hell rivers?'

'No, again, Erin. Like those less-in-cholesterol meals we're all supposed to eat.'

'I tried some of those on Paddy, and y'know what he told me? ... He told me he'd tell the Lord God himself – face to face, mind you – that if He didn't want his red-blooded boyos to eat porters, why the hell did He put them creatures on the earth for us to eat?'

'Did your husband ever get an answer?'

'By his lights, he did. Two years ago, thanks to Mr Pinkus, we visited our roots in Ireland, and Paddy got on his ass and kissed the Blarney Stone. When he got up he said to me, he said: "I got the message, wifey. Where porters are concerned, I'm the exception, and that's the holy truth!"'

'You accepted that?'

'Come now, lass,' replied Erin Lafferty, smiling sweetly, not necessarily innocently. 'He's my boyo, the only boyo I've ever wanted in m'life. After thirty-five years I'm going to question his visions?'

'Then give him his porters.'

'Oh, I do, Jenny, but I cut out all the fat and he screams like hell that the butcher's cheatin' us or I'm cookin' 'em wrong.'

'What do you do then?'

'An extra glass of whisky, lass, and maybe a few strokes where it takes his mind off his mouth.'

'You're a remarkable woman, Erin.'

'Oh, cut the bullshit, girl!' said Paddy Lafferty's wife, laughing as she chopped the lettuce for a salad. 'When you get a man of your own, you'll learn a few things. The first is to keep him alive; the second is to keep his batteries from goin' dead and that's all there is to it!'

'I envy you, Erin.' Redwing studied the fine-featured yet fleshed-out face of Mrs Lafferty. 'You have something I don't think I'll ever have.'

'Why not, girl?' Erin stopped chopping.

'I don't know . . . Perhaps I have to be stronger than any man that wants me in that way – the marriage bit, I mean. I won't be subjugated.'

'You mean like being below the guy what marries you, no dirty language intended?'

'Yes, I guess that's what I mean. I can't be subservient.'

'I'm not sure what sub – subservant means, but I figure it's like bein' low class, or no class, is that what you're sayin'?'

'That's exactly what I'm saying.'

'Well, ain't there a better way? Like what I do with Paddy – who I would care to spend the rest of my life with – by tellin' him that he can still have his porters, but *he* don't know I cut off the fat. He gets his steaks – so he stops complaining – but that fat crap goes away until he gets his teeth into the last quarter inch of the *bone*. Y'see what I mean? Give the gorilla the last small taste on the *bone* and he forgets the rest. He's happy.'

'Are you suggesting that we women manipulate our male counterparts?'

'What have we been doing for *years*? ... Until you screechers came along we had it right. Tell 'em anything, but give 'em yer own perfume.'

'Remarkable,' said the daughter of the Wopotamis pensively.

Suddenly, from the huge living room beyond the kitchen door, there were screams of anguish or exaltation, or both – it was impossible to differentiate. Jennifer dropped a potato on the floor as Erin involuntarily threw a head of lettuce up into a light fixture, smashing a long neon tube, the glass particles descending into her salad bowl. Desi the First appeared, crashing the door open with such force it slammed back from the wall into his face dislodging the temporary dentistry in his mouth.

'*Chu!*' he yelled. 'Come out here and look at thè *teledifusión*! Ees *loco* – ees crazy like *vacas* with *testículos!*'

Both women raced to the door, ran out into the living room, and stared in total bewilderment at the television screen. There were six obviously important visitors to Boston, all in formal clothes, some with short clipped beards, others clean shaven or with waxed moustaches, and each wearing a black homburg. They were being greeted by the mayor of Bean Town, who was equally obvious in his inability to express the city's greetings.

'So we welcome you to *Bahsten*, gentlemen of the *Noble* committee from Swedeland, and extend to you our *haartfelt* thanks for choosin' the great university of *Haavadd* for your seminal on international relatives and your search for the Soldier of the Century, namely a certain General MacKenzie Hawkings, who you presume to be in our far west frontiers and will hear or watch this broadcast – who wrote this shit?'

'We *break* away to bring you up to date!' intruded the voice of the announcer as the screen went mute. 'The illustrious Nobe*lll* committee has arrived in Boston to participate in Harvard's symposium on international *relations*, yet the spokesman, Sir Lars Olafer, stated upon arrival a few minutes ago that a secondary purpose was to determine the where-abouts of General MacKenzie *Hawkins*, twice recipient of the Congressional Medal of Honor and selected by the Nobel committee as the Soldier of the Century ... The mayor's motorcade will soon be off to the Four Seasons Hotel, where the *Swedish* committee will reside during the Harvard sympo-sium ... One minute, please. We have a call from the President of Harvard University ... *What* symposium? How the hell do *I* know, you run the place, not *me*! ... Sorry, folks, a minor communications glitch in Cambridge ... Now, back to our regular programme, a re-run of our most popular programme, *Watch Your Assets.*'

'*Somebody send in the dwarfs* ... !'

MacKenzie Hawkins got out of his chair and roared. '*Goddamn*, Soldier of the *Century*! Did you all *hear* that? ... Of course, it had to happen sooner or later, but the fact that it actually did makes me the proudest combat officer that ever lived! And let me tell you, boys and girls, I intend to share this great honour with every *grunt* who ever served under my command, because they're the *real* heroes and I want the world to *know* it!'

'General,' said the giant black mercenary calmly, even gently. 'You and I have to talk.'

'About what, Colonel?'

'I'm not a colonel and you're not the Soldier of the Century. This is the setup.'

CHAPTER TWENTY

The silence was both electric and affecting. It was as if all gathered were witnessing the pain of a large faithful animal being betrayed by some unseen master who had cast it aside, leaving it to the murderous whims of a wolf pack. Jennifer Redwing walked quietly to the television set and turned it off as MacKenzie Hawkins stared at Cyrus.

'I think you should explain yourself, Colonel,' said the general, his eyes conveying both astonishment and hurt. 'You and I just saw a network news programme and heard the words spoken by a distinguished foreign visitor, a spokesman for the Swedish Nobel committee; and unless my hearing is beyond repair, he announced that I was to be the recipient of the Soldier of the Century award. Since his broadcast, and the reporting of it, will undoubtedly be seen by millions of people throughout the civilized world, I submit that a fabrication is unthinkable.'

'The ultimate permanent sting,' said Cyrus M softly. 'I tried to explain that to your colleagues, Miss R and Mr D.'

'Try again with me, Colonel.'

'To repeat myself, I'm not a colonel, General –'

'And *I'm* not the Soldier of the Century,' broke in Hawkins. 'I assume you care to repeat that, too.'

'You may be entitled to that honour, sir, but it would never come from anyone associated with the Nobel committee.'

'*What?*'

'Let me spell it out for you so there's no misunderstanding.'

'Are you, by chance, an attorney?' interrupted Aaron Pinkus.

'No, but among other pursuits, I am a chemist.'

'A *chemist*?' asked the further-stunned Hawkins. 'Then what the hell do you know about *anything*?'

'Well, I'm certainly not in a class with Alfred Nobel, who was also a chemist, and who also invented dynamite, and who – many believe – to assuage his guilt over that invention, created the Nobel awards, not one of which would ever be associated with war. The concept of a Soldier of the Century would be an anathema to the Nobel committee.'

'So what precisely are you saying, Cyrus?' interjected Jennifer.

'An extension of what I told you this morning. *This* is the trap to pull in General Hawkins –'

'You know my *name*?' cried MacKenzie.

'He knows your name, Mac, let it go,' said Devereaux.

'*How*?'

'Forget it, General,' replied Redwing. 'For the moment, he's my witness ... Okay, Cyrus, it's a trap. What else? And from the tone of your voice, I'd say there *was* something else.'

'This isn't minor league lunatics with Alexander the Great complexes any longer. This operation is solo and comes from some son-of-a-bitch top gun in the government.'

'*Washington*?' asked an incredulous Aaron Pinkus.

'*Someone* in Washington,' refined the mercenary. 'Not a collective effort, too much danger of leaks for that, but a highly placed authority who can mount this on his own.'

'Why do you say that?' persisted Aaron.

'Because the Nobel committee in Sweden is pure, and to make it even temporarily impure would take the office of a very important person. After all, any respectable journalist could reach Stockholm and get a confirmation. I suspect that confirmation has already been given.'

'*Oh* boy!' exclaimed Sam Devereaux. 'This is hardball.'

'I believe I said as much this morning.'

'You also told me that you were thinking of pulling yourself and Roman Z out of here once those trip things with the lithium things were in place ... They're in place, Cyrus. What now? Are you going to leave us?'

'No, Counsellor, I've changed my mind. We're staying.'

'Why?' asked Jennifer Redwing.

'I suppose you expect some profound racial statement, like how we niggers had to survive the Klan by developing a sixth sense and get damned upset when the government behaves in like fashion. That's voodoo.'

'Hey, don't the big guy talk good?' interrupted Mrs Lafferty.

'Later, dear Erin,' said Redwing, her attention on Cyrus. 'All right, Mr Mercenary, no racial voodoo, which I know something about. Why are you staying?'

'Is it important?'

'It is to me.'

'I can understand that,' said Cyrus, smiling.

'*I* don't understand a goddamned thing!' exploded Mac-Kenzie Hawkins, crushing a cigar in his fingers as he put it into his mouth.

'Then let the gentleman answer,' rejoined Aaron Pinkus. 'If you'll forgive me, General, please *shut* the hell up.'

'One commander does *not* give such an order to *another*!'

'Oh, blow it out your ass,' said Aaron, suddenly shaking his head, as if wondering where the words had come from. 'Good heavens, I'm terribly sorry!'

'Don't be,' broke in Sam. 'You were saying, Cyrus?'

'Okay, Counsellor,' said the mercenary, looking at Devereaux. 'How much have you and the lady told the others?'

'Everything you told us, except it wasn't the others, just Aaron. We didn't include Mac or his "adjutants" or my mother here –'

'Why the hell *not* tell me?' shouted the general ' . . . whatever the hell it is you're not talking about!'

'We needed more to go on before you began issuing orders,' replied Sam curtly, then turning back to Cyrus. 'Also, we included your difficulties in Stuttgart and the aftereffects. Your "release" from prison, as it were.'

'It doesn't matter. If this is the mess I think it is and Roman Z and I can help you, I have an idea you won't use it against us.'

'You have my word on that,' insisted Redwing.

'I didn't hear a thing,' added Devereaux.

'You wouldn't have,' said the mercenary pointedly. 'Your questions were clumsy, while Miss R's were direct and made sense. She made it plain that in order to believe me, she needed some background credibility. I simply gave it to her.'

'It's all hearsay and inadmissible, as far as I'm concerned,' said Pinkus.

'My interrogations are never clumsy,' mumbled Sam.

'Well, you had a lot on your mind ... as well as your trousers,' said Jennifer quietly. 'You say your decision to stay isn't racial, Cyrus, but no one brought up that point but you. Are you protesting too much? You were a black man wrongfully convicted; if it happened to me, an Indian, I'd be mad as hell and stay mad for a long time. I'd want to strike back at any symbol of authority and I'm not sure the cause would matter. Is *that* why you're staying?'

'Your psychology's sound but it's not applicable. Basically, my plea of self-defence notwithstanding, I was put in jail, not because I was black, but because I was one hell of a chemical engineer. Now, maybe a few idiots in Stuttgart figured that a *Schwärzer* wasn't capable of analysing their final stage of synthesizing compounds –'

'Boy, he's *somethin'*!' cried Mrs Lafferty.

'Please, dear Erin.'

'Nevertheless,' continued Cyrus. 'The order for that end-user contract was approved by the head honcho of the Arms Control Commission, whom I had personally alerted in writing through a diplomatic relay I never met. One big lousy government appointee with his hand in the till never let my initial suspicions reach the rest of the commission. I was – forgive the term – blacked out, and it had nothing to do with my colour because analytical reports do not include such information.'

'How is your experience in Stuttgart related to this evening's press conference at Logan Airport?' asked Pinkus.

'Coupled with everything I told your associates about the strange circumstances of this assignment, I have to go back to that sixth sense I denied because this *isn't* race oriented – it's corruption oriented, *government* corruption. One powerful man in Arms Control was capable of getting my black butt out of a German prison, where it would have stayed for fifty years if it lasted a month, by pressuring the Bonn courts and cutting a deal with me. Suddenly, there was silence, the voice of the turtle was the only sound heard about that chemical plant, and my bargain was to draw five and serve maybe one if I kept my mouth shut – all for appearances. And don't tell me palms weren't greased.'

'But you *did* cut the deal,' said Jennifer, not kindly. 'A convenient plea bargain.'

'I wasn't too tickled over being the only black in a German prison where a lot of the inmates are skinhead maniacs waiting for Adolf to rise from the dead.'

'I'm sorry, I understand. We, too, have developed a sixth sense.'

'No, please, don't apologize,' protested the mercenary softly. 'When I saw those films on the prison television, all those people put down by the chemicals I knew about, I was ashamed of myself.'

'Hey, come on, Colonel –'

'For God's sake, stop that, Counsellor. I'm no colonel.'

'No, I mean it!' continued Devereaux rapidly. 'What could you have done being incarcerated for fifty years, if you'd lasted fifty minutes with the skinheads?'

'That was my rationalization, and it's also why I broke out with Roman Z. This kind of crap has got to *stop*, man!'

'And you believe a variation of what you experienced is happening now to General Hawkins?' asked Aaron, leaning forward in his chair. 'The evidence being the newscast we just witnessed.'

'I'll tell you what I won't and *can't* believe is that there'd ever be a Nobel prize for the Soldier of the Century. Secondly, why did this so-called committee fly into Boston, the only airport in the vicinity where you've already been attacked, which means you've been tracked by superior high-tech government intelligence. Thirdly, that quartet of confused psychopathic crazies who tried to take you in Hooksett were strictly out-of-sanction moronic lowlifes – someone you'll never find bribed a stockade warden is my guess. *You* figured that out by a stencilled prison laundry mark inside a pair of trousers and sent them back in body bags.'

'Goddamned slugs!' roared MacKenzie Hawkins. 'What we sent back was a *message*! . . . Will somebody tell me what we're *talking* about?'

'We'll fill you in later, Mac,' answered Sam, his hand on Cyrus's shoulder. 'If I read you right,' said Devereaux, 'we have to find out who's now running this operation, am I correct?'

'You've got it,' said the mercenary. 'Because the assault on you in New Hampshire may have the same origins but they've gone upscale – maybe too upscale, and that means they could be vulnerable.'

'Why do you say that?' asked Pinkus.

'These came in on Air Force Two,' replied Cyrus. 'They're foreign civilians accorded the second highest aircraft in the country, which means it has to be cleared by one of three sources: the White House, which we can dismiss because they've got enough trouble with that kid; the CIA, which we should reject out of hand, 'cause half the country rightfully thinks the initials mean *Caught In the Act*, and they probably wouldn't risk another embarrassment; and lastly the State Department, which nobody knows what the hell they're doing but they do it anyway. My guess is one of the last two; and if we can find out which it is, we'll narrow down the possible people who could order out that plane. Among them is the big bad cannon.'

'Perhaps both the Department of State *and* the CIA?' suggested Pinkus.

'No way. The Agency doesn't trust State and vice versa. Also, there's too much risk of leaks by combining forces.'

'Suppose we find out it's one or the other?' asked Sam. 'What then?'

'We shake the bones of every conceivable Washington big

shot until they rattle. We have to find out who's behind this operation – I mean really nail him or her down: name, rank and serial number – because it's the only way to insure your safety.'

'*How?*'

'Exposure, Sam,' said Jennifer. 'We're still a nation of laws, not maniacs in Washington.'

'Who says?'

'Moot point,' agreed Redwing. 'What should we do, Cyrus?'

'The optimum would be to send someone impersonating the general to that hotel they mentioned, with me and Roman Z as his civilian aides. It's standard that a retired general with two Congressionals would have aides.'

'What about Desis One and Two?' asked Aaron. 'They'll be hurt.'

'*Why*? They'd be with the real Hawkins.'

'Oh, of course. This feeble mind is ageing. Everything's happening so fast.'

'Also, they're good boys and you people should be covered here.' Cyrus stopped, suddenly aware of Eleanor Devereaux's withering stare from the couch. 'Man, that lady doesn't like me,' he whispered.

'She doesn't know you,' said Sam in a low voice. 'Once she does, she'll make a large donation to the United Negro College Fund, I promise.'

'Sure, a black mercenary is a terrible thing to waste . . . *Damn*, there's no one here who could pass for the general. We've got to think of something else.'

'Wait a minute!' broke in Pinkus. 'Shirley and I support the local theatre groups – she likes to have her picture taken at the opening nights. There's a particular favourite, an elderly performer who's been in a great many Broadway plays; he's in what you might say, semi-retirement. I'm sure I could convince him to help us out, for a fee, of course . . . But only, of course, if he was completely safe.'

'You have my word on that, sir,' said Cyrus. 'No possible

harm could come to him, because Roman Z and I will be on either side of him.'

'An *actor*?' exclaimed Devereaux. 'That's *crazy*!'

'In truth, he frequently appears a touch that way.' The telephone rang on the table beside Aaron's chair; instantly he picked it up. 'Yes? . . . It's for you, Sam. I believe it's your maid, cousin Cora.'

'Oh, my *God*, I forgot all about her!' said Devereaux, walking around the table to the phone.

'I didn't,' interrupted Eleanor. 'I spoke to her last night, but I didn't tell her where we were or give her this number.'

'*Cora*,' cried Sam. 'How are . . . you *talked* to her, Mother? Why didn't you tell me?'

'You didn't ask. However, everything's fine at the house. The police have been around constantly and I think she's been feeding the entire force.'

'Cora? Mother says everything's all right over there.'

'The hoity-toity's fulla tea, Sammy. The damn phone's been ringing off the hook all day and nobody could or would tell me where the hell you were.'

'How did you find out?'

'Paddy Lafferty's daughter Bridget. She said Erin gave her this number in case there was any trouble with the grandkids.'

'That makes sense. What is it? Who's been calling me?'

'Not *you*, Sambo – everyone *but* you!'

'*Who*?'

'First that nut general you're always talking about, then that long-legged Indian girl who shouldn't be let out in the streets. And I tell ya, there's been at least twenty calls for each of 'em, all from the same two fellas, like every half hour or so.'

'What are their names?'

'One wouldn't tell me and the other you wouldn't believe. The first sounded panicky as all blazes, kinda like you get sometimes, Sammy. He keeps screaming that his sister should call her brother right away.'

'Okay, I'll tell her. What about the other guy, the one for the general?'

'Well, yer gonna think I've been nippin' again when you

hear it, but I ain't 'cause there's been too many cops around
... Boy, what a butcher's bill yer gonna get –'

'The name, Cora?'

'Johnny *Calfnose*, can you swallow that, Sammy?'

'Johnny Calfnose?' said Devereaux softly.

'*Calfnose* ... ?' gasped Jennifer.

'*Calfnose*!' shouted the Hawk. 'My security's been trying to
reach me? Get off the phone, Lieutenant!'

'My former client's trying to reach *me*!' cried Redwing,
colliding with the general as each ran to Sam.

'No!' yelled Devereaux, turning and holding the phone out
of reach. 'Calfnose is for Mac. Your *brother* wants you to call
him.'

'Give me that phone, boy!'

'*No*, me first!'

'If you'll all calm *down*,' said Pinkus, raising his voice. 'My
brother-in-law has at least three, possibly four, lines on his
phones, two at least for Shirley's sister, and there are
telephones all over the place. Just find one, each of you, and
push an unlit button.'

It was like a brief pandemonium during a kindergarten
recess as the Hawk and Jennifer raced around looking for
separate phones. Mac spotted one on the redwood porch, ran
to a glass door and whipped it open with a vibrating crash;
Redwing saw another on an antique white desk against the
rear wall and pounced on it. The subsequent cacophony of
voices shattered the stillness of the Swampscott evening.

'Bye, Cora.'

'*Charlie*, it's me!'

'Calfnose, it's *Thunder Head*!'

'You're kidding, little brother, tell me you're *kidding*!'

'Goddamn, *zero* hour minus four days!'

'You're not kidding ... ?'

'Send back my acceptance and sign it T. C. Chief of This
Nation's Most Oppressed People!'

'Send me an airline ticket to American Samoa, Charlie. I'll
meet you there.'

One in triumph, the other in defeat, the Hawk and Jennifer

hung up their respective phones. The general strode through the porch door like a commander of a Roman legion entering the gates of Carthage, while Redwing turned away from the elegant white desk as might a lost, delicate bird buffeted by unfriendly winds.

'What is it, my dear?' asked Aaron gently, obviously touched by Jennifer's demeanour.

'The worst,' she replied, barely audible. 'The elevator to hell.'

'Come now, Jennifer –'

'Lear jets and limousines, oil wells on Lexington Avenue and distilleries in Saudi Arabia.'

'Oh, my *God* . . . ' whispered Sam. 'The Supreme Court.'

'*Bull's-eye!*' roared the Hawk. 'All rounds blowing out the centre of the target! The *Supreme Court*.'

'Chu sendin' us back to *jail*?' cried Desi-One.

'*H'enerale*, why chu do dat?' said the stunned Desi-Two.

'You've it wrong, Captains. You're on your way up the Ranger ropes to fine military careers.'

'Everybody be *quiet!*' yelled Devereaux, somewhat startled to see that he was obeyed. 'All right, Red, you first. What did your brother say?'

'What the Cro-Magnon just confirmed. Charlie called Johnny Calfnose to see if everything was okay back there, and Johnny was crawling up the walls trying to find your over-the-hill mutant. A telegram arrived yesterday morning requiring an immediate reply, by phone or fax . . . General Bomb Balls, alias Thunder Nuts, is to appear in the Court's chambers to certify his tribal authority in five days from yesterday at three o'clock in the afternoon and present his case. It's all over but the long agonizing process of watching a people being destroyed. The Court's arguments are going public.'

'We did it, Sam! The old team hasn't lost its touch.'

'*Nothing!*' screamed Devereaux. 'I did absolutely *nothing*! I haven't anything to *do* with you.'

'Well, I hate to contradict you, son –'

'I'm *not* your son!'

'No, he's mine,' said Eleanor. 'Anybody want him?'

' . . . you *are* the legal attorney-of-record,' completed Hawkins, somewhat less loudly than before.

'*Oh* no, that invitation was for you, *not* me!'

'Wrong again, Counsellor,' said Jennifer disconsolately. 'You've replaced not only my unauthorized brother but me at the whim of your Ape Man. Charlie was very clear, as well as personally relieved. The invitation included one Samuel L. Devereaux, Esquire, attorney for the Wopotami tribe.'

'They can't *do* that!'

'They did, and Charlie wants to thank whoever S. L. Devereaux is with all his heart. As he put it, "I'd love to buy that asshole a drink, but I don't think he's going to live long enough."'

'General,' said the quiet voice of Cyrus M, his following words like cracks of muted thunder. 'Do we forget the Soldier of the Century?'

The Hawk's face went white; his eyes roamed in short spastic movements seeing nothing, bespeaking only the furies of his inner conflict. 'Oh, Jesus and Caesar!' he murmured gutturally as he sank into the chair across from Pinkus. 'My God, what do I *do*?'

'It's a trap, sir, I sincerely believe that,' added the huge black mercenary.

'Suppose you're *wrong*?'

'There's nothing in the Nobel committee's history to support that kind of error.'

'*History*? For Christ's sake, man, there's nothing in the last forty years of history to support the tearing down of the Berlin Wall or the breaking up of the Eastern bloc! Things are changing everywhere.'

'Some things don't change. Stockholm doesn't change.'

'*Goddamn*, Colonel, I've given my life, *devoted* my life to the army and got screwed by the panty-laced, pricky-shit politicians! Do you know what that award would mean to me – to every man who served under me in three *wars*!'

'Just a minute, General.' Cyrus looked over at Devereaux. 'May I ask you a question – Sam . . . and may I call you Sam, since I think we're beyond the hired-guard situation.'

'"Massa" doesn't fit, from either side. Sure, what is it?'

'Does this trap, as I know damn well it is, have anything to do with this Supreme Court thing you're all yelling about? I understand your security, but you need my help, and in all conscience, I can't professionally give it without knowing more than I do. As a chemist, I demanded accurate component equations from my subordinates; as a merc, I have to know the fundamental components, period, in order to act accordingly.'

Devereaux turned first to Aaron, who nodded without hesitation, then looked at Jennifer, who paused, then nodded reluctantly. Finally, Sam walked over to Eleanor on the couch. 'Mother, it would please me greatly if you and Mrs Lafferty could find something to do in the kitchen.'

'Call Cora,' said the grande dame of Weston, Massachusetts, without moving.

'Hey, come on, fancy-dan girl!' cried Erin Lafferty. 'I gotta get rid of the salad bowl and you can make us some *tea*! Guess what I found, Mrs Great One? Hennessy, VSOP!'

'She's been talking to our shameless cousin,' said Eleanor, instantly rising. 'It *is* quite past time for tea, isn't it? Come along, Aaron, we'll do tea.'

'That's *Erin*, Missy –'

'Yes, of course, you don't look at all Jewish. Do you like camomile?'

'No, I like Hennessy.'

'Definitely, Cora. Have you known her long?'

'Well, she's from the Roman side and I'm the other, but we get together on this committee we formed to try to get those idiots together –'

'We'll discuss it all over tea, Errol, and perhaps I'll join your committee. Of course, I'm High Anglican.'

'Cora couldn't spell it.' The two ladies, arm in arm, walked through the kitchen door.

'*Desis* One and Two,' said Sam. 'Will you *stop* looking like that! Everything General Mac promised you will happen – believe me I know, both the good and the bad, and yours is only good.'

'*Privado*,' explained the Hawk. '*Confidencial, usted comprende?*'

'Sure, man, we go out with the *romano gitano*. He's crazy, y'know, man? He spins around a lot and always he's smiling. But, he's gotta be good in the streets, y'know what I mean? We could do good together.'

'*Bear* in mind, my *captains*!' shouted MacKenzie, 'You are now under *my* command! No more *streets*; no more muggings, no more thievery and no more hostility to civilians! Haven't you learned a goddamned *thing*?'

'Chu right, h'enerale,' answered Desi the First contritely. 'Sometimes we just slip back widdout t'inking. We're gentlemen an' h'officers now, so we godda t'ink different. Chu right . . . We go outside wid the *loco gitano*.' Desis One and Two walked into the tiled foyer and out the front door.

'What was that all about?' asked Cyrus, looking at the deserted foyer. 'I understood the Spanish, but not your "command" and the fact that they were captains? In what army?'

'In the *Army* of the United States, Colonel – oh, sorry, you don't like that . . . Let's say I'm training 'em up, because we could do a lot worse.'

'Never mind, General,' said the mercenary, shaking his head. 'It's beyond me, and at this moment, I'd rather concentrate on – this moment, on where we are. Will someone explain?'

Glances were exchanged, but it was Jennifer Redwing, daughter of the Wopotamis, who held up her hand and insisted on speaking. She described everything they knew about the Wopotami brief to the Supreme Court, then persuasively outlined what she believed was the forthcoming destruction of the Wopotamis as a result of the Court's action, whichever way it went.

'With merely the spectre of the suit, the entire federal government will react furiously, making our people out to be traitors and pariahs, and setting in motion the condemnation of our land, shutting down the reservation and dispersing all those living there. Washington *has* to, for the absolute preservation of the Strategic Air Command is uppermost, and not exactly secondmost is the army of defence contractors – hell, the Pentagon itself – who will be calling for our blood ... On the other side, there'll be hordes of carpetbaggers of every persuasion, descending on the tribe and corrupting everyone in sight, hoping for a hunk of the improbable but potential legal pie, or publicity, but all with their eyes on the bottom line. My God, there'll be more Rainbow Coalitions after a dollar than there are colours in a Jackson Pollock, and every bit as wild ... Finally, there'll be nothing left of us but censure and decadence, a people surfeited with slander, greed and rot, ultimately losing the no-win fight and discarded. That's not what I want for my brothers and sisters, whom I dearly love ... There, I've said it, and I hope you were listening, General Genghis Gun-in-the-Cookie-Jar.'

'Except for your final comment,' said Aaron Pinkus, riveted in his chair. 'That was a lovely summation ... I make no judgment about that comment, my dear, merely its effect on a jury which, I suspect, would be negative.'

'I don't know about that, Commander.' MacKenzie Hawkins sat motionless, his eyes locked with those of the Wopotami daughter. 'I figure I'm part of the jury here, and it had a pretty positive effect on me.'

'What do you mean, Mac?' asked Devereaux, from his expression obviously anticipating the unexpected.

'May I present my side, little lady,' said the Hawk, rising to his feet. ' ... Excuse me, you're not "little" in any sense, but you are a lady, and I mean no disrespect by the term.'

'Go ahead,' said Jennifer icily.

'I started this enterprise nearly three years ago with a few thoughts in my head, none of them too damned clear because I'm a soldier, not a thinker, except where military strategy's concerned. What I mean by that is I'm no intellectual, and I don't waste a lot of time trying to analyse things like motive or morality or justification and all the rest of that stuff. If I did, I would have lost a hell of a lot more fine young men in combat than my record shows ... Surely, I was looking for a magnificent score – I can't think small – because that kind of challenge appeals to this *discarded* old soldier. Also, it had to be fun and somebody who did or was doing something wrong should pick up the tab. I guess what I'm trying to say is that I never intended to hurt the *means* to the payoff, only those who found it necessary to *pay*, namely those who did something wrong.'

'But you *are* hurting the "means,"' interrupted Jennifer angrily. '*Namely*, my people and you damn well know it!'

'May I finish, please? ... When I learned what had happened to the Wopotamis over a hundred years ago, it kinda reminded me of what had happened to me – and with what I can piece together about Colonel Cyrus here – what happened to him ... We were all sacrificed by government big shots, who either had their hands in the *real* cookie jar or were furthering their own political ambitions, or who were just plain liars abusing the trust that had been placed in 'em! It doesn't matter whether it was a century ago, a decade ago, three months ago or yesterday. In the words of our mercenary friend here, it's got to *stop*! We've got the best system of living together the world has ever known, but there's always somebody trying to louse it up.'

'None of us is running in the angelic sweepstakes, Mac,' said Devereaux softly.

'Hell, no, Sam, but nobody elected us or appointed us and had us swear under oath to behave ourselves for the benefit of a couple of hundred million people we don't know. Now if the colonel here is right, there's somebody else way high up trying to stop a citizen – not just me, but a *citizen* – from carrying out his constitutional right to appear before the court. There we go again! ... And if our friend here who doesn't like to be called "Colonel" is wrong, and I really am the Soldier of the Century – well, I couldn't accept that grand award if I knew I walked away from finding out whether there *is* or there *isn't* some big government cannon trying to stop that citizen who happens to be me.'

'Rather well done, General,' said Aaron, leaning back in the chair. 'Actually, for a man unschooled in the law, quite remarkable.'

'What do you mean "unschooled," Mr Pinkus?' objected Jennifer, in her tone perhaps a touch of jealousy. 'He wrote the damned brief.'

'I submit he constructed it, my dear. Painstakingly adapting textbook terms and phrases to suit his points. That's translation, not creation.'

'And I submit,' said Sam, 'a certain ego aside, this is irrelevant.' He turned to the Hawk. 'But I'm puzzled by a few items you didn't bring up, and if they don't prove to you that somebody pretty damned important is trying to stop all of us, I don't know what the hell will. May I remind you –'

'*Son*, I'm way ahead of you,' interrupted Hawkins quickly, firmly. 'You're referring to the previous assaults.'

'Right on, Mac. The two hotels, a black Maria racing out to my house, and four armed-to-the-teeth military gorillas at the ski lodge. Who sent *them*? The tooth fairy?'

'We never would have found out, boy, take my word for it. You don't know how these things are put together – with mirrors and smoke and so many blind relays it'd take longer than the Iran-contra thing to find out who's where and what's his function. *Hell*, Sam, I invented those procedures behind half a hundred enemy lines. That's why I did what I did and in each case sent back the message that they couldn't *do* it!'

'I'm afraid I don't understand,' said a bewildered Aaron.

'Neither do I,' added a perplexed Jennifer.

'Are you people lawyers or *shoe* clerks?' cried MacKenzie in exasperation. 'If you're in the middle of a life-or-death trial and you need information you know is there but nobody wants to give it to you, how do you get it?'

'Vigorous cross-examination,' replied Pinkus.

'With heavy emphasis on perjury,' again added Redwing.

'Well, I suppose you've got your points, but we're not operating in a courtroom. There's another way –'

'You *provoke* it,' said Devereaux, interrupting, his eyes briefly, amusingly in contact with the Hawk's. 'You make an outrageous statement, or a series of statements, that elicit a hostile response that confirms the information.'

'*Goddamn*, Sam, I always said you were the best! Remember

London, in Belgrave Square, where I told you how to handle that scumbag traitor –'

'We will *not* refer to your previous relationship, General!' ordered Aaron. 'We don't care to hear a *thing* about it.'

'It's also irrelevant,' said a defensive Jennifer.

'Oh, *I* see!' exclaimed Sam, grinning falsely at his Indian Aphrodite. 'You can't *stand* it when I come up with something you haven't thought of!'

'*Irrelevant!*'

'When these two children stop squabbling,' said Pinkus, 'will you please explain your strategy, General?'

'If the colonel here – *my* colonel – is right, the explanation's sitting on a runway at Logan Airport. *Air Force Two*, Commander! Who sent it? . . . Unless, of course, I really am the Soldier of the Century, in which case we're back in an invasion landing craft without a motor, drifting into a heavily fortified beach without manoeuvrable protection.'

'I won't try to follow that, but –' Suddenly, Aaron stopped, turning his head in several directions until he saw what was missing. It was the mercenary, Cyrus M, his bulk filling an antique chair by the elegant antique white desk, his mouth gaping, his wide dark eyes staring at them. 'Oh, there you are, Colonel.'

'*What?*'

'Have you been listening?'

Cyrus nodded his large head and answered slowly, precisely. 'Yes, I've been listening, Mr Pinkus,' he began quietly, 'and I've just heard the most extraordinary story since a few clowns claimed nuclear fusion could be accomplished in ice water for twelve cents a gallon . . . You people are *nuts*! You're crazy, insane, *certifiable*! . . . Is any of this *true*?'

'It's all true, Cyrus,' said Devereaux.

'What the *fuck* have I gotten *into*?' roared the giant black chemist. ' . . . Excuse my language, Miss Redwing, I'm trying to put it all into an equation and it's not easy.'

'No apologies are necessary, Cyrus, and why don't you call me Jenny? I'm a little put off by the "Miss."'

'Voodoo,' said the mercenary, getting out of the chair, but

conscience stricken enough to look down and see if he had broken it. 'If it's true,' he continued, walking toward the trio of attorneys and the manic 'Soldier of the Century,' whose intense expression obviously caused Cyrus extreme discomfort. ' . . . if it *is* true, I don't think there's any alternative but to test out this Nobel committee. Hire your actor, Mr Pinkus. We're going on stage.'

CHAPTER TWENTY-ONE

Truce had descended on the beach house in Swampscott, Massachusetts, a fitting prelude to the battles ahead. Under the neutral guidance of Aaron Pinkus, a document was drawn up between General MacKenzie Hawkins, aka Thunder Head, current chief of the Wopotamis, and Sunrise Jennifer Redwing, ad hoc spokeswoman for said American Indian tribe, wherein all powers of attorney were transferred to Ms Redwing upon signatures and notarization. Samuel Lansing Devereaux, temporary attorney-of-record, consented to relinquish all duties following a joint appearance with the tribe's permanent attorney, the aforementioned Ms Redwing, before the Supreme Court of the United States, should such a joint appearance be required.

'I'm not sure I like the last part,' Jennifer had declared.

'I don't like it at all!' said Sam.

'Then I don't sign.' The Hawk had been adamant. 'To change attorneys at the last minute could be a glitch, a delay, and I've put too much blood, sweat, money and tolerance into this enterprise to accept that. Besides, Miss Red, I've given you full control over all negotiations, so *what* the – what the dickens *more* do you want?'

'What more? ... No appearance at all, no brief, no Supreme Court.'

'Come now, my dear,' said Aaron. 'It's too late for that. Not only is the hearing on the Court's calendar, but you could be losing a genuine opportunity for your people. Surely, with yourself in charge, that elevator to hell can be short-circuited.'

'Yes, of course,' agreed Jennifer. 'If there really is serious consideration, a quick settlement with the Bureau of Indian Affairs, perhaps two or three million dollars and life goes on, no waves. We could build four or five schools on the reservation and hire some fine teachers –'

'I *definitely* do not sign!' had roared the Hawk.

'Why, General? Isn't it enough to pay you off?'

'Pay me off? Who the hell said anything about paying me *anything*? I don't need money – Sam and I have more than we can ever spend in Switzerland!'

'*Mac*, shut *up*!'

' . . . all legally obtained from the scum of the earth who I can assure you will never sue us for it!'

'*Enough*, General!' Aaron Pinkus sprang – as best he could – to his feet. 'There'll be no further references, audible or written, to previous events of which we know nothing.'

'Fine by me, Commander, but I'll still make my position clear. I haven't spent three years of my life to settle for a few dollars any SAC supplier would give us out of petty cash.'

'*Us?*' exclaimed Jennifer. 'I thought you didn't want anything.'

'I'm not talking about me, I'm talking about the principle involved.'

'How do you spell that?' asked Redwing sarcastically. 'As in the interest on your principal?'

'You know what I mean, little lady. You're selling out the tribe – *my* tribe incidentally.'

'What did you have in mind, Mac?' had said Devereaux, knowing the futility of trying to change the Hawk's mind – in principle.

'We'll start at five hundred million, a nice round figure – nothing but spit to the Pentagon – and a hell of a cheap buy-out.'

'Five *hundred* –' Jennifer's bronzed face had grown darker as the blood rushed to her head. 'You're a *madman*!'

'You can always scale back your artillery, but you can't bring it up if there's none in reserve . . . Yup, five hundred mega-big ones or I don't sign. Maybe we should put that in there, Commander, like an addendum or whatever you call it.'

'That would be unwise, General,' said Pinkus, glancing at Sam. 'If ever examined, it could be construed as a precondition bordering on collusion.'

'Then I want a separate paper,' said MacKenzie, frowning. 'She's not going to sell *my* people down the dark river of the evil spirits.'

'*Your* . . . oh, my God!' Jennifer sank down on the couch. 'The dark river of the . . . oh, *shit*.'

'We elders strongly disapprove of such language from our squaws.'

'I'm *not* a . . . oh, forget it! . . . Five *hundred* – I can't even *think* about it! We'll be ruined, devastated, our land condemned and bought from us for nothing, taxpayers outraged, editorials in all the media denouncing us as ignorant savages and thieves –'

'Miss Redwing,' had interrupted Aaron, his use of the title, her last name, and his stern voice causing Jenny to look questioningly at the renowned attorney who had become so friendly to her.

'Yes . . . Mr Pinkus?'

'I shall prepare a Memorandum of Intent, stating quite clearly that you will, on a supreme best-efforts basis, initiate the negotiations – if and when such negotiations take place – according to the wishes of Chief Thunder Head, also known as General MacKenzie Hawkins. Do you accept this heavy responsibility?'

'*Hell* –' Jennifer was about to say *Hell, yes!*, but the glint in Aaron's eyes stopped her. 'Very well, sir, no more off-colour language. I know when I've been beaten by superior litigiousity. I'll sign both documents.'

'That's better, little lady,' said the Hawk, lighting a frayed cigar by lifting his leg and pulling a safety match against the right thigh of his buckskins. 'You'll see, Miss Red, the responsibility of command doesn't stop with a single victory. We go on and on and *on*, always looking after the fine troops who follow us!'

'That's very encouraging, General,' said Jennifer, smiling sweetly.

'You're both all hearts and smarts,' said Sam. 'Especially you, Pocahontas.'

So Aaron Pinkus had gone into his brother-in-law's office at the beach house and called his personal secretary, telling her to have Paddy Lafferty drive her out to Swampscott and to bring her notary seal. The grey-haired lady had arrived, her eyes red and heavy-lidded, no doubt the results of some rampant 'flu, and proceeded to type out the two documents. They were ceremoniously signed, and as Aaron courteously led his obviously ill secretary to the front door, thanking her for her acceding to his needs despite her condition, the slightly unfocused woman asked, 'Do you know someone named Bricky, Mr Pinkus? He's been asking for you.'

'Bricky? . . . Is there a last name?'

'I'm not sure I got it – it seemed to change.'

'You're not well, my dear. I want you to take several days off and I'll have my doctor look in on you. Abraham, forgive me, I *do* overwork you.'

'He was a very handsome young man. Shining dark hair, impeccably dressed –'

'Be careful now, watch your step.'

'He kept wanting to know where you were –'

'Easy now, there are two steps down to the flagstones . . . *Paddy*, are you there?'

'Right here, boss!' came Lafferty's reply from the circular drive as the chauffeur emerged from the shadows and ran up the path to the porch. 'Y'know, I think she's a bit under the weather, Mr Pinkus.'

'It's the 'flu, Paddy.'

'If you say so, sir.' Lafferty took the secretary, pulling her left arm around his shoulders as he helped her down toward the car.

'*Bricky is my darling, my darling, my darling . . . !*' The words floated up in song, fading into the tall pines that bordered the circular drive. ' *. . . he's the only boy for me – only boy for me!*'

Relieved, Aaron turned back to the front door, prepared to go inside, when he stopped, his head cocked in bewilderment . . . *Bricky?* . . . *Binky?* . . . Binghamton *Aldershot*, otherwise known as *Binky* on the Cape, the nearest thing Boston had to an international financier, hiding behind the iron gates of his Beacon Hill bank? ... Wasn't there a nephew somewhere? A youngish womanizer with a similar nickname, whom the Aldershots kept on a tenuous financial tether, if only to keep the idiot from embarrassing the family ... No, it was *impossible*. His personal secretary of fifteen years was a mature woman, previously a novitiate who had turned away from her vows, opting for a more worldly world, but withal a woman deeply committed to her faith. *Ridiculous*. A coincidence. Pinkus had opened the door and stepped into the foyer only to hear the telephone ring.

'*Okay*, Cyrus!' Sam Devereaux had yelled into the phone. 'Remember, he's an *actor*, so don't lose your temper, okay? Just bring him out here ... *What?* He wants a contract stipulating that he has star *billing*? ... With who – *what?* His name in print ... above and in equal size in type to that of the *title*? Holy shit! ... What about money, has he made any demands there? ... *Nothing*, just his *billing*? Christ, write out whatever he wants and get him here! ... A "run-of-the-play," no dismissal during rehearsals without full compensation? What the fuck does *that* mean? ... I don't know, either, but put it into his contract.'

An hour and twenty-two minutes later, the front door opened and the orange-shirted gypsy with the long blue sash around his waist lunged into the foyer, balletically spinning until he reached the entrance to the huge living room where the three attorneys and General MacKenzie Hawkins sat in a semi-circle. All heads turned as Roman Z made his announcement.

'Beautiful, *beautiful* lady, and you gentlemen of – well, adequate appearance. I now present to you Colonel Cyrus, a man with the strength of a Mediterranean tree, who has an announcement.'

'*Enough about him!*' came the whisper, hissed from the dark foyer. '*It's me, you bounder!*'

The enormous and embarrassed figure of the black mercenary appeared. 'Hi, there, folks,' said Cyrus, as tongue-tied as a normally confident man could be. 'I would like to introduce an artist who has appeared in many of the great Broadway shows of our time, whose brilliant reviews have been abash in our land –'

'*That's "awash," you idiot!*'

'An actor of supreme depth and widespread perversity –'

'*Di – dye – versity, you ass!*'

'Hell, man, I'm doing the best I *can* –'

'*Long introductions, inadequately presented, kill an entrance. Get out of my way!*'

The tall lean man swept down the short steps into the living room with a flair and an energy that belied his age. With grey, flowing hair, sharp features, and glaring eyes that bespoke a thousand such electric entrances on stage, he stunned the small group in front of him, as he had done with countless full houses in the past. His gaze settled upon Aaron Pinkus; he approached the attorney with a courtly bow.

'You have summoned me, sire, and I have obeyed. Your servant and boldest knight-errant, m'lord!'

'Why, *Henry*,' said Aaron, getting out of his chair and shaking hands with the actor. 'That was just wonderful! It reminded me of when you did your one-man show for Shirley's Hadassah, the excerpt from *The Student Prince*, I believe.'

'I don't remember too many of the smaller – forgive me – my out-of-town performances, dear boy . . . However, I think it must have been six and a half years ago roughly – on March twelfth, if I'm not mistaken, at two o'clock in the afternoon. I vaguely recall it for I don't believe I was in my best voice that day.'

'You certainly were, you were splendid . . . Here, let me introduce you to my friends –'

'My C-sharp wasn't full,' continued the actor, 'but then the piano player was dreadful . . . You were saying, Aaron?'

'My friends, I'd like you to meet them.'

'I certainly wish to, especially this adorable creature.' Sir Henry reached for Jennifer's left hand and brought it to his lips, his eyes looking into hers as he gently kissed the back of her palm. 'You make me immortal by your touch, sweet Helena . . . Have you ever thought of a theatrical career?'

'No, but I once did a little modelling,' replied Redwing, not only caught off guard but modestly enjoying the moment.

'A step, dear child, merely a step, but in the right direction. Perhaps we should lunch one day. I give private lessons, the fees in certain cases, shall we say, dismissible.'

'She's a lawyer, for God's sake!' said Sam, not entirely sure why he was so adamant.

'That's a terrible waste,' said the actor, slowly releasing the hand in his grip. 'As the Bard put it in Henry Six, Two, "First we kill all the lawyers" . . . Not you, of course, Aaron, for you have the soul of an artist.'

'Yes, well, let me introduce you, Henry. The actress – the *attorney* – is Miss Redwing.'

'*Enchantez encore, mademoiselle –*'

'Before you maul her hand again, I'm Sam Devereaux, and I'm also an attorney.'

'Shakespeare had his insights –'

'And this gentleman in Indian attire is General MacKenzie Hawkins –'

'Oh, *you're* the one!' exclaimed the performer, grabbing the Hawk's hand and shaking it firmly. 'I saw that film about you – how could you *stand* it? Didn't you have any control over the casting, the script? *My God*, man, that jackass playing you should have worn lipstick!'

'I think he did,' said the general warily, but not unimpressed.

'Everyone,' interrupted Pinkus. 'I want you to meet Henry Irving Sutton, as in England's Sutton Place, his ancestral home, and frequently referred to in the newspapers as Sir Henry Irving S, after the great Elizabethan actor to whom he's often compared. An outstanding artist of the stage –'

'Who says?' said Sam petulantly.

'Small minds make for large doubters,' answered Henry Irving Sutton, looking bemused at Devereaux.

'Who said *that*, Felix the Cat?'

'No, it was a French playwright named Anouilh. I doubt you've heard of him.'

'Oh *yeah*? How about "There's nothing left to do but scream!" ... *Huh?* How about that?'

'*Antigone*, but your translation's inaccurate.' Sutton turned to Hawkins. 'General, do me a favour – I ask it as a former second lieutenant in the African *TO* where I heard you speak many times, as often as not railing against Montgomery.'

'*You* were there?'

'Combat Intelligence, attached to OSS-Tobruk.'

'You boys were the *best*! You had those Krauts buffaloed in the big Sahara. They didn't know where our tanks were!'

'Most of us were actors who could speak a little German. Really, we were overrated – it was so easy to portray soldiers dying of thirst and sputtering wrong information while going into comas. Actually, very simple.'

'You were in the enemy's uniforms. You could have been *shot*!'

'Perhaps, but where do you get a chance to *play* such parts?'

'Well, I'll be goddamned! Whatever you want, soldier, I'll *do* it.'

'Screwed again,' mumbled Devereaux. 'He does this to me all the time.'

'I want you to speak, General, preferably reciting something we both might know, say a piece of doggerel or a poem, or perhaps the words of a song, repeating whatever you like. Also, talk normally or shout, whatever's natural.'

'Let's see, now,' said the Hawk, squinting. 'I've always been kinda partial to the old army standby, you know the one. "Over hill, over dale, we will hit the *dustee trail*" –'

'Don't *sing*, General, just talk it through,' ordered the actor, his facial expressions instantly parroting those of MacKenzie, sounds softly emerging as the old war-horse martially peeled off the words of 'The Caissons Go Rolling Along.' Then, suddenly, as though the two voices of a roundelay were merged, one fading, the other surviving, Henry Irving Sutton was speaking alone, his vocal tone and cadences, his body gestures and facial contortions, nearly indistinguishable from the Hawk's.

'*Goddamn!*' exclaimed the general, as bewildered as he was astonished.

'*Remarkable*, Henry!'

'Not bad, if I do say so.'

'You're a *terrific* actor, Mr Sutton!'

'Oh, no, dear child of Elysium,' protested Sir Henry Irving S modestly. 'That's not acting, it's merely mimicry, which any second-rate comic can do. You're fooled by the gestures and the expressions as much as you are by the vocal intonations ... I explain this thoroughly in my private lessons. Lunch?'

'Why the hell didn't they get *you* to play my part in that goddamn movie?'

'A dreadful agent, *mon general*, you have no idea what it's like ... Picture an outstanding staff officer who is not permitted to show his mettle in battle because his so-called superior is afraid his organization will fall apart – in my case it was a steady salary from a soap.'

'I'd have the bastard *shot!*'

'I tried that. Fortunately, I missed ... Lunch, Miss Redwing?'

'I think we should get down to the business at hand,' said Pinkus firmly, gesturing at the chairs and the sofa for everyone to use. They did so, Sam rushing to sit between Jennifer and Sutton.

'Of course, Aaron,' agreed the actor, glaring at the interloper. 'I merely wanted to assuage a small mind that apparently belongs in the Lesser Antilles, if you catch the mixed metaphor.'

'It's singularly apparent, Kermit the Frog,' said Devereaux. '*Sam!*'

'Okay, Jenny, I'm overreacting. I never do that in court.'

'*Business?*' Pinkus signalled Cyrus, who was purposely staying as far away from Henry Irving S as possible, the ride out from Boston with the actor having tried his patience, if not his sanity. 'Should your colleague join us?' asked Aaron.

'I'll tell him everything he should know,' said Cyrus quietly, sitting down. 'I'd like to keep this as simple as possible. Frankly, the combo of Roman Z and your new recruit doesn't appear to be the most stable. I'll handle it.'

'You have a fine deep voice, young man,' interrupted Sir Henry, obviously annoyed that he could not overhear Cyrus and the elderly attorney. 'Have you ever sung "Ole Man River"?'

'Get off my case, man,' said the mercenary.

'No, I'm quite serious. A revival of *Showboat* –'

'Henry, my friend, all that can come later,' Aaron broke in, holding up both hands in dissuasion. 'We haven't much time.'

'Of course, dear boy, the curtain must go up.'

'As soon as possible,' concurred Cyrus. 'Even tonight, *preferably* tonight, if we can.'

'How do you think we should proceed?' asked Jennifer.

'I can make contact with this so-called Nobel committee at that hotel as the general's civilian aide,' answered the mercenary. 'I've got decent clothes in my suitcase, but we've got to get something for Roman to wear.'

'My brother-in-law has a closet full of clothes and he's roughly your colleague's size – he lifts weights, even at his age. Also, Mrs Lafferty's an excellent seamstress –'

'Then that's settled,' interrupted the impatient Cyrus. 'We'd just have to refine my story for reaching those clowns from *Air Force Two*.'

'I've already done that,' said Mackenzie Hawkins, re-lighting his mangled cigar.

'*What?*'

'*How?*'

'*When?*'

The tumult of stunned voices assaulted the Hawk, who merely raised his bushy eyebrows and blew a circle of smoke above his face.

'*Please*, General!' pressed Cyrus. 'This is important. What did you *do*?'

'You lawyers and chemists think you're so smart, but you've got damn short memories.'

'Mac, for Christ's sake –'

'Especially you, Sam. You're the one who figured it out; of course, I was ahead of you but I was proud of your off-scene analysis.'

'What the hell are you talking about?'

'Little Joseph, boy! He's still there –'

'Who? . . . *Where?*'

'That hotel, the Four Seasons. I talked to him a half hour ago and he's on top of things.'

'On top of *what*? You can't trust that little bastard, Mac, you said so yourself!'

'I can now,' said the Hawk emphatically. 'He flagrantly abuses his per diem privileges, a sure sign of an independent subordinate, and he tries repeatedly to provoke me – that's a man you can have some faith in.'

'The logic escapes me,' said Pinkus.

'He's crazy,' said Jennifer softly, her wide, disbelieving eyes on the general.

'I'm not so sure about that,' said Cyrus. 'A hostile underling tells you where you stand. You're not likely to get fragged by him because he's done just that.'

'You're crazy, too,' observed Devereaux.

'Not really.' The mercenary shook his head. 'There's a maxim that goes back to the Cossack wars. "You kiss the boot before you hack it off with your sabre."'

'I like it, I *like* it,' cried the actor. 'A perfect second-act curtain!'

'Maybe I'm crazy, too,' added the daughter of the Wopotamis, 'but I think I understand that.'

'I would hope so,' said Sam sardonically. 'To clarify, Counsellor, one does not throw suspicion on oneself before committing a crime.'

'Smart ass,' muttered Redwing. 'I see your point, Cyrus, so what do we do?'

'The question is, what has the general *done*?'

'It's quite acceptable,' said the Hawk. 'And considering your background, I think you'll approve . . . I've instructed Little Joseph, who, although advanced in years, is a born infantry scout, to survey the situation from all points of the

352

battleground. He'll check out their bivouacs, the whereabouts of support troops and their firepower, if there are any, your escape routes, if necessary, and the best camouflage you can employ reaching zero target.'

'Zero *what?*' exclaimed Sir Henry.

'No, *no*, Henry, I'm sure the general's exaggerating!' interrupted Pinkus, staring at MacKenzie, then shifting his intense gaze to Cyrus. 'You guaranteed there'd be no violence, no lack of safety procedures!'

'There won't be, on either count, Mr Pinkus. The general's merely using military terms to describe this so-called committee's hotel rooms and the proper attire –'

'You misunderstood *me*, Aaron, dear boy!' The actor rose to his feet, his profile (that's 'profeel') to the right, his jaw firm, his eyes glowing. 'I welcome the assignment, a glorious pursuit – whatever it is. Remember, General, when we joined the Brits and slogged our way toward El Alamein!'

'Sure do, *Major* Sutton! . . . I just field-commissioned you up a couple of grades – command prerogative, of course.'

'I accept the rank, sir.' Sir Henry turned and saluted as the Hawk got out of his chair and did the same. 'Bring on the bastards! Once more into the breach and fill the walls up with our Equity dead – Screen Actors Guild and AFTRA, too, of course. We fear *no one* – gets the blood boiling, doesn't it, General?'

'You boys really *were* the best in the big Sahara. You had all the guts in the world, soldier.'

'Guts, be damned, it was the proper synthesis of classical technique and the best of Stanislavski, not that Method nonsense prescribed by fifth-rate gurus who teach that picking your nose is more acceptable than blowing it.'

'Whatever it was, Major, you survived. Do you recall outside Benghazi when the brigade –'

'They're *nuts!*' whispered Sam to Jennifer. 'They're in a typhoon paddling a canoe that's leaking.'

'Get hold of yourself, Sam! They're both . . . well, larger than life, and it's rather refreshing.'

'What do you mean by that?'

'Well, in a world of pin-striped legalizing wimps, it's nice to know there are men who can still hunt the killer tigers.'

'That's sophomoric, antediluvian bullshit!'

'Yes, I know,' said Redwing, smiling. 'Isn't it nice to see it's still around?'

'And you call yourself a liberated woman –'

'Although I am, I don't think I ever said it, *that's* antediluvian. These old men aren't, they're simply reliving a world as they knew it. I acknowledge that world and what they did to make it better, who wouldn't?'

'You're just brimming with Sunnybrook kindness, Rebecca!'

'Why not? The Court itself aside, I've won every point I raised. In fact, I won too damned much, which means *I'm* acknowledged.'

'With a little "mirrors and smoke," as our general called it. "Best efforts" is still euphemism for "Okay, I'll try, but if I don't get anywhere, I'll retreat. Fast."'

'You mention that and you'll find out how liberated I am, Counsellor,' said Jennifer quietly, again smiling. 'You won't have anything left to soil your trousers with . . . Let's break up the war stories, shall we?'

'*Mac!*' shouted Devereaux, causing both veterans of the North African campaign to look at him as though he were an ugly black worm emerging from a plate of red spaghetti. 'How do you really know this Little Joseph will do as you say? You've described a slime – maybe one who won't frag you – but still a *slime*. Suppose he tells you anything he figures you want to hear?'

'He couldn't do that, Sam. You see, I talked with his superior officer, who I can tell you is *very* superior, on a par with Commander Pinkus and myself – with maybe a mite more influence where it counts.'

'So what?'

'So this very important person has strong personal reasons for wanting us to complete our mission, which we can't do if we don't get to the Supreme Court in one piece eighty-seven hours from now and counting.'

'Eighty-seven what and what?' asked a confused Aaron.

'We're in the countdown, Commander. Ground zero in roughly eighty-seven hours minus.'

'Is that anything like "zero target"?' persisted the elderly lawyer.

'Can you imagine, Major Sutton, this fella was on Omaha Beach?'

'Probably an enlisted man, General –'

'Yes, I was, and I carried a rifle, not a code book.'

'Zero target, dear Aaron, is the immediate objective,' explained the actor. 'Ground zero, the zero not preceding, is the final objective. For instance, in the march to El Alamein we first had to take Tobruk, thus *it* was the zero target, Alamein ground zero. Actually, in the chronicles of Froissart – upon which Shakespeare based his Histories, along with Holinshed – mention is made of the terms –'

'Okay, *okay!*' cried an exasperated Devereaux. 'What the hell has all this crap got to do with some slime called Little Joseph at the Four Seasons? To repeat, Mac, what makes you think he'll do what you tell him to do? He's lied to you before.'

'Obviously different circumstances,' said Jennifer before the Hawk could reply. 'I gather he's beholden to his very important superior officer.'

'Bull's-eye, Miss Red. Like in whether Joseph goes on breathing or not.'

'Well, if that's the case –'

'It's the case, Sam,' confirmed Hawkins. 'As you well know, I don't make mistakes in that area. Outside of Belgrave Square in London, do I have to remind you of that country club on Long Island, or the chicken farm in Berlin, or that crazy sheik in Tizi Ouzou who wanted to buy my third wife for two camels and a small palace?'

'That will *do*, General!' said Pinkus firmly. 'I remind *you* that there'll be no reminiscing on such past events. Now, you and Henry sit down and let's continue with the business at hand.'

'Certainly, Commander.' The two veterans of El Alamein

sat down and the Hawk continued. 'But we can't do a hell of a lot until Little Joseph makes his report.'

'How's he going to do that?' asked Devereaux. 'Sending a coded message by a carrier pigeon that flies from his hotel window directly to the sheikdom of Tizi Ouzou?'

'No, son, by telephone.' And, as Sir Henry might say, on cue the telephone rang. 'I'll get it,' said the Hawk, rising and walking rapidly to the white antique desk against the wall. 'Base Camp Steaming Tepee,' he went on, the phone to his ear.

'Hey, *Fazool*,' came the excited voice of Little Joey the Shroud over the line. 'You ain't gonna *believe* the fuckin' pig-shit you walked into! I swear on the grave of my aunt Angelina, no shoe repair clown, including my uncle Guido, could scrape it off!'

'Calm down, Joseph, and speak clearly. Just give me the reconn ob-tech, on-scene factors.'

'What crazy language is that?'

'I'm surprised you don't remember it from the Italian campaign –'

'I was lower than sediment. What the hell you talkin' about?'

'The technical statistics as you observed them at the hotel –'

'No wonder you *fazools* are bleeding the taxpayers out of their corpuscles! No son of a bitch can understand you – you just scare the shit out of us!'

'What did you find *out*, Joseph?'

'For starters, if those jokers are Swedish, I never had a Norway meatball, which on occasion I have, 'cause this blonde bomberinna I used to go with a couple of centuries ago made 'em so to prove the Guinea variety wasn't so hotsy-totsy –'

'*Joseph*, is this going to be a long story? What did you *learn*?'

'Awright, awright . . . They got three suites, each with two bedrooms, and by spreading a little bread around with the maids and the waiters I found out they speak regular American, y'know English. Also, they're nuts, y'know real *fruitcakes*. They walk around lookin' in mirrors and talkin' funny to themselves, like they didn't know who they were lookin' at.'

'What about support troops, firepower?'

'They ain't got *nuthin*'! I checked out every staircase, even the nearby rooms with some enchilada named Raul who cost me two hundred little ones to check out the register – nobody nowhere around 'em could even be related by coincidence. The only possibility was some fruitcakereno asshole named Brickford Aldershotty, who it turned out was on a one-night stand.'

'Escape routes?'

'The exit signs to the staircases, what can I tell you?'

'So you're saying the beach is clear –'

'What beach?'

'Zero target, the *hotel*, Joseph!'

'Whoever you got can walk in like it was a church in Palermo on Easter Sunday.'

'Anything else?'

'Yeah, here are the room numbers.' The Shroud gave them, then added. 'Also, whoever you got should have muscle, y'know what I mean?'

'Explain that, Joseph.'

'Well, like a sharp-eyed maid named Beulah told me, these jokers break bottles with icicle points of glass stickin' up and do pushups over 'em, sometimes like two hundred. I mean they are *fruitcakes*!'

CHAPTER TWENTY-TWO

'Meat' D'Ambrosia walked through the swinging glass doors of the Axel-Burlap building on Wall Street, Manhattan, took the elevator up to the ninety-eighth floor, trudged his way through another pair of glass doors, and presented his card to a statuesque British receptionist.

Salvatore D'Ambrosia, Consultint. The card was printed by his cousin on a press in Rikers Island.

'I should like to have a meet with a certain Ivan Salamander,' said Salvatore.

'Is he expecting you, sir?'

'It don't make no never mind, call it in, pussycat.'

'I'm sorry, Mr D'Ambrosia, but one doesn't call the president of Axel-Burlap without prior notification, and certainly not in person without a previously scheduled appointment.'

'Try me, sweetheart, or maybe I have to break your desk.'

'*What?*'

'Just call, *capisce?*'

Mr D'Ambrosia was instantly admitted into the walnut-panelled sanctum sanctorum of one Ivan Salamander, president of Wall Street's third largest brokerage house.

'What ... *whaat?*' shrieked the gaunt bespectacled Salamander, wiping the perpetual sweat that kept oozing from his hairline. 'You gotta scare the shit out of some lousy receptionist who's got a ton of class for which I paid airfare, a Blackglama mink, and a salary my wife can no way find *out?*'

'We gotta talk, Mr Salamander, and more important, you gotta listen. Also, your private secaterry wasn't too perturbed.'

'Certainly, *certainly*, I told her to stay ice cold!' yelled Ivan the Terrible, as he was known on the Street. 'You think I'm *dumb*? ... Dumb I'm not, Mr Musclebound, and I would much prefer that whatever you have to say to me should be said in some rotten spaghetti dump in Brooklyn!'

'My associates and me ain't too partial to your smelly salami and your give-into-fish, either. Your delicatessens stink up the neighbourhoods.'

'So our culinary differences are settled, what've you got that I should waste my valuable time on a street soldier? Hahn, *hahn?*'

'Because what I've got for you comes from the big man himself, and if you've got a tape job in here, he'll rip your throat out. *Capisce?*'

'On my word, on my *word*, no such thing! You think I'm *crazy?* ... What does the big man say?'

'Buy defence, especially aircraft and related – wait a minute, I gotta read this.' D'Ambrosia reached into his pocket and pulled out a slip of paper. 'Yeah, here it is. Aircraft and every related supply component – that's it, component, that's the word I couldn't remember.'

'And that's crazy! Defence is going into the toilet, the budgets cut everywhere!'

'Here's the rest of it, and I repeat, if you gotta tape rollin', you're on a meat hook.'

'Never, are you *meshuga?*'

'Things have changed one whole hell of a lot.' Meat again looked at his instructions, for several moments reading silently with his lips. 'Okay, here it is ... Alarming events have tooken place,' continued D'Ambrosia, his voice as flat as his eyes, a man recalling from quasi-rote, 'which the country can't know too much about because of which the panic that might sue –'

'Maybe you mean *ensue?*'

'I'm on your side. Whatever.'

'Go ahead.'

'There has been a lot of interference with the sub ...

substratisforic military sattelactic transmissions which concludes high altitudenal aircraft are . . . fuckin' up the works.'

'High altitude – *U-2* types? The Russkies are going back on their nice words?'

'"The specific hostile equipment has not been firmly identified,"' replied Meat, now unfolding the paper and reading – as best he could. ' . . . "however, as the incidents have increased in numbers and fero-cosity, and the . . . Russian Kremlins . . . have secretly confirmed like events –"' Here, Salvatore D'Ambrosia, aka 'Meat,' refolded the paper and continued on his own. 'The whole fuckin' earth planet, especially the US of A, is on secret emergency alert. It could be the Chinks or the Arabs or the Hebes launching all that bullshit –'

'That's *cockamamie*!'

'*Or* . . . ' Salvatore D'Ambrosia lowered his voice and blessed himself, almost getting the sign of the cross correctly on his large chest, 'things we know nothin' about – from up *there*.' Meat raised his eyes to the ceiling, in his gaze a prayer, if not a plea for mercy.

'*Whaaat*?' shrieked Salamander. 'That's the biggest tube of Guinea cheese I ever heard of! It's full of . . . *hoo-hoo*, wait a minute . . . it's positively, absolutely *brilliant*. Like no junk bonder could ever come up with! . . . We got a whole new enemy we gotta arm the whole fuckin' world for. *UFOs!*'

'You got the big man's drift then?'

'Got it? I *love* it! . . . Hey, a sudden big thought. *What* big man? He's with the fishes!'

It was the moment Meat had been primed for, rehearsed until he could handle it with his head soaked in Chianti. He reached into another pocket and withdrew a small black-bordered envelope, in size and appearance similar to a funeral request. He handed it to the mesmerized Salamander with nine simple words, so ingrained by repetition Salvatore would no doubt say them on his deathbed. 'You breathe a word of this . . . no more breath.'

His eyes shifting warily between Meat's face and the ominous-looking envelope, Ivan the Terrible picked up his glistening brass letter-opener, inserted it beneath a sealed edge, slit the paper and extracted the message. The broker's gaze instantly dropped to the bottom of the page, to the scrawled familiar initials he knew so well. He gasped, his head snapping up, his wide eyes riveted on Salvatore D'Ambrosia. 'This is beyond *impossible!*' he whispered.

'Be careful,' said Meat, no louder than Salamander, as he drew his index finger slowly across his throat. 'Remember, no more breath. Read it.'

Fear paramount, a tremble developing in his hands, Ivan began at the top of the page. *Follow the instructions as delivered verbally to you by the courier. Don't even think about disobeying any aspect of them. We are in the midst of a maximum-classified, eyes only, top secret, black drape, need-to-know basis operation. Everything will be explained to you within a reasonable period of time. Now, in front of the courier, burn this message as well as the envelope, or, with love in his heart, he'll be forced to burn you. I shall return. VM* (illegibly scribbled).

'Gotta match?' asked the petrified Salamander quietly. 'I gave up cigarettes for my health. It'd be kinda dumb if I got burned because I don't smoke.'

'Sure,' said Meat, throwing a pack of matches on the desk. 'After you finish torching the paper, you got one other thing to do before I go.'

'Name it. When I get messages from beyond the grave, I don't quibble.'

'Pick up the phone and place an order for fifty thousand shares of Petrotoxic Amalgamated.'

'*Whaaat?*' shrieked Ivan the Terrible, his forehead drenched with beads of sweat. Then he watched in terror as D'Ambrosia's huge right hand reached under his jacket. 'So *certainly*, of course! So why *not?* Let's make it seventy-five, I mean, why *not?*'

Five other such courtesy calls were made by Meat the Courier, all with similar results – give or take a shriek or two – resulting in a *buy, buy, buy!* binge not seen since the DOW creased two thousand and was still climbing. As a natural consequence, in executive suites across the nation, the carrots led the asses (horses may not be bright but they're smarter than mules). Wild diversification and consummate over-supply were the orders of the day, and the orders went out by the billions. Something *really big* was going down and the smart money boys and the conglomerate fraternity were going to go up on that fantastical see-saw of economic balances.

Buy out those computer firms, screw the price!

Get control of all the subcontracting parts divisions in Georgia and don't bore me with figures!

We're dealing from strength, you idiot! I want the majority interest in McDonnell Douglas, Boeing, and Rolls-Royce Aero-engines, and for Christ's sake, don't stop bidding until you get them all!

Buy California!

So on the basis of an inflated fiction, shrouded in a mystery that would impress Little Joey, say nothing of Houdini and Rasputin, billions in debt were accrued by the enemies of Vincent Francis Assisi Mangecavallo, who sat under an umbrella in Miami Beach, Florida, a Monte Cristo cigar in his mouth, a cellular telephone at his side as well as a portable radio, a margarita on the plastic tray in front of him, and a wide grin on his face. 'Go with the big wave, you fancy country club cannolis,' he said to himself, reaching for his glass, his free hand adjusting his red-haired toupee. 'Wait'll the ocean dries up like that Moses made it do, may he rest in peace. You'll be sucked down into the sand, you *bastards*! Put out a contract on me, better you should read the small print. Cleaning urinals in *Cairo*, that's where all of you *belong*!'

Sir Henry Irving Sutton sat rigidly, angrily, in the kitchen chair while Erin Lafferty snipped away at his flowing crown of grey glory. '*Trim*, wench, merely a trim, or you'll spend the rest of your miserable life in the scullery!'

'Y' don't scare me, y' old fart,' said Erin. 'I seen ya in that afternoon programme *Forever All Our Forevers* fer – what was it? Ten years? – so I know all about *you*, boyo.'

'I beg your pardon?'

'You was always yellin' and caterwaulin' on those young kids until you was drivin' 'em nuts. Then you'd go into that big liberry and cry, sayin' to yerself that they had life too easy, and had to be brought up to snuff so they could face the terrible misfortunes that faced 'em – and by Jesus, Mary and Joseph, yer words were gospel! Such lousy *times* they had! I mean you was actually cryin', sorry for all the bad things you had to say to them, wishin' you didn't have to ... Nah, underneath you're a softie, Grandfather Weatherall!'

'I was merely playing a role, Mrs Lafferty.'

'Call it whatever you like, Mr Sutton, but for me and all the girls in Old Southy, you were the only reason we watched that stupid show. We was all in *love* with you, boyo.'

'I *knew* that son of a bitch never got me a decent contract!' spat out the actor under his breath.

'What was that, sir?'

'Nothing, dear lady, nothing. Cut away, cut away! You're obviously a woman of great taste.'

The kitchen door burst open, the hulk of Cyrus following, his dark face alive with anticipation. 'We're *on*, "General"!'

'Fine, young man! Where's my uniform? I was always a splendid figure in military plumage.'

'No plumes, no uniform, that's out of the question.'

'For God's sake, *why*?'

'To begin with, the general is no longer a general by request of the Pentagon and just about every other major influence in Washington, including the White House. Secondly, you'd call attention to us which isn't practical.'

'It's rather difficult to get into a role without proper accoutrements, which naturally presumes accurate clothing – as in a uniform ... Actually, as a general I outrank you, Colonel.'

'If you're going to play that game, Mr Actor, you're *playing* a general; you were field-commissioned a *major* and I was given the rank of *colonel*. You lose, Sir Henry.'

'Damned impertinent civilians –'

'Where the hell are you, still in World War Two?'

'No, I'm an artist! The rest of you are civilians ... and chemists.'

'Man, you and Hawkins got more in common than El Alamein. Then, most of the generals I've known were actors, too ... Come on, let's go. They expect us at twenty-two hundred.'

'Twenty-two hundred what?'

'*Hours*, Major, or General, if you prefer. It's military for ten o'clock at night.'

'Never could figure those damned numbers –'

The 'Nobel' committee's three hotel suites were adjacent to one another, the middle rooms designated as the meeting ground for the august General MacKenzie Hawkins, Soldier of the Century, and the distinguished 'visitors from Stockholm.' As negotiated by the general's aide-de-camp, one Colonel Cyrus Marshall, US Army, Retired, the conference was to be private, without press coverage or news releases. For as the colonel explained, although the celebrated warrior was immensely honoured by the award, he was currently in seclusion writing his memoirs, *Peace Through Blood*, and wished to know the extent of his travel and media commitments before rendering his decision to accept. The committee spokesman, one Lars Olafer, reacted to the secret meeting with such enthusiasm that Colonel Cyrus added gas-spraying weapons to the already complete arsenal on his and Roman Z's persons. A trap was to be reversed in the best tradition of subterranean rats and Cyrus knew exactly how to do it. Pull in the rodents, immobilize them, bring them to with bound hands and feet, then subject them to interrogation usually described as psychologically macabre but without physical harm. Like ice picks poised in front of their eyes.

'I'd be far more impressive in a uniform!' said Sutton angrily, walking down the hotel corridor in a pin-striped suit recruited from his Boston apartment. 'These damn clothes were appropriate for Shaw's *The Millionairess*, but *not* for the mission at hand.'

'Hey, you look terrific,' said Roman Z, pinching Sutton's

cheek to the astonishment of the actor. 'You should only have perhaps a flower in your lapel, it would have a certain somzing.'

'Cut it out, Roman,' said Cyrus quietly. 'He looks fine . . . Are you ready, *General*?'

'You're talking to a professional, dear boy. The adrenalin flows as we approach the moment. Now, the *magic* begins! . . . Knock on the door, precede me, as is proper, and I shall make my entrance.'

'Remember, Pops,' admonished the mercenary in front of the door. 'You're one hell of an actor, I'll give you that, but please don't get carried away and scare the hell out of them. We want to learn everything we can before we make our move.'

'Now you're a director, Colonel? . . . May I explain for your untutored frame of reference that there are three descending *t*'s in the theatre: talent, taste and tenacity, and within the second category is contained Hamlet's entire advice to the players. I remember one time in Poughkeepsie –'

'Tutor me some other time, Mr Sutton. Right now, let's just have the magic begin, okay?' Cyrus rapped on the door of the hotel suite, drawing himself up to his full military height and ramrod posture. The door was opened by a white-haired man with a salt and pepper chin beard and pince-nez spectacles looped over his nose. 'Colonel Marshall, sir,' continued Cyrus, introducing himself. 'Chief aide-de-camp to General MacKenzie Hawkins.'

'*Velkommen*, Colonel,' said the ersatz elderly delegate supposedly from Sweden; he also spoke in an extremely thick Scandinavian accent that made the travelled Cyrus wince. 'Vee are vid extreme pleasure to meet zee grand *ghy eneral*.' The delegate, bowing obsequiously, stepped backward so as to admit the celebrated Soldier of the Century, who strode through the door like an animated Colossus of Rhodes with an agitated Roman Z shuffling rapidly behind him.

'I am *deeply* honoured, gentlemen!' exclaimed the actor, his guttural bark extraordinarily close to that of MacKenzie Hawkins. 'Not only honoured but supremely humbled by your selection of this minor player in the major conflicts of our times. I have merely done my best, and as an old soldier tempered by battle, I can only say that we fill the wall up with our heroic dead, those brave souls surviving pressing ahead to victory!'

Suddenly, a rush of voices, the accents diverse and having nothing to do with Sweden, burst forth.

'Christ, it's *him*!'

'You forget your grammar, but by God, it *is!*'

'I don't believe it! I thought he died *years* ago!'

'Never on stage, he didn't! He never died on stage – he was always magnificent!'

'The finest character actor of our time! The Walter Abel of the seventies and eighties. *Brilliance* personified!'

'What the *hell* is going on?' shouted Colonel Cyrus, his naturally endowed but untrained voice no match for Ethelred Brokemichael's clandestine unit of actors. 'Will somebody *tell* me?' he yelled, trying to be heard above the din as the men of Suicidal Six crowded around 'General MacKenzie Hawkins' shaking his hand, patting him on the shoulders, and one overwrought man kissing his Players Club ring. '*Goddamn* it! Will someone explain what this is all *about*?'

'Let me try!' said Dustin, breaking away from the others, his eyes dazzled. 'You obviously were recruited late in this operation so you would have no way of knowing, but this *isn't* that clown Hawkins, but one of the theatre's most outstanding artists! We all saw him when we were younger, studied his performances, followed him into Joe Allen's – that's an actors' bar – and bombarded him with questions, trying to absorb whatever he could impart.'

'Impart *what*? What are you *talking* about?'

'This man is Henry Irving *Sutton*! *The* Sutton, *Sir* Henry –'

'Yes, I know,' interrupted Cyrus softly, in his voice the essence of abject defeat. 'After a long-gone English actor named Irving, who had nothing to do with the bank or a tailor on First Avenue ... Wait a *minute*!' yelled the mercenary suddenly. 'Who the hell are *you* people?'

'Each of us gives only his name, rank and serial number,'

replied Marion, overhearing Cyrus's question and reluctantly turning away from the adulated Sutton, who was accepting the accolades of his peers with brilliant humility. 'I say this in sadness, Colonel, for I once had a small role in a Sidney Poitier film and he, too, was and is a marvellous artist.'

'Name, rank and – what the *hell* are you *talking* about?'

'Just what I said, Colonel. Name, rank and serial number, according to the laws of the Geneva Convention. Nothing more.'

'You're *soldiers?*'

'Very accomplished ones,' answered Dustin, glancing over at his hero, namely Henry Irving Sutton, who was now holding his worshippers spellbound recounting past triumphs. 'We accept the risks of combat without uniforms, but to date it's never been a factor.'

'*Combat?*'

'Select covert activities, grey to black operations – the reference to "black" having nothing to do with race, of course.'

'I *know* what "black" operations are, I just don't know what the hell *you* are!'

'I just told you, we're a military unit specializing in clandestine activities, missions involving maximum security.'

'And this Nobel committee crap is one of those operations?'

'Between the two of us,' said Dustin confidentially, leaning toward Cyrus, 'you're lucky we are who we are or your pension might go down the tube. That man *isn't* General Hawkins! You were taken in, Colonel, flimflammed, if you know what I mean.'

'I was . . . ?' said Cyrus, staring, as if in a catatonic state.

'You certainly were, sir, as was obviously Mr Sutton – Sir Henry. He'd never tarnish his magnificent reputation by being involved in a global conspiracy to cripple this country's first line of defence. *Never!*'

'First line of defence – a global conspiracy . . . ?'

'That's as far as our briefing went, Colonel.'

'This is too fucking much!' said Cyrus, as if coming out of a trance. 'Just who *are* you and where do you come from?'

'Fort Benning, under the command of Brigadier General Ethelred Brokemichael. Our specific names are neither relevant nor called for at this juncture, but suffice it to say we're called the Suicidal Six.'

'The *Suicidal* –! My *God*, the Delta Force to the max? The most effective anti-terrorist unit ever put into the field!'

'Yes, that's what we've heard.'

'But you're . . . you're –'

'That's right, we're actors.'

'*Actors?*' yelled Cyrus in such a *scherzo fortissimo* that Henry Irving Sutton and the adoring crowd around him fell silent, staring at the mercenary in astonishment. 'You're – you're *all actors?*'

'And as splendid a group of conferees as I've met in years, Colonel. They play their parts to perfection. Notice the care they've taken with their clothing, the proper European cuts, the subdued colours as befits distinguished academics. You might also drink in the consummate attention they've given their tonsorial effects – flicks of grey, not overdone, to add a few years to their ages. And their postures, Colonel, the ever so slightly stooped shoulders and the minor concavities of their chests as we observed entering the room; and the pince-nez and the tortoiseshell glasses, all are marks of men in sedentary professions with strained eyes . . . Yes, Colonel, these are, indeed, actors – *fine* actors.'

'He notices everything!'

'Such observation!'

'Every minute detail –'

'*Details*, gentlemen,' proclaimed Sutton, 'are our secret weapons, never forget that.' A chorus of 'Never!' 'Certainly not!' and 'How could we?' followed the proclamation until the elderly actor held up his hands. 'But, of course, I don't really have to tell you that. I understand you convincingly deceived several million people with your performance at the airport . . . Well *done*, shepherds of Thespis! Now, I want to know each of you. Your names, please.'

'Well,' began the spokesman, Lars Olafer, none too subtly, nodding at the mercenaries, 'without certain people present we'd enthusiastically introduce ourselves by our real names, but our orders are to stay with our sobriquets, which is most embarrassing to me personally.'

'Why is that?'

'To be frank, an undeserved title, one you've earned but I haven't . . . I'm called "Sir Larry," for my first name is really Laurence.'

'With a *u*?'

'Oh, of course.'

'Then I say you *have* earned it. When Larry and Viv were together, we quaffed many an ale together, and in truth there's a certain similarity in your appearance to that skinny but terribly likeable fellow. I played the "First Knight" in his and Tony Quinn's *Becket*, of course.'

'I may die right here on the spot –'

'You were *great*!'

'*Magnificent!*'

'*Extraordinary!*'

'Passable, if I do say so.'

'Can we cut the bullshit, if *I* say so!' shouted Cyrus, the veins in his thick neck pronounced.

'I'm called The Duke.'

'I'm Sylvester –'

'Marlon's the name.'

'Dustin – y'know, y'know . . . am I, am I right, right, *right*?'

'Telly's the moniker, General, baby. Wanna lollipop?'

'You're all *superb*!'

'And this is all *preposterous*!' screamed Cyrus, clutching the lapels of Dustin and Sylvester. 'You bastards *listen* to me!'

'Hey, my black good buddy,' said Roman Z, softly patting the broad back of his recent cell mate. 'Don't shoot up your blood pressures, man!'

'Blood pressure, *hell*, I should shoot every one of these sons of bitches!'

'Now, Pilgrim, that downright primitive,' said The Duke. 'Y'see, mister, we don't believe in violence. It's actually just a state of mind.'

'State of *what*?' shrieked the dark-skinned mercenary.

'Of the mind,' explained The Duke. 'Freud called it the frenzied extension of the imagination – we use it a lot in acting classes, usually with improv, naturally.'

'*Naturally!*' Cyrus released his helpless hostages. 'I give up,' he mumbled, sitting down in the nearest chair as Roman Z massaged his shoulders. 'I give *up!*' he repeated, shouting, his wide eyes appraising the crowd of lunatics in front of him – and below him. 'You're the *Suicidal Six?* The anti-terrorist Delta Force unit *songs* have been written about? Nothing makes *sense!*'

'In some ways, you're right, Colonel,' said Sylvester in his normal Yale Drama School voice, 'for we've never had to fire a gun or basically injure anyone beyond a sprained wrist or, at worst, a cracked rib . . . We just don't work that way. You see, it's easier on everybody. We impersonate our way into and out of missions, frequently intimidating the targets, but every now and then making a friend or two.'

'You're breakouts from a funny farm,' said Cyrus, 'or maybe you're not really from this planet,' he added numbly.

'You're too hard on us, Colonel,' protested Telly in his normally cultured voice. 'If all the armies of the world were made up of actors, wars could be mounted as civilized productions, not uncivilized slaughters. Merits would be given for individual and collective performances – the best orations, the most convincing snarls, the finest crowd reactions –'

'Then, of course,' interrupted Marlon, 'there'd be points for costuming and set décoration, for the most creative props, as in weapons and *mise en scène* locations –'

'As well as plot and story development,' broke in The Duke. 'I suppose you could term them military tactics.'

'Let's not forget *direction*, for God's sake,' cried Sir Larry.

'And choreography,' added Sylvester. 'A choreographer would have to be an organic extension of *any* director under the circumstances.'

'Wonderful, simply *wonderful!*' exclaimed Henry Irving Sutton. 'An international academy of the theatrical arts could be set up to judge the forces in the field, in the air, and on the water. Naturally, military consultants would be included for semblances to authenticity, but their consultancy would be secondary, the primary judgements made on the basis of creativity – of conviction, characterization, *passion*! ... *Art!*'

'Right on, Pilgrim!'

'Hey, Stella, he got it right!'

'You ... you ... you are with ... with ... with it!'

'Speak the speech, I pray you –'

'Beautiful, sweetheart. Have a lollipop!'

'Yeah, yeah, we don' need no howitzers t' blow the gooks away!'

'*What?*'

'Well, he's gotta be right, y'know what I mean? Nobody gets *shot*. Nobody gets his face in a bucket!'

'*Eeeowweeah!*' bellowed Cyrus, his scream worthy of Anouilh's dictum. 'I've had it! I've really *had* it! ... *You*, Sir Henry *Horseshit!* You were military – I heard that certifiable Hawkins say you were a goddamned hero in North Africa! What happened to *that* man?'

'In a primitive sense, Colonel, all soldiers are actors. We're terrified, but we try to pretend we're not; we know that at any moment our precious lives may be taken from us, but we abandon that knowledge for the irrational reason that the immediate objective is paramount, although in the core of our minds, we understand that it's merely a statistic on a map. The problem with soldiers in combat is that they must *become* actors without proper training, proper professional training ... If all the drenched, mud-sunk foot soldiers understood the rules, they'd do as Telly says, and snarl viciously while firing above the heads of other young men they don't know but might have a drink with in some bar in another time and place.'

'*Bullshit!* What about values and beliefs? I've fought on different sides, but never against what I believed in!'

'Well, then, you're a moral man, Colonel, and I commend you. However, you also fight for the most questionable motive of all. Money.'

'What are *these* clowns fighting for?'

'I haven't the vaguest idea, but I doubt it's financial

remuneration. As I understand it, they're fulfilling their lifelong theatrical ambitions – in a rather unorthodox way, but obviously with considerable success.'

'I'll sure as hell give them that,' said Cyrus, turning to Roman Z. 'Have you got everything?' he asked.

'Everyz*ing* and everyone, my enduring friend.'

'Good.' The huge chemist turned back to the actors, singled out Dustin, and spoke. 'You, Shorty, come over here.' The diminutive performer looked questioningly at his comrades. 'For God's sake, man, I just want to talk to you privately. Do you think my friend and I would take on the entire Suicidal Six?'

'I wouldn't even think of "taking on" *him*, Pilgrim. He may not be your size but he's black belt karate to the tenth order, and they don't come no higher.'

'Oh, come on, Duke, I'd never use that stuff unless we were all in real trouble. And certainly not against a nice guy like the colonel. He's just upset, I can understand that ... Don't worry, Colonel, I wouldn't harm you. What is it?' Dustin walked with the stunned Cyrus to a far corner of the suite as the mercenary kept staring down – way down – at the actor. They stood next to a window, the night lights of Boston throwing a glow over the city, and Cyrus spoke quietly.

'You were probably right a few minutes ago when you said I could lose my pension. You see, I did come on late, actually only a few days ago, and I had no reason to think this man wasn't Hawkins. Hell, from what I've seen of him on television he looks like the general and sounds just like him – why wouldn't it *be* him? I'm really grateful, Dustin.'

'That's okay, Colonel. I'm sure you'd do the same for me if our positions were reversed – say somebody was impersonating Harry Belafonte and you being black knew he wasn't but I didn't.'

'What ... ? Oh, yes, I certainly would, Dusty, I certainly would. But just so I can get a clearer picture of this whole dirty business – officially, you understand, and since we're both on the same side – just what *was* your mission?'

'Well, as we're on a restricted, need-to-know basis and you

are a colonel, I'll tell you what I can, which is all we know. We're to make contact with General Hawkins, abduct him and everyone else around him, and drive to the SAC air base in Westover, that's here in Massachusetts.'

'Not back to Air Force Two on the Logan runway?'

'Oh, no, that was for the press conference ... You know, the Vice-President isn't really a bad guy. Of course, I don't think he can *act* –'

'*He* was on the plane?'

'Sure, but he wasn't allowed to get off until later.'

'Then why was he there?'

'Some gangsters stole one of his cars and it was somehow found here in Boston –'

'*Forget* it ... I mean it's not germane. So you kidnap the general and anyone accompanying him, drive to the SAC base in Westover, and then what?'

'*TBDL*, Colonel.'

'I beg your pardon?'

'"To be determined later," but we were told to carry sweaters and long johns in our duffels, which presumes the climate will be colder.'

'Sweden,' said the mercenary.

'That's what we figured, but then Sylvester, who was in an overseas tour of *Annie* in Scandinavia – we hear he was terrific, especially from him – said the summer weather wasn't that much different from ours.'

'It isn't.'

'So then we figured far more north –'

'Like in the ice fjords,' completed Cyrus.

'Wherever ... we'd receive further orders at that time.'

'Like depositing frozen bodies to be discovered in the year three thousand for medical research.'

'I wouldn't know anything about that, sir.'

'I would hope not ... And outside of this Brigadier General Broke ... Brokehethel –'

'That's Brokemichael, Colonel. Brigadier General Ethelred Brokemichael.'

'It's okay, I've got it. But outside of him, you have no idea who's responsible for this mission?'

'That's not in our purview, sir.'

'You can bet your ass it isn't.'

'Colonel . . . ?'

'We *split*, Roman,' said Cyrus abruptly, walking rapidly to the hotel door, the gypsy swiftly at his side, as a loud metallic slap was heard from behind his back. 'Don't try to follow us, it would be useless; we're as expert in our profession as you are on stage, *believe* me. And you, Mr Sutton, I don't know a hell of a lot about acting, but I suspect you're one of the best, so you can stay here and jaw with your buddies as long as you like . . . I'm afraid we used an old merc trick with you tonight. You may have wondered why my friend kept jumping around, studying each of you, so now I'll tell you. That red carnation in his lapel contains a miniaturized, high-speed camera; we have a minimum of a dozen photographs of each of your faces. And under my jacket I'm wired to max and still rolling; every word here this evening is recorded.'

'A moment, *please*!' exclaimed Sir Henry.

'*What?*' Cyrus reached between the folds of his coat and yanked out a large, ugly .357 Magnum as Roman Z whipped his hand from behind his back displaying a foot long switchblade knife.

'My *fee*,' said Sutton. 'Have Aaron send it around by messenger to my flat. And tack on several hundred more for I intend to take my newfound friends and associates to the finest restaurant in Boston.'

'Sir Henry!' said Sylvester, touching the great man's sleeve. 'Have you really retired?'

'Semi-retirement, dear boy. I do occasional stints for the locals, y'know, keeps the juices flowing. As it happens, I have a rather well-off son here in Boston from one of my marriages – can't remember which – who simply insisted I take one of the hundreds of condominiums he's built. He damn well should, of course; in the halcyon days I sent him through several universities for all those letters after his name. Sweet child, I must say, but *never* an actor! Damn disappointment, really.'

'How about the *army*? You could be our *director*! They'd probably make you a general right off!'

'Ah, but remember, my young cohort, what Napoleon said: "Give me enough medals and I'll win you any war." But for *actors* to get ahead, it's the billing, your name! Progressively larger until it equals the size of the play's title. Now, as you perform in secrecy, how could the army do that?'

'Oh, *shit*,' whispered Cyrus to Roman Z. 'Let's get the hell out of here!'

They left, and no one in the suite noticed.

CHAPTER TWENTY-THREE

'It's all *here!*' cried Jennifer, listening to the tape and looking at the enlarged photographs on the coffee table in the summer house on the beach in Swampscott. 'It *is* a conspiracy, a screwed-up conspiracy, but obviously involving the highest levels of the government!'

'There's no question about it,' agreed Aaron Pinkus from his chair, 'but whom do we go after? The "need-to-know" basis cuts off the trail.'

'What about this Brokemichael?' said Devereaux. 'He's the son of a bitch I caught in the Golden Triangle –'

'And got his first name mixed up with his cousin,' interjected Jennifer. '*Ass.*'

'Hey, look, how many times do you run into first names like Ethelred and Heseltine? They're both so weird it's hard *not* to get confused.'

'Not for an observant attorney –'

'Come on, Pocahontas, you couldn't differentiate between harsh cross-examination and extreme provocation!'

'Will you two stop it,' said an exasperated Pinkus.

'I only meant he could be after *me*,' explained Sam. 'Jesus, if he saw my name in the Hawk's file, his nostrils would outshoot two flamethrowers.'

'Since you're formally listed as the Wopotami attorney-of-record, I suppose that's entirely possible.' Aaron paused, frowning, his head tilted. 'On the other hand, Brokemichael couldn't order his rather unique unit into action by himself, and he certainly wouldn't have access to Air Force Two –'

'Which means he was so ordered himself by someone who

had both the authority as well as the access,' completed Redwing.

'Exactly, my dear, and therein lies our conundrum. For this Brokemichael certainly wouldn't reveal his superior, even if he could, and to paraphrase General Hawkins, the chain of command would be so convoluted as to be untraceable. At least within the time frame available to us – eighty-some hours and counting, as I understand it, but not actually.'

'We've got the evidence,' said Devereaux. 'The photographs, the tape in which the entire operation is outlined by two participants – perpetrators, if you like. We could go public, why not?'

'The stress has addled your normal perceptions, Sam,' answered Pinkus gently. 'Deniability is built into this whole operation. Just as our friend Cyrus, who is now on the beach with Roman Z no doubt consuming several quarts of vodka, put it – "they're all lunatics" ... *That's* the deniability. Lunacy, irrationality – crazy people. *Actors.*'

'Hold it, Aaron. They can't deny Air Force Two, that's too damned heavy.'

'He's got a point, Mr Pinkus. Clearance for the use of that plane has to come from on high.'

'Thank you, Princess.'

'I give when it's deserved.'

'*Wow*, what a prelude!'

'Oh, shut up.'

'My word, I called you addled, but I'm far worse. You have a glaringly obvious point –'

'No, he *doesn't*,' came the guttural voice of MacKenzie Hawkins from the darkened, partially opened door to the kitchen. It was pulled back and the figure of the Hawk emerged, clothed only in green and black camouflaged skivvies and T-shirt. 'Pardon my appearance, little ... Miss Redbird –'

'That's Redwing.'

'Sorry again, but when I hear voices on bivouac at three o'clock in the morning, my natural instinct is to prowl fast, not dress for the occasion of a dance at the officers' club.'

'You dance, Mac?'

'Check my fillies, son. I taught all of 'em everything from the mazurka to the true Viennese. Soldiers were always the best dancers; they have to make their moves on the ladies in quick fashion – leaves are short.'

'Please, Sam, the general's observation, if you will,' said Aaron, looking at the Hawk. 'Why is my learned employee wrong about the Vice-President's plane? It's the second-ranking aircraft in the country.'

'Because Air Force Two can be manipulated by a dozen agencies and departments for cosmetic reasons. Regardless of who it is, a Veep's staff jumps at every opportunity to bring its unnoticed merchandise out of the shadows, whether it's him or his benevolently provided equipment ... Hell, boy, remember when I landed at Travis from Beijing by way of the Philippines after the Chink trial, and gave that puke-inducing speech about "old, tired soldiers"? I had to include that I was eternally grateful to the Vice-President for sending his personal plane.'

'I remember, Mac.'

'You know where that Vice-President was, Sam?'

'No, I don't,' said Devereaux.

'He was holed up with one of my wives who wouldn't let him get to second base in LA, drunk as a flea in a bottle of bourbon and just about as equal to the task of his desires.'

'How do you know that?'

''Cause I smelled the whole China trial scam and wanted to know how high up it went in DC. I sent my girl to work to see if she could find out.'

'*Did* she?' asked an incredulous Pinkus.

'Sure as hell did, Commander. That tongue-twisting orator fell flat on his face with his trousers around his ankles, asking good old Ginny who I *was*! Then I knew just how tall the dirty dog was who had me by the tail, doing nasty things to this old soldier ... That's when I really made up my mind to pursue a different life and recruited you, Sam.'

'I'd rather you didn't remind me ... *Ginny* seduced the *Vice-President*?'

'You weren't listening, son. That girl's got taste, and his neutered fat face wasn't up to it.'

'Reminiscences aside,' broke in Aaron, shaking his head as if to erase forbidden images, 'what *exactly* are you saying, General?'

'I'm saying we've now got a direct counter for this counter-thrust strategy, Commander. It'll be a little tricky but we can manage it.'

'Speak English, Mac.'

'*Hell*, boy, it's worked from the Normandy coast to Saipan! From Pinchon to the Mekong – when the goddamned back-boiler brass didn't blow it with their big mouths.'

'I repeat, English.'

'*Disinformation*, Sam, within the holier-than-thou chain of command.'

'I mentioned that a moment ago,' interrupted Pinkus. 'The chain of command, I mean.'

'I know,' acknowledged the Hawk. 'I heard everything you all said for the past twenty minutes, taking a few moments off to bring Colonel Cyrus another bottle of vodka on the beach ... Those actor types really blew him into space, didn't they?'

'Your *disinformation*, General?' pressed Aaron.

'Well, I haven't actually worked it out yet, but the route's as clear as an oil slick in new-fallen snow ... Brokey the Deuce.'

'Who?'

'What?'

'I think I know,' said Jennifer. 'Brokemichael – not the Indian Affairs Heseltine, but the one who runs those faces on the table from Fort Benning. Ethelred.'

'The lady's right. Ethelred Brokemichael was about the poorest excuse for a West Pointer that ever was. He never should have been in the army, but it was on both sides of their families, you know, sons of army brothers. The crazy thing is that Ethelred was actually a more imaginative officer than Heseltine, but he had a weakness. He saw too many movies where generals lived like kings and he tried it on a general's salary, which doesn't allow for castles.'

'Then I was *right*,' said Devereaux. 'He was making bucks out of the Triangle.'

'Sure, you were, Sam, but he was no mastermind criminal; he was more of an unconscious middleman than anything else. It was like he was in a movie, being paid personal homage by a lot of people he couldn't understand but did minor favours for.'

'He pocketed the loot, Mac.'

'Some, not a hell of a bundle and nowheres near what you claimed. If the army could have proved that, he'd have been out on his duff. He gave a lot of it to the orphanages and the refugee camps. That's on the record and it's what saved his tail. There were others who did much worse.'

'That's hardly exculpatory,' said Pinkus.

'I guess not, but like Sam says, who's running in the angel sweepstakes?' The Hawk paused and walked to a beach front window in his camouflaged skivvies. 'Besides, it's history and I know Brokey the Deuce. He doesn't think too much of me because I knew Heseltine better and they didn't get along, but we talk . . . And we *will* talk and I'll goddamned well find out who's behind this whole fandango or the Deuce will be hung out to dry in public, and he can kiss his gold braid good-bye.'

'You're forgetting a negative or two, General,' interrupted Aaron. 'To begin with when word gets back that this "Suicidal Six" has failed, I'm sure Brokemichael will be placed beyond your reach, beyond anyone's, for the simple reason that through him the name of the high-ranking official who commandered Air Force Two might surface.'

'The word won't get back, Commander,' said Hawkins, turning away from the window. 'At least not for the next twenty-four hours, and I'm sure you can arrange for a private jet to fly me to Fort Benning first thing in the morning.'

'Twenty-four *hours*?' exclaimed Jennifer. 'You can't possibly guarantee that. Those actors may be lunatics, but they *are* covert operations professionals.'

'Let me explain, Miss Redwing. My adjutants, Desis One and Two, are in radio contact with me . . . Sir Henry Sutton and the so-called Suicidal Six are currently closing up Joseph's restaurant on Dartmouth Street, well oiled, and in great spirits. My adjutants will drive them – not to the hotel – but up to the ski lodge, where they'll remain for the day recovering. And when they've just about got their heads in place, Desi Two, who's not only a fine mechanic but also, I'm informed by Desi the First, an accomplished cook, will lace their chow with a pesto sauce comprised of tomatoes, tequila, gin, brandy, pharmaceutical grain alcohol and a liquid sedative of indeterminate potency that will provide us with Miss Redwing's guarantee. We may possibly have *more* than twenty-four hours, perhaps nearer a week, if it'd do us any good.'

'Really, General,' countered the daughter of the Wopotamis, 'even men crippled by drugs and alcohol – especially trained military personnel – find enough lucid moments to use the telephone.'

'The telephones won't be working – wires down, struck by lightning during the storm.'

'What storm?' asked Aaron.

'The storm that whipped up after they all fell into their sacks for some heavy snoring.'

'When they wake up they'll climb into the limo and get the hell out of there,' offered Devereaux.

'Rack and pinion steering will have been broken as a result of the rough country terrain.'

'They'll think they've been kidnapped and take appropriate measures, physical measures!' said Pinkus.

'There's some chance of that but not much. D-One will explain to them that you, Commander, in your wisdom, thought it might be wiser if the group slept off tonight's festivities at your vacation home rather than risking any embarrassment at the hotel.'

'What *about* the hotel, Mac?' said Sam anxiously. 'Broke-michael and his crowd will be checking in with the unit for progress reports, if nothing else.'

'Little Joseph's covering the phones in the middle suite as we speak.'

'What the hell's he going to *say*?' persisted Devereaux.

'"Hi, I'm the Suicidal Seventh and the rest of the boys are bombed out of their skulls at Joe's Bar"?'

'No, Sam, he's going to make it clear that he's been hired only to take messages and that his temporary employers were called out on business. Nothing more.'

'You seem to have thought everything through,' conceded Aaron, nodding. 'Quite remarkable.'

'Second nature, Commander. These kinds of counter-insurgency tactics are kindergarten stuff.'

'Oh, no, Mac, you *forgot* something.' Devereaux smiled a lawyer's smile of sardonic triumph. 'These days all the limousines have telephones.'

'Good thinking, son, but Desi the First thought of that a couple of hours ago –'

'Don't tell me he's going to snap off the antenna. That would be a little obvious, wouldn't it?'

'No need to. Hooksett, New Hampshire's out of the cellular range; the tower up there isn't completed. Desi-Two found out the hard way; he told us he had to drive twenty minutes down the highway to make contact with D-One in Boston the night before last – to tell him exactly where the lodge was.'

'Any other objections, Counsellor?' asked Redwing.

'Something terrible is going to happen,' squeaked Sam in a strained, piping voice. 'It always does when he thinks things *through*!'

The Rockwell jet soared over the Appalachian mountains preparing for its descent into the Fort Benning area, specifically a private airfield twelve miles north of the army base. The single passenger on board was the Hawk, once again dressed in his nondescript grey suit, wearing his steel-rimmed glasses, and with his grey, bristled brush-cut hair covered by his dull red wig now trimmed to perfection by Erin Lafferty. The former general had been on the telephone in Swampscott from roughly four o'clock in the morning until five-thirty making his arrangements. His first call he placed was to Heseltine Brokemichael, who was only ecstatic in any attempt whatsoever to 'screw the bejesus' out of his loathsome cousin, Ethelred. Seventeen calls later, all placed and received on the beach house lines, paved the way for a certain writer whose current research involved post-perestroika military adjustment to be admitted on to the base. At 0800 Brigadier General Ethelred Brokemichael, whose cover was Base Public Relations, had been alerted by Pentagon Public Relations to expect this *very* influential journalist and to act as his escort throughout the army complex. For Brokey the Deuce it was a relatively routine assignment that made good use of his minor theatrical talents, which, naturally, he did not consider minor at all. At ten hundred hours, Ethelred Brokemichael hung up his office phone, having instructed his WAC aide to show in the writer. The brigadier was fully prepared to repeat a PR performance he had done so successfully for a number of years.

What he was not prepared for was the sight of the large, somewhat stooped, bespectacled, red-haired elderly man, who walked shyly through his office door, profusely thanking the female sergeant who held it open for him. There was something vaguely familiar about the man, an aura, perhaps, that belied the image of solicitous courtesy; there was even an abstract sound of distant thunder, heard only by Brokey the Deuce but it was distinctly there. *What was it about this oddball character who might have walked right out of the movie* Great Expectations, *a large, awkward, downtrodden accounts clerk trying to assuage the old lady . . . or was he mixing the role up with that tall fellow on stage in* Nicholas Nickleby?

'It's very kind of you to spare your valuable time for my modest research, General,' said the journalist in a quiet if somewhat hoarse voice.

'It's my job,' said Brokemichael, flashing a sudden grin he felt would do justice to Kirk Douglas. 'We are the armed servants of the people and want them to fully understand our contributions to the defence of our country and the peace of the world . . . Please, sit down.'

'That's a wonderful and moving statement.' The red-headed writer sat down in front of the desk, pulled out a notepad and a ballpoint pen and proceeded to scribble a few words. 'Do you mind if I quote you? I'll ascribe it to an "authoritative source" if you prefer.'

'Certainly not – I mean, you may certainly ascribe it to me.' *This was the very influential journalist who had Pentagon PR running around in circles to accommodate him. Why? This ageing, gravel-voiced oddball was a certified civilian in awe of a uniform. The morning would be a snap.* 'We in the army don't hide behind secondary, unnamed sources, Mr ... Mr –'

'Harrison, General. Lex Harrison.'

'Rex *Harrison* ... ?'

'No, Alexander Harrison. My parents nicknamed me "Lex" many years ago, and my by-lines have always been under that name.'

'Oh, yes, of course – it's just kind of a jolt, if you know what I mean ... I mean, *Rex Harrison.*'

'Yes, Mr Harrison used to get quite a kick out of the similarity. He once asked me if we could change places – he'd write an article and I'd go on for him as "Henry Higgins." An untimely death; he was a lovely man.'

'You *knew* Rex Harrison?'

'Through mutual friends –'

'Mutual *friends*?'

'New York and LA are actually small towns if you're a writer or an actor ... but my publishers aren't interested in me and my Polo Lounge drinking companions, General.'

'*Polo* Lounge ... ?'

'It's a watering hole favoured by the rich and famous and everyone else in LA who wants to be ... Now back to my publishers, they're interested in the military and how it's reacting to the economies being imposed. May we start the interview?'

'Sure, yes ... of *course*. I'll tell you anything you like, it's just that I've always had a tremendous interest in the theatre and movies ... and even television.'

'My writing and performing friends would put television first, General. It's what they call "survival money." You can't make a living on the stage, and films are too few and far between.'

'Yes, I've heard that from – well, never mind – but this is real inside stuff from someone who really knows!'

'I haven't betrayed any secrets, take my word for it,' said the journalist. 'Even Greg, Mitch and Michael admit it.'

'Oh, my *God* ... naturally!' *No wonder Pentagon PR considered this old hoarse-voiced reporter very influential. He had obviously been around for years, and hobnobbed with famous people whom the Pentagon were always trying to cultivate for their TV commercials. Christ! Rex Harrison, Greg, Mitch and Michael – he knew everybody*! 'I frequently fly to ... LA ... Mr Harrison. Perhaps we might get together some time ... at the Polo Lounge.'

'Why not? I'm out there half the time, the other half in New York, but to tell you the truth, the action's on the Coast. When you're out there, just go to the Po-Lounge and tell Gus the bartender that you're looking for me. I always check in with him whether I'm staying at the Beverly Hills or not. That's how people know I'm in town – like Paul ... Newman, that is, and Joanne, and the Pecks, Mitchum, Caine and even a few newcomers like the Toms – Selleck and Cruise – and Meryl and Bruce – the good people.'

'The *good* people ... ?'

'Well, you know, the real ones, the guys and girls I get along with –'

'I'd *love* to *meet* them!' interrupted Brokemichael, his eyes two large white saucers with flashing brown cup rings. 'I can arrange my schedule *any* time!'

'Hey, whoa, General, whoa,' said the old reporter huskily. 'These people are pros in the business. They've been around the block, and don't necessarily like side streets to amateur-ville.'

'What do you mean?'

'Well, an *interest* in the movies or television or whatever isn't exactly being a member of the fraternity, if you see what I mean. Hell, everybody wants to meet these faces – sometimes they call themselves "faces," as though it's an insult to themselves – but underneath they're real people who know what goes with the territory, but put limits on the land grabs.'

'What does *that* mean?'

'In short words, you're not a pro, General, you're a *fan* – and that they can get on any street corner, more than they can handle. Pros don't socialize with fans, they tolerate 'em . . . May we get back to the interview, please?'

'Well, yes, of *course*,' cried the frustrated Brokemichael, 'but I think – I know damned *well* – that you're underestimating my commitment to the performing arts!'

'Oh, was your mother an actress in a community theatre, or did your father act in a high school play?'

'Neither one, although my mother always *wanted* to be an actress but her parents told her it would send her to hell, so she mimicked a lot . . . My father was a colonel – *goddamn*, I've outranked that son of a bitch! . . . But I've got the theatrical bloodline from my mother – I really *love* the theatre and good films and TV – especially the old movies. I feel electricity when I watch a show that moves me, really moves me. I cry, I laugh, I'm every *one* of those characters on the stage or on the screen. It's my alter *life*!'

'I'm afraid that's a fantasizing amateur's reaction,' said the gruff-voiced journalist, returning to his notebook.

'Oh, you *think* so?' protested Brokemichael, his own voice strained, cracked with emotion. 'Then let me *tell* you something – can we go off the record, no pen, no notebook – everything confidential?'

'Why not? I'm only here to get the overall military picture –'

'Be quiet!' whispered Brokey the Deuce, rising behind his desk, then crouching, slithering toward the door, listening as if playing a role in Bertolt Brecht's *Threepenny Opera*. 'I command the most elite acting repertory company in the annals of military history! I've trained them, guided them, brought them to the zenith of their talents, so that now they're considered a world-class, anti-terrorist unit that succeeds where everyone else fails! I ask you, is that *amateur-ville*?'

'Now, General, they're soldiers, trained for that sort of thing –'

'No, they're *not!*' exploded Brokemichael, his whisper growing into a near hiss. 'They're actors, real professional *actors*! When they enlisted as a group, I saw the opportunities right away. Who better to infiltrate and pull the plugs behind enemy lines than men trained to impersonate other people? And what better than a unit of actors familiar with one another's work, a *repertory* company capable of playing off one another to give the illusion of spontaneity, of naturalism – *reality?* . . . Clandestine Operations, Mr Harrison. They were born to it and *I* made it possible!'

The journalist's reaction was that of a curmudgeon grudgingly acknowledging a valid point where he had thought none existed. 'Well, I'll be damned . . . ! That's one hell of a concept, General – I might even go so far as to say it's brilliant.'

'Not exactly amateur-ville, is it? These days everyone wants their services. Even now, at this moment, they're on assignment for one of the most powerful men in the country.'

'Oh?' The man called Harrison frowned questioningly, a slight cynical smile shaping his lips. 'Then they're not on the premises so I can't meet them . . . and we *are* off the record so I can't write about them?'

'My God, way off the record, not a word!'

'Then, frankly, General, speaking as a reporter, I have only one source – you. No editor alive would accept a single source, and my friends in the Polo Lounge would laugh through their oat bran Eggs Benedict, saying it would make a hell of a screenplay if it were true – which it would if it was.'

'It *is!*'

'Who says besides you?'

'Well, I . . . I *can't!*'

'Too bad. If there was a shred of truth to the concept, you could probably sell an outline for a few hundred thousand. And with what they call a "screen treatment" – that's a half-assed summary like we all used to do in high school book reports – for maybe a half a million. You'd be the toast of Tinseltown.'

'Oh, my God, it *is* true! *Believe* me!'

'*I* may believe you, but my confidence wouldn't be worth a Pellegrino and lime in the Po-Lounge. For this kind of thing to fly, you need credibility . . . . Now, General, I really think we should return to the interview.'

'*No!* I'm too close to my dreams . . . Paul and Joanne, Greg and Mitch and Michael – all the *good* people!'

'That they are –'

'You *must* believe me!'

'How can I?' growled the old journalist. 'I can't even write down a word – we're off the record.'

'Well, try *this*,' cried Brokey the Deuce, his eyes on fire as the sweat rolled down his face. 'Within the next twenty-four hours, my anti-terrorist repertory company of actors will capture one of the most dangerous enemies our country has ever known.'

'That's a hell of a statement, General. Anything to back it up with that I can document?'

'Is there anything between off-the-record and on-the-record?'

'Well, I suppose there's confidential post-occurrence disclosure – that's to say nothing may be printed until the event takes place, and even then, only "on background."'

'What's *that*?'

'No specific names are used or revealed as sources.'

'I'll take it!'

'You'll get it,' muttered the journalist.

'I beg your pardon?'

'Nothing. Go ahead, General.'

'They're-in-Boston-Massachusetts,' said Brokemichael quickly in a monotone, his lips barely moving.

'That's nice.'

'Have you been reading the newspapers or watching television?' the general asked, again quickly, secretively.

'Off and on, you can't escape either one.'

'Did you read or hear about the Nobel committee that flew into Boston on the Vice-President's plane?'

'Yes, I think I did,' replied the journalist, scowling in thought. 'Something about an address at Harvard and announcing some award or other for a general . . . the Soldier of the Decade, or something like that. I saw it on the television news.'

'*Preet-tee* impressive, wouldn't you say?' said Brokey the Deuce, the question delivered in sing-song.

'Well, any committee representing the Nobel Foundation wouldn't be too tacky.'

'You agree then that they were a distinguished group of scholars and military historians, right?'

'Certainly. The Nobel boys don't mess around with bums, they don't have to. So what's all this got to do with your . . . your repertory company of anti-terrorists?'

'It's *them*!'

'What's them?'

'That Nobel committee! They're my men, my *actors*!'

'General, on this point I'll stay strictly off the record, but have you been dabbling in the sauce this morning? . . . Hey, look, I'm no young goober with newsprint stars in my eyes – like my friends at the Po-Lounge, I've been around the block, too, sometimes with a fifth in my pocket –'

'I'm telling you the *truth*!' fulminated Brokemichael, his harsh sotto voce so intense the veins in his throat turned purple. 'And I *never* have a drop of alcohol before the Officers' Club opens at noon. That "Nobel committee" is actually my clandestine unit, my *actors*!'

'Perhaps we should reschedule this interview –'

'I'll *prove* it to you!' The leader of Suicidal Six raced to a file cabinet, slapped open a drawer, and yanked out a number of manila folders. He ran back to his desk and threw them indiscriminately across the top, opening several and scattering dozens of photographs helter-skelter. 'There they *are*! We keep records of their various disguises so as not to duplicate them on succeeding operations in case of past photo surveillance . . . Here, *here*! These are the last pictures – the hair, a few short beards, the glasses and even the eyebrows. *These* are the men you saw on television in the press conference at Logan Airport in Boston! Look, *look!*'

'I'll be *damned*,' said the journalist, now standing and studying the eight-by-ten glossy photographs. 'I believe you're right.'

'I *am* right! These are the Suicidal Six, *my* creation!'

'But why are they in Boston?'

'It's top secret, max-classified to the zenith.'

'Well, General, I hate to tell you, but all you've shown me is disconnected visual possibilities. They're meaningless without an explanation. Remember, we're on "post-occurrence disclosure," so it's okay, you can tell me.'

'My name won't be mentioned – except perhaps to your "Po-Lounge" friends, who I'd *kill* to meet?'

'My word as a journalist,' agreed the man who called himself Harrison.

'Well, that general you mentioned – that disgraced *former* general – is a traitor to our country. I won't go into all the details, but if he carries out his plan, this nation stands to lose its primary first and second strike capabilities.'

'He's that – Soldier of the whatever?' interrupted Harrison.

'"Soldier of the Century," but it's all a hoax, a scam to pull him in and take him! And my men, my *actors* are doing that right now!'

'I'm genuinely sorry to hear that, General, *genuinely* sorry.'

'Why? He's demented.'

'He's *what*?'

'He's a screwball, a mental case –'

'Then why is he so goddamned important?'

'Because he and a criminal lawyer from Harvard, accent on criminal – who *I* know something about – have worked up some big fraud case against our perfect government that could cost us – especially the Pentagon – more millions than we could con from Congress in a hundred years!'

'What case?'

'I don't have the particulars, only the essence, and let me

tell you, it's a Rocky Horror Show – did you ever see that movie?'

'Sorry,' growled the journalist, his blatant hostility apparent, but apparently not to Brokey the Deuce. 'Who is this general?' asked the man called Harrison, choking out the question.

'A crazy son of a bitch named Hawkins, a real troublemaker, always has been.'

'I remember that name. Didn't he win the Congressional twice?'

'He's also a maniac. Eighty percent of the Congressionals get it after they're dead. How come he wasn't killed – maybe there's a story there?'

'*Auuaagh!*' coughed the journalist, the fire now in *his* eyes. 'How come Air Force Two carried these impostors to Boston?' he asked, resuming a semblance of control.

'Window dressing for the press conference. You can't ignore that aircraft.'

'You can't rent it from a Hertz counter, either. That plane's an untouchable.'

'Not for some people –'

'Oh, yes, you mentioned a big shot ... "one of the most powerful men in the country," I think you said.'

'Very high rank, damn near the highest. Max-classified.'

'Now that sort of confidential information would really impress my friends in Hollywood. They'd probably fly you out to the Coast for a couple of conferences – all very hush-hush, of course.'

'Conferences?'

'They look ahead, General, way down the road, they have to. A picture starts with a high concept; the development takes a couple of years. Good Lord, every major star in the industry would be at your feet – you'd have to meet 'em all for pre-casting purposes.'

'Meet them ... *all*?'

'Sure, but I guess it's out of the question since you can't tell me – on a confidential post-occurrence basis – who the big shot is. Later, any damn fool can reveal the name, and probably will; the time to strike for you is now. After the fact you won't be anything special ... Oh, well, win some, lose some. Let's get on with the interview, General. The cuts in defence spending directly affect the manpower situation, which has to in turn affect troop morale –'

'Wait a minute!' An apoplectic Brokey the Deuce paced back and forth, looking down at the photographs of his magnificent creation/obsession. 'As you say, when the story breaks – and it has to some day – I won't be anyone special, and any damn fool can take credit for what I've done. God, they *will*, too! They'll make a movie and I won't be any part of it. I'll have to pay probably fifty dollars just to sit in a theatre and watch what they've done to my masterpiece. Oh, Christ, it's terrible!'

'That's life, as Old Blue Eyes sings in that song,' said the journalist, his pen poised above his notepad. 'For a fact, though, Francis Albert is looking for a good character role – he might even play you.'

'Francis Albert ... ?'

'I mean Frank, naturally, Sinatra, of course.'

'*No!*' roared the brigadier general. 'I did all this and did it *my way!*'

'What was that?'

'All right, I'll tell you,' said the perspiring Brokemichael. 'Later on, down the road, he'll probably thank me, maybe find me another star, and even if he doesn't he can damn well pay fifty dollars himself and watch that movie, *my* movie.'

'I can't follow you, General.'

'The Secretary of State!' whispered Brokey the Deuce. '*He's* the one my Suicidal Six are on the Boston mission for. He arrived here yesterday incognito, nobody on the base knew who he was, his ID a processed fake!'

'*Bingo!*' shouted the Hawk, leaping up from the chair to his full height and ripping the dull red wig off his head. '*Gotcha*, Deucey!' he continued yelling as he tore apart his collar and tie while yanking the steel-rimmed glasses away from his face. 'How *are* ya, old buddy, you miserable son of a *bitch*?'

Ethelred Brokemichael was beyond speech; in a word, he

was paralysed. A series of deep-throated grunts combined with high-pitched nasal wheezes emerged from his gaped mouth in the lower middle of his contorted face. 'Ahhhh . . . *ahhhh*!'

'Is that any way to greet an old buddy, even if he is a mental case and a misfit who probably shouldn't have been given his Congressionals?'

'Aiya . . . *aiya*!'

'Oh, I forgot, he's also a traitor and a troublemaker, and maybe there's a story behind those medals like directing his own fire on himself, that might do it.'

'Nyahh . . . *nyahh*!'

'You mean you don't think that'd work, you *pissant*?'

'Mac, *stop* it!' cried Brokey the Deuce, recovering sufficiently to protest. 'You don't know what I've been going through . . . a divorce – the bitch is bleeding me dry – and fighting Washington for funds, and keeping my unit happy – Jesus, I have to arrange captive audiences for their goddamned staged readings when the recruits don't understand a word and smoke funny cigarettes to get through the ordeals . . . Have *mercy*, Mac, I'm just trying to survive! What would you have done, tell the Secretary of State to shove it?'

'I probably would have.'

'Yeah, well you never had to pay a dime in alimony.'

'Of course not. I taught my fillies how to take care of themselves and by God, they did. If I'm short, any one of 'em will ante up.'

'I'll never understand, never.'

'It's simple. I cared for each and every one and helped them to be better than they were. You didn't care and you didn't help.'

'Well, damn it, Mac, that wall-eyed Pease made a hell of a case against you! And when he told me that lousy punk lawyer Devereaux was involved, I went bananas – dedicated bananas.'

'That's kind of a shame, Deucey, because that "punk" Devereaux is the reason I'm here . . . to help you get your ass out of the biggest sling it could land in.'

'What?'

'It's time for *you* to have a little mercy, General. Sam Devereaux now knows he overstated his charges against you and wants to make up for his younger indiscretions. Do you think I'd risk coming down here and walk right into the enemy's camp if he hadn't insisted?'

'What the hell are you talking about?'

'You're being set up, Brokey. Sam found out and literally ordered me to fly down and warn you.'

'What? *How?*'

'There's this minor lawsuit against the government – someone's always suing the government – but this one is a major embarrassment to Warren Pease, and he's a very image-conscious politician. He wants it eliminated, so he enlists you and your team to do his dirty work, convincing you it's a big national crisis, and the minute you've done it, he doesn't *know* you! The lawsuit's thrown out of court 'cause the plaintiffs aren't there, somebody's bound to protest, and the elimination trail leads right to your Suicidal Six – and *you*. A general officer who only barely survived serious charges in the Golden Triangle. You're dead meat, Brokey.'

'Holy *shit*! Maybe I ought to call them back.'

'If I were you, I'd also insert an official memorandum in your files – dated yesterday – that upon reconsideration you withdrew your troops for you believed the mission was beyond military constitutional authority. If there's a congressional investigation, hang Pease, not yourself.'

'Goddamn, I will! . . . Mac, how did you know so much about LA – the Coast, and the Polo Lounge and all those other things you talked about?'

'You forget, old buddy, they did a movie about me. I was the consultant for ten crazy weeks out there, courtesy of the Pentagon pricky-shits who thought it would do wonders for recruitment quotas.'

'They took a nose dive, everyone knows that. It was the worse damn flick I ever saw and I'm something of an expert. I mean it was really terrible and even though I hated your guts, I bled for you.'

'I hated it too, but there were compensations as only that

place can provide . . . Call your troops back, Deucey. You're being led down the fall-guy path.'

'I will, I *will*. I just have to find a way.'

'Pick up the phone and give the order, that's all you have to do.'

'It's not as easy as that. Christ, I'm countermanding the Secretary of State! Maybe I'll just get sick –'

'You waffling, Deucey?'

'For God's sake, I've got to *think*!'

'Then while you're at it, think about this.' The Hawk unbuttoned his jacket and spread it open, revealing a tape recorder strapped to his chest. 'A colonel I recently field-commissioned suggested I be "wired," that's what he called it. Every word said in this room is recorded.'

'You're *scum*, Mac!'

'Come on, General, we're just a couple of old timers, and I've got to survive, too . . . What's that phrase? "If the devil don't get you, the big deep will"?'

'Never heard it before.'

'Neither have I, but it kinda fits, doesn't it?'

CHAPTER TWENTY-FOUR

Vincent Mangecavallo walked across the white marble floor of the condominium in Miami Beach on his way to the apartment's gym room. Once again he winced at the pink-coloured furniture that was everywhere, including the chairs, sofas, lamps, throw rugs, and even a living room chandelier made up of several hundred descending pink shells that looked like it was going to crash down on somebody's head any minute. Vinnie was no decorator, but the endless combination of pink and white did nothing for him except to figure that the big famous *decoratore* his cousin Ruggio hired was also very big on ballet.

'It ain't pink, Vin,' Ruge had said the day before yesterday over the telephone. 'It's peach, only you call it *pêche*.'

'Why?'

''Cause pink is low price, peach higher, and *pêche* goes through the fuckin' roof. Me, I can't tell the difference, and to be frank, I don't think Rose can either, but it makes her happy, y'know what I mean?'

'The way you live, Cugino, you should always make your wife happy. However, regardless, I appreciate your letting me use the place.'

'As long as you like, Vin. We can't get down there for at least a month, by which time you'll be back among the living. We got pressing business with the El Paso family – but, hey, look at the gym I built, steam bath and all.'

'At the moment, that's where I'm heading when I get off the phone – I'm even wearing a pink towel-type bathrobe, kinda short.'

'That's for the girls, I got blue ones in the gym.'

'What's with the El Paso boys, Ruge?' Vincent had asked.

'They want the whole fuckin' leather saddle market, which takes into account not only the fake dude ranches in New York and PA, but all the fancy fox hunt clubs in west Jersey and New England.'

'Well, with respect, Ruge, horses are like Western, y'know? And saddles maybe should be like cowboys, huh? Western, right?'

'That's bullshit, Vin. Most of that saddle stuff is made in Brooklyn and the Bronx. You give those paisan yippee-yie-yo-yos an inch, first thing you know they'll be into the tracks; and that we can't tolerate.'

'I see your point. I wouldn't on the breath of my dead mother interfere with you.'

'Your mama's not dead, Vinnie. She's in Lauderdale.'

'It's only an expression, Cousin.'

'Hey, Vin, guess what? Tomorrow I'm going to your memorial service! Ain't that *somethin'*?'

'You gonna speak on my behalf?'

'Hell, no, I'm lowlife. But the cardinal's gonna say a few words. Hey, a *cardinal*, Vinnie!'

'I don't know him.'

'Your mama called and cried a lot and made an impact on the collection plate. He'll speak.'

'She'll make a bigger impact when I'm resurrected ... Thanks again for the pad, Cugino.'

Mangecavallo paused beneath the pink-shelled chandelier, reflecting on the telephone conversation he had had with Ruggio two days ago. As then, he was on his way to the small elaborate gym, where he intended to studiously avoid the brand new Nautilus equipment, as if by touching it a person could catch the clap. The sudden memory of that phone conversation, brought on by the faggy Easter egg decor, reminded Vincent that it was time to make another call. It was not a call he was overjoyed to make but it was necessary, and perhaps the information he might be given would make him the happiest man this side of an honest amateur who broke a bank in Vegas. But there was a catch. The news of his being alive and well and pulling strings was restricted to a *very* few people, namely the scumball Wall Streeters on Meat's agenda who would have mouths sealed in cement or later face the rest of their lives in various slammers without the money they figured to make, and his cousin Ruggio. Ruge was also a necessity as Vincent needed a private residence where he could stay securely out of sight until the time came for Smythington-Fontini to pick him up and fly him to the point of his miraculous 'rescue' in the Dry Tortugas.

However, Abul Khaki was not on that exclusive list, nor should he have been, but he, too, was now a necessity. In the world of international finance, Abul was every bit as devious as Ivan Salamander; what made him more dangerous, or successful, depending on one's point of view, was the fact that he was not a citizen of the United States and had more offshore holding companies, like in the Bahamas and the Caymans, than anyone since the more successful pirates buried a couple of thousand trunks in the Caribbean. Also, as Khaki was an Arab from one of those sheikdoms that Washington was always trying to reach on the sly, he had certain built-in protections that came when the government concluded back-channel negotiations with politically unpopular people. People who, for instance, could broker a few thousand missiles and a King James' Bible for three convicts and a prostitute from Damascus. Abul Khaki had a walking case of immunity.

When Mangecavallo had learned of Abul's unadvertised credentials, he entered into a liaison with the Arab that was beneficial to both men. Khaki had numerous shipping interests and tankers pulling into waterfronts everywhere, sometimes carrying more than oil, and after a few embarrassing local busts, Vinnie let Abul know that he and his friends had not inconsiderable influence down at the docks . . . 'from New York to New Orleans and points in between – they're locked up, Mr Cocky.'

'That's Khaki, Mr Mangecuvulo.'

'That's Mangecavallo.'

'I'm sure we'll get to know each other's names.'

They did, and, as is said, one thing led to another, including certain financial services rendered by Abul to his friend Vincent. And when at the firm suggestion of the dons in the tri-state area and Palermo that Mangecavallo go after the directorship of the CIA, Vinnie went to Khaki.

'I gotta problem, Abul. The dons think big and that's good, but they're not much for details and that's bad.'

'The problem, please, my dear friend who has the eyes and the speed of the desert falcon – although, in truth, I've never been to the desert. Extremely hot, I'm told.'

'That's the problem, pal. The heat ... I've got a lot of bread buried in accounts all over the country under different names. Once I've got that job in Washington, and I'll get it, there's no way I can fly around some twenty-two states picking up my cash, a great deal of which I'd prefer to keep private.'

'An absolute, I should think.'

'Definitely.'

'Do you have your bank account books?'

'All four thousand two hundred and twelve.' Vinnie had permitted himself an indictable grin.

'*Ahh*, the gaze of the camel holds more than can be gathered by the rumblings of its several stomachs.'

'Something like that, I guess.'

'Do you trust me, Vincent?'

'Sure, I've got to – just like you've got to trust me, *capisce*?'

'With certainty. The tail of the Bedouin's dog wags in the triumph of its survival ... Have you ever met a Bedouin? No matter, but let me tell you, they smell to high heaven in the marketplace.'

'The bank accounts? The books?'

'Sign several dozen for closure and collection and bring all of them to me. I have on my payroll an artist, a man of extraordinary talent, who can duplicate the signatures of anyone, living or dead, and has done so many times for considerable profit. I shall handle your portfolio myself,

Vincent, a blind trust, as it were, under the aegis of one of the most respectable law firms in Manhattan.'

'*All* of it?'

'Don't be ridiculous. Only an amount commensurate with the estate of a rather successful importer. The remainder you'll really make money with, and I can assure you there'll be no paper trail.'

So Abul Khaki became Mangecavallo's ex officio personal manager with roughly four million in the market and seven times that amount in offshore holding companies. However, it was neither the serviceable friendship nor the service rendered that compelled Vincent to reach Abul. Quite simply, it was because Khaki had a greater in-depth knowledge of the global stock exchanges than any other person Mangecavallo knew, most of it garnered through illegal avenues, the rest through financial acumen. And of all men, Abul Khaki would keep his mouth shut. It was a given for his own survival eternally depended upon it, forget the Bedouin's dog.

'I can't *believe* this!' shrieked the Arab after Vincent had used one of the code names to get through to him – at the moment in Monte Carlo.

'Believe it, Abul, I'll fill you in later –'

'You don't *understand*. I wired ten thousand dollars' worth of floral wreaths for your memorial service yesterday and signed it on behalf of myself and the Israeli government through my offices in New York!'

'Why did you do that?'

'Well, I've made a shekel or two with the Likud, and coupling my name with theirs might lead to further arrangements.'

'It can't hurt,' said Vincent. 'I always got along with the Mossad.'

'I would expect so . . . but you've come back from the *dead*! I'm beside myself with shock, my entire body trembling – I'll lose every hand to the boot in baccarat, costing me hundreds of thousands!'

'Don't play.'

'With three Greeks at the table with whom I do business?

400

Are you *mad*! ... What are you *doing*, Vincent? What is *happening*? The swirling sands of the desert are blinding my universe!'

'You've never been to the desert, Abul.'

'I've seen photographs – appalling, just as your voice is appalling to me as you speak now, from where I know not but I must assume it isn't ethereal.'

'I told you, I'll explain later ... after I'm rescued.'

'*Rescued* ... ? Thank you, dear Vincent, but I don't care to hear another word. In fact, I insist upon it.'

'Then pretend it's not me, just an interested investor. How's the market doing in the States?'

'How is it doing? It's gone quietly *insane*. So much subterfuge, so many secret negotiations – mergers, buy-outs, controlling interests; it's started all over again! It's *madness*!'

'What do the oracles say?'

'They're not talking, even to me. Compared to the market, Alice's looking-glass world is a place of incontestable logic. Nothing makes sense – again even to me.'

'What about the defence-oriented companies?'

'As you Italianos say, they're *pazzo*! When they should be drying up, anticipating equipment conversions everywhere, they're reaching all-time highs. The Soviets called me, both furious and frightened, asking me what I thought, and I had no answers. And my contacts in the White House tell me the President's been on dozens of conference calls with everyone in the Kremlin, assuring them all that it must be the opening Eastern markets *and* the conversions because the Pentagon budget continues to be drastically cut ... I tell you, Vincent, everything is *pazzo*!'

'No, it's not, Abul. It's perfect ... I'll be in touch, I gotta take a steam.'

Warren Pease, Secretary of State, was beside himself, in the outer extremes of anxiety. His left eye was at the moment uncontrollable, racing back and forth like a laser blip trying to centre in on an illusive target. 'What do you mean you can't *find* General Ethelred Brokemichael?' he shouted into the telephone. 'He's under *my* orders – *strike* that – he's under the orders of the President of the United States who expects him to report to this max-classified phone number, which I have now *given* you at least a dozen times! How long do you expect the President of the United States to wait for a lousy brigadier general, *huh*?'

'We're doing the best we can, sir,' said the frightened, exhausted voice from Fort Benning. 'We can't produce what isn't here.'

'Have you sent out search teams?'

'To every movie theatre and restaurant from Cuthbert to Columbus up to Warm Springs. We've checked his logs, his outgoing calls –'

'Anything *there*?'

'Nothing productive but certainly unusual. General Broke-michael placed twenty-seven calls to a hotel in Boston over a two and a half hour period. Naturally we reached the hotel and asked whether the general had left any messages –'

'*Jesus*, you didn't say who you were, did you?'

'Only that it was official government business, nothing specific.'

'And?'

'They just laughed at the name – on four separate occasions. We were assured he wasn't there and that they'd never heard of him – if such a person with that name existed.'

'Keep *looking*!' Pease slammed the phone down on his console, got up from his desk, and began pacing angrily about his office in the State Department. What had that damn fool Brokemichael done, where had he *gone*? How dare he vanish into the military-intelligence woodwork where there were more cracks and knotholes than in the whole Sequoia National Park! What was he thinking of that permitted him to cut himself off from the Secretary of State? . . . Maybe he died, thought Pease. No, that wouldn't help and might only complicate matters – still, if anything had gone wrong, there was nothing to link *him* to the eccentric general who had created the lethal machine that was the Suicidal Six. Warren had arrived at the army base with the proper papers, of course, but they were not in *his* name, and besides, he had worn a short red toupee that covered his thinning hair. As far as the Fort Benning entry and departure logs were concerned, a nondescript lower level accountant from the Pentagon had dropped in to pay his respects to the general ... The red toupee, considered Pease, was really a stroke of genius, as even the political cartoonists made a point of his receding hairline. Where was that *son of a bitch*?

The telephone console interrupted his thoughts; he ran to it, seeing that three lines were lighted, then suddenly a fourth. He punched his secretary's blinking button and picked up the phone, hoping to hear the words 'Fort Benning calling on the relay!' His hopes, however, were dashed when after nearly thirty agonizing seconds, the bitch coolly informed him, 'You have three, now four, calls that I can only describe as being of a personal nature, Mr Secretary, as none cares to describe his business and I don't recognize the names – such as they are.'

'What are they?'

'Bricky, Froggie, Moose and –'

'All right, all *right*,' broke in Warren, not only confused but furious. They were, to a man, his social associates – social and then some – from the Fawning Hill Country Club! They were *never* to call him at his office, that was *bible*! But, of course, *they* were not calling: 'Bricky,' 'Froggie,' 'Moose,' and undoubtedly 'Doozie' had placed the calls. What in God's name had happened now that caused them all to reach him? 'I'll take them in sequence, Mother Tyrania,' he said, slapping his head to still his stressed left eye.

'I'm *not* Tyrania, Mr Secretary. I'm her youngest sister, Andromeda Trueheart.'

'Are you new?'

'As of yesterday, sir. The family felt that at the moment you needed extremely efficient service and Mother Trueheart's on vacation in Lebanon.'

'*Really?*' Visions of garter belts filled what air space was left in Pease's imagination. 'You're the youngest sister ... ?'

'Your calls, sir.'

'Yes, yes, of course. I'll start with the first – "Bricky," right?'

'Right, Mr Secretary. I'll tell the others to hold.'

'*Bricky*, what are you *doing* calling me here?'

'You old fox, Peasie,' said Bricky, the New England banker, oozing subterranean charm. 'I'm going to make you the most honoured alumnus at our class reunion.'

'I thought you said I couldn't go.'

'That's all changed, naturally. I had no idea what that incredible mind of yours was conjuring up. You're a credit to our class, old chum . . . I won't keep you, I know you're busy, but if you ever need a loan, the amount no object, just pick up the phone. Talk soon and let's have lunch – on me, of course.'

'*Froggie*, what the hell is going *on*? I just heard from Bricky –'

'I'm sure I don't have to tell *you*, you Midas incarnate, old sport, and certainly not on this phone,' replied the blond-haired cynic from Fawning Hill. 'We've all talked, and I want you to know that Daphne and I hope you and your dear wife will be our guests at the Debutantes' Cotillion in Fairfax next month. You'll be the guest of honour, of course.'

'I *will*?'

'Naturally. Can't do enough for one of our own, can we?'

'That's very kind –'

'*Kind*? The incredible kindness is yours, sport. You're simply *mahvullous*! Be in touch.'

'*Moose*, will you please tell me –'

'Goddamn, Pisser, you can play at my club any time you like!' cried the president of Petrotoxic Amalgamated. 'Forget what this dumb jackass said before, it'd be a privilege to swing a six iron with you.'

'I really don't understand –'

'Sure in hell you do, and I sure in hell know why you can't talk. Just let me say, my old good buddy-frat tie, you're number one in my social register, never forget it . . . Gotta go; just appointed myself chairman of the board, but if you want the job, it's yours.'

'*Doozie*, I've just spoken with Bricky, Froggie and Moose, and I must say I'm bewildered.'

'I understand, old chummy-chum-chum. There are people in your office, right? Just say "yes," and I'll speak accordingly.'

'I say "no," and you can say whatever you like!'

'What about taps on your phone?'

'Absolutely prohibited. The office is "swept" every morning and lead shields are externally positioned to block electronic surveillance.'

'Good-o, chummy, you've really got a hold on things down there.'

'Actually, it's standard procedure . . . Doozie, what the hell is going on?'

'Are you testing me, Pisser?'

The Secretary of State paused; since nothing else seemed to work, perhaps this was the way to go. 'Maybe I am, Doozie. Maybe I want to make sure you all understand.'

'Let's put it this way, *Mr* Secretary, old boy. You are the most creative thinker our crowd has put forth since we crushed the unions in the twenties. And you've done it through sheer imagination, not a shot fired against a rotten socialist or a left-wing congressman!'

'I must press you, Doozie,' said a stunned Warren Pease haltingly as the perspiration formed on his receding hairline. 'How exactly have I done that?'

'The *UFOs*!' exclaimed Doozie. 'As that socially unacceptable Ivan Salamander put it – very confidentially, of course – we'll now have to arm the entire world! Brilliant, Pisser, absolutely *brilliant*!'

'*UFOs*? What are you talking about?'

'Top drawer, chum, really top drawer.'

'UFOs . . . ? Oh, my *God*!'

The Rockwell jet carrying the Hawk landed at the airport in Manchester, New Hampshire, roughly ten miles south of Hooksett. The decision to bypass Boston and fly directly to Manchester had been Sam Devereaux's, his reasoning being that Mac had been picked up previously by *someone's* surveillance at Logan and it could happen again, so why chance the risk? Also, things were coming to a fast boil and if an hour or two of driving could be saved, do it. Mac's next move was to defuse the Suicidal Six, who, according to Desi the First, were in total disrepair thanks to Desi the Second's culinary talents; the rest was up to the Hawk's persuasive powers.

Paddy Lafferty, his chest bursting with pride and hero worship, picked up the general in the Pinkus limousine and, wonder of wonders, the great man himself chose once again to sit in front with Paddy.

'Tell me, Gunny,' said the Hawk as they sped north toward Hooksett, 'what do you know about actors, I mean real ones?'

'Outside of Sir Henry, not a hell of a lot, General.'

'Well, he's kinda special, I gather; he's got a track record. What about the ones who don't?'

'From everything I've read in the papers and them magazines that Mrs Pinkus leaves in the car, they're all waitin' to be discovered so they can *get* track records. Maybe that's not so bright, but it's what I figure.'

'It's very bright, Paddy. That's the answer.'

'To what, sir?'

'To get certain people to change their minds without thinking too much.'

Eight minutes later the Hawk walked into the ski lodge. It was a bright summer's afternoon and Desi-Two had just served a very late brunch; the results were all too apparent. The lethal members of Suicidal Six were as close to zombiland as corpses were to coffins. They sat around the lounge staring into their own personal horizons as upright dead fish might on a New Bedford dock. The single exception was Sir Henry Irving Sutton, who had obviously been around that block several times before, and was as disgustingly alive as a cawing black crow intruding on a massive collective hangover.

'*Come*, gentlemen!' cried Sir Henry, gently slapping several faces and prodding rib cages as he walked around the room. 'Our multi-decorated general from the North African campaign has come to speak with us!'

'Well said, Major,' said the Hawk approvingly. 'I won't take up much of your time, men, just enough to bring you up to date.'

'To date?'

'What date?'

'You got a date, Marlon?'

'I don't know what he means.'

'Who is he?'

'Give him a lollipop, baby.'

One by one the wide eyes of six intrepid fish focused on Hawkins, who walked to the staircase, climbed two steps, and addressed the members of the anti-terrorist unit. 'Gentlemen,' he began in his best stentorian tradition, 'and you *are* gentlemen as well as outstanding performers and soldiers, my name is Hawkins, MacKenzie Hawkins, the retired general who you were sent out to find and take into custody.'

'My God, it *is*?'

'He looks like the photographs –'

'Somebody *move* . . . !'

'Forget it.'

'My legs won't work, Pilgrim.'

'*Hold* it, men!' exclaimed the Hawk. 'Although I don't think that order's really necessary from what I can see before me. I've just returned from Benning, having conferred with my good friend and long time comrade in arms, General Ethelred Brokemichael, your commander. He sends you his congratulations for another job well done, along with new and concise instructions . . . This mission is cancelled, aborted, dropped into a shredder.'

'*Whoa*, Pilgrim!' said The Duke, rapping his knees to no effect. 'Who says so?'

'General Brokemichael.'

'Why doesn't he call us – us – us himself, himself, himself?'

'You must be that Dusty fella.'

'*I'm* not, ya *motha*!' said Sly menacingly. 'You stand there like a poor excuse for Rosencrantz at Elsinore, but why and how come and for what reason should we believe you, huh, *huh*? Why don't he call us his-self?'

'He – *we* – tried repeatedly from Fort Benning. The phones aren't working here.'

'How come, baby?'

'The storm?'

'What storm, dear boy? I recall no harsh winds or cracks of thunder across the moors.'

'Sir *Larry* . . . ?'

'Don't give me or Stella no crap, we got 'nuff problems!'

'*Marlon* . . . ?'

'The point, Pilgrim, is why should we believe you? Injuns play them games all the time. The war drums stop and you figure you got a break, then the blood-thirsty savages attack. That's when you gotta go for the slaughter.'

'You should work on that, Duke. I met the real one when they did that movie about me, and y'know something, he didn't have a hostile bone in his body.'

'You met The *Duke* . . . ?'

'Just *listen* up!' roared the Hawk, startling the men of Suicidal Six with his harsh command – at least sufficiently so as to catch their undivided attention, such as it was. 'General Brokemichael and I not only arrived at an honourable truce, but we reached a firm conclusion. In short words, men, we were both duped by corrupt politicians who were using your unique abilities to further their own ambitions. As you know, nothing is ever written down concerning your max-classified operations, your objectives delivered orally, and in line with that policy, I have been authorized by my good buddy, Brokey the Deuce – that's an affectionate term, incidentally – to tell you that this mission is cancelled and along with that order, and in light of your superb record over the past five years, he's arranged for all of you to be transferred to suites at the Waldorf-Astoria hotel in New York.'

'What's *there*?' asked Marlon without the slur.

'Why?' said Dusty without repeating himself.

'That's a pleasurable wrinkle,' added Sir Larry.

'It's really very simple,' said the Hawk. 'Your terms of enlistment are up in six months, and considering your extraordinary contributions to the military and the lessening of world tensions, General Brokemichael has arranged for all of you to interview the heads of several studios flying in from Hollywood. They're anxious to make your story into a motion picture.'

'What about *me*?' shouted a distraught Sir Henry.

'I suspect you'll play General Brokemichael.'

'That's better.'

'Goldang, I'm speechless, pilgrims,' said The Duke.

'It's everything we've ever wanted,' said Marlon in perfect English. 'Everything we've *dreamed* of!'

'It's *sensational* . . . !'

'*Stupendous* . . . !'

'We'll play ourselves . . . !'

'And be *together* . . . !'

'Hooray for *Holl-eee-wood* . . . !'

Like a pride of wounded lions delivered from torrential floods in the African veldt, the men of Suicidal Six struggled to their feet and unsteadily lurched toward one another, forming a less than perfect circle. And like weaving, disjointed marionettes, they started to dance around that imperfect circle, bodies colliding amid great if painful laughter. In the lounge of the former ski lodge, they created a *hora* born of a *tarantella* with generous portions of a drunken miners' camp thrown in for good measure. Crescendos of triumph filled the room as Desi the First walked to the staircase and spoke to the Hawk.

'Chu are really a great man, h'enerale! Look how happy they are – chu make them feel so wunnerful!'

'Yeah, well I'll tell you something, D-One,' said MacKenzie, removing a mutilated cigar from his pocket. 'I don't feel so wonderful myself. I feel about as big as a sewer rat and ten times dirtier.'

For the first time since their initial encounter in the men's room at Logan Airport, Desi the First looked disapprovingly at the Hawk. Long and hard.

Warren Pease flew down the stairs of his moderately elegant house in suburban Fairfax in his pyjamas. He raced across the living room in the wash of the hallway light, misjudged the door to his study and crashed into the wall, recouped in panic and ran inside to his blinking telephone. He punched three buttons until he found the right one, fumbled for his desk lamp and, turning it on, fell into the chair screaming.

'Where the hell have you *been*? It's four o'clock in the morning and no one's been able to find you all day and night! With every hour we're closer to catastrophe and you disappear. I demand an explanation!'

'It started with a tummy ache, sir.'

'*What?*' shrieked Pease.

'Stomach trouble. Gas, Mr Secretary.'

'I don't believe this! The country's facing disaster and you have *gas*?'

'It's not something you can control –'

'Where *were* you? Where's that goddamned unit of yours? What's *happening*?'

'Well, the answer to your first question is directly related to your second and third.'

'What did you say . . . ?'

'You see, my acidity – the gas – was brought on by my not being able to raise the unit in Boston, so I went undercover to find them.'

'Undercover *where*?'

'Boston, of course. I hitched a ride on an Air Force Reconn out of Macon and got there around three o'clock this afternoon – actually yesterday afternoon. Naturally, I went immediately to the hotel – it's a very nice hotel –'

'I'm so happy to hear that. What *then*?'

'Well, I had to be very careful, of course, because we wouldn't want any official linkage, I think you'll agree.'

'With every destroyed nerve in my body!' roared the Secretary of State. 'For God's sake, you didn't wear your *uniform*?'

'Please, Mr Secretary, I went undercover. I wore a civilian suit, and just in case I ran into any of our retired Pentagon procurement personnel working in the area, I had a splendid idea. I went through my unit's paraphernalia and found a wig that fit nicely. A touch too red for my taste, but with grey streaks –'

'All right, all right!' broke in Pease. 'What did you *find*?'

'A strange little man in one of the suites – I knew the room numbers, naturally. I recognized his voice immediately as I'd talked with him a number of times from Benning. He's a harmless old fellow the boys hired to take messages, which was very smart of them. He hasn't got much upstairs and that's a plus; he merely takes messages.'

'What did he *say*, for heaven's sake?'

'He repeated what he said to me over the phone from my office more times than I can count. His temporary employers had been called away on business; he didn't know any more than that.'

'That's it? They've simply *vanished*?'

'I have to assume they're zeroing in on the target, Mr Secretary. As I explained, they have broad parameters where the missions are concerned, for so much depends on instantaneous reactions which they're trained to invent.'

'Spook *babble*!' yelled Pease.

'No, sir, it's called improvisation – "improv," for short.'

'You're telling me you don't know what the hell is going on. There's no communication, for Christ's sake!'

'There are frequent occasions when the telephone equipment cannot be trusted, both civilian and government oriented.'

'Who made that up, the Pink *Panther*? Why didn't you return *my* calls?'

'On the Air Force Reconn which I took to Boston, Mr Secretary? You want the airbornes to have your relay number in their computers?'

'Hell, *no*!'

'And when I reached Boston I had no way of knowing you'd called –'

'Didn't you check your office to see if that out-of-sight unit of yours had called *you*?'

'We operate in black-drape deep cover. They have only two numbers: one to a line in my Benning office, which is in my bathroom but activates a light under my desk; and the other at my apartment, which is in my clothes closet and starts a tape of "There's No Business Like Show Business." Naturally, I have a remote for both answering machines and there was nothing on either.'

'I may just slit my wrists,' said the Secretary of State. 'All this high-tech crap means is that nobody can't talk to anybody who's got a pulse.'

'Once removed, sir, is twice removed from exposure ... That's a line from the movie *Thirty-Two Rue Madeleine*. Did you ever see it? Cagney and Abel, simply terrific.'

'I don't want to hear about any goddamned *movies*, soldier. I want to hear that your bunch of gorillas have captured Hawkins and taken him to the SAC base in Westover! That's *all* I want to hear, because if I don't hear that pretty goddamned soon, it could be the end for all of us! All it would take is two of those squirrelly justices on the Court sticking with those predictable left-wing radicals who won't die!'

'All of us, Mr Secretary, or just a few of us? Like a once demoted general of the Army and a very successful unit he created?'

'*What?* ... You don't carry your brass to play games with *me*, soldier!'

'Well, Mr Secretary, if I may ask you from a military point of view, why you're so concerned with Mac Hawkins's activities, whatever they are? The world's changing, becoming less hostile among the great powers, and among the lesser ones we can get together and blow them out of ground like we did with Iraq. Everywhere, on both sides, we're cutting back, our personnel and equipment reduced every day ... Why even yesterday morning a famous journalist flew down to interview me in Benning; he's doing an article on the army's reaction to the economies imposed on the military in the post-perestroika era.'

'P ... p ... post-*perestroika*?' stuttered the Secretary of State, lurching forward over the desk, his perspiration now further aggravating his pivoting left eye. 'Get *with* it, soldier!

What about a far more dangerous threat, the greatest threat we can *imagine*?'

'China, Libya, *Israel*?'

'No, you idiot! The weird people – who knows how far they'll go?'

'The *what*?'

'The . . . the . . . *UFOs!*'

CHAPTER TWENTY-FIVE

Jennifer Redwing rushed out of the morning surf at the beach house in Swampscott. She tugged at the straps of her bathing suit, one of many found in the guest cabanas, and dashed across the sand to the terrace steps where she had draped a towel over the railing. Vigorously, she dried her legs and arms, threw back her hair and massaged her scalp, only to open her eyes and find Sam Devereaux smiling down at her from a chair on the sun deck.

'You're a hell of a swimmer,' he said.

'We learned it luring settlers into the rapids and watching them drown as we swam across,' replied Jenny, laughing.

'You know, I can believe that.'

'You know, it's probably true.' Redwing climbed the steps and walked out on the deck wrapping the towel around her. 'How nice,' she added, looking at the round table of frosted Plexiglas. 'A pot of coffee and three cups.'

'Mugs, actually. I can't drink coffee from cups.'

'That's funny, neither can I,' said Jenny, sitting down. 'I guess that's why I call them cups; it's interchangeable. I must have a dozen in my apartment, very few the same.'

'I must have two dozen and only four are the same. Naturally, those are from mother and they're in some kind of green-coloured crystal, and I never use them.'

'It's called Irish glass, and it's terribly expensive and I've got two, and I never use them either.'

They both laughed and their eyes locked; it was a brief moment, yet not to be dismissed. 'Good Lord,' said Sam, 'we've talked for almost a minute and neither of us has thrown

414

a verbal blade. That calls for me to pour you a cup – a mug – of coffee.'

'Thanks. Just black, please.'

'That's helpful. I forgot the cream or milk or that white powder I avoid because it looks like you could end up in jail for possessing it.'

'Who's the third cup – mug – for?' asked the Indian Aphrodite, accepting the coffee.

'Aaron. My mother's upstairs; she's fallen in love with Roman Z, who said he'd make her a Gypsy breakfast and bring it to her, and Cyrus won't admit it, but he's nursing a hangover in the kitchen.'

'Don't you think he should keep his eye on Roman?'

'You don't know Mother.'

'I may know her better than you, that's why I asked.'

Again their eyes met and their laughter was louder ... warmer. 'You're a wicked Indian lady and I should take back your coffee.'

'The hell you will. Frankly, I think this is just about the best coffee I've ever had.'

'That's right, compound your statement. Roman Z made it. Of course, he combed the dunes and undoubtedly picked up slimy urchins from the ocean to mix in with the grounds, but if you start howling, I'll find a razor and shave off your beard.'

'Oh, *Sam*,' coughed Jenny, replacing her mug on the table. 'You can be amusing even if you're one of the most aggravating men I've ever known.'

'Aggravating? *Me*? Heaven forbid ... But does amusing mean in tepee terms we've got a truce?'

'Why not? I was thinking last night before falling asleep, we have a couple of rugged mountains to climb and we're not going to get over them sniping at each other. From here on the fire will be levelled at us, legally and probably otherwise, the otherwise doing nothing for my blood pressure.'

'Then why don't you let me "run point," as the Hawk would say? I won't cross you at the hearing.'

'I know you won't, but what makes you think you're more

capable of handling the "otherwise" than me? And if you say because you're a man, we're back to the sniping.'

'Well, sniping aside, I suppose that's a natural part of it, but it's minor. The larger part is that I know Mac Hawkins, know the way he reacts in tight situations. I can even anticipate him, and let me tell you, there's no one on earth I'd rather have on my side when the wickets get sticky than Mac.'

'What you're saying is you work well in tandem, as a team.'

'I'm the lesser horse but we have in the past. I've called him a devious son of a bitch more times than a computer could calculate, but when things get nasty, really nasty, I thank the moon and the stars for his God-given deviousness. I can even sense when he's going to pull something out of that incredible military knapsack of his. I sense it and go with the flow.'

'Then you'll have to teach me to do the same, Sam.'

Devereaux paused, his gaze on the mug of coffee; he looked up at her. 'Do you mind my saying that could be foolhardy – even an impediment?'

'You mean I'd get in the way of the good ole boys?'

'To be hard-nosed, you might.'

'Then we'll just have to risk my incompetence.'

'Sniper fire again?'

'Oh, come on, Sam, I know what you're doing and I appreciate it, even your latent heroics. Truthfully, it's tempting because I'm not a fool, I don't see myself as a female commando, but these are my *people*. I can't just fade; they have to know I'm there – was there. For them to listen to me, they have to respect me, and like it or not they won't if I hide while someone else does the legal work, the *tribe's* legal work.'

'I see your point, I don't like it but I see it.' There was the sound of a door opening and closing, followed by footsteps in the living room. Moments later Aaron Pinkus emerged from the house, his frail body encased in white walking shorts and a blue short-sleeved shirt, his head covered by a yellow golfing cap. He blinked at the bright sunlight and walked to the table. 'Morning, Benevolent Employer,' said Devereaux.

'Good morning, Sam, Jennifer,' replied Aaron, sitting down as Redwing poured him coffee. 'Thank you, my dear . . . I thought I heard voices out here, but as they were neither loud nor brimming with invective, I had no idea it was you two.'

'We negotiated a truce,' said Devereaux. 'I lost.'

'So far, things are looking up,' offered the venerated attorney, nodding and sipping from his mug. 'My, this is excellent coffee!'

'Brewed with jellyfish and filthy seaweed.'

'What?'

'Pay no attention, Mr Pinkus. Roman Z made it and Sam's jealous.'

'Why, because of Roman and my mother? Hey, I'm not that sort.'

'Roman Z and *Eleanor?*' Aaron's eyes widened beneath the visor of the yellow golfing cap. 'Perhaps I should go back inside and come out again. Things are a bit disjointed.'

'Never mind, it's silly small talk.'

'I don't know about small talk, my dear, but it's silly in the extreme ... It comes close to being as silly as the mental gymnastics our friend General Hawkins is going through. I just got off the phone with him.'

'What's happening?' asked Devereaux quickly. 'How are things at the lodge?'

'Apparently the ski lodge, or at least the problem contained therein, is moving its "bivouac" to three suites at the Waldorf-Astoria in New York.'

'*Huh?*'

'I was no more specific than you, Sam.'

'It means he's eliminated the problem,' said Jennifer brightly.

'And assumed several new ones, I gather,' added Pinkus, looking at Devereaux. 'He asked that you set up a line of credit at the Waldorf to the amount of one hundred thousand dollars and not to worry. Since it's his dilemma, he'll transfer funds from Berne to Geneva – which I care to know *nothing* about ... Can you *do* that, can *he?* Never mind, nothing!'

'Actually, it's a simple computer transfer, a bank draft to be drawn against by the assigned creditor –'

'I *know* how it's done, that wasn't the question! ... Never mind, *nothing!*'

'That's one problem,' said Redwing. 'What are the others?'

'I'm not entirely sure. He asked me if I knew any motion picture producers.'

'What for?'

'I have no idea. When I told him I once knew a young man at Temple – actually, he was thrown out of the Temple – who I later learned produced several triple X-rated films, but outside of that fellow, no one else in the industry, he said not to worry, he'd go in another direction.'

'This is one of those times when I sense a devious strategy in the making.'

'Devereaux's premonition?' asked Jenny.

'Devereaux's prophesy,' rejoined Sam. 'What else, Aaron?'

'Even odder. He wanted to know if we had any clients who had eye trouble, specifically straying left eyes, and preferably someone in need of an immediate infusion of money.'

'Odd?' questioned Redwing. 'It sounds crazy!'

'Never underestimate the devious, as the gospel according to Oliver North says with dripping sincerity.' Devereaux paused. 'I can't think of any such client, but if I could, I'd march him right into a Chapter Eleven for whatever Mac's got in his knapsack ... Other than that bit of useless trivia, what's our next move, Boss? Did you and the Hawk discuss it?'

'Briefly. We've got two and a half days to go before the hearing at which time you, Jennifer and the general must get out of a vehicle, or vehicles, and mount the steps to the Supreme Court building, be admitted beyond the lobby by the scheduling clerks, pass security and be taken to the chambers of the Chief Justice.'

'Oh, oh, I hear Mac talking,' interrupted Sam.

'Quite right,' agreed Pinkus. 'I believe those were his words, or an approximation thereof, minus a vulgarity or two – or three. He told me he had to approach the situation as if he were mounting a three-man insurgency strike behind enemy lines.'

'That's very comforting,' said Redwing, swallowing. 'What does he expect, a counter-insurgency interdiction where we get our heads blown off?'

'No, he ruled out overt violence, for it could be counter-productive since they might be caught.'

'Thank heaven for small favours,' added Jenny.

'But he did not rule out interdiction, you had that part right, even the word. He thinks the counter-strategy will be to "interdict" either himself or Sam or both from reaching the Chief Justice's chambers, for without them the hearing's a legal wash. Plaintiff and the attorney-of-record must appear together.'

'And *me*?'

'Your appearance, my dear, is by choice – insistence, if you like, as an interested party – and not a legal requirement. However, as you well know, your signed and notarized agreements with the general and Sam here are legally binding. In this situation the interested party controls the case for the plaintiff – not an unknown happenstance.'

'Read that as in mob trials where certain spectators hover around defendants' tables,' said Devereaux, addressing Jenny, his eyes then straying back to Pinkus. 'Why not stay here until around noon the day after tomorrow, take our own plane to Washington, then a couple of ordinary taxis to the Court? I can't see it as a problem. No one knows where we are except the man who hired Cyrus and Roman to join our guard detail, the one Mac spoke to. Even Cyrus agrees with the Hawk now; whoever that man is, he wants to keep us alive and well and heading directly into that hearing.'

'Cyrus also wants to know why,' said Redwing. 'Or didn't he mention that?'

'Mac told him; I was there. This "Commander Y" is settling a score with the people who want to stop the hearing, which means stopping us from getting there.'

'Apparently, my dear, our unknown benefactor was previously a staunch ally of those against us until he learned that these same people had other plans for him. Something in the order of a political sacrifice, if not a human one, neither of which is terribly unusual in Washington, according to the general.'

'But Mr Pinkus ... ' Jennifer squinted, pinching the features of her lovely face, part morning sunlight, part disturbing thought. 'Something's missing, something vital, I think. Perhaps I'm paranoid where Chief Thunder Head is concerned, and why shouldn't I be? But all Hawkins told us last night was that everything was under control – "under *control*." What does that mean? ... Okay, he's somehow called off these actor-guerrillas from blowing us away in ravines – it's always ravines, or cliffs, or whorehouses – but *how*? What happened in Fort Benning? We were all so relieved to hear we could sleep peacefully, we never *asked* him.'

'That's not quite accurate, Jennifer,' said Aaron. 'Prior to this morning, he and I agreed not to talk in specifics over the telephone, for as he pointed out, a previous assault team was sent after us in Hooksett, and a tap on the line would be routine.'

'I thought that line up there was cut,' interrupted Devereaux.

'In the telling, not the reality. He could not say last evening what he said this morning.'

'The tap was shut down? How could he know –'

'It wouldn't matter. This morning he was calling from a pay phone at Sophie's Diner on Route Ninety-three. He even extolled the kielbasy and eggs.'

'*Please*, Mr Pinkus,' said Redwing. 'What did he tell you about Fort Benning?'

'Maddeningly little, my dear, but enough to make this elderly lawyer wonder what happened to the rule of law among those guardians of the concept ... On second thought, I wonder why I'm even astonished any longer.'

'That's pretty heavy, Aaron.'

'What the general told me carries considerable tonnage, young man. To paraphrase our much-decorated soldier, the hostile action against us – essentially against the laws of airing public grievance – emanates from the office of one of our most powerful public figures who has covered his tracks to the point of nonexistence. He cannot be confronted, for there's nothing to confront him with –'

'*Goddamn* it!' exploded Devereaux.

'With everything that's happened, there must be *something*!' cried Jennifer. 'Wait a minute ... that gangster from Brooklyn, the one Hawkins knocked out at the hotel, Caesar somebody-or-other. He was taken into custody!'

'And traced to the deceased director of the Central Intelligence Agency,' said Pinkus.

'That has a familiar ring to it,' noted Sam.

'Those naked men at the Ritz ... ?'

'Disowned by all of Washington, including the zoo. Subsequently they were bailed out by someone claiming to be a member of a nudist cult in California and disappeared.'

'*Damn,*' said Jenny, discouragement as well as anger in the drawn-out expletive. 'We should never have permitted Hawkins to ship those four armed lunatics up at the ski lodge back to wherever it was. We had them for intended assault with deadly weapons, concealed invasion of property, masks, guns, grenades – even a tattooed forehead. We were *idiots* to let Thunder Cigar talk us into it!'

'My dear, they knew absolutely nothing; we questioned them at length – to no avail but incoherence. They, themselves, were maniacally programmed psychopaths, as deniable as the nudists. And to turn them over to the police would have revealed our whereabouts ... Worse, I'm embarrassed to say, since the lodge is in my firm's name, there would have been considerable media interest.'

'Also,' added Devereaux, 'and I'm not in the habit of throwing bouquets at Mac, but he was right. By sending them back, we created the climate that led directly to this crazy Suicidal Six flying into Boston.'

'*And* to General Ethelred Brokemichael,' said Aaron, smiling as wickedly as it was possible for him.

'What do you mean, Mr Pinkus? You made it clear yesterday that Brokemichael would be out of reach, shipped to an unmapped outpost, if he surfaces. You said Washington could not permit the name of the official who ordered up the Air Force Two – I remember because I agreed with you.'

'And we were both right, Jennifer, but we lacked the general's deviousness, as I believe Sam phrased it. That fine military tactician had a voice-activated recorder strapped to his chest during his entire interview with General Broke-michael. The Pentagon couldn't send "Brokey the Deuce" far enough away to be out of reach ... I must tell you, however, that General Hawkins wants it known that it was our mercenary-chemist, Colonel Cyrus, who suggested the device.'

'I assume the name of that powerful public figure is on the tape,' said Sam, controlled but dire hope on his face.

'Most definitely. Even to the fact that he got on the base without being recognized.'

'Who the hell *is* he?' pressed Devereaux.

'I'm afraid our general declines to reveal the name at this time.'

'He can't *do* that,' exclaimed Redwing. 'We're all in this together, we have to *know*!'

'He says if Sammy knew, he'd become a loose cannon and "... mount his high horse and take his personal cavalry into battle ... " to the detriment of Hawkins's next strategy. The "high horse cavalry" words were exact and accurate. I know, for I've lived through a number of Sam's legal indignations.'

'I'm *never* a loose cannon,' protested Devereaux.

'Should I remind you of several loud criticisms you've given the court?'

'They were entirely justified!'

'I never said they weren't; for if they weren't, you'd be with another firm. To your credit, you caused the retirement of at least four judges in the Boston district.'

'*There*, you see?'

'So does the general. He claimed you got on that high horse of yours – by way of bribed pilots and stolen helicopters – from some place in Switzerland to Rome, and he doesn't care for a repeat performance.'

'I *had* to!'

'Why, Sam?' asked Jennifer quietly. 'Why did you have to?'

'Because it was wrong. Morally and ethically wrong, against all the laws of civilized man.'

'Oh God, Devereaux, cut it out! You actually *can* turn me – forget it.'

'What?'

'*Forget* it! . . . So Thunder Trunk won't tell us, Mr Pinkus. What do we do now?'

'We wait. He's having a duplicate made of the tape, and Paddy Lafferty will bring it to us this evening. Then if we don't hear from the general within twenty-four hours, I'm to use whatever influence I have to reach the President of the United States and play the tape for him over the telephone.'

'Very heavy,' said Sam softly.

'The *heaviest*,' agreed Jennifer.

Although the trip south to New York City from Hooksett in Aaron Pinkus's limousine was somewhat cramped in the rear quarters – the Suicidal Six sat three facing three while the Hawk rode in front with Paddy Lafferty – several things were accomplished. The first was made possible by a brief stop at a shopping mall in Lowell, Massachusetts, where the general purchased two additional tape recorders and a carton of one-hour tapes, enough, he figured, for the trip to New York and then some. Along with these items Mac bought a small patch cord with a built-in attenuator that enabled him to transcribe the spoken material from one tape onto a new one in a second machine, thus duplicating whatever recorded dialogue was stored.

'Here, let me show you how it's done. It's really very simple,' the Radio Shack clerk said.

'Son,' replied the Hawk in haste, 'I was crosspatching prehistoric transmitters between the caves before you could turn on a radio.'

Back in the limousine, the first newly purchased tape recorder activated, Mac turned to Brokemichael's men in the rear of the vehicle. 'Gentlemen,' he began, 'since I'll be the liaison between you and these motion picture people you'll be meeting, your commander, my friend Brokey, suggested that you give me a complete rundown of your experiences, both as individuals and as members of your incredibly successful Suicidal Six. It will help me in my subsequent conversations with those big producers ... And don't be put off by the presence of Mr Lafferty here – Gunnery Sergeant Lafferty. We were comrades together at the Bulge.'

'I could die right here on the spot, me soul already sanctified!' choked Paddy under his breath.

'What was that, Gunny?'

'Nothin', General. I'll drive like you taught us to up through Roubaix. Greased lightnin', it was.'

As the huge automobile raced forward, there began an uninterrupted four hours of narrative, the complete history of the unit called the Suicidal Six – uninterrupted that was except when the members interrupted one another, which was frequently, with explosive energy incarnate. By the time they reached Bruckner Boulevard on their way across the bridge to Manhattan's East Side, the Hawk held up his left hand, his right turning off the tape recorder. 'That'll be fine, gentlemen,' he said, his ears ringing from the crescendos of melodramatics from the back seats. 'I've got the full picture now, and both your commander and I thank you.'

'Good *heavens*,' cried Sir Larry. 'I just remembered! Our clothes, the luggage your young adjutants picked up for us at the hotel last night, everything's badly in need of pressing. It would hardly be proper for us to be seen at the Waldorf walking around in wrinkled clothing. Or, God knows, into Sardi's!'

'Good point.' It was a wrinkle Hawkins had not considered, and it had nothing to do with clothes. The last thing they needed was for the exuberant actor-commandos to be parading around anywhere! Especially six high-spirited performers who believed they were on the edge of great success. *Christ!* thought MacKenzie, recalling his brief Hollywood days, all any actor – specifically any unemployed actor – needed was the slightest hint that a coveted role was in the offing and his or her personal network went to work. He never faulted the actors, for unrewarded talent needed all the confidence it could corral, but this was no time for the Suicidal Six to revert to their pre-clandestine lives. *Sardi's!* A theatrical institution! 'Tell you what,' the Hawk continued, 'the minute we get to the rooms we'll have everything sent out to the hotel cleaners.'

'How long will that take?' asked The Duke-cum-chairman of the board.

'Well, it doesn't really matter,' Mac had replied, 'at least not for tonight and maybe not even tomorrow.'

'What?' said Marlon.

'Hey, come on!' added Sylvester.

'I haven't seen the West Forties in years!' interrupted Dustin.

'And Mr Sardi is a close personal friend,' said Telly. 'He's the owner, an ex-marine, by the way –'

'Sorry, gentlemen,' broke in the Hawk. 'I'm afraid I wasn't clear about this bivouac, I just thought you'd naturally understand.'

'Understand what?' Sly spoke again, none too kindly. 'You sound like an agent.'

'Your upcoming conferences demand the ... utmost secrecy. Although your splendid commander, General Broke-michael, is going to bat for you with these Hollywood people, you're still in the army and everything could fall apart if word gets out. I mean really fall *apart*. Therefore, you're confined to quarters until he says otherwise.'

'We'll call him,' suggested Marlon.

'That's *out*! ... I mean all communications are on status "black drape."'

'That's for emergencies,' said Dustin. 'Frequency interception.'

'And that's what we're talking about. Those rotten politicians who tried to pit us against one another are out to wreck your film, your careers. They want it all for themselves!'

'Dirty *bastards*,' exclaimed The Duke. 'I won't deny a lot of them are actors but all their crap is shallow!'

'Not an honest spine in their motivations,' added Sylvester.

'Not an ounce of truth,' stated Marlon emphatically.

'You'll grant there's technique,' said Sir Larry. 'But it's Pavlovian, over-rehearsed, as it were.'

'As it *is*!' confirmed Telly. 'Sound bites, programmed expressions, and wrinkled eyebrows when they forget their lines – when will people wake up?'

'Well, they may *try* to act, but they're not *actors*!' cried The Duke. 'And I'll be damned if they take work away from *us*! . . . We'll confine ourselves to quarters and do whatever else you like, General!'

MacKenzie Hawkins, neat but less than impressive in his grey suit, steel-rimmed glasses, reddish toupee, and slightly stooped shoulders, walked across the carpeted, crowded lobby of the Waldorf, looking for a pay phone. It was shortly past one o'clock in the afternoon, the actor-soldiers of Suicidal Six safely ensconced in adjoining suites on the twelfth floor. Spared Desi the Second's more deleterious culinary fare, refreshed by large amounts of wholesome restorative food, exercise and a decent night's sleep without spiders crawling up the walls, all the members of the unit were fully recovered and in exuberant spirits.

The men had assured him that they had their combat fatigues with them – a vital component – and that they would stay in their suites and make no outside calls, no matter how tempting the urge. As they were getting settled, the Hawk had taken out the original tape recorder from Fort Benning, duplicated the entire conversation with Brokey the Deuce, given the duplicate to Paddy Lafferty and instructed him to take it to Swampscott. Now, bouncing several balls in the air at the same time, he had to make several untraceable calls – the first to Little Joseph in Boston; the second to a retired la-di-da admiral who had sold his soul to front for the State Department and who also owed Mac a favour for saving his miscalculating ass on an offshore battlewagon in Korea's Bay of Wonsan; and finally to one of his dearest old buddies, the first of his four delightful wives, Ginny, in Beverly Hills,

California. He dialled the zero code, entered his credit card number and dialled.

'Little Joseph, it's the general.'

'Hey, *fazool*, what took you so long? The big man wants to talk to you, but he don't want to call that swamp place 'cause he don't know what could be on the Ameches!'

'That dovetails with my strategy, Little Joseph. I want to talk with him.' The Hawk looked down at the number of the pay phone. 'Can you reach him?'

'Yeah. Every half hour he walks by a phone on Collins Avenue in Miami Beach. That's in about ten minutes from now.'

'Should I call him direct?'

'No win, place, or show, fazool. He calls you, not the revoice, that's the word.'

'All right, tell him to call this number in New York, but give me twenty minutes, I'll be here.' Mac gave the number of the Waldorf's pay phone and hung up. He then reached into his coat pocket and withdrew a small notebook; he fingered through the pages until he found the one he wanted. Again, he went through the credit card procedure. 'Hello there, Angus, how's the bull of the North Korean Pampas who just happened to blow up our buried beach radio stations in Wonsan?'

'Who the *hell* are you?' replied the harsh voice of a three-martinied former naval admiral.

'One guess, Frank. You want to go over the sixteen-incher coordinates?'

'*Hawk?* Is that *you*?'

'Who else, sailor?'

'You know damned *well* I had faulty intelligence –'

'Or you misread the figures – eyes-only figures, for you only, Frank.'

'Cut it out, Hawk! How the hell could I know you were there? Give or take a few miles or so, who knew, who *cared*?'

'My ass cared, Frank, along with my team. We were way behind the lines.'

'It's over! I'm *retired*!'

'But you're a consultant, Frank, a big respected expert to the State Department on Far East military affairs. All those parties, the perks, the private planes and vacations, courtesy of the contractors.'

'I'm damned well *worth* it!'

'Except that you can't tell one beach from the other – give or take a few miles or so. That's an expert?'

'Hawk, give me a break! Bringing up old stuff won't do either of us any good. *Jesus*, I saw on television that you were getting a big Swedish award, so what do you want from me? I pick up a few goodies and look after my garden – arthritis and all. So what?'

'So you talk to State.'

'That I do, and I give them my best input.'

'Here's additional input you're going to give them, Frank, or the Soldier of the Century is going to blow the whistle on one of the biggest military blunders in Korea.' The Hawk then detailed his addendum.

The call to Beverly Hills started off poorly. 'Mrs Greenberg, please?'

'There's no Mrs Greenberg at this residence,' said the cold male British voice from California.

'I must have dialled the wrong number –'

'No, you simply used the wrong name, sir. Mr Greenberg left over a year ago. Did you, by chance, care to speak with Lady Cavendish?'

'That's Ginny?'

'That's Lady Cavendish. May I ask who's calling?'

'Hawk's good enough.'

'"Hawk"? As in the revolting predatory bird, sir?'

'Very revolting and *very* predatory. Now tell Lady Caviar or whatever the hell her name is that I'm on the line!'

'I'll tell her but I guarantee nothing.'

The abrupt silence of a telephone on Hold was broken by the loud excited voice of Mac's first wife. '*Sweetie*, how *are* you?'

'I was better before I talked to that clown who should have his adenoids taken out. Who the hell *is* he?'

'Oh, he came with Chauncey; he's been the family butler for years.'

'Chauncey? ... Cavendish?'

'*Lord* Cavendish, sweetie. Oodles of money and everyone wants to meet him. He's on everybody's A list.'

'*A* list?'

'You know, *invitations*, sweetie.'

'What happened to Manny?'

'He got bored with an older woman so I set him free for a large hunk of change.'

'*Goddamn*, Ginny, you're not old!'

'In Manny's eyes, any girl over sixteen is also over the hill ... But enough about me, darling, *you're* the one. I'm so proud of you, Hawk – the Soldier of the Century! All the girls are proud of you!'

'Yeah, well hold up the parties, kid, it all could be a con.'

'*What?* I won't have it – *we* won't have it!'

'Ginny,' interrupted MacKenzie, 'I don't have time. The DC pricky-shits have got my ass in a sling again and I need help.'

'I'll call the girls together this afternoon. What can we do and whom can we do it to? ... Of course, I can't get hold of Annie; she's back in one of those leper colonies, I think, and Madge is on the East Coast – New York or Connecticut or someplace like that – but I'll get her and Lillian on a conference call.'

'I was really just calling you, Ginny, because I think you're the one who can help me.'

'Me, Hawk? Look, I appreciate your chivalry but I really *am* the oldest. It doesn't exactly thrill me to admit it, but Midgey and Lil are probably better suited to your needs. They're both still darling to look at. Of course, Annie remains the champ in that department, but I think the clothes she prefers these days would scare the hell out of anybody in a pair of vulnerable pants.'

'You're a fine and generous woman, Ginny, but it's nothing like that. ... Do you still talk to Manny?'

'Only through the lawyers. He wants some of the paintings

we bought, but I'll be damned if I let the horny little bastard scrape the paint off the cheapest frame.'

'*Goddamn*, there goes the shot I was hoping for!'

'Spell it out, Hawk. What is it that you need?'

'I need one of those screenwriters he hires at the studio to put something together for me.'

'Are they going to do another *movie* about you?'

'Hell, no. Never!'

'I'm relieved to hear it. So what do you need a writer for?'

'Some pretty incredible material, all true, that I want to dangle in front of those Hollywood buddhas, only it's got to look good and I've got to do it quickly. Like in a day, maybe.'

'A *day*?'

'Hell, boiled down it wouldn't be any more than five or ten pages, but pages of pure dynamite, Ginny. I've got it all on a few tapes. Manny would know someone who could do it –'

'So do *you*, sweetie! What about *Madge*?'

'Who?'

'Your number three, *mon général*.'

'Midgey? What about her?'

'Don't you read the trades?'

'The what?'

'The *Hollywood Reporter* and *Daily Variety*, those bibles of soaked-orange land.'

'I'm not so hot on the real Bible, either. What about them?'

'Madge is one of the hottest writers in town! She's so hot she can get *out* of town and write in New York or Connecticut. Her last screenplay, *Mutant Homicidal Lesbian Worms*, cleaned up!'

'I'll be damned. I always knew Midgey had a literary bent, but –'

'Don't *use* that word "literary"!' broke in Lady Cavendish. 'Out here it's death ... Here, I'll give you her telephone number, but you give me a couple of minutes to reach her first and tell her to expect your call. She'll be *so* excited!'

'Ginny, I'm in New York now.'

'Isn't she the lucky one! She's in two-O-three.'

'What's that?'

430

'The area code, a place called Greenwich, but not England. Call her in five minutes, sweetie. And when this is all over, whatever it is, you must come out and meet Chauncey. He'd really like that because he's a great admirer of yours – he was with the Fifth Grenadiers; the Fifth or Fifteenth or Fiftieth, I've never gotten it straight.'

'The Grenadiers were among the *finest*, Ginny! You've really bettered yourself and you can bet your nylons I'll be out to see both of you!'

The sun was briefly shining on MacKenzie Hawkins as he hung up the pay phone in the Waldorf lobby, having scratched his third wife's telephone number on the marblelite counter with the point of his penknife. He was so pleased with the turn of events that he reached into his jacket pocket, pulled out a cigar, masticated it until the proper juices flowed, then lighted it with a field match, also scratched on the counter. A matronly lady in a loud print summer dress at the wall pay phone to his left began coughing violently. She glared at the Hawk between seizures and managed to spew out.

'Such a proper looking man with such a despicable habit!'

'No worse than yours, madam. The management insists that you stop taking those young weight lifters up to the rooms.'

'Good God, who *told* . . . ?' The proper lady blanched and raced away in panic as Mac's phone rang.

'Commander Y?' said Hawkins quietly.

'General, it's time we met.'

'Optimum, sir! But if you're still dead, how can we?'

'I've got such a hell of a disguise my own mother wouldn't know me, may she rest in peace.'

'Sorry for your loss, fella. Always tough to lose your mother.'

'Yeah, she's in Lauderdale . . . Listen, I got a lot on my mind so we gotta talk fast, mainly how you get to that hearing two days from now. Have you got a plan?'

'One's forming up, Commander, that's why I wanted us to confer. I'm very impressed by the guard detail you sent us –'

'Detail? What details?'

'The mercs.'

'Who?'

'The two men you hired for our additional protection.'

'Oh, yeah, I gotta lot on my mind. Sorry about the Nazi, I figured he'd shave with pigshit if you ordered him to.'

'Nazi? What Nazi?'

'Oh, yeah, I forgot, he got lost. So what's this plan?'

'First, I'd like your permission to include the detail.'

'Include whatever you like – like what details are you referring to.'

'The *guards*, Commander.'

'Oh, yeah, sorry about the Kraut. Look, I gotta talk fast, and since your plan isn't solid, I'd feel one hell of a lot better if you and that nut lawyer of yours were in my immediate presence, if you know what I mean.'

'*Sam?* You've heard about Sam Devereaux?'

'Not pronounced that way, but I understand that when word was leaked to the Five-Sider brass at Defense that this Deveroxx was your lousy lawyer, they wanted blood, like with a grenade implanted in his haemorrhoids. It seems when he was with the IG he fingered the wrong army banana in Cambodia.'

'That's all been settled, Commander, the error's been rectified.'

'It may be from your mouth to God's ear, but it ain't reached the Joint Chiefs. A couple of those West Pointys want to hang the son of a bitch. He's up there with you on the most-wanted list.'

'I hadn't counted on that complication,' said the Hawk curtly. 'There's no cause for all this hostility, there really isn't.'

'*Hoo-hay*, as Little Joey would say,' yelled Vinnie the Bam-Bam. 'Maybe you forgot the end of the road with this scam of yours! *SAC* – in this case it's got nothin' to do with a bag of potatoes.'

'Yes, I understand that, Commander, but a nonviolent

resolution is still possible – not likely, but possible. It's worth a try.'

'Let me tell you what *I* got in mind,' interrupted Mangecavallo. 'I want you and the legal lasagna down in DC by tonight. I'll fly up, you fly down, and I'll put you in storage until we take you in an armoured car to the Court. What could be *better*?'

'You obviously have little experience in grey to black operations, Commander Y. Breaching the enemy's lines is simple; it's how you infiltrate beyond that counts. Each point to target-zero has to be calculated.'

'Speak fuckin' English, huh, pal!'

'Every barrier to the Chief Justice's chambers has to be surmounted. There's a way to do it – maybe.'

'*Maybe?* We got no time for maybes!'

'Maybe we do. And I agree with you we meet tonight in Washington, only I'll tell *you* where ... At the Lincoln Memorial, two hundred paces from the front and two hundred paces to the right. Eight o'clock sharp. *Got* it, Commander?'

'Got *what*? I got *bullshit*!'

'I have no time for hot-headed civilians,' said MacKenzie. 'I, too, have many things on my mind. *Be* there!'

'Brokey, this is Mac,' said Hawkins, retrieving his telephone credit card as the strains of 'There's No Business Like Show Business' were cut off by Brokemichael's voice.

'*Jesus*, you don't know what you've *done* to me, Mac! The goddamned Secretary of *State*, for Christ's sake. He wants my *ass*!'

'Trust me, Brokey, you may have his. Now listen to me and do exactly what I tell you to do. Catch a plane to Washington and ... '

'Frank, this is Hawk. Did you do it? Did you reach that wall-eyed son of a bitch, or are you *history* on Embassy Row?'

'I did it, you *bastard*, and all he wants are my stripes and my perks, you *deep sixer*! I'm dead in the basket!'

'*Au contraire*, Admiral, you may have upgraded your consultancy. He knows the time, the place?'

'He told me to shove it and never call him again!'

'Good. He'll be there.'

MacKenzie Hawkins stepped back from the pay phone, re-lit his cigar, and looked over at the open air bar across the crowded lobby. He had a pressing urge to go over to that shadowed sanctuary of long-ago memories when he was a young officer in love, always temporarily but genuinely in love with someone, but he knew there was no time for such indulgence – although he wished there were . . . *Madge*, his third wife, as lovely and as meaningful to him as the others; he had loved them all, not only for what they were, but for what they could become. Once, when he and an overeducated lieutenant hid out in a North Vietnamese cave off the Ho Chi Minh trail and there was nothing to fill the hours but whispered conversation, they had exchanged life stories. There was nothing else to do but be discovered and die.

'You know what you've got, Colonel?'

'What's that, boy?'

'A Galatea complex. You want to turn every beautiful stone image into a thing of reality and knowledge.'

'Wher'd you get that shit?'

'Psychology One, University of Michigan, sir.'

Was there anything wrong with that, whether the image was stone or flesh? But Madge, like the others, had a far-off dream – to be a writer. Mac had winced privately at her attempts, but there was no denying her ability to snap open one's eyes at her far-out characters and her wild stories . . . So Midgey's time had come. It was not exactly Tolstoy, but *Mutant Homicidal Lesbian Worms* had a place somewhere, and as barren as that place was, he was sure his third wife would keep it in amusing perspective. MacKenzie turned back to the pay phone, processed his credit card, and pushed the numbers. The ringing stopped; the phone was lifted off the hook and all that could be heard were screams of horror, of *terror*.

'Help, *help!*' shrieked the female voice over the line. 'The worms are slithering up from the floors and out of the walls! *Thousands* of them! They're *after* me! It's in their weaving heads! They're going to assault me!'

Abruptly there was silence, the silence of dread.

'Hold *on*, Midgey, I'm on my *way*! What's the goddamned *address?*'

'Oh, come on, Hawk,' said the calm voice suddenly over the line. 'That's only a promo tape.'

'*What* . . . ?'

'The thing they play on the radio and television commercials. The kids love it and their parents want me deported.'

'How'd you know it was *me?*'

'Ginny called a few minutes ago and nobody has this number but us girls and my agent, who never calls me unless there's a problem, and wouldn't you love it, but there never is! *You* did this for me, Mac, and I'll never know how to thank you enough.'

'Then Ginny didn't tell you?'

'Oh, the screen treatment thing, the ten-page proposal; sure she did. I've got the courier service on standby, waiting for your address. Just give the driver the tapes and you'll have something by morning. Good Lord, it's the *least* I can do!'

'You're a swell girl, Midgey, and I really appreciate this.'

'"Swell girl" – that's so like you, Hawk. But if the truth be told, you're the swellest guy any of us girls ever knew – except sometimes I think you went too far with Annie.'

'*I* didn't do it –'

'We know; she stays in touch and we've all promised not to say anything. My God, who'd *believe* it?'

'She's happy, Madge.'

'I know, Mac. That's your genius.'

'I'm no genius – except maybe in certain military situations.'

'Don't try to sell that to four girls who had nowhere to go until you came along.'

'I'm at the Waldorf,' said Hawkins abruptly as he wiped the start of a tear from his eye, revolted by its appearance. 'Tell your courier service to go directly to Suite Twelve A; it's in the name of Devereaux, in case he's stopped or questioned.'

'Devereaux? *Sam* Devereaux? That lovely delicious boy!'

'You stay in two-o-three, Midgey. He's aged considerably and has a wife and four kids now.'

'Son of a bitch, that's a *tragedy*!' cried the third ex-wife of MacKenzie Hawkins.

CHAPTER TWENTY-SIX

The day at Swampscott passed in ennui, the lack of activity causing the three attorneys to make constant calls to their offices in the hopes that someone wanted their individual judgments, expertise, decisions . . . *anything*. Unfortunately for each, as the games of summer were at full revel, no one seemed to require anything except bits of information relative to inconsequential problems. The idleness, compounded by the frustration of not knowing what the Hawk was doing, led to a degree of testiness, especially between Sam and Jennifer, the latter again ruminating on the whole insane situation.

'Why did you and your mental permutation of a general ever come *into* my life, *our* lives?'

'Hey, just wait a minute, I didn't come into your life, you took a taxi to my *house*!'

'I didn't have a choice –'

'No, of course not, the cab driver pulled out a gun and said that's where you're going –'

'I had to find Hawkins.'

'If I recall correctly, and I do, Charlie Sunset found him first; and instead of saying "No, you can't play in the tribe's sandbox," he said "Sure you can, old man, let's make a castle."'

'Unfair, *unfair*! He was tricked.'

'Then as a lawyer he'd better have the fastest feet in ambulance row because it's the only way he'll get clients.'

'I won't listen to you . . . you're a bigot.'

'Where feeble-minded apologists are concerned, I certainly am.'

'I'm going for a swim –'

'You shouldn't.'

'Why not? Aren't there enough frenzied sharks out there for you?'

'If there are, say adios to Aaron and my mother, as well as Cyrus and Roman Z.'

'They're all swimming?'

'Mother and Aaron wanted to and our mercs said they couldn't go alone.'

'That's sweet.'

'I don't think they get paid if people drown.'

'Why shouldn't I join them?'

'Because the giant Aaron Pinkus of Boston law said you ought to read and re-read Mac's brief until you can quote from it. As an *amicus curiae* you may be challenged by the Court.'

'I've read and re-read it and there's no section I can't quote from.'

'What did you think?'

'It's brilliant ... goddamned *brilliant* and I hate it!'

'Precisely my first reaction. He had no right being able to do it ... Is it true?'

'You know, it could well be. The legends we all heard growing up, passed from generation to generation and undoubtedly exaggerated and twisted in the process, have a lot of melodramatic correlations. Even symbolically.'

'What do you mean "symbolically"?'

'Fables of animals anthropomorphized. The cruel albino wolf tricking the dark-furred goats into grazing in a mountain pass from which there was no escape except through the flames of a forest fire, a fire that spread down from the pass and through the fields taking away their food, their homes, really.'

'The bank in Omaha that was torched?' asked Devereaux.

'Maybe. Who knows?'

'Let's both take a swim,' said Sam.

'Sorry I blew up –'

'An eruption now and then cools off the volcano. It's an old Indian proverb – Navajo, I think.'

'Forked-tongue lawman has horse tails for brains,' said Jennifer Redwing, laughing softly. 'The flatlands of the Navajo don't have mountains, much less volcanoes.'

'You never saw a Navajo brave pissed off because his wife gave a turquoise armband to the flasher in the next tepee?'

'You *are* incorrigible. Come on, let's get suits.'

'Let me take you to the cabana – it's not the Casbah, but it might do.'

'Let me give you a real Indian proverb. *Wanchogagog manchogagog* – oh, hell, in English since there are two cabanas, it sort of means one for the girls and one for the boys. "You fish on your side, I'll fish on my side, and nobody fishes in the middle."'

'How arcane, if not Victorian. No fun at all.'

The kitchen door swung open as Desis One and Two appeared, both obviously in a hurry. 'Where's d'big black Cyrus?' asked Desi the First. 'We gotta go!'

'Go where? Why?'

'Into Boston, Mr Sam,' replied D-Two. 'We got h'orders from the h'enerale!'

'You talked to the *general?*' said Redwing. 'I didn't hear the phone ring.'

'No *teléfono* ring here,' said D-One. 'We call the hotel every hour to check with José Pocito. He tells us what to do.'

'What are you going to Boston for?' asked Devereaux.

'To pick up dat crazy actor, Mr Major Sooton and drive him to dee h'airport. The great h'enerale has talked to him and he expects us quick.'

'What's *happening?*' asked Jennifer.

'I'm not sure you should ask,' cautioned Sam the lawyer.

'We gotta hurry,' said Desi the First. 'Major Sooton says he gotta stop at some big store for *correcto* "attire," which I don' t'ink is for an automobile . . . Where ees Colonel Cyrus?'

'On the beach,' replied a perplexed Redwing.

'You get d' car, D-Two,' ordered D-One. 'I'll tell d'colonel and meet you in the garage. *Pronto!*'

'*Sí, amigo!*'

The adjutants raced away, one out to the beach by way of the sundeck, the other through the foyer to the garage off the circular drive. Sam turned to Jenny. 'Did I say something about "Devereaux's prophesy"?'

'Why is he keeping us in the dark?'

'It's the devious part of his devious strategy.'

'What?'

'He doesn't tell you what it is until he's gone so far it's irreversible. You can't turn back.'

'Oh, that's wonderful!' exclaimed Redwing. 'Suppose he's all wet, all wrong?'

'He's convinced that's not possible.'

'And you?'

'If you take away his original premise, which is *always* wrong, his track record's not bad.'

'That's not good enough!'

'In fact, it's really terrific, goddamnit.'

'Why don't I feel more reassured?'

'Because the "goddamnit" means he drives you to the edge of oblivion and one day he'll take that extra step and we'll all go tumbling down.'

'He's going to have Mr Sutton impersonate him, isn't he?'

'Probably; he's seen him in action.'

'I wonder where.'

'Don't even think about it. It's easier that way.'

Johnny Calfnose, resplendent in his brightly beaded buckskins and jacket, stared forlornly at the sheets of rain beyond the admissions window in the Wopotami Welcome Wagon Wigwam, a large garishly painted structure in the shape of a covered wagon with the four sides of a colourful Indian tepee surging up from the centre of the ersatz layers of canvas. When Chief Thunder Head had designed the edifice and brought in carpenters from Omaha to build it, the inhabitants of the reservation had looked on in bewilderment. The Council of Elders' Eagle Eyes had asked Calfnose,

'What's that lunatic doing now? What's it supposed to be?'

'He says it represents the two images most associated with the old West. The pioneers' covered wagon and the symbolic tepee from which the savage tribes came out to slaughter them.'

'He's all heart and mashed brains. Tell him we need to rent a couple of Caterpillar backhoes, scything machines, a minimum of ten mustangs, and at least a dozen labourers.'

'What for?'

'He wants us to clear the north field and stage "raiding parties."'

'*Mustangs?*'

'Not the cars, horses. If we're going to gallop around the circled wagons, we'd better teach the younger ones how to ride, and the few nags we've got couldn't make it from one end of the field to the other.'

'Okay, but what's with the labourers?'

'We may be savages, Calfnose, but collectively we're the "Noble Savage." We don't do that kind of menial work. Or windows either.'

That was months ago and this was now, an afternoon drenched with rain and no summer tourists to buy a plethora of souvenirs made in Taiwan. Johnny Calfnose got up from his stool in front of the admissions window, walked through the narrow leather-sheeted entrance to his comfortable living quarters, and went to the television set. He turned it on, switched the cable channels to a ball game, and sat down in his Brincusi sling chair to enjoy the late afternoon watching a doubleheader. However, all was savagely interrupted by the ringing of a telephone – the *red phone*. Thunder Head!

'Here I *am*, Chief,' cried Johnny, grabbing the phone off the Adolfo parquet table.

'Plan A-one. *Execute.*'

'You're kidding – you gotta be *kidding*!'

'A general officer doesn't "kid" when the assault's in progress. It's code Bright Green! I've alerted the plane at the airport and the bus companies in Omaha and Washington. Everything's at the ready. You leave at dawn, so start spreading the word. All duffels are to be packed and checked by twenty-two hundred hours and the slop shoot's off-limits to the entire DC contingent. That's *gospel*, soldier. There'll be no red-eyed redskins in my brigade. We *march*!'

'Are you sure you don't want to think about this for a couple of weeks, TH?'

'You've got your orders, Sergeant Calfnose. Swift execution is paramount!'

'That's kinda what's bothering me, Big Fella.'

Sundown had come and gone, the massive awe-inspiring statue of Lincoln bathed in floodlights as hushed, mesmerized tourists weaved around one another for differing views of the masterpiece. An odd exception was a strange-looking man who seemed furtively occupied with the shadowed grass beneath his feet. He kept walking directly away from the memorial's steps in a straight line, under his breath verbally abusing the sightseers he collided with, and every now and then thrusting his hands out into the stomachs and cameras of the offending intruders as he adjusted the red wig that kept falling over his ears and his neck.

Vincent Mangecavallo had not been born and brought up in Brooklyn's *Mondo Italiano* without learning a few things. He knew when it was preferable to arrive at a 'meet' long before the appointed hour because a 'meet' could be spelled differently, like in a carcase on a hook in a slaughterhouse. The problem Vinnie the Bam-Bam had was in the plural word 'paces' – what the hell was a pace? Was it a foot, a yard, a yard and a half, or something in between? He had heard the stories from the old days in Sicily where duels were fought with *Lupo* guns, the firing marked off by paces as the enemies walked in short steps or long steps, all counted off by a referee, or sometimes by a drum, and nobody paid much attention because the one who cheated always won. But this was *America*. 'Paces' should be more specific in the interests of fairness and honesty.

Also, how the *hell* could he keep an accurate count while walking through the crowds at night? He would reach like number sixty-three, bump into some clowns causing his wig to sideslip on his head and blinding him, resume his 'pacing' and forget the number he had reached. So it was back to the steps and start again! *Shit!* On the sixth attempt, hanging a right for the final yardage, he reached a large tree that had a brass plate on the trunk spelling out the date it was planted by some president in the year one and who could care less, but there was a circular bench around the goddamned tree that made a little more sense. He could sit down and his face not necessarily be seen by the nut general he was to meet for the purpose of exchanging information.

Naturally, Vincent decided to walk away from the tree and wait in the shadows of another – who knew how many lousy *paces* away. But he knew what to watch for: a tall old joker hanging around that brass-plaqued tree and probably wearing feathers in his head.

Watching the obese figure circling the rendezvous, the uniformed General Ethelred Brokemichael was astonished! He had never liked MacKenzie Hawkins; in fact, quite the opposite since Mac was the despised Heseltine's buddy, but he had always respected the tough old soldier's abilities. At the moment, however, he had to question all those years of silent admiration. What he had just witnessed was a ridiculous exercise in covert rendezvous procedures – ridiculous, hell, it was grotesque! Hawkins had obviously borrowed or bought a jacket designed for a heavyset man, filled it with stuffing, and to conceal his natural height he walked, or rather half-prowled unnaturally like an ape, through the crowds in front of the Lincoln Memorial – back and forth, *back* and *forth* – a grunting gorilla foraging for berries in the underbrush. It was a sight to sicken the creator of the Suicidal Six! And there could be no error in Brokey the Deuce's recognizing him, for the Hawk still wore his stupid red wig, only here in the warm, humid Washington night it kept falling over his eyes. He obviously had never heard of liquid adhesive, which *anyone* familiar with the theatre would know about; talk of amateur-ville, MacKenzie Hawkins was a novice's neophyte!

Now Brokey's wig, by sheer coincidence only *slightly* red –

auburn, really – was held in place by a Max Factor flesh-toned base tape that was indistinguishable from his hairline, especially in soft light, a low 'muted amber' in theatrical parlance. Professionalism would take the day, thought Brokemichael, deciding to surprise the Hawk who had retreated to a surveillance position beneath a large spreading Japanese maple thirty-odd feet from the rendezvous. The Deuce was exhilarated; Mac had made an ass of him in Benning and now he would return the favour.

He made a wide circle, skirting the edge of the crowds in the diminishing wash of the memorial's floodlights, every once in a while passing another uniform whose arm instantly responded with a salute to his rank. As he approached the maple tree from the eastern flank, the intermittent salutes caused Brokey to wonder again why the Hawk insisted that he wear his uniform for such a covert rendezvous. When he had repeatedly asked why, the only reply he got was:

'Just do it, and wear every goddamned medal you ever won or issued yourself! Remember, everything we talked about down in Benning is on tape. *My* tape.'

The Deuce reached the maple tree and slowly, his back against the trunk, sidestepped his way around the bark until he stood silently next to the *really* amateur former soldier who had made a fool of him and who was now staring intensely at the rendezvous ground. The really *stupid* thing was that instead of standing up straight for a better view, the idiot continued to buckle his knees and hunch over the stuffing in his coat, thus maintaining the short stature of his disguise in the dark *shadows* of the spreading maple. Amateur-ville!

'You expecting somebody?' said Brokey quietly.

'Holy *shit*!' exploded the disguised civilian, whipping his head around with such force his red wig spun ninety degrees to the left, the sideburns descending over his forehead. 'It's *you*? . . . Sure, it's you, you got on the brass threads!'

'You can stand up now, Mac.'

'Stand up on what?'

'Nobody can see us here for God's sake. I can barely see my

feet, but I sure as hell can see that dumb wig of yours. I think it's on backwards.'

'Yeah, well yours ain't so totally perfect, GI Joe!' said the civilian, adjusting his hairpiece. 'A lot of the bald older dons wear that shit with the Max Factor tape that suddenly takes the top wrinkles away from your forehead – you can always tell, but, naturally, we don't say a word.'

'What do you mean "tell"? How can you *tell* in this light?'

'Because, you jerk, the light reflects off clear tape.'

'Okay, okay, Mac. Now stand up so we can talk.'

'So you're a couple of inches taller, what d'ya want from me? Go downtown and buy a pair of elevator shoes or maybe a couple of stilts? What's with you?'

'You mean you . . . ?' Brokey the Deuce leaned over, his neck thrust forward. '*You're* not Hawkins!'

'*Hold* it, pal!' cried Mangecavallo. '*You're* not Hawkins! I got photographs!'

'Who are *you?*'

'Who the fuck are *you?*'

'I'm to meet the Hawk – over *there!*' exclaimed Broke-michael.

'So am *I!*'

'You're wearing a red wig –'

'So the hell are you –'

'He wore one in Benning!'

'I got mine in Miami Beach –'

'I got mine from my unit's extensive wardrobe.'

'You like *pêche*, too, huh?'

'What are you talking about?'

'What are *you* talking about?'

'*Wait* a minute!' Brokemichael's eyes had been drawn in exasperation to the brass-plaqued rendezvous tree. '*Look!* Over there! Do you see what I see?'

'You mean the skinny priest in the black suit and collar sniffing around the meet like a Doberman who's gotta take a piss?'

'That's exactly who I mean.'

'So what? Maybe he wants to sit down on the bench – there's like a bunch of slats that go around the tree –'

'I *know* that,' said Brokey the Deuce, squinting in the shadows of the maple. '*Now*, look,' he continued as the cleric came into the western wash of the distant floodlights. 'What do you see?'

'The collar, the suit, and he's got red hair, so *what*?'

'Amateur-ville,' determined the creator of the Suicidal Six. 'It's not hair, it's a wig; and like yours, very badly done. Too long in the nape and too wide at the temples . . . Odd, I seem to recall seeing him before.'

'What Nate and whose temple? What's religion got to do with anything?'

'Not religion, the *wig*. It's not properly fitted.'

'Oh, I forgot, *pêche*. I gotta find me a soldier *poofereeno* at the biggest conference of my life – not that I personally got a problem, you understand – only that this is *no* time for unholy tolerances!'

'Perhaps the wigs are the symbols . . . ?'

'Of *what*, for Christ's sake? We gonna join a protest?'

'Don't you see? He had all of us wear red wigs!'

'He didn't have me do a goddamned thing. I told you, I got mine in Miami Beach at a weirdo shop near the Fontanbloo.'

'And I found mine in my unit's wardrobe room –'

'Some unit –'

'But *he* wore a red wig when he came to see *me* . . . My God, it was subliminal motivation directed at *improv*!'

'Sub-*who* to *what*?'

'Did he ever use the word "red" to you – use it more than once?'

'Maybe, I don't know. The whole *deal's* about Indians – Redskins, you know what I mean? Maybe he said "Redskins," y'know? But I never saw him, only talked on the phone.'

'That's it! He used his voice as the subconsciously motivating force of conviction. Stanislavski wrote extensively about that.'

'He's a Commie?'

'No, *Stanislavski*, a god of the theatre.'

446

'Oh, Polish, huh? Well, you gotta make allowances.'

'What *deal*?' asked Brokey the Deuce suddenly, snapping his head down at the red-wigged stranger. 'What "deal" are you talking about?'

'That Wop tribe's suit that's in the Supreme Court, what else?'

'In the military, sir,' said Brokemichael firmly and standing tall, 'we do not permit code words that connote ethnic slurs. This nation's outstanding Italian-American citizenry, the sons and daughters of Leonardo Michelangelo and Rocco Machiavelli, are to be treated with the greatest respect for their contributions. The Capones and the Valachis were aberrations.'

'I'll go to Mass tomorrow and light a candle on your behalf for your survival should you meet the sons and daughters of the last two mentioned. In the meantime, what do we do right *now*?'

'I think we should have a conversation with our red-headed priest.'

'Good point. Let's go.'

'Not *yet*!' broke in the deep harsh voice behind them. 'Glad you could make it, gentlemen,' continued the Hawk, coming around the trunk of the maple tree, his trimmed red wig catching the filtered light from the leaves. 'Good to see you again, Brokey . . . and you, sir, I assume, are Commander Y. It's a distinct pleasure to meet you, whoever you are.'

As much as his fear would permit, Warren Pease, Secretary of State, was pleased with himself, even impressed. When he had seen that priest swearing at a cab driver over a fare outside the Hay-Adams hotel, he was struck with an inspiration – he would go to the rendezvous as a man of the cloth! If he did not like what he saw or heard, he could walk away with impunity. After all, nobody gets rough with a priest or a minister in public, it simply was not proper, and more to the point, drew attention.

And, of course, not to go to the rendezvous would be crazy in spite of what he told that dreadful admiral who was forever submitting expense vouchers for places he never went, to see people he never saw on State Department business that did not exist. Pease had soundly berated him over the phone, not to rectify the admiral's abuses, but to learn how much he really knew ... and how he knew it. The answers to both questions were minimal, confused, and disturbing enough to convince Warren to clear the evening's calendar and procure a clerical collar and *rabat*. He had a black suit for state funerals and the inspired reddish toupee completed his outfit.

As he now walked among the crowds at the Lincoln Memorial, the admiral's words rang in his ears.

'Mr Secretary, I've been asked by an old comrade of many years to relay a message to you, a message that could lead to the solution of your most pressing problem – a crisis was the way he described it.'

'What are you talking about? The Department of State has scores of crises every day, and as my time is the most valuable in Washington, I'll thank you to be specific.'

'I'm afraid I can't *be* specific. My old comrade made it clear that it was beyond my clearance, way beyond.'

'That doesn't tell me anything. Be clearer, sailor.'

'He said it had something to do with a group of original Americans – whatever that means – and certain military installations, whatever *they* are.'

'Oh, my God! What *else* did he say?'

'He was very top-max, but he said there was a solution that could weather-wax your skis.'

'Could weather my *who*?'

'Skis ... Frankly, Mr Secretary, I'm not into winter sports, but militarily speaking, I must assume that the code reference means you can reach your objective far more quickly by meeting with him as soon as possible, which is basically his message.'

'What's his name, Admiral?'

'To reveal that would implicate me in a situation I have nothing to do with. I'm only a conduit, Mr Secretary, nothing more. He could have chosen a dozen other ex-militaries, and I wish he had.'

'And *I* could choose to question a large percentage of your expense vouchers and the propriety of those cosy trips you take on diplomatic aircraft! How does that grab you, sailor?'

'I'm only delivering a message, Mr Secretary, I'm not *involved*!'

'Not involved, huh? That's what you say, but why should I believe you? Maybe you're a part of this evil, malicious conspiracy.'

'*What* conspiracy, for Christ's sake?'

'Oh, you'd like that, wouldn't you? You'd like nothing better than for me to spell out the whole horrible mess so you can write a book like all those fine, selfless public servants who were unjustly indicted for doing nothing more than anyone else would do while giving up their stock options by coming down here.'

'I don't know what the hell you're *talking* about!'

'The name, sailor, the *name*!'

'So *you* can write a book and put *me* in it? No way!'

'Well, since you've wasted my time this long, you might as well deliver the rest of your rotten message. Where and when does this unnamed monster think I'll meet him?' The admiral had told him. 'Good, *fine*! I've already forgotten whatever you said. Now, shove it, sailor, and never call me again unless it's to tell me you're resigning from your consultant's contract!'

'Hey, come on, Mr Secretary, I don't want any trouble, honest to God! ... Look, I'll talk to the Prez's buddy, Subagaloo, and he'll tell you –'

'To *Arnold*? No, don't talk to Arnold, *never* talk to Arnold! He'll put you on a list, he'll have you on a list – a list, a list, a horrible, intolerable *list*!'

'Are you all right, Mr Secretary?'

'I'm fine, I'm fine, I really will be fine, but do not do and never do call Arnold Subagaloo. He'll get you on his list, his list, a fretful, dreadful, executionary *list*! ... Over and out, sailor, or whatever you stupid soldiers say!'

He had told off that awful leech, all right, mused Pease, smiling sweetly at an overly made-up little old lady who looked adoringly at him as he approached the maple tree. The rendezvous had to be the tree up ahead, he thought. It was hardly an inspired location and Warren wondered why MacKenzie Hawkins, aka Chief Thunder Head of the nefarious Wopotamis, had chosen it. The light was poor, but perhaps that was good, and there were crowds barely a hundred feet away ... that wasn't bad either, he supposed; there was protection in numbers. Of course, the maniac Hawkins was taking these precautions for his *own* safekeeping, not for the benefit of the Secretary of State. He undoubtedly thought the government would have troops throughout the area hoping to capture him, but that kind of show of force was the last thing all the President's men wanted. It would be terrible PR if the media found out they had set a trap for a two-time winner of the Congressional Medal of Honor. Pease squinted in the dim light under the tree and looked at his watch; he was nearly thirty minutes early. Good, fine; he would walk off to the side and wait – and watch. He rounded the trunk, then stopped, annoyed to see that the little old lady with the garishly rouged cheeks was waiting for him.

'Bless me, Father, for I have sinned,' she said in a high-pitched tremulous voice, standing in front of him under the overhanging maple blocking his way.

'Yes, well ... *vox populi* and all that sort of thing. Some of you aren't perfect but that's the way it goes –'

'I'd like to confess, Father. I *must* confess!'

'That's probably very commendable but I don't think this is the place for it. Besides, I'm in a hurry.'

'The Bible says that in the eyes of the Lord a desert can be the House of God if a sinner's spirit wills it.'

'Hogwash aside, I told you I'm in a hurry.'

'And *I'm* telling you to get your ass behind the tree.'

'Oh, very well, you're forgiven whatever you're capable of doing – *what* did you say?'

'You heard me, Angel Puss!' whispered the now grotesque harridan, her voice abruptly lower, harsher, as she withdrew a straight razor from the folds of her dress and whipped it open. 'Now get behind the tree or the last thing you'll worry about is your vow of chastity.'

'Oh, my *God* – you're not a woman, you're a *man*!'

'It's debatable on both counts, but what I am is a cutter – I love to *cut*. Now, move!'

'Please, *please* don't hurt me, don't . . . oh, my God . . . don't *cut* me!' His whole body trembling, the Secretary of State stepped awkwardly back into the shadows of the tree. 'You really shouldn't, you know. Cutting a priest is a very, *very* big sin.'

'I had you marked fifteen minutes ago, Angel Puss,' hissed the man/woman, his or her wrinkled scarlet lips and swollen purple eyelids revolting in the dim light. 'You and that ugly rug on your head, you're a disgrace to honest deviants everywhere!'

'What . . . ?'

'How *dare* you walk around like that? Looking for little boys, you *creep*? And dressed like a priest? That's *disgusting*!'

'Now, really, madam – mister, whatever you are –'

'What was that? You insulting me, Snake Face?'

'On my word, *never*!' Pease's left eye was in pivotal-orbit. 'I'm only telling you that you don't understand –'

'*I* understand, all right! Creeps like you carry lots of bread in case somebody blows a whistle. Up with it, you *pervert*!'

'Money, you mean *money*? For God's sake, take everything I've got!' The Secretary dug into his pockets and pulled out a number of folded bills. 'Here, *here*, take it!'

'Take what? That's *chickenshit*. I'll have to slash your pockets before I start the *real* cutting!' The androgynous monster forced Pease behind the tree. 'You make a sound, your lips are on the ground, you dirty, *dirty* boy!'

'*Please!*' begged the Secretary of State. 'You don't know who I *am* –'

'But *we* do!' interrupted the strange deep voice from the shadows beyond. 'All right, Brokey . . . you, too, Commander Y, disarm the assault! *Now!*' As one, the elderly West Pointer and the portly middle-aged capo supremo from Brooklyn attacked, the former wrenching the razor away from the hand that clutched it, the latter tackling the legs encased in a wide flowery skirt.

'It's a fuckin' *broad*!' yelled Mangecavallo.

'The *hell* he is!' shouted Brokemichael, yanking the grey-haired wig off the wrinkle-faced, rouge-faced mugger.

Vinnie the Bam-Bam saw his error instantly, and instantly began pummelling the ugly cosmeticized figure that was falling to the ground. 'You no good piece of rotten *mozzerell*!' he roared.

'Let him go, Commander!' ordered the Hawk.

'*Why?*' asked Brokey the Deuce. 'The scumbag should be behind bars!'

'With his fuckin' legs broken!' added the presumably deceased director of the CIA.

'Are *we* going to press charge, gentlemen?'

'What . . . ?' Brokemichael stepped back as Mangecavallo snapped his head up, his red wig once more askew, a sideburn now partially covering his nose, his eyes barely seen. 'He's got a point, Commander whoever-you-are,' said the Deuce.

'Yeah, well maybe he does,' agreed Vincent, administering a last knee into the rib cage of the mugger. 'Pound sand and get outta here, you lowlife!'

'Hey, *fellas*!' shrieked the perpetrator, grinning exuberantly as he grabbed his wig and got to his feet. 'You wanna come to my place? We could *really* have a ball!'

'Get *outta* here.'

'I'm going, I'm *going*.' Skirt flying, the mugger ran across the lawn and disappeared into the crowds.

'Oh, my God, oh, my *God* . . . !' came the quivering sounds from the prone figure on the ground beside Hawkins, his head face down in the grass, his hands gripped above that head. 'Thank you, *thank* you! I might have been *killed*!'

'Why don't you turn over and get up and see if you want to live?' said the Hawk gently, reaching into his pocket and withdrawing a tape recorder.

'What? . . . What are you talking about?' Slowly, Warren Pease pushed himself off the ground, pivoted painfully on his buttocks, and from his sitting position, saw first the resplendent uniform on his right, then, in shock, the face. '*Brokemichael!* What are *you* doing here?'

At that moment, MacKenzie activated his recorder and the sound of Brokemichael's voice filled the enclave. '*The Secretary of State. He's the one my Suicidal Six are on the Boston mission for! . . . That wall-eyed Pease made a hell of a case against you!*'

'Only it wasn't a legitimate case, was it, Mr Secretary?' said General Brokemichael as the Hawk turned off the machine. 'It was a sacrifice. One exonerated old soldier who could never get out from under that cloud of suspicion and his unit of fine young men. We were as expendable as Mac here, not my closest old buddy, but he doesn't deserve to be dropped into an arctic ice floe, either.'

'What are you *talking* about?'

'Perhaps I didn't introduce him. This is the former General MacKenzie Hawkins, twice winner of the Congressional Medal of Honor, who you first tried to have . . . let's say "neutralized" . . . and then ordered my unit to kidnap, destination TBDL, "to be determined later," but definitely north, way far north.'

'Not too terribly pleased to make your acquaintance, Mr Secretary,' said the Hawk. 'You'll forgive me if I don't offer my hand.'

'This is insane, absolutely *insane*! Great issues are at stake, the ultimate strength, the *strike* force of the nation is in the balance!'

'And the only way to put it right is to get rid of those complaining?' asked MacKenzie. 'You can't talk, you can only get rid of the nuisances, who, incidentally, have a *very* legitimate case.'

'You're twisting everything! There are other issues, economic issues, gargantuan financial losses – my God, my *boat*, the *Metropolitan* Club, my class *reunion*, the life I deserve, I was *born* to! You don't understand!'

'*I* do, you smelly *prichute*,' said Vincent Mangecavallo, walking forward in the dull wash of light. 'Like certain people can be useful to you, but you got no use for *them*!'

'Who are *you*? I've seen you before, I know your voice, but I can't . . . I can't –'

'Maybe because my own mother, may she rest in peace in Lauderdale, wouldn't know me, either, due to my one terrific disguise.' Vinnie removed his red wig and squatted in front of the Secretary of State. 'Hello, fazool, how *are* ya? Maybe your country club boys blew up the wrong boat, wadd'ya think of that?'

'*Mangecavallo!* . . . No, *no!* I went to your memorial service the other day! You're gone, you're *dead!* This isn't *happening* to me!'

'Maybe it isn't, you big *diplomático*, maybe it's all a bad dream brought on by the evil in your rotten soul. Maybe I just rose from the arms of Morphine –'

'Morpheus, Commander Y, *Morpheus.*'

'Yeah, him . . . Like from the dead across that big river, come back to haunt you pricks who think you're so *superiore*, like what goes through your stomachs comes out vanilla ice cream. Yeah, fazool, I'm back from the fishes, and the sharks came with me. They give me respect; you never did.'

'*Auggh!*' Suddenly, with a shriek that pierced the night and over the floodlit crowds at the Lincoln Memorial, the Secretary of State wriggled like a trapped reptile, sprang to his feet and raced screaming hysterically across the grounds.

'I gotta *catch* that son of a .bitch!' yelled Mangecavallo, getting up, but not easily due to his weight. 'He'll spill everything!'

'*Forget* it!' cried the Hawk, tripping over the CIA director. 'He's finished, he's out.'

'Wadd'ya talkin'? He's *seen* me!'

'It won't matter. No one will believe him.'

'Mac, you're not making sense!' insisted Brokey the Deuce. 'Do you know who this man *is?*'

'Sure I do, and I'm making sense, too . . . So you're really that Italian fella who ran the Agency?'

'Yeah, it's a long story and I don't like long stories. I got carried away. *Shit!*'

'Melodramatic emotionalism is one of the finest gifts of your race, signore. Think of the great operas – no one could have created them but yourselves. *Capisce Italiano?*'

'Sure, I speak.'

'*Lo capisce inoltre.*'

'That's beautiful, but that cannoli is going to blow apart the whole fuckin' ball of wax!'

'No, he's not, Signor Mangecavallo ... Brokey, do you remember Frank Heffelfinger?'

'"Finger Frank" with his digits on the wrong six-inchers? Who the hell wouldn't? He blew up the wrong beaches in Wonsan. Naturally, none of us ever say anything, especially now since he's the President's clown prince in the navy stag department.'

'I spoke to Frank. That's why Pease was here.'

'So?'

'The Finger's waiting by his phone now. He's got one other call to make. To his buddy, the President.'

'About *what*?'

'About Pease's state of mind, which is the result of a very strange telephone conversation Frank had with the Secretary this afternoon. After thinking about that call all day, he's decided to tell his friend in the White House about his concerns ... Come on, we've got to find a phone booth. And damn quick, too, I've got to catch the shuttle back to New York.'

'Hey, GI Joe!' cried Mangecavallo. 'What about you and me and you getting to that hearing?'

'That's under control, Commander Y. You'll be with the Wopotamis. Naturally, I'll have to get your measurements, but we can do that quickly. The squaws are excellent seamstresses – almost as good as Mrs Lafferty.'

'*Squaws*? We got Irish-American *Indians*? This guy's *pazzo*!'

'Have faith, Mr Director. The Hawk moves in mysterious ways.'

'Come, gentlemen,' ordered MacKenzie. 'Triple quick-march. There's a phone booth at the edge of the parking lot. Let's roll!'

The three red-wigged men ran across the grounds in varying degrees of breathlessness, the only words, however, from Vinnie the Bam-Bam, who kept repeating. '*Manage, manage! It's all crazy! Pazzo, pazzo, pazzo!*'

The Washington Post

SECRETARY OF STATE HOSPITALIZED TAKEN TO PSYCHIATRIC WARD AT WALTER REED HOSPITAL

Warren Pease, Secretary of State, wearing the garb of a Catholic priest, was taken into custody last evening while running amok through the crowds at the Lincoln Memorial. According to the police, as well as witnesses, Mr Pease kept screaming that some 'specter' he could not or would not identify had 'risen from the dead' and had 'come back to haunt his rotten soul,' He also claimed that a 'painted hermaphrodite from hell' had threatened to slash his 'pockets and his throat' because he/ she determined he was an (expletive deleted) which he kept screaming he was not because 'he forgave her her sins.'

The Secretary has no history of being an ordained priest or minister, and would therefore have no powers of religious absolution. (Our editors have diligently researched this fact.)

A late report from the White House, however, may shed light on this incredible event. Maurice Fitzpeddler, the press secretary, said that the nation should have only great sympathy for the stressed, overburdened Mr Pease and his family, although when questioned, Mr Fitzpeddler admitted that the divorced Secretary Pease had no family. Adding to this, the President allowed, through Mr Fitzpeddler, that he had received a telephone call yesterday calling into question the state of the Secretary's extreme stress under the pressures of his office. He asked that the nation pray for Mr Pease's recuperation and 'his release from a straitjacket.'

It should be noted here that the President's Chief of Staff, Arnold Subagaloo, smiled throughout the press conference. When questioned about his expression, the Chief of Staff gave the press an erect middle finger.

CHAPTER TWENTY-SEVEN

It was shortly past midnight when MacKenzie Hawkins walked into the lobby of the Waldorf-Astoria and, as arranged, went to the front desk to pick up whatever messages were left for Suite 12A – no names, merely the room number. There were two.

> *Call Beverly Hills.*
> *Reach Worm City.*

As it was three hours earlier in California, he decided to call Madge first in Greenwich, Connecticut. He recrossed the lobby to a pay phone.

'Midgey, I'm sorry it's so late but I just got in.'

'No sweat, Mac dear, I'm still working on the outline. I'll have it finished in less than an hour, and the courier service will bring it down right away; you should have it by two-thirty. Hawk, it's *terrific*! Straight boffo box office across all markets!'

'Now, Midge, don't go sounding too Hollywood, it gets a mite hard.'

'Sorry, you're right, darling. It's just that everyone talks like that to work up enthusiasm for a project. The more the hype, the better the pitch.'

'March to your own drummer, girl. You've got too much class for that.'

'With *worms*, Mac?'

'Well, you were fashioning a commodity.'

'You can bank on it and I have.'

'But I'm pleased you think the Suicidal thing's got possibilities ... frankly, I did, too.'

'Darling, it's pure *gelt*! ... Gold, Mac, I mean gold. *Actors* travelling the world over as an anti-terrorist unit, and it's *real*!'

'You think I could get a couple of West Coast types interested –'

'*Interested?*' she interrupted. 'Then you haven't talked to Ginny yet, have you?'

'No, I figured it was early out there, so I called you first.'

'I spoke to her late this afternoon, after I listened to the tapes, and we had a long talk. You're in for a surprise, Mac. She's been networking since three-thirty, California time.'

'"Networking"? Midgey, you're picking up some very odd language and I'm not sure I approve. It sounds coarse.'

'No, darling, that one's okay, it's really standard. It's just taking a noun and turning it into a verb.'

'That sounds better –'

'But, Hawk, you *listen* to me,' broke in Madge of Worm City. 'I know you sometimes get a little overprotective about us girls, and we love you for it, but you've got to promise me something.'

'What is it?'

'Don't beat the shit out of Manny Greenberg. Don't give him the deal, but don't break his face.'

'Now, *Midgey*, that's plain vulgar –'

'Gotta go, Mac. I'm getting near the finish line here and my word processor's smoking. Call Ginny, darling. Love, as always.'

'The residence of Lord and Lady Cavendish,' announced the adenoidal Anglican on the line from California. 'The name, please?'

'Guy Burgess calling from Moscow.'

'It's all right, I've got it!' Ginny broke in quickly. 'He's such an old tease, Basil.'

'Yes, madam,' said the butler in a devastating monotone as he hung up the phone.

'Mac, sweetie, I've been waiting hours for your call. I've got wonderful news!'

'Which, I gather from Madge, includes not engaging Manny in hand-to-hand combat.'

'Oh, him – no, don't, he can be useful in an auction but not if he's in the hospital. To tell you the truth, I started with Manny, breaking my rule never to talk to ex-husbands while my lawyers are talking to their lawyers, and it worked.'

'What worked? What's an auction?'

'Midgey says the concept is not only *sensational*, it's a landmark in the worldwide gold stakes! She says it's all *there*, everything – and it's *got* everything! Actors – *hunks*, six of them – flying all over freeing hostages, capturing terrorists, and its all *true*! I gave Manny just a hint . . . after he agreed to leave the paintings alone, naturally . . . and when I told him that Chauncey was reaching some "*cinema* chaps" in London, Manny screamed for his secretary to schedule the studio plane.'

'Ginny, for God's sake, slow down! You're grasshopping from one thing to another and not making sense, at least not to me . . . Now what's Manny doing and what did this "Chauncey" do and who the hell is he?'

'My husband, Mac!'

'Oh, the Grenadier, yes, I remember now. Damn fine regiments, all of 'em; first rate in combat. What *did* he do?'

'I told you, he's a great admirer of yours, and when Madge called and began explaining what you had on those tapes, I asked him to get on the line – what with his being so military and everything.'

'What did he think?'

'He said it was similar to the Fourth or Fortieth Royal Commandos who were recruited from the Old Vic and had what he called "only marginal success," because they kept "breaking silence." He wants to talk to you about it and compare notes.'

'*Goddamn*, put him on the phone, Ginny!'

'*No*, Mac, there isn't time. Besides, he's not here. He's over at the armoury in Santa Barbara playing polo with the British colony.'

'So what did he *do*?'

'Hawk, you must be tired and need to have your shoulders massaged. I *told* you. He thought the whole thing Midgey's putting together for you has the earmarks of a megahit and called some friends of his in London to let them know about it.'

'So?'

'They're taking the early morning Concorde and will be here before they took off from London.'

'Be where?'

'In New York. To see you.'

'Tomorrow ... *today*?'

'Where you are, yes.'

'And your ex, Greenberg?'

'Tomorrow morning – *this* morning for you. Also, since I had Manny and Chauncey's friends on the record – out here everyone checks out everything, including airline passenger lists and the schedules of studio planes – I called a few other hot shots who want Chauncey at their dinner tables, and gave out a little inside information. You're going to have a busy day, sweetie.'

'By Caesar, you're on the mark, it *is* wonderful! But frankly, Gin-Gin, I knew you girls would come through for me except I sort of figured later on, like early next week – not Friday to Monday, of course, because I'm kind of tied up with other endeavours –'

'*Mac*, you said, and I quote! "In a *day*"'

'Well, surely I did, but that was to get the writing stuff out of the way and somehow have it in the hands of those Beverly Hills Buddhas over the weekend and get things rolling on Monday or Tuesday.'

'Look here, once-great husband of mine and the dearest friend I've ever had, what the hell are you trying to tell me?'

'Well, Gin-Gin –'

'Cut the "Gin-Gin" crap, Hawk. When you found Lillian in that run-down gym and decided she needed more help than me, that's how you started with us, with the Gin-Gin. Then Lil told me that when you ran across Midgey in that coke bust where you wondered where the cola was, she said you began by saying "Lilly-Lilly." What is it, Mac? We *love* you, you know that. Why is tomorrow morning a problem? If it's another wife, we'll understand and take her under our wings when the time comes.'

'It's nothing like that, Ginny. But it's goddamned important – for a lot of people, a lot of underprivileged people.'

'You're tilting at windmills again, aren't you, my dearest friend?' said Lady Cavendish softly. 'I'll call everything off, if you like. I can do it – actually, you can do it by not answering the phone or the door. The vultures have only a room number, Suite Twelve A, no name, no identification.'

'No, no, I'll handle it – we'll handle it.'

'*We?*'

'I've got the boys all here. I just figured on keeping them here until my other problem is solved.'

'The *Suicidal Six?*' cried Ginny. 'They're there at the *Waldorf?*'

'The whole half dozen, kid.'

'Are they *hunks?*'

'They're that and more than that in varying sizes. What's more important, they expect something from me.'

Then deliver, Mac. You never failed any of us.'

'One, maybe.'

'Annie? . . . Get off it, Hawk. She got through to me last week on some radio phone with a lot of static. She managed to fly out a dozen really sick children from an island in the Pacific for treatment in Brisbane. She's happy as can be. Isn't that what it's all about? Being happy with yourself? That's what you taught us.'

'Tell me, does she ever mention Sam Devereaux?'

'*Sam . . . ?*'

'You heard me, Ginny.'

'Well, yes, she does, but I don't think you want to hear it, Mac. Leave it lie.'

'I want to hear it. He's my friend.'

'*Still?*'

'By circumstance, yes.'

'All right . . . She says she remembers him as the only man she ever slept with for it was – "a communion of love" – that's the way she put it. All the others are forgotten.'

'Will she ever come back?'

'No, Mac. She's found what you wanted her to find – what you wanted all of us to find. Comfort in our own skins, remember telling us that?'

'Damned psycho-*bullshit*!' exclaimed Hawkins, once again wiping a tear from his eye in front of a pay telephone. 'I'm no goddamned saviour of goddamned souls, I just know who the hell I like and who the hell I don't like. Don't put *me* on any goddamned pedestal!'

'Whatever you say, Hawk, and anyway, you'd crush it.'

'Crush what?'

'The pedestal. What about tomorrow morning?'

'I'll handle it.'

'Be kind to the vultures, Mac, kind and noncommittal, they can't stand that.'

'What do you mean?'

'The nicer you are, the more they sweat, the more they sweat, the better off you are.'

'Kinda like facing down enemy intelligence personnel in Istanbul, right?'

'That's Hollywood, Mac.'

Morning came, barely dawn to be precise, and the phone in Suite 12A began ringing. Hawkins, who lay supine on the floor of the living room area, was prepared for it. He had received Madge's 'Concept Treatment' at 2:03 a.m., finished reading, re-reading, and absorbing the eighteen pages of high tension fashioned by his third wife by three o'clock, had taken the telephone off the desk and placed it on the carpet next to his head, and bivouacked for a few hours of sleep. Rest was a weapon for impending combat, as necessary as superior firepower. However, Midgey had done such a superb job – the narrative explosive, each page dynamic in terms of energy, action and diversified character sketches – that much-needed sleep was postponed for nearly thirty minutes while the Hawk considered becoming a motion picture producer.

Hell, no! Omaha and the Wopotamis will take up all of my time. Stick to priorities, soldier! Suddenly, the abrasive ringing echoed off the walls of the room.

'Yes?' said Mac, the phone at his left ear on the floor.

'Andrew Ogilvie here, General.'

'*What?*'

'Yes, I said "General," chap. I'm afraid my old Grenadier comrade broke the rules and told me who you were. You had a splendid war, old boy. Much impressed, much impressed.'

'Much early, too,' said Hawkins. 'You really were with the Grenadiers?'

'A callow youth, to be sure, as was Cavvy.'

'*Cavvy?*'

'Lord Cavendish, of course. He, too, had a *fine* war. Got right into the mud and the mortars and never "lorded" it over anyone, if you catch my meaning.'

'Yeah, it's splendid, real fine. It's also real early and my troops aren't ready for muster. Have some morning tea and come up in an hour. You're first, I'll give you that.'

The phone replaced, there was a rapid knocking at the corridor door. Mac got to his feet, and in his camouflaged skivvies walked over to it. 'Yes?'

'Hey, who *else*?' shouted the intruder in the hallway. 'I knew it was you, I'd know that growl anywhere!'

'*Greenberg?*'

'Hey, baby, who else? My lovely, adorable wife, who threw me out of the house for no reason whatsoever and took me for a bundle – but who cares, she's a doll – gave me a rundown and I *knew* it was you! Lemme in, pal, okay, *okay*? A deal we can make!'

'You're second in line, Manny.'

'You got some phonies in there *awready*? Hey, listen, sweetheart, I gotta whole studio behind me, the big *megillah*! Wadd'ya want to deal with second-raters for, huh?'

'Because they own England, that's why.'

'That's crapolla! They make those dumb movies where everybody's talking and nobody knows what they're saying because they got gefilte fish in their mouths!'

'Others think otherwise.'

'*What* others? For every *Jimmy Bond*, they got fifty underwear *Gandhis* which never made back their negative costs, and don't let 'em tell you they did!'

'Others say otherwise.'

'Who you gonna believe? The rotten Red Coats who talk funny or the pure Paul Reveres?'

'Come back in three hours, Manny, and call first from the lobby.'

'Mac, give me a break! The whole studio's got the big eye on me!'

'I'm giving you a break, you horny toad. Maybe you'll find a none too discriminating sixteen-year-old hooker in the lobby.'

'Hey, that's libel! I'll sue the bitch!'

'Just leave now, Manny, or don't bother to come back.'

'Awright, *awright*.' The telephone rang again, pulling Hawkins away from the door although he would have preferred to wait and make sure Greenberg had really left.

'Yes?' said the Hawk, picking the phone up off the floor.

'Suite Twelve A?'

'So?'

'This is Arthur Scrimshaw, head of development for Holly Rock Productions, the rock of Hollywood, with worldwide grosses that would stagger the imagination if I were at liberty to disclose them, and, furthermore, the recipient of a total of sixteen Oscar nominations over the past ... *harrumph* ... years.'

'How many Oscars did you win, Mr Scrimshaw?'

'Very close, *very* close. Could have gone either way each time. And speaking of time, I've found some in my unbelievably hectic schedule for us to have breakfast – shall I say a *power* breakfast?'

'Come back in four hours –'

'I *beg* your pardon. Perhaps I didn't make clear my position –'

464

'You made everything perfectly clear, Scrimmy, and so did I. You're third on the list and that means four hours, leaving an hour for my people to prepare for muster.'

'Are you quite sure you want to treat the chief of Holly Rock's division of development in this manner?'

'Don't have a choice, Artie boy. The schedule's been set.'

'Well . . . *harrumph* . . . in that case, and since you're in a suite, would you perchance have an extra bed?'

'A *bed*?'

'It's the damned bookkeepers, you understand. I should fire them all . . . They seem to frown upon spontaneous reservations, and I never sleep a *wink* on the Red Eye from LA. I tell you, I'm *exhausted*!'

'Try the Salvation Army mission down in the Bowery. They take all contributions over a dime . . . *Four* hours!' The Hawk slammed down the phone, placed it on the hotel desk, and as he turned to head for the nearest bedroom, it rang again. 'Goddamn, what *is* it?' he roared.

'Emerald Cathedral Studios, heah,' began the mellifluous voice in a thick Southern accent. 'A God-fearin' patriotic bird flew some information down here regardin' some great patriotic movie you want to get made, a movie based on real facts! And let me tell ya', boy, we ain't no part of those *Hebes* and *Nigras* that's runnin' the filum industry. We'ah simon-pure Christian, flag-wavin' real *Amerucuns* who believe that might is fuckin' right, and we want to tell the story of real Amerucuns doin' God's work. We also got lots of dollars – quite a few million fer a fact. Our Sunday telecasts and used car lots where every salesman's a Christian minister are weekly uranium mines.'

'Be at the Lincoln Memorial in Washington, DC at midnight tonight,' ordered Hawkins quietly. 'And wear white hoods over your heads so I'll know you!'

'Ain't that kinda obvious?'

'Are you gutless, antimilitary, anti-American *liberal* types?'

'Hell, *no*! We put our money where our mouths are, and we got plenty of both. We'ah Jesse's boys!'

'If it's the right Jesse, catch a plane and be in Washington tonight. Four hundred feet from the front of the statue and six hundred to the oblique right. You'll reach the honour guard house and the men inside will tell you where we are.'

'We got a deal then?'

'A deal you couldn't imagine. Remember the hoods. They're *vital*!'

'Gotcha, boy!'

The phone replaced, MacKenzie walked to the nearest bedroom door and knocked. '*Reveille*, troops! You've got an hour for spit, polish, and mess before engagement. Don't forget, you're in combat fatigues and side arms. Place your orders with room service.'

'We did that last night, General,' shouted the voice of Sly from inside. 'It'll be here in twenty minutes.'

'You mean you're up?'

'Of course, sir,' replied Marlon. 'We've already been out and run forty or fifty blocks.'

'You don't have doors to the hallway.'

'That's right, sir,' agreed Sylvester.

'*I* didn't hear you leave and I hear everything!'

'We can be very quiet, General,' added Marlon. 'And you must have been very tired. You didn't even move ... We're all meeting here for *petit déjeuner* ... early mess, sir.'

'*Goddamn!*'

To the Hawk's annoyance, the telephone rang again. Angry but resigned, he returned to the desk and picked up the shrill instrument. 'Yes?'

'*Ahh*, it is most pleasurable to hear your beautiful voice,' said the obviously Oriental male on the line. 'This most unworthy soul is most rucky to make your acquaintance.'

'Nice to meet you, too, and who the hell are you?'

'Yakataki Motoboto, but my rovery friends in Horrywood call me "Cruiser."'

'I can understand that. Come back in five hours and call from the lobby first.'

'*Ahh*, yes, you are being friverous, no doubt, but perhaps I can irriminate your conditions since I believe we now own this beautiful hotel and its robby.'

'What are you talking about, Motorboat?'

'We also own three of the rargest studios in Horrywood, most worthy person. I suggest you see me first, or perhaps most unfortunatry we must evict you instantry.'

'No can do, Tojo. Your front desk has a line of credit on our behalf to the tune of a hundred thousand. Until that's in jeopardy you can't move our asses anywhere. That's the law, Banzai, *our* law.'

'*Aiyee!* You try the patience of this unworthy soul. I represent the *Toyhondahai Enterprises, USA* Motion Picture Operations!'

'Good for you. I represent six warriors that make your samurai look like chickenshit purveyors . . . Five hours, Slope, or I'll call my buddies in the Tokyo Diet and they'll take away your tax exempt company expense accounts for reasons of corruption!'

'*Aiyee!*'

'On the other hand, come back in five hours and all is forgiven.' The Hawk hung up the phone and went to his open duffel bag on the couch. It was time to dress. The grey suit, not the buckskins.

Nineteen minutes and thirty-two seconds later the men of the Suicidal Six stood rigidly at attention, a line of superbly conditioned stalwarts impressively filling out their camouflaged combat fatigues, their .45 calibre side arms holstered and strapped tightly around their enviously slim waists. Gone were the theatrical manifestations of their currently assumed 'names'; the slouches, swaggers and vocal imitations had vanished. In their places were rock-hard faces, sharp, precise language, and the concrete postures of relatively young but experienced *soldiers*, each with striking features and clear, unblinking eyes that held both intensity and perception. At the moment they were passing inspection for their surrogate commander.

'That's *it*, boys, you've got it!' cried the Hawk approvingly. 'Remember, this is the image you want to give 'em when they first take a look at you. Tough but smart, battle-scarred but human, above the crowd but with the common touch. *God*, I love it when men look like you! Damn it to hell, we *need* heroes! We crave brave souls who'll ride into the mouth of death, into the jaws of *hell* –'

'You've got it backwards, General, it's the other way around.'

'Same damn *thing*.'

'Not really.'

'He wants William Holden in the last scenes of *Kwai*.'

'Or John Ireland in *O.K. Corral*.'

'How about Dick Burton and Big Clint in *Eagles Dare*?'

'Or Errol Flynn in anything.'

'Don't forget Connery in *The Untouchables*.'

'Hey, fellas, what about Sir Henry Sutton as the knight in *Becket*?'

'Absolutely!'

'Hey, what *about* Sir Henry, General? We're here, but where is *he*? We consider him a part of us now, especially where our movie's concerned.'

'On another assignment, men. A very vital assignment; he'll meet up with you later ... Now, back to the engagement facing us.'

'Can we relax, sir?'

'Yes, yes, of course, but don't lose that, that ... '

'*Collective* image, General?' asked Telly gently.

'Yeah, that's what I mean – I think.'

'And you'd be quite right, sir,' added the Yale-trained Sly. 'You see, we're basically ensemble players. It's largely improv and goes with the interacting totality, as it were.'

'*Totality* ... ? Yeah, sure ... Now, listen up. The Hollywood types and the London film types you're going to meet don't know what to expect, but when they see six military *hunks* – as a dear friend of mine who understands their mentalities put it – they'll see bucketfuls of bucks. Especially because you're the real thing, and that's where you're different. You don't have to sell yourselves, they've got to sell *themselves*. You're the choosers, not the choosees; they may want to buy, but you may not want to sell. You've got certain standards.'

'Isn't that a dangerous position?' asked The Duke. 'Producers hold the purse strings, not actors, especially not actors like us who haven't exactly set Broadway on fire, say nothing of Hollywood.'

'*Gentlemen*,' said the Hawk. 'Forget your previous lives and whatever marks you made or didn't make. As of now, who and what you are is setting the *world* on fire! That's what these people will see flowing into their cash registers. You're not only professional actors, you're soldiers, *commandos* in various disguises to achieve your missions!'

'Oh, hell,' said Dustin, shrugging. 'Anyone with advanced acting techniques under his belt could do it –'

'Don't *ever* say that!' shouted MacKenzie.

'Sorry, General, but I think it's the truth.'

'Then keep it a secret, son!' said the Hawk. 'We're dealing with "high concept" here. We keep it big, not small.'

'What does that mean?' asked Sly.

'Don't bring in details; their attention spans can't handle it.' MacKenzie walked to the desk and picked up the clipped pages of his third wife's literary labours; he turned back to the unit. 'This is what's known as an outline, or a "treatment" or something just as dumb-sounding, and there's only one copy – that's to keep its security at a maximum. It's a high-powered summary of your activities over the past few years, and let me tell you, it's a nuclear missile. When each of these vultures arrives, I'll give him this single copy and tell him he's got fifteen minutes to read it and then ask whatever questions he likes, the answers to which will be subject to national security. I want you to sit in those chairs over there that I've placed in a semicircle maintaining that collective – whatever you call it.'

'Collective image of silent strength with an admixture of intelligence and perception?' suggested Telly the professor.

'Yeah, that one. And maybe it wouldn't hurt if a couple of you slap the holsters of your forty-fives whenever I say "national security."'

'You, Sly; then you, Marlon,' ordered The Duke.

'Got it.'

'Got it.'

'Now, here's the kicker,' continued the Hawk quickly. 'At first, you answer the clowns' questions in your normal regular voices, then when I nod at each of you, you switch to the impersonations of the people – the *actors* – you imitated for me and Colonel Cyrus.'

'We've got lots of others,' said Dustin.

'Those will do,' replied Hawkins. 'They were damned convincing.'

'What's the point?' asked the sceptical Marlon.

'I'd think you'd see that right off. We *prove* that you're real talented professionals, that you've done what you've done because you *are* actors.'

'That can't hurt us, Pilgrims,' said The Duke, reverting to his *persona imitazione*. 'What the hell, not too many other honchos in the business ever listened to us.'

'*Confidence*, men. You've got it *all*!' The telephone rang again. 'Chow down, gentlemen,' went on MacKenzie, reaching for the phone as the Suicidal Six rushed to the room-service tables. 'Yes, who's this?'

'The twelfth son of the sheik of Tizi Ouzou by his twenty-second wife,' said the soft voice over the line. 'Thirty thousand camels may be yours if our talk bears fruit, otherwise a hundred thousand Western dogs may die if the fruits are barren.'

'Ream it! Come back in six hours or go bury your balls in the desert sand!'

Seven hours later, the good ship, *Hawk's Assault*, had made its initial foray into the turbulent waters of the motion picture industry. In its treacherous wake and struggling to keep from drowning were a former British Grenadier named Ogilvie, who blustered about thankless *wog* colonials; one Emmanuel Greenberg, whose copious weeping touched all but one MacKenzie Hawkins; a certain exhausted head of Holly Rock's development named Scrimshaw, who finally said he'd temporarily settle for a bed he didn't have to pay for; a shrieking 'Cruiser' Motoboto, who made it abundantly clear that prison camps in 'Horrywood' were not entirely out of the question; and lastly, a snarling Sheik Mustacha Hafaiyabeaka, in flowing robes, who made constant and odious comparisons between camel droppings and the American dollar. Nevertheless, to a man and his corporate entity, each profoundly hoped to be chosen as the producing force behind the most spectacular motion picture to be made in modern times, and each, stunned speechless by the six extraordinary actor-commandos, agreed without reservation that they would portray themselves in the film of their exploits. Only Greenberg offered the suggestion: 'Maybe a little skin, fellas? Y'know, a few girlies so there shouldn't be any questions, y'know?' The Suicidal Six agreed enthusiastically, especially Marlon, Sly and Dustin. 'Thirty-six carat *gelt*!' whispered Manny, even more enthusiastically.

Business cards were proffered, but Hawkins was clear: no decision would be made until early the following week. When the last of the supplicants left, namely the growling twelfth son of the sheik of Tizi Ouzou by his twenty-second wife, MacKenzie turned to his elite Delta Force by way of the footlights and rendered his judgement. 'You were *great*, every one of you. They were hypnotized, blown out of their foxholes – you *did* it!'

'Outside of putting on a pretty good show,' said the erudite Telly, 'I'm not exactly sure what we did.'

'Did you just lose your flak jacket, son?' broke in the startled Hawkins. 'Didn't you hear what they *said*? To a sweaty palm they want this project so bad they drooled!'

'Well,' observed Dustin, 'I heard a lot of noise, a lot of shouting and pleading, especially Mr Greenberg's crying – he was especially effective, very much like a Greek chorus – but I'm not sure what it all meant.'

'We didn't see anyone pulling out a contract,' said Marlon.

'We don't *want* any contracts. Not yet.'

'When's "yet," General?' said Sir Larry. 'You see, we've been through all this before. There's always a great deal of talk but very few pieces of paper. Paper is a commitment, sir, the rest is just ... well, talk.'

'If I remember correctly, gentlemen, negotiations are left to the negotiators. We're the *creative* side; we do and they haggle.'

'Who negotiates for us, if anybody really wants us ... Pilgrim?'

'Good point, Duke. Maybe I'd better make a phone call.'

'I'll pay for it,' said Sly.

Instead, the Waldorf-Astoria's telephone rang. The Hawk crossed to the desk. 'Yes, who the hell is *this*?'

'Sweetie, I couldn't wait any longer! How's everything going?'

'Oh, hi, Ginny, everything went fine, but as the boys explained to me, we may have a problem.'

'*Manny?* ... You didn't *kill* him, did you, Mac?'

'Hell, no. As a fact, the boys were kinda taken by him.'

'The crying bit, huh?'

'You got it.'

'He's very good at that, the *bastard* ... Then what's the problem?'

'Well, as the men say, it's real splendid that these vultures liked us, or pretended to like us, but how do we get anything on paper –'

'It's all arranged, Mac. The William Morris Agency is handling everything – right up at the top. Robbins and Martin themselves.'

'Robbins and Martin? Sounds like a classy men's shop.'

'Class they are, and we should all have their brains, sweetie. Not only brains, they speak English you can understand, not Hollywood crapola. That's why they confuse everybody and take home the bread. They'll go to work when I tell them.'

'Make it early next week, okay, Ginny?'

'Sure. Where can I reach you, and who exactly besides Manny showed up?'

'Here, I've got their cards.' The Hawk picked up the business cards on the desk and read each off to his former wife.

'Wasn't there a nut studio in Georgia or Florida? Of course, no legitimate company in the South will deal with them, but they've got several cathedrals full of money and can push up the bids.'

'I have an idea they may run into a bit of trouble tonight in Washington.'

'*What?*'

'Let it pass, Ginny.'

'I know that tone; it's passed. Now how about you? Where will you be?'

'Call a Johnny Calfnose at the Wopotami reservation outside of Omaha, he'll know where to find me. Here's his private number.' Hawkins gave it to her. 'Got it?'

'Sure, but what's a Calfnose, and what the *hell* is a Wopotami?'

'He's a disenfranchised member of that downtrodden people.'

'The windmills, Mac?'

'We do what we can, little lady.'

'Who to this time, sweetie?'

'Bad protectors of the republic with very bad attitudes.'

'Oh, the DC pricky-shits?'

'And their forebears, Ginny, going back over a hundred years.'

'How delicious! ... But how did you ever get Sam involved?'

'He's a very principled man – far more mature than he was and with seven children – but he knows right from wrong.'

'That's what I *mean*! How did you get him back? That beautiful boy thinks you're Ali Baba's forty thieves all walking around on one pair of legs.'

'Well, as I say, he's changed, mellowed over the years. Probably goes with his haggard looks and the arthritis that kinda makes him stoop ... I guess nine kids would do that to anybody.'

'*Nine?* I thought you said seven?'

'I get mixed up, but then so does he. I'll say this, though, he's become a far more tolerant man.'

'Thank heavens he got over Annie. We were all worried

about him . . . *Wait* a minute! Seven kids . . . *nine?* What did his wife do, drop two and three at a *time?*'

'Well, we haven't really –' Fortunately for MacKenzie Hawkins, there were several clicks on the line followed by the excited voice of an interrupting operator.

'Suite Twelve A, you have an emergency call! Please terminate your current conversation so I can connect you.'

'Bye, Ginny girl, we'll make contact later.' MacKenzie slammed down the phone and held it in place; it rang three seconds later and he yanked it up. 'This is Suite Twelve A. Who's this?'

'*Redwing*, you prehistoric monster!' roared Jennifer from Swampscott, Massachusetts. 'Sam heard the Brokemichael tape last night, and it was all Cyrus, Roman, and our two Desis could do to hold him down! Finally, Cyrus managed to get practically a whole bottle of whisky into him –'

'When he sobers up, he'll come to his senses,' interrupted the Hawk. 'He usually does.'

'Nice of you to say so, but, of course, we'll never know.'

'What do you mean?'

'He's *gone!*'

'That's impossible! With my adjutants and Roman Z and the colonel all *there?*'

'He's one sneaky son of a bitch, Thunder Ass. His door was closed and we figured he was still sleeping it off, then five minutes ago Roman was patrolling the beach when he saw a speedboat pull close to the shore about a quarter of a mile away and a figure running from the dunes into the water, and get on board!'

'*Sam?*'

'Binoculars don't lie and Roman Z's eyesight's got to be damn sharp or he'd have a much longer record than he has.'

'Goddamn, there he goes again! It's Switzerland all *over* again!'

'You mean when Sam tried to stop you –'

'Damn near did,' broke in MacKenzie, furiously checking his pockets with his free hand for his pacifier, namely a mutilated cigar. 'He must have used a phone and called somebody.'

'Obviously, but who?'

'How would *I* know? I haven't seen him in years ... still, what can he do?'

'Last night he kept shouting about the manipulators in high places, how the corruptors were selling out the country and should be exposed and he was going to expose them –'

'Yeah, he goes on a lot about that stuff, believes it, too.'

'Don't *you*? I think I heard you say practically the same thing at the Ritz-Carlton, General.'

'Yeah, I believe it, but there's a time and place to act on those principles and this isn't *it*! ... Yet what can he really *do*? A hysterical lawyer with bloodshot eyes and wet clothes running to a newspaper, like he suggested, with a story like ours? There's no way they could confirm it; they'd call a truck from a funny farm.'

'I think I left out something,' said Jennifer.

'What?'

'He's got the Brokemichael tape.'

'Sherman in Atlanta, you've got to be *kidding*, Redskin lady!'

'With all my Redskin heart, I wish I were. We can't find it anywhere.'

'Holy pistols of Georgie Patton! He could nuke the whole enterprise. We've got to *stop* him!'

'*How?*'

'Call the Boston papers, the radio and television stations and tell 'em all a lunatic's escaped from the biggest mental institution in Massachusetts.'

'That won't do much good when they hear the tape. The first thing they'll do is make copies, then voice print scans and match them with your friend General Brokemichael, either from newsreel tapes or just over the telephone.'

'I'll call Brokemichael and tell him to stay off the phone!'

'The phone ... ?' said Jennifer pensively. 'That's *it*! All telephone companies have computerized printouts of every number called; it's standard billing procedure. I'm sure Mr Pinkus can get an immediate police order.'

'For what?'

'The number Sam called from the Birnbaum phone here! Except when you reached us early this morning, no one's used that phone.'

'Someone did, and his name is Devereaux.'

Thanks to Aaron Pinkus's exemplary relations with the authorities, Redwing's suggestion was swiftly effective. 'Counsellor, this is Lieutenant Cafferty, Boston PD. We have the information you want.'

'Thank you so much, Lieutenant Cafferty. Had there not been an emergency, I would never have prevailed upon your office or your kindness.'

'Hey, come on, no trouble, sir. After all, every year at the department's annual dinner it's always "Pinkus's Corn Beef and Cabbage."'

'An insignificant contribution compared to the services you render to our fair city.'

'Well, you just call us any time . . . Here's what we got from the telephone company. During the past twelve hours there've been only four calls made from the Swampscott number, the last being six minutes ago to New York City –'

'Yes, we're aware of that one, Lieutenant. The other three, please.'

'Two were to your own house, Mr Pinkus. The first at six-thirty-three last night and then this morning –'

'Oh, yes, I was reaching Shirley, that's my wife. I forgot.'

'We've all met the missus, Counsellor, and a grand lady she is. So tall and graceful, sir.'

'Tall? No, actually she's quite short; it's her hairdo. Never mind, what's the fourth call, please?'

'It was made on the unlisted number out there at seven-twelve this morning to the residence of Geoffrey Frazier –'

'*Frazier?*' interrupted Aaron involuntarily. 'How extraordinary . . . !'

'He's a lot of things, if you don't mind my saying so, Mr

Pinkus, including a royal pain in the arse, forgive my language, sir.'

'I'm sure his grandfather employs far worse, Lieutenant Cafferty.'

'Oh, I've heard him, Counsellor! Whenever we pull the lad into the tank, the old man asks if we can't keep him a few more days.'

'Thank you very much, Lieutenant, you've been a great help.'

'Any time, sir.'

Aaron replaced the phone and looked quizzically at Jennifer. 'At least we know how Sam found the tape; he used Sidney's private line in the study. That's where we played it last night.'

'But that's not what's shocked you, is it? It's someone named Frazier, right?'

'Exactly. He's one of the most charming – I might even say lovable – men you could ever meet. A totally nice person whose parents died years ago in a plane crash when the inebriated Frazier, Senior, tried to land his seaplane on the Grand Corniche in Monte Carlo. Geoffrey was a classmate of Sam's at Andover.'

'Then that's why he called him.'

'I doubt it. Sam doesn't hate people, that's not in him, really, even MacKenzie Hawkins, as you've seen. But he does disapprove, disapprove deeply.'

'Disapprove – in what way, and why this Frazier.'

'Because Geoffrey's abused and wasted his privileges. He's a functioning alcoholic whose only purpose in life is the pursuit of pleasure and the avoidance of pain . . . And Sam has absolutely no use for him.'

'He did today – about ten minutes ago on the beach.'

'The general's right, we have to stop him!' said Aaron suddenly, turning back to the phone.

'How?'

'If we knew where he went in the boat, it'd be a place to start.'

'That could be *anywhere*.'

'No, not really,' said Aaron. 'Things have changed along the shoreline; the Coast Guard and the Power Squadrons are constantly on the alert, not only for reckless boaters, but for people bringing in illegal substances from other craft farther out. Those with houses on the beach are asked to report any suspicious activity on their water frontages.'

'Someone may have called already then,' interrupted Jennifer. 'That boat came *up* to the beach.'

'Yes, but Sam went out to get on board, no one got off.'

'Then we have the why-get-involved syndrome?' concluded Jennifer.

'Exactly.'

'Still, why not call the Coast Guard?'

'I would in a second if I knew what kind of boat it was, even its size or shape or colour or the marina where it's berthed.' Pinkus reached for the telephone, adding as he dialled. 'But I just remembered, I do know something else, *someone* else.'

One of the secluded crowns of Boston is an isolated patch of ground on top of Beacon Hill called Louisburg Square. It is a compound of elegant town houses originally built in the 1840s, its small manicured park guarded at the north end by a statue of Columbus, at the south by a monument to Aristides the Just. It is not isolated physically, of course, for mail must be delivered, garbage picked up, and the daytime servants have to get there as best they can without leaving their distressed vehicles among the Rolls-Royces, Porsches, and whatever cute, new American pretenders catch the fancy of the lairds of Louisburg. These lairds, however, are demographically semi-democratic – small *d*, presumably – for there is old, old money, old money, first generation money and newly acquired cash. There are inheritors, stockbrokers, lawyers, several CEOs, and doctors, especially one doctor who is also a major American novelist whom the medical profession would like to put into a coma, but he's too good at both professions.

However, again, demographics notwithstanding, only one telephone rang at this moment, and it was in the tastefully ornate town house of the oldest old money in Boston, specifically the residence of R. Cookson Frazier. As the phone rang, the spry elderly gentleman in red sweat-stained gym shorts sank a basketball accurately into the net of the small court he had built for himself on the top floor of his home. His sneakers squeaking on the hard wood beneath, he turned quizzically at the shrill intrusion. The momentary indecision ended when he remembered on the third ring that his housekeeper was down at the market. Wiping his brow beneath his white hair, he walked over to the wall phone and picked it up. 'Yes?' he said, partially out of breath.

'Mr Frazier?'

'This is he.'

'It's Aaron Pinkus, Mr Frazier. We've met several times, the last being at the Fogg Museum charity ball, I believe.'

'It was, indeed, Aaron, and why the "Mr Frazier"? You're damn near as old as I am and *I* believe we both agreed you wouldn't look it if you exercised more.'

'Too true, too true, Cookson. There never seems to be enough time.'

'There won't be for you, although you'll probably be the richest man in the graveyard.'

'I've long since given up such ambitions.'

'I know that, I'm just goading you because I'm sweating like a pig, which is a poor metaphor because I'm told that pigs don't sweat ... What can I do for you, old fellow?'

'It concerns your grandson, I'm afraid –'

'*You're* afraid?' interrupted Frazier. 'I'm terrified! What *now*?' Pinkus started to tell his story but within eight seconds, at the mention of the speedboat, the old man broke in, shouting triumphantly. 'That's it! I've *got* him!'

'I beg your pardon, Cookson?'

'I can put him away!'

'What ... ?'

'He's not permitted by law to drive his boat – *or* his car *or* his motorcycle *or* his snowmobile. He's been deemed a menace on land, sea and snow!'

'You'd have him sent to jail?'

'*Jail?* Good Lord, no. Simply to one of those places that can straighten the boy out! My attorneys have already arranged it. If he's caught in even one of the violations, and there've been no injuries or legal redress from second parties, the court will permit me to take my own custodial measures.'

'You want to place him in a sanatorium?'

'I'd prefer to use another term, like a "rehabilitation centre" or whatever the code words are.'

'To go that far, he really has grieved you then.'

'He certainly has, but perhaps not in the way you think. I know that boy and love him dearly – my *God*, he's the last of the male Fraziers!'

'I understand, Cookson.'

'I don't think you do. You see, whatever he is, *we* made him that way, our family did, just as I did with my own son and I'm far worse because at least I was around, alive. But, as I say, I *know* him, and underneath that besotted exterior oozing with charm is a *brain*, Aaron! There's another *man* beneath the overindulged boy, I sense it, I truly *believe* it!'

'He's a very likeable person and I certainly couldn't contradict you.'

'You don't believe me, either, do you?'

'I don't know him that well, Cookson.'

'The newspapers and the television people obviously think they do. With every scrape he gets into, the labels are there. "Scion of wealth in drunk tank again," and "Playboy of Boston a disgrace to the city," et cetera, et cetera, *et cetera*.'

'The events apparently took place –'

'Of *course*, they did! That's why your news is the greatest gift you could give me. I can now take control of that overage delinquent!'

'How? His speedboat's on the water and we don't know where he's going.'

'You said he pulled up to the Swampscott beach about twenty minutes ago –'

'Or slightly less.'

'To get back to the marina will take him at least forty to forty-five minutes –'

'Suppose he's not heading for the marina? Suppose he's going the other way?'

'North of Swampscott, the nearest refuelling dock that permits outsiders is at Gloucester, and those cigarette boats drink fuel like six Arabs with straws in a single pot of tea. Gloucester's about a half hour away.'

'You know all this?'

'I was commander of Boston's Power Squadron for five consecutive terms; of course I know it. We're wasting time, Aaron! I've got to call the squadron and our friends in the Coast Guard. They'll find him.'

'One thing, Cookson. On board is an employee of mine named Devereaux, Samuel Devereaux, and it's imperative that he be held by the authorities for me.'

'Bad business, eh?'

'No, not bad at all, merely impetuous. But it's vital that he be held. I'll explain later.'

'Devereaux? Any relation to Lansing Devereaux?'

'His son, actually.'

'Damn fine man, Lansing. Died much too young for a fellow of his abilities. For a fact, he led me into several lucrative investments.'

'Tell me, Cookson. After he died, did you ever make contact with his widow?'

'Could I do otherwise? *He* was the brains, I was merely some minor money. I transferred my profits to her accounts. As I say, who could do otherwise?'

'Apparently a number of people.'

'Damned thieving bloodsuckers ... I've got to get off the phone and make some calls, Aaron, but now that we've talked, let's have dinner some evening.'

'A great pleasure.'

'With your lovely wife, Shelly – such a tall and graceful woman.'

'It's Shirley, and, actually, she's not tall, it's her – never mind.'

CHAPTER TWENTY-EIGHT

The sky grew suddenly grey and the dark clouds above swelled in direct proportion to the angry ocean below. And off the coast of Massachusetts, Sam Devereaux held on to the stainless steel railing of the speedboat wondering what had possessed him to call Geoff Frazier, a man he thoroughly disliked . . . Well, perhaps 'disliked' was too strong. Nobody who knew 'Crazy Frazie,' as he was sometimes affectionately called, could really *dislike* him because the 'Spaced Cadet,' as he was frequently referred to, had a heart as big as his monthly inheritance stipend, which he would willingly give to anyone he knew to be in distressful circumstances. What disturbed Sam at the moment was Frazie's maniacal man-oeuvres that sent the narrow, sleek, twin-engined cigarette boat intentionally into the monstrous waves.

'Have to do it, old sport!' shouted the grinning skipper, his braided captain's hat askew. 'These thin things can go belly-up if you don't take the water on head first!'

'You mean we could *sink?*'

'Actually, I'm not sure; never happened!' A gigantic spray washed over the boat's windshield, soaking both men. 'Damned *exhilarating*, isn't it, sport?'

'Geoff, are you *sober?*'

'Perhaps a touch, old boy, but it won't interfere!' yelled Frazier. 'The sauce always makes one better in these sudden squalls! Gives you the edge over nature, if you know what I mean . . . Can you *hear* me, Devvy?'

'Unfortunately yes, *Frazie.*'

'Not to worry. These billy-blows kick up quickly but they can go away sometimes just as fast!'

'How *long*?'

'No more than an hour or so,' shouted the happily grinning Frazier. 'Our only problem will be finding a basin until then.'

'A *basin*?'

'Can't head in till we find a cosy nook, as it were.'

'Speak *English*!'

'Just did, sport. An inlet that reduces the wind and the water, and there's damn few along the shoreline.'

'Go into the beach!'

'There are a lot of rocks and jetties, Devvy, and these sweet things aren't the easiest to control in weather.'

'Whether what . . . ?'

'Never mind –'

'Damn it, go into the *beach*! There's a whole stretch up ahead without a rock in sight and I've got important things to do!'

'Well, rocks and shoals aren't the only impediments, old fellow,' yelled Frazier. 'Boats like this one beaching on private property aren't exactly welcome sights, and if you'll look closer, there's nothing but dune houses as far as you can see!'

'You went in almost a half hour ago down in Swampscott!'

'Down there people like me pay for beachfront they never use so the neighbours can't hear us or pollute our waters. Also, everyone knows the Birnbaums' house and anyone who reads the society pages knows they're at the estate auctions in London. I took a chance, Devvy, but not up here – not with this squall and not with my past boo-boos!'

'*Boo-boos* . . . ?'

'Just silly little traffic violations, you might say, old boy. Nothing to worry about, but there *are* rotten apples in every decent barrel, you know!'

'What apples? *What* barrels?' roared Sam as harsh, simultaneous sprays from both port and starboard overwhelmed him, drenching him to the skin.

'Grandpapa's stupid Power Squadron – snitches, all of

them, and they hate me because my boat's faster than any of theirs!'

'What the *hell* are you talking about, Frazie?' A tremendous midair lurch and subsequent pounding return into an onrushing wave caused Devereaux to lose his grip; he crashed to the deck, grabbing the handle of a stow-away cabinet and yanking it down, the force propelling his head inside. '*Help!*' he screamed. 'I'm *stuck* somewhere!'

'Can't hear you, Devvy, but not to worry, chum! I can see the Gloucester markers up ahead. "Red right return," as they say.'

'Red ... *mftt* ... *mfttt!*'

'You'll have to be *clearer*, Devvy! Can't make you out in this wind, but I'd be most grateful if you'd uncork a bottle of Dom Perry for me. There's an iced case in the aft locker, that's a good fellow! ... Just spin it up on the deck the way we used to do with the girls from Holyoke, *remember*? The centrifugal motion loses only half the precious liquid. Physics One-Two at dear old Andover! Most vital thing I ever learned!'

'*Mfttt* ... *oww* ... *ouch!*' shrieked Sam, pulling his head out of the deck recess, a coil of white rope around his skull. 'You want a bottle of wine when we're in the middle of a *hurricane*? You're *certifiable*, Frazie, absolutely *nuts!*'

'Come now, sport, this is merely a heavy squall, that's all.' The grinning captain, the visor of his cap of authority now over his right ear, turned and looked at his deck-prone passenger with the rope around his head. 'Oh, come now, old boy, is that your crown of thorns?' he roared, laughing.

'I will *not* get you a bottle of champagne, and I *demand* that you get me on shore, or I'll personally wax your tail as an officer of the court with regard to your incapacity on the high seas!'

'Two hundred yards offshore?'

'*You* know what I mean!' As Devereaux rose to his knees, another massive wave crashed over his shoulders, splaying him back on the deck. '*Frazier!*' screamed Sam, once more gripping the stainless steel railing on the gunwale. 'Don't you care about *anything* but yourself?'

'That in itself – or myself – is a very large territory, chum, but, of course, I do. I care about old friends who still call me a friend. I care about you because you called me in need!'

'I can't deny that,' said Devereaux, deciding to open the stern ice cabinet, suddenly thinking that Frazie might need that 'edge over nature' after all.

'*Oh*, oh!' roared the captain of the Swampscott rescue mission. 'We've got a problem, Devvy!'

'What?'

'One of those snitches from Grandpapa's dumb Power Squadron must have spotted us!'

'*What?*'

'There's a CG cutter on our tail, old friend! Turn aft and look!'

'Holy *shit*!' whispered Sam to himself as he saw the sharp-bladed bow of a white Coast Guard patrol boat with red stripes leaping over the waves several hundred yards behind them. Then through the erratic bursts of wind he heard the sound of a siren. 'Are they trying to *stop* us?' he roared.

'Let's put it this way, sport, it's not a courtesy call!'

'But I *can't* be stopped!' yelled Devereaux, uncorking a bottle and spinning it across the wet deck. 'I have to get to the authorities – the police, the FBI, *The Boston Globe, somebody*! I have to expose one of the most powerful men in Washington who's done a terrible thing! I *have* to *do* it! If the Coast Guard or anyone in the government finds my evidence, they'll *stop* me!'

'That's sounds heavy, old boy!' shouted Frazier, his voice carrying over the wind and through the sprays of the waves as he picked up the bottle. 'But I have to ask you a question! You're not carrying anything like little pills or packets of powder or anything like that, are you, sport?'

'Christ, no!'

'I really have to be sure, Devvy, please understand that!'

'*Believe* me, Frazie,' screamed Sam over the now thunderous sounds of the New England squall. 'We're talking about a man who can shape the nation's policies, who next to the President is considered the most powerful man in our government! He's a liar and a crook and he hires killers! I've got it all in my pocket!'

'Someone's *confession*?'

'No, on a *tape* that confirms the whole conspiracy!'

'That's *really* heavy, isn't it?'

'Get me on shore, Frazie!'

'Then I'd suggest you really do hold on, chum!'

The next minutes, the approximate number a hysterical Devereaux would never know, were like plunging, swirling, plummeting submersions into all of Dante's circles of hell. Crazy Frazie suddenly became a maniacal Ahab, but instead of attempting to kill the great beast, he was doing his God-commanded damnedest to avoid its massive jaws. Like a satanic captain from the netherworld, a grinning Geoffrey Frazier, the bottle of Dom Perignon sporadically at his lips, whipped and thrashed the machine beneath him to obey his commands as he spun the wheel repeatedly back and forth, expertly crashing into and ebbing away from the angry swells on all sides.

The less manoeuvrable patrol boat behind was obviously skippered by a furious Coast Guard officer. Joining the bursts of the wailing siren came indignant, commanding words shouted over a loudspeaker. '*Cut back your engines and head for marker seven due northwest! Repeat, you maniac, marker seven and knock off the horseshit!*'

'We couldn't ask for anything better,' yelled Captain Crazy Frazie to his stunned passenger. 'He's a fine fellow!'

'What are you *saying*?' screamed Sam. 'They'll board us with cutlasses and knives and guns and *capture* us!'

'Capture me, no doubt, old sport, but not you if you do as I tell you.' Frazier did not reduce his twin engines, but he did wave-tack against the squall until he was heading roughly northwest. 'Now, listen to me, Devvy! I haven't been up this way in a while, but the "marker seven" jogged my memory. It's about a hundred and fifty yards to the left of a rather large rock formation that juts out of the water, a small land mass that cuts down the wind – the sails frequently complain it's four hundred feet of dead air.'

'*Rocks*? Dead *air*! . . . For Christ's sake, Frazie, I'm fighting for my sanity, for my country's *integrity*!'

'Just a sec, old boy!' shouted Devereaux's rescuing skipper as he bounced the bottle of champagne against the top of his dashboard. 'You broke the cork, chum, and it's choking the neck!' The Dom Perignon back to his lips, he added. 'There, that's better! Now, what was it, sport?'

'Oh, my God, you're *impossible*!'

'Seems I've heard that before –' Frazier's words were interrupted by a starboard lurch with its subsequent spray catching him directly in the face. '*Damn!* Salt water never did mix with the bubbly!'

'*Frazie* . . . *!*'

'Oh, yes, now listen up, Devvy! . . . We'll reach marker seven where I'll throttle back in the calmer stretch – that's your signal to prepare to abandon ship, as it were.'

'You mean like in "man overboard" where those navy fascists behind us can pick me *up*?'

'I said "*prepare*," not execute –'

'For Christ's sake, use another word!'

'When I slow down, get to the starboard but stay below the gunwale, then I'll suddenly hit full throttle and make a large arc to port bringing you within forty or fifty yards of the beach. *That's* when you slip over the side – the spray will cover your disappearance – and I'll continue to give our water commandos a merry chase!'

'Good *Lord*, Frazie! You'd do this for *me*?'

'You asked for my help, Devvy –'

'Sure, but that's because I knew you had a fast boat and . . . and . . . well, I sort of thought . . . '

'That "Crazy Frazie" might just be your man, being the man he was?'

'I'm *sorry*, Geoff. I don't really know what to say.'

'Don't bother, sport, it's all fun!'

'You could get in a great deal of trouble, Geoff, and I never counted on that, honest I didn't!'

'Of course, you didn't. You're the most irritatingly honest

person I've ever known! *Hang* on, now, Devvy, we're going in.'

They entered the narrow channel that held the red marker seven, the reedlike cigarette boat abruptly slowed down in the smoother waters. The Coast Guard patrol approached within thirty yards aft.

'*Hear this, and hear me well!*' came the agitated voice over the loudspeaker. '*You have been identified as one Geoffrey Frazier and your passenger is a man named Samuel Devereaux, and you are both now under arrest. Hold to, as three of my crew board your craft and take full control.*'

'Geoff!' cried Sam Devereaux, lying prone on the starboard deck. 'I really didn't expect anything like this to happen –'

'Oh, shut *up*, old boy! Another few moments – as soon as they lower their dinghy – I'll start up and swing toward the beach. I'll signal you when I think we're as close as we can get and that's when you slip over. *Got* it?'

'Got it and I'll never forget it! Not only that, I'll defend you in court with all the legal expertise Aaron Pinkus Associates has!'

'That's terribly considerate, sport . . . all right, Devvy, here we *go*!' With those words the powerful speedboat lurched forward with such force its bow sprang out of the water like an ascending egret. The roar of the engines muted all other sounds as the craft sped out of the briefly sheltered area back into the angry waves past marker seven. Then, true to his word, Frazier went into a wide steep bank to the left, sending up a huge sheet of ocean spray to the starboard, a continuous wall of dense foam and sea that provided complete cover for any activity in front of or behind it – such as a prone figure rolling over the side into the water.

Which was precisely what a determined if anxiety-prone Sam Devereaux did, hardly buoyed by his captain's last words, shouted as he waved his hand. '*Now*, old chum, and I know you can *do* it. You were on the school's swimming team!'

'*No*, Frazie! It was tennis! I didn't *make* the swimming team!'

'Oh, sorry . . . *over* you go!'

Buffeted by waves, Sam kept his head half submerged as the Coast Guard patrol boat whipped to the left in pursuit of his former classmate, its loudspeaker blaring. '*You can run but you can't hide, you swizzling son of a bitch! We've got you this time – resisting arrest, drinking while piloting your craft, recklessly endangering the life of your passenger who's also under arrest! Oh boy, I'm gonna ream you!*'

Suddenly, further stunning the bobbing Devereaux, who gasped for air, came the sound of a much more powerful loudspeaker – from *Frazie's* boat. The noise it emitted could best be described as that of a blaring seagoing whoopie cushion.

' ... *who's also under arrest ... a man named Samuel Devereaux and you are both under arrest.*' Under *arrest*? *He* was under *arrest*? He had vaguely heard the words while clinging to the deck, but in his own personal hysteria they had not registered. *Arrest!* By *name*! *Oh, my God, I'm a fugitive!* They were searching for him; there was probably a dragnet! It had to mean that Aaron and Jenny and Cyrus and Roman and the two Desis had been taken – taken and *broken*, forced to confess everything! And Mac – he'd probably be executed! ... And Jenny, the new love of his life – they would hurt her, maybe do terrible things to her. The desperate men in Washington would stop at nothing!

Well, they hadn't figured on Samuel Lansing Devereaux, attorney of consequence, avenger of the mistreated, and the scourge of corruptors everywhere! And he had learned from a master – a misguided, antediluvian master, to be sure – but nevertheless a *master*! Of lies and theft and trickery, all those fine attributes that made him the Soldier of the Century! Sam would use every devious device, every nefarious deception he had learned from the Hawk to spread the truth and free his comrades. Not only free his comrades but save his country from the grip of the insidious manipulators. Not only free his comrades and save his country, but bring the glorious Sunrise Jennifer Redwing permanently into his life! He'd do it all with a voice tape securely locked in a finger-sealed plastic bag he had found in the Birnbaum kitchen and was now in his deepest pocket. Coughing and swallowing sea water, Devereaux struggled with all his strength against the tide and the chopping waves toward the beach. He had to prime the inventive part of his brain and, as Mac had frequently made clear, be prepared to instantly create whatever fiction he could think of to support the false facts. Like: 'Wow, am I glad to be on land! My boat capsized!'

'Hey, there, mister!' cried the teenage girl who had run down from the house to greet him at the water's edge. 'I'll bet you're glad you got here, on land, I mean. Did your boat capsize in the squall?'

'Yes ... well, yes it did. Pretty rough out there.'

'Not if you've got a decent keel. Or if you're a pot, just get to mark seven.'

'Young lady, I'm not in the habit of smoking such substances.'

'What?'

'Simply put, I don't use pot, as you call it.'

'Pot ... ? You mean "grass"? Nobody I go out with does, either! I meant "pot" like in pot-sailor. You know, engines and oil leaks that mess up the water.'

'Oh, of course! I'm just a little disoriented from the swim.' Sam rose unsteadily to his feet, his right hand checking his trousers' pocket. The sealed tape was there. 'As it happens, I'm in a great hurry –'

'I'll bet,' interrupted the girl. 'You want to call your marina or the CG or probably your insurance company. You can use our phone.'

'Aren't you a bit too trusting?' asked Devereaux, the attorney in him demanding the question. 'I'm a stranger washed up on your beach.'

'And my older brother is the wrestling champ of New England. There he is!'

'Oh?' Sam raised his eyes to the house. Walking down the beach steps was a handsome crew-cut white gorilla whose muscular arms were inordinately long, rather near or below his knees. 'Fine-looking young man.'

'Oh, sure, all the girls are crazy about him but wait'll they find out!'

'Find *out*?' Devereaux had the sinking feeling that some terribly intimate family secret was about to be divulged. 'Some people are merely different, my dear, but we're all God's children, as the prophets say. Be tolerant.'

'Why? He wants to be a *lawyer*! I mean, is that nerdsville to the max, or what?'

'To the max,' muttered Sam as the champion wrestler of New England approached. 'Sorry to bother you,' said Devereaux. 'My heel – *keel* – wasn't decent enough and I capsized.'

'Probably winded into a forced jibe,' said the young man pleasantly, 'and it's also probably your first boat!'

'How did you *know*?'

'Pretty obvious. Long pants, oxford shirt, black socks, and one brown leather loafer – how that stayed on, darned if I know.'

Devereaux looked down at his feet. Indeed the wrestler was right, he had only one shoe. 'I guess it was foolish of me, I should have worn sneakers.'

'Topsiders, mister,' corrected the girl.

'Naturally, I forgot, and it *was* my first boat.'

'Sail?' asked the young man.

'Yes, sail – two sails, one big one and small one in front.'

'Oh, *wow*,' said the teenage sister. 'It sure was his first boat, Boomer!'

'Be tolerant, kid. Everybody has a first boat. I had to swim out and get you in your first Comet at mark three, remember?'

'You big sludge, you *promised* –'

'Cool it . . . Come on in, mister. You can dry off and use the phone.'

'Actually, I'm in a terrible hurry . . . Frankly, I have to reach the authorities on a very urgent matter, and the phone won't help. I have to be there in person.'

'Are you a *narc*?' asked the young man sharply. 'You sure as hell aren't a sailor.'

'No, I'm *not* a narc. I'm simply a man with information that's needed urgently.'

'Do you have identification –'

'Is that necessary? I'll pay you for getting me where I have to go.'

'Definitely identification. I'm pre-law at Tufts and it goes with Initial Procedures One. Who are you?'

'All right, all right!' Sam reached into his drenched, buttoned rear left pocket and managed to extricate his wet, swollen wallet. It was not likely that the dragnet for him had gone public; the dirty bastards in Washington would be too cautious for that. 'Here's my driver's licence,' he added, suctioning out the plastic card from its slot and handing it to the wrestler.

'*Devereaux!*' cried the young man. 'You're Samuel *Devereaux!*'

'It's been broadcast then?' said Sam, holding his breath, trying desperately to invent a fiction according to the Hawk. 'Then I must explain to you the other side of the story and you *must* listen to me.'

'I don't know about any broadcasting, sir, but I'll listen to anything you say! You're the guy who got those rotten judges thrown out. You're a legend – kind of a new legend – for all of us going into law. I mean, you built the malfeasance charges against those judicial creeps like they were textbook cases! And every one held up to the last indictment!'

'Well, I was kind of pissed off –'

'Sis, hold the fort,' broke in the future attorney, grinning broadly. 'When Mom and Dad get back, tell 'em I'm driving a man who's going to be on the Supreme Court someday to wherever he wants to go.'

'The FBI would probably be best,' suggested Sam quickly. 'Do you know where the local office is?'

'There's one in Cape Ann. They're in the papers a lot – you know, the narc boats.'

'How long will it take to get there?'

'No more than ten or fifteen minutes.'

'Let's go!'

'Are you sure you don't want to go into the house and get into some dry clothes? My father's kind of skinny like you.'

'There's no *time*. The issues at stake are momentous, believe me!'

'Oh, boy, let's take off! The Jeep's in front.'

'Nerdsville,' said the teenage girl.

'*Abchoo!*'

'Bless ya,' said Tadeusz Mikulski, Special Agent, Federal Bureau of Investigation, his flat voice and dour expression conveying far less than a benediction. In truth, as he studied the strange figure seated in front of his desk, a man with one shoe who was obviously under severe stress and whose wet clothes were making puddles on his floor, Agent Mikulski reminded himself that his retirement was only eight months, four days, and six hours away, not that he was counting. 'Okay, Mr Deverooox,' he continued, looking down at the various soaked articles of identification extracted from the subject's wallet. 'Let's start again.'

'That's Devereaux,' said Sam.

'Look, Mr Devereaux, I speak English, Polish, Russian, Lithuanian, Czech, and would you believe Finnish, due to the Estonian influence on the language, but French has always eluded me. Perhaps it's a natural aversion; my wife and I spent a week in Paris and *she* spent the better part of my annual salary while we were there . . . Now, my error explained, may we start over again?'

'You mean you *don't* know my name?'

'I'm sure it's my loss, but then I doubt you've heard of Casimir the Third, also known as Charles the Great, King of Poland in the fourteenth century.'

'Are you *crazy*?' cried Sam. 'He was one of the most brilliant diplomat-rulers of his time! His sister was on the throne of Hungary and he learned from her court the expertise he needed to unify Poland. His treaties with Silesia and Pomorze were models of legal temperance.'

'All right, all *right*! Then maybe I've heard your name or read it in the papers, okay?'

'That's not what I'm asking, Agent Mikulski.' Devereaux leaned forward in the chair, a small bubble of water in his shirt unfortunately bursting through the buttons. 'I'm talking about the *dragnet*,' he whispered.

'The old television show?'

'No, *me*! . . . I have to assume it's been spread by those bastards in Washington because my associates were obviously taken – probably *tortured* to find out about Frazie's boat – but there are times when subordinates must learn the lesson of "I was only following orders!" . . . You *can't* take me in, Mikulski, you must *hear* what I have to tell you and listen to the tape recording that confirms everything I *say*!'

'You haven't told me anything. All you've done is wet my floor and ask me if my office is tapped.'

'Because the arm of this conspiratorial government-within-the-government is evil incarnate! They – *it* – will stop at *nothing*! They stole half of Nebraska!'

'*Nebraska?*'

'Over a hundred years ago!'

'A hundred . . . no *fooling?*'

'Tragically, obscenely, Mikulski! We have the proof and they'll do anything to stop us from being at the Supreme Court tomorrow to present ourselves *personae delectae!*'

'Oh, yeah, that,' said the FBI agent, pressing a button on his telephone console. 'Prepare psychiatric,' he said quietly into the intercom.

'*No!*' screamed Sam, yanking the sealed plastic bag from his pocket. '*Listen* to this!' he demanded.

Agent Mikulski took the plastic bag, which dripped, profusely soaking his clean blotter, removed the tape, and placed it into his desk recorder. He pressed the button; there was a sudden eruption of static followed by a spinning circle of water that splashed across the faces of both men as the thin black tape exploded from the machine, reeling across the room in splintered fragments. Whatever was on the tape had been obliterated.

'I don't *believe* it!' shouted Devereaux. 'I matched the yellow

494

and the blue lines to reach green on that pouch and sealed it! Those commercials are bullshit!'

'Maybe your eyesight's not so good,' said Mikulski, 'although I've got to agree with you, I can't freeze a kielbasy in one of these mothers.'

'It was all there – *everything*! The general, the Secretary of *State*, the whole conspiracy!'

'To steal Nebraska?'

'No, that was a hundred and twelve years ago. Federal agents burned the bank where the Wopotami treaties were kept.'

'Not *me*, pal. My grandparents were still slinging cowshit over in Poznán . . . Woppa-*who*?'

'Another general, *my* general, pieced it all together from the records in the archives – records and missing records which he *knew* were missing!'

'Archives . . . ?'

'The Bureau of Indian Affairs, naturally.'

'Oh, naturally.'

'You see, he was able to do it because there's *another* general with the same name as the general who was viciously conscripted by the Secretary of State. He retired from the army because the names got mixed up when I pressed drug-running charges against his cousin –'

'Speaking of such matters,' interrupted Mikulski. 'What brand of cigarettes do you smoke?'

'I'm trying to give them up, you should, too . . . Anyway, it was a big mistake, and this other general was given the job at Indian Affairs and *my* general, who's a friend of his, got to invade the sealed archives and wrote the brief based on those documents. It's all really very simple.'

'Absolutely fundamental,' said Mikulski in a monotone, nodding his head slowly, his wide eyes riveted on Sam as his hand inched back to his console and the intercom.

'You see, the Wopotami tribe could actually own all the territory in and around Omaha.'

'Of course . . . Omaha.'

'*SAC*, Agent Mikulski! The Strategic Air Command!

According to law, illegally usurped property that's been reclaimed by its rightful owners, the said criminally injured owners are entitled to whatever developments have been made on said usurped property. That's basic.'

'Real basic, oh, *real* basic.'

'And because certain corrupt persons in the government refuse to negotiate, they intend to eliminate the whole problem by *eliminating* the plaintiffs to the Supreme Court, which has recognized the Wopotami brief for argument and may just possibly adjudicate in its favour.'

'It might do that . . . ?'

'It's entirely possible – remote but possible. The dirty bastards in Washington hired someone named Goldfarb and fielded the Filthy Four and the Suicidal Six to stop us!'

'Someone named Goldfarb . . . ?' muttered the mesmerized Mikulski, his wide sad eyes briefly closing. ' . . . the Filthy Four and the Suicide-whatever?'

'We sent the Filthy Four back to their base in body bags.'

'You *killed* them?'

'No, Desi Arnaz the Second laced their food with sleep-inducing ingredients and there were air holes in the body bags.'

'Desi Arnaz the . . . ?' Special Agent Mikulski could not continue; he was a defeated man.

'It's now obviously clear to you, or *should* be, that we must move quickly and expeditiously to expose the Secretary of State and all those around him who would deny by violence the fundamental rights of the Wopotami tribe!'

Silence.

Finally.

'Let me tell you something, Mr Devereaux,' said the FBI man quietly, bringing to the fore what immediate resources he had left. 'What's obvious to me is that you are a troubled man beyond my ability to help you. Now, we have three choices. One, I can call the hospital in Gloucester and recommend psychiatric counselling; two, I can phone our friends at the police department and ask them to take you into custody until whatever you've been on wears off; or, three, I can forget you walked into my office, dripping wet with one shoe and flooding my floor, and let you walk out, trusting that your imaginative powers will lead you to friends who can assist you.'

'You don't *believe* me!' yelled Sam.

'Where do you want to start? With Desi Arnaz the Second and someone named Goldfarb? Or body bags with air holes and three generals who wouldn't last two minutes in the Pentagon without being put in straitjackets?'

'Everything I've told you is *true!*'

'I'm sure it is for you and I wish you well. Also, if you like, I'll call you a cab. You've got sufficient money in your wallet to get you to Rhode Island and another FBI office out of state.'

'You're derelict in your duty, Agent Mikulski.'

'My wife says the same thing where the bills are concerned. What can I say? I'm a failure.'

'You are a snivelling bureaucrat afraid to stand up to those who would trash our country's laws and constitutional rights!'

'Hey, you've got Desi Arnaz, this guy Goldfarb and three squirrelly generals on your side. What do you need me for?'

'You're a *disgrace*.'

'I'll buy that ... Now, unless you're going to mop up my floor and wipe down my desk, please get the hell out of here, huh? I've got work to do. The first-grade class at the Cape Ann grammar school is marching on City Hall, demanding equal voting rights.'

'Funny, *funny!*'

'I thought it was pretty cute.'

'It wasn't, and I don't need your help for transportation. My driver happens to be the champion wrestler of New England!'

'If you're selling tickets, I'll buy one if you'll only please just leave,' said the FBI agent, gathering up Devereaux's belongings and handing them to him.

'I won't forget this, Mikulski,' rejoined Sam, rising with all the dripping dignity he could summon to his one-shoed feet. 'As an officer of the court, I intend to file charges at the

Justice Department. Your dereliction of duty cannot be tolerated.'

'You do that, pal, only get the name right, okay? I mean, we wouldn't want a screw-up like you did with those two generals, would we? There are a lot of Mikulskis around here.'

'You think I'm *crazy*, don't you?'

'That's for the doctors to say, not me, but frankly I'm leaning in that direction.'

'*You'll* see!' said Sam the Avenger, turning and hobbling to the door, twice skidding on the wet floor. 'You'll *hear* from me!' he added, going into the outer office and slamming the door behind him.

Unfortunately, Special Agent Mikulski did hear about Sam precisely three minutes and twenty-one seconds after his departure. As the FBI man swallowed his fourth gulp of Maalox, the priority line on his telephone console rang; he pressed the button and picked up the phone. 'Mikulski, FBI.'

'Hey, Teddy, it's Gerard over at the base,' said the commander of the 10th District Massachusetts Coast Guard station.

'What can I do for you, sailor?'

'I called on a hunch that you could fill me in on the Frazier-Devereaux alert.'

'What ... ?' asked the special agent, barely audible. '*Devereaux*, you said?'

'Yeah, we got that cork-popping loon Frazier but no Devereaux, and Frazier didn't tell us a thing. He just sat there with an ass-eating grin and made his phone call.'

'"Didn't?" "Sat?" ... Past tense?'

'It's *nuts*, Teddy. We had to let him go and that's what we can't understand. What was that stupid alert about anyway? We damn near burned out an engine, stranded three men in a dinghy, and crashed five marina buoys which we have to pay for, all for nothing! Devereaux disappeared and we don't even know what he was *wanted* for. I figured you federals could fill us in.'

'We never even got the alert,' said Mikulski forlornly. 'Tell me what happened, Gere.' Commander Gerard did so and the special agent blanched, reaching for his Maalox. 'That son-of-bitch Devereaux just left here a few minutes ago. He's a walking banana barge! What the hell have I *done*?'

'If you didn't get the alert, you didn't do anything, Teddy. We teletyped out our report and that's all *we* could do ... Hold it, I just got handed a note. A shaver named Cafferty from the Boston PD is on the phone. Do you know him?'

'Never heard of him.'

'*Wait* a minute. PD-Boston is where that goddamn alert originated! I'm going to give that bastard a salvo he'll never forget! Talk to you later, Teddy.'

'Eight months, four days, and five and a half hours,' mumbled Mikulski, opening his top drawer and looking at his marked-off retirement calendar.

CHAPTER TWENTY-NINE

The champion wrestler of New England drove his Jeep into the Birnbaum driveway in Swampscott. 'Here we are, Mr Devereaux. I've seen this place from the water but never from inland. Some joint, huh?'

'I'd ask you in, Boomer, but the conversation's going to be pretty heavy and very confidential.'

'I'll bet it is! You land up on our beach, then the FBI, then here – *wow*. But don't mistake me, sir, I wasn't hinting, honest. I'll split fast and if anybody without legal authority asks me, I never saw you.'

'Well put – legally. However, I insist on paying you.'

'No *way*, Mr Devereaux, it's been an honour. But if you don't mind, I took the liberty of writing out my name in case – in a couple of years from now maybe – you might at least consider me for a clerking position. No special privileges, I wouldn't want that.'

'No, I don't think you would, Boomer,' said Sam, taking the piece of paper and looking into the clear, earnest eyes of the pre-law student. 'But if I want to grant them, there's nothing you can do about it.'

'Sorry, sir, I have to be good enough. You learn that in weight-class wrestling.'

'Let's put it this way. With that statement you won't have to look for us, we'll find you ... Thanks, Boomer.'

'Good luck, sir!' Devereaux climbed out of the Jeep; it spun around the drive and disappeared through the gates. Sam looked at the imposing brick entrance to the Birnbaum beach house, took a deep breath, and hobbled up the flagstone path

500

to the door. Things would be so much simpler if he had both shoes, he considered as he rang the bell.

'I'll be *damned*!' roared the huge black mercenary-chemist, Cyrus, as he pulled back the door. 'I don't know whether to hug you or to slug you, but get the hell in here, Sam!'

Devereaux trudged sheepishly into the foyer, his blotted clothes, matted hair, and shoeless foot apparent for all to see. The 'all' consisted of Cyrus, Aaron Pinkus . . . and the love of his eternal existence, Jennifer Redwing, who stood in the far corner of the room staring at him. What was in her alert – angry? – eyes, he could not tell.

'Sammy, we've heard *everything*!' shouted Aaron, who rarely if ever shouted, as he rose from the couch and spryly ran around it to greet his employee by gripping both Devereaux's arms and placing his elderly head against Sam's left cheek. 'Thank Abraham, you're alive!'

'It wasn't that hard,' said Devereaux. 'Frazie may be a maniac, but he sure knows how to drive a boat, and then there was this kid who's the champion wrestler of New England –'

'We know what you've *been* through, Sammy,' exclaimed Pinkus. 'Such courage, such *chutzpah*. All because you acted on principle!'

'It was dumb, Devereaux,' said Cyrus, 'but you got guts, man, I'll give you that.'

'Where's Mother?' asked the avenger, avoiding Jenny's eyes.

'She and Erin went back to Weston,' answered Aaron. 'Apparently cousin Cora fell into some teapots.'

'And Desis One and Two are on beach patrol with Roman Z,' added Cyrus.

'They let in Boomer's Jeep – the car I was in,' said Sam, disapproval in his statement.

'Not exactly,' countered the mercenary. 'Why do you think I was at the door? Desi the First radioed that the tall *loco-gringo* was back.'

'He's always had a way with words,' said Devereaux, slowly turning his head and looking over at Jenny. 'Hi,' he said cautiously.

It was like a pavane filmed in slow motion, as Aaron Pinkus and Cyrus M gracefully moved away from the line of contact. Tears flowing from her eyes, Sunrise Jennifer Redwing ran across the carpeted floor as Sam walked gallantly, if unsteadily, down the marble steps into the living room. Devereaux held his place as she rushed into his arms; they embraced, their lips meeting in swollen agony and delight.

'*Sam*,' she cried, holding him fiercely. 'Oh, Sam, Sam, *Sam*! It was Switzerland all over again, wasn't it? Mac *told* me! You did what you did because you knew it was *right*. It was the legal, *moral* thing to do! Leaping off a boat and swimming miles and miles in a storm to right the wrong! Oh, God, I *do* love you!'

'Well, it wasn't that many miles, maybe four or five –'

'But you *did* it! I'm so *proud*!'

'It was nothing.'

'It was *everything*!'

'I failed. The tape was drowned.'

'But you weren't, my darling, *you* weren't!'

Suddenly, there was the eruption of static and a squawking Hispanic voice over Cyrus's radio. 'Hey, *mon*! A big *leemoseeno* ees racing into dee house! You want me to blow it away?'

'Not yet, Desi!' ordered the mercenary. 'Cover the door; and you, Roman, come to the front, all weapons ready!'

Moments later, the middle-European voice of Roman Z could be heard. 'It iss only one old man weez white hair walking to the door. Iss driver inside turning on raadio. Iss lousy music.'

'Stand to,' ordered Cyrus, removing his gun from his shoulder holster. 'If I have to fire, converge.'

'Was dat? Con-sompding?'

'Iss no problem. Old man don' go for pockets or gun.'

'Out. Stay at the ready!'

'Reddy wad . . . ?'

'*Out!*'

'Wad . . . ?'

The doorbell rang as Cyrus waved Pinkus, Jenny and Devereaux away from any conceivable line of gunfire. He yanked the door open, his weapon at his side, only to be faced by a tall, slender, elderly gentleman.

'You're the butler, I presume,' said R. Cookson Frazier, his anxiety in no way mitigating his genuine courtesy. 'I must see your employer immediately, it's of the utmost urgency.'

'*Cookson!*' cried Aaron Pinkus, emerging from a curtained beach window. 'What are you *doing* here?'

'It's unbelievable, Aaron, absolutely *unbelievable!*' said Frazier, clutching a paper in his hand and rushing down the marble steps, his arms upright in apoplectic disbelief. 'You and I and all of Boston have been *gulled*, old fellow, positively *caged!*'

'What is that in English, Cookson?'

'Here, *look!*' Again, suddenly, the entangled figures of Jennifer and Sam came out of the far right shadowed corner. 'Who the hell are *they?*' yelled Frazier.

'The young man with one shoe and rather distressed clothing is Samuel Devereaux, Cookson –'

'Oh, you're Lansing's son. Damn fine man, your father. Damn shame he was taken so early.'

'And our lady friend is Jennifer, Jennifer Redwing ... Cookson Frazier.'

'Lovely tan, my child. Caribbean, no doubt. I've a house in Barbados – I think. You and Lansing's son must go down and enjoy it – haven't been there in years.'

'What's so unbelievable, Cookson?'

'As I say, *here* ... look!' The old gentleman thrust out the paper in his hand. 'This came to my house over the fax machine that has a noninterceptor, nonmemory line confirmed by Washington – just a moment, old boy, can everyone here be trusted?'

'My word on it, Cookson. What does it say?'

'*You* read it. I'm still in a state of shock.'

Aaron took the thin fax paper, scanned it, and slowly, in bewilderment, lowered himself into the nearest chair. 'It's beyond my understanding,' he said.

'What *is* it?' asked Devereaux, his arm protectively around Jennifer's shoulders.

'It says, and I quote: "This communiqué is top secret and must be destroyed upon perusal, its contents restricted to the highest levels of law enforcement. Geoffrey C. Frazier, code name Rumdum, is a highly effective and covertly much-decorated undercover agent for the federal government. Proceed accordingly with maximum regard for Officer Frazier's cover, credibility and safety" . . . It's signed by the director of the Drug Enforcement Agency. My *word*!'

'The boy's a damned Scarlet Pimpernel!' cried Cookson Frazier, throwing himself into the chair next to Aaron. 'What in heaven's name am I to *do*?'

'To begin with, I'd say you should be enormously proud as well as relieved. You yourself said there was another man inside your grandson and you were right. Instead of a wastrel, he's a highly successful, highly decorated professional.'

'Yes, but good God, old boy, the only way he can continue to be successful without being killed is to bring further disrepute on the family!'

'I hadn't considered that,' said Pinkus, frowning and nodding in agreement. 'But surely one day the truth will be revealed and all manner of praise will be heaped on the Boston Fraziers.'

'If that day comes, Aaron, the last male Boston Frazier will have to skip to Tasmania or Tierra del Fuego and assume another name. He'll be a marked man!'

'That, too, I had not considered.'

'Protection,' said Cyrus, walking down the steps, 'and extremely thorough protection can be purchased, Mr Frazier.'

'Oh, forgive me, Cookson, this is . . . Colonel Cyrus, an expert in security.'

'Good Lord, forgive *me*, Colonel! Damned stupid of me at the door. I *do* apologize.'

'No offence. In this neighbourhood, it's a perfectly understandable mistake. However, I'm not really a colonel.'

'I beg your pardon?'

'What he *means*,' cried Sam, his eyes boring in on the mercenary, 'is that he's retired from the military. He's not with any army – *the* Army, that is.'

'Oh, I see,' said Frazier, turning back to a bewildered Cyrus. 'Well, obviously, your expertise in security matters serves you well. Aaron only hires the finest. As a matter of fact, although it's probably too minor for your time, I've an alarm system in my house that confuses the hell out of me. I keep setting it off.'

'The pinpoints either aren't clean or they overlap in the circuitry,' said Cyrus offhandedly, frowning at Devereaux. 'Call your alarm's service department and tell them to check the point relays.'

'Really? Just like that?'

'It's common in house systems,' replied the mercenary, trying to read Sam's nodding expressions. 'Even a momentary power shortage can louse up those firefly circuits.'

'I'm sure the colonel would be happy to take a look at it, *wouldn't* you, Colonel?' said Devereaux, his nods now jackhammering behind Cookson Frazier's head.

'When my work for Mr Pinkus's security concerns are over . . . certainly,' answered the hesitant soldier-of-fortune-chemist, definitely confused. 'Perhaps some time next week,' he concluded weakly.

'*Good* fellow!' exclaimed Frazier, slapping his hand on the arm of the chair, then suddenly reverting to his previous state of quandary. 'I can't get over my grandson. It's positively *incredible*.'

'Why do I conjure up the image of a winking Crazie Frazie, his captain's hat lopsided and drinking from a champagne bottle probably filled with seltzer,' said Sam. 'But then I've never seen anyone drive a boat like that even in the movies.'

And then, as if evoked by the mention of motion pictures, the telephone rang, answered quickly by Colonel Cyrus, who was standing next to the antique white table. 'Yes?' said the mercenary softly.

'We *roll*, soldier,' said the voice of MacKenzie Hawkins from New York. 'We've scratched Plan A – it's too risky now – going with Plan B as we discussed an hour ago. Any news about Lieutenant Devereaux?'

'He's here, General,' replied Cyrus quietly, cupping the

phone as the others excitedly discussed Sam's seagoing revels with Secret Agent Geoffrey Frazier. 'He just arrived a few minutes ago and he's a mess. Do you want to talk to him?'

'*Christ*, no! I know that phase he's in; I call it Righteous Rabbit. What's the damage?'

'None that we can tell; no one believed him. Apparently the tape was destroyed.'

'Thank Hannibal for favours, big and small, but I knew he'd show up; he never does that sort of thing right . . . Then you haven't gone over either of the plans with him yet?'

'I haven't gone over them with anybody; no time. Mr Pinkus has been on the phone with the Boston police ever since the Coast Guard radioed that they'd spotted the boat Sam was on.'

'A boat? The *Coast Guard?*'

'We gather it was a hell of a chase and the sight of your lieutenant confirms it, wet clothes, one shoe, and all.'

'Switzerland again, goddamnit!'

'We gathered that, too, at least his girlfriend did. She's all over him like he was Johnny-come-marching-home with one leg – probably because of his one shoe.'

'Good! Work on the filly when you explain the plan, Colonel. She'll convince him if *you* convince her. I know that boy when he's got the hots, all my wives told me.'

'I'm not following you, General.'

'It's not important. Just remember, our enemies are desperate and the only way they can short circuit us is to stop us from getting into the Supreme Court. *That's* where Sam can climb up on his pulpit and say whatever he wants to say, expose whomever he wants to expose, yell as loud as he likes. But *only* there, Colonel. He wouldn't get to first base with anyone else in Dizzy City. They protect their turfs, and they'd blow him out of the Beltway if only because he makes too much noise.'

'Since I can personally vouch for that Washington reaction, it won't be difficult to be convincing,' said Cyrus. 'But how come Plan B? I thought you and I agreed that *A* was perfectly feasible.'

'I don't know who the inside contact is but my informant, the one I told you about –'

'The government honcho everyone thinks is dead,' interrupted the mercenary.

'That's the one, and let me tell you, he's out for blood. Speaking of which, he made it goddamned clear that we're facing termination with extreme prejudice – and I mean *real* extreme, Colonel.'

'My *God*, they'd go that *far*?'

'They haven't got a choice, soldier. Through mergers and megabuy-outs, that whole crowd owns seventy percent of the defence industries and is so many billions in debt it would take World War Three to bail 'em out, if it lasted that long, which it wouldn't.'

'How do you read the strategy, General?'

'I don't have to read it, I know it! They've hired the scum of the earth to stop us: head-bashing gunslingers, union-busters-for-hire, probably meres like you looking for bucks.'

'It's a free economy,' said Cyrus, now whispering as he glanced over at Aaron, Jenny and Sam, who, in turn, were glancing over at him. 'And there's a lot of economics involved ... I can't talk much longer. Did your supposedly deceased informant tell you when and how all those nasty people will get in place?'

'They'll be everywhere! In the crowds, among the Court guards, even up into the outer chambers!'

'That's a rough call, General.'

'Plan B creates the diversion we need, Colonel. Nobody's happy about it, especially the Wopotamis, but it's in place. They're all ready to do their thing.'

'How's that fruitcake Sutton taking all this?' asked Cyrus. 'That son of a bitch isn't my favourite person, but I'll grant you he's a hell of an actor.'

'What can I tell you? He says he'll give the greatest performance of his life!'

'If he lives to read the reviews ... Over and out, General, see you in the morning.'

'What about our Desis and Roman Z?' broke in Hawkins

suddenly. 'What with my Suicidal Six business, I hadn't factored them into the scenario.'

'If you think I'm leaving them out, you should be cleaning latrines, General.'

'I like your response, Colonel!'

'Out.'

A shell-shocked R. Cookson Frazier returned to Louisburg Square in his limousine, and at the beach house a stunned sextet faced Cyrus, who stood in front of the white antique table. Jennifer Redwing sat between Aaron Pinkus and Sam Devereaux on the couch, while Desis One and Two stood behind them, flanking their new friend, Roman Z. All mouths were gaped, all eyes riveted on the field-commissioned colonel.

'That's the scenario everybody,' said the imposing black mercenary, 'and speaking as the liaison to the general, if any of you wish to back out, you may. However, I should tell you that as someone who's been exposed to a great many infiltration strategies, they don't come much better than this. General Hawkins didn't become a legend because of press releases – he's the real thing and he's damn good and I don't say that lightly.'

'Hey, like Miss Erin say, he talk real good for a black brother, yeah, D-One?'

'Shaddup, D-Two.'

Thank you for the gratulatory comment, Desi.'

'See wad I mean?'

'If I may,' said Aaron Pinkus, inching forward on the couch, 'this highly complicated charade, as ingenious as it may be, strikes me as being – well, too complicated, too theatrical, as it were. Is it really necessary?'

'To answer your questions in generic terms, Mr Pinkus, complicated theatrics are the best diversion.'

'We can understand that, Cyrus,' said Jennifer, her left hand gripping Devereaux's right. 'But, as Mr Pinkus says, is it really *necessary*? I think Sam's idea of simply getting off the plane and taking a taxi to the Supreme Court – no limousine, no calling attention to ourselves – would be quite sufficient.'

'Under normal circumstances it would be, but these are not normal circumstances. You have powerful and very capable enemies. *Very* capable, the kind your friend Sam wants to expel from the government, even at the risk of his life, as we all witnessed today.'

'He was wonderful!' cried Jennifer, pressing her lips into Devereaux's left cheek. 'Swimming all those miles in a storm –'

'It was nothing,' said Sam. 'Only six or seven, maybe eight . . . If I understand you, Cyrus, you're saying this "diversion," as you call it, is necessary because these very capable enemies of ours intend to physically intercept us before we can get into the building, is that right?'

'Basically, yes.'

'Basically? What else is there?'

'With ramifications,' answered the mercenary curtly.

'I won't pretend to understand that but if we have reason to believe a threat exists, we can request police protection. Coupled with you fellas, if you guys are with us, what else could we possibly need?'

'An item or two I haven't mentioned.'

'*What?*'

'Look, you three are the lawyers, I'm not, and Washington isn't Boston where Mr Pinkus's corn beef and cabbage have a positive effect on the police department. In DC, when you request blue-coat protection, you'd better show justifiable cause. Hell, those jackets can't handle what they've got.'

'And "justifiable cause" would naturally entail naming names in the highest places,' broke in Jenny, 'and even if we got another copy of the tape, we wouldn't dare play it for evidence.'

'Why *not?*' exclaimed Devereaux furiously. 'I'm damn sick and tired of pussyfooting around! Public trusts have been violated, laws broken – why the *hell* not?'

'The paws of the cat were created for a purpose, Sam,' said Pinkus.

'Oh, that's all I *need*. My boss, the Punjabi prophet from the Himalayas! Would you mind coming off the mountain and explaining that, Aaron?'

'You're upset, my darling –'

'Tell me something I don't know! ... Maybe it was ten miles and that storm was really closer to a hurricane – say Force Ninety-nine, or whatever they call it.'

'I'm trying to tell you,' said Pinkus, his voice calm, his electric eyes on Devereaux, 'that a quiet approach to catch a quarry is usually more effective than setting off alarms.'

'I'll put it another way,' added Cyrus. 'No precinct in Washington – tape or no tape – is going to take on someone like the Secretary of State.'

'He's in a *funny house!*'

'All the more reason for State to maintain an equilibrium,' said the mercenary-chemist. 'Believe me, I know.'

'It's all *corruption!*' roared Sam.

'Only a few,' insisted Jennifer. 'The vast majority are overworked, underpaid, dedicated bureaucrats – bureaucrats in the best sense, men and women who try their best to sort out the problems of their myriad departments brought on by politicians waffling for votes. It ain't easy, darling.'

Devereaux unclasped his hand from Redwing's, brought it to his forehead, and leaned back on the couch. 'All right,' he said wearily. 'I'm the dumbest kid on the block. People do terrible things and everybody shuts up; accountability's out the window!'

'Not true, Sam,' corrected Aaron. 'You'd never build a case that way, I know you. You'd cover every escape route before you made either your initial presentation to a jury or whatever subsequent counter arguments. That's why you're the finest attorney in my firm – when you're all together.'

'All right, all *right*. We're clowns in a three-ring circus tomorrow! ... What were the items you hadn't mentioned, Cyrus?'

'Bulletproof jackets and steel helmets under your head-gear,' replied the mercenary as if he had just enumerated the ingredients for chocolate chip cookies.

'*What?*'

'You heard me. We're talking hardball now, Counsellor. There are more billions – yes, *billions* – riding on your appearance tomorrow afternoon than you can conjure in your out-of-orbit imagination.'

'*Caramba!*' yelled Desi the Second. 'Don' he talk good!'

'*Shaddup!* We could be *muerto*!'

'H'ye don' care! Ees right!'

'So I agree wid chu, so *wad*? So we're *loco*!'

'Iss in the Romany tarot cards, my frenz!' shouted Roman Z, twirling in place, his flowing blue sash over his orange shirt covering the withdrawal of his long-bladed knife. 'The blade of the Romany will cut the throats of any who attack our holy cause – whatever it iss.'

'Hey, come on, Cyrus!' roared Devereaux. 'Under these circumstances, I will *not* permit Jenny or Aaron to be any part of it!'

'You don't speak for *me*!' cried the Aphrodite of Sam's dreams.

'Nor me, young man!' said Pinkus, getting up from the couch. 'You forget, I was on Omaha Beach. I may not have been significant, but I've still got the shrapnel as proof of my efforts. It was, indeed, a holy cause then and there's a distinct parallel here. When men deny by force the rights of others, the only result is tyranny. And I will not *tolerate* that for this country of ours!'

'*Ahchoo, ahchoo,* ahchoo!'

CHAPTER THIRTY

5:45 A.M. As dawn broke over the Washington skyline, a russet mantle in the making, the silent marble halls of the Supreme Court came quietly alive as teams of cleaning women pushed their maintenance carts from one doorway to another. The tiers of trays held new boxed soap, fresh towels, tissue replacements, and in front of each dolly, a suspended plastic trash bag for yesterday's refuse.

One cart, however, differed from all the others in the magnificent structure dedicated to laws of God and nation. So did the elderly grey-haired lady pushing it; she was *distinctly* different from her counterparts throughout the building. For upon closer examination, her grey locks were perfectly coiffed, her blue eye shadow subtly apparent, and by mistake she wore a diamond and emerald bracelet around her wrist that was in value many times the annual salary of the other ladies. She also wore a large plastic label clipped to the pocket of her uniform that read: *Temporary. Cleared.*

What made her cart different was the suspended plastic bag designed for refuse. It was full before she reached the first office on her assigned route – an office she disdained to enter as her mumbled words confirmed while she passed the door.

'*Escremento!* ... Vincenzo, you *pazzo*. My best and most loved child of my dearest sister should be in an *istituzione*! I could buy every statue in dissa whole building! ... So why do I *do*? ... Because my beloved nephew means my no-good husband don' have to work. *Manage!* ... Oh, here it is, the closet. *Bene!* I leave everything here, go home, watch a little TV, then with girls a little shopping. *Molto bene!*'

8:15 A.M. Four nondescript brown and black automobiles pulled up swiftly on First Street near the corner of Capitol Street. Three dark-suited men got out of each, their brows furrowed, all eyes robotically centred; they were the 'gunslingers' hired for a job, and to fail meant going back to the most menial of their former union tasks – a fate worse than death. Twelve dedicated professionals, who had no idea what they were dedicated to, except that the two men in the photographs they carried in their pockets must never enter the Supreme Court across the street. No sweat. Nobody ever found Jimmy Hoffa.

9:12 A.M. Two vehicles with government licence plates parked briefly in front of the Supreme Court. Under the instruction of the Attorney General, the eight men who emerged were to take into custody two individuals wanted for outrageous crimes against the country. Each FBI agent had a photograph of the former and thoroughly discredited General MacKenzie Hawkins and his accomplice, an underworld lawyer named Samuel Lansing Devereaux still wanted for treasonous activities during his tour of duty in the last days of the Vietnam action. There was no statute of limitation on his crimes. He had impugned the reputations of his superiors while profiting from their disgrace. Federal agents *hated* guys like that – how did they *do* it?

10:22 A.M. A dark blue van veered into the kerb on Capitol Street at the side of the Supreme Court. Its rear doors opened and seven Ranger Commandos in camouflaged green and black combat fatigues leaped out, their weapons concealed in their wide pockets. After all, they did not want to appear conspicuous. Their covert mission had been defined by the diminutive Secretary of Defense himself – orally, not in writing. 'Gentlemen, these two scum would cripple the first line of America's airborne forces, that's all I can tell you. They must be stopped at all costs. In the words of that great commander, "Beam 'em up, Scotty," – *way* up, out of *sight*!' ... Commandos *hated* scum like that! If anyone was going to dump on the sky jocks, it would be *them*. The fly-boys grabbed all the headlines and still flew home for a steak while *they* were in the mud! *No!* If anybody was going to blitz the 'airborne,' *they* would do it!

12:03 P.M. MacKenzie Hawkins, arms akimbo, studied the figure of Henry Irving Sutton in the hotel room, nodding his approval. '*Goddamn*, Mr Actor, you could be me!'

'It wasn't difficult, *mon général*,' said Sutton, removing his gold-braided officer's cap, revealing a head of close-cropped grey hair. 'The uniform fits superbly and the ribbons are, indeed, impressive. The rest is merely vocal intonation, which is simple. My voice-over commercials, including one for a rotten cat, sent one of my children through college – damned if I can remember which one.'

'I still want you to wear a combat helmet –'

'Don't be ridiculous, it would spoil the effect and defeat the purpose. My role is to draw men out, not frighten them away. A battle helmet telegraphs impending conflict and that connotes defence measures such as armed concealed personnel for protection. One's motivation must be clean and consistent, General, not muddled, you lose your audience that way.'

'You could also lose – well, you could be a target, too, you know.'

'I really don't think so,' said the actor, his eyes twinkling at the Hawk's unfinished statement. 'Not with what you've got going out there. Compared to the sands of North Africa, this is practically off stage. At any rate, it's a minor risk for which I'm being well compensated . . . Incidentally, how goes it with our Stanislavski warriors of the Suicidal Six?'

'There's been a change of plans –'

'*Oh?*' interrupted Sir Henry sharply, suspiciously.

'All to the good for everybody,' said Hawkins quickly, instantly recognizing the quasi panic of the actor's expression, a custom of a trade where *you got it, sweetheart, you're teriff!* frequently meant *the bum's a loser, get me some class like Sonny Tufts*. 'They'll be in Los Angeles by four o'clock this afternoon. My wife, my former wife – one of 'em, that is, the first, actually – wanted them out there so she could keep a motherly eye on all six.'

'How very sweet.' The actor touched the two stars on his collar. 'However, to be blunt, nothing's changed with regard to my appearance in the film?'

'Hell, no. The boys want you and whatever they want they're going to get.'

'Are you certain? They have no recognition quotient, you realize.'

'Whatever it is, they don't need it. They control the "hottest boffo-box-office-mega-buster" – whatever *that* is – anyone in Dizzy City, West, can remember. In any event, everything's in the hands of the William Morris Agency and –'

'William *Morris*?'

'Isn't that the name?'

'It certainly is! I think one of my daughters is an attorney in their legal department – probably got the job because she's my daughter. What *is* her name; I see her every Christmas.'

'The deal's being handled by two men named Robbins and Martin, and my wife, my former – you know what I mean – says they're the best.'

'Yes, yes, of course, I've read about them in the trades. I believe my daughter – Becky or Betty ... whatever – was engaged to that Robbins fellow, or was it Martin? Yes, they really must be splendid, for she's a very bright girl – *Antoinette*, that's her name! She always gives me a sweater three sizes too big, but then I've always appeared extremely large on stage – it's called presence, you know.'

'I guess I do now. The boys are heading out to the coast, everything's first class, my Ginny told me.'

'Naturally. One doesn't send six quarts of diamonds on a subway unattended. I'm surprised they didn't hire their own jet.'

'My ex-wife explained that. She said all the studios and the agents out there hire people who do nothing but monitor corporate aircraft, and if anything looks suspicious, they bribe the pilots. She told me a Lear was lost in the Alaskan tundra three weeks ago and was just found yesterday, two hours after a rival studio signed some guy named Warner Batty to a contract.'

The hotel room doorbell rang, startling both men. 'Who the hell could *that* be?' whispered the Hawk. 'Henry, did you tell anybody –'

'Absolutely *no one*!' replied the actor, also whispering, but far more emphatically. 'I followed the script, dear boy, not a single variation in the stage directions! I registered quite respectably as a pipe salesman from Akron – proper polyester suit, weary slouch . . . damn fine performance, if I do say so.'

'Who could it *be*?'

'Leave it to me, *mon général*.' Sutton walked to the door and assumed the weaving posture of a drunken man, loosening his tie and partially unbuttoning his tunic. 'Hide in the *closet*, MacKenzie!' he said quietly, then raising his timbre, he spoke in a loud inebriated voice. '*Yesh*, wassit it? Dish is a personal party, and me and my broad don' want no extra guests!'

'Hey, *fazool*!' came the gruff reply through the door. 'If you think you're playin' one of your fuckin' games like you did when we was in Bean Town, ferget it! Lemme *in*!'

Sir Henry snapped his head around; the closet door opened simultaneously, the face of MacKenzie Hawkins pinched in shock. 'Oh, my *God*, it's Little Joseph! . . . Let him in, goddamnit.'

'*So?*' said Joey, his hands clasped behind him as the door closed and standing as high as his five foot, three inches permitted. 'If the head of that *fazool* peekin' out of the closet is your broad, soldier boy, you got *big* troubles in the military.'

'Who is this *dwarf* who obviously speaks dwarf-talk?' asked the actor, his indignation scathing.

'You're an easy mark, fazool number *two*. Once you made contact with the big fazool on F Street and Tenth, what with your right shoulder twitching and your left hand jabbing south like you got the *dt's*, I knew you was the contact. You couldn't fool nobody.'

'Are you questioning my *technique*, sir? I, who have

garnered the approbation of a thousand critics across the land!'

'Who's the hot fudge sundae?' asked Little Joey as a perplexed Hawk walked out of the clothes closet. 'I think maybe Bam-Bam and me should know, y'know what I mean?'

'*Joseph*, what are you *doing* here?' roared MacKenzie, his astonishment receding and veering to menace.

'Cool it, fazool. Vinnie has your best interests at heart, you gotta know that. Remember, I'm the Shroud. I can be anywhere, move anywhere, nobody notices me. Like you didn't notice me when you flew into National Airport from New York this morning and I was right on your ass.'

'*So?*'

'A couple of things, maybe. Bam-Bam wants to know if he should call in a squad of torpedos from Toronto.'

'Absolutely *not!*'

'He figured; there's no time . . . Awright, then he wants you to know that his blessed aunt Angelina has done like you wished her to do because her husband, Rocco, is a no-good son of a bitch and she loves her nephew, Vincenzo. The stuff you wanted is in the second closet in the hallway to the right.'

'*Good!*'

'All is not so good. Bam-Bam is a proud man, fazool, and your original American buddies are not so good to him. He says they treat him like garbage and the feathers around his head don't fit!'

12:18 P.M. The manager of the Embassy Row Hotel on Massachusetts Avenue was not prepared for the current behaviour of one of his favoured guests, namely Aaron Pinkus, attorney-at-law. As usual, whenever the celebrated lawyer journeyed to Washington, it was a given that his stay was confidential, as, indeed, was the case with any guest who requested the same, but this afternoon Mr Pinkus had carried confidentiality to its extreme. He had insisted that he and his party use the delivery entrance and ascend to their adjoining suites – on the freight elevator. Furthermore, only the manager himself was to be aware of the attorney's presence;

fictitious names were to be entered into the register and, therefore, should any telephone calls come for him, those callers would naturally be told that no Aaron Pinkus was registered, for indeed he was not. However, should calls come specifying only the room numbers, they should be put through.

It was not like Pinkus to issue such vigilant instructions, considered the manager, but he thought he knew why. Washington was a zoo these days, and no doubt a lawyer of his expertise had been called to testify before Congress on some complicated points of law about a bill fraught with special interests. Obviously, Pinkus had brought down a contingent of the brightest attorneys in his firm to advise him during the hearings.

Which was why the manager was bewildered when, as he routinely checked the front desk, a man in an orange silk shirt, a blue silk sash and a gold earring swinging from his left lobe came up to the counter and asked where the 'droogy store' was.

'Are you a guest of the hotel, sir?' asked the suspicious clerk.

'Wat *alse*?' replied Roman Z, displaying his room key. The manager glanced at it. It was the number of a Pinkus suite.

'Over there, sir,' said the mortified clerk, pointing across the lobby.

'Iss *good*! I need new cologne! I *charge*, no?'

Only seconds later, two swarthy men dressed in uniforms the manager did not recognize, apparently from some South American revolution, he thought, rushed up to the desk.

'Where'd he *go*, man?' cried the taller of the two, several gaps in his teeth.

'Who?' asked the clerk, backing away from the counter.

'The *gitano* wid d'gold earring!' said the second Hispanic. 'He got the key to d'room but my amigo pressed d'wrong button on the h'evelator. We went up, he wen' down!'

'*Two* elevators?'

'Ees *seguridad*, chu know wad I mean?'

'Security?'

'Dad's it, gringo,' answered the man with the missing teeth as he studied the formally dressed clerk in the cutaway. 'Chu got nice clothes like I got *vispera* – dee odder day ago. Chu bring 'em back in d'morning, chu no pay so much rent. I read dat on a sign.'

'Yes, well, these are not rented, sir.'

'Chu *buy* dem? *Madre de Dios*, you gotta good chob!'

'A lovely job, sir,' said the astonished clerk, glancing over at the even more astonished manager. 'Your friend went to the "droogy" – the drugstore, sir. It's over there.'

'*Gracias*, amigo. Chu keep dis nice rich chob!'

'Indeed, sir,' mumbled the clerk as Desis One and Two raced across the lobby after Roman Z. 'Who *are* those people?' asked the hotel clerk, turning to the hotel manager. 'That room key was for one of our better suites.'

'Witnesses?' said the appalled manager, a ray of hope in his reply. 'Yes, of course, they could *only* be witnesses. It's probably a hearing about the mentally impaired.'

'What is?'

'Never mind, they'll be gone by the day after tomorrow.'

Upstairs in the suite Aaron Pinkus had reserved for Jennifer, Sam and himself, the vaunted attorney was explaining the hotel of his choice. 'One can usually repel curiosity by confronting it and discouraging it,' he said, 'especially if you're dealing with an institution that profits from your patronage. If I had made our requests to an unfamiliar hotel, the rumours would fly.'

'And you're not an unknown in this city,' added Devereaux. 'Can you trust the manager?'

'I would in any event; he's a fine man. However, since all flesh has its weaknesses and the muckrakers in this town are vultures constantly in search of informational carrion, I made it plain that he was the only person who knew we were here. I felt bad doing so; it wasn't necessary.'

'There's "safe" and there's "sorry," Mr Pinkus,' said Redwing, walking to a window and looking down at the street below. 'We're so close – to what I don't know, but it frightens me. Within a matter of days my people will either be patriots or pariahs, and right now my money's on pariahdom.'

'Jenny,' began Aaron, a muted sadness in his voice. 'I didn't wish to alarm you, but upon reflection, I think you'd never forgive me if I didn't tell you now.'

'Tell me what?' Redwing turned away from the window, staring at Pinkus, then glancing at Sam, who shook his head conveying no knowledge of Aaron's statement.

'I spoke with an old friend of mine this morning, a colleague from the early days, in fact, who's now a member of the Court.'

'*Aaron!*' cried Devereaux. 'You didn't mention anything about this *afternoon*, did you?'

'Of course not. It was merely a social call. I said I had business here and perhaps we might have dinner.'

'Thank *heavens*!' said Jenny.

'He was the one who brought up this afternoon,' said Pinkus quietly.

'What?'

'*What?*'

'Not in terms of specifics, mind you, only with regards to our proposed dinner . . . He said that it was quite possible he wouldn't be able to make it for he might be hiding and under guard in the cellars of the Supreme Court.'

'*What?*'

'That's what I said –'

'*And?*'

'He said today was one of the strangest in the annals of Supreme Court history. They're holding a special session in chambers with plaintiffs over a case that has acrimoniously divided the justices. None of them knows how the others will ultimately vote, but they're determined to dispose of their initial responsibility, which is to make public a rather momentous suit against the government. They'll do so immediately after the hearing is over.'

'*What?*' screamed Redwing. 'This *afternoon*?'

'Originally, they kept it off the Court calendar for reasons of national security and the possibility of reprisals against the litigants – the Wopotamis, I presume; then, apparently, the administration demanded that news of the suit be kept secret for an extended period of time.'

'Thank heavens for *somebody*!' cried Jennifer.

'For Chief Justice Reebock,' explained Aaron, 'who's not the most likeable fellow in the world, albeit quite bright. Unaccountably, and contrary to his normal disposition, Reebock went along with the White House. When the rest of the justices learned this, the majority simply revolted, including my friend. He made it clear that along with the others, even those ideologically opposed to him, the Executive had no constitutional right to impose restrictions on the Judicial ... Sometimes it all comes down to ego, doesn't it? Forget checks and balances, ego's the great equalizer.'

'Mr *Pinkus*, my people will be in the streets, on the steps of the Supreme Court! They'll be *slaughtered*!'

'Not if the general plays his cards right, my dear.'

'If there was a *wrong* card to show, he'd *show* it!' yelled Redwing. 'That man is instant hate! There's no one on earth he's incapable of offending!'

'But *you* hold the deck,' interrupted Devereaux. 'He can't legally do a damn thing without your approval; your contract with him is binding.'

'Has that ever stopped him *before*? From all I've learned about your prehistoric *dinosaur*, he tramples over the international laws of behaviour, his own government, the Joint Chiefs, the Catholic Church, the universal concepts of morality, and even *you*, Sam, whom he professes to love like his own son! It's not *you* who'll climb up on that sacrosanct bully pulpit to denounce injustice, it'll be *him*, and to make his case he'll nuke the whole goddamn system and turn the Wopotamis into the biggest threat this nation has faced since Munich in 'thirty-nine! He'll be a bolt of lightning that has to be shorted out, *grounded*, before a hundred other minorities think they see how *they've* been screwed by a government and there'll be riots in the streets everywhere ... We can correct these things with time and prudence, but not *his* way, which is chaos!'

'She's got a point, Aaron.'

'Again, a brilliant summary, my dear, but you overlook a fundamental law of nature.'

'What the hell is *that*, Mr Pinkus?'

'Wrapped in a bagel, he can be stopped.'

'For God's sake, *how*?'

At that moment, the door of the suite burst open, crashing against the wall as a furious Cyrus stood in the frame. But it was a different Cyrus; he was dressed in an extravagantly expensive pin-striped suit, Bally shoes and a foulard tie. 'Those sons of *bitches* got out!' he yelled. 'Are they *here*?'

'You mean Roman and our two Desis?' said Sam, holding his breath. 'They've *deserted*?'

'Hell, no, they're like kids at Disneyland; they've got to explore. They'll be back but they disobeyed orders.'

'What do you mean, Colonel?' asked Pinkus.

'Well, I went to – I went to the can and told them to stay put, and when I got out they were gone!'

'You just said they'd be back,' offered Devereaux. 'So what's the problem?'

'You want those grinder monkeys running around in the *lobby*?'

'It might be rather refreshing actually,' said Aaron, chuckling. 'Give a little life to the army of diplomats here who walk around so rigidly you'd think they were containing severe cases of duodenal gas – forgive me, my dear.'

'Once again, no apologies are necessary, Mr Pinkus,' said Jennifer, her gaze on the huge mercenary. 'Cyrus,' she continued, 'you look so – oh, I don't know what the word is – but so . . . I guess, *distinguished*.'

'It's the threads, Jenny. I haven't worn a suit like this since forty-six relatives in Georgia got together and bought me one at the Peachtree Center when I got my doctorate. Couldn't afford one before then and certainly not afterward. Glad you like it; me, too. It's courtesy of Mr Pinkus, whose tailors jump through the eyes of needles when he sneezes.'

'Not true, my friend,' said Aaron. 'They simply understand

the meaning of emergency . . . Isn't our colonel a magnificent sight?'

'Awesome,' agreed Sam reluctantly.

'The Colossus of Rhodes dressed for an IBM board of directors' meeting,' added Redwing, nodding approvingly.

'Then, perhaps, I should introduce you to your new associate at the hearing this afternoon . . . May I present Judge Cornelius Oldsmobile, who will accompany you into the chambers as a visiting *amicus curiae* extraordinaire, courtesy of my old friend who's a member of the Court. He is not permitted to speak, only observe, but he will be sitting next to General Hawkins, who logically thinks he's there as military security. At the conclusion of the hearing, should our general be determined to add inflammatory comments, "Judge Oldsmobile" has assured me that there are a number of ways to prevent him from doing so, including a metabolic seizure that for one of the general's age would mandate his immediate removal.'

'*Aaron*, you old fox!' cried Sam, leaping up from his chair.

'It pained me to even conceive of such an action, but one must consider the alternative, as the lovely Jennifer suggests.'

'*God*, I wish you were thirty years younger!' cried Redwing. 'Hell, even *twenty*!'

'So do I, my child, but I'd be grateful if you never mentioned such a thought to Shirley.'

'Maybe *I* will, if Pocahontas doesn't behave,' said Devereaux. 'You know, it could have been ten, maybe fifteen, miles in the storm, but I'm too modest to talk about it.'

Arnold Subagaloo wriggled his broad beam into the captain's chair, secure in the knowledge that the tight-fitting arms would hold his body firm as he indulged in his favourite office pastime. For when he raised his arm to throw his darts, his pear-shaped frame was confined to the parameters imposed, thus ensuring a better aim as there was a minimum of lower lateral movement. After all, he was an engineer *par excellence*, with an IQ of 185, and knew everything there was to know about everything except real politik, courtesy, and a diet.

He had pressed the button that pulled back the flushed curtain on the wall, revealing an enormous photographic tableau stretching from corner-to-corner with the enlarged faces of one hundred six men and women – *enemies* all! *Liberals* in both parties, *environmentalist* loonies who could never understand a profit and loss statement, *Feminazis* who were forever trying to emasculate God's order of masculine superiority, and, above all, those senators and congressmen who had the temerity to tell him he *wasn't* the President! . . . Well, maybe he wasn't, actually, but who the hell did they think *thought* for the President? Every hour, every minute!

As Subagaloo began to throw his first dart, his private telephone rang, causing the sharp, pointed missile to deviate and go through an open window on the left, resulting in a loud scream from a landscaper in the Rose Garden.

'That motherfucker's at it again! I *quit*!'

Arnold dismissed the gratuitous remark out of hand; he should have hit the man between the eyes – obviously a member of some socialist-communist union expecting two weeks' severance pay for a lousy twenty years on the job. Unfortunately, Subagaloo could not get out of the chair; his swollen hips were unable to negotiate the tight-fitting arms. As there was no other choice, he waddled across the floor, chair and rump temporarily attached, to the incessantly ringing phone.

'Who are you and how did you get this *number*?' yelled the chief of staff.

'Easy, Arnold, it's Reebock, and we're on the same side on this one.'

'Oh, *Mister* Chief Justice! Are you about to give me another big problem I don't need?'

'No, I just solved the biggest one you've got.'

'The *Wopotamis*?'

'They can starve to death on their stupid reservation, who cares? I had a little barbecue at my house last night, the whole Court. Naturally, as my wine cellar is the finest in Washington, everyone got pissed to the antlers except the lady, and now she doesn't count. We had a very American, *intellectual*, conversation around the pool. Very erudite, very judicial.'

'*So?*'

'Six to three against the Wopotami savages, guaranteed. Two of our brethren wavered, but they saw the light when our nubile lady caterers took off their clothes and went for a swim. Our two would-be bleeding hearts claimed they were pushed into the pool, but the photographs don't show that. Such injudicious behaviour – the tabloids would go wild, I made that rather clear.'

'Reebock, you're a *genius*! Not on my level, of course, but not bad, not bad at all ... But let's keep this between ourselves, all right?'

'We speak the same language, Subagaloo. Our job is to keep the un-American deviates out of the mainstream. They're dangerous, every *one* of them. Can you imagine where we'd all be without the income tax and those civil rights laws?'

'In heaven, Reebock, in heaven! ... Remember, we never talked.'

'Why do you think I called you on this number?'

'How'd you get it?'

'I've got a mole in the White House.'

'*Who*, for Christ's sake?'

'Come on, Arnold, that's not fair.'

'I guess it isn't, because I've got one in the Court.'

'*Stare decisis*, my friend.'

'What else is new?' said Arnold Subagaloo.

12:37 P.M. The huge Trailblaze bus, leased and paid for by no one the company had ever heard of, stopped in front of the imposing entrance to the Supreme Court. The driver fell over the large circular steering wheel, anguished tears flowing from his eyes, grateful that his full load of passengers was about to depart. Miles back he had yelled, screamed, and finally shrieked in panic that 'Fire – *cooking* – is not permitted inside the bus!'

'We're not cooking, man,' had said a firm voice behind

him. 'We're mixing the colours which means you've got to melt the wax.'

'What?'

'*See?*' Suddenly a grotesquely painted face had been thrust in front of his eyes, causing the driver to lurch across the Virginia highway, slipping between the onrushing vehicles until he managed to return to his lane.

There followed what could only be described as a series of events that justified the screams of the owner of the Last Ditch Motel outside of Arlington when he had roared from behind a mountain of duffel bags:

'I'll blow the fucking place up before I let 'em back in! Holy *shit*! Fuckin' war dances around a fuckin' bonfire in the parking lot! Everybody else in all the other rooms left – *running* – without a nickel in my till!'

'You got it wrong, man! They were supplication chants. You know, like prayers for rain and deliverance, even sometimes broads.'

'*Out, out, out!*'

Once the duffel bags had been loaded, by necessity a number strapped on top of the bus, the series of intolerable events continued amid the smoke and the stench of melted-down Crayola crayons. 'You see, man, when you mix it with paraffin and press it into your skin, it conforms and slowly drips down your face with the body heat. Scares the hell out of palefaces . . . *see?*' The driver saw. Weeping streaks of bright colours slowly crawling down the face of someone named Calfnose. The bus had nearly crashed into the rear of a diplomatic limousine bearing the flags of Tanzania; instead, it merely dented the bumper, then skirted to the left, passing it and removing a side mirror as several wide-eyed black faces stared up at their more colourful counterparts in the windows of the bus.

Then came the audibles, initially the slow, bass-toned *boom*-booms of at least a dozen drums. *Boom*-boom, *boom*-boom, *boom*-boom – *boom-boom, boom-boom!* '*Hai-ya, hai-ya, hai-ya!*' The fanatical chorus built to a hysterical crescendo as the driver's head shot back and forth over the wheel like a rooster in heat in time with the beat. Relief had suddenly come as the drums and the chanting abruptly stopped, apparently by command.

'I think we got that one wrong, guys and girls!' shouted the terrorist named Calfnose. 'Isn't that the wedding night celebration?'

'Beats the hell out of Ravel's "Bolero"!' replied a male voice at the rear of the crowded bus.

'Who'd know the difference?' yelled another, now a woman.

'I don't know,' answered Calfnose, 'but Thunder Head said Indian Affairs might send down a couple of experts 'cause nobody expects us or knows why we're there.'

'If they're Mohawks, they'll crap on us!' shouted yet another, by his voice an elderly member of the tribe. 'Legend has it that they threw us out of our wigwams whenever it snowed!'

'Well, just in case, let's rehearse the one that greets the sunrise; that'd be applicable.'

'Which one is that, Johnny?' Another woman.

'The one that sounds like a tarantella –'

'Only when sung *vivace*, Calfy,' corrected a painted brave in front. 'When it's adagio, it could be a dirge out of Sibelius.'

'So we go with the *balachy* bit. All right, girls, into the aisle and rehearse your thing. And remember, Thunder Head wants some legs for the TV cameras but no garter belt stuff. We gotta be squeaky clean.'

'*Awe, awe, awe* . . . shit!' came the male voices.

'Here we go – *now!*'

The drums and the vocal chorus had begun again, compounded by the beating of female feet in the aisle, as the driver tried to concentrate on the growing traffic in the District of Columbia. Unfortunately, a Sterno can under a boiling pot of bright red Crayolas overturned, setting fire to the beaded skirt of a dancer. Several braves were quick to extinguish the flames.

'Get your *hands* out of there!' screamed the offended Indian lass.

The driver's head had whipped around as the bus skidded into a fire hydrant, snapping off the top and sending a gusher of water into Independence Avenue, drenching all the cars and pedestrians in the vicinity. Company regulations required that the operator of any vehicle involved in such an incident stop immediately, radio his dispatcher, and await the police. It was a corporate policy that absolutely, positively did *not* apply to *him*! concluded the driver of the bus filled with savage terrorists who wore dripping waxed paint on their faces. He was five blocks from his destination, and the moment his load of Sterno-burning, foot-stomping barbarians in their leather and their beads got off his vehicle with their duffel bags and their card-board signs, he would race back to the depot, hand in a hastily scribbled resignation, drive home, grab his wife, and together they would take the next plane to as far away as possible. Fortunately, their only son was a lawyer; the hot-shot lawyer could take care of the aftereffects. What the *hell*, he had put the snotty little bastard through law school! . . . Thirty-six years behind a wheel driving the pigs of humanity, a man had to know when the critical sign of acceptance stopped. It was like when he was in France in WW II, and they were taking a pounding from the Krauts, and that great man, General Hawkins, took over the division and shouted the words out.

'There comes a time, soldiers, when we either cut bait or go after the big ones! I say we go on! I say we *attack*!'

And by God, they did. The great man had been right then, but here and now there was nothing to attack, no armed enemy intent on killing you, just armies of lunatics wanting to climb into your bus and drive you crazy! Thirty-six years; a good life, a productive life – *outside* the bus. But now, at this critical moment, there was nothing left, nothing to attack. It was time to cut bait . . . He wondered what the great General Hawkins would say. He thought he knew.

'If the enemy isn't worth it, find another!'

The driver would cut bait. The enemy was not worth it.

The last terrorist off the bus was the one they called Calfnose, the maniac with the grotesque waxed streaks of bright colours dripping down his face. 'Here, man,' said the savage, handing the driver a small metal coin of no discernible value. 'Chief Thunder Head wanted this to be presented to the one who took us to our "point of destiny." Damned if I know what he meant, but it's yours, buddy.' Calfnose leaped down the steps to the pavement, his cardboard placard which was nailed to a tree branch, balanced over his right shoulder.

' . . . *our point of destiny. Nothing will be the same after the action we take. We attack!*' General MacKenzie Hawkins in France forty years ago.

The driver stared at the metal coin in his hand and gasped. It was a replica of their division's insignia . . . forty years ago. A sign from heaven? Hardly likely, as he and his wife had long ago managed to avoid church. Sunday mornings were for all those television programmes where politicians fuelled his anger and his wife reduced it by a pitcher of Tabasco-laced Bloody Marys. Good woman, his wife . . . But *this*! His old division, and the words of the finest commanding officer that ever lived! *Christ*, he had to get out of there. It was *weird*!

The driver restarted the engine, jammed his foot on the accelerator and sped down First Street, only to see in his rearview mirror a crowd of painted faces racing after him. '*Fuck* you!' he cried out loud. 'I'm out, *finished*! Me and my girl are heading west – maybe so far west it's east, maybe someplace like that American Samoa!'

What the driver had overlooked was that there were thirty-seven duffel bags strapped to his roof.

CHAPTER THIRTY-ONE

1:06 P.M. The doorbell of the suite rang and as Aaron and Sam slipped into a bedroom to avoid any possible recognition, Jennifer walked across the room, glanced behind her, then said: 'Yes, who is it?'

'Pliss, Miss Janey!' replied the unmistakable voice of Roman Z. 'Thiss thing iss havvy!'

Redwing opened the door to be greeted by Roman standing in front of the two Desis who held the handles of an enormous steamer trunk, perspiration forming over their foreheads. 'Good heavens, why didn't you have the bell captain send it up?'

'My dearest fren who now happens to be a brutal and deranged "colonel" said we had to bring it up ourselves.' The gypsy walked into the room. 'Otherwise, in case it fell open, I should slit the throats of any who saw its contents . . . Come, my second and third dearest frens. In here!'

'I can't believe Cyrus would give such an order,' protested Jennifer as Desis One and Two struggled with the outsized trunk, carrying it into the suite and setting it upright. 'At least you could have used a dolly.'

'Was dat?' asked Desi the Second, wiping his brow.

'A small platform with wheels but large enough for heavy luggage.'

'Chu said we shouldn't use one of dem!' yelled D-One at Roman.

''Cause the magnificent *colonel* wass talkin' to the crazy peoples on the truck an' all he said was "take it up an' hurry!" He didn't say "take it up on thiss machine an' hurry." My

530

dearest fren iss smart; you never know when one of those things iss a trap. You ever try to run out of a big supermarket pushing a cart without paying? Zee bells go off, right, Miss Janey?'

'Well, there are codes on merchandise that are neutralized by passing over the paycheck grids –'

'*See!* My dearest fren saved our *lives*?'

'You will be well compensated for your labours,' said Aaron Pinkus, rushing out of the bedroom, Devereaux behind him. 'Somebody open it,' he added, staring at the trunk.

'There iss no key,' said Roman. 'Only leetle numbers on zee locks.'

'*I* have the numbers,' announced the impeccably, expensively dressed Cyrus, walking through the open door and immediately closing it. 'I'm afraid I had to sign an additional bill-of-delivery with my firm, Mr Pinkus.'

'You gave them my *name*?'

'Hell, no, but the original contractor may go after you if this whole thing comes out in the wash.'

'I'll handle *that*!' exclaimed Sam. 'Hiring escaped prisoners and wanted mercenaries to do their dirty work. *Hah!* A piece of cake!'

'Darling, we're doing the same,' said Jennifer.

'Oh?'

'For heaven's sake, open the trunk! I can feel Shirley breathing down my spine, a not altogether pleasant sensation. I haven't called her since yesterday morning.'

'Giff me her number,' said Roman Z, twirling his blue silk sash around his right arm in front of his silk orange shirt. 'There iss women and then there iss *women*, and very few can resist my charms. Iss so, my dearest frens?'

'Shirley would have you committed,' replied Pinkus. 'I doubt your Dunn and Bradstreet would meet her standards.'

'*There!*' said Cyrus, having manipulated the locks and pulling apart the trunk.

'My *God!*' cried Sunrise Jennifer Redwing. 'All that metal!'

'I told you, Jenny,' said Cyrus, looking at the profusion of steel breastplates and skullcaps on hangers in front of receding racks of odd clothing. 'This is hardball.'

1:32 P.M. The contents of the huge steamer trunk were distributed and the process of infiltration-camouflage began. According to the Hawk's orders (several points added or refined by his now senior military aide, Cyrus), the initial objective was to deceive the enemy scouts searching for them in the crowds outside and by deceiving them, gain entrance to the great hall of the Supreme Court. Once inside, the second goal was to pass through security without Sam, Aaron, the Hawk and very possibly Jenny revealing their identities. MacKenzie was convinced the guards had been given ident-alerts, certainly specifying Devereaux and himself, and as Sam was Pinkus's employee, probably Aaron, and since S.J. Redwing had previously argued before the Court *and* if someone had done his homework and learned she was a member of the Wopotami tribe, she, too, could be on the list. Granted, Jenny's inclusion was farfetched, but so were the untold billions of dollars owed by the greedy enemies of the 'deceased' Vincent Mangecavallo.

The third hurdle depended solely on Sam, Aaron and Hawkins finding a men's room and Jennifer locating a ladies' room prior to being admitted into the august chambers. According to the detailed building plans secured somehow by 'relatives' of Vinnie the Bam-Bam and confirmed by his favourite aunt, Angelina the Go-Go, the hallway on the second floor, where the chambers were, had two such conveniences – at opposite ends of the marble hall. The reason for the necessity of the rest rooms takes us back to the initial objective of deceiving the Supreme Court guards and gaining entry into the chambers. The contents of the steamer trunk, however, caused Jenny to scream from her bedroom.

'*Sam, this is impossible!*'

'What is?' said Devereaux, walking awkwardly out of the second bedroom dressed in a bulky chequered suit with puffed trousers, altogether adding the appearance of seventy pounds to his slender frame. What was even more bizarre was his head. His skull was covered by a knotted brown wig, the free-flowing ringlets falling below a hat best described as a 'porkpie,' the favoured headpiece of the raccoon-coated collegiates of the twenties. He pushed Redwing's partially open door and stood in the frame. 'Can I help?'

'*Yahhh!*'

'You're screaming. Is that a yes or a no?'

'Who are *you* supposed to be?'

'According to the driver's licence and the voter's registration card provided with the clothes, my name is Alby-Joe Scrubb, and I run a chicken-breeding farm somewhere ... Who the hell are *you*?'

'An ex-*chorus* girl!' replied Jenny, trying once more to clamp the steel breastplate not quite over her generous chest. '*There!* Never mind, I've got it! ... Now for this stupid kelly green peasant blouse that wouldn't excite a sex-starved gorilla.'

'It excites me,' said Sam.

'You're one step below a gorilla and more easily aroused.'

'Hey, come on, we're on the same side. No kidding, who *are* you supposed to be?'

'Let's say a loose woman whose bulging topside under this bulletproof corset will hopefully take the guards' attention away from the admission procedures.'

'The Hawk thinks of everything.'

'Right down to the libido,' agreed Redwing, slipping the bright green blouse over her head and tugging it into shape above her yellow miniskirt. She bent partially forward, glancing at the swell of her breasts within the loose hanging blouse. 'That's the best I can do,' she said with a sigh.

'Let's work on it –'

'Down, Rover ... Now comes the worst part. The "headgear," as a friend of mine on the Forty-niners calls it.'

'*That's* what's different,' observed Devereaux. 'Your hair looks funny; it's all pinned back or something.'

'In preparation for your neanderthal's pluperfect revenge.' Jenny reached for a large square box on the bed and pulled out a platinum blonde wig that rested on a steel helmet. 'That bulletproof skullcap is so heavy I'll have a stiff neck for the rest of the year, if I see the year through.'

'Yeah, I've got one, too,' said Sam as Redwing placed the helmeted wig over her hair. 'Shaking your head's okay, but if you nod, you could break your nose.'

'Shaking my head doesn't go with this image.'

'I see what you mean. If this is Mac's pluperfect revenge, what's perfect?'

'I should think it would be obvious. He'll set me up with a vice squad "john" and I'll be arrested as a hooker.'

'*Sam!*' cried Aaron Pinkus from the living room. 'I need help!'

'I'm in demand.' Devereaux rushed out of the bedroom, Jenny at his heels. What they saw was as improbable a sight that either could hope to see with the possible exception of looking at themselves in a mirror. Gone was the slight but nevertheless distinguished figure of Boston's foremost attorney. In his place, dressed in a long black frock coat and wearing a flat black hat below which hung two strands of braided black hair was a Hasidic rabbi. 'Are you soliciting confessions or don't you people do that sort of thing?' said Sam.

'You're not remotely amusing,' replied Aaron, taking several tentative steps forward, then growing unsteady, grabbed the fringe of a table lamp which naturally crashed to the floor. 'My whole body is encased in *iron!*' he cried angrily.

'It's for your own protection, Mr Pinkus,' said Jennifer, dashing around Devereaux and holding the old man's arms. 'Cyrus made it clear, you have to protect yourself.'

'The protection will *kill* me, my child. On Omaha Beach I carried a forty-pound pack on my back that nearly caused me to drown in four feet of water, and I was much younger then. This metal underwear is much heavier and I'm much, much older.'

'The only really difficult time for you will be the steps outside the Court, and since we have to separate, I'll have Johnny Calfnose find someone to help you.'

534

'Calfnose? I seem to recall that name; it's not a name one easily forgets.'

'He's Mac's honcho at the tribe,' said Sam.

'Oh, yes, he called Sidney's house, and Jennifer and our general had a shouting match, as I recall.'

'Johnny Calfnose and MacKenzie Hawkins make a perfect team. Slime and Sludge. Calfnose still owes me bail money, and Hawkins owes me my soul as well as my career ... Regardless, Johnny will get someone to help you. He'd better or I'll have him indicted for skimming thousands from General Thunder Nut's bribe money to the Council.'

'He *did* that?' asked Devereaux.

'Actually, I have no idea, but it would be perfectly natural for him to try.'

There was a rapid knocking at the door. Sam walked over and opened it, again mildly startled by the huge elegance of Cyrus. 'Come on in, Colonel, although frankly you look more like a darker version of Daddy Warbucks.'

'That's the idea, Sam, and to broaden your horizons even further, I'd like you to meet two friends of mine, or I should say of "Judge Oldsmobile."' Cyrus stepped inside and gestured for Desis One and Two to do the same. However, they were not the Desi Arnazes anyone in the room had seen before. D-One, his false teeth in place, was dressed in a conservative grey suit and an oxford blue shirt that emphasized his white clerical collar. D-Two, a religious kin but of a different faith, wore the black suit and collar of a priest along with a gold cross that fell over his *rabat*. 'May I present Reverend Elmer Pristin, an Episcopalian minister, and his comrade-in-protest, Monsignor Hector Alizongo of some Catholic diocese in the Rocky Mountains.'

'Good heavens!' said Aaron, clanking down in the chair.

'My God!' added the platinum-haired hooker, who was Jenny.

'*He* hears chu,' said D-Two, blessing himself, then correcting his benediction and blessing all those in the room – backwards.

'Don' be *blasfemor*,' mumbled Desi the First.

'Chu *loco*. I include chu an' chu are a dumb *Protestante*!'

'It's okay, fellas,' said Devereaux. 'We get the message . . . Cyrus, what's this all about?'

'First, let me ask if each of you found everything. There was a check list for your items.' Jennifer, Sam, and Aaron nodded, considerable doubt in each face. 'Good,' continued the mercenary. 'Is there any trouble with the camo-ex equipment?'

'What's that?' asked Pinkus from the chair.

'Short for camouflage externals – our disguises. We want you to be as comfortable as possible under the circumstances. Any problems?'

'To be honest, Colonel,' answered Aaron, 'perhaps you should lease a derrick to move me around.'

'It's not a problem, Cyrus,' said Redwing. 'I'll get a member of the tribe to help Mr Pinkus.'

'Sorry, Jenny, there can't be any communication whatsoever with the Wopotamis. Also, it's not necessary.'

'Now, wait a minute,' broke in Devereaux. 'My revered boss can barely walk in that medieval flak suit!'

'He'll be flanked and assisted by our two men of the cloth every step of the way.'

'Our *Desis*?' said Jennifer.

'Exactly. It's Hawkins's idea and it's a beaut . . . The "Reverend Pristin" and "Monsignor Alizongo" have joined with "Chief Rabbi Rabinowitz" in a religious protest to the Supreme Court over recent decisions they consider to be both anti-Christian and anti-Semitic. You can't beat that rap unless you throw in antiblack, which would naturally diminish the television coverage.'

'It's certainly unique,' admitted Sam. 'By the way, where's Roman Z?'

'I hate to think,' replied Cyrus.

'He hasn't *deserted*, has he?' said Jenny.

'Not for a minute. There's an old Gypsy proverb stolen from the Chinese that says that a man who saves the life of another can live off that person or persons for the rest of *his* life.'

'I'm not sure he's got that right,' said Aaron. 'I believe it's the other way around.'

'Of course it is,' agreed Cyrus, 'but the Gypsies changed it and that's all he has to know.'

'So where is he?' asked Redwing.

'I gave him money to rent a video camera. At this moment I suspect he's stealing one from an unsuspecting clerk by telling him he just wants to check the lens refraction in the sunlight. I could be wrong but I doubt it. He hates to pay for anything – I think he really believes it's unethical.'

'He should run for Congress,' said Sam.

'But why a camera?' asked Redwing.

'It's my idea. I think we should have an audiovisual record of the Wopotami protest, as extensive as possible, including any attempts by specific individuals to interfere, harass, or prevent citizens from the exercise of free assembly and their rights of petition.'

'I knew it,' exclaimed Pinkus weakly in the chair. 'He may be a professional soldier and a chemist, but he's also a lawyer.'

'Not so, sir,' contradicted Cyrus. 'Due to the confusion of an early turbulent youth, I – we – had to understand certain basic constitutional rights.'

'Wait a minute,' said Devereaux, a note of scepticism in his quiet voice. 'Let's dispense with "We Shall Overcome" for a moment, and carry this where I think you're taking it. An unedited videotape, the date and time counted off by seconds in every frame, is generally conceded to be irrefutable evidence, right?'

'I'd think a number of congressmen and senators and a mayor or two would agree with you, Sam,' agreed the mercenary, the hint of a smile on his face. 'Especially those who've temporarily given up eggs Benedict for the powdered variety on less than elegant china.'

'Yes, and if we have such a tape featuring "specific individuals" engaged in unlawful behaviour of a violent nature during the Wopotami protest –'

'*And*,' interrupted Redwing, glancing at Devereaux, who nodded, as if to say be-my-guest, 'if those nasty individuals were identified as being under the orders of one government agency or another, we'd have considerable legal leverage.'

'Not just government oriented,' said Cyrus. 'There are a bunch of goons in that crowd who've been paid to stop you. Their employers are so much in debt that even the thought of you has them chewing rugs while soiling their trousers.'

'Violent obstruction of the legal process,' added Sam. 'Facing ten years in jail, there's not one of those thugs who wouldn't break.'

'Colonel, I *salute* you!' said Aaron, struggling forward in the chair, the sound of metal against metal heard in the room. 'Even if everything goes wrong, we've got secondary positions of defence.'

'I call it frying the asses of those who would fry yours first, Mr Pinkus.'

'Indeed! You know, law degree or no, I wish you'd consider a position in my firm, say as a strategist in the criminal law department.'

'I'm flattered, sir, but I think you'd better talk with your friend, Cookson Frazier. Apparently he has a home in the Caribbean, two in France, a flat in London, and several he can't remember in the ski country of Utah or Colorado. They've all been broken into, and he wants me to take over his far-flung security.'

'My word, how wonderful for you! You'd be terribly well paid. You'll accept, of course.'

'Perhaps for a few weeks, but if there's any way I can work it out, I'd like to get back to the laboratory. I'm a chemical engineer; that's where the real excitement is.'

'Now I've heard everything,' said Devereaux, shaking his head, his 'porkpie' hat above his chequered suit swivelling.

There was a furious burst of knocking at the door. 'Stay where you are,' said Cyrus calmly as the others reacted in shock. 'It's Roman. He thinks his entrance into any room is a command performance – especially when the 'police are chasing him.' The mercenary opened the door; the figure standing in the corridor was, indeed, Roman Z, but instead of a single video camera, he held two in each hand, as well as a large nylon case suspended from his broad shoulder by a thick strap. Also, gone were the silk orange shirt, the blue silk sash, the tight black trousers and the dangling gold earring. Instead, he was the image of a working media stiff, the kind one sees climbing out of television news vans at the scene of an accident or a fire. He wore neat but abused Levis below a white T-shirt on which was printed in large letters:

WFOG-TV
PRESS

'Zee mission is accomplished, my dearest best fren . . . Colonel,' announced Roman, walking into the room, his words trailing off as his eyes absorbed the sight of Sam, Jenny and Aaron. 'Iss zerr a dancing bear somewhere?'

'If there is, it's you,' said Cyrus. 'Bears forage . . . Why four camcorders?'

'Maybe one get hurt,' replied the gypsy, grinning. 'Also plenty of tape,' he added, gesturing at his case.

'Where's the receipt?'

'Zee what?'

'The paper that shows the amount of the rental and the deposit you gave the store.'

'Oh, zey don't want it. They hoppy to cooperate.'

'What are you talking about, Roman?' asked Redwing.

'I *charge* it, Miss Janey – if you are Miss Janey under zat beautiful dress.'

'To whom?' said Devereaux.

'Zeez people!' The gypsy pointed with pride to his T-shirt. 'I wass in a great hurry and they understand.'

'There *are* no such people!' cried Cyrus.

'I write them a letter sometime. I tell them how sorry I am.'

'Please, Colonel,' said Pinkus, struggling out of the chair with Jenny's help. 'We haven't time for an audit. What do we do now?'

'It's simple,' answered Cyrus.

It wasn't.

2:16 P.M. Boom-boom, *boom*-boom, *boom*-boom-*boom-boom*, *boom-boom, boom-boom!* . . . *Hai-ya, hai-ya, hai-ya – hai-ya, hai-ya, hai-ya!* The drums went bang while the stompers sang, and the signs were raised and the crowds were hazed, and the steps of the Supreme Court were Wopotami madness. The tourists were furious, wives more than husbands, as the dancing-girl protestors were to a dancer inordinately attractive and their skirts flew high.

'Jebediah, we can't get *through*!'
    'Right.'
    'Where are the *police*?'
    'Right.'

'Olaf, these crazy people won't let us by!'
    'Right.'
    'There should be *laws*!'
    'Right.'

'Stavros, this never happened at the temple of Athena!'
    'Right.'
    'Stop staring!'
    'Wrong – oh, sorry, Olympia.'

Around the corner on Capitol Street, concealed in a recessed doorway, were two tall men. One was resplendent in the full dress uniform of an army general, the other in the ragged clothes of a tramp. The tramp rushed out of their sanctuary, peered around the edge of the building and then ran back to the general.

'Things are progressing, Henry,' said MacKenzie Hawkins. 'They're really getting hot!'

'Have the media arrived?' asked Sutton, the actor. 'I made it perfectly clear to you, I don't make my appearance until the cameras are there.'

'A couple of radio stations have come. You can tell by the people with microphones.'

'Not good enough, dear boy. I specifically said *cameras*.'

540

'All right, all *right!*' The Hawk raced out again, looked again and raced back. 'A TV crew just got here!'

'What station? Is it a network?'

'How the hell do *I* know?'

'Find out, *mon général*. I have my standards.'

'Christ on a *seesaw!*'

'Blasphemy isn't called for, MacKenzie. Look again.'

'You're *impossible*, Henry!'

'I hope so. It's the only way you get anywhere in this business. Hurry up, now. I feel the urge to perform; it's the stimulus of a growing audience as you hear them flocking into a theatre.'

'Don't you ever get stage fright?'

'My good fellow, I've never been afraid of the stage, *it* is afraid of me. I tread across it like thunder.'

'*Shit!*' The Hawk rushed out again, but instead of racing back to the actor, held his place and saw what he hoped to see. Four taxis pulled up on the other side of First Street only moments apart. Out of the one in front stepped three men of the cloth: a priest, a minister and an elderly rabbi helped by the two Christians. From the second, emerged the Marilyn Monroe of hookers, hips swaying – somewhat awkwardly – but who was examining? The third cab deposited the maximum rube of the Ozark's backcountry, with the image of chicken shit dripping from his porkpie hat and over his ballooned chequered suit. The fourth taxi made up for the banality of the three fares ahead. An immense, elegantly dressed black man stepped out on the kerb, his huge sculptured head and giant body nearly dwarfing the vehicle.

As programmed, Jennifer, Sam and Cyrus walked in different directions, no acknowledgment among them, but none crossed the street to the Court. The three religious zealots stayed on the pavement, bickering among themselves, the rabbi's head pecking forward as the two opposing Christians alternately nodded and shook their heads disapprovingly. The Hawk reached into his ragged pocket and withdrew his walkie-talkie. 'Calfnose, come in. Come in, Calfnose!' (There was no need for a code name.)

'Don't shout, T.H., this thing's in my ear!'

'Our contingent's arrived –'

'So have half the horny population of Washington! And I *do* mean just half – the other half would like to scalp our girls!'

'Tell 'em to keep it up.'

'How high? Are we up to garter belts?'

'That's *not* what I mean! Just keep up the chants and make the drums louder. I need the next ten minutes.'

'You got it, T.H.!'

The Hawk ran back to the recessed doorway. 'Another ten minutes, Henry, and you make your entrance!'

'That *long*?'

'I have a few things to do, and when I return, we'll go out together.'

'What do you have to do?'

'Eliminate some of the enemy.'

'*What?*'

'Nothing to be concerned about. They're young and inexperienced.' MacKenzie raced out in his dishevelled tramp's clothing.

And one by one four of the Ranger commandos in their camouflaged green and black fatigues were tapped on the shoulder and subsequently rendered unconscious by an old hobo. Each was dragged to a kerb, his face doused with several ounces of Southern Comfort, and laid to rest until revived.

However, and adding to Sir Henry's anxiety, the 'ten minutes' became twelve, then twenty, and finally, nearly a half hour! The Hawk had spotted five buttoned-down, stern-faced federal agents and six gentlemen whose squinting frowns and large foreheads were barely above and perhaps also below the gorillas-in-the-mist. He dispatched them in like fashion. '*Amateurs!*' whispered the Hawk to himself. 'What kind of commanders do they *have*?' . . . Whoever they were, they sure had the PR covered! Some son of a bitch in a T-shirt kept his video camera rolling, focused on the counterprotestors, obviously for the benefit of those who had given them their orders. *Ha!* A *joke*! But every time Mac tried to grab the bastard with the camera, he pivoted like a goddamn ballet dancer and disappeared in the crowds.

And crowds there were en masse, as Mac ran back to the doorway. Sir Henry Irving Sutton was not *there*! Where the hell *was* he? ... The actor was ten feet away at the edge of the building, stunned, studying the mêlée at the steps of the Supreme Court. Fights had broken out in front of the forty-odd stamping, chanting, drumming, sign-jerking Wopotami protestors, but the violent altercations seemed to have nothing to do with the Indians.

'Oh, my God!' said Hawkins, his hand on Sutton's shoulder. 'I'm not as young as I used to be!'

'Neither am I. So what?'

'A few years ago, none of those bastards would have got up. Or there were a hell of a lot more of them than I saw.'

'*Who?*'

'Those clowns who are beating the shit out of one another in the crowd of tourists.'

And, indeed, they were. The buttoned-down collars were screaming at the camouflaged commandos, who proceeded to throw them over their shoulders, as the goons of the world, figuring that any fight meant they had to be the victors or it was back to the union shop, jumped in with brass knuckles and leaded blackjacks. A full-fledged riot was not merely in the making, it was made. Angry tourists, pummelled and tripped by the combatants, screamed; those in mortal combat, bewildered by the lack of uniforms or any identification of their enemies, kept hammering away at anything that moved near them, and the idiot with the video camera kept yelling '*Glorioso!*' as he pranced around.

'*Go*, Buttercup!' shouted Hawkins into his radio.

'Right, Daffodil, but we've got a problem,' came the voice of Colonel Cyrus.

'*What* problem?'

'We're okay with the religious trio, but we've lost the hooker and the rube!'

'What *happened*?'

'Pocahontas got mad when some female tourist threw a

bunch of firecrackers at the feet of the dancers and screamed something in Greek. Our girl went after the bitch and Sam went after *her*!'

'Get them back, for God's sake!'

'Do you really want Judge Oldsmobile to go into that mess and bash heads?'

'Damn it, we don't have much *time*! It's almost quarter to three and we've got to get inside, change our clothes, and present ourselves to the praetors of the chambers by three o'clock!'

'We may have a few minutes of flexibility there,' interrupted Cyrus. 'Even the judges have to know about the chaos out here.'

'A *Wopotami* chaos, Buttercup! Let's say that's not to our benefit, even though it's necessary.'

'*Hold* it! Our chickenshit rube is bringing back Pocahontas – in a hammerlock, I might add.'

'Every once in a while that boy comes through! . . . Detail the situation and let's *move*!'

'Will do. When does our general walk out?'

'As soon as I see the rube and the princess cross the street, separately, and make sure *she* goes first . . . Where are the three holy joes? I can't see 'em.'

'You couldn't. They're on this side, making their way through the riot. You'd think people would have more respect for religious types. Desis One and Two have already clobbered a dozen yahoos, and I swear I saw D-One rip off five watches!'

'That's all we need, a preacher-mugger!'

'That's what we got, Daffodil . . . *Out*, here come our two attorneys, Punch and Judy.'

'Whip 'em into shape, Colonel. That's an order!'

'Listen, massa, you're lucky I'm smarter than you or I'd take offence.'

'Huh?'

'Never mind, your instincts are right. *Out*.'

The Hawk put his walkie-talkie back in his distressed

overcoat pocket and turned to Sutton. 'Only a couple of minutes now, Henry. Are you ready?'

'*Ready?*' said the actor, controlled fury in his voice. 'You idiot! How can I possibly command the stage with that fracas going on?'

'Come on, Hank, you told me only a couple of hours ago that this thing was practically "off-stage."'

'That was an objective analysis, not a subjective interpretation. There are no small parts, only small players.'

'Huh?'

'You're extremely insensitive where the arts are concerned, MacKenzie.'

'Yeah?'

'The lovely Jennifer is crossing the street – God, the wardrobe mistress should be fired *forthwith*! She's a *harlot*!'

'That's the idea ... There goes Sam –'

'*Where?*'

'The guy in the chequered suit –'

'Wearing that ridiculous hat?'

'Looks different, doesn't he?'

'He looks positively stupid!'

'That's what we want. No smart lawyer there.'

'Good *Lord*!' exclaimed the actor. 'Did you see *that*?'

'See what?'

'The minister in the grey suit – over there – the one climbing the steps with a priest and what appears to be an old rabbi between them.'

'Oh, oh ... What happened?'

'I swear to you the vicar just punched a man and stole his watch. Ripped it right off his wrist!'

'*Damnation!* I told the colonel that's all we needed, a preacher who's stealing his flock blind.'

'You know ... ? Oh, my word, of course you do. The elderly man in the rabbinical clothes is *Aaron*! And the two others are those fellows from Argentina or Mexico!'

'Puerto Rico, but that's not important. They've reached the top, they'll get *in*! ... You're *on*, General!'

Static erupted from the Hawk's radio; he yanked it out of

his pocket as the voice of Cyrus burst forth. 'I'm crossing the street. Wish me luck!'

'All systems are *go*, Colonel . . . Calfnose, come in!'

'I'm here, don't shout. What is it?'

'Cut the Indian stuff and go into the national anthem.'

'Ours is better, you can sing it.'

'*Now*, Johnny! Our general's going out!'

'You got it, paleface.'

'This is it, Henry! Make it *good*!

'I've never made it bad, you jackass,' said the actor as he took several deep breaths, pulled himself up to his full imposing height, and strode out toward the rioting crowd and the sudden Wopotami rendering of 'The Star Spangled Banner.' The chorus was in a word, spectacular. Voices rose to the heavens and the sight of forty painted, weeping faces of America's original inhabitants had a striking effect on the crowd. Even the fiercely aggressive commandos, in deadly combat with the union-busting thugs, held their adversaries off with straight-arms and hands around throats. The goons dropped their brass knuckles and their blackjacks, and all stared at the tragic figures singing their hearts out in devotion to a land that had been stolen from them. Many tears were starting to cloud the eyes of the onlookers.

'*Now* is the winter of our *discontent*!' roared Sir Henry Irving Sutton in his most stentorian voice as he climbed to the fourth step and turned to the crowd. 'Dogs may *bark* at us but our vision is clear. A dreadful wrong has been done and we are here to *right* it! To *be* or not to be, that is the question . . . '

'That son of a bitch can go on for an hour,' whispered MacKenzie Hawkins into his radio. 'Where is everybody? Answer by your numbers!'

'We are in dee big stone hall, but chu don' unnerstand, h'enerale –'

'I've got the princess and the rube with me,' said Cyrus, 'and you *really* don't understand!'

'What the hell are you two talking about?'

'A little number you hadn't figured on,' explained the mercenary. 'They've got metal detectors in here and if Jenny or Sam or Mr Pinkus passes through, they'll set off every alarm in the building and probably most of Washington.'

'Oh, m'God! What's this country coming to?'

'I suppose I should say something like "look to the root causes," but right now we're screwed.'

'Not yet, Buttercup,' yelled the Hawk. 'Calfnose, are you on the line?'

'Sure am, T.H., and we've also got a problem. Our people have had it with your friend Vinnie. I mean he's one big pain in the ass.'

'What's he done? You've only had him since this morning – what *could* he do?'

'*Kvetch, kvetch, kvetch*, that's all he does! Then *his* friend shows up, the little guy who talks like a chicken, and before you can say Geronimo, we've got a dozen crap games going on all over the motel with Joey something-or-other running from room to room to catch the action. Catch it, I might add, with very funny dice. He cleaned up and a lot of our braves were cleaned out.'

'We don't have *time* for this!'

'Make it, T.H., while your general, who I've got to admit looks like you, is still yelling his head off. Our boys and girls are mad as hell and they're not going to take it any more. They want those two scumballs out and their money back!'

'They'll get their money back fifty times over, I *promise!*'

'Holy *shit!* Do you see what I see, T.H.?'

'I'm at the edge of this building and there's too much going on –'

'A bunch of guys in funny green and black suits are breaking through our ranks ... wait a second! Now some others – either linebackers or apes in business suits – are joining them. They're going after your *general!*'

'Execute Plan B, Number One priority! Get him out of there! We can't let him be hurt ... Start the chanting and the dancing. *Now!*

'What about the two scumballs, Vinnie and the chicken?'

'Sit on 'em!'

'We did that on the bus. The little guy bit Eagle Eye's ass.'

'*Execute*. I'm heading over!'

Colonel Tom Deerfoot, arguably the smartest officer in the United States Air Force and certainly in line down the line for the chairmanship of the Joint Chiefs, was strolling through the streets of Washington, showing his niece and nephew the usual sights. As the trio turned right off Constitution Avenue toward the Supreme Court, Deerfoot's ears picked up various familiar sounds stored somewhere in his memory banks; chants that went back to his childhood forty-odd years ago in upper New York State near the Canadian border. For Tom Deerfoot was a full-blooded Mohawk and the words and rhythms he heard were a slight variation of his own tribe's language.

'Hey, Uncle Tommy!' cried his nephew, a boy of sixteen. 'There's a riot over there!'

'Maybe we should go back to the hotel,' suggested his niece, a young lady of fourteen.

'No, you're perfectly safe,' said the uncle. 'Wait here, I'll be right back. Something crazy's going on.' Deerfoot, as his name implied, was a splendid runner, and in less than thirty seconds he reached the outskirts of the confused, rebellious crowd at the steps of the Supreme Court. It *was* crazy! *Indians – their* Indians – were in full war paint, stamping and dancing, and yelling their heads off in some fanatical protest, the nature of which was hard to determine.

Then the memories came back, the legends passed down by the old men of the tribe, from one generation to another. The language he was hearing was similar but different, the pounding feet of the dancing chants imitative, yet not authentic. Good *God*, they were the Wopotamis of old! The ancient stories abounded with tales of how they stole everything in sight, so why not most of the language, and they never left their tepees whenever it snowed! Colonel Deerfoot bent over in laughter, holding his stomach so as not to collapse to the pavement in hysterics. The wild frenzy of the protesting chant with its highly suggestive dance movement was the 'Celebration of the Wedding Night.'

The Wopotamis never got *anything* right!

'*Calfnose*, hear me and execute!' whispered Hawkins harshly into his radio as he threaded his way through the dancers to the entrance of the Court.

'What *now?* We got your general out, who kept screaming that he "wasn't finished!" Little Joey's right, he's a *fazool!*'

'Little *Joey?* . . . *Fazool?*'

'Yeah, well we made a deal. He'll give back half the money and I collect twenty-per of his take for arbitration.'

'Johnny, we're in a *crisis!*'

'No, we're not, the two scumbuckets are in a bar down the street. You know, Vinnie's red wig doesn't do anything for our image. Real tacky, y'know what I mean?'

'Oh, Christ, you're talking like *him!*'

'Actually, he's not a bad guy when you get to know him. Did you realize that ethnic Indian types are very respected in Las Vegas? Nevada was big redskin territory, y'know.'

'I'm talking about right *now!* Plan *B* priority *Two* – the peaceful storming of the Court!'

'You're out of your fucking mind! We could get *shot!*'

'Not if you all fall on your knees and do the wailing bit once you're inside. It's un-American to shoot anybody on his knees.'

'Who says?'

'It's right there in the Constitution. You don't shoot anyone on his knees because he's praying and will die in a state of grace while you get shafted by God.'

'No kidding?'

'No fooling. *Go!*'

The Hawk replaced the radio in the pocket of his distressed overcoat inside the great hall of the Supreme Court as Cyrus kept Aaron, Jenny, Sam and the two Desis off to the side, away from the arched metal detectors. 'Now listen up, folks,' said the mercenary-chemist. 'When the Wopotamis crash in here, D-One and D-Two will raise the cordons and you – Sam, Jenny and Mr Pinkus – will slip under them and head to the second floor. Use the stairs or the elevators, whatever, and go to the second closet on the right. Your other clothes are there in a plastic bag. Change in the ladies' and men's rooms and meet at the chambers at the west end of the hall, I'll be waiting for you.'

'What about Mac?' asked Devereaux.

'If I know him, and by now I think I do, he'll be at that closet before you distributing the merchandise. *Man*, I wish that cat had been running a few campaigns I've been in. I'm good, but he's the max – I mean really *evil!*'

'That's a recommendation, Cyrus?' asked Pinkus.

'You better believe it, Rabbi. I'd follow him to hell and back because I'd know I'd *get* back.'

'Well, he never swam twenty miles in a hurricane –'

'Oh, be quiet, Sam ... Oh, oh, here they *come!*'

'Great *Abraham!*' whispered Aaron Pinkus as a horde of Wopotamis, their painted, waxed faces grotesquely weeping, burst through the doors and instantly fell on their knees, singing in unison, their heads raised to the ceiling, imploring their gods for deliverance. (If anyone knew, and they did not, it was still the 'Celebration of the Wedding Night.')

The weapons of a dozen guards were unholstered, their guns aimed at the heads of the protestors. None was fired. Somehow, it was in the Constitution, or at least in the minds of the Supreme Court police, that one did not fire on people who were in the act of prayer. Instead, alarms were heard, not from the detectors but from within the building itself. In seconds additional guards, clerks and maintenance personnel streamed into the great hall. Pandemonium prevailed.

'*Now!*' whispered Cyrus as Desis One and Two raised the thick velvet cords while Aaron, Sam and Jenny swept underneath during the insanity that faced the Supreme Court police and staffers.

During this new and totally unexpected chaos, MacKenzie Hawkins walked through the interior metal detectors, thanked nobody in evidence, and raced to the stairway that led to the second floor.

A problem. Naturally. Vinnie the Bam-Bam's Aunt Angelina

the Go Go had confused the second closet on the right with an air-conditioning machine room and for several precious minutes the black plastic bag holding their clothes was not found. Suddenly, there was a muted explosion that none of them really noticed.

'I've *got* it!' yelled Sam, in his excitement pushing a lever and shorting out the air-conditioning. 'Everything stopped,' he added, bewildered by the cessation of the huge machinery.

'Who *cares*?' cried Jennifer, holding up Pinkus as the Hawk came running down the corridor, throwing off his tramp's overcoat.

'*There* you are!' he roared. 'The goddamned staircase was locked from the outside!'

'How'd you get in?' asked Devereaux, pulling Redwing's clothes out of the bag.

'I always carry a little plastic explosive – you never know.'

'I thought I heard a boom,' said the exhausted Pinkus.

'You did,' admitted Hawkins. 'Let's *go*.'

'Where's the ladies' room?' asked Redwing.

'Down at that end,' answered MacKenzie, pointing east.

'Where's *our* room?' asked Sam.

'Much nearer, right over there on the left.'

They scattered and suddenly Jennifer turned and shouted. '*Sam!* Can I dress with you? We've only got three minutes and that door's two football fields away!'

'Boy, have I been waiting for those words!'

The platinum-helmeted hooker raced back to the chicken-breeding 'Alby-Joe Scrubb' and together they followed Pinkus and the Hawk into the rest room. Jenny ran into a stall as the men shed their clothes and wigs for the more dignified attire they wore under their outlandish 'cam-ex equipment.'

Except for the Hawk. For at the bottom of the large refuse bag, layered neatly for easy removal, were the massive full ceremonial garments of Thunder Head, chief of the Wopotamis, including the longest, most flamboyant feathered head-dress since the Okeechobees greeted a misguided cosmetician named Ponce de León on the shores of the future Miami Beach. He swiftly removed his tramp's trousers and soiled shirt, replacing them with his buckskins and his beaded buffalo jacket. Then, under the stunned gazes of Aaron and Sam, he carefully placed the gargantuan trail of feathers over his head. It reached down all six feet three inches to the tiled floor.

A minute later Redwing walked out of the stall in a smart dark tailored suit, the image of a cool successful lady lawyer totally unafraid of facing the male dominated Supreme Court. What momentarily terrified her, however, was the sight of MacKenzie Hawkins. '*Ahh!*' she screamed.

'My sentiments exactly,' said Devereaux.

'*General,*' added Pinkus, in the title a soft but earnest plea. 'This is not a costume parade at Pasadena's Rose Bowl. These proceedings are among the most serious and venerable of our legal system, and your outfit, as splendid as it is, is hardly in keeping with the occasion.'

'What's the occasion, Commander?'

'Only the future of the Wopotami tribe and a large segment of the nation's defence structure.'

'I'll go with the first part. Case closed. Besides, it's all I've got unless you want me to walk in like a member of Hoboes Anonymous – which from another point of view *isn't* a bad idea.'

'We'll go with the feathers, General,' said Jennifer quickly.

'That filthy overcoat's probably still in the hallway,' mused Hawkins. 'There's no one up here to find it; everybody's downstairs ... Think of it, a downtrodden indigent from a disenfranchised people – in rags and maybe holding my stomach from hunger.'

'*No,* Mac!' yelled Sam. 'They'd drag you out to be deloused.'

'I suppose that's a possibility,' said the Hawk, frowning. 'This is a heartless city.'

'Thirty-five seconds,' announced Redwing, glancing at her watch. 'We'd better go.'

'I can't imagine that a minute or two of tardiness would matter,' said Aaron. 'I mean, that's a veritable insurrection downstairs, the masses storming the barricades, as it were.'

'Not storming, Commander, but *praying*. There's a difference.'

'He's right, Aaron, and that's not to our benefit,' said Devereaux. 'As soon as the guards realize it's basically a peaceful demonstration, the alert will be called off and all the others will return to their posts ... You've been to these examinations before, haven't you, boss?'

'Three or four times,' replied Pinkus. 'Authenticity is established of the plaintiff's identity, as well as that of the attorney-of-record, and those of whatever *amicus curiae* are in attendance. Then the arguments are presented.'

'Who's at the chambers' doors, Commander?'

'An assigned guard and a law clerk, General.'

'*Bingo!*' roared the Hawk. 'One of 'em or *both* of 'em will have our names on a list. They'll get on a radio and a dozen others will come out of the woodwork and haul us away. We'll never get in!'

'You can't be serious,' said Jennifer. 'This is the Supreme Court. No one can buy guards and law clerks to do that sort of thing.'

'Try billions in debt and red faces at the Pentagon, as well as State, Justice and several dozen leeches in Congress who vacation on barrels filled with pork, against a few hundred thousand dollars spread through these hallowed halls!'

'Mac's got a point,' said Sam.

'Flesh is weak,' observed Aaron.

'Let's get the hell out of here!' concluded Redwing.

They did, all four hastening with as much decorum as possible toward the huge carved doors of the chambers. To their relief, they saw the massive figure of Cyrus standing in front of them; to their astonishment, they also saw the two Desis, kneeling on either side of him in their clerical garbs.

'Colonel, what are my adjutants *doing* here?'

'General, what the hell are you *wearing*?'

'The mantle of my tribal office, of course. Now, answer my question!'

'It was Desi the First's idea. He said they'd gone this far and although they're not sure what it's all about, they figured you should have additional protection. It was no problem for them to get up here – it's an insane asylum in revolt downstairs.'

'How sweet,' said Jennifer.

'How *dumb*!' cried Devereaux. 'They'll be spotted, arrested, and questioned, and our whole illegal entry will be front page news!'

'Chu don' unnerstand,' said D-One, raising his head, his palms still matched in prayer. '*Número uno*, we never say nodding. *Número dos*, we are *misioneros* who convert the poor *bárbaros* to dee ways of Christ. Who can arrest such padres? Also, if dey try, dey don' walk for a couple of months, and nobody goes inside but chu.'

'I'll be *damned*,' mumbled Hawkins, affection in his eyes as he looked down at his two aides-de-camp. 'I brought you boys up right. In dark operations one should always have secondary egress personnel; they're usually the first to take the fire. We hesitate to assign them because we know the odds, but you didn't hesitate to volunteer. Fine show, men.'

'Daz nice, h'enerale,' said D-Two, 'but chu not be damned. I can straighten dat out myself, not my amigo. Chu see, I'm *católico*, he ees only a *protestante* – it don' count.'

The thundering sound of pounding footsteps in the long hallway caused all of them to whip their heads around in shock. It diminished quickly as the running figure of Roman Z, a camcorder in each hand, his shoulder-strapped nylon pouch bouncing off his hips, came rushing down to them, his WFOG T-shirt drenched with sweat. 'My dearest, most loving *frenz*!' he cried, stopping breathlessly. 'You could not *believe* how magnificent I was! I got pictures of efferyone, including three peoples who were convinced by my blade to say they were sent here by a "general-attorney," and by a leetle man secretary in somzing they call "defance," and a beeg soccer player who told me he was only an ignorant represansive of somzing he call zee "Fanny Hill Society" – some society, we got better in Serbo-Croatia.'

'That's terrific!' said Sam. 'But how did you get up here?'

'Iss easy! Down in zee big marble hall, efferybody iss

dancing and singing and laughing and crying like zee best of my Gypsy ancestors. Men in crazy clothes and painted faces are passing around bottles of fruity juice and efferybody is so happy and so sad it remind me of our camps in zee Moravian mountains. It iss all *glorioso*!'

'Oh, my *God*!' exclaimed Jennifer. 'The yaw-yaw stills!'

'The what, my dear?'

'*Stills*, Mr Pinkus. The most intoxicating drink ever devised by civilized or uncivilized man. The Mohawks say they invented it but *we* refined it and made it twenty times more potent. It's totally banned on the reservation, but if anyone could find those stills and put them to use it would be that bastard, Johnny Calfnose!'

'I'd say at this moment, he's totally legitimate, both in birth and in timing,' said Devereaux.

'So that's how you – *we* – people swindled the Western settlers,' said the Hawk.

'That's irrelevant, General.'

'Yes, but interesting –'

'Let's go *in*,' said Cyrus, his voice now commanding. 'That kind of juice has two effects – oblivion and the sudden recognition of remembered responsibilities which brings on panic, which we don't need. I'll open the door.' He did so and added. 'You first, General.'

'Quite correct, Colonel.'

MacKenzie Hawkins strode into the large mahogany-panelled room, his feathers flying, his supporting contingent following in dignity, when suddenly the blaring, deafening sounds of a frenzied Indian war chant, drums and voices, filled the sacrosanct enclosure. Up on the semicircular dais, the previously stern-faced judges reacted in panic, as to a man and a woman, they fell below the surface, one by one emerging, wide-eyed and terrified, but relieved that no violence had ensued. Mouths gaped at the feathered monster below them; they did not rise, but remained, their faces in shock.

'What the hell have you *done*?' whispered Sam behind the Hawk.

'Little trick I learned in Hollywood,' answered MacKenzie

under his breath. 'A soundtrack heightens a climax when the words don't do it. I've got a triple-volume, high-impedance tape recorder in my pocket.'

'Shut the fucking thing off!'

'I will just as soon as those quivering pumpkins recognize that Thunder Head, chief of the Wopotamis, is in their presence and his tribal position demands respect.'

And once again, one by one, the stunned justices of the Supreme Court rose slowly off their knees, no one, however, above his and her chest. The music diminished and then stopped. The justices looked questioningly at one another and returned to their chairs.

'*Hear* me, you wise elders of this nation's justice!' roared Thunder Head, his voice echoing off the walls. 'Your people have been caught in an insidious conspiracy to defraud us of our rights of proprietorship, to take from us our fields and our mountains and our rivers that provide us with the necessities of life and survival. You have confined us to the ghettos of barren forests and unwatered ground from which nothing grows but the most unwanted weeds. Was this not *our* nation? Our nation in which a thousand tribes existed both in peace and war as you did with us, and with the Spanish, then the French and the English, and then finally among *yourselves*? Have we no more privileges than those you conquered and then forgave, absorbing them into your culture? The blacks of this country have gone through two hundred years of servitude; we have endured *five* hundred. Will you now in this day and age permit that to continue?'

'Not me,' said one justice quickly.

'Nor me,' said another, even more quickly.

'Certainly not *I*,' protested yet another, violently shaking his head, his jowls jiggling.

'Oh, Lord, I've read that brief ten times and each time I cried,' said the lady justice.

'You're not supposed to *do* that,' said the Chief Justice, glaring at the woman, then instantly turning off the microphones so the Court could confer in quiet.

'I *love* him,' whispered Jennifer in Sam's ear. 'Mac said it *all* in a few sentences!'

'He never swam thirty-seven miles through a hurricane at sea!'

'Our general is very eloquent,' whispered Pinkus. 'He knows his subject well.'

'I'm not too happy about his black comparison,' said Cyrus, also whispering. 'Hell, his Indian brothers and sisters weren't put in chains and sold, but his thrust was right.'

'No, Cyrus, we weren't,' added Redwing. 'We were merely slaughtered or driven to places where we starved to death.'

'Okay, Jenny. Checkmate.'

The microphones were turned on again. 'Yes, well, *ahem*!' said a justice from the right end of the Court. 'As the distinguished attorney from Boston, Counsellor Pinkus, is in attendance with you, we certainly accept your credentials, but are you aware of the magnitude of your suit?'

'We want only what is ours. Everything else is negotiable – anything else is intolerable.'

'That wasn't necessarily clear in the brief, Chief Thunder Head,' said the black justice, in his eyes a glaring disapproval as he picked up a single page of paper. 'Your attorney-of-record is one Samuel Lansing Devereaux, is that correct?'

'It is and I'm he, sir,' replied Sam, stepping forward beside Hawkins.

'A hell of a brief, young man.'

'Thank you, sir, but in all fairness –'

'You'll probably be shot in the head for it,' continued the judge, as if Devereaux had not spoken. 'However, throughout I find an underlying streak of vitriol, as if you were not so much interested in justice but in vengeance.'

'In retrospect, I was offended, sir, at the *injustice*.'

'You're not paid to be offended, Counsellor,' said a justice on the left side. 'You're paid to present the truth of your petition. Without the many long-since deceased alive to defend themselves, you've made startling insinuations.'

'Based on the evidentiary materials uncovered, sir, and they were, indeed, insinuations, or, if you like, speculations. None, however, were without corroborative historical foundation.'

'You're a professional historian, Mr Devereaux?' asked another.

'No, Mr Justice, I'm a professional lawyer who can read and follow lines of evidence, as I'm sure you can, sir.'

'Nice of you to grant our colleague that ability,' said yet another.

'I meant no offence, sir.'

'Yet, in your own words, you're capable of being offended, Counsellor,' observed the lady justice. 'So I must assume it follows that you can give offence.'

'Where I believe it's justified, madam.'

'That's what I meant, Mr Devereaux, when I mentioned that streak of vitriol in your brief. It didn't strike me that you wanted anything less than abject surrender on the part of the government, a total capitulation that would place an extraordinary burden on every taxpayer in this country. A liability far beyond the nation's ability to absorb.'

'If the Court will allow me to interrupt,' broke in Thunder Head, chief of the Wopotamis. 'My brilliant young counsel here has a reputation of righteous indignation when he feels a cause is just –'

'*What?*' whispered Sam, his elbow crashing into Hawkins's ribs. 'Don't you *dare* –'

'He *dares* to tread where angels fear to, but who among us can fault the truly honest man who passionately believes in justice for the disenfranchised? You, sir, stated that he's not paid to be offended – you're only half right, sir, for he's not paid at all, merely offended on his own time, no reward in the future for his passionate beliefs ... And what are those beliefs that drive him so on our behalf? Let me try to explain. Or better yet, rather than any explanation on my part, have each of you visit a dozen reservations on which our people live. See for yourselves what the white man has done to our once proud Indian nations. See our poverty, our squalor, our – yes, our *impotence*. Ask yourselves if you could live that way *without* being offended. This land was *our* land, and when you took it from us, we somehow understood that even a greater, *single* nation could evolve, and that we would be a part of it . . . But no, that wasn't to be. You cast us off, shunted us aside, consigned us to isolated reservations without any share in your progress. That is documented history, and no one can dispute it . . . . Therefore, if our learned counsel has filled his brief with a certain anger – "vitriol," if you like – he'll go down in the chronicles of twentieth-century law as the Clarence Darrow of our day. Speaking for the victimized Wopotamis, we *worship* him.'

'Worship, Chief Thunder Head, is no part of this Court,' said the large black justice, scowling. 'One can worship his god, or a bull or an icon or the newest guru, but it has no influence in a court of law, nor should it have. We here worship only the law. We adjudicate on the basis of provable fact, not on convincing speculation derived from unsubstantiated records of over a hundred years ago.'

'*Hey*, now just wait a minute!' cried Sam. 'I *read* that brief –'

'We thought you *wrote* it, Counsellor,' interrupted the lady justice. '*Didn't* you?'

'Yes – well, that's another story, but let me tell you, I'm one hell of a lawyer and I've scrutinized that brief, and the historical evidentiary materials that support it are damn near *irrefutable*! Furthermore, if this Court disregards that evidence for pragmatic concerns, you're a bunch of – of . . . '

'Of *what*, Counsellor?' asked a justice on the left side of the bench.

'Goddamnit, I'll say it – *cowards!*'

'I *love* you, Sam,' whispered Jennifer.

The voluble astonishment of the entire Court was broken by the stentorian tones of Chief Thunder Head, aka MacKenzie Lochinvar Hawkins. '*Please*, great deliberators of justice in this stolen land of ours, may I *speak*?'

'*What*, you feathered *termite*?' shrieked Chief Justice Reebock.

'You have just witnessed the outrage of an honest man, an outstanding attorney who's willing to throw away a brilliant career because he found the *truth* within the hidden tran-scripts that were never meant to see the light of day. Such uncompromising men have made this country great, for they faced the truth and understood its majesty. The *truth*, both good and bad, had to be accepted in all its glory and all the sacrifices it demanded, a shining light that led a new nation into its own majesty, its own *glory*. All he seeks, all *we* seek, all the Indian nations seek, is to be a *part* of that great land we once called ours. Is that so difficult for you?'

'There are grave national considerations, sir,' said the black justice, his scowl receding. 'Extraordinary costs, severe taxes upon the body politic that may not be tolerated. As many have said before us, it is all too frequently an unfair world.'

'Then *negotiate*, sir!' cried Thunder Head. 'The eagle does not stoop to destroy the wounded sparrow. Instead, as our young counsel phrased it, that mighty eagle soars through the skies, a marvel of flight but far more important, a constant symbol of the power of freedom.'

'*I* said that –'

'*Shut* up! . . . Oh, ye judges, let that wounded sparrow find a measure of hope in the shadow of the great eagle. Do not cast us out again for there is no place left for us to wander. Give us the respect that is long overdue – give us the hope we need to survive. Without it we die, our slaughter complete. Do you wish this on your hands – are they not bloody *enough*?'

Silence. Everywhere. Except:

'Hey, Mac, not bad,' whispered Sam, from the left side of his mouth. And:

'*Magnificent!*' whispered Jennifer from behind.

'Hold it, little filly,' replied the Hawk, in hushed tones, turning his head. 'Now comes the crunch, like when my buddy, General McAuliffe, said "Nuts" to the Krauts in the Battle of the Bulge.'

'What do you mean?' asked Aaron Pinkus.

'Listen up,' whispered Cyrus. 'I know where the general's coming from. Now he's got to sting 'em where it really hurts. Right in their own bladders. That'll put the bullshit in concrete.'

'It wasn't bullshit,' protested Redwing. 'It's the *truth*!'

'For them it's inescapable *truthful* bullshit, Jenny, because they're between a rock and a very hard 'nother rock.'

The microphones were turned off once again while the justices conferred. At last, the seemingly emaciated judge from New England spoke. 'That was a moving peroration, Chief Thunder Head,' he said quietly, 'but such accusations could be made on behalf of numerous minorities everywhere. History isn't kind to these people, much to my personal regret. As one of our presidents said, "Life isn't fair," but it must go on for the betterment of the majority, not the unfortunate minorities who suffer. We all wish with all our hearts that we could change that scenario, but it's beyond our providence. The "brutality of history" was the way Schopenhauer described it. I loathe his conclusion but I recognize its reality. You could open floodgates that might drown whole communities across the country far, far in excess of the litigants.'

'Your point, sir?'

'Considering everything that's involved, what would be your response if the Court in its wisdom decided against you?'

'Quite simple,' replied Chief Thunder Head. 'We would declare war against the United States of America, knowing we'd have the sympathy of our Indian brothers across the land. Many thousands of white men would not survive. We would lose, but so would you.'

'Holy *shit*,' intoned the nasal-twanged Chief Justice Reebock. 'I have a house in New Mexico –'

'The land of the warlike Apaches, sir?' asked the Hawk innocently.

'Two and a half miles from the reservation,' answered the justice, swallowing.

'The Apache is our brother in blood. May the Great Spirit grant you a swift and relatively painless death.'

'What about Palm Beach?' asked another member of the Court, his brows arched.

'The Seminoles are our cousins. They boil the blood of the

white man to remove its impurities – while the blood is still in the body, of course; it tenderizes the meat.'

'Aspen . . . ?' said yet another haltingly. 'Who's there?'

'The impetuous Cherokee, sir. They're even closer cousins due to the geography. However, we've frequently voiced disapproval over their primary method of retribution. They strap their enemies face down over killer anthills.'

'*Augh!*' gasped Jennifer.

'Lake . . . Lake George?' asked a pale-faced justice on the left, his expression conveying sudden fear. 'I have a lovely summer home there.'

'Upper New York State, sir? Need you ask?' MacKenzie lowered his voice, as if to confirm the unspoken terror. 'The hunting and *burial* grounds of the Mohawk?'

'Something like that . . . I imagine.'

'Our tribe is an offspring of the Mohawks, sir, but in all honesty, we felt we had to flee and travel west, away from our closest blood brothers.'

'Why was that?'

'The Mohawk brave is perhaps the most ferocious and daring of us all – but, well, I'm sure you understand.'

'Understand . . . *what?*'

'When provoked they torch their enemy's tepees at night, as well as setting fire to all their enemy's property. It is a scorched earth policy that we found too severe for our branch. Of course, the Mohawks still consider us one with them. The ties of blood are not easily washed away. Without question, they would join our struggle.'

'I think we should *confer* again!' snapped the Chief Justice as the microphones went silent and the entire Court, their heads whipping back and forth, whispered among themselves.

'*Mac!*' hissed Redwing. 'None of what you said is *true*! The Apaches are from the Athabaskan people and are no part of us, and the Cherokees wouldn't strap anybody over an anthill, that's preposterous, *and* the Seminoles are the most peaceful tribe of all the nations! . . . The Mohawks, well, they like to shoot craps because it brings in money, but they never attacked anyone who didn't attack or steal from them first, and they certainly would *never* scorch the land because then you can't grow anything on it!'

'*Please*, daughter of the Wopotamis,' said the Hawk, standing imperiously in his feathered headdress and looking down at Jennifer. 'What do the dumb palefaces know?'

'You're besmirching all the Indian nations!'

'What have these people been doing to us all these years?'

'*Us?*'

The microphones crackled on again, and again the sniffling, nasally inclined voice of the Chief Justice shot out of the speakers. 'Let the record show that the Court will recommend to the government of the United States that it will enter into immediate negotiations with the Wopotami nations to seek a reasonable solution for past malfeasances. Without argument, the Court upholds the plaintiff's case. It will be announced forthwith. *Sine die*, we are adjourned!' And then, without realizing that the microphone was still operative, the Chief Justice added, 'Someone call the White House and tell Subagaloo to shove it! That son of a bitch got us into this mess, he *always* does. He probably had our goddamned air-conditioning shut off, too. I'm sweating right down to the crack in my ass! ... Sorry, dear.'

News of the Wopotami triumph reached the lobby and the steps of the Supreme Court in a matter of minutes. Chief Thunder Head, in full regalia, strode down the marble corridor toward the great hall expecting the adulation and the celebration of his people. A celebration was, indeed, in progress, but what the celebration was about appeared somewhat irrelevant to the celebrants. The huge gallery was filled with dancing, prancing men and women of all ages, from awkward waltzes to hard rock, the participants whirling and wiggling to the recorded sounds of up-graded, speeded-up versions of original Indian chants from enormous speakers. Even the guards, the tourists and the DC police joined partners hither and yon; the revered great hall was the scene of a wild carnival.

'Oh, good *God*!' exclaimed Sunrise Jennifer Redwing as she

walked out of the elevator with Sam and Aaron on the first floor.

'It's a joyous occasion,' said Pinkus. 'Your people are rightfully jubilant.'

'*My* people? Those aren't my people!'

'What do you mean?' asked Devereaux.

'*Look!* Do you see a single Wopotami, a single painted face or Indian skirt dancing or singing or shouting?'

'No, but I see a lot of Wopotamis out on the floor.'

'So do I, but I can't understand what they're doing.'

'Well, they seem to be going from group to group encouraging ... *oh*, oh, they're carrying –'

'Paper *cups*! And plastic bottles – it's what Roman told us. They're passing out yaw-yaw juice!'

'Slight correction,' said Sam. 'They're selling it.'

'I'll *murder* that Calfnose!'

'Second suggestion, Jennifer,' said Aaron, chuckling. 'Instead, put him on your finance committee.'

EPILOGUE

The New York Daily News

WOPS TAKE SAC

Washington, DC, Friday – In a stunning decision the Supreme Court has upheld the legitimacy of a suit brought by the Wopotami tribe of Nebraska against the government of the United States. The Court, in a unanimous decision, held that a territory of several hundred square miles in and around Omaha is the rightful property of the Wopotamis according to a treaty affirmed by the fourteenth Congress in 1878. This land includes the headquarters of the Strategic Air Command. The Senate and the House of Representatives have been called back into emergency session, and attorneys from several thousand law firms have expressed interest in the forthcoming negotiations.

Il Progresso Italiano

Questo giornale muove obiezione all 'insensibilita' del Daily News *facendo uso di un' espressione denigratoria nella testata di ieri. Noi non siamo dei 'pellerossa selvaggi!'*
This newspaper takes great exception to the insensitivity of the Daily News *by the use of a derogatory ethnic slur in its headline of yesterday. We are not redskinned savages!*

Hollywood Variety

Beverly Hills, Wednesday – Messrs Robbins and Martin, top execs at the William Morris Agency, have announced that a *major deal has been concluded between their clients, known at this juncture only as six terrif actors who've been toiling for the government as an antiterrorist unit for the past five years, and Consolidated-Colossal Studios, Emmanuel Greenberg, producer, for a $100,000,000 pic starring their clients who'll be 'picting themselves. At the press conference held at Merv's place, that great legit character actor Henry Irving Sutton made an appearance, stating that he was so moved by the property he was coming out of retirement to play a major role. Apparently Greenberg was also mucho moved for he intermittently weeped, too choked up to speak. Many at the press outing said it was because he was so proud, but others maintained it was due to the negotiations. Greenberg's former wife, Lady Cavendish, was also present. She kept smiling.*

The New York Times

CIA DIRECTOR FOUND ALIVE
RESCUED FROM AN ISLAND IN THE DRY
TORTUGAS

Miami, Thursday – A fishing yacht, the Contessa, owned by the international industrialist Smythington-Fontini, spotted smoke from a fire on the beach of an uninhabited out island in the Dry Tortugas. As the Contessa drew in to shore, the crew and passengers heard loud cries for help both in English and Spanish and saw three men racing into the water, giving thanks for having been found. One of the three was Vincent F.A. Mangecavallo, director of the Central Intelligence Agency, until this morning presumed lost at sea last week. The presumption was based on the debris of the yacht Gotcha Baby, on which Mr Mangecavallo was a passenger and which was wrecked in a tropical storm. The debris included several personal effects of the director.

The story of survival is one of extraordinary heroism on the part of Mr Mangecavallo. According to the two Argentinian crew, who've been flown back to their families in Rio de Janeiro, the director literally dragged them through shark-

infested waters by their holding on to his legs as Mr Mangecavallo swam to the uninhabited island. Upon hearing the news, the President said, 'I knew my old Navy buddy would pull through!' As previously noted, the Navy Department had no comment other than to say, 'That's nice.'

In Brooklyn, New York, one Rocco Sabatini, upon reading the account of the rescue, said to his wife over the breakfast table. 'Hey, what the hell's going on here? Bam-Bam can't swim.'

The Wall Street Journal

RASH OF BANKRUPTCIES SHOCKS FINANCIAL AMERICA

New York, Friday – Lawyers are scurrying throughout the corridors of corporate America today, rushing in and out of executive suites and board meetings, trying to put scores of conglomerate Humpty Dumpties back together again. The conventional wisdom is that it's impossible as massive overextensions of debt incurred in the recent frenzy of buy-outs, and block stock purchases have left many of the nation's industrial giants, both corporate and individual, jointly and severally, with empty pockets, red faces, and in a number of cases, a sudden desire to leave the country.

It was reported that at Kennedy International Airport one such company president was heard to shout hysterically. 'Anywhere but Cairo! I will not clean urinals!' The significance of the remark is unclear.

Stars and Stripes
The Newspaper of the US Army

DEFECTORS FROM CUBA COMMISSIONED

Fort Benning, Saturday – In a first for the Army, two highly regarded former officers in Castro's military machine, experts in sabotage, espionage, covert operation, intelligence and counter-intelligence, have been commissioned with the ranks of First Lieutenant at this base, announced General Ethelred Broke-michael, chief of Information and Public Affairs.

Desi Romero and his cousin, Desi Gonzalez, who defected from 'the intolerable situation in our homeland,' will head up a Special Forces unit being formed at Benning after linguistic indoctrination and orthodontal treatment.

The Army welcomes such brave and experienced men who risked their lives to seek freedom and honour. In the words of General Brokemichael, 'A great motion picture could be made of their exploits, we should look into that.'

Summer was fading, lethargy receding, each a prelude to the energized games of autumn. The north winds grew chillier in the mornings, reminding the residents of Nebraska that soon they would become colder, then very cold, finally numbing the skin; another prelude, this to the winter snows. However, such thoughts were far from the minds of the Wopotami nation, for as the negotiations with the United States Government continued, Washington saw fit to send two hundred and twelve state-of-the-art trailer homes to the reservation, replacing the wigwams and the ramshackle structures previously used for communal gatherings and shelter for many against the winter snows. Of course, what Washington did not know was that several hundred perfectly adequate cabins had been bulldozed only weeks previously and that the tepees, or wigwams, were previously an un-familiar sight on the reservation except for a few around the tourists' gate. MacKenzie Hawkins was not one to overlook either the subtleties or the inconsistencies of observable terrain, no trained military man would. It was all part of the strategy, and no battle was ever won without a plan.

'I still can't believe it,' said Jennifer, walking hand in hand with Sam down a dirt road on the reservation, the field to their right dotted with huge, extravagant trailers, each with a satellite television dish attached to the roof. 'It's all coming out the way Mac thought it would.'

'The negotiations are going well then?'

'Incredibly. If we frown simply because something's not clear, they fuss and backtrack and make a better offer. Several times I've had to interrupt the government people and explain that the financial aspects were perfectly satisfactory, I just wanted a legal point clarified. One lawyer from the GAO shouted, "You don't like it, don't worry, it's *out*"!'

'That's a nice position to be in.'

'I was merely excusing myself to go to the ladies' room.'

'Strike my comment . . . But why are you being so gentle?'

'Come on, Sam, what they've offered is so outrageously beyond our wildest dreams it would be criminal to argue.'

'Then why even negotiate? What are you after?'

'To begin with, a legally binding guaranteed timetable for our immediate needs, such as good housing, fine schools, paved roads, a real honest-to-God village with seed money for stores and shops so decent livings can be made right here legitimately. Then maybe a few goodies like a couple of community pools and clearing Eagle Eye Mountain for ski lifts and a restaurant – but, of course, the latter could be considered part of our commerce. It was Charlie's idea; he loves to ski.'

'How's he doing?'

'Darling, I diapered that kid and now I sometimes feel almost incestuous.'

'*Huh?*'

'He's so much like *you*! He's quick and smart and, yes, funny –'

'I'm a very serious officer of the court,' broke in Devereaux, grinning.

'You're a lunatic and so is he, both your lunacies mitigated by quick perceptions, irritating memories, and reducing complexities to fundamental simplicities.'

'I don't even know what that means.'

'Neither does he, but you both do it. Did you know that he came up with an insane, insignificant blemish on our history of jurisprudence called *non nomen amicus curiae* when Hawkins filed his brief? Who would ever know what it is, much less *remember* it?'

'I do. Eighteen twenty-seven, Jackson versus Buckley, one stole pigs from the other –'

'Oh, shut up!' Jenny released his hand, then immediately grabbed it back.

'What's Charlie going to do when this is over?'

'I'm making him the attorney-of-record for the tribe. He can run the ski resort in winter at the same time.'

'Isn't that terribly limiting?'

'Perhaps, but I don't think so. Someone has to be here to make damn sure Washington lives up to every article of the reconstruction agreement. When you're involved with building on this scale, you'd better have a lawyer at your beck and call. Ever put an addition on your house that was completed on time? And I should add that I've placed heavy penalty clauses on every aspect of the construction.'

'Charlie will have his hands full. What else did you get from Dizzy City, as Mac calls it? I mean beside your "immediate needs"?'

'Very simple. An uninvadable, irrevocable trust based on irreversible guarantees by the Treasury Department that the tribe will receive a basic two million dollars a year, adjusted for inflation, for the next twenty years.'

'That's *chickenshit*, Jenny!' cried Sam.

'No, it's not, darling. If we can't make it by then, we don't deserve to. We don't want a free ride, we simply want the opportunity to get in the mainstream. And knowing my Wopotamis, we'll take you palefaces for just about every nickel you've got. If I also know my tribe, and surely I do, in twenty years your president will probably have a surname like "Sundown" or "Moonbeam," take my word for it. We didn't refine the yaw-yaw juice for nothing.'

'And now what?' asked Devereaux.

'And now what *what*?'

'What about us?'

'Did you have to bring that up?'

'Isn't it about time?'

'Of course it is, but I'm afraid.'

'I'll protect you.'

'From whom? *You?*'

'If need be. Actually, it's very simple, and as you've pointed out, Charlie and I can reduce complex matters into simple issues anyone can understand.'

'What the hell are you talking about, Sam?'

'Reducing a complicated situation into a very simple problem.'

'What, may I ask, is that?'

'I refuse to live the rest of my life without you, and somehow I get the idea that you might feel the same way.'

'Say there's a grain of truth in what you say, just a grain, even a large kernel, how is it possible? I'm in San Francisco and you're in Boston. That's not a good arrangement.'

'With your credentials, Aaron would hire you in a minute at a terrific salary.'

'With your record, Springtree, Basl and Karpas of San Francisco would make you a partner before me.'

'I could never leave Aaron, you know that, but you've already left one firm in Omaha. So you see it's been reduced to a simple either/or, based on the assumption that we'd both take the gas pipe if we couldn't be together.'

'I didn't go that far.'

'I did. Can't you?'

'I refuse to answer on the grounds that it may incriminate me.'

'Still, I have a solution.'

'What is it?'

'Mac gave me a medallion of his old division from World War Two, the one that broke through the Bulge, and I always keep it on me for good luck.' Devereaux reached into his pocket and withdrew an outsized, lightweight, ersatz coin with the face of MacKenzie Hawkins etched in the centre. 'I'll flip it up and let it land on the road. I'll take heads, you take tails. If it's tails, you'll go back to San Francisco and we'll both suffer the tortures of the damned. If it's heads, you'll come to Boston with me.'

'*Agreed.*' The medallion spun end-over-end in the air and fell on the dirt road. Jennifer bent down. 'Good heavens, it's heads.' She started to pick up the ersatz coin when Sam's hand clamped over hers.

'*No*, Jenny, you mustn't lean over like that!'

'Like what?'

'It's very bad for your sacroiliac!' Devereaux pulled her up while clutching the medallion in his right hand.

'Sam, what are you *saying*?'

'The husband's first job is to protect his wife.'

'From *what*?'

'Bad sacroiliacs.' Devereaux manipulated the medallion in his fingers and scaled it into the pasture on their left. 'I don't need any lucky pieces anymore,' he said, embracing Jenny. 'I have you and that's all the luck I ever wanted or needed.'

'Or maybe you didn't want me to see the other side of the coin,' whispered Redwing into his ear while softly biting it. 'The Hawk gave me one of those in Hooksett. His face is on both sides. If you had said tails, I would have killed you.'

'Wanton *bitch*,' whispered Sam, nibbling her lips like a chimpanzee finding peanuts. 'Is there a secluded field we might wander into?'

'Not now, Rover, Mac's expecting us.'

'He's *out* of my life; this is the *end*!'

'I sincerely hope so, my darling, but being a realist, I wonder for how long?'

They rounded the corner of the dirt road where the huge multicoloured, multilayered tepee of polyester imitation animal skins flapped down from the apex to the widespread stakes in the ground. Smoke emerged from the opening above.

'He's there,' said Devereaux. 'Let's make the good-byes quick and simple, like in nice-to-know-you-stay-the-hell-away-from-our-lives!'

'That's a bit harsh, Sam. Look what he's done for my people.'

'It's all a game for him, Jenny, don't you understand that?'

'Then it's a good game he plays, darling, can't *you* see that?'

'I don't know, he always confuses me –'

'Never mind,' said Redwing. 'He's coming out. Good Lord, *look* at him!'

Sam stared in disbelief. General MacKenzie Lochinvar Hawkins, aka Thunder Head, chief of the Wopotamis, bore absolutely no resemblance whatsoever to either alleged person. There was not an inkling of the military, much less the majesty of the American Indian; in fact, there was no dignity properly attributed to either image. Instead, regality had been replaced by gaucherie, the flamboyance of the shallow man, which somehow was more solid, more convincing. Partially covering his bristling close-cropped grey hair was a yellow beret, and below his strong nose a thin, blackened moustache, and below that a purple ascot that was in flaming contrast to his pink silk shirt, which was colour-coordinated with his tight-fitting bright red trousers, the cuffs lopping over a pair of white Gucci loafers. Naturally, the suitcase he was carrying was a Louis Vuitton.

'Mac, who the hell are you supposed to *be*?' yelled Devereaux.

'Oh, there you two are,' said the Hawk, without answering the question. 'I thought I'd have to leave without seeing you. I'm in a dreadful hurry.'

'"A dreadful hurry"?' said Jennifer.

'Mac, who *are* you?'

'Mackintosh Quartermain,' replied the Hawk sheepishly, 'veteran of the Scots Grenadiers. It was Gin-Gin's idea.'

'*What?*'

'Off to Hollywood,' mumbled Hawkins. 'I'm a co-producer and technical adviser on Greenberg's flick.'

'"Flick" . . . ?'

'Just to keep an eye on Manny's financial imagination . . . and maybe a few other things, if they crop up. Hollywood's in a mess, you know. It needs some clear-thinking innovators . . . Look, it was terrif seeing you two sweethearts, but I'm really in a hurry. I'm meeting my new adjutant – *assistant* – Colonel

573

Roman Zabritski, late of the Soviet military cinema, at the airport. Our plane goes on to the coast.'

'Roman *Z*?' asked a stunned Redwing.

'What happened to Cyrus?' said Sam.

'He's somewhere in the south of France, checking on one of Frazier's châteaux. It was vandalized.'

'I thought he wanted to go back to the laboratory.'

'Oh, well, what with his prison record and everything . . . well, Cookson's buying a chemical plant . . . Look, it was great. you dolls came out to see me but I've really got to dash-bash. Give us a kiss, sweetheart, and if you ever want a screen test, you know where to jingle me.' The astonished Redwing accepted the Hawk's embrace.

'And you, Lieutenant,' continued MacKenzie, throwing his arms around Devereaux, 'you're still the best legal skull on the planet, except maybe for Commander Pinkus and the little lady here.'

'*Mac!*' cried Sam. 'Don't you *see*? You're starting all over again! There'll be nothing left of Los Angeles!'

'No, not true, son, not true at all. We'll bring back the glory days.' The Hawk picked up his Louis Vuitton suitcase, stifling the emergence of tears. '*Ciao*, babes,' he said, quickly turning away and hurrying up the dirt road, a man with a mission.

'Why do I have the idea that sometime, somewhere in Boston, the telephone will ring and at the other end will be Mackintosh Quartermain?' said Devereaux, his arm around Jennifer as they watched the figure of the Hawk grow smaller in the distance.

'Because it's inevitable, my darling, and we wouldn't have it any other way.'